Praise for the authors of

# HOLIDAY BLESSINGS

*New York Times* bestselling author

## DEBBIE MACOMBER

"Debbie Macomber has a gift
for evoking emotions."
—*Publishers Weekly*

The internationally acclaimed author's first book, a Silhouette Inspiration titled *Heartsong,* was the first romance ever to be reviewed in *Publishers Weekly.*

## JANE PEART

"Interesting and likeable characters
will keep readers well entertained."
—*Romantic Times Magazine*

Award-winning author of more than 20 books, including the bestselling Orphan Train West series, Jane has brought readers timeless themes of family, faith and love.

## IRENE HANNON

"A poignant, touching story."
—*Rendezvous*

A prolific author of inspirational and traditional romances, Irene began her writing career at the age of ten when she won a story contest in a national children's magazine.

JANE PEART

IRENE HANNON

DEBBIE MACOMBER

# HOLIDAY BLESSINGS

Love Inspired®

Published by Steeple Hill Books™

Steeple Hill™

STEEPLE HILL BOOKS

RECYCLED PAPER

ISBN 0-373-87130-9

HOLIDAY BLESSINGS



This edition published by arrangement with Steeple Hill Books.



Visit us at www.steeplehill.com

**Printed in U.S.A.**

# CONTENTS

# THANKSGIVING PRAYER
## Debbie Macomber

# Chapter One

The radiant blue heavens wooed Claudia Masters as she boarded the jet for Nome, Alaska. Her heart rate accelerated with excitement. In less than two hours she would be with Seth—manly, self-assured, masterful Seth. She made herself comfortable and secured the seat belt, anticipating the rumble of the mighty engines that would thrust the plane into the welcoming sky.

There had been some uncertainty when Claudia boarded the plane that morning in Seattle. But a hastily placed phone call from Anchorage, and she'd been assured by Seth's secretary that yes, he had received her message, and yes, he would meet her at the airport. Again confident, Claudia relaxed and idly flipped through a magazine.

A warmth, a feeling of contentment encompassed her. Cooper's doubts and the last-ditch effort to change her mind were behind her now, and she was free to make her life with Seth.

Cooper had been furious with her decision to leave

medical school. But Cooper was only her uncle, even if he was the same age as Seth. He hadn't understood her love for the itinerant oilman, just as he couldn't understand her faith in the Lord.

A smile briefly curved her soft mouth upward. Cooper had shown more emotion in that brief twenty-minute visit to his office than she'd seen in all her twenty-two years.

"Quitting med school is the most stupid idea I've ever heard," he'd growled, the keen brown eyes challenging the serene blue of hers.

"Sometimes loving someone calls for unusual behavior," she had countered. Anything impractical was foreign to her uncle.

For a moment all Cooper could do was stare at her. She could sense the anger drain from him as he lowered himself into the desk chair.

"Contrary to what you may believe, I have your best interests at heart. I see you throwing away years of study for some ignorant lumberjack. Can you blame me for doubting your sanity?"

"Seth's an oilman, not a lumberjack. There aren't any trees in Nome." It was easier to correct Cooper than to answer the questions that had plagued her with doubts. The choice hadn't been easy; indecision had tormented her for months. Now that she'd decided to marry Seth and share his life in the Alaskan wilderness, a sense of joy and release came to her.

"It's taken me two miserable months to realize that my future isn't in any hospital," she continued. "I'd be a rotten doctor if I couldn't be a woman first. I love Seth. Someday I'll finish medical school, but if a decision has to be made, I'll choose Seth Lessinger every time.''

But Cooper had never been easily won over. The tense atmosphere became suddenly quiet as he digested the thought. He expelled his breath, but it was several seconds before he spoke. ''I'm not thinking of myself, Claudia. I want you to be absolutely sure you know what you're doing.''

''I am.'' She smiled reassuringly, and for the first time since entering his office, she sat.

Now, flying high above the lonely, barren land of the Alaska tundra, Claudia was confident she was doing the right thing. God had confirmed the decision. It had taken her much longer to realize the truth, but Seth had known from the beginning.

Gazing out the plane window, she viewed miles upon miles of the frozen, snow-covered tundra. It was just as Seth had described: treeless plains of crystalline purity. There would be a summer, Seth promised, days firmly united when the sun would never set. Flowers would blossom, and for a short time the tundra would explode into a grassy pasture. Seth had explained many things about life in the North. At first she'd resented his letters, full of enticements to lure her to Nome. If he really loved her, he should be willing to relocate in Seattle until she'd completed her studies. It wasn't so much to ask. But as she came to know and love Seth, it became evident that Nome was more than the location of his business; it was a way of life, Seth's life. Crowded cities, traffic jams, shopping malls would suffocate him.

She should have known that the minute she pushed

the cleaning cart into the motel room. Her being at the Wilderness Motel, cleaning rooms, was something of a miracle in itself.

Leaning back, Claudia slowly lowered her lashes as the memories washed over her.

Ashley Robbins, her lifetime friend and roommate, had been ill—far too sick to spend the day cleaning rooms. By the time Ashley had admitted as much, it was too late to call the motel and tell them she wouldn't be coming. Claudia had volunteered to go for her.

Claudia had known from the moment she slid the pass key into the lock. There was something special, something different about this room.

Her hands rested on slender hips as she surveyed the quarters. A single man slept here. A smile had trembled on her soft mouth as she thought of how accurate she was becoming at predicting the occupants of each room she cleaned. It had become a game to speculate who was here and why. Whoever had this room had rested uneasily. The sheet and blankets were ripped from the mattress and dumped haphazardly at the foot of the king-size bed.

As she stripped the sheets, Claudia couldn't help wondering what Cooper would think if he could see her now. He would be aghast to know she was doing menial work.

She lifted the corner of the mattress to tuck in the blanket, then felt as if someone had entered the room. As she turned around, a smile lit up the sky-blue eyes. But her welcome died: no one was there.

Finishing the bed, she plugged in the vacuum. With

the flip of the switch the motor roared to life. Again the sensation came and she turned off the machine. But when she turned, Claudia discovered she was alone.

Pausing, she studied the room. Silence encompassed her as she stood in the middle of the floor. There was something about this place: not the room itself, but the occupant. She could sense it, feel it, a depression, a sadness that seemed to reach out and touch her, wrap itself around her. Claudia wondered why she should be receiving these strange sensations. Nothing like this had ever happened to her before.

A prayer came to her lips as she silently petitioned God for whoever occupied this bed, this room. When she finished she released a soft sigh. Once, a long time ago, she remembered reading that no one could come to the Lord unless someone first prayed. Claudia wasn't sure how scriptural that was, but the thought had stuck with her. Often she found herself murmuring silent prayers for virtual strangers.

After cleaning the bathroom and placing fresh towels on the rack, she began to wheel the cleaning cart into the hallway. Again she paused, brushing wisps of copper-colored hair from her forehead as she examined the room. She hadn't forgotten anything, had she? Everything looked right. But again that terrible sadness seemed to reach out to her.

Leaving the cart, she moved to the desk and took out a postcard and a pen from the drawer. In large, bold letters she printed one of her favorite verses from Psalms. It read: "May the Lord give you the desire of your heart and make all your plans succeed." Psalm

20:4. She didn't question why that particular verse came to mind. It didn't offer solace, and yet it was unhappiness that she had felt. Perplexed and a little unsure, she placed the card in the metal prong that held the dresser mirror in place.

Outside, she checked to be sure the door had completely closed and locked. Her back ached. Ashley hadn't been teasing when she said this was hard work. It was that and more. A thin sheen of perspiration wetted Claudia's brow, and she pushed the thick, naturally curly hair from her face. Her attention was focused on the door when she began wheeling the cart. She hadn't gone more than a few feet when she struck something. A quick glance upward told her she'd run into a man.

"Oh, sorry," she apologized immediately. "I wasn't watching where I was going." Her first impression was that this was the largest, most imposing man she'd ever seen. He loomed above her, easily a foot taller than her five-foot-five frame. His shoulders were wide, his waist and hips lean, and he was so muscular that the material of his shirt was pulled taut across the broad chest. He was handsome in a reckless-looking way, his hair magnificently dark. The full, well-trimmed beard was a shade lighter.

"No problem." The stranger smiled, his mouth sensuous and appealing, his eyes warm.

Claudia liked that. He might be big, but one look told her he was a gentle giant.

Not until she was in her car did Claudia realize she hadn't watched to see if the giant had entered the last special room.

By the time Claudia returned to the apartment, Ashley looked better. Propped against the arm of the sofa, Ashley's back was cushioned with several pillows. A hand-knit afghan covered her legs and torso. A box of tissues sat on the coffee table, with crumpled ones littering the polished mahogany surface.

"How'd it go?" Ashley queried, her voice scratchy and unnatural. "Were you able to figure out one end of the vacuum from the other?"

"Of course." Claudia laughed. "I had fun playing the domestic, but next time warn me—I broke my longest nail."

"That's the price you pay for being so stubborn," Ashley scolded and grabbed a tissue, anticipating a sneeze. "I...I told you it was a crazy idea. Did old Burns say anything?"

"No, she was too grateful. Finding a replacement this late in the day would have been difficult."

Fall classes at the University of Washington had resumed that Monday, and Ashley had worked at the motel only a couple of weeks. Her friend hated to make a bad impression by calling in sick, so Claudia had offered to fill in for her at the last minute.

Claudia was pleased to help her friend. Her own school expenses were paid by a trust fund her father had established before his death. But Ashley maintained two part-time jobs to earn enough to stay in school. Claudia had offered to lend her friend money on numerous occasions, but Ashley had stubbornly refused. Ashley believed that if God wanted for her to have a teaching degree, then He would provide the necessary money. Apparently He did want that for her, because the funds were always there when she needed them.

Ashley's unshakable faith had taught Claudia valuable lessons. She had been blessed with material wealth while Ashley struggled from one month to the next. But of the two, Claudia considered Ashley the richer.

Often Claudia marveled at her friend's faith. Everything had been well taken care of in her own life. Decisions had been made for her. As for her career, she'd known from the time she was in grade school she would be a doctor. That dream had been shared by her father. The last Christmas before his death he'd given her a stethoscope. Later she realized that her father must have known he wouldn't be alive to see their dream fulfilled. Now there was only Cooper, her pompous, dignified uncle.

"How are you feeling?"

Ashley sneezed into the tissue that did little to muffle the sound. "Better," she murmured, her eyes red and watery. "I should be fine by tomorrow. I don't want you to have to fill in for me again."

"We'll see," Claudia said, hands on her hips and shaking her head. Stubborn Ashley, Claudia mused—she seemed to be surrounded by strong-willed, obstinate people.

Later that night, Claudia lay in bed unable to sleep. She hadn't told Ashley about what had happened in the last room she'd cleaned. She didn't know how she could explain it to anyone. Now she wished she'd waited to see if the stranger outside had been the one occupying that room. The day had been unusual in more ways than one. With a yawn, she rolled over and forced herself to relax and go to sleep.

The clouds were gray and thick the next morning. Claudia was up and reading over some material from one of her classes when Ashley strolled into the living room.

"Don't you ever let up?" she complained with a long yawn. "I swear all you do is study. Take a break, kid. You've got all quarter to hit the books."

With deliberate slowness Claudia closed the volume. "Do you always wake up so cheerful?"

"Yes," Ashley snapped. "Especially when I feel I could be dying. You're going to be a doctor—do something!"

Claudia picked up the thick book on psychology. "All right," she agreed. "Take two aspirin, drink lots of liquids and stay in bed. I'll check on you later."

"Wonderful," Ashley murmured sarcastically as she stumbled back into her bedroom. "And for this she goes to medical school."

A half hour later, Claudia tapped lightly before letting herself into Ashley's bedroom. "Feel any better?"

"A little." Ashley spoke in a tight voice. She was curled into a ball as if every bone ached.

"You probably have a touch of flu to go along with that rotten cold."

"This isn't a touch," she denied vehemently. "This is a full-scale attack. Why does this have to happen to me now?"

"Don't ask me," Claudia said as she set a tray of tea and toast on the nightstand. "But have you ever stopped to think that maybe your body has decided it needs a rest? You're going to kill yourself working at the motel and the bookstore, plus everything else. Something's got to give, and in this instance it's your health. I think you should take warning."

"Oh dear, here it comes." Ashley groaned and rolled over, placing the back of her hand to her forehead. "I wondered how long it would take to pull your corny doctor routine on me."

"It's not corny." The blue eyes flashed. "Don't you recognize good advice when you hear it?"

Ashley gestured weakly with her hand. "That's the problem, I guess. I don't."

"That's it," Claudia said and fluffed up a pillow so Ashley could sit up comfortably.

"I'm better, honest," Ashley said and coughed. "Good enough to work. I hate the thought of your breaking another fingernail."

"Sure you do, Ash, sure you do."

Claudia wheeled the cleaning cart from one room to the next without incident. The small of her back ached, and she paused to rub it. She hadn't done much housecleaning in her life. Ashley's mother had been their housekeeper and cook from the time Claudia was small.

Her fingers trembled when she inserted the pass key into the final room—the same one she had finished with yesterday. Would she feel the same sensations as before? Or had it all been her imagination? The room looked almost identical to the way it had been. The sheets and blankets were rumpled at the foot of the bed as if the man had slept restlessly.

Her attention flew to the mirror and she noted that the card was gone. Well, at least the occupant had discovered that. Slowly she walked around the quarters, waiting to feel the sensations she'd had yesterday. Whatever it had been was gone. Maybe she had conjured up the whole thing in her mind. The brain could do things like that. She should know. She'd studied enough about the human mind these past couple of days.

Claudia was placing the fresh white towels in the bathroom when a clicking noise was followed by the sound of the front door opening.

She stiffened as her fingers nervously toyed with the towel, pretending to straighten it.

"Hello." The male voice came from behind her, rich and deep.

"Hello," she mumbled and managed a smile. The man she had bumped into yesterday was framed in the doorway. Somehow Claudia had known he was the one occupying this room. "I'll be out of your way in a minute."

"No," he insisted. "Don't go, I want to talk to you."

Turning away from him, Claudia moistened her suddenly parched lips.

"Do I frighten you?" he asked.

Claudia realized that his size might intimidate many people. "No," she answered honestly. This man could probably lift a refrigerator by himself, yet he wouldn't hurt an ant. She wasn't sure how she knew this, but she did.

"Are you the one who left this?" He pulled the card she'd placed in the mirror from his shirt pocket.

Numbly she nodded. She didn't know anything about motel policy. This type of thing could possibly get Ashley into trouble.

His thick brows lifted as if he expected more than a simple shake of her head. "Why?" The single word seemed to be hurled at her.

"I...I don't really know," she began weakly, surprised at how feeble her voice sounded. "If it offended you, then please accept my apology."

"I wasn't displeased," he assured her. "But I was a little curious about the reasons why." He released her gaze as he put the card back into his shirt pocket. "Do you do this often?"

Claudia looked away uneasily. "No. Never before."

His dark eyes narrowed on her. "Do you think we could have a cup of coffee somewhere when you're through? I really would like to talk to you."

"I..." She looked down on the uniform skirt the motel had provided and noted a couple of smudges.

"You look fine."

This stranger assumed she was a penniless motel maid. So many times Claudia had wished she could meet someone without the fear of intimidating him with her brains and position. Although she wasn't an heir to millions, she would receive a large cash settlement at age twenty-five, or the day she married—whichever came first.

"I'd like that." Obviously this stranger needed to speak to someone. The open Bible on his nightstand had convinced her he was a Christian. Was it because he was lonely that she had felt that terrible sadness in the room? No, she was sure it was more than loneliness—a lot more.

"Can we meet someplace?" he suggested. "There's a coffee shop around the corner."

"Fine," she said and nodded, knowing he had set the meeting in a public place so she would feel safe. Cooper would have a fit if he knew what she was doing. "I can be ready in about twenty minutes."

"I'll see you there." He stepped aside and Claudia could feel him studying her as she moved out of the bathroom. What was the matter with her? Never had she done anything so impulsive as meet a stranger like this.

With the room assignments finished, Claudia returned the cart to Mrs. Burns, who again thanked her. Next she made a stop in the ladies' room. One glance in the mirror and she groaned at the reflection. Her hair was an unruly mass of auburn curls. Taking the brush from her purse, she ran it through the long tresses until they sparked with electricity. Her thick, naturally curly hair had always been a problem. For several years now she had kept it long and pulled away from her face with a ribbon tied at the base of her neck. When she first applied and was accepted into medical school, she'd been determined to play down her femininity. Women weren't the rarity that they once were, but her sex combined with the money was sure to prejudice many of her classmates. There might have been some ill feelings her first year of medical school, but she had long since proved herself.

The coffee shop was crowded, but Claudia's searching gaze instantly located the stranger, who towered head and shoulders above the other patrons. Even when sitting, his large, imposing build couldn't be disguised. Weaving her way between chairs, Claudia sauntered toward him.

The welcome in his smile broke the smooth slant of his mouth. He stood and pulled out a chair for her. She noticed that he chose the one beside him as if he wanted her as close as possible. The thought didn't disturb Claudia, but her reaction to him troubled her. She wanted to be close to him.

"I suddenly realized I don't know your name," she said after sitting down.

"Seth Lessinger." A thick eyebrow arched in silent inquiry. "And yours?"

"Claudia Masters."

"I'm surprised they don't call you Red with that hair."

In any other family she might well have been tagged with the name, but not in hers. "No, I never was." Her voice contained a husky quality. To hide her discomfort, she lifted the menu and began studying its contents, although she didn't want anything more than coffee.

The waitress arrived and Claudia placed her order. Seth asked for a club sandwich.

"What brings you to Seattle?" she asked and absently smoothed a wrinkle from the skirt.

"A conference."

"Are you enjoying the Emerald City?" She was making small talk to cover up her nervousness. Maybe meeting a strange man like this wasn't such a good idea.

"Very much. It's my first visit to the Northwest, and I'll admit it's nicer than I expected. Big cities tend to intimidate me. I never have understood how anyone can live like this, among so many people."

Claudia didn't mean to smile, but amusement played at the edges of her mouth. "Where are you from? Alaska?" She'd meant it as a joke, but he nodded in confirmation.

"Nome," he supplied. "Where the air is pure and the skies are blue."

"You make it sound lovely."

"It's not," he told her with a half-smile. "It can be dingy and gray and miserable, but it's home."

Her coffee arrived and she cupped the mug, grateful to have something to do with her hands.

His eyes seemed to study her, and when their gazes clashed, a lazy smile flickered from the dark depths.

"What do you do in Nome?" His look was a gentle caress that Claudia found disturbing. Not that it made her uncomfortable: the effect was quite the opposite. He touched a softness in her, a longing to be the woman she had denied for so long.

"I'm a commissioning agent for a major oil company."

"That sounds interesting." She knew the words came out stiff and stilted.

"It's more than that. What about you?"

"Student at the University of Washington." She didn't elaborate.

A frown creased the wide brow. "You look older than a college student."

"I'm twenty-two." She concentrated her gaze on the black coffee. "How long will you be in Seattle?" If he noticed she was disinclined to talk about herself, he didn't say anything.

"I'll be flying back in a few days. I'd like to be home at the end of the week."

A few days, her mind echoed. She would remember to pray for him. Claudia believed that God brought everyone into her life for a specific reason. The purpose of her meeting Seth might be for her to remember to pray for him. He certainly had made an impression on her.

"How long have you been a Christian?" Seth inquired.

"Five years." That was another thing Cooper had never understood. He found this "religious interest" of hers amusing. "And you?" Again she directed the conversation away from herself.

"Six months. I'm still an infant in the Lord, although my size disputes that!" He smiled, and Claudia felt mesmerized by the warmth in his eyes.

She returned his smile, aware he was as defensive about his size as she was about her money and her brains.

"Why'd you leave the Bible verse in the mirror?"

This was the crux of his wanting to talk to her. How could she explain? She didn't know why she'd done it. "Listen, I've already apologized for that. I realize it's probably against the motel policy."

A hand twice the size of her own reached over the

table and trapped hers. "Claudia." The sound of her name was low-pitched and reassuring. "Don't apologize. The message meant more to me than you can possibly realize. My intention is to thank you for it."

The dark, mysterious eyes studied hers. Again Claudia sensed more than saw a sadness, a loneliness there. She made a show of glancing at her watch. "I…I really should be going."

"Can I see you again? Tomorrow?"

Claudia was afraid he was going to ask her that. Afraid he would, afraid he wouldn't.

"I was planning on doing some grocery shopping at the Pike Place Market tomorrow," she said without accepting or refusing.

"We could meet somewhere." His tone was clipped with a faint challenge. He sounded almost unsure. Claudia had the impression there wasn't much that unsettled this man. She wondered what it was about herself that caused him to be uncertain.

"All right," she found herself agreeing. "But I feel I must warn you, if you find large cities stifling, downtown Seattle at that time of the day may be an experience you'd wish to avoid."

"Not this time," he said with a chuckle.

They set a time and place as Seth walked her back to the motel and her car. Claudia drove a silver compact. Cooper had generously given her a fancy sports car when she was accepted into medical school. She'd never driven it around school and kept it in one of Cooper's garages. Not that she didn't appreciate the gift. The car was beautiful, and a dream to drive, but she already had her compact and couldn't see the need for two cars. Not when one of them would make her stand out and give her unnecessary and unwanted attention on campus. She told Cooper she couldn't keep it at the apartment because the color clashed with those of all the other cars in the parking lot. He had nodded in agreement. Cooper's whole life was color-coordinated, poor man.

"Hi." Claudia floated into the apartment, a Cheshire cat grin gently lifting her mouth into a smile.

"My heavens," Ashley groaned from the sofa. "You look like you've just met Prince Charming."

"I have." She dropped her purse on the end table and jumped up on the sofa arm the opposite end from Ashley. "He's about this tall." She held her hand high above her head. "With shoulders this wide." Her hands extended as far as they could reach from her sides. "And he has the most incredible dark eyes."

"Oh, honestly, Claudia, that's not Prince Charming. That's the Incredible Hunk," Ashley admonished on a sigh.

Claudia tilted her head to one side, a slow smile spreading over her features. "Incredible is the word all right."

Not until the following morning, when Claudia dressed in her best designer jeans and cashmere sweater, with knee-high leather boots, did Ashley take her seriously.

"You really did meet someone yesterday, didn't you?"

Claudia nodded, pouring steaming cocoa into a mug. "Want some?"

"Sure," Ashley said and hesitated. "When did you have the chance? The only place you've been is school and—" she paused, her sky-blue eyes rounding "—the Wilderness and back. Claudia," she gasped, "It isn't someone from the motel, is it?"

Two pieces of toast blasted from the toaster with the force of a skyrocket. Deftly Claudia caught them in the air. "Yup."

For the first time in recent history, Ashley was speechless. "But, Claudia, you can't...I mean...all kinds of people stay there. He could be anyone..."

"Seth isn't just anyone. He's large, so large he may shock you. But he's gentle and kind. I like him."

"I can tell," Ashley murmured with a worried look pinching her face.

"Don't look so shocked. Women have met men in stranger ways. I'm seeing him this afternoon. I told him I have some grocery shopping to do." At the glare Ashley was giving her, Claudia felt obliged to add, "Well, I do. I wanted to pick up some fresh vegetables. I was just reading an article on the importance of fiber in the diet."

"We bought a whole month's worth of food last Saturday," Ashley mumbled under her breath.

"True." Claudia shrugged. "But I think we could use some fresh produce. I'll be sure and pick up some prunes for you."

Seth was standing on the library steps waiting when Claudia arrived. Again she noted the compelling male virility. She waited on the bottom stairs for Seth to join her. A balmy September breeze coming off Puget

Sound teased her hair, blowing the auburn curls across her cheek. Seth paused, standing in front of her, his eyes smiling deeply into hers.

The mesmerizing quality of his gaze held her motionless. Her hand was halfway lifted to her face to remove the lock of maverick hair, but it, too, was frozen by the warmth in his look, which seemed to reach out and caress her. Claudia had neither the will nor the desire to glance away.

The rough feel of his callused hand removing the hair brought her out of the trance. ''Hello, Claudia.''

''Seth.''

''You're beautiful.'' The words appeared to come involuntarily.

''So are you,'' she joked. The musky scent of his cologne drifted pleasantly toward her, and an unwilling sigh broke from between her slightly parted lips.

Someone on the busy sidewalk bumped into Claudia, throwing her off balance. Immediately Seth's hand moved around her protectively. The iron band of his arm continued to hold her close, far longer than necessary. His touch warmed her through the thin jacket. No man had ever been able to produce this kind of feeling within her. This was uncanny, unreal.

# Chapter Two

"Are you ready to call it quits?" Claudia questioned. Seth had placed a guiding hand at the base of her neck, and she wondered how long this touch would continue to produce the warm, glowing sensation that spread down her spine.

"More than ready," Seth confirmed.

The Pike Place Market in the heart of downtown Seattle had always been a hub of activity as tourists and everyday shoppers vied for the attention of the vendors who displayed their wares. Claudia and Seth strolled through the market, their hands entwined. Vegetables that had been hand-picked that morning were displayed on long tables, while the farmers shouted, enticing customers to their booths. The odd but pleasant smell of tangy spices and fresh fish drifted agreeably around them.

"I did warn you," she said with a small laugh. "What's the life expectancy rate of someone from Nome, Alaska, in crowds like this?"

Seth glanced at his wristwatch. ‘‘About two hours,’’ he murmured. ‘‘And we’ve been at it nearly that. Let’s take a break.’’

‘‘I agree.’’

‘‘Lunch?’’

Claudia nodded. She hadn’t eaten after her last class, hurrying instead to meet Seth. Now she realized she was hungry. ‘‘Sounds good.’’

‘‘Chinese okay?’’

For once it was a pleasure to have someone take her out and not try to impress her with the best restaurant in town, or how much money he could spend. ‘‘Yes, that’s fine.’’

Seth paused. ‘‘You sure?’’

She squeezed his hand. ‘‘Very sure.’’

They rode the city bus to Seattle’s International Settlement and stepped off into another world. Seth looked around him in surprise. ‘‘I didn’t know Seattle had a Chinatown.’’

‘‘Chinatown, Little Italy, Mexico, all within a few blocks. Interesting, isn’t it?’’

‘‘Very.’’

They lingered over the tea, delaying as long as possible their return to the hectic pace of the world outside.

‘‘Why do you have a beard?’’ Claudia asked curiously. She didn’t mean to be abrupt, but beards had always fascinated her.

Seth looked surprised by the question, rubbing both sides of the dark hair with one hand. ‘‘Does it bother you? I can shave it off if you like.’’

‘‘Oh, no,’’ she protested instantly. ‘‘I like it. Very

much. But I've always been curious why men sometimes chose to leave their beards.''

''I can't speak for others, but growing one offers some protection to my face during the long winter months,'' he explained.

His quick offer to shave it off for her had faintly shocked Claudia. She couldn't understand his eagerness.

''I'm about finished my shopping. What about you?'' She hated to torture him further.

The tiny teacup was dwarfed in his massive hands. ''I was finished a long time ago.''

''Want to take a walk along the waterfront and ride the trolley?'' Claudia suggested, looking for reasons to prolong their time together.

''I'd like that.''

While Seth paid for their meal she excused herself to reapply her lipstick and comb her hair. Then, hand in hand, they walked the short distance back to the heart of downtown Seattle. They paused at a major department store to study a window display in autumn colors.

Her eyes were laughing into his when Seth placed a possessive hand around her waist, drawing her close to his side. They stepped away from the window and started down the street toward the waterfront.

It was then that Claudia spotted Cooper walking across the opposite street. Even from this distance she could see the disapproving scowl on her uncle's face. The differences between these two men were so striking that to make a comparison would be ludicrous.

''I'll get us a taxi,'' Seth suggested, his eyes showing concern. "I've been walking your legs off." Apparently he thought her pale face was the result of the brisk pace he'd set.

"No, I'd rather walk," she insisted and reached for his hand. "If we hurry, we can make this light."

Their hands were linked when she began to run. There had never been any chance of their reaching the street before the light changed, but Claudia still proceeded to push between the busy shoppers.

"Claudia." Seth stopped, placing his arm over her shoulders, his wide brow creased with concern. "What's the matter?"

"Nothing," she said hesitantly, looking around her. She was certain Cooper had seen them. For once she didn't want him to ruin things. "Really, let's go." Her voice was raised and anxious.

"Claudia."

Cooper's voice behind her stopped her heart.

"Introduce me to your friend," Cooper requested in a crisp, businesslike tone.

Frustration washed over her. Cooper would take one look at Seth and judge him as one of the fortune hunters he was always warning her about.

"Cooper Masters, this is Seth Lessinger." The introduction was made grudgingly.

The two men eyed each other shrewdly while exchanging handshakes.

"Masters," Seth repeated. "Are you related to Claudia?"

Cooper ignored the question, instead turning toward Claudia. "I'll pick you up for dinner Sunday at about two. If that's convenient?"

"It was fine last week and the week before, so why should it be any different this week?"

Her uncle flashed her an impatient glance.

"Who is this man?" Seth questioned, the look in his eyes almost frightening. Anger darkened his face. He dropped his hand to his side, and she noted how his fist was clenched until the huge knuckles turned white.

Claudia watched, stunned. He thinks I'm Cooper's wife. Placing a hand on his forearm, she implored, "Seth, let me explain."

He shook his arm free. "You don't need to say anything more. I understand. Do you do this kind of thing often? Is this how you get your thrills?"

For a moment Claudia was speechless, the muscles of her throat paralyzed with anger. "You don't understand. Cooper's my uncle."

"And I believe in Santa Claus," Seth returned sarcastically.

"I've warned you about men like this." Cooper began speaking to her at the same time, confusing her.

"Will you please be quiet!" she shouted at her uncle.

"There's no excuse for you to talk to me in such a tone," Cooper countered in a huff.

People were beginning to stare, but Claudia didn't care. "He really is my uncle." Desperately her eyes pleaded with Seth, hers asking for understanding and the chance to explain. His were dark, clouded and unreasonable.

"You don't want to hear, do you?"

"We definitely need to have a discussion, Claudia," Cooper interrupted again.

"You're right, I don't." Seth took a step away from her.

Claudia breathed in sharply, the rush of oxygen inhaled so quickly her lungs hurt. She bit into her lip as Seth turned and walked away. His stride was filled with purpose, as if he couldn't get away from her fast enough.

"You've really done it this time," she flared at her uncle.

"Really, Claudia," he said with a relieved look. "That type of man is most undesirable."

"That man—" she pointed at Seth's retreating figure "—is one of the most desirable men I've ever known," she cried, stalking away.

An hour later, Claudia was banging pans around in the kitchen. Ashley came through the front door and paused, watching her for a moment. "What's wrong?"

"Nothing," Claudia responded shortly.

"Oh, come on. I always know when you're upset because you bake something."

"That's so I can eat it."

Ashley scanned the ingredients that lined the counter. "Chocolate chip cookies," she murmured. "This must really be bad. Obviously you had another run-in with Cooper?"

"Right again," Claudia snapped.

"You don't want to talk about it?"

"That's a brilliant deduction." With unnecessary force she cracked two eggs against the mixing bowl.

"You want me to leave?"

Claudia paused, closing her eyes as the waves of impatience rippled over her. "Ashley, please."

"All right, all right. I'm leaving."

Soon the aroma of freshly baked cookies filled the apartment, though Claudia didn't notice. Almost automatically she lifted the cookies from the baking sheet and placed them on a wire rack to cool.

"I can't stand it anymore." Ashley stumbled into the kitchen dramatically. "If you don't want to talk, fine, but at least let me have a cookie."

Claudia sighed, placed four on a plate and set it on the kitchen table.

Ashley poured herself a tall glass of milk and sat down, her eyes following Claudia's movements. "Feel like talking now?" she asked several minutes later. There was a sympathetic tone in her voice that came from many years of friendship.

Ashley had been Claudia's only friend as a child. Ashley's mother had been Claud Masters's cook and housekeeper. The woman had brought her daughter with her when she came to work, to keep the lonely Claudia company, and the two girls had been best friends ever since.

"It's Seth," Claudia admitted and sighed, taking a chair opposite Ashley.

"Seth? Oh, the guy you met at the motel. What happened?"

"We ran into Cooper, and he had a fit of righteous indignation to see me with someone not wearing a business suit and silk tie. To complicate matters, Seth apparently thought Cooper and I were married, or at least divorced. He didn't wait for an explanation."

Ashley's look was thoughtful. "You really like him, don't you?"

Claudia worried the soft flesh of her bottom lip. "Yes," she said simply. "I like him very much."

"If he's so arrogant that he wouldn't wait for you to explain, then I'd say it was his loss," Ashley attempted to assure her.

"No." Claudia shook her head and lowered her gaze to the tabletop. "In this case, I think I'm the one to lose."

"I don't think I've ever heard you talk this way about a man...anyone. What makes him so special?"

Claudia's brow knit in concentration. "I'm not really sure. He's more attractive than any man I can remember, but I'm not talking about looks. Although I think most women would think he was attractive. He's a rare man." She paused to formulate her thoughts. "Strong and intelligent."

"You know all this and you've only seen him twice?" Ashley sounded shocked.

"No." Claudia hung her head, and the long auburn curls fell forward. "I sensed more than saw, and even then that's only skimming the surface. This man is deep."

"If he's so willing to jump to conclusions, I'd say it's his own fault—"

"Ashley, please," Claudia interrupted. "Don't. I know you're trying to make me feel better, but I'd appreciate it if you didn't."

"All right." Ashley was quiet for a long time. After

a while she took a chocolate chip cookie and handed it to Claudia.

With a weak smile, Claudia accepted the cookie. "Now, that's what I need."

They talked for a while, but it wasn't until Claudia entered the living room that she noticed Ashley's suitcase in front of the door.

"You're going away?"

"Oh, I almost forgot. I talked to Mom this morning, and she wants me home for a few days. Jeff and John have the flu and she needs someone there so she can go to work. I shouldn't be any more than a couple of days. You don't mind, do you?"

"Not at all," Claudia said with a smile. Although Ashley's family lived in the nearby suburb of Kent, Ashley lived with Claudia because it was easier for her to commute to school and back. But several times during the year she would move back home for a few days when her family needed her.

"You'll be all right, won't you?"

"Are you kidding?" Claudia joked. "The kitchen's full of cookies!"

Ashley laughed, but her large blue eyes contained a knowing look. "Don't be too hard on Cooper," she said and gave Claudia a small hug before she left.

What good would it do to be angry with her uncle? He was reacting the only way he knew how. Anger wouldn't help the situation.

The apartment felt large and lonely with Ashley gone. Claudia turned on the television and flipped through the channels, hoping to find something interesting, feeling guilty because she was ignoring schoolwork. Nothing. Good, she decided, and forced herself to hit the books. This quarter wasn't going to be easy, and the sooner she sharpened her study habits the better.

Two hours later she took a leisurely bath, dressed in a long purple velvet robe, curled up on the sofa and engrossed herself in a good book. Long ago she'd recognized that reading was her escape. When things were really bothering her, she'd plow through one mystery after another, not really caring about the characters or the plot so long as it was strong enough to distract her from her troubles.

The alarm rang at six and she stumbled out of bed, plugging in the coffeepot before stepping into the shower. As she rotated under the hot spray, her thoughts again drifted to Seth Lessinger. She felt some regrets. She would have liked to get to know him better. On Sunday she'd definitely have a talk with Cooper. She was twenty-two, old enough to choose who she wanted to date without his interference. It was bad enough being forced to endure a stilted dinner with him every Sunday afternoon.

She dressed in jeans, a plaid long-sleeved blouse and red sweater vest. Pouring herself a cup of coffee, she wondered how long she would have to force thoughts of Seth from her mind. The mystery novel had diverted her attention last night, but she couldn't live her life with her nose in a book. Today and tomorrow she would be busy with school, but it was Thursday and she wasn't looking forward to spending the evenings and weekend alone. She'd ask a friend at school if she'd like to go to a movie tonight.

She sat sipping from her mug at the kitchen table, her feet propped against the opposite chair, and read the morning paper. A quick look at her wristwatch and she placed the cup in the sink and hurried out the door for school.

Claudia pulled into the apartment parking lot later that afternoon. It seemed everyone had already made plans for this evening. Several of her friends were attending the Seahawk football game. Claudia loved football and decided to pop popcorn and stay at home and watch the game on television. She had no sooner let herself into the apartment and hung up her jacket when the doorbell rang.

The peephole in the door showed no one. It could be the neighbor's boy collecting for the jogathon. Claudia had sponsored the ten-year-old, who was trying to earn enough money for a soccer uniform. Todd had probably seen her pull into the parking lot. She opened the door and focused her gaze on the hallway.

"Claudia." Her name was breathed in surprise.

"Seth." Her heart tripped over itself.

"What are you doing here?" They both asked the question at the same time.

Claudia smiled. It was so good to see him, it didn't matter what the reason.

"I was looking for Ashley Robbins, the motel maid," he told her, the surprise leaving his eyes, to be replaced by a mocking glint.

"Ashley?" A pleasant warmth filled her. "Come in," she invited and closed the door after him. "Ashley's gone home for a few days to be with her parents. You don't know Ashley, do you?"

"No." One hand stroked the side of his beard. "But I was hoping she could tell me how to find you."

"We're roommates," Claudia explained unnecessarily. "You were looking for me? Why?"

Again Seth looked slightly ill at ease. "I wanted to apologize for yesterday. I could at least have stayed and listened to an explanation."

"Cooper is my uncle."

"I should have known that. It wasn't until later that I realized I'd behaved like an idiot," Seth said, his face tight and drawn. "If I hadn't reacted like a jealous fool, I would have realized you would never lead anyone on like that."

"I know what you thought." She paused and glanced away. "I know how it looked, how Cooper wanted it to look."

Seth ran a self-derisive hand over his face. "Your uncle." He chuckled. Wrapping his arms around her, he lifted her off the ground and swung her around. Hands resting on the hard muscles of his shoulders, Claudia threw back her head and laughed.

Soon the amusement died as their gazes met and held. Slowly Seth released her until her feet had securely settled on the carpet. With an infinite gentleness, his hand brushed her face, caressing her smooth skin. It was so beautiful, so sweet, that Claudia closed her eyes to the sensuous assault. Her fingers clung to his arms as he drew her into his embrace, and her lips trembled, anticipating his kiss.

Seth didn't disappoint either of them as his mouth

settled firmly over hers. His hand slid down her back, molding her against him, arching her upward to meet the demand of his kiss.

Claudia felt her limbs grow weak as she surrendered to the sensations swirling inside her. Her hands spread over his chest, but there was no resistance, only a rightness in the feel of his arms.

When he freed her mouth, his lips caressed the sensitive cord along the side of her neck.

"Does this mean you'll give me another chance?" He murmured the question, his voice faintly husky from the effects of the kiss.

"I'd say the prognosis is excellent," Claudia replied, her breathing still affected. "But I'd like to explain a few things."

She led the way into the kitchen, poured mugs of coffee and added sugar to his the way she'd seen him do. When she set his cup on the table, Seth reached for her hand and kissed her fingers.

"Your family has money?" he asked.

"Not me," she explained, "at least not yet. Cooper controls the purse strings for a little while yet. My father was Claud Masters; you may or may not have heard of him. He established a business supply corporation that has branch offices in five states. Dad died when I was in high school. Cooper is president of the company now, and my legal guardian." Her soft mouth quirked to one side. "He takes his responsibility seriously. I apologize if he offended you yesterday."

Humor glinted briefly in his expression. "The only thing that could possibly offend me is if you were married." He laughed and Claudia stared at him curiously. "I'll never wear five-hundred-dollar business suits. You understand that?"

Nodding, she smiled. "I can't imagine you in a suit at all."

"Oh, I've been known to wear one, but I hate it."

Again, Claudia smiled.

"Do you hate having money?" Seth was regarding her steadily, his wide brow creased.

"No," she replied honestly. "I can't say I dislike money when I need it. What I hate is being different from others, like Ashley and you. I have a hard time trusting people. I'm never really sure they like me. I find myself looking at a relationship with a jaundiced eye, wondering what the other person is expecting to receive from my friendship." She lowered her gaze, her fingers circling the top of the mug. "My father was the same way. Consequently he closed himself off from the world. I was brought up in a protected environment. I fought tooth and nail to convince Cooper I should attend the University of Washington. He wanted to send me to study at a private university in Switzerland."

"I'm glad you're here."

Claudia watched as Seth clenched and unclenched his hands.

"Do you think the reason I came back is because you obviously have money?" he asked.

Something in his voice conveyed the seriousness of the question. "No, I don't think you're the type of person to be impressed by wealth. Just knowing you this little while, I believe if you wanted money, you'd have it. You're that type of man.'' Having stated her feelings, Claudia fell silent.

''God gives the very best.'' The throaty whisper was barely discernible, and Claudia glanced up, her blue eyes questioning.

''Pardon?''

Seth took her hand and carried it to his lips. The coarse hairs of his beard prickled her fingertips. ''Nothing,'' he murmured. ''I'll explain it to you later.''

''I was going to fix myself a sandwich. Would you like one?'' she offered. ''I guess I'm like a little kid coming home from school, needing my afternoon snack.'' Claudia had skipped lunch and suddenly realized she was hungry.

''I'd like that. You don't need to ask, I'm always hungry. Let me help,'' Seth volunteered. ''Believe it or not, I'm a darn good cook.''

''You can slice the cheese if you like.'' She flashed him a happy smile.

''I hope you don't have any plans for the evening,'' he said, easing a knife through the slab of cheese. ''I've got tickets for the football game. The Seahawks are playing tonight and I...'' He paused, his look brooding, disconcerted.

''What's wrong?''

Seth sighed, walked to the other side of the small kitchen and stuck his huge hands inside his pants pockets. ''Football isn't much of a woman's sport, is it?''

''What makes you say that?'' Claudia loved football.

''I mean...'' He looked around uneasily. ''You

don't have to go. It's not that important. I know that someone like you isn't—''

Claudia didn't give him the chance to finish. ''Someone like me,'' she repeated, ''would love going to that game more than anything else.'' Her eyes were smiling into his.

Amusement dominated his face as he slid his arms around her waist. One hand toyed with a strand of her hair. ''We'll eat a sandwich first, then grab something for dinner after the game. All right, Red?'' He said the name as if it was an endearment. ''You don't mind if I call you that, do you?''

''Only you,'' she murmured just before his mouth claimed hers. ''Only you.''

The day was wonderful. They spent a good portion of the afternoon talking, almost nonstop for two hours. Claudia, who normally didn't drink more than a cup or two of coffee, shared two pots with Seth. She told him things she had never shared with anyone: her feelings during her father's short illness and after his death; the ache, the void in her life afterward; and how the loss and the sadness had led her to Christ. She told him about her lifelong friendship with Ashley, the mother she had never known, medical school and her struggle for acceptance. There didn't seem to be anything she couldn't discuss with Seth.

In return he talked about his oil business, life in Nome and his own faith.

Before they knew it, the afternoon was gone. Claudia hurried to freshen up, but took the time to add a light perfume at her pulse points. Running a comb through the unruly curls that framed her face, she tied back the curls at the base of her neck with a silk scarf. Seth was waiting for her in the living room. Checking her appearance one last time, she noted the happy sparkle in her eyes and paused to murmur a special thank-you that God had sent Seth back into her life.

Seth helped her into her jacket. A rough hand ran lovingly up and down her arm as he brought her even closer to his side.

"I don't know when I've enjoyed an afternoon more," he told her. "Thank you."

"I should be the one to thank you, Seth." She avoided eye contact, afraid how much her look would reveal.

"I knew the minute I saw you that you were someone very special. I didn't realize until today how right my hunch was." Seth looked down at her gently. "It wasn't so long ago that I believed Christians were a bunch of do-gooders. Not long ago I thought religion was for the weak-minded. But I didn't know people like you. Now I wonder how I managed to live my life without Christ."

A hand tugged Seth's as Claudia excitedly walked up the cement ramp of the Kingdome. "The game's about to start." They'd parked on the street, walking the few blocks to the stadium, hurrying up First Avenue. The traffic was so heavy that they were a few minutes late. The Seahawks were playing nationally televised games Monday nights, but this was Thursday. Claudia never hoped to understand the network's reasoning.

"I love football," she said, her voice unnaturally high with enthusiasm.

"Look at all these people." Seth stopped and looked around him in amazement.

"Seth," she groaned. "I don't want to miss the kickoff."

Because the football game was being televised back East, the kickoff time was slated for five o'clock Pacific time. More than sixty thousand fans filled the Kingdome to capacity. Seahawk fever ran high and the entire stadium was on its feet for the kickoff. In the beginning, Claudia applauded politely so she wouldn't embarrass Seth with her enthusiasm. But when it came to her favorite sport, no one could accuse her of being phlegmatic. Within minutes she was totally involved with the action of the players on the field. She'd cheer wildly, then shout at the officials in protest.

Seth's reaction was much more subdued, and several times when Claudia complained to him about a certain play or the refereeing, she found that Seth seemed to be watching her more closely than the game.

There was something about football which allowed her to be herself, something which broke down that natural reserve about her. With her school schedule, she couldn't take the time to attend the games. But if at all possible she watched them on TV, jumping on the furniture in exaltation, or pounding the carpet in despair. Most of her classmates wouldn't have believed it was the same girl. At school she was as serious as a schoolmarm, since she still felt the need to prove herself to her classmates. Although she had won respect from most of the other students, some still believed the only reason she had been accepted was her name and her sex.

"Touchdown!" Her arms flew into the air and she leaped to her feet.

For the first time since the game had started, Seth showed as much emotion as Claudia. Lifting her high, he held her tight against him. Her hands framed his face and it seemed the most natural thing in the world, staring into the dark, hungry eyes, to press her lips to his. Immediately Seth deepened the kiss, wrapping his arms around her, lifting her higher off the ground.

The cheering died to an excited chatter before either was aware of the crowd.

"We have an audience," Seth murmured huskily in her ear.

"It's just as well, don't you think?" Her face was flushed lightly. Claudia had known almost from the beginning that the attraction between them was stronger than anything she had experienced with another man. Seth seemed to have recognized this as well. The effect they had on each other was strong and disturbing. Seth had kissed her only three times, and already they were aware of how easy it would be to let their attraction rage out of control. It was exciting, but in another sense it was frightening.

After the game they stopped for hamburgers. When Seth had finished his meal, he returned to the counter and bought them each an ice cream sundae.

"When you come to Alaska, I'll have my Inuit friends make you some of their ice cream," he said. His eyes flashed her a look of amusement.

Claudia's stomach tightened. *When* she came to

Alaska? She hadn't stopped to think about ever visiting America's last frontier. From the beginning she had known that Seth would be in Seattle only a few days. She had known and accepted that as best she could.

Deciding it was best to ignore the comment, she cocked her head to one side. "Okay, I'll play your little game. What's Inuit ice cream?"

"Berries, snow and rancid seal oil."

"Well, at least it's organic."

Seth chuckled. "It's that all right."

Claudia twisted the red plastic spoon, making circles in the soft ice cream. She avoided Seth's gaze, just as she had been eluding facing the inevitable.

Gathering her resolve, she raised her face, her eyes meeting his. "When will you be returning to Nome?"

Seth pushed his dessert aside, his hand reaching for hers. "My flight's booked for tomorrow afternoon."

# Chapter Three

The muscles of Claudia's throat constricted. "Tomorrow," she repeated, knowing she sounded like a parrot. Lowering her gaze, she continued, "That doesn't leave us much time, does it?" She'd thought she was prepared. Hadn't she known from the beginning that Seth would only be in Seattle for a few days?

Lifting her eyes to his watchful gaze, she offered him a weak smile. "I know this sounds selfish, but I don't want you to go."

"Then I won't," he announced casually.

Claudia's head shot up. "What do you mean?"

The full force of his magnetic eyes was resting on her. "I mean I'll stay a few more days."

Claudia's heart seemed to burst into song. "Over the weekend?" Eyes as blue as the Caribbean Sea implored him. "My only obligation is dinner Sunday with Cooper, but you could come. In fact, I'd like it if you did. My uncle will probably bore you to tears, but I'd like you to get to know each other. Won't you stay that long?'' She tilted her head questioningly, hopefully.

Seth chuckled. Claudia loved the sound of his laugh. The loud, robust sound seemed to roll from deep within his chest. She'd watched him during the football game and couldn't help laughing with him.

''Will you?'' She repeated the question.

''I have the feeling your uncle isn't going to welcome me with open arms.''

''No.'' She smiled beguilingly. ''But I will.''

The restaurant seemed to go still, quiet. Seth's gaze was penetrating, his voice slightly husky. ''Then I'll stay, but no longer than Monday.''

''Okay.'' She was more than glad, she was jubilant. There hadn't been time to question this magnetic attraction that had captured them, and deep down Claudia didn't want to investigate her feelings, even though this was all happening too fast.

Seth's arm slipped around her waist as they walked to the car. He held open the door for her and waited until she was seated. Unconsciously her fingers smoothed the plush sheepskin cushions, their texture smooth against the tips of her fingers. The vehicle had surprised her. Seth didn't fit the luxury-car image.

''This thing is a bit much, isn't it?'' His gaze briefly scanned the interior. The limousine was fitted with every convenience, from the automatic sunroof to a stereo system that must have cost thousands. Such opulence was an embarrassment to him. Claudia had seen her share of luxury cars, but this one surprised even her.

''Did you rent it?'' she felt obliged to ask.

"Heavens, no! This is all part of the sisters' efforts to get me to sign the contract."

"The sisters?"

"That's a slang expression for the major oil conglomerates. They seem to feel the need to impress me. My original hotel reservation was at the Four Seasons, in a suite that was three hundred dollars a night. I wouldn't put up with that, and found my own place. But I couldn't refuse the car without offending some important people."

"We all get caught in that sometimes."

Seth agreed with a short, preoccupied nod. Although the football game had finished over an hour before, the downtown traffic was at a standstill. Cautiously Seth eased the limousine into the heavy flow of bumper-to-bumper traffic.

While they were caught in the snarl of impatient drivers, Claudia watched Seth's strong profile. Several times his mouth tightened and he shook his head in disgust.

"I'm sorry, Seth," she said solemnly and smiled lamely when he glanced at her.

He arched thick brows. "You're sorry? Why?"

"The traffic. I should have known to wait another hour, until things had thinned out a bit more."

"It's not your fault." His enormous hand squeezed hers reassuringly.

"Don't you have traffic jams in Nome?" she asked, partly to keep the conversation flowing, and partly to counteract the crazy reaction her heart seemed to have every time he touched her.

"Traffic jams in Nome?" He smiled. "Red, Nome's

population is barely three thousand. On certain days my car is the only one on the road."

Claudia's eyes narrowed suspiciously. "You're teasing? I thought Nome was a major Alaskan city."

He returned both hands to the wheel and Claudia's heartbeat relaxed. "The population of the entire state is only 400,000, a mere fraction of Washington's four million." A smile softened the rugged features. "Anchorage is the largest city in Alaska, with about 200,000 residents."

"Washington's the closest state to Alaska, and even I didn't know that. I must have been daydreaming during geography class in the fifth grade."

An impatient motorist honked and Seth pulled forward onto the freeway entrance ramp. The traffic remained heavy but was moving at a steady pace.

"I couldn't live like this," he said and expelled his breath forcefully. "Too many people, too many buildings and," he added with a wry grin, "too many cars."

"Don't worry. You won't have to put up with it much longer," she countered with a smile.

Seth scowled thoughtfully and didn't reply.

He parked the car in the lot outside her apartment building and refused the invitation to come in for coffee. "I have a meeting in the morning that shouldn't go any longer than noon. Can I see you then?"

She nodded, pleased. "Of course." Every minute left would be treasured. "Shall I phone Cooper and tell him you're coming for dinner Sunday?"

"He won't mind?" Seth queried.

"Oh, I'm sure he will, but if he objects too strongly, we'll have our own dinner."

His hand reached out to caress the delicate curve of her cheek and entwine with the auburn curls along the nape of her neck. ''Would it be considered bad manners to hope he objects strenuously?'' he asked.

''Cooper's not so bad.'' Claudia felt as if she should at least make the effort to explain her uncle. ''I don't think he means to come off so pompous, he just doesn't know how else to act. What he needs is a woman to love.'' She smiled inwardly. ''I can just hear him cough and sputter if I were to tell him that.''

''I need a woman to love,'' Seth whispered as his mouth found hers. The kiss was deep and intense, as if to convince her of the truth of his words.

Claudia wound her arms around his neck, surrendering to the mastery of his kiss. He's serious, her mind repeated, dead serious. Not that it mattered, not when she was in his arms. The whole world seemed right when Seth was holding her like this. He covered her neck and the hollow of her throat with light, tiny kisses. Claudia tilted her head at an angle reveling in the warm feel of his lips against the creamy smoothness of her skin. A shudder of desire ran through her, and she bit into her bottom lip to conceal the effect he had on her senses.

Taking in a deep breath, Seth straightened. ''Let's get you inside before this gets out of hand.'' His voice sounded raw and slightly uneven.

He kissed her again outside her apartment door, but this one lacked the ardor of a few minutes earlier. ''I'll see you about noon tomorrow.''

With a trembling smile she nodded.

''Don't look at me like that,'' he groaned. His strong

hands stroked the length of her arms as he edged her body closer. "It's difficult enough to say good night."

Standing on tiptoe, she lightly brushed her mouth over his.

"Claudia," he growled in warning.

She placed her fingertips over her moist lips, then over his, to share the mock kiss with him.

Seth closed his eyes as if waging some deep inner battle, then covered her fingers with his own.

"Good night," she whispered, glorying in the way he reacted to her.

"I'll see you tomorrow."

"Tomorrow," she repeated dreamily.

Dressed in her pajamas and housecoat, Claudia sat on top of her bed an hour later, reading her Bible. Her concentration drifted to the events of the past week and all the foreign emotions she had encountered. This thing with Seth was happening too fast, far too fast. No man had ever created such an intensity of emotion within her. No man had made her feel the things he did. Love, real love, didn't happen like this. The timing was all wrong. She couldn't fall in love—not now. Not with a man who was only going to be in Seattle for a few days. But why had God sent Seth into her life when it would be so easy to fall in love with him? Was it a test? A lesson in faith? She was going to be a doctor. The Lord had led her to that decision, and there wasn't anything in her life she was more sure of. Falling in love with Seth Lessinger could ruin that. Still troubled, she turned off the light and attempted to sleep.

* * *

Claudia was ready at noon, but for what she wasn't sure. Dressed casually in jeans and a sweater, she thought she might suggest a drive to Snoqualmie Falls. And if Seth felt ambitious, maybe a hike around Mount Si. Claudia didn't have the time to do much hiking herself, but she enjoyed the outdoors whenever possible. The mental picture of idly strolling with Seth, appreciating the beautiful world God had given, was an appealing one. Doing anything with Seth was appealing.

When he hadn't shown by one, Claudia became worried. Every minute seemed interminable, and she glanced at her watch repeatedly. When the phone rang at one-thirty, she grabbed the receiver after only one chime.

"Hello," she said anxiously.

"Red?" Seth asked.

"Yes, it's me." He didn't sound right; he seemed tired, impatient.

"I've been held up here. There's not much chance of my getting out of this meeting until late afternoon."

"Oh." She tried to hide the disappointment in her voice.

"I know, honey, I feel the same way." The depth of his tone relayed his own frustration. "I'll make it up to you tonight. Can you be ready around seven for dinner? Wear something fancy."

"Sure." She forced a cheerful note in her voice. "I'll see you then. Take care."

"I've got to get back inside. If you happen to think of me, say a prayer. I want this business over so we can enjoy what's left of our time."

If she thought of him? Claudia nearly laughed out loud. "I will," she promised, and did.

Cooper phoned about ten minutes later. "You left a message for me to call?" he began with a question.

Claudia half suspected Cooper wanted her to apologize for the little scene downtown with Seth. "Yes," she replied evenly. "I'm inviting a guest for dinner Sunday."

"Who?" he asked, and Claudia could almost picture him bracing himself because he knew the answer.

"Seth Lessinger. You met him already once this week."

The line seemed to crackle with a lengthy silence. "As you wish," he said tightly.

A mental picture formed of Cooper writing down Seth's name. Undoubtedly, before Sunday, her uncle would know everything there was about Seth, from his birth weight to his high school grade point average.

"We'll see you then."

"Claudia," Cooper said and hesitated. Her uncle didn't often hesitate. Usually he knew his mind and wasn't afraid to speak it. "You're not serious about this—" he searched for the right word "—man, are you?"

"Why?" It felt good to turn the tables, answering her cagey uncle with a question of her own. Why should he be so concerned? She was twenty-two, old enough to do anything she pleased.

Cooper allowed an unprecedented second pause. "No reason. I'll see you Sunday."

Thoughtfully Claudia replaced the receiver and released her breath in a slow sigh. Cooper sounded different, on edge, not like his normal self at all. Her mouth quivered with a suppressed smile. Cooper was worried; she'd heard the concern in his voice. For the first time since he'd been appointed her guardian, he had showed some paternal feelings toward her. The smile grew. Cooper wasn't such a bad fellow after all.

Scanning the contents of her closet later that afternoon, Claudia chose a black lace dress she had bought on impulse the winter before. This wasn't the type of dress she'd wear to church, although it wasn't low-cut or revealing. Made of Cluny lace, the one-piece outfit had a three-tiered skirt. Claudia had seen it displayed in an exclusive boutique, but was angry with herself at the time for buying something so extravagant. She was unlikely to find a reason to wear a dress this elegant, but she'd loved it and couldn't resist. Even Ashley had been surprised when Claudia had showed it to her. No one could deny that it was a beautiful, romantic dress.

The auburn curls were formed into a loose chignon at the top of her head, with tiny ringlets falling at the sides of her face. The diamond earrings had been her mother's, and Claudia had worn them only a couple of times. Seth had said fancy, he was going to get fancy!

He arrived promptly at seven. One look at Claudia and his eyes showed surprise, then astonishment, then something else she couldn't decipher.

Slowly his gaze traveled over her face and figure, openly admiring the curved hips and slender legs.

"Wow."

"Wow yourself," she returned, equally impressed.

Claudia saw him as a virile and intriguing male without the rich dark wool suit. But now he was compelling and so attractive she could hardly take her eyes off him.

"Turn around, I want to look at you," he requested, his attention centered on her. His voice sounded ragged, as if seeing her had stolen away his breath.

Claudia did as he asked, slowly twirling around. "Now you."

"Me?" He looked stunned.

"You." She laughed, her hands directing his movements. Self-consciously he turned, his movements abrupt and awkward. "Where are we going?"

"The Space Needle." He took the white coat out of her hands and held it open for her. Claudia turned and slid her arm into the satin-lined sleeves. Seth guided it over her shoulders, and his hands lingered there as he brought her back against him. She heard him inhale sharply before kissing the gentle slope of her neck.

"Let's go," he murmured, "while I'm able to resist other temptations."

Seth parked outside the Seattle Center and they walked hand in hand toward the city's most famous landmark.

"Next summer we'll go to the Food Circus," she mentioned casually. If he could say things that spoke of her visiting Alaska, she could toss out the same things at him.

Seth didn't miss a step, but his hand tightened over hers. "Why next summer? Why not now?"

"Because you've promised me dinner on top of the city, and I'm not about to let you out of that. But anyone visiting Seattle shouldn't miss the Food Circus. A multitude of booths serve exotic dishes from all over the world. The worst part is having to make a decision. When Ashley and I go there, we each buy something different and divide it. That way we both get a taste of something new.'' She stopped talking and smiled. ''I'm chattering, aren't I?''

''A little.'' She could hear the amusement in his voice.

The outside elevators whisked them up the Space Needle to the observation deck 607 feet above the ground. The night was glorious; brilliant lights lit up the world below. Seth stood behind her, his arms looped over her shoulders, pressing her close.

''I think my favorite time to see this view is at night. I love watching all those lights. I've never stopped to wonder why the night lights enthrall me the way they do. But I think it's probably because Jesus told us we were the light of the world, and from up here I can see how much one tiny light can illuminate.''

''I hadn't thought of it like that,'' Seth murmured close to her ear. ''But you have to remember I'm a new Christian. There are a lot of things I haven't discovered yet.''

''That's a wonderful part, too.''

''How do you mean?''

She shrugged lightly. ''God doesn't throw all this knowledge and insight at us at once. He lets us digest it little by little, as we're able.''

''Just as any loving father would do,'' Seth said quietly.

They stood for several minutes until a chill ran over Claudia's arms.

"Cold?" he questioned.

"Only a little. It's so lovely out here, I don't want to leave."

"It's beautiful all right, but it's more the woman I'm with than the scenery."

"Thank you," Claudia murmured, pleased by his words.

Seth was still behind her. "You're blushing." The pressure of his arms turned her around. "I don't believe it—you're blushing."

Embarrassed, Claudia looked away. "Men don't usually say those things to me."

"Why not? You're a beautiful woman. By now you should have heard those words a thousand times over."

"Not really." The color was creeping up her neck. "That's the floating bridge over there." She pointed into the distance, attempting to change the subject. "It's the largest concrete pontoon bridge in the world. It connects Mercer Island and Seattle."

"Claudia," Seth murmured, his voice dipping slightly, "you are a delight. If we weren't out here with the whole city looking on, I'd take you in my arms and kiss you senseless."

"Promises, promises," she teased and hurried inside before he could make good his words.

They ate a leisurely meal and talked over coffee so long that Claudia looked around guiltily. Friday night was one of the busiest nights for the restaurant business.

"I'll make us another cup at my place," she volunteered.

Seth didn't argue.

The aroma of fresh-brewed coffee filled the apartment. Claudia poured them each a cup and carried it into the living room.

Seth sat on the long, green couch, flipping through the pages of one of the medical journals Claudia had stacked on the end table.

"Are you planning on specializing?"

She nodded. "Probably pediatrics."

His dark brown eyes became intent. "Do you enjoy children that much, Red?"

"Oh, yes," she said fervently. "Maybe it's because I was an only child and never got my fill. I can remember lining up my dolls and playing house."

"I thought every little girl did that?"

"At sixteen?" she teased, then laughed at the expression on his masculine face. "The last two summers I've worked part-time in a day care center to see how I'd interact with children. The experience convinced me to go into pediatrics. But that's a long ways down the road. I'm only a first-year medical student."

When they'd finished the coffee, she carried their cups to the kitchen sink. Seth followed her, slipping his hands around her waist. All her senses reacted to his touch.

"Can I see you in the morning?"

She nodded, afraid her voice would tremble if she spoke. His finger traced the line of her cheek and Claudia held her breath, bracing herself as it trailed over her soft lips. Instinctively her arms reached for him, gliding up his chest and over the corded muscles of his shoulders. The steel fibers flexed beneath her exploring fingers. He rasped her name before his mouth hungrily descended on hers. A heady excitement engulfed her. Never had there been a time in her life when she was more gloriously happy. The kiss was searing, turbulent, wrenching her heart and touching her soul.

"Red?" His hold relaxed and with infinite care he studied her soft, yielding eyes, filled with the depth of her emotions. "Oh, Red?" He inhaled several sharp breaths and pressed his forehead to hers. "Don't tempt me like this." The words were a plea that seemed to come deep from within him.

"You're doing the same thing to me," she whispered softly, having trouble with her own breathing.

"We should stop now."

"I know," she agreed, but neither pulled away from the other.

How could she think reasonable thoughts when he was so close? A violent eruption of Mount St. Helens couldn't compare with the ferocity of her emotions.

Slowly she pulled back, easing herself from his arms.

He dropped his hands limply to his sides. "We have to be careful, Red. My desire for you is strong, but I want us to be good. I don't think I could ever forgive myself if I were to lead us into sin."

"Oh, Seth," she whispered, her blue eyes shimmering with tears. "It's not all you. I'm feeling these things just as strongly. Maybe it's not such a good idea for us to be alone anymore."

''No.'' His husky voice rumbled with turmoil. A tortured silence followed. He paced the floor, raking his fingers through his thick brown hair. ''It's selfish, I know, but there's so little time left. We'll be careful and help one another. It won't be much longer that we'll be able...'' He let the rest of the sentence fade.

Not much longer, her mind repeated.

He picked up the jacket he'd discarded over the back of a chair and held out a hand to her. ''Walk me to the door.''

Linking her fingers with his, she did as he asked. He paused at the door, his hand on the knob. ''Good night.''

''Good night,'' she responded with a weak smile.

He bent downward and gently brushed her lips. Although the contact was light, almost teasing, Claudia's response was immediate. She yearned for the feel of his arms again and felt painfully empty when he turned away and closed the door behind him.

They spent almost every minute of Saturday together, their day full and varied. In the morning Seth drove them to Snoqualmie Falls and they ate a picnic lunch, then took a leisurely stroll along the trails leading to the water. Later in the day they visited the Seattle Aquarium on the waterfront and ate a dinner of fresh fish and crusty, deep-fried potatoes.

Cooper phoned to tell her Seth was welcome for Sunday dinner, a gesture that surprised her.

''He's a good man,'' Cooper announced. ''I've been hearing quite a few impressive things about your lumberjack.''

"Oilman," she corrected, amused.

"I'll apologize for my behavior the other day," Cooper continued.

"I'm sure Seth understands," she assured him.

Six days. She had known Seth for a total of six days, and yet it felt like a lifetime. Her feelings for him were well defined now. Other than a few cases of puppy love, she had never experienced the deep womanly yearnings Seth created within her. The attraction was sometimes so strong that it shocked them. Aware of their physical weaknesses, they'd carefully avoided situations that would tempt them both. Now, although Seth touched her often and made excuses to caress her, he was cautious, and their kisses were never allowed to deepen into the passion they'd shared the night they dined at the Space Needle.

On Sunday morning Claudia woke early, with the eagerness of a child. The past week had been her happiest since before her father's death.

Claudia and Seth attended the early morning church service together, and she introduced him to her Christian family. Her heart filled with emotion as Seth sat beside her in the wooden pew. There could be nothing more she would ask in a man than a deep, committed faith in the Lord.

Afterward they went back to her apartment. The table was set with her best dishes and linen. Now she set out fresh-squeezed orange juice and delicate butter croissants on china plates. A single candle and dried-flower centerpiece decorated the table.

Claudia had chosen a pink dress and piled her hair high upon her head, with tiny curls falling free to frame her face. Although Seth would be leaving tomorrow, she didn't want to face that now, and quickly dismissed the thought. Today was special, their last day together, and she refused to let the reality of a long separation trouble her.

"I hope you're up to my cooking," she said to him as she tied the apron around her waist and took the special egg casserole from the oven.

Seth stood framed in the doorway, handsome and vital. He still wore a dark wool suit but held the restraining tie in one hand as if he didn't want the confining material around his neck any longer than absolutely necessary.

Just having him this close made all her senses pulsate with happiness, and a warm glow stole over her.

"You don't need to worry. My stomach can handle just about anything," he teased gently. He studied her for a moment. "I can't call you Red in a dress like that." He came to her and kissed her lightly. Claudia sighed at the sweetness of his caress.

"I hope I don't have to wait much longer; I'm starved."

"You're always hungry," she admonished. "Besides, how can you think about food when I'm here to tempt you?"

"It's more difficult than you know," he said with a smile. "Can I do anything?"

Claudia answered him with a short shake of her head.

"Well, are you going to feed me or not?" His roguish smile revealed stark masculinity.

The special baked egg recipe was one Ashley's

mother had given her. Claudia was pleased when Seth asked for seconds.

''Here.'' Seth took a small package from his coat pocket. ''This thing has been burning a hole in my pocket all morning. Open it now.''

Claudia took the package and shook it, holding it close to her ear. ''For me?'' she asked, her eyes sparkling with excitement.

''I brought it with me from Nome.''

From Nome? her mind questioned. Carefully she untied the bow and removed the red foil paper, revealing a black velvet jeweler's box.

''Before you open it, I want to explain something.'' He leaned forward, resting his elbows on the table. ''For a long time I've been married to my job, building my company. It wasn't until...'' He hesitated. ''I won't go into the reason, but I decided I wanted a wife. Whenever I needed anything in the past, I simply went out and bought it. I didn't think finding a good woman would work like that. It had to be someone special, someone I could love and respect, someone who shared my faith. The more I thought about the complexities of finding a wife, the more I realized how difficult it would be.''

''Seth—''

''No, let me explain,'' he continued, reaching for her hand. He gripped it hard, his gaze studying her intently. ''I was reading my Bible one night and came across the story of Abraham sending a servant to find a wife for Isaac. Do you remember the story?''

Claudia nodded, color draining from her features. ''Seth, please—''

"There's more; bear with me." He raised her hand to his lips and very gently kissed her fingers. "If you remember, the servant did as Abraham bid and traveled to the land of his master's family. But he was uncertain, the weight of his responsibility bore heavily upon him. So the servant prayed, asking God to give him a sign. God answered that prayer and showed the servant that Rebekah was the right woman for Isaac. Scripture says how much Isaac loved his wife, and how she comforted him after the death of his mother, Sarah."

"Seth, please, I know what you're going to say—"

"Be patient, my love," he interrupted her again. "After reading that account, I decided to trust the Lord to give me a wife. I was also traveling to the land of my family. Both my mother and father originally came from Washington State. I prayed about it. I also purchased the engagement ring before I left Nome. And I, too, asked God for a sign. I was beginning to lose hope; I'd already been here several days before you placed the card with the verse in the mirror. You can't imagine how excited I was when I found it."

Claudia swallowed tightly, recalling his telling her that the message had meant more to him than she'd ever know. She wanted to stop him, but the lump in her throat had grown so large that speaking was impossible.

"I want you to come back to Nome with me tomorrow, Red. We can be married a few days later."

# Chapter Four

Claudia's eyes widened with incredulous disbelief. ''Married in a few days?'' she repeated. ''But, Seth, we've only been together six days! We can't—''

''Sure we can,'' he countered, his eyes serious. ''I knew even before I found the Bible verse in the mirror that it was you. Do you remember how you bumped into me that first day in the outside corridor?'' Although he asked the question, he didn't wait for the answer. ''I was stunned. Didn't you notice how my eyes followed you? Something came over me right then. I had to force myself not to run and stop you. At the time I assumed I was physically reacting to a beautiful woman. But once I found the Bible verse on the mirror, I knew.''

''What about school?'' Somehow the words made it past the large knot constricting her throat.

A troubled look pinched his mouth. ''I've done a lot of thinking about that, it's weighed heavily on me. I know how much getting your degree means to you.''

He caught her hand and gently kissed the palm. ''Someday, Red, we'll be able to move to Anchorage and you can finish your schooling. I promise you that.''

Taking her hand from his, Claudia closed the jeweler's box. The clicking sound seemed to be magnified a thousand times, a cacophony of sound echoing around the room.

''Seth, we've only known one another a short time. So much more goes into building the foundation for a relationship that will support a marriage. It takes more than a few days.''

''Rebekah didn't even meet Isaac, she responded in faith, going with the servant to a faraway land to a man she had never seen. Yet she went,'' Seth argued.

''You're being unfair,'' Claudia said as she stood and walked to the other side of the room. Her heart was pounding so hard she could feel the blood pulsating through her veins. ''We live in the twentieth century, not biblical times. How do we know what Rebekah was feeling? Her father was probably the one who said she would go. More than likely, Rebekah didn't have any choice in the matter.''

''You don't know that,'' Seth said.

''You don't either,'' she shot back. ''We hardly know each other.''

''You keep saying that! What more do you need to know?''

Claudia gestured weakly with her hands. ''Everything.''

''Come on, Red. You're overreacting. You know more about me than any other woman ever has. We've done nothing but talk every day. I'm thirty-six, own and operate the Arctic Barge Company, wear size thirteen shoes, like ketchup on my fried eggs and peanut butter on my pancakes. My tastes are simple, my needs few. I tend to be impatient, but God and I are working on that. Usually I don't anger quickly, but when I do, stay clear. After we're married, there will probably be several things we'll need to discuss, but nothing we shouldn't be able to settle."

"Seth, I—"

"Let me see," he continued undaunted. "Did I leave anything out?" He paused again. "Oh yes. The most important part is that I love you, Claudia Masters."

The sincerity with which he said the words trapped the oxygen in her lungs, leaving her speechless.

"This is the point where you're supposed to say, 'And I love you, Seth.'" He rose, coming to stand directly in front of her. His hands cupped her shoulders as his gaze fell lovingly upon her. "Now repeat after me: *I...love...you.*"

Claudia couldn't. She tried to say something, but nothing would come. "I can't." She choked out the words. "It's unfair to ask me to give up everything I've worked so hard for. I'm sorry, Seth, really sorry."

"Claudia!" His mouth was strained and tight; there was no disguising the bitter disappointment in his voice. "Don't say no, not yet. Think about it. I'm not leaving until tomorrow morning."

"Tomorrow morning." She closed her eyes. "I'm supposed to know by then?"

"You should know now," he whispered.

"But I don't," she snapped. "You say that God gave you a sign that I was to be the wife He had chosen for you. Don't you find it the least bit suspicious that God would say something to you and *nothing* to me?"

"Rebekah didn't receive the sign," he explained rationally. "The servant was the one. She followed in faith."

"You're comparing two entirely different times and situations."

"What about the verse you stuck in the mirror. Haven't you ever wondered about that? You told me you'd never done anything like that before."

"But..."

"You have no argument, Red."

"I most certainly do."

"Can you honestly say you don't feel the electricity between us?"

How could she? "I can't deny it, but it doesn't change anything."

Seth smoothed a coppery curl from her forehead, his touch gentle, his eyes imploring. "Of course it does. I think that once you come to Nome you'll understand."

"I'm not going to Nome," she reiterated forcefully. "If you want to marry me, then you'll have to move to Seattle. I won't give up my dreams because of a six-day courtship and the whim that you received a sign from God."

Seth looked shocked for a moment, but recovered quickly. "I can't move to Seattle. My business, my home, my whole life are in Nome."

"But don't you understand that's exactly what you're asking me to do? My schooling, my home, my friends are in Seattle."

Seth glanced uncomfortably around the room, then directed his gaze back to her. His dark eyes were filled with such deep emotion, it nearly took Claudia's breath away. Tears shimmered in her eyes, and his tall, masculine figure blurred as the moisture welled.

Gently Seth took her in his arms, holding her head to his shoulder. His jacket felt smooth and comforting against her cheek. Taking in a quivering breath, she tried to stop the tears before they ruined her makeup.

Tenderly his hand caressed her neck and she could feel his breath against her hair. "Red, I'm sorry," he whispered with such love that fresh tears weaved a crooked course down her wan cheek. "I've known all this from the first day. It's unfair to spring it on you at the last minute. I know it must sound crazy to you now. But think about what I've said. And remember that I love you, nothing's going to change that. Now dry your eyes and we'll visit your uncle; I promise not to mention it again today." He kissed the top of her head and gently pulled away.

"Here." She handed him the jeweler's box.

"No." He shook his head. "I want you to keep the ring. You may not feel like you want it now, but you will soon. I have to believe that, Red."

Her face twisted with pain. "I don't know that I should."

"Yes." Brief anger flared in his eyes. "Please."

Because she couldn't refuse without hurting him more, Claudia agreed with an abrupt shake of her head.

Since she didn't feel as if she could wear the ring, she placed the velvet box in a drawer. Her hand trembled when she pushed the drawer back into the dresser, but she put on a brave smile when she turned toward Seth.

To her dismay, his returning smile was just as weak.

Cooper knew something was wrong almost immediately. That surprised Claudia, who hadn't expected her uncle to be sensitive to her moods. But when he asked what was troubling her, she quickly denied that there was anything. Claudia couldn't expect Cooper to understand what was happening.

The two men eyed each other like wary dogs who had crossed paths unexpectedly. Cooper, for his part, was welcoming, but Seth was brooding and distant most of the day.

When they sat down to dinner, Seth smiled ruefully.

"What's wrong?" Claudia asked.

"Nothing," he said, shaking his head. "It's just this is the first time I've needed three spoons to eat one meal."

Cooper arched thick brows expressively, as if to say he didn't know how anyone could possibly do without three spoons for anything.

Claudia looked from one to the other, noting the differences. Two men from separate worlds. Although she found Cooper's attitudes and demeanor often boring and stringent, she was, after all, his own flesh and blood. If she were to marry Seth, give up everything that was important to her and move to Alaska, could she adjust to his way of life?

During the remainder of the afternoon, Claudia often found her gaze drawn to Seth. Cooper and Seth played a quiet game of chess in Cooper's den. Claudia sat opposite them, studying the two men.

Seth was the kind of man to thrive on challenges; he wasn't afraid of hardships. He was self-assured, and although she had never seen the ruthless side of his nature, Claudia didn't doubt that it existed. In the few days they had spent together she had been witness to the underlying thread of tenderness that ran through this man's heart. Seth thrived on hardships and challenges, but would she?

Resting her head against the velvet swivel rocker, she slowly lowered her gaze. The problem was she also knew that Seth was the type of man who loved intensely. His love hadn't been offered lightly; he wanted her forever. But most of all, he wanted her now—today. At thirty-six he had waited a long time to find a wife. His commitment was complete. He had looked almost disbelieving when she hadn't felt the same way.

Or did she? She couldn't deny that the attraction was powerful, almost overwhelming. But that had been physical, and there was so much more to love than the physical aspect. Spiritually they shared the same faith. To Claudia that was vital; she wouldn't share her life with a man who didn't believe as she did. But mentally they were miles apart. Each had goals and dreams that the other would never share. Seth seemed to believe medical school was a pastime, a hobby, with her. He had no comprehension of the years of hard work and study that had gotten her this far. The dream had been ingrained in her too long for her to relinquish it on the basis of a six-day courtship. And it wasn't only her dream, but one her beloved father had shared.

Seth hadn't understood any of this. Otherwise he wouldn't have asked her to give it all up without a question or thought. He believed that God had shown him she was to be his wife. If only life were that simple! Seth was a new Christian, eager, enthusiastic, but also a bit immature—not that she was a tower of wisdom and discernment. But Claudia would never have prayed anything so crazy. She was too down to earth, like Cooper. She hated to compare herself with her uncle, but in this instance it was justified.

Cooper's smile became faintly smug, and Claudia realized he was close to putting Seth in check, if not checkmate. Claudia didn't need to be told that Seth's mind was preoccupied with their conversation this morning and not on the chess game. Several times in the last hour he had lifted his gaze to hers. One look could reveal so much. Until that day, Claudia had never been aware how much Seth's eyes could say. He wanted her so much, more than he would ever tell. Guiltily her lashes fluttered downward; watching him was hurting them both too much.

He kissed her good night outside her apartment, thanking her for the day. A lump blocked her throat from thanking him for the beautiful solitaire diamond she would probably never wear.

"My flight's due to take off at seven," he said without looking at her.

"I'll be there," she whispered.

He held her then, so tight, that for a moment it was

impossible to breathe. She felt him shudder, and tears prickled her eyes as he whispered, ''I love you, Red.''

She couldn't say it; couldn't repeat the words he desperately longed to hear. She bit into her tongue to keep from sobbing. She longed to tell him how she felt, but the words wouldn't come. They stuck in her throat until it constricted painfully and felt raw. Why had God given her a man who could love her so completely, when she was so wary?

Claudia set the alarm for five. If Seth's flight took off at seven, then she should meet him at the airport at six. She'd volunteered to drive him there, but he declined the invitation. He would take a taxi, somehow she knew it. Meeting him at Sea-Tac International would be far easier for Seth than her driving him there.

Sleep didn't come easily, and when it did, her dreams were filled with questions. Although she searched everywhere, she couldn't find the answers.

Her blue eyes looked haunted and slightly red the next morning. Claudia tried to camouflage the effects of the restless night with cosmetics.

The morning was dark and drizzly as she climbed inside her compact and started the engine. The car heater soon took the bite out of early morning, and she pulled onto the street. With every mile her heart grew heavier. A prayer came automatically to her lips. She desperately wanted to do the right thing: right for Seth, right for her. She prayed that if her heavenly Father wanted her to marry Seth, then He would make the signs as clear for her as He'd apparently done for Seth. Did she lack faith?

''No,'' she answered her own question aloud. But

her heart seemed to respond with a distant ''yes'' that echoed through her ears.

She parked in the garage, pulled her purse strap over her shoulder and hurried along the concourse. ''I'm doing the right thing,'' she mentally repeated with each step. Her heels clicked against the marble floor, seeming to pound out the message—right thing, right thing, right thing.

After she'd passed through the metal detector and was free to join Seth, her pace quickened. She paused when she saw him and the dejected figure he made. Biting into her lip, she whispered a prayer, seeking strength and wisdom.

''Morning, Seth,'' she greeted him, forcing herself to smile.

His expression remained bland as he purposely looked away from her.

This was going to be more difficult than she imagined. The atmosphere was so tense and strained, Claudia couldn't tolerate it. ''You're angry, aren't you?''

''No,'' he responded dryly. ''I've gone beyond the anger stage. Disillusioned, perhaps. You must think I'm a crazy man, showing up with an engagement ring and the belief that God had given me this wonderful message that we were to marry.''

''Seth, no.'' She placed a hand on his forearm.

He looked down at it and moved his arm, breaking her light hold. It was almost as if he couldn't tolerate her touch.

''The funny thing is,'' he continued, his expression stoic, ''until this minute I didn't accept that I'd be returning to Alaska alone. Even as late as this morning

I believed that something would happen and you'd decide to come with me.'' He took in a deep breath, his gaze avoiding hers. ''I've behaved like a fool.''

''Don't say that,'' she pleaded.

He glanced at her then; regret, doubt and a deep sadness touched his face. ''We would have had beautiful children, Red.'' A hand lightly caressed her cheek.

''Will you stop talking like that,'' she demanded, becoming angry. ''You're being unfair.''

He quirked his head at an angle and shrugged his massive shoulders. ''I know. You love me, Red, you haven't admitted it to yourself yet, but you do. The time will come when you can, but I doubt that even then it will make much difference. Because, although you love me, you don't love me enough to leave all this behind.'' His face scanned the airport interior, looking far beyond the glass, marble and concrete.

She wanted to argue with him, but couldn't. Unbidden tears welled in the blue depths of her eyes, and she lowered her head, blinking frantically to still their fall.

''Until you can admit your love for me, or anyone else, you'll only be half a woman. And when you stop putting your own dreams above everyone and everything—including God—then there's the chance you'll be a complete person.''

The words seemed to reach out and physically slap Claudia. Her eyes widened incredulously, knowing they had been spoken with the intent to cause her pain.

She held her head high and glared at him with all the anguish in her eyes for him to see. ''I'm going to forgive you for that, Seth, because I know you don't mean it. You're hurting, and because of that you want me to suffer, too.'' Tugging the leather purse strap over her shoulder, she took a step in retreat. ''I can't see that my being here is doing either of us any good. I wish you well and thank you for six of the most wonderful days of my life. God bless you, Seth.'' She pivoted and stalked down the corridor. For several moments she was lost in a painful void. Somehow she managed to make it to a ladies' rest room.

Avoiding the curious stares of others, she wiped the moisture from her face and blew her nose. Seth had been cold and cruel, offering neither comfort nor understanding. Before, Claudia had recognized that his capacity for ruthlessness was as strong as his capability for tenderness. How sad that they must part like this. There'd been so much Claudia had longed to say, yet maybe it was better left unsaid.

When she felt composed enough to face the outside world, she moved with quick, purposeful steps toward the parking area.

She had only gone a few feet when a hand gripped her shoulder and whirled her around. A cry of alarm was muffled as she was dragged against Seth's muscular chest.

''I thought you'd gone,'' he whispered into her hair, a desperate edge to his voice. ''I'm sorry, Red. You're right, I didn't mean that, none of it.''

She was squeezed so tight her ribs ached. Seth raised his head and looked around at the attention they were receiving. A hand tugged her elbow and she was half dragged, half pulled into an area reserved for traveling servicemen. Thankfully it was empty. The minute he was assured they were alone, his mouth sought hers, fusing them together with a fiery kiss filled with such emotion that Claudia was left weak and lightheaded.

"I need you," he whispered hoarsely against the delicate hollow of her throat. "God help me, I need you." He lifted his face and smoothed a curl from her forehead, his eyes pleading with her.

Claudia was deluged with fresh pain. She needed him too, but here in Seattle. She couldn't leave everything behind, not now, when she was so close.

"No, don't say it." He placed a finger over her mouth to prevent the words of regret from spilling out. "I understand, Red. Or at least I'm trying to understand." He sighed heavily and gently kissed her again. "I have to go—it's time to board the plane." His voice was low and troubled.

He sounded so final, as if everything between them was over. Claudia blinked away the tears that were burning her eyes. No sound came from her parched throat as she was gently eased from his embrace. Her heart hammered furiously as they returned to the departure gate.

A feeling of panic overcame her when she saw that Seth's plane was already being boarded. The time was fast approaching when he would be gone.

Once again he gently caressed her face, his dark eyes burning into hers.

"Goodbye, Red." His lips covered hers very gently. In the next instant, Seth Lessinger turned and strolled out of Claudia's world.

Part of her screamed silently in tortured protest as she watched him go, offering no resistance. The other part, the more level-headed, sensible part, recognized that there was nothing she could do to change his leaving. But all of Claudia suffered. Instantly she felt regret, remorse and self-reproach, but she found very little solace in her decision.

The days passed slowly and painfully. Ashley grew watchful over Claudia's loss of appetite and the dark shadows beneath her eyes. She spent more time in her room alone, blocking out the world, but closing the door on reality didn't keep away the image or the memories of Seth at bay. He was in her thoughts continually, haunting her dreams, obsessing her days, preying on her mind.

She threw herself into her studies with a ferocity that surprised even Ashley. The days she could handle, but not the nights. Often she lay awake for hours, wide-eyed and frustrated, afraid that once she did sleep her dreams would be haunted by Seth. She prayed every minute, it seemed, harder than she had about anything in her life. But no answer came: no flash of lightning, no writing on the wall, not even a Bible verse stuck to a mirror. Nothing. Wasn't God listening? Didn't He know that this indecision was tormenting her?

Two weeks after Seth's departure, she still hadn't heard from him. Claudia was hollow-eyed and her cheeks were beginning to look gaunt. Many times she saw Ashley glance at her with concern, but Claudia put on a weak smile and dismissed her friend's worries. No, she was fine. Really.

The next Saturday, Ashley was getting ready to go to work at the University Book Store near the U. of W. campus when one of the girls Ashley worked with, Sandy Hoover, waltzed into the apartment.

"Look." She proudly beamed and held out her hand, displaying a small diamond.

"You're engaged!" Ashley squealed with delight.

"Jon asked me last night," Sandy burst out. "I was so excited I could hardly talk. First, like an idiot, I started to cry, and Jon didn't know what to think. But I was so happy, I couldn't help it, and then I wasn't even able to talk and Jon finally asked me if I wanted to marry him or not and all I could do was emphatically nod my head."

"Oh, Sandy, I'm so happy for you." Ashley threw her arms around her friend and hugged her. "You've been in love with Jon for so long."

Her happy smile was animated. "I didn't ever think he'd ask me to marry him. I've known so much longer than Jon how I felt, and it was so hard to wait for him to feel the same things." She sighed, and a dreamy look stole over the pert face. "I love Jon so much it almost frightens me. He's with me even when he isn't with me." She giggled. "I know that sounds crazy."

It didn't sound so crazy to Claudia. Seth was thousands of miles away, but in some ways he had never left. If anything was crazy, it was the way she could close her eyes and feel the taste of his mouth over hers. It was the memory of that last gentle caress and the sweet kiss that was supposed to say goodbye.

Claudia was so caught up in her thoughts she hadn't noticed that Sandy had left.

"I wish you could look at yourself," Ashley said impatiently, her look thoughtful. "You look so miserable that I'm beginning to think you should see a doctor."

"A doctor isn't going to be able to help me," she mumbled.

"You've got to do something; you can't sit around here moping like this. It isn't like you, Claudia. Either you settle whatever's wrong between you and Seth or I'll contact him myself."

"You wouldn't," Claudia insisted.

"Don't count on it. Cooper's as worried about you as I am. If I don't do anything, he might."

"It isn't going to do any good." She tucked her chin into her neck. "I simply can't do what Seth wants. Not now."

"And what does he want?"

"He wants me to marry him and move to Nome," she whispered weakly. "But I can't give up my dream of a medical degree and move to some forsaken no-man's-land. And Seth just as adamantly refuses to move to Seattle. As far as I can see, there's no solution."

"You ninny," Ashley flared incredulously. "The pair of you! You're both behaving like spoiled children, each wanting your own way. For heaven's sake, does it have to be so intense? You've only known each other a few days. It would be absurd to make such a drastic change in your life on such a short acquaintance. And the same thing goes for Seth. The first thing to do is be sure of your feelings—both of you. Get to know each other better and establish a friendship, then you'll know what you want."

"Good idea. But Seth's three thousand miles away, in case you'd forgotten, and forming a relationship thousands of miles apart isn't going to be easy."

"How did you ever make the dean's list, girl?" Ashley questioned in a scathing tone. "Ever hear of letters? Some people have been known to faithfully deliver those white envelopes and fill their appointed rounds—through snow, through rain—"

"I get the picture," Claudia interrupted.

She had thought about writing Seth, but didn't know his address and didn't know what she could say. One thing she was certain, the next move must come from her. Seth was a proud man. He had made his position clear. The next move was hers.

Ashley left for work a few minutes later, and Claudia mentally toyed with the idea of writing Seth. She didn't need to say anything about his proposal. As usual, her level-headed friend had put things into perspective. Ashley was right. She couldn't make such a major decision without there being more of a basis for their relationship than six days. They could write, phone and even visit each other until Claudia was sure of her feelings. And most of all, she recognized that she couldn't go on living like this.

The letter wasn't easy. Crumpled pieces of paper littered the living room floor. When it got to the point that the carpet had all but disappeared under discarded sheets, Claudia paused and decided it would go better if she ate something. She stood, stretched and was making herself a sandwich when she realized that, for the first time since Seth left, she was actually hungry. A pleased smile spread slowly across her face.

Once she'd eaten, the letter flowed smoothly. She wrote about the weather and her classes, a couple of idiosyncrasies of her professors. She asked him questions about Nome and his business. Finally there were two sheets of neat, orderly handwriting, and she signed it simply: Claudia. Reading it over, she realized so much had been left unsaid. Chewing on the end of her pen, she scribbled in a postscript that said she missed him. Would he understand?

The letter was almost memorized by the time she dropped it into the mailbox an hour later. Purposely she walked it there, afraid she'd change her mind if the letter lay around all weekend. Because she had no address, she wrote his name and Nome, Alaska. If it arrived, then it would be God's doing. This whole relationship was God's doing.

Calculating roughly that the letter would arrive on Wednesday or Thursday, she guessed that, if he wrote back right away, she could have something from him by the following week. That night she crawled into bed and, for the first time in two and a half desolate weeks, slept peacefully.

All day Thursday, Claudia was fidgety. Seth would get her letter today. How would he react to it? Would he be glad, or had he given up on her completely? How much longer would it be before she knew? How long would it be before she could expect an answer? She smiled as she let herself into the apartment; it was as if she expected something monumental to happen. By ten she'd finished her studies, and after a leisurely bath she read her Bible and went to bed, unreasonably disappointed.

Nothing happened Friday, either. Steve Kali, another medical student, asked her out for coffee after their lab class and Claudia accepted, pleased at the invitation. Steve was nice. He wasn't Seth, but he was nice.

The phone rang Saturday afternoon. Claudia was bringing in the groceries and dropped a bag of oranges as she rushed across the carpet to answer it.

"Hello." She sounded out of breath.

"Hello, Red," Seth's deep, rich voice returned.

Claudia's hand tightened on the receiver and her heartbeat accelerated wildly. "You got my letter?" Her voice remained breathless, but it had nothing to do with hurrying to answer the phone.

"About time. I didn't know if I'd ever hear from you," he admonished gently.

Claudia suddenly felt so weak that she sat on a chair. "How are you?"

"Miserable," he admitted harshly. "Your letter sounded so bright and newsy. If you hadn't added that note on the bottom, I don't know what I would have thought."

"Oh, Seth," she breathed into the phone. "I've been wretched. I really do miss you."

"It's about time you admitted as much. I had no idea it would take you this long to realize I was right. Do you want me to fly down there? Alaska requires blood tests."

"Blood tests?"

"Yes, silly woman, they're required for a marriage license."

# Chapter Five

"Marriage license? I didn't write because I was ready to change my mind," she denied. Did Seth believe this separation was a battle of wills and she was the first to surrender? "I'm staying here in Seattle, I thought you understood that."

Her announcement was followed by a lengthy pause. Claudia could hear Seth's anger, and the effort he made to control his breathing. "Then why did you write the letter?"

"You still don't understand, do you?" She threw the words at him. "Someday, Seth Lessinger, I'm going to be a fabulous doctor. This has been my dream from the time I was a little girl." She took a calming breath; she didn't want to argue with him. "Seth, I wrote you because I've been miserable. I've missed you more than I believed possible. I thought it might work if you and I got to know one another better. We can write and—"

"I'm not interested in a pen pal." His laugh was harsh and bitter.

"Neither am I," she returned sharply. "You're being unfair again. Can't we compromise? Do we have to do everything your way? Give me time, that's all I'm asking."

Her words were met with another long silence, and for an apprehensive second Claudia thought he might have hung up on her. "Seth," she whispered, "give me more time, is that so unreasonable?"

"All right, Red, we'll do this your way," he conceded. "But I'm not much for letter writing, and this is a busy time of the year for me, so don't expect much."

Claudia breathed in happily. "I won't." It was a beginning.

Seth's first letter arrived four days later. Home from her classes before Ashley, Claudia stopped to pick up the mail in the apartment vestibule. There was only one letter, with large, bold handwriting. Claudia stared at it with the instant knowledge it was from Seth. Clutching the envelope tightly, she rushed up the stairs, fumbled with the apartment lock and barged in the front door. She tossed her coat and books haphazardly on the couch before tearing open the letter. His, too, was newsy, full of tidbits of information about his job and what this new contract would do for his business, Arctic Barge Company. He told a little about the city of Nome and about what she should expect when she came.

Claudia couldn't prevent the smile that trembled across her lips. When she came, indeed! He also explained that when she packed her things she'd have to ship everything she couldn't bring in her suitcases. Arrangements would need to be made to have her belongings transported on a barge headed North. The only way into Nome was either by air or by sea, and access by sea was limited to a few short weeks in the summer before the water froze again. The pressure for her to make her decision soon was subtle. He concluded by saying that he missed her and, just in case she'd forgotten, he loved her. She read the words and closed her eyes to the flood of emotions that swirled about her.

She answered the letter that night and sent off another two days later. A week passed, and Claudia received another long response from Seth, with an added postscript that there was a possibility he would be in Seattle at the end of October for two days of meetings. He didn't know how much unscheduled time he'd have, but he was hoping to come a day early. Then would be the time for them to sit down and talk, because letters only made him miss her more. He gave her the dates and promised he'd contact her when he knew more. Again he told her he loved her and needed her.

Claudia savored each letter, reading them so many times she knew each one by heart. In some ways, corresponding was building a more solid relationship than having him in Seattle. If he'd been here, Claudia would have been more easily swayed by her physical response to him. This way she could carefully weigh each aspect of her decision and give Seth and the move to Nome prayerful consideration. And she did pray, fervently, every day. But after so many weeks she was beginning to believe God wasn't ever going to answer.

Ashley saw her reading over one of Seth's letters for the tenth time and laughingly threw a decorator pillow at her.

"Hey," Claudia snapped, "what did you do that for?"

"Because I couldn't stand to see you look so miserable!"

"I'm not miserable," Claudia denied. "I'm happy. There's another letter from Seth and...and he told me again how much he wants me to marry him and..." Her voice cracked and she swallowed back tears that burned for release. "I...didn't know I would cry about it."

"You still don't know what you want, do you?"

Claudia shook her head. "I pray and pray and pray, and God doesn't seem to hear me. He gave Seth a sign, but there's nothing for me. It's unfair!"

"What kind of confirmation are you looking for?" Ashley sat beside Claudia and handed her a tissue.

Claudia sniffled and waved her hand dramatically. "I don't know. Just something, anything! When I made my commitment to Christ, I told Him my life was no longer my own but His. If He wants me digging ditches, then I'd dig ditches. If He wants me to give up medical school and marry Seth, then I'd do so in a minute. Seth seems so positive, and I'm so unsure."

Ashley pinched her lips together for a moment, and went into her bedroom returning a minute later with her Bible. "Do you remember the story of Elijah?"

"I think so. Wasn't he an Old Testament prophet?"

Ashley nodded as she flipped through the worn pages of her Bible. "As I recall, Elijah was hiding from the wicked Jezebel. God sent the angel of the Lord, who led Elijah into a cave. He told him to stay there and wait, because God was coming to speak to him. Elijah waited and waited. When a strong wind came, he rushed from the cave and cried out, but the wind wasn't God. An earthquake followed, and again Elijah hurried outside, certain this time that the earthquake was God speaking to him. But it wasn't the earthquake. Next came a fire, and again Elijah was positive that the fire was God speaking to him. But it wasn't. Finally, when everything was quiet, Elijah heard a soft, gentle whisper. That was the Lord." Ashley transferred the open Bible to Claudia's lap. "Here, read the story yourself."

Thoughtfully Claudia read over the chapter before looking up. "You're telling me I should stop looking for that bolt of lightning in the sky that spells out: *Marry Seth.*"

"Or the handwriting on the wall," Ashley added with a laugh.

"God is answering my prayers—all I need to do is listen?"

"I think so."

"It sounds too simple," Claudia said with a sigh.

"I don't know that it is. But you've got to quit looking for the strong wind, the earthquake and the fire and listen instead to your heart."

"I'm not even positively sure I love him." The magnetic physical attraction between them was overwhelming, but there was so much more to love and a lifetime commitment.

''You'll know,'' Ashley assured her confidently. ''I don't doubt that for a second. When the timing is right, you'll know.''

Claudia felt as if a weight had been lifted from her, and she sighed deeply before forcefully expelling her breath. ''Hey, do you know what today is?'' she asked, then answered before Ashley had the opportunity, ''Columbus Day. A day worthy enough to celebrate with something special.'' Carefully she tucked Seth's letter back inside the envelope. ''Let's bring home Chinese food and drown our doubts in pork fried rice.''

''And egg rolls,'' Ashley added. ''Lots of egg rolls.''

By the time they returned to the apartment, Claudia and Ashley had collected more than dinner. Claudia met Steve Kali and a friend of his at the restaurant, and after quick introductions, the four decided they could get two extra items off the menu if they ordered together.

They sat on the floor in a large circle at Ashley and Claudia's apartment, eating their meal with chopsticks out of the white carry-out boxes. Everything was passed around the circle.

Steve's friend, Dave Kimball, was a law student who immediately showed a keen interest in Ashley. Claudia watched with an amused smile as Ashley responded with some flirtations of her own.

The chopsticks were soon abandoned in favor of more common utensils, but the laughter continued.

"You know what we're celebrating, don't you?" Ashley questioned between bites of ginger-spiced beef and tomato.

"No." Both men shook their heads, glancing from one girl to the other.

"Columbus Day," Claudia supplied.

"'Columbus sailed the ocean blue'?" Steve jumped up and danced around the room singing.

Everyone laughed.

The phone rang and Steve picked up the receiver. "I'll answer that," he volunteered, "it might be a phone call." He promptly dropped the phone. "Oops, sorry," he apologized into the receiver.

Claudia couldn't help smiling. Steve didn't mean to be flip, he was just having a good time. She was, too; it felt good to laugh again. Ashley was right, this whole thing with Seth was too intense. She needed to relax. Her decision must be based on the quiet knowledge that marriage to Seth was what God had ordained.

"I'm sorry, would you mind repeating that?" Steve said into the earpiece. "Claudia? Yeah, she's here." He covered the receiver with the palm of his hand. "Are you here, Claudia?" he asked with a satisfied smirk.

"You nut. Give me that." She stood and took the phone. "Hello." Just her luck, it'd be Cooper, who'd demand to know what a man was doing in her apartment. "This is Claudia."

"What's going on?"

The color drained out of her flushed cheeks. "Seth?" she asked incredulously. Breathlessly, she repeated herself. "Seth, it is really you?"

"It's me," he confirmed, his tone brittle. "Who's the guy who answered the phone."

"Oh." She swallowed, and turned her back to the others. "That's Steve Kali, a friend of mine from school. There are several friends here," she explained, stretching the truth. She didn't want Seth to get the wrong impression. "We're celebrating Columbus Day...you know, Columbus, the man who sailed the three ships across the blue Atlantic looking for India and discovered America instead. Do you celebrate that day in Alaska?" She continued to babble.

"I know what day it is. You sound like you've been drinking."

"Not unless the Chinese tea's got something in it I don't know about."

"Who's the guy who answered the phone?"

The last thing Claudia wanted to do was make explanations to Seth with everyone listening to the conversation. There'd never been any need for more than one phone before. "It really would be better if we talked later," she said, stammering slightly.

"Everyone's there listening, right?" Seth guessed.

"Right," she confirmed on a soft sigh. "Do you mind?"

"No, but before you hang up, answer me one thing. Have you been thinking about how much I love you and want you here with me?"

"Oh, Seth," she murmured miserably. "Yes, I've thought of little else."

"And you still don't know?" he asked, his voice heavy with exasperation.

"Not yet."

''All right, Red. I'll call back in an hour.''

Actually, it was almost two hours before the phone rang again. Steve and Dave had left an hour before, and Ashley had made a flimsy excuse about needing to do some research work at the library. Claudia didn't question her and appreciated the privacy.

She answered the phone on the first ring. ''Hello.''

''Now tell me who the guy was who picked up the phone the first time,'' Seth demanded.

Claudia's light laugh drifted pleasantly into the receiver. ''Seth Lessinger, you sound almost jealous.''

''Almost?'' he shouted back.

''His name's Steve Kali, we have several classes together, that's all,'' she explained, pleased at his small display of concern. ''I didn't know you were the jealous sort,'' she admonished gently.

''I never have been before. I don't like the way it feels either, if that makes you any happier.''

''I'd feel the same way,'' she admitted. ''I wish you were here, Seth. Ashley and I walked by a skating rink tonight and stopped to watch some couples skating together. Do you realize that you and I have never skated? If I close my eyes, I can almost feel your arm around me.''

Seth sucked in his breath. ''Why do you say things like that when we're separated by thousands of miles? Your sense of timing is sadly misplaced. Besides, we don't need skating as an excuse for me to be near you,'' he murmured, his voice disturbed and low. ''Listen, honey, I'll be in Seattle a week from Saturday.''

"Saturday? Oh, Seth!" She was too happy to express her thoughts. "It'll be so good to see you!"

"My plane arrives early that morning. I'll phone you as soon as I can review the conference schedule."

"I won't plan a thing. No," she said, laughing, "I'll plan everything. Can you stay over until Monday? I'll skip classes and we could have a whole extra day alone."

"I can't." He sounded as disappointed as she.

They talked for an hour, and Claudia felt guilty at the thought of his phone bill, but the conversation had been wonderful.

Did she love him? The question kept repeating itself all the next week. If she could truthfully answer that one question, then the other would answer itself. Just talking to him over the phone had lifted her spirits dramatically. But could she leave school and everything, everyone, she had ever known and follow him to a harsh, cruel land?

Her last class Friday of the following week was a disaster. Her attention span was no longer than a four-year-old's. Time and time again she was forced to bring herself back into reality. So many conflicting emotions seemed to be coming at her. The first big tests of the quarter, Seth's visit. She felt pounded and burdened from every side, tormented by her own indecision.

Steve walked out of the building with her.

"Why so glum?" he asked. "If anyone's got complaints, it should be me." They continued down the stairs, and Claudia cast him a sidelong glance.

"What have you got to complain about?"

"Plenty," he began in an irritated tone. "You remember Dave Kimball?"

Claudia nodded, recalling Steve's tall, sandy-haired friend who had flirted so outrageously with Ashley. "Sure, I remember Dave."

"We got picked up by the police a couple of nights ago."

Claudia glanced apprehensively at her friend. "What happened?"

"Nothing, really. We'd both been having a good time and decided to walk home after several beers. About halfway to the dorm, Dave starts with the crazies. He was climbing up the streetlights, jumping on parked cars. I wasn't doing any of this, but we were both brought into the police station for disorderly conduct."

Claudia's blue eyes rounded incredulously. Steve was one of the straightest, most clean-cut men she had met. This was so unlike anything she'd suspect from him, she didn't know how to react.

"That's not the half of it," Steve continued. "Once we were at the police station, Dave kept insisting that he was a law student and knew his rights. He demanded his one phone call."

"Well, it's probably a good thing he did know what to do," Claudia said.

"Dave made his one call all right." Steve inhaled a shaky breath. "And twenty minutes later the desk sergeant came in to ask which one of us ordered the pizza."

Claudia burst into giggles, but it wasn't long before Steve joined her. He placed a friendly arm around her shoulders as their laughter faded. Together they strolled toward the parking lot.

"I do feel bad about the police thing..." Before she could complete her thought, she caught sight of a broad-shouldered man walking toward her with crisp strides. She knew immediately it was Seth.

His look of contempt was aimed directly at her, his rough features darkened by a fierce frown. Even from the narrowing distance, she recognized the tight set of his mouth as he glared at her.

Steve's arm resting lightly across her shoulders felt as if it weighed a thousand pounds.

# *Chapter Six*

Claudia's mouth became dry as she quickened her pace and rushed forward to meet Seth. If his look hadn't been so angry and forbidding, she would have walked directly into his arms. "When—how did you get here? I thought you couldn't come until tomorrow?" Only now was she recovering from the shock of seeing him.

An unwilling smile broke his stern expression as he pulled her to him and crushed her in his embrace.

Half lifted from the sidewalk, Claudia linked her hands behind his neck and felt his warm breath in her hair. "Oh, Seth," she mumbled, close to tears, "you idiot, why didn't you say something?"

So many emotions came at her at once. She felt crushed yet protected, jubilant yet tearful, excited but afraid. To each sensation she responded with equal fervor by spreading eager kisses over his face.

Slowly he released her and the two men eyed each other skeptically.

Seth extended his hand. "I'm Seth Lessinger, Claudia's fiancé."

Claudia had to bite into her lip to keep from correcting him, but she wouldn't say anything that could destroy this minute.

Steve's eyes rounded with immediate surprise, but he managed to mumble a greeting and exchange handshakes. He made some excuse about catching the bus and was gone.

"Who's that?"

"Steve," she replied, too happy to see him to question the way he had introduced himself to her fellow student. "He answered the phone the other night when you called. He's just a friend, don't worry."

"Then why did he have his arm around you?" Seth demanded with growing impatience.

Claudia ignored the question, instead standing on the tips of her toes and lightly brushing her mouth over his. His whiskers tickled her face, and she lifted both hands to his dark beard, framing his lips so she could kiss him soundly.

Seth's response was immediate as he pulled her into his arms. "I've missed you. I won't be able to wait much longer. Who would believe this little slip of nothing could bring this giant to his knees? Literally," he added.

Claudia's eyes widened with feigned offense. "Little slip of nothing? Come now, you make me sound like a young Shirley Temple!"

He laughed; it was the robust, deep laugh that she loved. "Compared to me, you're pint-size." Looping his arm around her waist, he walked beside her. Again

Claudia felt cradled and loved beyond anything she had known. She smiled up at him, and his eyes drank deeply from hers as a slow grin spread over his face, crinkling tiny lines at his eyes. "You may be small, but you hold powers over me I don't think I'll ever understand."

Leaning her head against the crook of his arm, Claudia relaxed. "Why didn't you say anything about coming today?"

"I didn't know that I was going to make the flight until the last minute. As it was, I hired a pilot out of Nome to make the connection with Alaska Airlines in Fairbanks."

"How'd you know where to find me?"

"I met Ashley at your apartment. She drew me a map of the campus and told me where you'd be. You don't mind?"

"Of course not," she assured him with a smile and a shake of her head. "I just wish I'd known. I could have met you at the airport."

She gave him her car keys and he drove the silver compact, but it wasn't until they were in heavy afternoon traffic that she noticed Seth was heading in the opposite direction from her apartment.

"Where are we going?" She looked down at her navy-blue cords and Irish cable-knit sweater. She wasn't dressed for anything but a casual outing.

"My hotel," he answered without looking at her, focusing his attention on the freeway. "I wanted to talk to you privately, and from the look of things at your place, Ashley is going to be around for a while."

Ashley was involved in a project that she'd been

working on for two nights. Magazines, newspapers and several loose sheets of written notes were scattered over the living room floor.

"I know what you mean about the apartment." She laughed softly in understanding. Most likely Ashley had been engrossed in it all when Seth arrived. "Did you get a chance to talk to my roommate?"

"Not too much." He slowed the car as he pulled off the freeway and onto Mercer Avenue. "She's a nice girl. I like her. Those blue eyes are almost as beautiful as yours."

Something twitched in Claudia's stomach. Jealousy—over Ashley? She was her best friend! Quickly she tossed the thought aside.

Seth's hand reached for hers. Linking their fingers, he carried her hand to his mouth and gently kissed her knuckles. Shivers tingled up her arm and she smiled contentedly.

The downtown hotel lobby was bristling with activity. Suitcases littered the richly carpeted floor, while the continuous ringing of bells alerted the bellhops to where they were needed. In contrast, Seth's room was quiet and serene. Situated high above the city, the large suite displayed a sweeping view of Puget Sound and the landmarks Seattle was famous for: the Pacific Science Center, the Space Needle and the Kingdome.

The king-size bed was bordered on each side by oak nightstands with white ceramic lamps. Two easy chairs were set obliquely in front of a color television. Claudia glanced uneasily over the room, feeling slightly uncomfortable.

The door had no sooner closed when Seth placed a

hand on her shoulder and turned her around to face him. Their eyes met, hers uncertain and a little afraid, his warm and reassuring. When he slipped his arms around her, she came willingly, fitting herself against the hard contours of his solid length. Relaxing, she savored the fiery warmth of his kiss. She slipped her hands behind his neck and yielded with the knowledge that she wanted him to kiss her, needed his kisses. Nothing on earth had been so close to heaven than being cradled in his arms.

Arms of corded steel locked her, held her close. Yet he was gentle, as if she was the most precious thing in the world. With a muted groan, he dragged his mouth from hers and showered the side of her neck with urgent kisses.

"I shouldn't be doing this," he moaned hoarsely. "But I don't know if I have the will to stop." One hand continued down her back, arching her upward while the fingers of the other hand played havoc with her hair.

Claudia's mind was caught in a whirl of desire and need. This shouldn't be happening, but it felt so right. For a moment she wanted to question him. They should wait until they were married. But she couldn't speak. Seth pulled away and paused, his eyes searching hers. His breath came in uneven gasps.

This was the time to stop, to back away, but she couldn't. The long weeks of separation, the doubts, the uncertainties that had plagued her night and day, the restless dreams all exploded in her mind as she lifted her arms to him. It had been like this between them almost from the beginning, this magnetic, overpowering attraction.

Seth released a shuddering sigh as he slipped a hand under her sweater. His hands roved the soft skin of her bare back, soothing and caressing.

A rush of cold air hit her and Claudia inhaled a slow breath. She closed her eyes, suddenly frightened by the hungry look in his eyes.

Slowly Seth lowered his mouth to hers until their breaths merged, and the kiss that followed sent her world in a crazy spin.

"I can't do it." The bitter words were whispered hoarsely in her ear, barely distinct. "I can't," he repeated and broke the embrace.

The words flittered through her consciousness and Claudia forced her eyes open. Seth was standing away from her. He wasn't smiling now, and the troubled, almost tormented expression puzzled her all the more.

"Seth," she whispered, "what is it?"

"I'm sorry." He crossed his arms and turned his back, as if offering her the chance to escape.

Her arms felt as if they'd been weighed down with lead, and her heart felt numb, as if she'd been exposed to the Arctic cold without the proper protective gear.

"Forgive me, Red." Seth covered his eyes with a weary hand and walked across the room to stand before the window. "I brought you here with the worst of intentions," he began. "I thought if we were to make love, then all your doubts would be gone." He paused to take in a labored breath. "I knew you'd marry me then without question."

Understanding burned like a laser beam searing

through her mind, and she half moaned, half cried. Her arms cradled her stomach as the pain washed over her. Color blazed in her cheeks at how close she had come to letting their passion rage out of control. It had been a trick, a farce, in order for Seth to exert his will over her.

Several minutes passed in silence. Claudia turned to Seth, his profile was outlined by the dim light of dusk. He seemed to be struggling for control of his emotions.

"I wouldn't blame you if you hated me after this," he spoke at last.

"I...I don't hate you." Her voice was unsteady, soft and trembling.

"You don't love me either, do you?" He hurled the words at her accusingly and turned to face her.

The muscles in her throat constricted painfully. "I don't know. I just don't know."

"Will you ever be completely sure?" he questioned her with thinning patience

Claudia buried her face in her hands, defeated and miserable.

"Red, please don't cry. I'm sorry." The anger was gone and he spoke softly, reassuringly.

She shivered with reaction. "If...if we did get married, could I stay here until I finished my schooling?"

"No," he returned adamantly. "I want a wife and children. Look at me, Red. I'm thirty-six; I can't wait another five, six years for a family. And I work too hard to divide my life between Nome and Seattle."

Wasn't there any compromise? Did everything have to be his way? "You're asking for so much," she cried.

"But I'm offering even more," he countered.

"You don't understand," she told him. "If I give up school now, I'll probably never be able to finish. Especially if I won't be able to come back for several years."

"There isn't any compromise," he said with a note of finality. "If God wants you to be a doctor, He'll provide the way later. We both have to trust Him for that."

"I can't give it all up. It's not that easy," she whispered.

"Then there's nothing left to say, is there?" Dark shadows of doubt clouded his face, and he turned sharply and resumed his position in front of the window.

There didn't seem to be anything left to do but to leave quietly. She forced herself to open the door, but knew she couldn't let it end like this. Softly the door clicked shut.

At the sound Seth slammed his fist against the window ledge. Claudia gave a small cry of alarm and he pivoted to face her. His rugged features were contorted with anger as he stared at her. But one look told Claudia the anger was directed at himself and not her.

"I thought you'd gone." His gaze held hers.

"I couldn't," she whispered.

He stared deeply into her liquid blue eyes and paused as if he wanted to say something, but instead shook his head in defeat.

Claudia's eyes were red and haunted as she covered the distance between them. She slid her hands around his waist, hugging him while she rested a tearstained cheek against his back.

"We have something very special, Red, but it's not going to work." The dejected tone of his voice stabbed at her heart.

"It'll work. I know it will. Everything's my fault, I know that. But I want to be sure, very sure, before I make such a drastic change in my life. Give me time, that's all I'm asking."

"You've had almost six weeks."

"It's not enough."

He tried to remove her hands, but she squeezed all the tighter. "We're both hurt and angry tonight, but that doesn't mean things between us won't work."

"I could almost believe you," Seth murmured and altered their position so that she was securely wrapped in his arms.

She met his penetrating gaze and answered in a soft, throbbing voice, "Believe me, Seth. Please believe me."

His gaze slid to her lips before his mouth claimed hers in a fierce and flaming kiss that was almost savage, as if to punish her for the torment she had caused him. But it didn't matter how he kissed her as long as she hadn't lost him.

They had dinner at the hotel, but didn't return to Seth's room. They discussed his conference schedule, which included several meetings the following day. His plane left early Sunday afternoon. They made plans for Seth to attend the Sunday morning church service with Claudia and for her to drive him to the airport afterward.

Claudia's heart was heavy all the next day. Several times she wished she could talk to Seth, clear away the ghosts of yesterday. For those long, miserable weeks she had missed him so much that she could hardly function. Then at the first chance to see each other again, they had ended up fighting. Why didn't she know what to do? Was this torment her heart suffered love?

The question remained unanswered as they sat together in church Sunday morning. It felt so right to have Seth by her side. Claudia closed her eyes to pray, fervently asking God to guide her. She paused, recalling the verses she had found in the Gospel of Matthew about asking, seeking, knocking. God had promised that anyone who asks receives, and anyone who seeks finds. It had all sounded so simple and straightforward when she read it, but it wasn't—not for her.

When she finished her prayer and opened her eyes, she felt Seth's gaze burn over her, searching her face. She longed to reassure him, but could find no words. Gently she reached for his hand and squeezed it.

They rode to the airport in an uneasy silence. Their time had been wasted for the most part. What Claudia had hoped would be a time to settle doubts had only raised more.

"You don't need to come inside with me." Seth said as they neared the airport. His words sliced into her troubled thoughts.

"What?" she asked, confused and hurt. "But I want to be with you as long as possible."

He didn't look pleased with her decision. "Fine, if that's what you want."

The set of his mouth was angry and impatient, but Claudia didn't know why. "You don't want me there, do you?" She tried to hide the hurt in her voice.

His cool eyes met her look of defiance. "Oh, for goodness' sake, settle down, Red. I take it all back. Come in if you want. I didn't mean to make a federal case out of this." The appeasement was issued in a rumbling tone.

Claudia didn't want to argue again, not in their last minutes together. Seth continued to look withdrawn. They parked in the cement garage and walked into the main terminal to check his luggage.

Tentatively her hand reached out to rest on his arm. "Friends?" she asked and offered him a smile.

He returned the gesture and tenderly squeezed her delicate hand. "Friends."

The thick atmosphere melted and the tension eased as she waited while Seth reported to the airline desk with his ticket and suitcases. He returned with a wry grin.

"The flight's been delayed an hour. How about some lunch?"

Claudia couldn't prevent the smile that softly curved her mouth. Her eyes reflected her pleasure at the unexpected time together.

They ate at an airport restaurant, but Claudia noted that Seth barely touched his meal. Her appetite wasn't up to par, either. Another separation loomed before them.

"How long will it be before you'll be back?" Claudia asked as they walked toward the departure gate.

There was a moment of grim hesitation before Seth answered. "I don't know. Months probably. This conference wasn't necessary. If it hadn't been for you, I wouldn't have attended. I can't afford to take time away from my business like this."

Claudia swallowed at the lump forming in her throat. "Thanksgiving break is coming soon. Maybe I could fly up and visit you. I'd like to see for myself the beauty of Alaska. You've told me so much about it already." Just for a moment, for a fleeting second, she was tempted to drop everything and leave with him now. Quickly she buried the impulsive thought and clenched her fists together inside the pockets of her wool coat.

Seth didn't respond either way to her suggestion that she come and visit him.

"What do you think?" she prompted.

Seth inclined his head and nodded faintly. "If that's what you'd like."

Claudia had the feeling he hadn't understood any of what she'd been saying.

When the time came for him to board the plane, her façade of composure began to slip. It was difficult to restrain her tears, and she blinked several times, not wanting Seth to remember her with tears shimmering in her eyes. With a proud lift of her chin she offered him a brave smile.

He studied her unhappy face. "Goodbye, Red." His eyes continued to hold hers.

The hesitation before her answer emphasized all the

more her inner turmoil. "Goodbye, Seth," she whispered softly, a slight catch to her voice.

The palm of his hand cupped her face and his thumb gently wiped away a single tear that was weaving a slow course down her pale face. Claudia buried her chin in his hand and gently kissed the calloused palm.

Gathering her into his embrace, Seth wrapped his arms around her as he buried his face in her neck and breathed deeply. When his mouth found hers, the kiss was gentle and sweet and so full of love that fresh tears misted her eyes. She sniffed to abate their fall.

His hold relaxed and he began to pull away, but she wouldn't let him. "Seth." She murmured his name urgently. She had meant to let him go, relinquish him without a word, but somehow she couldn't.

He scooped her in his arms, crushing her against him with a fierceness that stole her breath away. "I'm a man," he bit out in an impatient tremor, "and I can't take much more of this." He released her enough to study her face. His dark eyes clearly revealed his needs. "I'm asking you again, Claudia. Marry me and come to Nome. I promise you a good life. I need you."

Claudia felt raw. The soft, womanly core of her cried out a resounding yes, but the decision would be based on the emotion of the moment. She didn't want to decide something so important to both of them on the basis of feelings. Indecision and uncertainty raced through her mind, and she could neither deny nor accept him. Unable to formulate words, she found a low, protesting groan slipping from her throat. Her brimming blue eyes pleaded with him for understanding.

Seth's gaze sliced into her as a hardness stole into

his features, narrowing his mouth. Forcefully he turned and with quick, impatient steps made for the plane.

Unable to do anything more, Claudia watched him enter the jetway. Still crushed by her emotions, she stood by the large windows waiting until the plane was in the sky.

The following week was wretched. At times Claudia thought it would have been easier not to have seen Seth again than endure the misery of another parting. To complicate her life further, it was the week of mid-term exams. Never had she felt less like studying. Each night she wrote Seth long, flowing letters. School had always come first, but suddenly writing letters to Seth was more important. When she did study, her concentration waned and her mind wandered to the hurt look on Seth's face before he'd entered the plane. The look haunted her all week. She did poorly on the first test, her drive to excel weakening to lack of interest. Determined to do better on the next series of exams, Claudia forced herself to study. The textbooks lay open on top of the kitchen table, and Claudia's chin was propped on both hands as she stared into space. Her thoughts weren't on school but on Seth. The illogical meanderings of her mind continued to haunt her with the burning question of her future. Was being a pediatrician so important if it meant losing Seth?

"You look like a lovesick calf," Ashley commented as she strolled into the kitchen to pour herself a glass of milk.

"I feel like one," Claudia returned miserably.

"There's something different about you since Seth's gone back to Alaska."

"No there isn't," she denied. "It's all the hassles of these tests." Why did she feel the need to make excuses? She'd always been able to talk to Ashley about anything.

Her roommate gave her a funny look, but didn't say anything. A minute later she returned to the living room.

Angry with herself and the world, Claudia studied half the night, finally staggering into her bedroom at about three. That was another thing. She hadn't been sleeping well since Seth had gone.

Ashley was cooking dinner when Claudia arrived home the next afternoon. She'd gone to the library, hoping to keep her mind off Seth and concentrate on her schoolwork.

"You had company," Ashley announced casually, but she looked a bit flushed and slightly uneasy.

Claudia's heart stopped. Seth. Seth had come back for her. She needed so desperately to see him again, to talk to him.

"Seth?" she questioned breathlessly.

"No, Cooper. I didn't know what time you were going to be home, so instead of waiting here, he decided to run an errand and come back later," Ashley explained.

"Oh." Claudia didn't even try to disguise the disappointment in her voice. "I can do without another unpleasant confrontation with my uncle. I wonder how he found out about that awful test grade so early."

"Why do you always assume the worse with Cooper?'' Ashley demanded with a sharp edge of impatience. ''I, for one, happen to think he's nice. I don't think I've ever seen him treat anyone unfairly. It seems to me that you're the one who—'' She stopped abruptly and turned back toward the stove, stirring the frying hamburger with unnecessary vigor. ''I hope spaghetti sounds good.''

''Sure,'' Claudia responded. ''Anything.''

Cooper didn't arrive until they had eaten and were clearing off the table. Claudia made a pot of coffee and brought him a cup in the living room. She could feel his gaze studying her.

''You don't look so good,'' he commented, taking the cup and saucer out of her hand. Most men would have preferred a mug, but not Cooper.

''So Ashley keeps telling me.'' She sat opposite him. ''Don't do the dishes, Ash,'' she called into the kitchen. ''Wait until later and I'll help.''

''No need.'' Ashley stuck her head around the kitchen door. ''You go ahead and visit. Call if you need anything.''

''No, Ashley,'' Cooper stood as he spoke. ''I think that it might be beneficial if you were here, too.''

Ashley looked from one to the other, dried her hands on a towel and came into the room.

''I don't mean to embarrass you, Ashley, but in all fairness I think Claudia should know that you were the one to contact me.''

Claudia's gaze shot accusingly across the room. ''What do you mean?''

Ashley shrugged. ''I've been so worried about you lately. You're hardly yourself anymore. I thought if you talked to Cooper, it might help you make up your mind. You can't go on like this, Claudia.'' Her voice was gentle and stern all at the same time.

''What do you mean?'' She vaulted to her feet. ''This is unfair, both of you against me.''

''Against you?'' Cooper echoed. ''Come now, Claudia, you seem to have misjudged everything.''

''No I haven't.'' Tears threatened her eyes, burning for release.

''I think it would probably be best if I left the two of you alone.'' Ashley stood and excused herself, returning to the kitchen.

Claudia hurled her an angry glare as she stepped past. Some friend!

''I hope you'll talk honestly with me, Claudia,'' Cooper began. ''I'd like to know what's got you so upset that you're a stranger to your own best friend.''

''Nothing,'' she denied adamantly, but her voice cracked and the first tears began spilling down her cheek.

Claudia was sure Cooper had never seen her cry. He looked at a loss as he stood and searched hurriedly through his suit coat for a handkerchief. Just watching him made Claudia want to laugh, and she hiccuped in an attempt to restrain tears and laughter.

''Here.'' He handed her a white linen cloth, crisply pressed. Claudia didn't care, she wiped her eyes and blew her nose. ''I'm fine, really,'' she declared in a wavering voice.

''It's about Seth, isn't it?'' Cooper prompted.

She nodded, blowing her nose again. ''He wants me to marry him and move to Alaska.''

The room suddenly became still as Cooper digested the information. ''Are you going to do it?'' he asked in a quiet voice she had long ago learned to decipher as a warning.

''If I knew that, I wouldn't be here blubbering like an idiot,'' she returned defensively.

''I can't help but believe it would be a mistake,'' Cooper continued. ''Lessinger's a good man, don't misunderstand me, but I don't think you'd be happy in Alaska. Where did you say he was from again?'' he asked.

''Nome.''

''I don't suppose there's a university in Nome for you to continue your studies?''

''No.'' The word was clipped, impatient.

Cooper nodded. ''You were meant to be a doctor,'' he said confidently as he rose to his feet. ''You'll get over Seth. There's probably a fine young man you'll meet later.''

''Sure,'' she agreed without enthusiasm.

Cooper left a few minutes later, and at the sound of the door closing, Ashley stepped out of the kitchen. ''You aren't mad, are you?''

At first Claudia had been, but not now. At least she knew where Cooper stood on the subject and what she would face if she did decide to marry Seth.

''Oh, Seth,'' she whispered that night, sitting up in bed. He hadn't contacted her since his return, not even answering her long letters. Eagerly Claudia had checked the mail every day. After several days she understood that the next move would have to be from her. Her Bible rested on her knees, and she opened it for her devotional reading in Hebrews. She read Chapter 11 twice, the famous chapter on faith. Had Rebekah acted in faith when the servant had come to her family, claiming God had given him a sign? Flipping through the pages of her Bible, she turned to Genesis to reread the story Seth had quoted. When Seth had given her the engagement ring they had argued. Claudia had said Rebekah probably didn't have any choice in the matter, but reading the story now, Claudia noted that the Bible said she did. Rebekah's family asked her if she was willing to go with Abraham's servant, and she'd replied that she would.

Rebekah went willingly! Claudia reread the verses again as a sense of release came over her. Her hands trembled with excitement as she closed the Bible and stopped to pray. The prayer was so familiar: asking God's guidance and stating her willingness to do as He wished. But there was a difference this time. The peace she had so desperately sought was there, and she knew that she, too, would answer Seth in faith and respond willingly.

Slipping out of the sheets, she opened the drawer that contained the jeweler's box and the engagement ring. With a contented, happy sigh, she hugged it to her breast. The temptation was to slip the ring on her finger now. But she'd wait until Seth could do it.

Claudia slept peacefully that night for the first time since Seth had left. She didn't go to classes the next morning.

Ashley looked at her with surprise. Claudia was still in her pajamas when she was dressed and ready to go out the front door. ''Did you oversleep? I'm sorry I didn't wake you, but I thought I heard you moving around in your room.''

''You did,'' she answered cheerfully, but her eyes grew serious as her gaze sought Ashley's. ''I've decided what to do, Ash,'' she announced solemnly. ''I love Seth. I'm going to him as fast as I can make the arrangements.''

Ashley's blue eyes widened with joy as she laughed and hugged her friend. ''It's about time. You nut, I knew all along that the two of you belonged together! I'm so happy for you.''

Once the decision was made, there seemed to be a hundred things to be dealt with all at once. Claudia phoned Nome almost immediately, her fingers trembling and reached Seth's secretary, who told her Seth had flown to Kotzebue on an emergency. She didn't know when he would be returning, but would give him the message as soon as he walked in the door. Releasing a sigh of disappointment, Claudia replaced the phone in its cradle.

Undaunted by the uncertainties, Claudia drove to the university and officially withdrew from school. Next she purchased several outfits she would be needing to face an Arctic winter, and a beautiful wedding dress. Lastly she stopped off at Cooper's office.

He smiled broadly when she entered his office. ''You look in better spirits today,'' he greeted. ''I knew our little talk would help.''

''You'd better sit down, Cooper,'' she said and smiled. ''I've made my decision. I love Seth. I've withdrawn from school and have made arrangements for my things to be shipped North when possible. I'm marrying Seth Lessinger.''

Cooper stood, his eyes raking over her. ''That's what you think.''

# Chapter Seven

It was dark and stormy when the plane made a jerky landing on the Nome runway. Claudia shifted to relieve her muscles, tired and stiff from the bouncing ride. The aircraft had hit turbulent weather shortly after takeoff from Anchorage, and the remainder of the flight could be compared to a roller-coaster ride. More than once Claudia had felt the pricklings of fear, but none of the other passengers showed any concern, so she had accepted the jarring ride as a normal part of flying in Alaska.

Her blue eyes glinted with excitement as she stood and gathered the small bag stored in the compartment above the seat. There wasn't a jetway to usher her into a dry, warm airport. When she stepped from the cozy interior of the plane, she was greeted by a solid blast of Arctic wind. The bitter iciness stole her breath, and she groped for the handrail to maintain her balance. Halfway down the stairs, she was nearly ripped away by a fresh gust of wind. Her hair flew into her face, blinding her vision. Unable to move either up or down, she stood stationary until the force of the wind decreased.

Unexpectedly the small bag was wrenched from her numb fingers and she was pulled into the protective hold of a solid form.

He shouted something at her, but the wind carried his voice into the night and there was no distinguishing the message.

Claudia tried to speak, but soon realized the uselessness of talking. She was half carried, half dragged down the remainder of the steps. Once on solid ground, they both struggled against the ferocity of the wind as it whipped and lashed against them. If the man hadn't taken the brunt of the force, Claudia might not have made it inside.

As they came close to the terminal, the door was opened by someone who'd been standing by, watching. The welcoming warmth immediately stirred life into Claudia's frozen body. Nothing could have prepared her for the intensity of the Arctic cold. Even before she could turn and thank her rescuer she was pulled into his arms and crushed in a smothering embrace.

''Seth?'' Her arms slid around his thick-coated waist as she returned the urgency of his hug.

He buried his face in her neck and breathed her name. His hold was punishing, and when he spoke, his voice was tight and worried.

''Are you all right?'' Gently his hands framed her face, pushing back the strands of hair that had been whipped across her cheek. His eyes searched her features as if looking for any sign of harm.

"I'm fine," she assured him and, wrapping her arms around him a second time, pressed her face into his coat. "I'm so glad to be here."

"I've been sick with worry," he ground out hoarsely. "The storm hit here several hours ago, and there wasn't any way your flight could avoid the worst of it."

"I'm fine, really." Her voice wobbled, not because she was shaky from the flight, but from the effect of being in Seth's arms.

"I was with the air traffic controller when he first made contact with your pilot and heard the pilot claim that your plane was being batted around like a tennis ball. If anything had happened to you, I don't know..." He let the rest fade, and tightened his already secure hold.

"Now that you mention it, I do feel something like a tennis ball," she teased with a happy look and lightly touched her lips to the corner of his mouth.

Seth released her. The worried look in his eyes had diminished now that he knew she was safe. "Let's get out of here," he said abruptly and left her standing alone as he secured her luggage.

The suitcases contained only a small part of her possessions. In the days preceding her flight she'd packed her things and made arrangements to have them shipped to her in the spring. Everything she could possibly get into the three large suitcases would have to see her through until the freight barge arrived.

They rode to the hotel in a four-wheel-drive vehicle.

Neither spoke as Seth gave his full attention to manipulating the car through the streets. Claudia looked around her in awe. The barren land was covered with snow. The road was merely compact dirt and snow. The buildings were a dingy gray color. In her dreams she had conjured up romantic pictures of Seth's life in Nome. Reality shattered the vision as the winds buffeted the large car.

The hotel room was neat and clean—not elegant, but she hadn't expected the homey, welcoming appeal. It contained a bed with a plain white bedspread, a small nightstand, a lamp, a telephone and one chair. Seth followed her in, managing the suitcases.

"You packed enough," he said with a sarcastic undertone. Claudia ignored the comment and busied herself by removing her coat to hang it in the bare closet. She gave him a puzzled look. Something was wrong. He had hardly spoken to her since they'd left the airport. At first she'd assumed the tight set of his mouth was a result of the storm, but not now, when she was safe and ready for his love. Her heart ached for him to hold her. Every part of her longed to have him slip the engagement ring onto the third finger of her left hand.

"How's school?" Again the inflection in his voice was derisive.

"Fine."

He remained on the far side of the room, his hands clenched at his sides.

"Let me take your coat?" she offered. As she studied him, the gnawing sensation that something wasn't right increased. Seth unfastened the coat opening, but he didn't remove his thick parka. He sat at the end of the bed, his face tight and drawn. Claudia wasn't sure he'd heard her.

Resting his elbows on his knees, he leaned forward and buried his face in his hands.

"Seth, what's wrong?" she asked calmly, although she was far from feeling self-possessed.

"I've only had eight hours' sleep in the last four days. A tanker caught fire in port at Kotzebue, and I've been there doing what I could for the past week. You certainly couldn't have chosen a worse time for a visit. Isn't it a little early for Thanksgiving?"

Claudia wanted to scream that this wasn't a visit, she'd come to stay, to be his wife and share his world. But again she remained quiet, guided by the same inner sense. Seth's manner, once he'd been assured she was safe, had been distant, even aloof.

Quietly Seth stood and stalked to the far side of the small room. He seemed to be limping slightly. He paused and glanced over his shoulder, but didn't return to her.

Uncertainty clouded her deep blue eyes and her mind raced with a thousand questions.

"I'm flying back to Kotzebue as soon as possible. I shouldn't have taken the time away as it is." He turned around and his eyes burned her with the intensity of his glare. His mouth was drawn, hard and inflexible. "I'll have one of my men drive you back to the airport for the first available flight to Anchorage." There was no apology, no explanation, no regrets.

Claudia stared back at him in shocked disbelief.

Even if he had assumed she was here for a short visit, he was treating her as he would unwanted baggage.

Belying the hurt, she smiled lamely. "I can't see why I have to leave. Even if you aren't here, this would be a good opportunity for me to see Nome. I'd like to—"

"Can't you do as I ask, just once?" he shouted.

She lowered her gaze to fight the anger building within her. Squaring her shoulders, she prepared for the worst. "There's something I don't know, isn't there?" she asked in quiet challenge. She wanted to hear the truth, even at the risk of being hurt.

Her question was followed by a moment of grim silence. "I don't want you here."

"I believe you've made that obvious." Her fingers trembled, and she mentally chided herself for the telltale mannerism.

"I tried to reach you before you left." He gestured defeatedly with his hand.

She didn't comment but continued to stare at him with round, questioning eyes.

"It's not going to work between us, Claudia," he announced solemnly. "I think I realized as much when you didn't return with me when I gave you the ring. You must think I was a fool to propose to you the way I did."

"You know I didn't, I—"

He interrupted her again. "I want a wife, Claudia, not some virtuous doctor out to heal the world. I need a woman, not an insecure, immature little girl who can't decide what she wants in life."

White-lipped, Claudia stiffened her back and met

the building rage with feigned control. ''Do you want me to hate you, Seth?'' she asked softly as her fingers picked an imaginary piece of lint from the sleeve of her thick sweater.

He released a bitter sigh. ''Yes. It would make things between us a lot easier if you hated me,'' he replied flatly. He walked away as if he couldn't bear to see the pain he was causing her. ''Even if you were to change your mind and relinquish your lofty dreams to marry me, I doubt that we could make a marriage work. You've been tossing on a wave of indecision for so long, I don't think you'll ever decide what you really want.''

Claudia studied the pattern of the worn carpet, biting her tongue to keep from crying out that she knew what she wanted now. But Seth had witnessed her struggle in the sea of uncertainty. He would assume that her decision was as fickle as the turning tide.

''If we married, what's there to say you wouldn't regret it later?'' he went on. ''You've wanted to be a doctor for so many years, and frankly, I don't know if my love could satisfy you. Someday you might have been able to return to medical school—I would have wanted that for you—but my life, my business, everything I need is here in Nome. It's where I belong. But not you, Red.'' The affectionate endearment rolled easily from his lips, seemingly without thought. ''We live in two different worlds. And my world will never satisfy you.''

''What about all this business about the sign from God? You were the one who was so sure. You were the one who claimed this deep, undying love.'' She hurled the words at him bitterly, intent on hurting him as much as he was hurting her.

"I was wrong. I don't know how I could have done anything so stupid."

Again she had to restrain herself from crying out that it had never been absurd, it was wonderful. The Bible verse in the mirror had meant so much to them both. But she refused to plead, and the dull ache in her heart took on a throbbing intensity.

"That's not all," he added with a cruel twist. "There's someone else now."

Nothing could have shocked her more. "Don't lie to me, Seth. Anything but that!"

"Believe it, because it's true. My situation hasn't changed. I need a wife, someone to share my life. There's—" he hesitated "—someone I was seeing before I met you. I was going to ask her to marry me as soon as I got the engagement ring back from you."

"You're lucky I brought it with me," she shouted as she tore open her purse and dumped the contents over the bedspread. Carelessly she sorted through her things. It took only a couple of seconds to locate the velvet box, turn around and viciously hurl it at Seth.

Instinctively he brought his hands up and caught the box. Their eyes met for a moment, then without another word he tucked it in his coat pocket.

A searing pain burned through her heart and she bit her lower lip.

Seth seemed to hesitate. He hovered for a moment by the door. "I didn't mean to hurt you." Slowly he lowered his gaze to meet hers.

She avoided his look. Nothing would be worse than

to have him offer her sympathy. "I'm sure you didn't," she whispered on a bitter note, and her voice cracked. "Please leave," she requested urgently.

Without another word, Seth opened the door and walked away.

Numb with shock, Claudia couldn't cry, couldn't move. Holding up her head became an impossible task. A low, protesting cry came from deep within her throat, and she covered her mouth with the palm of one hand. Somehow she made it to the bed, collapsing on the mattress.

Claudia woke the next morning, and a quick lump of pain formed in her throat at the memory of her encounter with Seth. For a while she tried to force herself to return to the black cloud of mindless sleep, but to no avail.

She dressed and stared miserably out the window. The winds were blustery, but nothing compared to yesterday's gales. Seth would have returned to Kotzebue. Her world had died, but Nome lived. The city appeared calm; people were walking, laughing and talking. Claudia wondered if she would ever laugh again. What had gone wrong? Hadn't she trusted God, trusted in Seth's love? How could her world dissolve like this? The tightness in her throat grew and grew.

The small room became her prison. She waited an impatient hour, wondering what she should do, until further lingering became intolerable. Since she was here, she might as well explore the city Seth loved.

The people were friendly and offered an easy smile and a cheery good morning as she passed. There weren't any large stores, nothing to compete with Seattle. She strolled down the walkway, following the only paved road she could see. Not caring where her feet took her, she continued until she saw the sign ARCTIC BARGE COMPANY—Seth's business. A wave of fresh pain swamped her fragile composure and she turned and briskly walked in the opposite direction. Ahead, she spotted a picturesque white church with bell and steeple. Claudia sought peace inside.

The interior was dark as she slipped quietly into the back pew. Thanksgiving would be at the end of the month—a time for sharing God's goodness with family and friends. She was trapped in Nome with neither. When she'd left Seattle, her heart had nearly burst with praise for God. Now it was ready to burst with the pain of Seth's rejection.

Claudia didn't mean to cry, but there was something so peaceful and restful about the quiet church. A tear slipped from the corner of her eye and Claudia wiped it aside. She'd left Seattle so sure of Seth's love and the joy of her newfound discovery. She'd come in faith. And this was where faith had led her. To an empty church, with a heart burdened by bitter memories.

She'd painted herself into a dark corner. She'd lost her apartment. Ashley had found herself a cheaper place and a new roommate. If she did return to school, she would be forced to repeat the quarter, and there wasn't any guarantee she would be admitted back into the medical program. Every possession she owned had been carefully packed and loaded onto a barge that wouldn't arrive in Nome for months.

Claudia poured out her complications in prayer. She

had come, following what she thought was God's leading, and now it seemed she had made a terrible mistake. Lifting the Bible from the pew, she sat and read, desperately seeking guidance, until she caught a movement from the corner of her eye. A stocky middle-aged man was approaching.

"Can I help you?" the man asked her softly.

Claudia looked up blankly.

He read the confusion in her eyes. "I'm Paul Reeder, the pastor," he said to identify himself, and sat beside her in the pew.

She held out her hand and smiled weakly. "Claudia Masters."

"Your first visit to Nome?" His voice was gentle and inquiring.

"Yes, how'd you know?" she couldn't help but wonder aloud.

He grinned and his brown eyes sparkled. "Easy, I know everyone in town, and either you're a visitor or I've fallen down on my duties."

Claudia nodded and hung her head at the reminder of why and for whom she had come to Nome.

"Is there something I can do for you, child?" he asked thoughtfully.

"I don't think there's much anyone can do anymore." Her voice shook slightly, and she lowered her lashes in an effort to conceal the desperation in her eyes.

"Things are rarely as difficult as they seem. Remember, God doesn't close a door without opening a window," he said in kind understanding.

Claudia attempted a smile. "I guess I need someone to point to the window."

"Would you feel better if you confided in someone?" he urged gently.

She didn't feel up to explanations, but knew she should say something. "I quit school and moved to Alaska expecting...a job." The pastor was sure to know Seth, and she didn't want to involve the good man in her relationship with Seth. "I...I assumed wrong...and now..."

"You need a job and place to live," he concluded for her. A light gleamed in the clear depths of the older man's eyes. "There's an apartment for rent near here. Since it belongs to the church, the payments are reasonable. As for the other problem..." He paused thoughtfully. "You're trained in a specific skill?"

"No, not really." The words were heavy and bare. "I have a college degree in premed and have completed one year of medical school, but other than that—"

"My dear girl!" Pastor Reeder clenched his hands in excitement. "You are the answer to our prayers. Nome desperately needs medical assistants. We've advertised for months for another doctor—"

"Oh, please understand," Claudia cried, "I'm not a doctor. I'm not even qualified to work in the medical profession. All I have is the book knowledge, but little practical experience."

Disregarding her objections, Pastor Reeder stood and anxiously moved into the wide aisle. "There's someone you must meet."

A worried frown marred Claudia's smooth brow.

She licked her dry lips and followed the tall man as he briskly stepped from the church and into the street.

They stopped a block or two later. ‘‘While we're here, I'll show you the apartment.'' He unlocked the door to a small house and Claudia stepped inside.

‘‘Tiny'' wasn't the word; it was the most compact space Claudia had ever seen: living room, miniature kitchen and a very small bathroom.

‘‘It's perfect,'' she stated positively. Perfect if she didn't have to return to Seattle and face Cooper. Perfect if she could show Seth she wasn't like a wave tossed to and fro by the sea. She had made her decision and was here to stay, with or without him. She had responded in faith; God was her guide.

‘‘The apartment isn't on the sewer,'' the pastor added. ‘‘I hope that won't inconvenience you.''

‘‘Of course not.'' Claudia smiled. It didn't matter to her if she had a septic tank.

He nodded approvingly. ‘‘I'll arrange for water delivery, then.''

Claudia didn't understand, but let the comment pass as he locked the door.

He led her down the street. ‘‘I'm taking you to meet a friend of mine, Dr. Jim Coleman. I'm sure Jim will share my enthusiasm when I tell him about your medical background.''

‘‘Shouldn't I sign something and make a deposit on the apartment first?''

Pastor Reeder's eyes twinkled. ‘‘We'll settle that later. Thanksgiving has arrived early in Nome. I can't see going through the rigmarole of deposits when God

Himself has sent you to us." He handed her the key and smiled contentedly.

The doctor's waiting room was crowded with people when Claudia and Pastor Reeder entered. Every chair was taken, and small children played on the floor.

The receptionist greeted them warmly. "Good morning, Pastor. What can I do for you? Not another emergency, I hope."

"Quite the opposite. Tell Jim I'd like to see him, right away, if possible. I promise to take only a few minutes of his time."

They were ushered into a private office. The large desk was covered with correspondence, magazines and medical journals. A pair of glasses had been carelessly tossed on top of the pile.

A young-looking doctor entered the room fifteen minutes later and skeptically eyed Claudia, dark eyes narrowed fractionally.

Eagerly Paul Reeder stood and beamed a smile toward Claudia. "Jim, I'd like to introduce you to God's Thanksgiving present to you."

Claudia stood and extended her hand. The smile on her face died as she noted the frown that flitted across the young doctor's brow.

The handshake was barely civil. "Listen, Paul, I haven't the time for your matchmaking efforts today—no matter who the young lady is. There are fifteen people in my waiting room and the hospital just phoned. Mary Fulton's in labor."

If he hadn't spoken so gruffly, Claudia could have forgiven the bad manners, but now her eyes snapped with blue sparks at the affront.

"Let me assure you, Dr. Coleman, that you are the last man I'd care to be matched with!"

A wild light flashed in Jim's eyes and it looked as if he would have stormed a reply if Pastor Reeder hadn't scrambled to his feet.

"I'll not have you insulting the woman the good Lord sent to help you. And you, Claudia—" he turned to her, waving his finger "—don't be offended. Jim made an honest mistake. He's simply overworked and rushed."

Confusion and embarrassment played rapidly over the physician's face. "The Lord sent?" he repeated. "You're a nurse?"

Sadly Claudia shook her head. "Medical student. Ex-medical student," she corrected. "I don't know if I'll be much help; I don't have much practical skill."

"If you work with me, you'll gain that fast enough." He looked at her as if she had suddenly descended from heaven. "I've been urgently looking for someone to train to work on an emergency medical team. With your background and a few months of on-the-job training, you can take the paramedic test and easily qualify. What do you say, Claudia? Can we start again?" His boyish grin lent reassurance.

Claudia smiled reluctantly, not knowing what to say. Only minutes before, she'd claimed to be following God, responding to faith. Did He always move so quickly? "Why not?" she said with a laugh.

"Can you start tomorrow?"

"Sure," she confirmed, grateful that she would be kept so busy she wouldn't have time to remember that the reason she had come to Nome had nothing to do with paramedic training.

A message was waiting for her when she returned to the hotel. It gave a phone number and name, with information for the flights leaving Nome for Anchorage. Crumpling the paper, Claudia checked out of the hotel.

The rest of the afternoon was spent unpacking and settling in the tiny apartment. If Cooper could only see her now!

Hunger pangs interrupted her work, and Claudia realized she hadn't eaten all day. Just as she was beginning to wonder about dinner, there was a knock on the door. Her immediate thought was that Seth had somehow learned she hadn't returned to Seattle. Though it was unlikely, she realized, since Seth was in Kotzebue.

Opening the door, she found a petite blond with warm blue eyes and a friendly smile. "Welcome to Nome! I'm Barbara Reeder," she said and handed Claudia a warm plate covered with aluminum foil.

"Dad's been talking about his miracle ever since I walked in the door this afternoon, and I decided to meet this Joan of Arc myself." Her laugh was free and easy.

Claudia liked her immediately. Barbara's personality was similar to Ashley's, and the two women fell into ready conversation. Claudia let Barbara do most of the talking. She learned that the woman was close to her own age, worked as a legal secretary and was engaged to a man named Teddy. Claudia felt she needed a friend, someone bright and cheerful to lift her spirits from a tangled web of self-pity.

"Barbara, while you're here, would you mind explaining about the bathroom?" Claudia had been shocked to discover the room was missing the most important appliance.

Barbara's eyes rounded derisively. "You mean Dad didn't explain that you aren't on the sewer?"

"Yes, but—"

"Only houses on the sewers have flush toilets, plumbing and the rest. You, my newfound friend, have your very own 'honey bucket.' It's like having an indoor outhouse. When you need to use it, just open the door in the wall, pull it inside and—*voilà.*"

Claudia looked up shocked. "Yes, but—"

"You'll need to get yourself a fuzzy cover, because the seat is freezing. When you're through, open the door, replace it outside and it'll freeze almost immediately."

"Yes, but—"

"Oh, and the water is delivered on Monday, Wednesday and Friday. Garbage is picked up once a week, but be sure and keep it inside the house because wild dogs will get into it if it's outside."

"Yes, but—"

"And I don't suppose Dad explained about ordering food supplies, either. Don't worry, I'll get you an order from the catalog and you'll have plenty of time to decide what you need. Grocery prices are sometimes as much as four times higher than Seattle, so we order the nonperishables once a year. The barge from Seattle arrives before winter."

Claudia breathed in deeply. The concepts of honey buckets, no plumbing and wild dogs were almost too much to grasp in one lump. This lifestyle was primitive compared to that of Seattle. But she would grow stronger from the challenges, grow or falter and break.

Concern clouded Barbara's countenance. "Have I discouraged you?"

Pride and inner strength shimmered in Claudia's eyes. "No, Nome is where I belong," she stated firmly.

Jim Coleman proved to be an excellent teacher. Her admiration for him grew with every day and every patient. At the end of her first week, Claudia was exhausted. Together they had examined and treated a steady flow of the sick and injured, eating quick lunches when they could between patients and small emergencies. At the end of the ten-to-twelve-hour day, Jim was sometimes due to report to the hospital. Claudia spent her evenings studying a huge pile of material he had given her to prepare for the paramedic exam that spring. Claudia marveled at how hard he drove himself, but Jim explained his work load wasn't by choice. Few medical staff were willing to set up practices in the frozen North.

Barbara stopped by during Claudia's second week in Nome with an invitation for Thanksgiving Day. Jim had also been invited, along with Barbara's fiancé and another couple. Claudia thanked her, accepted and might have appeared preoccupied, because Barbara left soon afterward. Claudia closed the door, leaning against the wood frame and swallowed back the bitter hurt. When she'd left Seattle, she told Ashley that she was hoping the wedding would be around Thanksgiving. Now she would spend the day with strangers.

"Good morning, Jim," she greeted the doctor cheerfully the next day. "And you, too, Mrs. Lucy."

The receptionist glanced up, grinning sheepishly to herself.

"Something funny?" Jim demanded brusquely.

"Did either of you get a chance to read Pastor Reeder's sign in front of the church this morning?" she asked.

Claudia shook her head and waited.

"What did he say this time?" Jim asked, his interest aroused.

"The sign reads: God Wants Spiritual Fruit, Not Religious Nuts."

Jim Coleman tipped his head back and chuckled, but his face soon grew serious. "I suggest we get moving," he said. "We've got a full schedule."

Jim was right. The pace at which he drove himself and his staff left little time for chatting or visiting. With so many people in need of medical attention and only two doctors dividing the load, they had to work as efficiently as possible. At six, Claudia had barely had time to grab a sandwich. She was bandaging a badly cut hand after Jim had stitched it when he stuck his head around the corner.

"I want you to check the man in the first room. Let me know what you think. I've got a phone call waiting for me. I'll take it in my office and join you in a few minutes."

A stray curl of rich auburn hair fell haphazardly

across her face, and Claudia paused long enough to tuck it around her ear and straighten the white smock.

Tapping lightly, her smile warm and automatic, she entered the room. "Good afternoon, my name's—"

Stopping short, she felt her stomach pitch wildly. Seth. His eyes were cold and hard. The thin line of his mouth tightened ominously.

"What are you doing here?"

# *Chapter Eight*

"I work here," Claudia returned, outwardly calm, although her heartbeat was racing frantically. She had realized it would only be a matter of time before she ran into Seth, and had in fact been mildly surprised it hadn't happened before now. But nothing could have prepared her for the impact of seeing him again.

Seth's mouth tightened grimly. "Why aren't you in Seattle?" he demanded in a low growl.

"Because I'm here," she countered logically. "Why should you care if I'm in Seattle or Timbuktu? As I recall, you'd washed your hands of me," she replied defensively.

Her answer didn't please him, and Seth propelled himself from the examination table in one angry movement. But he couldn't conceal the wince of pain as he placed his weight on the injured leg.

For the first time Claudia realized he was hurt. "Jim asked me to look at that leg—now get back on the table."

"Jim?" Seth murmured the name derisively. "You seem to have come to a first-name basis pretty quickly."

Pinching her lips tightly together, she ignored the implication. "I'm going to check you whether you like it or not," she commanded with authority few would question.

Seth's dark eyes narrowed mutinously at her demand.

Winning any kind of verbal confrontation with Seth would be almost impossible. She wouldn't have been surprised if he'd stalked from the office limping rather than follow her demand. He might well have if Jim Coleman hadn't entered the cubicle at that precise minute.

"I've been talking to the hospital," he remarked, handing Claudia the medical chart. Sheer reflex prevented the folder from falling as it slipped through her fingers. She caught it and glanced up guiltily.

Jim seemed oblivious to the thick atmosphere between the two. "Have you examined the wound?" he questioned and motioned for Seth to return to the table.

Seth hesitated for a moment before repositioning himself on the table. With another flick of his hand, Jim directed Seth to lie down. Again he paused before lowering his back onto the red vinyl cushion. He lay with his eyes closed, and Claudia thought her heart would burst. She loved this man, even when he had cast her from his life, tossing out cruel words in an attempt to make her hate him. Still, she couldn't.

Jim lifted the large bandage, allowing Claudia the first look at the angry wound. Festering with yellow pus, the cut must have been the source of constant, throbbing pain. Gently testing the skin around the infection brought a deathly pallor to Seth's face as he battled to disguise the intense pain. A faint but nonetheless distinct red line followed the cut, reaching halfway up his thigh.

"Blood poisoning," Claudia murmured gravely. She could almost feel his agony and paled slightly. Anxiously she glanced at Jim.

"Blood poisoning or not, just give me the medicine and let me out of here. I've got a business to run. I can't be held up here all day while you two ohh and ahh over a minor cut." The sharp words burst impatiently from Seth as he struggled to sit upright.

"You seem to think you can work with that wound," Jim shot back angrily. "Go ahead if you fancy strapping a wooden peg to your hip the rest of your life. You need to be in the hospital."

"So you keep saying," Seth retorted.

Stiff with concern, Claudia stepped forward when Seth let out a low moan and lay back down.

"Do whatever you have to," he said in a resigned tone.

"I'd like to talk to you in my office a minute, Claudia. Go ahead and wait for me there."

The request surprised her, but she did as Jim asked. He joined her a moment later, a frown of concern twisted his brow.

"I've already spoken to the hospital," he announced and slumped defeatedly into his chair. "There aren't any beds available." He ran a hand over his face and looked up at her with unseeing eyes. "It's times like these that make me wonder why I chose to work in Nome. Inadequate facilities, no private nurses, overworked staff...I don't know how much more of these hours my health will take.''

Claudia hadn't known Jim long, but she had never seen him more frustrated or angry.

''I've contacted the airport to have him flown out by a charter plane, but there's a storm coming and flying for the next twelve hours would be suicidal,'' Jim continued. ''His leg can't wait that long. Something's got to be done before that infection spreads any farther.'' He straightened and released a bitter sigh. ''I don't have any choice but to send you home with him, Claudia. He's going to need constant care, or he could lose that leg. I can't do it myself, and there's no one else I would trust.''

Claudia leaned against the door, needing its support as the weight of responsibility pressed heavily upon her shoulders. She couldn't refuse.

Patiently Jim outlined the treatment for the infection. His eyes studied Claudia for a sign of confusion or misunderstanding. He gave her the supplies and reminded her of the seriousness of the infection.

An hour later, with Seth strongly protesting, Claudia managed to get him into his home and into his bed. Propping his leg up with a pillow, she removed the bandage to view the open wound a second time. She cringed at the sight of the rotting flesh and fought back revulsion.

Her eyes clouded with worry as she worked gently and efficiently to make him as comfortable as possible.

Purposefully she avoided his gaze in an attempt to mask her concern.

He appeared somewhat more comfortable as he rested his head against the pillow. The only sign of pain he allowed to show on the ruggedly carved features was the tightly clenched mouth. Beads of perspiration wetted his brow. Claudia didn't need to see his agony to know he was in intense pain.

"Why are you here?" He repeated his earlier question, his eyes closed.

"I'm taking care of your leg," she replied gently. "Don't talk now, try and sleep if you can." Deftly she opened the bag of supplies and laid them out on the dresser table.

Standing above him, she rested her cool hand against his heated brow.

At the tender touch of her fingers, he raised his hand and gripped her wrist. "Don't play games with me, Red." He opened his eyes to hold her gaze. "Why are you in Nome?" The words were weak; there wasn't any fight left in him. Protesting Jim's arrangements had depleted him of strength. Now every effort was used to disguise his pain. "Have you come back to torment me?"

"I never left," she answered and touched a finger to his lips to prevent his questions. "Not now," she whispered. "We'll talk later and I'll explain then."

He nodded almost imperceptibly and rolled his head to the side.

Examining the cut brought a liquid sheen to her eyes. "How could you have let this go so long?" she protested. Jim had explained to her earlier that Seth had fallen against a cargo crate while in Kotzebue. Claudia recalled that he had a slight limp the day he had picked her up from the airport. He had let the injury go untreated all that time. Was he crazy?

He didn't respond to her question, but exhaled a sharp breath as she gently began swabbing the wound. To cause him the least amount of pain, she probed the wound patiently. She bit into her lip when he winced again, but it was important to clean the cut and check the possibility of foreign matter imbedded in the flesh. Jim had given Seth antibiotics and painkillers before leaving the office, but their effect had been minor.

When she'd finished, she heated hot water in the kitchen, steeping strips of cloth in the clean water. Allowing them to cool slightly, she placed the cloths over his thigh. His body jerked taut and his mouth tightened with the renewed effort to conceal his torment. The process was repeated until the wound was thoroughly cleansed. Claudia returned to the kitchen.

"I'm going to lose this leg," Seth mumbled as she walked into the bedroom.

"Not if I can help it," she said with a determination that produced a weak smile from him.

"I'm glad you're here," he said, his voice fading.

Claudia gently squeezed his hand. "I'm glad I'm here, too." Even if she did return to Seattle, there would always be the satisfaction of having been able to help Seth.

He rested fitfully. Some time later, she again heated water, adding the medicine Jim had given her to the steaming water. A pungent odor filled the room. As quietly as possible, so not to disturb him, she again steeped the strips. Cautiously she draped them around the swollen leg, securing them with a large plastic bag to keep them moist and warm as long as possible. When the second stage of Jim's instructions had been completed, she slumped wearily into a chair at Seth's bedside.

Two hours later she repeated the process, and again after another two-hour interval. Claudia didn't know what time it was when Jim came. But there didn't seem to be any noticeable improvement in Seth's condition.

"How's the fever?" Jim asked as he checked the sleeping man's pulse.

"High," Claudia replied, unable to conceal her worry.

"Give him time," Jim cautioned. He gave Seth another injection and glanced at his watch. "I'm due at the hospital. I'll see what I can do to find someone to replace you."

"No!" she said abruptly, too abruptly. "I'll stay."

Jim eyed her curiously, his gaze searching. "You've been at this several hours now. The next few could be crucial, and I don't want you working yourself sick."

"I'm going to see him through this," she said with marked determination. Avoiding the question in his eyes, she made busy work around the room. She would answer him later if she must, but now all that mattered was Seth and getting him well.

Jim left a few minutes later, and Claudia paused to fix herself something to eat. She would need her strength, but although she tried to force herself to eat, her fears mounted, dispelling her appetite.

The ache in the small of her back throbbed as she continued to labor through the night. Again and again she applied the hot cloths to draw out the poison.

Claudia bit at her lip anxiously when she took his temperature and discovered the fever continued to rage, despite her efforts. Her fingers gently tested the flesh surrounding the infection, and she frowned heavily.

Waves of panic mounted again a few minutes later when Seth stirred restlessly in his sleep. He rolled his head slowly from side to side as the pain disturbed his sleep.

"Jesus, please help us," Claudia prayed as she grew more dismayed. Nothing she did seemed to be able to control Seth's fever.

Repeatedly she'd heard the importance of remaining calm and clear-headed when treating a patient. But her heart was filled with dread as the hours passed, each one interminable, and still his fever raged. If she couldn't lower Seth's fever, he might lose his leg.

His Bible lay on the nightstand and Claudia picked it up, holding it in both hands. She brought the leather-bound book to her breast and lifted her eyes to heaven, murmuring a fervent prayer.

Another hour passed and he began to moan and mumble incoherently as he slipped into a feverish delirium. He tossed his head and Claudia was forced to hold him down as he struggled, flinging out his arms.

He quieted and Claudia tenderly stroked his brow while whispering soothing words of comfort in an attempt to quiet him.

Unexpectedly, with an amazing strength, Seth jerked

upright and cried out in anguish, ‘‘John...watch out...no...no...’’

Gently but firmly she laid him back against the pillow, murmuring softly in an effort to calm him. Absently she wondered who John was. She couldn’t remember Seth ever mentioning anyone by that name.

Repeatedly he mumbled something about John. Once he even laughed, the laugh she loved so much. But only seconds later he again cried out in anguish.

Tears that had been lingering so close to the surface quickly welled. Loving someone, as she loved Seth, made that person’s torment one’s own. Never had she loved this completely, this strongly.

‘‘Hush, my darling,’’ she murmured softly.

She was afraid to leave him, even for a moment, so she pulled the chair as close as she could to his bedside and sank wearily into it. Exhaustion claimed her mind to everything but prayer.

Toward daylight, Seth seemed to be resting more comfortably and Claudia slipped into a light sleep.

Someone spoke her name and she shifted from her uncomfortable position to find Seth, eyes open, regarding her steadily.

‘‘Good morning,’’ he whispered weakly. His forehead and face were beaded with sweat, his shirt damp with perspiration. The fever, at last, had broken.

A lump of happiness formed in Claudia’s throat and she offered an immediate prayer of thanksgiving.

‘‘Good morning,’’ she returned the greeting, her voice light as relief washed over her. She beamed with joy as she tested his forehead. It felt moist and cool, and she stood to wipe the sweat from his face with a fresh washcloth.

His hand stopped her action and closed over her fingers, as if touching her would prove she was real. "I'm not dreaming, it is you."

She laughed softly. "The one and only." Suddenly conscious of her disheveled appearance, Claudia ran her fingers through her tangled hair and straightened her blouse.

His warm gaze watched her movements and Claudia felt unexpectedly shy.

"You told me you never left Nome." The inflection in his voice made the statement a question.

"I didn't come here to turn around and go back home," she said and smiled, allowing all the pent-up love to burn in her eyes.

His eyes questioned her as she examined his leg. The improvement was remarkable. She smiled, remembering her frantic prayers during the night. Only the Great Physician could have worked this quickly.

She helped Seth sit up and removed his damp shirt. They worked together silently as she wiped him down and slipped a fresh shirt over his head. Taking the bowl, and tucking his shirt under her arm, she smiled at him and walked toward the door.

"Red, don't go," he called urgently.

"I'll be right back," she assured him. "I'm just going to take these into the kitchen and fix you something to eat."

"Not now." He extended his hand to her, his look intense. "We need to talk."

Claudia walked back to the dresser to deposit the

bowl before moving to the bed. Their eyes locked as they studied one another. A radiant glow of love seemed to reach out to her. She took his hand in her own and, raising it to her face, rested it against her cheek and closed her eyes. She didn't resist as the pressure of his arm pulled her downward. She knelt on the carpet beside the bed and was wrapped in his embrace.

Seth's breathing was heavy and labored as he buried his face in the gentle slope of her neck. This was what she'd needed, what she'd yearned for from the minute she stepped off the plane—Seth and the assurance of his love.

"I've been a fool," he muttered thickly.

"We both have. But I'm here now, and it's going to take a lot more than some angry words to pry me out of your arms." She pulled slightly away so she'd be able to look at him as she spoke. "If there's anyone to blame, then it's me," she murmured and brushed the hair from the sides of his face. He captured her hand and pressed a kiss against her palm. "I'd never once told you I loved you."

His hand tightened around hers punishingly. "You love me?"

"Very much." She confirmed her words with a nod of her head. "You told me so many times that you needed me, but I discovered it was I who needed you."

"Why didn't you tell me when you arrived that you intended to stay?" He met her eyes, and she watched as his eyes filled with regret. "I thought this was another one of your pen-pal ideas."

"I'm a little slow sometimes," she said. She sat in

the chair but continued to hold his hand in hers. "I couldn't seem to understand why God would give you a sign and me nothing. I was miserable—the indecision was disrupting my whole life. Then one day I decided to read the passage you'd talked about in Genesis. I read about Abraham's servant and learned that Rebekah had come by her choice. It was as if God was offering me the same type of decision and asking that I respond in faith. It didn't take me long to recognize how much I loved you. I can't understand why I fought it so long. Once I admitted it to myself, quitting school and leaving Seattle became secondary."

"You quit school?"

"Without even hesitation." She laughed with sudden amusement. "I'd make a rotten doctor. Haven't you noticed that I become emotionally involved with my patients?"

"What about your uncle?" Seth questioned wryly.

"He's accepted my decision. He's not happy about it, but I think he understands more than he lets on."

"We'll make him godfather to our first son," Seth said and slipped a large hand around her nape, pulling her trembling, soft mouth across the narrow distance to meet his. The kiss was so gentle that tears misted her eyes. Seth's hands framed each side of her face as his mouth slanted across hers, the contact deepening until he seemed capable of drawing out her soul.

Jim Coleman stopped by later. But only long enough to quickly check Seth's leg and give him another injection of antibiotic. He spoke frankly with Seth and warned him it would take weeks to regain the full use of the leg.

He hesitated once, apparently noticing the silent communication and love that flashed between Seth and Claudia. His eyes narrowed and the corner of his mouth twitched. For a fleeting moment Claudia thought the look was filled with contempt. She dismissed the idea as part of a long night and an overactive imagination. Jim left shortly afterward and promised to return that evening.

Claudia heated a lunch for both Seth and herself and waited until he had eaten. He fell asleep while she washed the dishes. When she checked on him later, Claudia's heart swelled with the wonder and joy of their love. How many other married couples had such a profound confirmation of their lives together as Seth and she did? Seth had spoken of a son, and Claudia realized how much she wanted this man's child.

Smiling, she rested her hands lightly on the flat surface of her stomach and again entertained the thought of children. They would have tall lean sons with thick dark hair, and perhaps a daughter. A glorious happiness stole through her.

Content that Seth would sleep, she opened the other bedroom door, crawled into the bed and drifted into a deep sleep. Her dreams were happy, confident of the many years she would share with Seth.

When she awoke later, she rolled over and glanced at the clock. Seven. She had slept almost five hours. Sitting up, she stretched, lifting her arms high above her head, and rotated her neck to ease the tired muscles.

The house was quiet as she threw back the covers and walked back to Seth's room. He was awake, his face turned toward the wall. Something prevented her from speaking and drawing attention to herself. He looked troubled, worried. His face was tight. Was he in pain? Was there something to cause him concern about his business?

As if feeling her regard, Seth turned his head and their eyes met. The look was gone immediately, replaced by a loving glance that sent waves of happiness through her.

"Hello. Have you been awake long?" she asked softly.

"About an hour. What about you?"

"Just a few minutes." She moved inside the room. "Is something troubling you, Seth? You had a strange look just now, I don't exactly know how to describe it...a sadness?"

His hand reached for hers. "It's nothing, my love."

Her fingers tested his brow, which was cool, and she smiled contentedly. "I don't know about you, but I'm starved. I think I'll see what I can dig up in the kitchen."

Seth nodded absently.

As Claudia left the room, she couldn't help glancing over her shoulder. Her instincts told her that something wasn't right. But what?

A freshly baked pie was on the kitchen table, and Claudia glanced at it curiously. When did that appear? She shrugged her shoulders and opened the refrigerator. Maybe Seth had some eggs and she could make an omelette. There weren't any eggs, but a gelatin salad sat prominently on the top shelf. Again Claudia felt a prickling of something out of place. When she turned around, she noted that the oven light was on, and a quick look through the glass door showed a casserole dish warming. Someone had been to the house when she'd been asleep and brought Seth a meal. How thoughtful.

"You didn't tell me you had company," she said as she carried a tray into the bedroom for Seth.

He was sitting on the edge of the mattress and she could see him tightly grit his teeth as he attempted to stand.

"Seth, don't," she cried and quickly set the tray down to hurry to his side. "You shouldn't be out of bed."

He sank back onto the side of the mattress and closed his eyes to mask an influx of pain. "You know, I think you're right about that."

"Here, let me help you." With an arm around his shoulders, she gently lifted the injured leg and propped it against a thick pillow. When she'd finished, she turned to Seth and smiled. She couldn't hide the soft glow that warmed her eyes as she looked upon this man she loved.

Sitting up, his back supported by pillows, Seth held his arms out to her and drew her into his embrace. His mouth sought hers, and the kisses spoke more of passion than gentleness. But Claudia didn't care. She returned his kisses, linking her hands around his neck, her fingers exploring the black hair at the base of his head. His hands moved intimately over her back as if he couldn't have enough of her.

"I think your recovery will impress Dr. Coleman, especially if he could see us now," she teased and tried to laugh. But the husky tone betrayed the extent of her arousal. When Seth kissed her again, hard and long, she offered no resistance.

Crushed in his embrace, held immobile by the steel band that circled her waist, she submitted happily to the mastery of his kisses.

Claudia smiled happily into his gleaming eyes. "There are only a few more days before Thanksgiving," she murmured and kissed his brow. "I have so much to thank God for this year—more happiness than one woman was ever meant to have. I had hoped when I first came that we might be married Thanksgiving week; it seemed fitting somehow." There were no more doubts, she was utterly his.

Although Seth continued to hold her, she felt again the stirring sense of something amiss. When she leaned her head back to glance at him, she noted that his look was distant, preoccupied.

"Seth, is something wrong?" she asked a second time.

A smile of reassurance touched his lips, but Claudia noted that it didn't reach his eyes. "Everything's fine."

"Are you hungry?"

He nodded eagerly and straightened so that she could bring him the tray. "I'm always hungry."

But he hardly touched his meal.

She brought him a cup of coffee from the kitchen

after taking away the dinner tray. She sat beside him in the chair, her hands cupping the hot mug.

"If you don't object, I'd like Pastor Reeder to marry us," she said and took a sip of the hot liquid.

"You know Paul Reeder?" His eyes shot over her curiously.

Claudia nodded. "I'm very grateful for his friendship. He's the one who introduced mc to Jim Coleman. He also rented me the apartment the church owns—honey bucket and all," she said with a tender smile. "I'm going to like Nome. There are some wonderful people here. I found the dinner in the kitchen; it wouldn't surprise me if Pastor Reeder had something to do with that."

"He did," Seth confirmed. "Paul's the one who talked to me about Christ and salvation. I greatly respect the man."

"I suspected as much." Claudia recalled Seth's telling her about the pastor who had led him to Christ. From the first day, Claudia had suspected it was Pastor Reeder. "I didn't get to church last Sunday to hear him preach, but I bet he packs a powerful sermon."

"He does," Seth said and looked away.

Claudia's gaze followed his and she noticed that Jim Coleman had let himself into the house. The two men eyed each other and an icy stillness seemed to fill the room. Claudia looked from one man to the other and lightly shook her head, sure she was imagining things.

"I think you'll be impressed with how well Seth is doing," she said and moved aside so Jim could examine the cut himself.

Neither man spoke and the tension in the room was

so thick that Claudia found herself stiffening. Something was wrong between these two, something was very wrong.

Claudia walked Jim to the front door. Again he praised her efforts. "He might have lost that leg if it hadn't been for you."

"I was glad to help," she said, studying him a second time. "But I feel God had more to do with the improvement than I did."

"That could be." He shrugged and expelled a long, tired sigh. "He should be okay by himself tonight if you want to go home and get a good night's sleep."

"I might," she responded noncommittally.

Jim nodded and turned to leave. Claudia stopped him with a hand on his arm. "Jim, something's going on between you and Seth."

"Did he tell you that?"

"No."

"Then ask him," he said, casting a wary glance in Seth's direction.

"I will," she replied, determined to do just that.

Seth's eyes were closed when she returned to his room, but she wasn't fooled. "Don't you like Jim Coleman?" she asked right out.

"He's a fine Christian man. There aren't many doctors as dedicated as he is."

"But you don't like him, do you?"

Seth closed his eyes again and let out a sharp breath. "I don't think it's a question of my friendship. Jim doesn't like me and at the moment I can't blame him," he responded cryptically.

Claudia didn't know what to say. It was obvious

Seth didn't want to talk about it, and she didn't feel she should pry. It hurt a little that he wouldn't confide in her. There wasn't anything she would ever keep from him. But she couldn't and wouldn't force it, not if he wasn't ready.

An hour later she checked on Seth, who appeared to be asleep. Leaning down, she kissed his brow. She was undecided about spending another night. A hot shower and a fresh change of clothes sounded tempting.

"Seth," she whispered, and he stirred. "I'm going home for the night. I'll see you early tomorrow morning."

"No." He sat up and winced, seeming to have forgotten his leg. "Don't go, Red. Stay tonight. You can leave in the morning if you want." He reached for her, holding her so tight she ached.

"Okay, my love," she whispered tenderly. "Just call if you need me."

"I'll need you all my life. Don't ever forget that, Red."

He sounded so adamant that she frowned, drawing her delicate brows together. "I won't forget."

Claudia woke before Seth the next morning. She was in the kitchen putting on a pot of coffee when she heard a car pull up outside the kitchen door.

Barbara Reeder slammed the car door closed and waved. Claudia returned the wave and opened the door for her friend.

"You're out bright and early this morning," she said cheerfully. "I just put on coffee."

"Morning." Barbara returned the smile. "How's the patient?"

"Great. It's amazing how much better he is from just two days ago."

"I was sorry to miss you yesterday." Barbara pulled out a chair and set her purse on the table while she unbuttoned her parka.

"Miss me?" Claudia quizzed.

"Yes, I brought by dinner, and you were in the bedroom sound asleep. From what I understand, you were up all night. You must have been exhausted. I didn't want to wake you."

"Funny Seth didn't say anything." Claudia spoke her thoughts out loud.

Barbara's look showed mild surprise. "You don't know, do you?"

"Know what?"

"That man, honestly!" A bright bubble of happiness gleamed from her eyes. "You'd think it was top secret or something." She held out her left hand for Claudia to admire the sparkling diamond. "Teddy and I are going to be married next month."

# Chapter Nine

"Teddy?" Claudia repeated. Her stomach felt as if someone had kicked her. Somehow she managed to conceal her shock.

"It's confusing, I know," Barbara responded with a happy laugh. "But Seth has always reminded me of a teddy bear. He's so big and cuddly, it seemed only natural to call him Teddy."

Claudia's hand shook as she poured coffee into two mugs. Barbara continued to chat excitedly about her wedding plans, stating they'd hoped to have the wedding before Christmas.

Strangely, Claudia felt no emotion. She sipped her coffee, adding little to the conversation. Barbara didn't seem to notice.

"Teddy changed after John's death," Barbara added and blew into the side of her mug.

"John," Claudia repeated the name. Seth had called out the name several times while his fever raged.

"John was his younger brother, and partner in Arctic Barge. There was some kind of accident on a barge—I'm not sure I ever got the story straight. Seth was with John when it happened. Something fell on top of him and ruptured his heart. He died in Seth's arms."

Claudia stared into the coffee. From that first day she'd walked into the Wilderness Motel, she'd known there was a terrible sadness in Seth's life. She'd felt it even then. But he had never shared his grief with her. As much as he professed to love her and want her for his wife, he hadn't shared the deepest part of himself. Knowing this hurt as much as his engagement to Barbara.

"Could I ask a favor of you?" Claudia said and stood, placing her mug in the kitchen sink. "Would you mind dropping me off at my apartment? I don't want to take Seth's car, since I don't know when I'll be back. It should only take a minute."

"Of course. Then I'll come back and surprise Seth with breakfast."

He'd be amazed all right, Claudia couldn't help musing.

She managed to maintain a fragile poise until Barbara dropped her off. Waving her thanks, she entered her tiny home. She looked around the room that had so quickly become her own and bit the inside of her cheek. With purposeful strides she opened the lone closet and pulled out her suitcases. She folded each garment with unhurried care and placed it neatly inside the leather luggage.

Someone knocked at the door, but Claudia obstinately ignored the repeated raps.

"Open up, Claudia, I know you're in there. I saw Barbara drop you off." It was Jim Coleman.

"Go away," she cried, and her voice cracked. A tear squeezed past her determination not to cry, and she angrily wiped it away with the back of her hand.

Ignoring her lack of welcome, Jim pushed open the door and stepped inside the room.

"I like the way people respect my privacy around here," she bit out sarcastically. "I don't feel up to company at the moment, Jim. Another time, maybe." She turned around and continued packing.

"I want you to listen to me for a minute." Clearly he was angry.

"No, I won't listen. Not to anyone. Go away, just go away." She pulled the drawer from the dresser, flipped it over and emptied the contents into the last suitcase.

"Will you stop acting like a lunatic and listen? You can't leave now."

She whirled around and placed both hands challengingly on her hips. "Can't leave? You just watch me. I don't care where the next plane's going, I'll be on it," she shot out, then choked on a sob.

Jim took her in his arms. Claudia struggled at first, but he deflected her hands and held her gently. "Let it out," he whispered soothingly.

Again she tried to jerk away, but, undeterred, Jim held her fast, murmuring comforting words.

"You knew all along, didn't you?" Hurt, questioning eyes lifted to search his face.

Jim arched one brow and shrugged his shoulders. "Not until yesterday. No one could help looking at the two of you without knowing you're in love. I was on my way to his house this morning when I saw Barbara with you. Something about the way you were tilting your head told me you must have found out the truth. Did you say anything to Barbara?''

Claudia shook her head. ''No. I couldn't. Why does it have to be Barbara?'' she asked unreasonably. ''Why couldn't it be some anonymous soul I could hate? But she's bright and cheerful, fun to be around. And she's so in love with him. You should have heard her talk about the wedding.''

''I have,'' Jim stated and rammed his hands into his pockets. He walked to the other side of the couch that served as Claudia's bed.

''I'm not going to burst that bubble of happiness. I don't think Seth knows what he wants. He's confused and unsure. The only thing I can do is leave.''

Jim turned and regarded her steadily. ''You can't go now. You don't seem to understand what having you in Nome means to me, to all of us. When Pastor Reeder said you were God's Thanksgiving gift to us, he wasn't teasing. I've been praying for someone like you for months.'' He heaved a sigh, his eyes pleading with hers. ''For the first time in weeks I've been able to do some of the paperwork that's cluttering my desk. And I was planning to take a day off next week, the first one in three months.''

''But you don't know what you're asking.'' Haunted eyes returned his pleading look.

''I do. Listen, if it will make things easier, I could marry you.''

The proposal was issued sincerely, and his gaze didn't waver as he waited for her reaction.

Claudia smiled her appreciation. "Now you're being ridiculous."

Jim's taut features relaxed, and Claudia laughed outright at how relieved he looked.

"Will you stay a bit longer, at least until someone answers our advertisements in the medical journal? Two, three months at the most."

Gesturing weakly with one hand, Claudia nodded. She was in an impossible position. She couldn't stay, and she couldn't leave. And still there was Seth to face.

Jim sighed gratefully and smoothed the hair at the side of his head. "Thank you. I promise you won't regret it." He glanced at his watch. "I'm going to talk to Seth. Something's got to be done."

Claudia walked him to the door. "Why haven't you married?" His proposal prompted the question.

"Too busy in medical school," he explained. "And since I've been here, there hasn't been the time to date the one I wanted." He pulled his car keys from his pocket.

There was something strange about the way he spoke, or maybe it was the look in his eyes. Claudia stopped him by placing a hand on his arm. "You're in love with Barbara, aren't you?" If she hadn't been caught in her own problems, she would have realized it long before. Whenever Jim talked about Barbara there had been a softness in his tone.

He began to deny his feelings, but seemed to notice the knowing look in Claudia's blue eyes. "A lot of good it's done me.'' His shoulders slouched forward in defeat. ''I'm nothing more than a family friend. Barbara's been in love with Seth for so long, she doesn't even know I'm around. And with the hours I'm forced to work, there hasn't been time to let her know how I feel.''

''Does Seth love her?'' Pride demanded that she hold her chin high.

''I don't know. But he must have some genuine affection for her or he wouldn't have proposed.''

Both became introspective, unable to find the words to comfort each other. Jim walked out the door a minute later and Claudia stood at the window watching him go.

Clothes were scattered across the carpeted floor and she bent down to clean away the mess she'd made. As she replaced each item in the closet or the drawers, Claudia tried to pray. God had brought her to Nome. She had come believing she would marry Seth. Did God have other plans for her now that she was here? How could she bear to live in the same city when she loved Seth so completely? How could she bear seeing him married to another?

No sooner had the last suitcase been tucked away when there was another knock at the door.

Barbara's cheerful smile greeted her as she stuck her head in the front door. ''Are you busy?''

Claudia had her back turned and bit into her lip. Barbara was the last person she wanted to see. It would almost be preferable to face Seth. Inwardly she groaned as she turned, forcing a smile onto her frozen lips.

"Sure, come in."

Barbara let herself in and held out a large gift-wrapped box to Claudia. "I know you're probably exhausted and this is a bad time, but I wanted to give this to you now, before I went back to Teddy's."

Numbly Claudia took the gift, unable to look higher than the bright pink bow that decorated the box. Words seemed to knot in her throat.

"I'll only stay a minute," Barbara confirmed. "Jim Coleman came by. It looked like he wanted to see Teddy alone for a few minutes, and I thought this was the perfect time to run this over."

"What is it?" The words sounded strange even to herself.

"Just a little something to show my appreciation for all you've done for Teddy. All along, Dad's said that God sent you to us. You've only been here a short time and already you've affected all our lives. Teddy could have lost his leg if it hadn't been for you. And Dad said your being here will save Jim from work exhaustion. All that aside, I see you as a very special sister the Lord sent to me. I can't remember a time I've felt closer to anyone more quickly." She ended with a shaky laugh. "Look at me," she mumbled, wiping a tear from the corner of her eye. "I'm going to start crying in a minute, and that's all we both need. Now go ahead and open the gift."

Claudia sat and rested the large box on her knees. Carefully she tore away the ribbon and paper. The ever tightening lump in her throat constricted painfully. Lifting the lid, she discovered a beautiful hand-crocheted afghan in bold autumn colors of gold, orange, yellow and brown. She couldn't restrain the gasp of pleasure. "Oh, Barbara!" She lifted it from the box and marveled at the weeks of work that had gone into its making. "I can't accept this—it's too much." She blinked rapidly in an effort to forestall the tears.

"It's hardly enough," Barbara contradicted. "God sent you to Nome as a helper to Jim, a friend to me and a nurse for my Teddy."

A low moan of protest and guilt escaped Claudia's parched throat. She couldn't refuse the gift, just as she couldn't explain why she'd come to Nome.

"How…how long have you been engaged?" she asked in a choked whisper.

"Only a short time. In fact, Teddy didn't give me the ring until a few days ago."

Claudia's gaze lowered to rest on the sparkling rainbow-hued diamond. She felt a sense of release that it wasn't the same ring he'd offered her.

"His proposal had to be about the most unromantic you can imagine," she said with a girlish smile. "I didn't need a fortune-teller to realize he's in love with someone else."

Claudia's breathing became shallow. "Why would you marry someone when he…" She couldn't finish the sentence and, unable to meet Barbara's gaze, she fingered the afghan on her lap.

"It sounds strange, doesn't it?" Barbara answered with a question. "But I love him, I have for years. We've talked about this other girl. She's someone he met on a business trip. She wasn't willing to leave everything behind for Teddy and Nome. Whoever she is, she's a fool. The affection Teddy has for me will grow, and together we'll build a good marriage. He wants children right away.''

With a determined effort Claudia was able to smile. ''You'll make him a wonderful wife. And you're right, the other girl was a terrible fool.'' Her mouth twitched with the effort of maintaining a smile.

Again Barbara misread the look of strain in Claudia's pale face as fatigue. Standing, she slipped her arms into the thick coat. ''I imagine Jim's done by now. I'd better go, but we'll get together soon. And don't forget Thanksgiving dinner. You're our guest of honor.''

Claudia felt sick to her stomach and stood unsteadily. The guest of honor? This was too much.

Together they walked the short space to the door.

''Thank you again for the beautiful gift,'' Claudia murmured in a wavering breath.

''No, Claudia, I need to thank you. And for so much—you saved the leg of the man I love.''

''You should thank God for that, not me.''

''I do!''

Barbara was halfway out the door when Claudia blurted out, ''What do you think of Jim Coleman?'' She hadn't meant to be so abrupt and quickly averted her face.

To her surprise, Barbara stepped inside the door and laughed softly. ''I told Dad a romance would soon be brewing between the two of you. It's inevitable, I suppose, working together every day. The attraction between you must be a natural thing. I think Jim's a great guy, not that I fancy his sort. He's too arrogant for my tastes. But you two are exactly right for one another.

Jim needs someone like you to mellow his attitudes.'' A smile twinkled from the blue eyes. ''We'll talk more about Jim later. I've got to get back, Teddy will be wondering what's going on. He hadn't wakened when Jim arrived, and I haven't had a chance to talk to him yet.''

That afternoon Jim phoned and asked if Claudia could meet him at the office. An outbreak of flu had apparently hit Nome and several families had been affected. He needed her help immediately.

Several hours later, Claudia was exhausted. She came home and cooked a meal, then didn't eat. She washed the already clean dishes and listened to a radio broadcast until she realized it wasn't in English.

The hot water in her bathtub was steaming when there was yet another knock at her door. The temptation to let it pass and pretend she hadn't heard was strong. She didn't feel up to another chat with either Barbara or Jim. Again the knock came, this time more insistent.

Impatiently she stalked across the floor and jerked open the door. Her irritation died the minute she saw that it was Seth. He was leaning heavily on a cane, his leg causing him obvious pain.

''What are you doing here?'' she demanded. ''Oh, you fool!'' she cried in alarm. ''You shouldn't be walking on that leg.''

Lines of strain were etched beside his mouth. ''Then invite me inside so I can sit down.'' He spoke tightly and Claudia moved aside, a hand at his elbow as she helped him to the couch.

Relief was evident when he lowered himself onto it. ‘‘We have to talk, Red,’’ he whispered coaxingly, his eyes seeking hers.

Fearing the powerful pull of his gaze, she turned away. The control he had over her senses was frightening.

‘‘No, I think I understand everything.’’

‘‘You couldn’t possibly understand,’’ Seth countered.

‘‘Talk all you like, but it isn’t going to change things.’’ She moved to the tiny kitchen and poured water into the kettle to heat. He stood and followed her, unable to hide the grimace of pain as he moved.

‘‘Where are you going?’’ he demanded.

‘‘Sit down, Superman,’’ she snapped. The sign of his pain upset her more than she cared to reveal. ‘‘I’m making us something to drink; it looks like we can both use it.’’ She moved across the room and gestured toward the bathroom door. ‘‘Now I’m going to get a pair of slippers. My feet are cold.’’ She’d taken off her shoes and the floor was chilly against her bare feet. ‘‘Any objections?’’

‘‘Plenty, but I doubt that they’ll do any good.’’

Claudia was glad for the respite as she slipped her feet into the shoes. She felt defenseless and naked. Seth knew her too well. The room was quiet and still and she paused to pray. Her mind was crowded with a thousand questions.

‘‘Are you coming out of there, or do I have to knock that door down?’’ he demanded in a harsh tone.

‘‘I’m coming.’’ A few seconds later she left the bathroom and entered the kitchen to pour their coffee.

His cane hit the floor. "I can't take this. Yell, scream, rant, rave, call me names, but for goodness' sake, don't treat me like this. As if you didn't care, as if you weren't dying on the inside, when I know you must be."

She licked her dry lips and handed him the steaming cup. "I don't need to yell, or scream. I admit I might have done so this morning when I talked to Barbara, but not now. I have a fairly good understanding of the situation. I don't blame you, there was no way for you to know I was coming to Nome to stay." Purposely she sat across the room from him, her composure stilted as her fingers hugged the hot mug.

"Look at me, Red," he ordered softly.

She raised unsure eyes to meet his, and all time came to a halt. The unquestionable love that glowed in his dark eyes was her undoing. Claudia vaulted to her feet and turned away from him before the anguish of her own eyes became readable.

"No," she murmured brokenly.

His large hand reached for her, but she easily side-stepped his arm.

"Don't touch me, Seth."

"I love you, Claudia Masters." His words were coaxing and low.

"Don't say that!" she burst out in a half-sob.

"Don't look! Don't touch! Don't love!" His voice was sharp and marked with determination. "You're mine. I'm not going to let you go."

"I'm not yours," she cut in swiftly. "You don't own me. What about Barbara? I won't see you hurt her like this. She loves you, she'll make you a good wife. You were right about me. I don't belong here. I should be in Seattle with my family, back in medical school. I should never have come."

"That's not true and you know it," he said harshly.

"Answer me something, Seth." She paused and her lips trembled. For a moment she found it difficult to continue. "Why didn't you tell me about your brother?"

If possible, Seth paled all the more. "How do you know about John? Barbara?"

Claudia shook her head. "You called out to him in your fever the first night I tended your leg. Then Barbara said something later and I asked her."

He covered his face with his hands. "I don't like to talk about it, Red. It's something I want to forget. That feeling of utter helplessness, watching the life flow out of John. I would have told you in time. To be frank, it hasn't been a year and I still have trouble talking about it." He straightened and wiped a hand across his face. "In some ways John's death has been one of the most influential events of my life. Later, I could find no reason why I should live and my brother die. It didn't make sense. Other than the business, my life lacked purpose. I sought only personal gain and satisfaction. That was when I talked to Pastor Reeder to seek some answers and later accepted Jesus Christ. It was one of the things that made me decide it was time to get married and have a family."

Unable to speak, Claudia nodded. She had been with him that night as he relived the torment of his brother's death. She had witnessed just a little of the effect it had had upon his life.

"I'll be leaving Nome in a couple of months. I want—"

"No," Seth objected strenuously.

"I'm going back to Seattle," she continued. "And someday, with God's help, I'll be one of Washington's finest pediatricians."

"Red, I admit I've made a terrible mess of this thing. When I told you God and I were working on the patience part of me, I wasn't kidding." His voice was low and tense. "But I can't let you go, not when I love you. Not when..."

"Not when Barbara's wearing your ring," she finished for him.

"Barbara..." he began heatedly, then stopped, defeated. "I have to talk to her. She's a wonderful woman, and I don't want to hurt her."

Claudia laughed softly. "We're both fools, aren't we? I think that at the end of three months we'd be at each other's throats." She marveled at how calm she sounded.

"You're going to marry me." Hard resolve flashed from his eyes.

"No, Seth, I'm not. There's nothing anyone can say that will prevent me from leaving."

Seth met her look and for the first time Claudia noticed the red stain on his pant leg. Her composure flew. "Your wound has opened. It was crazy for you to have come here," she cried in a shrill voice. "I've got to get you home and back into bed."

"You enjoy giving orders, don't you?" He bit out savagely. "Marry Barbara. Go home. Stay in bed." He sounded suddenly weary, as if the effort had become too much. ''I'll leave, but you can be sure that we're not through discussing the subject.''

''As far as I'm concerned, we are.'' She ripped her coat off the hanger and got her purse.

''What are you doing now?''

''Taking you home, and if necessary putting you back in bed.''

Carefully Seth lifted himself off the couch. The pain the movement caused him was mirrored in his eyes. Standing, he leaned heavily on the cane and dragged his leg as he walked.

''Let me help.'' She hastened to his side.

''I'm perfectly fine without you,'' he insisted.

Claudia paused and stepped back. ''Isn't that the point of this conversation?''

The next days were exhausting. The strain of flu reached epidemic proportions. Both Jim and Claudia were on their feet eighteen hours a day. Claudia traveled from house to house with Jim because the sick were often too ill to come into the city.

When the alarm sounded early the morning of the fifth day, Claudia rolled over and groaned. Every muscle ached, her head throbbed and it hurt to breathe. As she stirred from the bed, her stomach twisted into tight cramps. She forced herself to sit on the edge of the extended hideaway bed, but her head swam and waves of nausea gripped her. A low moan escaped her parted lips and she laid her head back on the pillow. Her fingers groped for the telephone, which sat on the end table beside the bed, and she sluggishly dialed Jim's number to tell him she was the latest flu victim.

Jim promised to check on her later, but Claudia assured him she'd be fine. She just needed rest and some sleep.

After struggling into the bathroom and downing some aspirin, she floated naturally into a blissful sleep.

Suddenly she was chilled to the bone and shivered uncontrollably, incorporating the iciness into her dreams. She was lost on the tundra in a heavy snowstorm, searching frantically for Seth. He was lost, and now she was, too. Then it was warm, the snowflakes ceased and the warmest summer sun stole through her until she was comfortable once again.

"Red?" A voice sliced into her consciousness.

Gasping, Claudia's eyes flew to the one chair in the living room. Seth sat with his leg propped on the ottoman. A worried frown furrowed his brow. Struggling to a sitting position, Claudia pulled the covers against her breast and flashed him a chilling glint. "How'd you get in here?" Her voice came in a hoarse whisper. The lingering tightness in her chest remained painfully constant.

"Jim Coleman let me in. He was concerned about you. I thought it was only right that I volunteer. I owe you one."

"You don't owe me anything, Seth Lessinger, except the right to leave here when the time comes."

He responded with a gentle smile. "I'm not going to argue with you. How are you feeling?"

"Like someone ran over me with a two-ton truck." She leaned against the pillow. The pain in her chest continued, but it hurt less to breathe if she was propped up against something solid. Her stomach felt better, and the desperate fatigue had fled.

"I haven't had a chance to talk to Barbara," he said as his gaze searched her face. "She's been helping Jim and her father the last couple of days. But I'm going to explain things. We're having dinner tonight."

"Seth, please." She looked away. "Barbara loves you, while I..."

"You love me, too."

"I'm going back to Seattle, Seth. I was wrong to have ever come North."

"Don't say that, Red. Please."

She slid down into the bed and pulled the covers over her shoulders. Closing her eyes, she hoped to convince him she was going back to sleep.

When she opened her eyes again, the room was dark and Seth was gone. A tray had been placed on the table and she saw that it was a light meal he had apparently fixed for her.

Although she tried to eat, she couldn't force anything down. Her wristwatch had stopped; the world outside her door was dark. There was very little sunlight during the days now, making it almost impossible to predict time accurately. The sun did rise, but only for a few short hours, and it was never any brighter than the light of dusk or dawn.

Claudia was awake when Seth returned. His limp was less pronounced as he let himself into her apartment.

"What are you doing here?" She was shocked at how weak her voice sounded.

"Barbara's got the flu," he murmured defeatedly.

"I didn't get to see her for more than a couple of minutes." He sighed heavily as he lowered himself into the chair.

Instantly Claudia was angry. "You beast! You don't have any business here! You should be with her, not me. She's the one who needs you, not me."

"Barbara's got her father. You've only got me," he countered gently.

"Don't you have any more concern for her than this? What if she found out you were here taking care of me? How do you think she'd feel? You can't do this to her—" A tight cough gripped her chest and she shook violently with the spasm. The exertion drained her of what little strength she possessed. Wearily she slumped back and closed her eyes, trying to ignore the throbbing pain in her chest.

Cool fingers rested on her forehead. "Would you like something to drink?"

Nodding was almost more than she could manage. The feeble attempt brought a light of concern to Seth's eyes.

The tea hurt to swallow and she shook her head after the first few sips.

"I'm phoning Jim. You've got something more than the flu." A scowl darkened his face.

"Don't," she whispered. "I'm all right, and Jim's so busy. He said he'd stop by later. Don't bother him, he's overworked enough as it is." Her heavy eyelids drooped, and Claudia returned to a fitful slumber.

Again the warming rays of the sun reappeared in her dream, but this time in a fiery intensity. She thrashed, kicking away the blankets, fighting off imaginary foes who wanted to take her captive.

Faintly she could hear Jim's voice, as if he were speaking in the distance.

"I'm glad you phoned." His tone was anxious.

Gently she was rolled to her side and an icy-cold stethoscope was placed against her bare back. "Do you hear me, Claudia?" Jim's voice asked.

"Of course I hear you." Her voice was shockingly weak and strained.

"I want you to take deep breaths."

Every inhalation burned like fire, searing a path through her lungs. Moaning, she tried to speak and found the effort too much.

"What is it, man?" Seth was standing above her, his face twisted in grim concern.

Jim Coleman stood at his side and sighed heavily. "Pneumonia."

# Chapter Ten

"Am I dying?" Claudia whispered weakly. Cooper and Ashley stood looking down at her from opposite sides of the hospital bed.

Cooper's mouth tightened into a hard line as his gaze traveled over her, the oxygen tubes and intravenous bottles that lined the wall.

"You'll live," Ashley said and responded to the weak smile with one of her own.

"You fool. Why didn't you let me know things hadn't worked out here?" Cooper demanded. "Are you so full of pride that you couldn't come to me and admit I was right?"

Sparks of irritation flashed from Claudia's blue eyes. "Don't you ever give up? I'm practically on my deathbed and you're preaching at me!"

"I am not preaching," he denied quickly. "I'm only stating the facts."

Jim Coleman chuckled, and for the first time Claudia noticed that he had entered the room. "It's beginning to sound like you're back among the living, and sooner than we expected.'' Standing at the foot of her bed, he read the chart and smiled wryly. ''You're looking better all the time. But save your strength to talk some sense into these folks. They seem to think they're going to take you back to Seattle.''

Claudia rolled her head away so that she faced the wall and wouldn't need to look at Jim. ''I am going back,'' she mumbled in a low voice, knowing how desperately Jim wanted her to stay.

A short silence followed. Claudia could feel Cooper's eyes boring holes into her back, but to his credit he didn't say anything.

''You've got to do what you think is right,'' Jim said at last.

''All I want is to go home. And the sooner the better.'' Oddly, she had never considered Cooper's penthouse condominium home until now. She'd return to Seattle and rebuild her life. Maybe this was the time to investigate the fancy Swiss medical school her uncle had been so keen about.

''I don't think it's such a good idea to rush out of here,'' Jim said, and Claudia could tell by the tone of his voice that he'd accepted her decision. ''I want you to gain back some of your strength before you go.''

''Pastor Reeder introduced himself to us when we arrived. He's kindly offered to have you stay and recuperate at his home until you feel up to traveling,'' Ashley added.

''No.'' Claudia's response was adamant. ''I want to go back to Seattle as soon as possible. Cooper was right, I don't belong in Nome. I shouldn't have come in the first place."

The words produced a strained silence around the small room. "When will I be discharged, Jim?" Her questioning eyes sought his troubled ones.

"Tomorrow, if you like," he said solemnly.

"I would."

"Thanksgiving Day," Ashley announced.

Claudia's eyes clashed with her friend's. Ashley knew. The day she'd left Seattle, Claudia had told Ashley to expect the wedding around Thanksgiving. And Ashley had teased her, saying Claudia was making sure their anniversary was at a time no one would forget. Recalling the conversation brought a physical ache to her heart. No, she'd said, she wanted to be married around Thanksgiving because she wanted to praise God for giving her such a wonderful man as Seth. Now there would be no wedding. She would never have Seth.

"If you feel she needs more time, Doctor," Cooper began, "Ashley and I could stay a few days."

"No," Claudia interrupted abruptly. "I don't want to stay any longer than necessary." Remaining even one extra day was intolerable.

Claudia closed her yes, blotting out the world. Maybe she could fool the others, but not Ashley, who gently squeezed her hand. Shortly afterward Claudia heard the sound of hushed voices and retreating footsteps.

The stay in the hospital had been a nightmare from the beginning. Seth had insisted upon flying in another doctor from Anchorage. As weak as she'd been, Claudia had refused to have anyone but Jim Coleman. Jim and Seth had faced each other, their eyes filled with bitter anger. Claudia was sure they'd argued later when she wasn't there to watch.

She had seen Seth only once since that scene, and only to say goodbye. The relationship was over, finished, and Seth had accepted the futility of trying to change her mind.

Pastor Recder had been a regular visitor. He tried to talk to her about the relationship between Seth, Barbara and herself, but Claudia had stated forcefully that she really didn't want to talk about it. He hadn't brought up the subject again.

Barbara had come once, but Claudia had pretended she was asleep, not wishing to face the woman who would share Seth's life, or make explanations that would only embarrass them.

Claudia relaxed against the pillows, weak after the short visit. Without meaning to, she slipped into a restful slumber.

When she awoke an hour later, Seth was sitting at her bedside. Somehow she had hoped not to see him again. But she felt no overwhelming surprise as she lifted her lashes and their eyes met.

''Hello, Seth,'' she whispered. Her fingers longed to reach out and touch his haggard face. He looked as if he hadn't slept in several days.

''Hello, Red.'' He paused and looked away. ''Claudia,'' he corrected. ''Cooper and Ashley arrived okay?''

She nodded. ''They were here this morning.''

''I thought you might want someone with you.'' He

said this with the understanding she wouldn't ever rely on him.

"Thank you. They said you were the one who phoned." Claudia didn't know how she could be so calm. She felt like she had in the dream, lost and wandering aimlessly on the frozen tundra.

Seth shrugged his shoulders, dismissing her gratitude.

"You'll marry Barbara, won't you?"

The hesitation was only slight. "If she'll have me."

Claudia put on a brave smile. "I'm sure she will. She loves you. You'll have a good life together."

Seth neither agreed with nor denied the statement. "And you?"

"I'm going back to school." The smile on her face died and she took in a quivering breath.

He stood and walked across the room to stare out the window, his back to her. He seemed to be gathering his resolve. "I couldn't let you go without telling you how desperately sorry I am," he began before returning to the chair at her side. "It was never my intention to hurt you. I can only beg your forgiveness."

"Don't, please." Her voice wobbled with the effort to suppress tears. Seeing Seth humble himself this way was her undoing. "It's not your fault. Really, there's no one to blame. We've both learned a valuable lesson in this. We should never have sought a supernatural confirmation from God. Faith comes from walking daily with our Lord until we're so close to Him we don't need anything more to know His will."

Until then Seth had avoided touching her, but now

he took her hand and gently held it between his two large ones. ''When do you leave?''

Even the slight touch of his fingers caused shivers to shoot up her arm. She struggled not to withdraw her hand. ''Tomorrow.''

He nodded, accepting her decision. ''I won't see you again,'' he said and breathed in deeply. Very gently he lifted her fingers to his lips and kissed the back of her hand. ''God go with you, Red, and may your life be full and rewarding.'' His eyes were haunted as he stood, looked down on her one last time, turned around and walked from the room.

''Goodbye, Seth.'' Her voice was throbbing and she closed her eyes unable to watch him leave.

''Honestly, Cooper, I don't need that.'' She was dressed and ready to leave the hospital when Cooper came into her room wheeling a chair. ''I'm not an invalid!''

Jim Coleman rounded the corner into her room. ''No backtalk, Claudia. You have to let us wheel you out for insurance purposes.''

''That's a likely story,'' she returned irritably. Cooper gave her a hand and helped her off the bed. ''Oh, all right, I don't care what you use, just get me to the plane on time.'' It should be the church, she reminded herself bitterly.

Jim drove the three of them to the airport. Ashley sat in the back seat with Claudia. The two men occupied the front seat.

''This place is something!'' Cooper looked around

him curiously. "Aren't there any paved roads in Nome?"

"Two," Jim answered as he pulled onto the dirt road that was covered by compacted snow. Although it was almost noon, he used the car headlights. "The road leading to the airport is paved."

"I wish I'd seen the tundra in springtime. From what everyone says, it's a magnificent sight," Claudia murmured to no one in particular. "The northern lights are fantastic. I was up half one night watching them. Some people claim they can hear the northern lights. The stars here are breathtaking. Millions and millions, like I've never seen before. I…I guess I'd never noticed them in Seattle."

"The city obliterates their light," Jim explained.

Cooper turned around to look at Claudia. She met his worried look and gave a poor replica of a smile.

"Is the government planning to build any kind of road into Nome?" Ashley questioned. "I was surprised to learn we could only come by plane."

"Rumors float around all the time. The last thing I heard was the possibility of a highway system eventually reaching Nome."

No one spoke again until the airport was in sight. "You love it here, don't you?" Ashley looked at her with renewed concern, and Claudia glanced out the side window, afraid what her eyes would reveal if she glanced at her friend.

"It's okay," she said, doubting that she'd fooled anyone.

As soon as they arrived, Cooper got out of the car

and removed the suitcases from the trunk. Ashley helped him carry the luggage inside.

Jim opened the back door and gave Claudia a hand, quickly ushering her inside the warm terminal. His fingers held hers longer than necessary. ''I've got to get back to the office.''

''I know. Thank you, Jim. I'll always remember you,'' she said in a shaky voice. ''You're the kind of doctor I hope to be: dedicated, gentle, compassionate. I deeply regret letting you down.''

Jim hugged her fiercely. ''No, don't. You're doing what you must. Goodbye. I'm sorry things didn't work out for you here. Maybe we'll meet again someday.'' He returned to the car, pausing to wave before he climbed inside and started the engine.

''Goodbye, Jim.'' The ache in her throat was almost unbearable.

Ashley was at her side immediately. ''You made some good friends in the short time you were here, didn't you?''

Claudia nodded rather than make an explanation that would destroy the fragile control of her composure.

A few minutes later, Claudia watched as the incoming aircraft circled the airstrip. She was so intent that she didn't notice Barbara open the terminal door and walk inside.

''Claudia,'' she called softly and hurried forward to meet her.

Claudia turned around, shock depleting her face of color.

''Don't leave,'' Barbara said breathlessly, her hands clenched at her sides.

"Please don't say that," Claudia pleaded. "Seth's yours. This whole thing is a terrible misunderstanding that everyone regrets."

"Seth will never be mine," Barbara countered swiftly. "It's you he loves, it'll always be you."

"I didn't mean for you ever to know."

"If I hadn't been so blind, so stupid, I would have guessed right away. I thank God I found out."

"Did...Seth tell you?" she asked in an accusing voice.

Barbara shook her head. "He didn't need to. From the moment Jim brought you into the hospital, Seth was like a madman. He wouldn't leave, and when Jim literally escorted him out of your room, Seth stood in the hallway grilling anyone who went in or out."

For a moment Claudia couldn't speak. A hoarseness was blocking her throat. She put on a false smile and gently shook her head. "Good heavens, you're more upset about my leaving than I am. Things will work out between you and Seth once I'm gone."

"Are you crazy? Do you think I could marry him now? He loves you so much it's almost killing him. How can you be so calm? Don't you care? Don't you honestly care?" Barbara argued desperately. "I can't understand either of you. Seth is tearing himself apart, but he wouldn't ask you to stay if his life depended on it." She stalked a few feet away and pivoted sharply. "It's Thanksgiving," she cried. "You should be thanking God that someone like Seth loves you."

Claudia closed her eyes to the shooting pain that pierced her heart.

"I once said, without knowing it was you, that the

girl in Seattle was a fool. If you fly out of here, you're a bigger fool than I thought.''

Paralyzed by indecision, Claudia turned to Cooper, her eyes filled with doubt.

''Don't look at me,'' he told her. ''This has got to be your own choice.''

''Do you love him, honestly love him?'' Ashley asked her gently.

''Yes, oh yes.''

Ashley smiled and inclined her head toward the door. ''Then what are you doing standing around here?''

Claudia spun around to Barbara. ''What about you?'' she asked softly.

''I'll be all right. Seth was never mine, I'm only returning what is rightfully yours. Hurry, Claudia, go to him. He's at the office. He needs you.'' She handed Claudia her car keys and smiled broadly through her tears.

Claudia took a step backward. ''Ashley...Cooper, thank you. I love you both.''

''I'd better be godmother to your first child,'' Ashley called after her as Claudia rushed out the door.

Seth's building was deserted when Claudia entered. The door leading to his office was tightly shut. She tapped lightly, then turned the handle and stepped inside.

Seth stood with his back to her, his attention centered on an airplane making its way into the darkening sky.

"If you don't mind, Barbara, I'd rather be alone right now." His voice was filled with stark pain.

"It isn't Barbara," she whispered softly.

Seth spun around, his eyes wide with disbelief. "What are you doing here?"

Instead of answering him with words, she moved slowly across the room until she was standing directly in front of him. Gently she glided her fingers over the stiff muscles of his chest. He continued to hold himself rigid with pride. "I love you, Seth Lessinger. I'm yours now and for all our lives."

Groaning, he hauled her fiercely into his arms. "You'd better not change your mind, Red. I don't have the strength to let you go a second time." His mouth burned a trail of kisses down her neck and throat. Claudia surrendered willingly to each caress, savoring each kiss, oblivious to the pain of his punishing hold.

# Epilogue

"Honey, what are you doing up?" Seth tied the sash to his robe and wandered sleepily from the master bedroom. Claudia watched her husband with a translucent happiness, her heart swelling with pride and love. They'd been married almost a year now: the happiest twelve months of her life.

Seth moved behind her; his hand closed over her hip before sliding around the full swell of her stomach. "Is the baby keeping you awake?"

Claudia relaxed against him, savoring the gentle feel of his touch. "No, I was just thinking how good God has been to us. A verse I'd read in the Psalms the other day kept running through my mind."

"Did you look it up?"

She nodded, reaching for her Bible. "It's Psalm 16:11.

"Thou wilt make known to me the path of life; in Thy presence is fullness of joy; in Thy right hand there are pleasures forever.""

Seth tenderly kissed the side of her creamy, smooth neck. ''God has done that for us, hasn't He? He made known to us that our paths in life were linked, and together we've known His joy.''

Claudia nodded happily, rested the back of her head against his shoulder and sighed softly. ''You know what tomorrow is, don't you?''

Seth gave an exaggerated sigh. ''It couldn't be our anniversary. That isn't until the end of the month.''

''No, silly, it's Thanksgiving.''

''Barbara and Jim are coming, aren't they?''

''Yes, but she insisted on bringing the turkey. You'd think just because I was going to have a baby I was helpless.''

''Those two are getting pretty serious, aren't they?''

''I think it's more than serious. It wouldn't surprise me if they got married before Christmas.''

''It may be sooner than that. Jim's already asked me to be his best man,'' Seth murmured and his mouth nibbled at her earlobe with little kisses. The two men had long before settled their differences and had become good friends. Claudia had worked for Jim until two additional doctors had set up practice in Nome. The timing had been perfect. Claudia had just learned she was pregnant and she was ready to settle into the role of homemaker and mother.

''I don't know how you can love me in this condition.'' She turned and slipped her arms around his middle.

''You're not so bad-looking from the neck up,'' he teased affectionately and kissed the tip of her nose. ''Has it been a year, Red?'' His gaze grew serious.

She nodded happily and her eyes became tender pools of love. "There's no better time to thank God for each other, and for His love."

"No better time," Seth agreed, his arm cradling her close to his side. "When I thought I had lost you forever, God gave you back to me."

"It was fitting that it should have been Thanksgiving Day, wasn't it?"

"Very fitting," he murmured huskily in her ear, leading her back into their room.

* * * * *

Dearest Friends,

What you hold in your hands is one of my earliest books, originally published in the mid-eighties, when my dream of becoming a published writer was only in its infancy. *Thanksgiving Prayer* is a special book. I hope you will enjoy the story of Claudia and Seth and the lessons God has in store for them.

At the time I wrote this story, my husband had recently returned from working on the Alaskan pipeline. He delighted in telling me wonderful tales of life in the frozen North. It was from him that my fascination with Alaska began. Several years later Wayne and I did an extended research trip in Alaska for my six-book series MIDNIGHT SONS, but it all began with this inspirational romance.

I'm pleased that Steeple Hill has decided to reissue *Thanksgiving Prayer.* May this story remind us all of the power of prayer and the often unplanned surprises God sends into our lives.

In His love,

Debbie Macomber

# THE RISK OF LOVING

Jane Peart

# *November*

# Chapter One

On a rain-swept night the weekend before Thanksgiving, holiday travelers thronged San Francisco International Airport.

In the passenger lounge of Westair's northbound Flight 84 Mark Emery glanced over the top of his *Newsweek* as a slender brunette came through the security check enclosure. She wore a belted raincoat and high-heeled boots. Her dark, shoulder-length hair glistened with raindrops. She stood for a minute looking around for an empty seat.

Mark watched as she made her way across the crowded waiting room. She had a confident, graceful walk. Stepping over assorted baggage cluttering the aisles, she took a seat opposite his. There was something familiar about her but he couldn't place her. Could he have seen her at some local function he'd covered for the *Daily Sentinel?* He'd been to dozens of them. Community and political affairs were newsworthy events in the small northern California town of

Rockport. Still, he couldn't recall where or when they might have met. He returned to the article on the Middle East.

Coryn Dodge stared blankly through the plate-glass window out to the landing field. Planes taxied into position, lights glowing on the rain-slick tarmac. Carts piled with luggage swerved and snaked toward yawning cargo bins. Planes took off. Planes going different places carrying people to happy homecomings.

Coryn knew she should feel happy, too, and be looking forward to spending Thanksgiving with her parents. She felt guilty that she didn't.

If her father hadn't phoned, she might have waited to see if Jason called from Detroit. But there had been something in her father's voice, an uncharacteristic tension in his tone. When he reminded her she had not been home since last spring, a sliver of guilt had pricked Coryn, and she'd quickly agreed to come for Thanksgiving.

She'd been lucky to get a reservation at this time of year. There was only one available seat on the flight to San Francisco. In order to make the connecting flight to Rockport she'd had to leave L.A. right away. Before she left for the airport she'd called Jason but only got his message machine. She hated leaving with so many unresolved questions about their relationship. But what relationship? Jason had never made any commitment. They'd never discussed a future together. The enduring love Coryn had always secretly hoped to find was probably a dream. Not a nineties kind of thing.

Impatient with herself, Coryn dug into her tote bag

and pulled out the magazine she'd bought at the airport newsstand. She slipped on her glasses and started flipping through the pages, hoping to find an article to distract her.

Mark Emery stirred restlessly in the vinyl chair and glanced at his watch. The flight to Rockport took an hour and forty-five minutes. He'd get home around ten. Home. Alone.

Mark felt the old bitterness twist within, as it always did when he thought about it. It wasn't fair. But whoever said life was fair?

He looked around the waiting room at the various groups of happy people bound for family gatherings. Even crowded airports were strangely lonely places. It didn't really matter where he was. He could spend Thanksgiving in the airport for all he cared.

At that moment the young woman seated across from him lifted her head from the magazine she was reading. Their gazes met. Even with her glasses on she was amazingly attractive. The lenses magnified the size and color of her intensely blue eyes.

Their look held for a minute. Coryn wondered where she had seen the man across the aisle before. He was good-looking in a tweedy sort of way. His thick brown hair was salted with some gray at the temples. His features were good, his eyes thoughtful, his expression held both intelligence and humor. His destination must be Rockport. She searched her memory. Could she possibly have met him somewhere when she was home last spring?

Just then the PA system crackled to life: "Attention,

all passengers ticketed for Westair Airlines Flight 84 to Rockport. We are overbooked for this flight. If two passengers will volunteer to give up their seats they will be placed on the next available flight and receive a voucher for a free trip anywhere on our route.''

An uncomfortable silence spread throughout the waiting room. People stirred in their seats. The low murmur of voices followed. Still, no one got up and moved to the ticket counter. Most of the assembled passengers were on their way home from college or business trips, eagerly awaiting the flight home to be with family and friends. Nobody wanted to give up their seat.

Coryn was aware of the uneasy pall that fell on the holiday mood in the room after the announcement. A few hours' difference in *her* arrival time would not matter that much, she reflected. Her parents had a social engagement anyway and would be gone all evening. Why not give up her seat on this flight and take the next one?

Mark folded his *Newsweek,* stuffed it into the pocket of his duffel bag, got up and ambled over to the ticket counter. He was certainly in no hurry to get home. Without Ginny the weekend loomed dismal. He'd given Mrs. Aguilar, the housekeeper, the holiday weekend off. Why not give up his seat?

At the ticket counter, Mark was rewarded with a big smile of relief from the harried-looking agent behind the desk. He waited while his ticket was rewritten and his travel voucher made out. Mark became aware of movement beside him. He turned. The young woman who'd been sitting near him now stood beside him.

"I guess we're the altruistic ones in the bunch. Or maybe just the only ones with no holiday plans." Immediately he realized the remark he had meant jokingly did not amuse her.

She inclined her head slightly, forced a smile. He was grateful for the ticket agent's interruption, "Here you are, Mr. Emery, and many thanks."

Mark pocketed his ticket and voucher. As he walked back to his seat, he heard the agent say, "Good evening, Miss Dodge."

Dodge? That was the name of the Rockport man rumored to be challenging the incumbent for an assembly seat in the next election. Neil Dodge, a successful contractor and civic leader. Was that his wife? No, too young. Besides, the agent had called her *Miss* Dodge. Maybe she wasn't related to Neil Dodge at all. Still, he may have seen her before at some fund-raising event or other.

He felt a little sheepish for the remark he had made to her. He was not good at small talk or socializing. Out of practice. Even among his colleagues at the newspaper he had a reputation for being a loner. A curmudgeon? Shari had been the one who was outgoing, friendly, vivacious. Everyone loved Shari. She made friends easily. Since she was gone, everything had changed.

Flight 84 was called and passengers gathered up packages, bundles, belongings and trooped out through the gate to board the plane. Mark watched them go, grimly wishing he hadn't been so impulsive. The next flight north wasn't due for at least two hours. He looked around uneasily. Suddenly, the waiting room, filled with people and voices a few minutes before, was quiet and empty. Except for two. Himself and Miss Dodge. He glanced over at her, seated on the opposite side of the room, apparently preoccupied with her own thoughts.

Mark stood up. He'd read his magazine cover to cover. He thought he'd better get something else to read until the next flight north arrived. He strolled out to the corridor, passed people worriedly studying posted arrival and departure bulletins. Weather seemed to be affecting all eastbound flights originating in San Francisco, as well as those due. A long list of "delayed" or "canceled" notices followed destination names and numbered flights. It might be a long night.

Mark checked out the newsstand but nothing appealed to him so he strolled the labyrinthine halls of the airport, leisurely browsing the gift-shop windows. Something for Ginny for Christmas? No. Too early. Anyway, he wasn't sure what she'd like this year.

At the entrance of one of the airport restaurants, Mark stopped to examine the menu on the door. Knowing the best he could expect on the flight was a soft drink and small bag of peanuts, he decided he might as well eat. There was a line, made up, he guessed, of stranded passengers. He took a place at the end of it. Overheard snatches of conversations relayed the usual horror stories of delayed plans and canceled flights. He listened with sympathetic amusement. A few minutes later someone stepped in behind him. When he turned his head, he saw it was her, his fellow passenger from Flight 84.

Remembering her lack of response to his first attempt at conversation, he hesitated. Yet, he couldn't ignore her. He nodded and said, ''Hi.''

This time she smiled—an astonishingly lovely smile. ''When in doubt, eat, right?''

He grinned. ''Well, I've taken the flight to Rockport before and I can guarantee you that we won't get fed on the plane. And who knows how long we'll be delayed here. Might as well take advantage of being in San Francisco.''

''At least they'll probably have sourdough French bread.''

The line moved slowly ahead of them. A hostess escorted people to the few vacated tables. Obviously other passengers were using their waiting time by lingering over dinner and coffee.

''I'm Mark Emery. I'm a reporter on the *Rockport Times.*''

''I'm Coryn Dodge. I've seen your byline. My mother sends me the hometown paper.''

''You live in San Francisco?''

''In L.A. At least, I work in L.A.''

''Are you on your way home?''

''Yes, I'm spending Thanksgiving with my parents.''

They were now at the head of the line. The hostess threaded her way through the tables, approaching them. ''Table for two?'' she asked, and not waiting to be corrected, ''This way, please.''

Mark glanced at Coryn and back at the hostess. ''Well, we're not—together.''

The hostess's arched eyebrows lifted, her forehead puckered. Pursing her lips, she looked around the restaurant with an annoyed expression. "Well...it might be a long wait..." Turning back to them, she asked, "Would you mind sharing a table?"

Mark looked at Coryn, "Would you?"

With only the slightest hesitation, she answered, "No, not at all."

Her problem solved, the hostess smiled. "Good. Please come this way." She moved swiftly over to a corner table a busboy had just cleared.

They sat down and a waiter handed them menus and went away. For a few minutes they studied the selections.

"See anything you like?" Mark asked.

"I'm not really all that hungry. I just thought it would take up some time... Oh, a Cobb salad, I guess."

"I think I'll try the scallops." Mark said. The waiter came back and Mark ordered for them both. "Coffee first?" he asked Coryn. When she nodded, the waiter poured them each a cup then left again.

As she sipped her coffee, Coryn took a good look at the man across the table. He had an intelligent, pleasant expression and might have been downright handsome had it not been that his nose was the slightest bit crooked. However, instead of detracting from his looks, Coryn thought the slight flaw lent a certain ruggedness to his features that she found quite attractive. Suddenly she realized that he was also regarding her thoughtfully. All at once, she felt a little self-conscious. Here they were, two complete strangers, now what?

Mark did not want to force conversation. Yet it

seemed worse not to say anything. Besides, he felt obligated. He had been the one to suggest they share a table. He could always employ his reportorial skills. His comfort zone. He cleared his throat.

"Do you like L.A.?"

"Like it?" Her eyes widened as if she was caught off guard by the question. "Actually, I hadn't intended to stay there. The summer after I graduated I went to visit a girlfriend, someone I knew from college. It just sort of happened…I got a job and…"

What had *really* happened was she had met Jason Kramer. They had met at a party, a housewarming for one of Sheila's friends who had just moved into a new condo in Santa Monica. Someone introduced them. One thing had led to another. It was as simple as that. And as complicated.

"What do you do in L.A.?" Mark continued, feeling he was on safe ground. He *was* curious. She had a certain style, a class-act look.

"I work for a public relations firm."

"That sounds interesting."

"Interesting?" She paused as if not quite knowing how to answer him. "That's what I thought, at first. At least my job isn't. We're assigned to certain accounts. What it actually amounts to is a clipping service."

"I gather you're not planning to make a career of it?"

"Hardly."

"What would you rather be doing?"

She looked at him steadily for a full minute as if she didn't quite understand the question.

"I meant," he explained, "if you aren't that sold on your job, there must be some other interest you'd like to pursue. Unless something else is keeping you in L.A.?"

To her relief the waiter reappeared with their order. She had no intention of telling him what kept her in L.A. Or that she might be on the brink of making a change. In her job and her lifestyle. But you don't pour out your heart to a perfect stranger. At least, she'd never been the type to do so. Besides, she wasn't sure just what she was going to do about anything.

After the waiter left, she asked Mark, "What about you? Were you always interested in newspaper work?"

"Yes. I worked on the school paper in high school, worked as a stringer and in the summer at a local paper. In college, I took a double major in journalism and economics. When I graduated, I got the first job I interviewed for, and that was that. For a year." He smiled. "Ironically, one of the good or bad aspects of being a newspaperman is the urge to move on to another town, a bigger paper."

"How did you happen to come to Rockport?" Coryn found herself curious to know. There was a certain sophistication about Mark that hardly seemed small-town. "The *Times* isn't exactly a metropolitan newspaper."

"Rockport seemed a good place to bring up children."

"You have children?" Coryn felt surprised. It had not occurred to her that Mark Emery was married or a father.

"A little girl. Ginny. Six."

"Does your wife like Rockport?"

His expression changed. He took a sip of coffee. "My wife's dead."

"Oh, I'm sorry, I—"

"Don't apologize. You couldn't have known. It was three years ago. A skiing accident." He paused. "Being a single parent, you have to weigh everything. The job itself isn't the priority. Where it's located is sometimes more important. Now I consider things I might not otherwise, take fewer risks."

Coryn could think of nothing to say to that. Marriage, children, death, all things she had not experienced. She picked up her fork and began to eat.

In a few minutes, Mark commented thoughtfully, "Strange, isn't it? You moved from the north coast to L.A. and I moved from southern California to Rockport."

"The heart has its reasons, as someone said."

Her remark begged exploring. His reporter's instinct prompted, but this time Mark decided against acting upon it. There was a remoteness about her that discouraged intimacy. He studied the young woman sitting opposite him. She had slipped the raincoat off her shoulders and underneath she wore a royal blue cowl-necked sweater that deepened the color of her eyes. Her dark hair waved softly back from ears where small gold hoops swung.

The waiter appeared, refilled their coffee cups. When he left, Mark brought the conversation back to himself.

"Well, *my* reason to move to an area like Rockport

was practical. Ginny started first grade this year. I wanted her to grow up in a small community, go to school with the same kids through her school life, kids whose parents I'd know. I wanted to know her teachers, have neighbors who cared about her... In the city, I didn't even know my neighbors' names."

"There's some value in anonymity. In a town like Rockport, there are no secrets. In L.A., nobody knows what you do or cares."

He raised his eyebrows. "And you like that?"

"We're coming from opposite perspectives, as you pointed out. I grew up in Rockport."

"And don't you think small towns have advantages?"

"Sure. But they also have their downside. A town like Rockport doesn't prepare you for another kind of life. It's a real reality shift to move to a big city." Coryn thought of her own naiveté when she'd arrived in L.A. Her expectations had ended in disillusionment. But that wasn't something she wanted to talk about, either. Mark was looking at her intently as if waiting for her to go on.

Suddenly Coryn thought, *I'm talking too much.* That was the danger with as good a listener as Mark Emery. Talking to a stranger was easier than to a friend. Safer. Chances were they'd never see each other again after tonight.

The waiter returned to see if they wanted dessert. They refused, but asked for coffee refills. Coryn had indicated separate checks when their order was taken, so when they finished their coffee and got up to leave, there was no discussion about who paid what. They both used credit cards and made their way out of the restaurant.

Coryn told Mark she wanted to make a phone call and added that she'd see him back in the waiting room.

"See you later," he replied. "And thanks for the company at dinner," he added.

Coryn smiled as they parted. He was merely being polite, she told herself. But it was nice of him to say, nonetheless.

In the phone booth, she dialed her L.A. number. She wanted to see if Jason had left any message on her answering machine since her last check. There was none.

Coryn sat there for a full minute, got her phone card out of her wallet and dialed Jason's number. It rang and rang, then his taped message came on. "Jason Kramer. Leave a message. If it seems important, I'll get back to you. Cheers."

As she listened for the message to finish, a mixture of emotions swept over Coryn. Recorded, Jason's self-confident manner came off as arrogant. Hadn't her roommate, Sheila, often complained that Jason's tendency for put-downs was offensive? She had defended him, saying, "Oh, he's only kidding." But maybe Sheila was right. She didn't leave a message. She knew he wasn't home, but he sometimes left a personal message for her on his greeting. Coryn replaced the receiver and sat there for another moment. Well, he hadn't left a message for her. It had happened before. Later, he'd offhandedly apologize. But that was Jason. Take it or leave it. Coryn opened the folding doors of the phone booth to take a deep breath just in time to hear the PA announce her flight.

She hurried toward the waiting room. Mark was standing at the entrance. He motioned her forward. He held open the door to the field for her and together they went down the steps out to where the plane was loading.

The wind was fierce as they walked across the wet tarmac to board. Coryn hurried up the small metal steps and into the plane. She immediately noticed that the plane was nearly full with passengers who had boarded in Sacramento. At the door, the flight attendant, taking them for a couple, said, ''Sorry, there are no two seats together, just singles.''

Coryn moved down the aisle to an empty seat. She stowed her luggage in the overhead compartment then got settled, safety belt fastened, as the plane taxied down the runway for takeoff. Finally, they were airborne. Without wanting to, her thoughts returned to Jason. For months he'd occupied so much of her life. She was beginning to realize their whole relationship might have been a waste of time. It would be a relief to be away from L.A. for a while.

Mark pushed the lever at the side of his seat to move it into a reclining position. At last he was on his way home. Home? Without Ginny.

He'd left Ginny in San Rafael to spend the holidays with Shari's parents. They'd always spent Thanksgiving with the Bartons. This year he'd used work as his excuse not to stay over. They accepted that. He wasn't sure they believed it, but he knew they understood. In three years he'd made a lot of progress, but there were still too many memories of other Thanksgivings spent there when Shari was alive.

She'd been their pride and joy, the light of their lives. All those clichés people use to describe the feelings of doting parents of an only daughter fit the Bartons. Since her death, their house had become a kind of shrine to her memory with photos of her everywhere. Shari in her cheerleader outfit, as homecoming queen in high school, at her senior prom and as a bride. Shari had done it all. The only thing she hadn't been able to do was have a baby.

They had adopted Ginny. Then their happiness was complete. For a while at least. He felt a deep, familiar sadness well up in him. It was so unfair. But it had been three years ago. He should be getting over it, shouldn't he?

At Rockport Airport the terminal clock read 2:20 a.m. Too late certainly to call home. Coryn walked outside into the foggy night in hopes of finding a cab or maybe one of the hotel-shuttle vans. Neither was in sight. She'd have to go back inside, phone for a cab. Just then, Mark Emery emerged through the glass doors, carrying his overnight bag and briefcase.

"No one to meet you?"

"I didn't really expect anyone this late."

"I left my car parked here Friday. I'd be glad to drive you home."

Coryn hesitated. "You're sure? It might be out of your way. My parents live in Chestnut Hills, that's quite a way on the other side of town."

"No problem. We live in Kensington Park." He looked at her carry-on and overarm leather tote. "Is that all you have?"

"Yes, I'm only staying through Thanksgiving," she explained as they started walking toward the parking lot.

The night air was damp and smelled of fog. He unlocked his car, a station wagon, and held the door open for her to get into the passenger seat. He went around, got in the other side, turned on the ignition. They pulled out into the curved road leading from the airport.

Fog drifted in eerie yellow swirls in the headlights as they merged onto the freeway. "Looks as though it just opened up enough so we could land, now it's closed down again," Mark said.

"Typical north-coast November," Coryn replied.

"I'm getting used to it. In fact, I like it. The rain, the fog. There's a kind of feeling of being sheltered, protected from the outside world."

"Some call it the Redwood curtain." Coryn glanced at him. "You don't feel confined? I mean, after working in the city I would think you might find living up here too insulated."

"No, not at all. It's better for Ginny. And it's what Shari wanted...what we planned to do if she had lived."

Coryn murmured something she hoped sounded sympathetic.

"It's working out just fine. Great, in fact," he said firmly. He sounded as if he was convincing himself.

They drove the rest of the way mostly in silence,

each locked into private thoughts. Mark took the turn-off to Chestnut Hills, one of Rockport's prestigious residential areas. They wound up the twisting tree-lined road.

"Next right, number 183." Coryn directed and Mark swerved into a gravel driveway and pulled to a stop in front of a rambling stucco and timbered house. An old-fashioned lamppost lit the way to an arched stone entrance.

Coryn slung the strap of her tote over her shoulder and opened the car door. "Don't bother to get out. I can manage. Thanks for the ride."

"My pleasure," Mark said. "Good night and have a nice visit with your folks." He watched her until she had opened the door, turned back and waved and gone inside.

The minute Mark turned the key in the lock of his front door he was hit by the emptiness. He quickly switched on the light in the hall, set his suitcase down and stood there for a minute. It still happened, that wave of depression crashing down on him, knowing there was no one to welcome him.

He looked through the mail Mrs. Aguilar had left neatly stacked on the hall table. Nothing important. Mark felt tired but not sleepy.

He went into the kitchen, turned on the light, went to the refrigerator. Ginny's last drawing brought home from school adorned the front of it. A smiling Pilgrim family, complete with a huge orange cat. A Thanksgiving art project, or was this her way of persisting in her plea for a pet? "Just a little kitten, Daddy, please.

I'll take care of it, I promise!" Mark smiled. Even at six Ginny knew how to get to him.

Shari would have let her have a kitten. That's for sure. The sharp sensation of loneliness came again. The realization of not having things like this to share with someone. Sometimes the pain was sharp and sudden. Other times just a dull ache.

Somehow, he and Ginny had managed to survive. They had a housekeeper, the efficient Mrs. Aguilar, who adored Ginny, cooked good meals and kept the house, saw that their clothes were washed and ironed. The first year had been the hardest. Now going on three since Shari's accident, they'd managed. Just.

Maybe it was wandering around the San Francisco airport waiting for the next flight north that had put him in this strange mood. The unexpected meeting with Neil Dodge's daughter. He had seen the quick brightening of her eyes in sympathy when he'd told her about Shari. It was as if she'd wanted to say something comforting but was too shy. Sensing that in her had sharpened his own need to share his heart with someone again. Someone who would understand. It might be crazy. He might be way off base, but he had sensed a vulnerability in Coryn Dodge under her poised surface.

He'd like a chance to get to know her better...but that took time and effort. He'd tried going out after the first year. Friends had fixed him up with someone they "knew" he'd like. But nothing had ever worked out. He knew there was a void in his life, but relationships took time and effort.

Coryn Dodge might be someone he could be interested in. She had been easy to talk to, had listened with warm empathy...as if she understood.

Mark opened the refrigerator, got out a quart of milk, poured himself a glass. Coryn Dodge. There had been something about her, something elusive that lingered in his mind. Like the scent of her perfume had lingered in the heated car after she got out.

He drained the glass, rinsed it and left it on the drainboard. That kind of thinking was going nowhere. Theirs had been one of those chance meetings. After Thanksgiving she'd be back in L.A. His life here would go on. He had a long weekend to get through somehow, alone.

Coryn let herself in the house. The lamp on the hall table shed a rosy glow, touching the gold frame of the mirror on the wall above and gilding the bronze chrysanthemums in the vase beside it. A note was propped against the base of the lamp:

> Welcome home, darling! We called the airport and were told your connecting flight had been delayed in Sacramento. Hope it wasn't too awful. There's an apple pie on the kitchen counter. We'll see you in the morning.
>
> Love,
> Mother and Dad

Coryn removed her coat, flung it on one of the Queen Anne chairs that flanked the table. She dropped her bag and set down her carry-on, took off her boots and walked stocking-footed down the hall to the kitchen. She heard a low whimpering and the sound of scratching from behind the closed utility-room door. Smiling, she opened it. Ranger, their fourteen-year-old black Lab, came out sniffing and whining deep in his throat.

"Hello, old fella. How are you?" she whispered, bending over to rub his head, scratch his ears. His thick tail swung like a heavy whip as he circled her. He moved stiffly. Coryn realized Ranger was getting older. His arthritis was worse, there was gray around his muzzle. "Good boy." She nestled his head against her shoulder and hugged him. "I know, it's been a long time. I'm glad to see you, too."

Her throat constricted suddenly. She hadn't realized. Away from home, in her mind, everything remained the same. The picture held constant, secure, reassuring. But Ranger was visibly changed. What other changes would she find here?

# Chapter Two

Coryn opened her eyes and looked around the bedroom. It had been redecorated for her sixteenth birthday. The furniture was the ivory French Provincial she had requested. Wallpaper, curtains, pillows on the curved window seat were all in her favorite color, blue.

The room had suited her perfectly when she was a teenager. But even when she came home from college on spring break or summer vacations, it had seemed juvenile, though she had not spent much time in it. There was always too much to do. Friends to see, places to go. It had just been a place to sleep or change clothes, to come to and leave from.

Everything in the bedroom was familiar. As if she'd never been away. Yet everything *had* changed. *She* most of all. From sixteen to twenty-six.

Faintly she heard muted sounds, movement, voices from downstairs. Her parents were probably already up, knew she was home.

She got out of bed and looked out the window. Fog

dripped from the Douglas firs surrounding the house. She thought of the days of endless smog-hazy sunshine in L.A. and shivered. She was back in "God's country," as natives of the area called it.

In the adjoining pink-tiled bathroom, she splashed water on her face, scrubbed her teeth, brushed and tied her hair back with a ribbon she found in the vanity drawer.

At the doorway of the kitchen, Coryn hesitated a moment, taking in the scene. Cheerful yellow walls, daisy-print café curtains accented the oak cabinets. Pots of red geraniums on the windowsill brightened the gray day outside. Her father stood at the counter, holding the morning paper, scanning the headlines. Her mother sat in the curved breakfast nook sipping a cup of coffee. Coryn realized anew what an extraordinarily good-looking couple her parents were.

Neil Dodge, six-foot and broad-shouldered with iron-gray hair that was perhaps receding a bit these days, was still a handsome man at fifty-five. He had strong features. A prominent nose and high cheekbones in a face tanned from weekends on the golf course or on fishing trips.

Her mother was...well, the only way you could describe Clare Dodge was beautiful, even at this hour of the morning, without makeup. Her silver-blond hair fell in natural waves around her slim shoulders.

"Good morning!" Coryn said as she stepped into the room.

"Darling!" Her mother greeted her happily and got up to hug her. "It's so good to have you home."

Coryn returned the hug and over her mother's shoulder, smiled at her father saying, "Hi, Dad."

"Good to have you home, honey. How was the trip?"

"Not bad at all. Just late." She went over to kiss him. Ranger struggled to his feet from where he had been sprawled on the floor looking up at her hopefully and Coryn bent over and rubbed his ears affectionately. "The flight was overbooked and I had to take the later one."

"I'm not surprised. This time of year," her father said. "I've cooled my heels at San Francisco International myself plenty of times waiting for the fog to lift. It's to be expected coming up the coast. I thought you might have to stay overnight at one of the airport hotels."

"Did you see anyone you know from Rockport in the airport or on the plane?" her mother asked. "Your father usually runs into someone."

"Not exactly. No one I knew. But I did get to have some company in the waiting room. Someone named Mark Emery. He's a reporter for the *Times.* We had dinner together while waiting for our flight. He drove me home."

"Mark Emery, the columnist?" Her father looked interested. "He writes fine, incisive articles. Pulls no punches."

"Sit down and have some breakfast, darling," her mother urged. "What would you like? Waffles? Muffins? Bacon and eggs."

"Just coffee for now. Thanks, Mom."

"That's no breakfast for a growing girl," her father

teased. It was a family joke. He'd made the same comment for years at breakfast. "Better eat something. You're too thin."

"Didn't someone say you can't be too thin or too rich?" Coryn slid into the built-in cushioned seat of the breakfast nook.

"I don't know about the too thin but maybe I agree about the too rich." Her father pretended to scowl.

Her mother set down a cup of coffee in front of Coryn. "There's so much to talk about. You never write and when you phone, well, you always seem in a hurry. Tell us all about everything."

"That's a tall order. Can it wait until I get my daily dose of caffeine?" Coryn smiled. Taking a sip, she regarded her mother affectionately, noticing that she seemed a little pale. Still, no one would ever guess her to be fifty-three.

Her mother sat down opposite her and reached over to pat her arm. "I'm so glad you're here. There is so much I want us to do. We'll have to go Christmas shopping, of course, and I'd like to do something special for you while you're here. Wouldn't you like to have a little get-together with some of your old friends? Lora and Cindy both want to see you and—"

"Mom, I'm going to be here only a few days. There won't be much time."

"Clare," her father's voice cut into the conversation. "Are you planning to cook something? All the burners on the stove are on *high.*"

"Are they?" Sounding startled, her mother jumped up. "Oh, dear, I didn't realize—" She looked flustered and went over to the stove, snapped the buttons off.

Her face was flushed, she darted a quick anxious look at her husband. ''I'm sorry—''

''It's okay, dear. You probably were just excited at Coryn's being here.'' Although her father spoke quietly, obviously checking his irritation, his words had seemed like a reprimand. ''Just be careful, won't you? The other night when I couldn't sleep, I came down to make some cocoa and I found the burners had been left on.''

''Oh, my, I didn't know. How could I have done that?''

Coryn's father put his arm around her mother's shoulders. ''It's okay, dear, it won't happen again, I'm sure, with Coryn here to check up on you.'' His attempt at humor didn't quite come off.

Coryn put her cup down slowly. *What was going on here?* There was a disturbing friction between her parents. A definite undercurrent.

''Well, ladies, I better be on my way.'' Neil reached for his raincoat, which was hanging on the peg by the back door that led into the garage. ''I have some bids to go over. You two have a good day catching up. See you later.''

''What time will you be home for dinner, Neil?''

He halted, as if considering. ''What say we go out to dinner tonight? Celebrate Coryn's homecoming? That way you won't have to worry about shopping or cooking.''

Coryn saw her mother's smile fade. Clare was a gourmet cook. At other times Coryn had come home she had taken delight in preparing a special dinner with all her daughter's favorite dishes. It was almost a tradition. Had her father forgotten that? Or was there some hidden meaning in her father's words?

"Of course, dear," Clare replied. "That will be fine."

Neil left, and her mother came back to the table, a bewildered frown creasing her smooth forehead. It was quickly replaced by a bright smile as she said, "That will be fun, the three of us going out. Won't it? Remember we used to do that Friday nights when you were little. Meet Daddy downtown for dinner? An adventure." She glanced at Coryn fondly. "We've missed you so much."

An anxiousness came into her mother's eyes. She seemed about to say something else then changed her mind. "Now, what shall we do today?"

# Chapter Three

The Grill Room of the Highland Inn was fashioned after an English pub with low-beamed ceilings, latticed amber windows, round tables and Windsor chairs. Along one side was a curved bar with high leather stools studded with brass nail heads. As Coryn and her parents entered, a heavyset man at the bar set down his drink and came over to Coryn's father.

"Bryson Falvey," the man said, holding out his large hand. "Falvey Heavy Equipment. We hear you're thinking of unseating old Mason Bigelow. That's good news." He pumped Neil's hand. "We need someone like you in Sacramento."

"Well, thank you. Very kind of you to say so. Nothing's definite yet..."

The man didn't seem to hear her father's words, just clapped him on the shoulder and went back to his seat at the bar.

When they were at their own table, Coryn asked her

father, "Are you seriously considering running for the assembly, Dad?"

"Several people are urging me to think about it. It's mostly talk. Nothing's been decided."

Coryn noticed her mother nervously rearranging silver at her plate. Didn't she like the idea?

Neil opened the glossy red menu. "Now, what would you ladies enjoy tonight? How about a nice sirloin, or fresh salmon fillet?"

The next few minutes were spent choosing their dinner entrées. Coryn's father exchanged a few friendly remarks with the waitress, who evidently knew him, then gave her their order.

When they were alone again, Neil looked at Coryn and picked up the conversation where they'd left off. "However, if I *did* decide to run, how about going to work for me on my campaign committee? With your PR experience, you could contribute a great deal. I'd pay you—match your salary in L.A. or more. And—" he laughed "— you wouldn't have any living expenses. Free room and board."

Coryn didn't have a chance to reply because the waitress came with their shrimp cocktails and her father did not return to the subject.

As soon as they got home, Clare told them she was going to take a long, leisurely bath and go to bed. Her father had some work to do and went to his den. Coryn went upstairs to her bedroom.

All through dinner she had felt restless. A couple of times she had completely lost track of the conversation. That hadn't mattered so much because several people had stopped by their table to engage her father in conversation. Over and over, the subject of his running for office had come up, but he had dismissed it lightly. It bothered Coryn that her mother had seemed so detached from it all. More than detached, she reflected, the subject seemed to make Clare anxious, though she did her best to hide it.

Coryn shut the door of her room and glared at the phone—the blue Princess one, her parents' gift to her on her fourteenth birthday. Her own line, her own number. She had been ecstatic.

She sat down on the side of the bed and stared at it. Maybe she'd just call her apartment in L.A., check the message machine. No harm in that. She heard the prerequisite six rings, the click of the recording machine. There was no message from Jason. Just her roommate Sheila's voice saying she'd gone to San Leandro to her folks' home for Thanksgiving.

Disappointed, Coryn put down the phone. Why hadn't Jason called from Detroit? She knew the name of the hotel where he said he'd be staying. It was one of the chain the company account executives used. She could call him there. What would be wrong with that? She could make it sound casual. Ask him how the sales presentation went. After all, they had discussed nothing else for weeks. They had brainstormed ideas together. He seemed to think some of hers were good. Had he used them? Wouldn't it seem natural she'd be interested to hear how his presentation had gone?

She picked up the receiver and dialed the long-distance number. As she waited, she caught a glimpse of herself in the dressing-table mirror. It brought a sudden flashback. She remembered how many nights she had glared at this same phone when she was a teenager, waiting for a certain boy to call. Ironic, ten years later, she was doing the same thing. Almost.

The hotel switchboard operator came on the line and Coryn asked to be connected to Jason Kramer's room.

The phone rang several times. Then, ''Jason Kramer here.'' His voice sounded crisp, businesslike.

''Jason, it's Coryn. How did it go? I've been thinking about you and—'' She stopped. She sounded overeager, gushy.

''Coryn. Oh, well. Yes, it went well.'' Was he annoyed or was that her imagination?

Coryn twisted the phone cord through her fingers. She hadn't meant to say it, but she gave in, couldn't stop herself. ''Why didn't you call? Why didn't you let me know?''

She was sure she could hear someone moving around in the background. ''Jason?'' Coryn heard a distinctly feminine voice call.

She closed her eyes, drew a deep breath. Had she no pride?

She clutched the receiver, which slipped a little in her clammy palm.

''I told you I'd be busy here,'' he snapped.

She clenched her teeth. What was that she heard? Had he put his hand over the mouthpiece, was he speaking to someone there in the room with him? He came back on the line. He seemed a little impatient. ''I'll have to go, Coryn. There're some people I've got to meet downstairs in the lounge.''

She waited, holding her breath a few seconds longer, idiotically, not wanting to hang up. Surely he would say something about her input. Tell her some of her ideas had helped?

Jason's voice came on again, a little bored. Indifferent? "I'll be in L.A. on the first. I'll call you then."

Her fingers tightened on the receiver. *No, you won't,* a voice in her head said.

There was definite irritation in Jason's tone now. "I better wrap this up, Coryn. I'll see you back in L.A."

Coryn did not answer. Slowly she put down the phone.

After she'd hung up, she sat perfectly still for a long time. Why had she been such a fool? Why hadn't she resisted the urge to call him. She had a feeling of finality. All her nagging doubts and questions about Jason came rushing for confirmation. Little cracks in his veneer had appeared months ago. She just hadn't wanted to see them. He was the reason she'd stayed in L.A. Long after she was bored with her job, disliked the lifestyle around her. She should have come home months ago when she first realized who and what Jason was.

The irrefutable truth descended like an icy cloak. Whatever she had felt for Jason or he for her was over. Whatever purpose she'd had in his life had been served. He didn't need her anymore. It was humiliating to admit. The truth might be best but it also could be ugly. She sat there perfectly still while her conviction took hold. She drew a long, shaky breath.

She wasn't going back to L.A.

She didn't want to face Jason. Or, everyone at the office. They would all know how he'd made a fool of her. Maybe they knew already, she grimly reflected.

Besides, she didn't care about that job. But if she didn't go back, what would she do? She'd figure that out later. Once that was decided, there were other things to do to make it stick. To make it so she couldn't change her mind.

First, she had to resign her job. That wouldn't cause any waves. It was an entry-level position. If she had potential, she could move up they'd told her. Her potential had been given to feeding Jason ideas for him to present. She'd never learned to be assertive enough. She'd trusted him to give her credit. It hadn't happened.

The following day when she made the call to the office it was as she'd expected. No one asked her many questions.

Next, she had to call Sheila to let her know she'd have to look for another roommate. That was a lot harder. But Sheila was a friend and very understanding. Good apartments at reasonable rents in safe neighborhoods were at a premium in L.A. Before she could allow herself to have any second thoughts she dialed Sheila at her parents' house, where she was visiting for the holiday.

Sheila was disappointed that Coryn wasn't coming back but surprised her by saying, "Actually, I think I saw it coming. You've been so depressed. Sure, you did a good job of covering it, but I could see you'd lost your enthusiasm."

"It was that obvious, huh?"

"Well, you know me," Sheila laughed. "I should hang out my shingle. Like Lucy in the Peanuts cartoon strip. 'The Doctor is In'." She laughed, "I guess you could say, I saw the handwriting on the wall."

"You did? Well, you were ahead of me. I just woke up." Coryn's voice was tinged with irony. There was a slight pause, then Sheila asked, "What about Jason?"

"What about him?"

"Does he know you're not coming back?"

"I told him."

"Is he the reason?"

"Partly."

"I hope you're okay about it."

"I can't discuss it right now. I'll fill you in another time, okay?"

"Sure." Sheila agreed. Then they'd launched into a discussion of the best way to send Coryn's belongings. The things she had purchased for their common use at the apartment—the iron and toaster, for instance—she told Sheila to keep. Her clothes were the main items that would have to be shipped.

"I'm sorry you have to do all this, Sheila. I know it's an awful lot to ask," Coryn said. "I feel I've let you down. I'll pay my part of next month's rent if you have trouble finding someone to share the apartment."

"No way."

Sheila assured her things could be worked out. She had lots of friends and was great at networking. Before they hung up Sheila said, "If you want my advice, which you probably don't, forget Jason Kramer. He isn't worth it."

"Thanks, Anne Landers."

Sheila's words reaffirmed what Coryn had concluded herself. Although forgetting Jason might be easier said than done. However, Coryn was determined to do it. He'd taken up too much of her time, energy, life already.

After she put the phone down Coryn just sat there. With two calls she had changed the direction of her life. Now what?

Even a bad experience can teach something if one is willing to learn. Maybe every woman has to have one disastrous romance in her life so that she can at least know what she doesn't want. The question in Coryn's heart was were her dreams of an enduring love too idealistic? Had she expected too much, trusted too much? Was there such a thing anymore as true love? Or did she cling to a hope that could never be fulfilled?

# *Chapter Four*

Thanksgiving came as a welcome distraction. It took her mind off what she'd done. If she'd had time to think about it she might have regretted her impulsive decision. She was sure she'd been right about Jason. Breaking off would have eventually happened anyway. What bothered her was, now what? Not knowing the answer, helping her mother gave her a chance to put off making any immediate decisions about her future.

This year for Thanksgiving, besides Coryn's aunts, her father's two sisters and their husbands from Redding, her father's lawyer Martin Prentis and his wife Lucille, old time friends, several other local couples had been invited. When Coryn asked her mother why some of these were being included in what had always been a family occasion, the answer was, "Well, Neil wanted some of the people that are urging him to run for the assembly. Actually as a kind of courtesy." That was also the reason her mother gave for having the turkey and most of the trimmings catered.

"But what about your famous candied sweet potato casserole and creamed onions?" asked Coryn in surprise. These were two of her mother's specialties.

"Oh, everyone's on a diet these days," was the offhanded reply. "With the extra people Neil invited, it just seemed—" she paused, "I haven't been doing much entertaining lately..."

Coryn accepted the explanation. Preoccupied with her own new problems it sounded reasonable enough. She pitched in to help with some of the details of preparing for her parents' guests. These mainly consisted of polishing the silver, arranging the flowers, and creating a cornucopia of fruit as a centerpiece for the buffet table.

Coryn moved through the day itself as if playing a role, smiling, chatting, answering questions about her life in L.A. casually. She was glad when evening came and all the guests had left. It was only when she was alone in her own room that she then faced the decisions she had made, the steps she had taken and confronted what she would do next.

Thanksgiving morning Mark got up late. The day was gloomy and windy. The sky dark, heavy with clouds threatening rain. He got up, put on his bathrobe and slippers. As he passed through the living room, he flipped on the TV. In the kitchen he dumped some cornflakes into a bowl, then clicked on the automatic coffeemaker.

The sound of the TV blared and he went to turn it down. The famous New York Thanksgiving Day parade was being telecast with its marching bands, floating air-balloon figures, baton twirlers and horseback riders. He watched for a few minutes, hoping the Bartons had turned it on for Ginny. She loved it. She recognized all the cartoon characters and called out their names, clapping her hands happily. His heart twisted. He missed her. Maybe he should have stayed in San Raphael with her, in spite of the memories.

The scene changed to a commercial and Mark went back out to the kitchen. His coffee was ready and he poured some into a mug. Gulping it, he stood staring out the window over the sink. It was beginning to rain. A gray steady rain that he knew would last all day.

Good thing there'd be marathon football. From California to Florida some of the biggest college teams would be playing. It would fill up the empty hours of this long day yawning ahead.

Noon found him still in his bathrobe in front of the TV, not knowing which team was even playing, which was winning or losing. Mindlessly watching the constantly moving figures on the screen, Mark's thoughts were far from points and scores.

He used the remote to change channels. Sleet fell heavily at the traditional Army-Navy game. The players battled through the soggy turf. Click, click. Sunshine in Florida. Click. In Michigan snow fell.

Mark's finger poised above the button, mesmerized by the picture of snow flurries. Snow. Always reminded him. How could it not? Squaw Valley nearly four years ago.

They'd been on one of their favorite vacations, their first since adopting Ginny. A ski weekend. It was wonderful. Ginny at two was fun, easy to take with them, enjoying everything. Shari was the skier. It was a sport she loved, and she was a good skier. Mark was a klutz on skis and had taken Ginny sledding so Shari could be free to run the slopes.

Then the unexpected, the unthinkable, happened. A freak accident. The ski lift broke, tumbling skiers thirty feet. Shari had hit her head and had been killed instantly.

A minute before, she had been laughing, waving down at him as he held Ginny in his arms. "Just one more time," she had pleaded when he suggested they call it a day, go back to the lodge. She had been having such a good time...

Click, click, Mark switched channels. Then he stood up, turned off the set. He looked out the window. A gray veil of rain darkened the afternoon. He turned abruptly and hurried to his bedroom, flinging off robe, pajamas as he did. Couldn't stay holed up like this another minute. Rain or no rain, he was going jogging. He pulled on his sweats, tied his running shoes and left the house.

Stepping outside on the porch, the cold, wet wind stung his face. He warmed up by running in place a few minutes, then set out through the misty rain.

An hour later he was back, blood tingling, muscles aching, but feeling better. After a long shower, he shoved a frozen pizza into the microwave and studied the TV listings. The movie channel was playing a John Wayne retrospective. *The Quiet Man* was scheduled next. Why not? Mark got the pizza out, put it on a tray and carried it into the living room and settled down in his easy chair. Some Thanksgiving, he thought with grim humor. Next year, it would be different. He'd make sure of it.

He settled back to lose himself in the movie. In two more days he'd go back to San Rafael, bring Ginny home and life would get back to normal.

Yet, it would never seem the same without Shari. Ginny needed a father *and* a mother.

For some reason, Coryn Dodge came into his mind. Her eyes, so clear and candid, yet still holding a kind of mystery. What was she really like when you got to know her? Mark had the impression there were layers to her personality. Things he would find interesting, intriguing, exciting. Not that he'd ever know. She was going back to L.A. after the holiday.

The morning after Thanksgiving Coryn awoke at seven. Her inner alarm clock working, she guessed, it was the time she usually got up to get ready to leave for the office.

It took her a few minutes to compute that she didn't have an office to go to, didn't have to fight the early-morning freeway traffic. L.A. and everything there was now history.

Tossing aside the covers, she got out of bed. Outside, early-morning fog swirled. She pulled on a sweater and an old pair of jeans she found in her closet and went out into the hall.

The house was quiet. On her way downstairs she passed her parents' closed bedroom door. They must be still asleep.

To her surprise her father was in the kitchen, making himself a cup of coffee, something she had rarely seen him do. He looked preoccupied. When he saw her, he lifted his eyebrows.

"You're up early. Thought you'd sleep in this morning after being up so late last night."

"I was awake. I thought I might as well get up," Coryn said. Ranger rose from his place under the table and, tail wagging like a metronome, came stiffly over to her. She rubbed his head, "Mornin', old fella."

"'Fraid you'll have to make coffee. I settled for instant," her father said. He glanced down at the newspaper on the table. "I've got an early meeting and didn't want to take the time."

"That's okay." She moved past him, got the canister of coffee down and started to measure it into the paper-filter cup. She gave him a curious look. He seemed on edge, as if something troubling was on his mind.

"By the way, Coryn, I haven't told you how glad I am you decided not to go back to L.A." He folded the paper and pushed it aside on the table. "I hope you won't try to get another job for a while. I was serious when I suggested you help with my campaign, if there is one. But aside from that, it would be nice for you to be here, keep your mother company. I think she gets pretty lonesome. Not good for her." He paused. "Your mother misses you, honey. You know, the only chick, the empty nest syndrome. She'd love to have you home for a while. We both would."

That her self-confident, self-absorbed father *needed* her had never occurred to Coryn before. That he would verbalize it caused a little pinch of anxiety.

Her father glanced at his watch, took a final sip of

his coffee, then set down his coffee mug. "Got to be off. Meeting at eight." He put his hand on her shoulder, kissed her cheek. "Think about it, honey. We really love having you home."

After her father left, Coryn felt puzzled. She thought of the subtle tension she had been aware of between him and her mother. Did he think her presence would act as a buffer somehow? Distracted by the thought, she plugged in the coffeemaker, and shoved two pieces of wholewheat bread into the toaster. While waiting, she stood at the sink staring out at the gloomy landscape. Wind tossed the limbs of the tall pines in a wild dance against the pewter sky. She had forgotten how long, dreary Rockport winters could be and suddenly felt depressed. Sometimes she had also been depressed in L.A. sunshine. So how she felt had nothing to do with the weather. Rather, she had shut one door of her life, slammed it actually, and she couldn't see another door to enter yet. The sound of the toast popping up diverted her attention. Enough of this, she told herself, as she buttered it. She'd read somewhere that physical activity was the best antidote for depression. As soon as she'd had some coffee she would take a walk.

Still, she couldn't shake the conviction that something was wrong here. Terribly wrong. Maybe this was just some sort of temporary phase. She'd noticed her mother's reaction to that Falvey man talking to her father about running for the assembly. Maybe they'd disagreed over the possibility of his going into politics. Whatever it was, it was upsetting the usual smooth surface of the Dodges' home.

A walk, that's what she needed. A long walk. She

took down her jacket from the peg near the back door and put it on. Ranger's tail began to thump. His leash hung on one of the other pegs. All she had ever had to do was rattle it and Ranger was up and ready to go.

"Want to go, fella?" Coryn asked, automatically reaching for the leash. Ranger tried to get to his feet, slipped on the vinyl floor. He sank back down, put his muzzle between his front paws, looked up at Coryn, as if to say, *Sorry, these old bones won't take me where I used to run.*

Coryn replaced the leash, stooped down to caress the dog affectionately, kiss the top of his head. "It's okay, boy. Another time."

Outside it was damp with the chill of a typical north-coast winter day. Hands deep in her flannel-lined pockets, head bent against the wind, Coryn quickened her pace. Gradually, new energy kicked in. She felt a tingling sensation in her arms and legs. Her heart rate increased.

She walked on mindlessly in the chill air, paying little attention to where she was going. Fog dripped from the tall Douglas firs along the way, she felt it beading her scarf. She tugged up the collar of her jacket, looked around. She had come much farther than she had meant to, preoccupied with thoughts that tumbled like a child's alphabet blocks, the numbers and letters on them making no sense. She stopped, shivering with cold, to get her bearings. She had walked out of the familiar residential area into an older section of town. In the distance, through the fog, she saw the blurry lights of a neon sign spelling out the words Al's Diner. It had been a favorite hangout in her teen years.

She was about two blocks from the high school. She hurried toward the diner. She decided a cup of hot coffee would warm her up for the homeward trek.

The air inside the diner was steamy, thick with the smell of frying bacon and sausage from the grill. She ordered a coffee at the counter then slipped into one of the red-vinyl booths.

The waitress brought the coffee in a thick white mug, set it down in front of her and whipped out an order pad. "Our special today is potato pancakes or apple turnovers with sausage."

Coryn stared at the woman for a stunned moment. It was like being in a time warp. The same red V-shaped apron and headband. She must be a hundred years old. Hadn't she worked here when Coryn was in high school?

The waitress waited, her pencil poised. "So which will it be?"

Coryn shook her head and said, "Just this coffee, thanks."

The waitress looked a little offended then went off, pocketing her order pad.

Still feeling somewhat dazed, Coryn wrapped both hands around the mug to warm them and cautiously took a sip of the scalding-hot coffee.

"Coryn."

Hearing her name made her jump. She set down the mug, spilling a little, and looked up, right into Mark Emery's warm brown eyes.

"Sorry, I didn't mean to startle you." He stood beside her table. "I was just surprised to see you. I mean,

I thought you were going back to L.A. after Thanksgiving."

"That's okay. It was just that I was sort of spaced out." She mopped up the spill with the edge of a paper napkin.

"May I join you? Or would you rather be alone?"

"No. I mean, fine. Please do."

Mark slid into the seat opposite her. "I always stop here to get coffee to go and a doughnut to take to the office with me. I was surprised to see you here."

"This used to be an old high-school haunt. I was out walking, and just thought I'd drop in to warm up."

He opened the top of the plastic coffee container he'd been holding and spooned in some sugar from the dispenser. He stirred his coffee for a minute while looking across the table at her.

Even at this early hour, Coryn Dodge looked undeniably attractive. Her eyes bright, her skin glowing from the outdoor exercise.

"I thought you'd be back in L.A. by now."

Coryn shook her head. "Not yet. I'm staying through Christmas. Maybe longer. It depends."

Her vague answer seemed to puzzle him. He gave her a quizzical look, then said, "I'm afraid I have disturbed you."

"Not at all," she quickly protested.

"You sure? You seem..."

"I'm sorry. I guess I was just doing some heavy thinking. Not advisable this early in the morning." She gave a small laugh. "I guess if I decide to stay in Rockport, I have to figure out what I'll do. I'll have to find a job of some kind. I don't even know where to look. This town has changed a great deal since I lived here.''

''For the better?''

''I don't know. I'm not sure. It seems like I've been away for a long time. At least it feels that way.

''Meaning L.A. is light years from Rockport.'' He sounded amused but his eyes were sympathetic. ''It does take getting used to. But I'm finding I like the slower pace, the laid-back lifestyle.''

Mark checked his watch. ''Gotta run. I've an appointment out in Field's Landing. I'm doing a feature on seniors. It's turned out to be fascinating. Each person I've interviewed is different. Some regard old age as the end, while others are like kids, enthusiastic, looking forward, trying new things.'' Mark shook his head. ''Funny, some people are old at fifty, others young at eighty.'' Mark took a final sip of his coffee and stood up. ''It was nice seeing you again. Now that you're staying, maybe we'll see each other again.''

''It's a possibility.'' She smiled. ''It's a small town.''

He smiled then, too. A smile that brought a warm light to his deep brown eyes and caused Coryn's pulse to quicken. Then, with a wave of his hand, he was gone.

Coryn remained a few minutes thinking about the coincidence of running into Mark so soon after their encounter in San Francisco. It *was* a small world. Chances are they would see each other somewhere again. That is if she *really* decided to stay in Rockport.

She left the diner and started back toward home. So many jumbled thoughts crowded into her mind. She knew she had made the right decision about Jason. That wasn't what troubled her. What she should do next was the problem. Her father's words this morning *had* bothered her. There was something beneath his casual suggestion that she stay home for a while. But what?

Her parents had always seemed completely content together. In fact, sometimes she had even felt they didn't need anyone else—not even *her*—to be happy. The ideal couple. That's how she had always thought of them. That's why it seemed so odd—Coryn brushed aside the worrying thoughts that crept back. Was her parents' perfect marriage coming apart?

She turned in the driveway and saw the kitchen light was on and her mother was standing at the window. When she saw Coryn she smiled and waved. Coryn waved back, feeling reassured. Maybe she had let her imagination run away with her. Everything was fine. Just as it had always been.

# *December*

# Chapter Five

Coryn's parents expressed their satisfaction that she had given up her job in L.A. and decided to remain in Rockport.

"At least until after the first of the year," she said cautiously not wanting to make any promise she couldn't keep. "I have many things to figure out."

They accepted that without comment whatever they secretly hoped she might decide to do.

"Oh, it will be marvelous having you here for Christmas," her mother said. "I do think you should call Cindy and make some plans since you're going to be here longer than you thought."

So the first week of December, heeding her mother's urging, Coryn finally called her childhood friend Cindy Barnes, now Cindy Lowell. There was no excuse for not letting people know she was back in Rockport. At least temporarily.

"Coryn, how great!" Cindy exclaimed when Coryn called to make a date for lunch. "Lora will be so excited. You can't imagine how often we talk about you. About all the things the three of us used to do."

"There's a lot to catch up on," Coryn answered, "Where shall we meet?"

"There's a new restaurant in Old Town I've been dying to try, the Seafarer. Tuesday's best for me. That's Benjy's day at nursery school. I'll contact Lora so she can work on getting a sitter."

Hearing this Coryn remembered with a shock that her two best friends were now mothers. Of course, she'd sent baby gifts. But she'd almost forgotten. The people she knew in L.A. were mostly single.

"Can't wait to see you," Cindy said gaily before she hung up.

Suddenly Coryn had mixed feelings about the upcoming reunion. She wasn't sure if she really wanted to stroll down memory lane. Would she feel completely out of touch? Would the three of them, who once were so close, have much in common after all this time? Would it feel strange now that their lives were so different? Well, it was too late to worry about that.

Old Town had once been a run-down waterfront area, lined with derelict buildings, empty storefronts with broken windows, seedy bars and dilapidated Victorian houses in various degrees of decay. Most people had avoided walking along the grim streets even in broad daylight, afraid of being panhandled by disheveled drunks, or confronted by loudly arguing tavern patrons standing outside the dingy entrances.

About six years earlier, a group of civic-minded

merchants, retailers, businessmen and city officials decided to clean up Old Town. They'd transformed it by turning what was already there into tourist-attractive places. They'd restored, renovated, repaired the buildings, leaving their unique architecture intact. The streets with brick walkways and old-fashioned lampposts established a nineteenth-century atmosphere. Boutiques, bookstores, toy shops, art galleries, restaurants, all conforming to the theme, gradually opened. Soon shoppers and tourists were flocking to Old Town.

During the pre-Christmas season, Old Town was a magic place. Uniquely trimmed Christmas trees stood in front of every shop and store. Swags of evergreen and twists of laurel leaves studded with bunches of bright red holly berries, draped from lamppost to lamppost. From the gazebo in the center of Old Town, a carillon played Christmas music, lifting spirits into the holiday mood and motivating shoppers to even more gift buying.

An old-fashioned horse and carriage with a driver dressed in appropriate garb provided an authentic Dickensian touch to the scene.

The Seafarer was one of the newer restaurants, decorated with nostalgic touches of the 1800s. On the walls were framed photographs of early woodsmen standing proudly on huge felled timber, and of the large cargo ships that used to sail into Rockport Bay when it was a thriving seaport of fishing boats, their nets bulging with their catch. Bentwood chairs were placed at round tables covered with red-checked cloths. Baskets of ferns hung at the windows, which offered scenic views of the wharf. This had become the favorite eatery for women shoppers and it was always busy.

Cindy and Lora were already seated when Coryn arrived after leaving her mother at the beauty salon. Both women greeted her warmly and rose to give her hugs, declaring she looked wonderful.

"It's that Beverly Hills touch." Lora sighed dramatically.

"Definitely," Cindy agreed, laughing. "So tell us all about life in the fast track."

"Hardly life in the fast track," she said. "Fighting freeway traffic, work, frozen dinners..."

"Oh, come on! Surely there's some glitter in all this!" Cindy looked skeptical. "A man?"

"No one special," Coryn said, and knew it was now true. She was glad the waitress came to take their order.

Decisions were made with much ado about dieting and calorie counting, exchange of quotes from the health-food-nut instructor of the aerobics class they were taking.

Finally, the patient waitress left with their menus and the conversation immediately turned to reminiscing. Coryn felt herself drifting off from the conversation. She couldn't remember half the things they were recalling. If she stayed in Rockport, would she fit in again? The only one of the trio, not married? Could she find a place here again, a lifestyle that would work?

Coryn looked at her two friends. The three of them had grown up together, sleeping over at one another's homes nearly every weekend, sharing dates, proms, opinions. They had been secure in their friendship. One by one they had paired off, gone steady, fallen in love. The spring they had all graduated college she had been a bridesmaid in both weddings. That summer, she had gone to L.A.

Their seafood salads were served and they chatted about mutual friends and whatever-happened-to-so-and-so. The waitress reappeared and rattled off the day's list of delectable dessert possibilities. Reluctantly they passed on it.

"I feel so virtuous I think we should go shopping," Cindy declared, laughing.

"Sure, why not?" Lora agreed as she got out her compact to freshen her lipstick. "I've got a sitter for the rest of the afternoon."

Lora glanced at Coryn, "How about you? It's not Rodeo Drive but they do have some new stores at the mall."

Coryn checked her watch. She had more than an hour to spare before she was supposed to meet her mother. Yet, she didn't want to extend the visit with her old girlfriends a minute longer. "I'm sorry, I can't join you this time," Coryn said. "I'm meeting Mom after her hair appointment. I promised I'd help her Christmas shop, she has a list a yard long."

"She does?" Cindy looked surprised. "That's funny, I ran into your mom in October. I remember because I was getting Halloween things for the kids. She joked about having nearly all her Christmas shopping done."

"That's another thing I always admired about your mother, Coryn," Lora commented. "Besides being gorgeous. She was always so organized, on top of things.''

Coryn felt a small flutter in her stomach. That was the reputation her mother had. But since she'd been at home, there had been a series of incidents that troubled Coryn. Sometimes Clare seemed vague, forgetful, confused. Doing things like leaving the stove burners turned on, as her father had pointed out. And there had been other things. For a moment, she considered what Lora had just said. Something kept her from making the glib comments she might have given ordinarily.

Coryn left the Seafarer with a sense of relief. She said goodbye to the other two, making some noncommittal remarks about getting together again. As she walked in the direction of the beauty salon her mother patronized, she saw a man and a little girl coming toward her. As they got closer, she saw the man was Mark Emery. The child with him must be his daughter.

They saw each other almost at the same time. She looked as surprised as he was. Coryn Dodge was even prettier than he remembered. In sunlight her hair had mahogany lights, her blue eyes seemed bluer. She was dressed in a blazer, pants, a silk scarf patterned with vivid autumn leaves was knotted casually at her neck.

''Hello there,'' he greeted her. ''What a wonderful surprise.'' The warm look in his eyes made her heart skip a beat.

Coryn smiled. ''Good to see you again, Mark.''

He turned to the little girl beside him, ''Coryn, I'd like you to meet Ginny. Ginny, this lady is Coryn Dodge. We came up on the same plane from San Francisco after I left you at Nana's and Grampa's.''

The child regarded Coryn with wide curious eyes. She had a spray of golden freckles across a small button nose and round, rosy cheeks.

Coryn held out her hand. "I'm happy to meet you, Ginny."

Ginny smiled, shook Coryn's hand. She was not at all shy, but she had a sweetness about her that suggested the security of being well-loved.

"Are you Christmas shopping?" Coryn asked.

"Sort of." Ginny glanced at Mark, as if for confirmation. "We shopped for the Three Wise Men."

Puzzled, Coryn looked first at Mark then back at Ginny.

"See, first we got the stable scene, where the Baby Jesus was born, and the angels. Last year, we got the shepherds and some of the sheep. So *this* year we get the Three Kings," Ginny explained.

"Shari, Ginny's mother, always wanted Ginny to understand Christmas wasn't just presents and Santa Claus, so we started celebrating 'little Christmas,' too. January sixth commemorating the arrival of the Magi."

"How lovely," Coryn said, touched by this unique family custom. "So, did you find them?"

"Yes, they're great! They've got crowns and gold trimmed robes and all." Ginny smiled happily. "Now we're going for a carriage ride, aren't we, Daddy?"

Mark nodded. "A promise is a promise."

"That should be fun."

The carriage was just turning the corner at the end of the street. It came to a stop a few yards from where they were standing. As the driver helped down the couple who had been riding, Mark raised his hand to signal that they wanted to hire the carriage next. Coryn walked over to the curb with them.

Ginny gave a little skip, swinging Mark's hand, then she glanced up at Coryn. "Want to come with us?"

The driver stepped forward and said with a grin, "Same price, one or two adults with a child."

"How about it?" Mark asked Coryn. "Would you like to?"

Riding in a carriage with Mark and Ginny would certainly beat waiting in a beauty salon for her mother, she thought. "Why not?" she replied with a smile. "How long will it take?"

"Fifteen minutes is the ride, miss." The driver tipped his stovepipe hat, opened the carriage door.

Coryn looked at Mark, Ginny and the carriage. It did look like fun. "Okay, I'd love to."

The next thing she knew, she was being helped up into the carriage. With a flick of the driver's whip, they started off. Coryn glanced at Mark. He looked different this afternoon. Younger, handsomer, his hair was tousled by the brisk wind off the bay. He was wearing a creamy Irish-knit sweater, corduroy pants. He was obviously more relaxed and enjoyed being with his child.

The horses' hooves clip-clopped on the brick streets as they rolled through Old Town. People walking along the sidewalks looked at them, smiled and waved. Ginny giggled.

"Let's wave back like the English royals I've seen on TV!" Coryn suggested. She fluttered her hand in the famous back-hand wave Queen Elizabeth gave while riding in *her* carriage.

"Yes! Let's!" said Ginny as she bounced happily and followed suit.

Mark looked a little embarrassed, but grinned indulgently at both of them.

The wind was strong, cold. Coryn pulled her silk scarf from around her neck and tied it under her chin to keep her hair from blowing into her face.

Coryn enjoyed the ride thoroughly. Seeing Rockport from the vantage of a carriage was like being transported back in time. She glanced at Mark, smiling. "This is *really* fun!"

He grinned back. Coryn *was* having a good time. Her eyes were sparkling, and her smile—why, she looked really beautiful.

They went up Viewmont Hill to its crest, where Highland Inn stood, then back, and circled the little park in the center of Old Town. The driver shouted "Whoa!" to his compliant horse, and pulled to a stop.

Ginny looked disappointed

"It was too short, wasn't it?" Coryn said understandingly.

"Well, maybe we'll do it again," Mark said, getting out, then turned back to lift Ginny down. "But now we're going for our treat, remember?"

"Oh, yes! We're going to have a frozen-yogurt cone," Ginny told Coryn. "Pumpkin flavor. It's my favorite."

"For the time being, right?" Mark laughed. "Would you like to come with us?"

Coryn again glanced at her watch and hesitated. She still had a half hour before she had arranged to meet her mother. She would like to stretch this time with

Mark Emery and his little girl longer. She made up her mind quickly, ''Okay, I will. A frozen-yogurt cone sounds just great!''

With perfect naturalness, Ginny took Coryn's hand and the three of them walked down the street together to Old Town's Old Fashioned Ice Cream Parlor. On the way Ginny chattered happily. The pink-and-white-striped awnings outside the shop matched the ruffled aprons and headbands on the girls behind the counter. Inside, the decor was so deliberately nostalgic, with curlicued metal chairs and faux-marble-top round tables that Coryn and Mark exchanged an amused look. But it was also charming and since Ginny was enjoying herself completely, their amusement remained shared but unspoken.

Ginny had a little trouble with the generous double-dip serving. The creamy substance melted away faster than her small tongue could lick it up. Ginny fretted a bit as it started to drip down the side of the cone and onto her hands, but Coryn quickly came to the rescue. She took some packaged handi-wipes from her purse and she deftly cleaned Ginny's chin and sticky fingers.

''You must have been a Girl Scout. Always prepared.'' Mark commented, his eyes amused. Coryn smiled.

''I'm going to be a Brownie. Next year when I'm seven,'' announced Ginny.

Coryn saw the look of tenderness on Mark's face and was touched. It was clear he adored his little girl.

Coryn checked her watch again and said, ''Sorry, but I have to hurry. I really do need to meet up with my mother.'' She got up to leave; ''Thanks for inviting me to your party. I really enjoyed myself.''

Their gazes met. Mark smiled and she caught her breath.

''We enjoyed having you along,'' Mark told her.

''It was fun waving in the carriage,'' Ginny added.

They said goodbye and Coryn hurried away in the opposite direction. She felt happy and lighthearted. Meeting up with Mark and his child had been a most pleasant surprise. She liked what she'd seen. He was a real hands-on Daddy.

As Mark and Ginny came out of the ice-cream parlor and were walking back down the street, they were hailed by the driver who was standing by his mount and carriage waiting for customers.

''Sir! The lady forgot her scarf,'' the carriage driver said, handing Mark the length of silk. Mark took it, held it for a second, breathing in the scent that clung to it. He recognized it. It was the same distinctive perfume he had noticed the night he had driven her home from the airport.

''It's pretty, isn't it, Daddy?'' Ginny asked, fingering the edge of the scarf. ''Like Coryn. She's pretty, too, isn't she?''

''Yes, very,'' Mark answered, folding the scarf and putting it in his jacket pocket. ''She'll be sorry she lost it. We'll have to return it to her, won't we?''

# Chapter Six

Coryn stepped inside LaMode Beauty Salon and was immediately swept into a pink perfumed world. The assorted fragrances of lotions, cosmetics and shampoo mingled in the warm air. Blow-dryers whirred and women's voices murmured. A constant hum of conversation flowed from the pink-leather quilted booths and manicure tables.

A high-fashioned coiffeured blonde with vividly blue-shadowed eyes and incredible long, curved false eyelashes sat behind the reception desk. She was new since Coryn had last been here, and when Coryn asked if her mother was finished, the young woman ran long sequin-lacquered fingernails down the page of her open appointment book.

"Mrs. Dodge? Oh, yes. Are you her daughter? Well, she left a little while ago."

"Are you sure? I was to meet her here."

"I'll ask Justine, her stylist. But I'm almost certain...I'll find out,'' she said, and got up and moved into one of the nearby booths.

Coryn recognized the woman who followed the receptionist back to the desk as her mother's regular hairstylist.

''Hi, Coryn. Your mom wasn't feeling so well when we finished and I called a cab to take her home. She left her keys and said you could drive her car home.'' With her free hand she dug into her pink nylon smock pocket, brought out a set of keys and gave them to Coryn. ''Has your mom been sick? I didn't think she looked good when she came in...pale, sort of shaky. I thought maybe she'd had flu or was coming down with it.''

''I don't know. I hope not,'' Coryn said.

Justine tapped the hairbrush she was holding against her palm. ''Lately she's seemed...I don't know...not quite herself.''

Hearing someone else put into words what Coryn had felt about her mother since coming home made her suddenly tense. ''Thanks, Justine. I'll go right home and see how she is.''

Coryn drove home quickly, her heart beating hard, her breathing shallow. Something was wrong with her mother. But what?

She didn't know what prompted her to do it. But when she pulled into the garage, before going into the house, she unlocked the trunk of the car. Inside she found two large shopping bags filled with beautifully wrapped Christmas packages. The tags bore the same names of the friends and relatives her mother had put on her list to buy gifts for that very morning at the breakfast table.

But when had her mother bought these gifts? She'd been in the beauty parlor all morning, Coryn realized. She must have purchased the gifts days ago—and forgotten.

After staring at the presents for a few stunned minutes, Coryn slammed down the trunk and went into the house.

Rita, their weekly housecleaner, was vacuuming in the living room. In a hushed tone of voice she told Coryn her mother was napping.

"How did she look when she came home?" Coryn asked.

Rita frowned, leaned on the vacuum handle. "Not good. When I seen the cab pull up front, I looked out the window, not expecting anyone since you both were gone. Then I saw your mom come up the walk, ever so slow. I went right to the door and opened it. 'Mrs. Dodge, you look beat and that's for sure,' I told her. She said something about not feeling well, so I helped her up to her bedroom. She said she'd be all right if she'd just lie down for a bit. I took her up a cup of tea later but she had a cloth over her eyes and was just stretched out on the bed. I pulled the quilt over her and just tiptoed out." Rita shook her head. "Never saw her look that bad before."

"Maybe it's the flu," Coryn said through stiff lips, fearing it was something much worse than that.

Still shaken by the discovery of the Christmas presents in the car, Coryn went upstairs. She opened her mother's closed bedroom door, peeked in, saw she was sleeping and went on into her own.

What should she do? Ask her mother about the wrapped gifts, tagged and ready to give? Could her mother possibly have forgotten? She seemed to forget so many things these days.

Was something seriously wrong with her? All sorts of possibilities crowded into Coryn's mind. Some kind of emotional break? Some kind of amnesia?

She still hadn't decided whether to bring up the subject an hour later when her mother emerged from her bedroom, refreshed and fragrant from her rest and bath. She seemed perfectly fine. The explanation she gave for leaving the beauty salon early seemed perfectly logical.

"I should have eaten something before I went there. I rushed around shopping and then—it was so hot in there with all the steam and the smells of nail polish and blow-dryers going, I just felt faint. I didn't want to spoil your luncheon with Cindy and Lora, so it was simpler for me to come home in a cab."

Momentarily Coryn felt better. That evening, even with Coryn's observation, her mother seemed her usual self. They watched TV together, a Christmas program. It was like a hundred other evenings Coryn remembered at home. But she couldn't forget those packages in the trunk of the car. There *was* something going on here she didn't understand. But what?

# *Chapter Seven*

The next afternoon Coryn helped her mother with the holiday ritual of baking dozens of sugar cookies. Clare was in a holiday mood, full of plans for Christmas. Her mother loved Christmas, everything about it, gave dozens of presents to people Coryn did not even know. She decided not to ask her about the gifts in the car. It didn't seem that important right now. Just as long as her mother was happy.

Wasn't it enough that her father was sometimes short with Clare? Reminding her of errands, phone calls, questioning her. Coryn saw how upset this made her mother. She considered asking her father about Clare's forgetfulness, but she knew the conversation would disturb him. It could even make things worse between them and she just didn't want to add to her mother's distress. She'd just let it go. For now.

As Clare slid the baked cookies off the sheet onto the wax paper on the counter, the doorbell chimed, and she looked up. "Who could that be?"

"I'll go see, Mom."

When she opened the front door, Mark Emery and Ginny stood on the doorstep. "Why, hello."

"We just stopped by to bring you this." Mark held out her scarf. "You left it in the carriage yesterday."

"How kind of you. I didn't miss it." She took it. "Thank you."

Clare had followed her from the kitchen and was standing a little distance behind her. "Mom, I'd like you to meet Mark Emery and his little girl, Ginny. Mark, this is my mother, Clare Dodge."

"Well, I'm delighted to meet you, Mark. We read your byline regularly. My husband thinks you're doing a great job." Coryn's mother stepped forward, held out her hand to Mark. Then she looked down at Ginny. "And this is Ginny. Do come in, won't you? We've just been baking Christmas cookies. You can be our taste testers."

"Oh, I don't know, Mrs. Dodge. We wouldn't want to—"

Ginny tugged on Mark's hand, her upturned face eager.

"You won't be. Not at all. Come on in," Clare urged.

Coryn opened the door wider for them to enter.

"Here, let me take off your coat, Ginny, and you come along out to the kitchen with me," Clare said. "The little bell on the oven is about to ring that tells us the next batch is ready to take out. Then you can help decorate them, would you like that?"

The bonding was almost immediate. Ginny seemed to feel perfectly at ease with Coryn's mother. Without a backward look at her father, Ginny went down the hall to the kitchen with Clare, the two chatting like old friends.

Mark shook his head in wonder. ''That's amazing. Ginny's not shy, but I've never seen her take to someone that quickly.''

''My mother's always had a magic touch with children. All my friends adored her.''

''She seems to be one of those rare people who has somehow managed to retain enough of the best elements of childhood so she can relate to children without talking down to them.''

''Like Glynda, the Good Witch, in the *Wizard of Oz?* When I used to watch it on TV every year, I always thought my mother looked exactly like her.'' Coryn smiled, remembering what a magical childhood her mother had given her.

Mark grinned. ''She does, sort of, doesn't she?''

''Here, let me take your jacket.'' Coryn took it and hung it up beside Ginny's little red parka. ''Let's join them. Are you good at decorating cookies?''

''It's a skill I haven't really acquired.''

''There's always a first time.'' She smiled again.

By the time they got to the kitchen, Coryn's mother had tied an apron around Ginny's neck. It covered her completely. A high stool at the kitchen counter provided her easy access to a number of small glass containers filled with tinted sugar, raisins, jellied candies and chocolate sprinkles. Coryn's mother then placed a tray of freshly-baked cookies in front of her.

''Look, Daddy, what I'm doing. See?'' Her little hands moved swiftly. Tiny fingers curved delicately as she used them to dip into the various toppings. "This one's going to be a Christmas tree, so I'll use the green sugar and..." She went on happily talking, intent on the task at hand.

Coryn's mother was beside her, gently coaching but letting Ginny do the selecting and actual decorating. Coryn thought how happy she looked and was glad she hadn't mentioned the packages in the car. She saw Mark glance in the direction of her mother and Ginny as the animated chatting continued at the counter. An expression of tender amusement gave his strong-featured face a softness she hadn't noticed before. What a wonderful father he must be.

Just then the kitchen phone rang and her mother asked, "Will you get it, dear? My hands are all gooey." She held them up, wiggling her fingers.

Coryn picked up the phone, listened for a few minutes then said, "Just a minute, please." Holding the receiver against her shoulder she mouthed, "It's Mrs. Prentis, Mom. Something about the Christmas Tea at the club."

Mrs. Dodge made a little face, then whispered, "All right, I'll take it in the other room. Okay, honey?" she turned to the little girl. "I'll be back as soon as I can," she said as she left the room.

Coryn replaced the receiver then moved over to the counter, taking her mother's place beside Ginny. Ginny's face had a smudge of flour on both cheeks but she was smiling happily. "You come, too, Daddy!" she motioned to Mark.

"I don't know—" Mark shook his head.

"Yes you can, Daddy, I'll show you," Ginny urged.

"Come on, Mark, like the Little Red Hen, if you don't help you don't get to taste!" Coryn teased, winking at Ginny.

"That's right, Daddy." Ginny giggled.

There were lots of laughs and comments as Mark began to clumsily form the dough, use a cookie cutter to stamp out various shapes then decorate them. Urged on by Ginny he made clown faces and sprinkled colored sugar with abandon. The effects were greeted with enthusiastic praise by Ginny and Coryn.

"I may have missed my calling." Mark grinned as their batch of a dozen cookies was placed in the oven.

By the time Coryn's mother returned they were done and the baked results were viewed. Mark looked dubious as Ginny renewed her compliments. "I don't know. Mine get mixed reviews, I'm afraid."

"Never mind. They all taste the same." Coryn's mother comforted him. "We've got enough batter for another batch. So Ginny and I will finish up on these. Maybe you could make us some tea to have with them, Coryn?"

While Coryn put the kettle on to boil, got out cups and saucers, she asked Mark to choose the kind of tea from an assortment in a glass jar on the counter.

As Coryn poured some milk into a small ceramic creamer she saw Mark glance in the direction of her mother and Ginny as their cookie decorating and animated chatting continued at the counter.

"Your mother's awfully kind," he said, smiling at her.

"She loves children," Coryn said, then asked, "How is it you're not at the paper this time of day?"

''Ginny had an appointment with the optometrist so I took off some time to take her.''

''I hope it's not anything serious. Does she have to wear glasses?''

''I don't think so. The school nurse noticed something while doing routine testing. She suggested a doctor should look at Ginny's eyes. She has something called a lazy eye.'' He lowered his voice, ''She'll probably have to wear a patch over it a couple of days a week until it strengthens itself. The doctor gave me some stuff to read that explains the condition in layman's terms. Which I haven't had a chance to do yet.''

The sound of laughter from the other two broke into their conversation. Coryn's mother called gaily, ''Your daughter has a great sense of humor, Mr. Emery.''

''I know, and please call me Mark, Mrs. Dodge.''

''All right, I shall. Are you ready for these delicious and artistically decorated creations?'' She slipped down from her stool and brought a plate of cookies over to the table. Ginny jumped down and ran over, too.

Ginny seemed so proud of her handiwork, Coryn found her sweet expression touching as she pointed out the cookies she'd decorated. ''Oh, my—these are too beautiful to eat,'' Coryn told her. The little girl flushed with pleasure at the compliment.

The cookies were sampled and complimented lavishly. Then they were eaten along with the tea and a glass of milk for Ginny.

When Mark finally said they'd have to leave, Clare insisted Ginny select a dozen cookies to take home. Coryn put them in a plastic bag for her to carry.

Coryn walked to the door with them. In the front hall, Mark held Ginny's parka for her, zipped it up, then handed her a knitted cap saying, "Thanks for a great time."

"And for the cookies." Ginny held up the bag, smiling.

"You did a wonderful job decorating," Coryn told her.

"So did *you.* I liked your Christmas tree the best." Ginny said.

"Thank you." Coryn looked over Ginny's head and met Mark's amused expression.

He took Ginny's hand and said, "Well, thanks again."

As he started out the door, Coryn said, "By the way, Mark, we always have an open house on New Year's Day starting around five. Stop by if you're free."

Seeming surprised, Mark halted and then said, "Why, thank you very much."

As she closed the door behind them Coryn wondered, *would* he come? She realized she hoped he would. She would like to see Mark Emery again.

# *Chapter Eight*

"Coryn! Wake up, dear."

Her mother's voice and her hand gently shaking her shoulder roused Coryn from a deep slumber. Coryn sat up, blinking sleepily. When she saw her mother standing by the side of her bed, she came immediately wide-awake. Clare was deathly pale, deep shadows circled her eyes, her expression was pained.

"Mom! What's wrong?"

"I'm sorry to waken you, dear, but I have a beastly headache, probably a migraine. The medicine, the only one that touches this kind, is starting to have some effect, but it will keep me in bed for most of the day, I'm afraid. That's why I had to wake you up. I need to ask a favor."

"Sure, Mom, anything. An ice bag for your head? Some tea?"

"No, thanks, dear. Nothing like that. I'll just have to sleep this off for a couple of hours. What I need you to do is go to the church in my place. I volunteered to help pack Christmas baskets for the needy.''

Coryn reached for her robe, threw back the covers and searched for her slippers.

''Of course, Mom. What time should I be there?''

''At ten. It's just a little after nine now.''

''I can make that. I'll jump in the shower and be ready in a jiff. Are you sure there isn't something I can do for you before I leave?''

Her mother shook her head. ''No, dear, that's all. That relieves me. I dislike not fulfilling a commitment. It's such a worthy cause and so few show up to do the job. I hate to let them down. Now that you're going, I can rest easy. Thank you, Coryn,'' she said as she left the room.

''No problem, Mom.''

Coryn showered quickly, dressed in sweater, slacks. She peeked in her mother's bedroom before she went downstairs and saw her lying with an eye mask on, already asleep. Good. In the past, Clare occasionally had this sort of debilitating headache, but Coryn didn't recall ever seeing her look that bad. Could something more serious be the cause? Coupled with some of the other things she'd noticed about her mother, Coryn couldn't help worrying. A slow-growing tumor? That could account for some of it. Heavens, but she hoped it was nothing as serious as that! Only a headache, she assured herself.

In the kitchen she drank some juice and poured herself a cup of coffee. Then took her mother's car keys off the peg where she kept them and went out to the garage.

Good Shepherd Church was only a short drive. Her mother was a faithful member of the congregation. Coryn had gone to Sunday school here and had belonged to the youth group in high school. At college Coryn had gone to chapel service but in the last few years she had not regularly attended church. Certainly not in L.A. There, Sundays were usually spent around the pool of their apartment complex or at brunch parties that had become a trendy way to entertain. As she pulled into a space in the parking lot, Coryn felt a little guilty, like the black sheep turning up at the fold.

There were four ladies already working in the parish hall when Coryn entered. They looked at her curiously as she came in the door. Then one, a stout, gray-haired woman with sparkling brown eyes and a generous smile, greeted her, "Why, it's Coryn Dodge, isn't it? Hello there, I'm Mildred McCurry." She came over, both hands extended. "Your mother called earlier to say you'd be coming." Then she said sympathetically, "I hope she'll be feeling better. Those headaches are awful."

She took Coryn by the arm and led her over to a long table where the other volunteers were working and introduced her. They were busy filling baskets from cardboard cartons filled with canned food, bakery goods, boxes of cereal and dry milk, bags of flour and other groceries.

"You can work beside me, Coryn," Mrs. McCurry told her. "I'll show you the order in which we pack the baskets, staples on the bottom, crushables and perishables on top. Later, we check our lists. Families with children get a few extras, little toys, candy, some special sort of treat.''

Coryn took off her jacket, hung it up and got to work.

It was slow going at first, moving down the table following instructions as to what and how much went into each basket. She soon caught on and got into the rhythm. She had been working steadily for some time when one of the ladies called, ''Break time.'' The smell of fresh coffee permeated the room and someone had set up a delicious buffet lunch for the workers.

''One thing about working for the church, you always get fed!'' joked Mrs. McCurry.

''It's scriptural even,'' declared a lady Coryn had been introduced to as Emily Austin. ''Cast your bread on the water and it returns to you buttered.''

*''Emily!''* remonstrated another volunteer. ''That's not out of the Bible!''

''I'm paraphrasing,'' retorted Emily, and they all laughed.

Whatever the theological truth, there was indeed not only buttered bread, but a platter of cold cuts, three different kinds of salad, two pies and a maple-walnut layer cake.

''Virtue rewarded,'' commented Mrs. McCurry as she refilled everyone's coffee mug.

Although all the volunteers were her mother's age or older, Coryn felt welcome and comfortable in this group. She knew they were all committed Christians and that a great deal of their life was centered in their church activities. She wondered how big a part this played in her mother's life. It was something they had never really discussed. Clare just quietly lived her faith in everything. It was so much a part of her.

Coryn felt a kind of emptiness inside, realizing that she had not developed more of those values her mother had tried to instill in her. She had neglected that part of her life during the last few years. No wonder she had made such poor choices, such wrong decisions, hadn't been able to tell the difference between the counterfeit and the real.

"All right, ladies, back to work. We've only got a few more baskets to go," Mrs. McCurry announced.

Shortly after they all returned to their posts, they heard dozens of feet scuffling along the corridor outside and children's voices. Soon, from an adjoining room, came the slightly off-key singing of Christmas carols.

"Hark, the herald angels sing!" quipped the irrepressible Emily.

"The junior choir rehearsing for the Christmas program," Dorothy, one of the other volunteers, explained to Coryn.

It did seem to add a special touch to their work hearing them. Finally all the baskets were filled, tagged, ready to go to another set of volunteers who would deliver them on Christmas Eve.

As Coryn got ready to leave, Mrs. McCurry said, "Thank you so much for coming to help us. It would have taken us much longer if you hadn't pitched in with your young energy and willing hands."

"I really enjoyed it, Mrs. McCurry," Coryn told her, realizing she really had.

Outside, the wind was cold and Coryn hurried to

her car. She was just unlocking her door, when she heard a horn tapped lightly. Turning, she saw Mark Emery sitting behind the wheel of his station wagon. He rolled down the window and called, "Hi!"

She turned and waved. "What are you doing here?"

"Waiting for Ginny. She's practicing for her big moment as an angel in the Christmas program."

"She won't have to practice very hard, she *is* one." Coryn smiled.

"Thanks. I could ask you the same question, I mean, what you're doing here?"

"Actually, filling in for my mother," she said. "Of course, we used to come here as a family." She paused. "I always wanted to be an angel in the Christmas program but they always picked the girls with long blond curls."

"They're more liberal about angels nowadays." Mark grinned.

"I certainly hope so." Coryn stood there for a minute. But there really wasn't anything more to say. "Well, I'm off. Merry Christmas," she said, and got in her car.

Mark watched her thinking he wished he'd said something more. Asked her for a date. *Date!* He hated that word. It seemed so juvenile somehow. But what else could he call it? He liked Coryn Dodge, he'd thought from the beginning she was someone he'd like to know. She was—well, a lot of things, and how else could he find out more unless he called her and asked her out?

Coryn waved to him again after she'd backed out and passed his car. Funny, running into him again.

Here, of all places. And to find out Ginny attended Sunday school at the same church Coryn had as a child. And that she was in the Christmas pageant.

What a special guy Mark Emery must be. Obviously a great father. She remembered the reasons he'd told her for moving to Rockport. His values were certainly in the right place. Tragic about his wife. As she drove home, Coryn wondered what his wife had been like, Ginny's mother. It must be hard for Mark doing the things alone that ought to be shared.

From deep inside of Coryn came a longing for something, for someone to love, some fulfilling purpose to her life.

# *January*

# Chapter Nine

Christmas came. Coryn tried to enter into the spirit of it but it seemed to come and go before she could grasp the real meaning under all the glitter, the music, the presents. She had received invitations to parties to which she went, some given by her parents' friends and some by her contemporaries. She had a detached sense of not really belonging anymore. If she stayed in Rockport she would have to make more of an effort. But she wasn't sure yet if that's what she was going to do. She felt as if she was waiting for something. Direction?

Underneath it all she found herself wondering what kind of Christmas Mark and Ginny were having. Had Ginny received what she wanted from Santa? Were the Three Wise Men in place? Had it been a day of sad memories for Mark?

Preparations for her parents' New Year's Day party filled the week after Christmas. Her father had added several dozen people to the guest list. Names Coryn couldn't place. When she asked her mother about them, she received a vague answer.

"They're mostly people he knows through Rotary and in business. I don't know some of them. He wanted them invited so—" She smiled. "He's testing the political waters, you know."

Coryn frowned. The idea that her father might run for the state assembly still seemed strange. He had a great personality for it—outgoing, gregarious, positive. But if elected, it would mean spending most of his time in Sacramento. She couldn't imagine her parents giving up their home, their friends, their pleasant lifestyle here in Rockport.

Well, it wasn't her decision to make. The week passed quickly and suddenly it was the day of the open house.

Coryn had a new dress—a rich blue velour with an empire waist, a scoop neck, long sleeves and a flowing ankle-length skirt—for which she had paid far too much. She had bought it thinking she would wear it to celebrate the new year with Jason. In the shop's dressing room she had known it was the most becoming dress she had ever owned. But now Jason would never see her in it. To her surprise, she realized she didn't care very much.

She brushed her freshly shampooed hair to a polished sheen, applied mascara and sprayed on perfume. She gave herself a final check in the mirror and went across the hall and tapped on her mother's bedroom door. To her surprise, Clare was still in her bathrobe, standing uncertainly in front of her open closet. She turned as Coryn came into the room. Her smile was brief, tentative, her eyes anxious. "It's the silliest thing, but I can't remember what I planned to wear."

"I thought you said you had a new dress."

"Oh, yes, *of course.* How stupid." Her mother laughed. "I'd forget my head if it wasn't attached. I suppose it's all the excitement of you coming home and all the fuss of getting ready for the holidays and this party that's rattled me."

Clare gave a nervous little laugh. "Did I tell you what happened downtown the other day when I was shopping? I went to write a check and couldn't find my checkbook. My credit cards and driver's license and everything. Imagine! I'd changed purses, taken it out and left it..." Her voice trailed off indecisively.

"Sounds like something I might do!" Coryn said quickly, but her stomach tightened. It was an uncharacteristic thing for her mother to have done. Her mother was organized about everything. Take her clothes closet. Everything arranged in perfect order by coordinating colors, shoes neatly stored in shoe trees, matching handbags on the shelves above in zippered plastic bags. It was her modeling training. Clare Dodge had been a model before her marriage. Her career had gotten off to a promising start, but she'd given it all up once she married Coryn's father simply because he'd asked her to.

Thrusting back a prickle of anxiety, Coryn said briskly, "Well, you better get ready, Mom. Dad will be pacing if you're not downstairs to greet guests with him."

Coryn stepped inside the walk-in closet and looked around. She spotted a creamy silk dress, its draped bodice and long sleeves scattered with silver star-shaped sequins. She took it off the clothes rack and held it up. "Is this what you planned to wear?"

"Of course! How clever of you, darling."

Coryn had the awful feeling that unless *she* had found it, her mother would not *really* have known if this was the dress or not.

Clare put on her dress and Coryn zipped up the back. Then her mother seated herself at her dressing table to put on her makeup. Standing behind her, Coryn watched as graceful hands expertly dusted on blusher, applied mascara to her eyelashes. As her mother picked up her brush to give a final touch to her silver-blond hair, her eyes met Coryn's in the mirror. Almost as if her mother were waiting for her to say something, Coryn exclaimed, "You look beautiful, Mom."

A strangely pensive expression crossed Clare's face. A rather wistful smile lifted the corners of her mouth. "Beauty is in the eye of the beholder, don't they say? My stepfather didn't value beauty much. That's why he didn't feel they should spend the money to send me to college. 'She's got nothing going for her but her looks,' I overheard him tell my mother. You know, that devastated me." Clare shrugged. "Most teenage girls would have died for what I had then. But I wanted something more. I wasn't sure just what...but I believed eventually I would know." She sighed. "That's why I wanted to succeed at modeling, I guess. To show my stepfather. I guess I'm still trying to prove something to him."

Coryn didn't know how to respond. She had never

heard about this incident before. So she said nothing. Her mother stood up, moved away from the mirror. She did a model's pirouette in the center of the floor then and cupped Coryn's chin lightly with cool fingers. "Thank you, darling, for your help. Come on, let's go downstairs and do your father proud. He's always happy to show off his wife and daughter."

Coryn was cheered by the lilt in her mother's voice. The sadness was gone from her eyes, the radiant smile was in place. Everything was all right again. Everything was fine. *Wasn't it?*

It was frightening to think anything was wrong with her mother. Her mother so confident, so charming, so with it. Ah, but there was something definitely missing now...something vital and important. Coryn just wasn't sure what.

As they went down the curving stairway together, Coryn thought of the memory her mother had just shared. Although it had happened years ago, it had shaped the direction of Clare's life. Her mother had never talked much about her childhood or her parents. Coryn had never known either of them, both had died before she was born.

In the front hall stood a glittering decorated Christmas tree. Gold and white angels, gilded pinecones, silvery bows and frosted bells hung from sweeping branches. Another example of her mother's artistry. Each of the rooms looked like a picture in one of those glossy-paged architectural magazines. The house smelled of cedar, cinnamon and some kind of spicy potpourri placed in porcelain bowls on tabletops and other surfaces in the spacious living room and dining room. The scent of burning apple logs crackling in the open fireplace mingled with scented candles alight on the mantelpiece and buffet table.

Door chimes began to ring with frequency. For the next hour, guests arrived, and flowed in chattering clusters through the festively decorated rooms.

Coryn dutifully circulated, stopping to speak to people who had not seen her for months, answered questions about her job, her life in L.A., smiling.

The buzz of conversation, the clink of glasses and sounds of laughter, merged around her. Groups of well-dressed people milled through the house, helping themselves to the plentiful food and drinks. The atmosphere was festive, but instead of making Coryn feel happy, she became increasingly anxious. It was ridiculous to feel depressed in the midst of all this gaiety, but she couldn't seem to help it. Then, as though she was expecting him, she turned toward the front door just as Mark Emery walked into the house.

Mark had sat in his car out in the driveway for a good ten minutes before getting out and going up to the house. He'd sat there asking himself why he had come to the Dodges' open house. The minute he had driven up the hill and seen the lights blazing out into the winter darkness, cars parked along the parkway and on either side of the street, he had almost turned around and gone home. From the number of cars, he realized it must be a big party. Judging from the make of the cars outside, he guessed that their owners, and the guests, must be some of Rockport's most affluent. His economy station wagon was hardly in the same league. Why hadn't he turned around and left? Because Coryn had asked him and because he wanted to see her again.

When he saw her, something happened. That same sense of recognition that he had felt in the S.F. Airport. Only then, they'd never met before. It was an uncanny sensation. It had been more than momentary attraction. What it might become, he didn't know.

As he walked into the house, he spotted her immediately, standing by the Christmas tree in the foyer. The lights sent sparkles glinting through her hair. When she saw him, her eyes lit up, too, and she smiled—almost as if she were waiting for him.

Suddenly there seemed to be no one else in the room, just the two of them.

Mark was a little stunned by his own reaction as Coryn moved gracefully toward him. He noticed she was wearing her hair differently tonight, swept up from her slender neck and back from her ears where blue pendant earrings swung. She looked altogether lovely.

"Hello, Mark, I'm glad you came," she said.

For a minute they'd just stood there smiling at each other. He was aware how blue her eyes were and of the perfume he remembered that seemed to move with her like a lovely cloud. Then Coryn's father came up and greeted him heartily. Coryn made the introductions.

"Good to meet you, Emery. My wife mentioned you might stop by. Come with me, there are some people you ought to meet," and he took Mark's arm and walked him away to introduce him to a group of guests.

Some time later Mark found his way back to Coryn. ''Can we find someplace to talk? I came to see *you.*''

''Dad has a way of taking over.'' She smiled.

''He'll make a good politician.''

''You think so?''

''Has all the right stuff.'' Mark grinned.

Coryn led him to a windowed alcove in the living room and they sat down. ''I guess that remains to be seen. I don't think he's decided. I'm not sure my mother is that for it.''

''Politics is hard on families. I saw that when I worked at the *Sacramento Bee.* Sometimes a choice has to be made and the families get the short end.''

''Families mean a great deal to you, don't they?''

''Yes. I think they *are* important. Growing up in a solid family is everything for a child.''

''That's what you're doing for Ginny, isn't it?''

''Trying to.''

''She's a sweet child. You must be doing it right,'' Coryn said then changed the subject. ''Have you had something to eat, to drink?''

He shook his head.

''Let me get you something.'' She got up, saying, ''I'll be right back.''

All around him the party sounds swirled. Mark glanced around the room. This was a part of Rockport he'd only seen from a distance, as a reporter covering fancy fund-raising dinners and political events. He was sure the movers and shakers of the town were here tonight, with their expensively gowned wives. The Dodges belonged to this social scene. He didn't. Did Coryn? When they had dinner together in the airport restaurant, he had sensed, under her composure, a restlessness, a longing for something more. Her discontent with her job in L.A. had evidently resulted in her decision not to return. What would she do now? He knew he wanted to find out. To do that he'd have to get to know her better. Where that would lead was the question.

In a few minutes Coryn was back with a plate of sandwiches, deviled eggs, and balancing two cups of punch.

"So how does it feel being back in Rockport?" Mark asked.

"I don't think it seems real yet. I made the decision and I have to live with it but I'm not sure what comes next."

"The new year is always a good time for new beginnings, isn't it? Or at least it's supposed to be. Making resolutions and all that."

She made a small groan. "Making resolutions has never been my strong suit. It brings a lot of stuff to the surface. Old mistakes you don't want to repeat."

"New Year's resolutions can be sobering. I mean that in the most literal sense. I always think I'm going to make some. I rarely do." He paused, "I guess Rockport seems awfully provincial to you after L.A.?"

"No, I don't think that's my problem." She attempted a laugh. "If you could say I *have* a problem."

"Has it changed much?"

"I suppose. It's different. There's more going on now…culturally, I mean. The Civic Light Opera, Old Town, the Nautical Museum, the Repertory Theater…"

"Speaking of which—" Mark reached into his jacket pocket and held up two tickets. "The newspaper gets courtesy tickets. These are for their opening production of the year. Chekov's *Uncle Vanya.* Would you like to go?"

"Chekov? That's awfully ambitious for an amateur group, isn't it?"

"They're pretty good. I saw their last performance. Maybe you don't like Russian plays?"

"They do tend to be somewhat dark. All heavy drama, family secrets, hidden motives. Whatever happened to local theaters putting on *Charlie's Aunt* or *A Christmas Carol?*"

They both laughed.

"Ironic, isn't it that Dickens wrote so often about the ideal, happy family when his own home life was so terrible."

"Maybe everyone has his or her own fantasy of what constitutes a happy family," Coryn suggested.

"Tolstoy wrote, 'All families are unhappy in their own way.' In modern terms...all families are dysfunctional in their own style. What's dysfunctional to one person may seem normal to another, depending on the circumstances."

Coryn did not comment. Her idea of a happy family had always been her own. Now she wasn't so sure. It was like seeing a distorted image reflected in a mirror. That's how she'd felt since she came home. It had not shattered, thank God. But there was definitely a crack in the mirror.

Their conversation turned to lighter things yet Mark had the feeling that there was so much more they had to talk about. He had the strong sensation something was on the brink of happening between them. A man who knew Mark came up to discuss some current local event and claimed his attention. Coryn excused herself.

At length he felt he had stayed long enough, especially since he knew he and Coryn wouldn't have another chance to talk alone. He felt a little lift, thinking she looked somewhat disappointed when he told her he was leaving.

"Well, this has been very enjoyable but I better go. I told Mrs. Aguilar I'd be home by eight. In time to read Ginny her story and tuck her in." Mark grinned. "Start the new year right by being on time for work tomorrow morning."

"I'm glad you could come, Mark," Coryn said as she accompanied him into the hall. At the door she said, "Tell Ginny 'hi' for me."

"I'll do that. She's talked a lot about the day here with you and your mother, baking cookies and all." He halted a second then asked, "So, would you like to go with me next Thursday?"

"To the play?"

"Yes, *Uncle Vanya.*"

"Yes, thank you. I'd like to, very much."

"Thursday night, then. I'll pick you up at seven-thirty. Curtain's at eight."

All the way home Mark thought about Coryn. He hadn't been sure about asking her out but when the conversation had turned to talk of plays, it just seemed natural to do so. Well, it wasn't a big deal. He'd found Coryn Dodge interesting, intelligent, a good conversationalist. And it would be interesting to see how a local group handled Chekov.

Okay, cut out the rationalization. Admit it. He was attracted to Coryn Dodge. No doubt about that. Furthermore, she was the first woman he'd felt that kind of attraction for since Shari. It wasn't as though he was falling in love or anything.

And yet, there was a kind of truth stirring. Unsettling. If this did develop into something serious, how would he feel? How would he handle it?

Was it too soon?

Soon? It had been three years. Three years was a long time to be alone. He knew his life was incomplete. He knew Ginny needed a mother. They both needed to be a family. But he didn't want to make a mistake. Loneliness wasn't sufficient reason to marry again.

He pulled into his driveway. Mrs. Aguilar had left the porch light on for him, otherwise the house was dark. He felt letdown somehow. It would be nice to have someone to come home to again.

Sighing heavily, he got out of the car. He better get to bed, he was due at the paper at seven-thirty.

# *Chapter Ten*

Coryn had mentioned her theater date with Mark Emery to her parents. Casually. But inside she felt excited. With Mark she was on new ground. That he was such a contrast to Jason made it even better. It proved something. In fact, Jason was becoming more and more a thing of the past. A bad mistake she wanted to forget.

A recent phone conversation with Sheila had confirmed the wisdom of her decision not to go back to L.A., to break with him.

They had finished discussing the disposal of some of Coryn's belongings she didn't want shipped when Sheila said, "Oh, by the way, Jason phoned asking about some CDs of his that were missing from his collection. Wanted me to check if they were among ours, see if you'd taken them with you. Get that? What a nerve! I told him off but good. He didn't even ask about you, if you were coming back or what." Coryn felt the sting of humiliation but only said, "It doesn't matter, it was over between us even before I left."

"I never could understand what you saw in him. Shallow, arrogant jerk," Sheila retorted.

They talked a little longer before hanging up. Yet Jason's indifference hurt. Hadn't she meant anything to him? She had been so foolish. Echoing Sheila's question, what *had* she ever seen in Jason?

Thursday evening Coryn dressed with special care. She put on the new pink cashmere sweater her mother had given her for Christmas, and fastened in the pearl studs, her father's present. When she was ready a full half hour before he was due, she realized how much she was looking forward to being with Mark.

The play was labored, but the cast tried hard.

Mark and Coryn were swept into the vestibule of the theater with the flow of the departing audience. They stood for a minute near the box office.

"*Heavy,*" Mark said.

"*Very,*" she replied.

"I should have known what we were in for. Did it seem as long to you as that summer did to Uncle Vanya?"

Coryn laughed. They started walking across the street to where Mark had parked his car.

"Still," Coryn said, "I must say it was well done, for a nonprofessional cast."

"You're right. I guess you saw a lot of theater when you were in L.A."

"Actually not," Coryn replied, recalling that Jason liked to go to high-visibility restaurants or dinner clubs where he could see and be seen. By whom, she never really knew. Jason often table-hopped when he was with her, rarely introducing her to anyone. She had been so naive. Taking him at his own estimation. Simply glad to be with him. She had liked the feeling of other women's envious gazes following them. Who were these people he had tried so hard to impress? Probably only self-important climbers like himself.

"I'm glad I don't have to write the review," Mark said as he unlocked the passenger-side door and opened it for her to get in. He got in the driver's side. "I don't know why, but I am hungry. At least my stomach didn't fall asleep. How about you?"

"That sounds great."

"Al's?" he asked.

"Sure, why not?" They both laughed.

A sign boasted: Breakfast Served 24 Hours. Once in the red-vinyl booth Mark asked her, "What will you have—the Lumberjack, or the Woodsman's Special?"

"What's the difference?" She looked for a clue in the menu description.

"Lumberjack has hotcakes on the side, the Woodsman hash browns."

"The Woodsman then."

Their order given, the waitress left. For a minute they were quiet. Mark looked over at her. Coryn looked prettier than ever tonight. Pink was becoming to her, gave her skin delicacy and warmth. As if conscious of his regard, she lowered her eyes and her long lashes made tiny crescent shadows on her cheeks. She asked, "How is Ginny's eye?"

Mark grimaced. "It's an every morning hassle," he said in a low voice. "She doesn't like to wear the patch to school. Says the kids make fun of her. It always seems to disappear just as we're getting ready to leave.'' He shook his head. ''I don't understand it. I'm sure Mrs. Aguilar puts it out in plain sight along with her clothes the night before. It's a mystery.''

''Probably *The Borrowers.*'' Coryn smiled.

Mark frowned. ''The Borrowers?''

She laughed. ''It's a famous book series for children. I used to love it when I was Ginny's age. It explained all the things that disappear in a household. No one can ever find what happens. But the secret is there is a tiny family that lives behind the walls that take things—put them to their own use...''

Mark still looked puzzled.

''Oh, well, scratch that!'' Coryn laughed. ''It's probably not a 'guy thing'.''

Their orders came, heaped plates smelling deliciously, were set in front of them. For a few minutes conversation slowed while they ate hearty food. Then they talked about all sorts of things.

Mark was easy to talk to. He was knowledgeable about what was current in books and films, politics. He was matter-of-fact, not arrogant, and clearly interested in hearing her opinion on various subjects. Coryn realized this was a different kind of date. She felt relaxed, instead of trying to make an impression, she was being herself. It was like talking to someone she had known for a long time, a friend. Coryn had never had a man friend. The idea intrigued her.

Over coffee Mark asked, ''So, what is the real reason you decided not to go back to L.A.? When we were in San Francisco, I got the idea you felt you'd outgrown a small town like Rockport.''

Coryn hesitated. Tell Mark the truth? Yes, she could

trust him to fill in the blanks. He was perceptive enough.

"I was in a dead-end job and a dead-end relationship. I thought I'd give myself a new start."

"Sometimes the best thing you can do is just that. And don't look back. Clean slate." He paused, then said almost shyly, "I'm glad you decided to stay in Rockport."

Coryn felt inordinately pleased by the way he said it and by the way he was looking at her.

The waitress came with their check and to refill their coffee cups.

Mark told Coryn the subject of his next feature story, coastal lighthouses. "They're almost obsolete now, I mean, the romantic idea of the lone lighthouse keeper keeping the light burning for lost ships at sea, that sort of thing. But they've got a great history, one that shouldn't be forgotten. It means making some short trips to Mendocino and up the coast of Oregon. They're beautiful drives, and talking to some of the old-timers should be fascinating."

It was nearly one o'clock in the morning when they left the diner.

In the car, Mark turned on the car radio and as they drove along the winding roads to the Dodges' house in Chestnut Hills, they listened to a concert of semi-classical music with lots of strings.

Coryn felt a little tension start to creep over her. The other times she'd been with Mark they'd met by chance. This was their first real date. A *date* date.

The moment she always dreaded on "first dates"

was fast approaching. Would he or wouldn't he? And should she or not?

When Mark turned in the driveway, the piece hadn't quite finished. They sat there listening until it ended. Coryn mentally held her breath.

The decision was made for her. Mark got out of the car, came around, opened the door on the passenger side for Coryn. They walked up to the front door and Coryn put her key in the lock. "Thanks, Mark, I enjoyed the evening."

"Next time we'll try for lighter entertainment," he said.

Coryn felt pleased. There would be a *next* time then. She pushed open the door and stepped inside the entryway. As she turned, he took her hand and drew her back. With one hand he brushed back her hair, then leaned toward her and kissed her.

Her hair was silky against his hand, her mouth was soft.

The kiss, light and very sweet, surprised her a little. Yet she returned it.

"Good night, Coryn," he said quietly. "I really enjoyed being with you. I'll call you soon."

"That would be great," Coryn replied realizing she meant it.

She stood there as he walked back to his car, got in, backed out of the driveway. She felt a little ripple of happiness. A feeling she almost didn't recognize. It had been so long since she had felt this way. And Mark's kiss. Had that really happened? Had she liked it as much as she thought she did?

# *Chapter Eleven*

In the first weeks of the new year, Coryn often asked herself why had she never asked her mother about the Christmas presents in the trunk of her car? Coryn had gone along on another shopping trip with her mother, helping her pick out gifts for the same people whose presents were already wrapped, tagged. Was it just because she loved her mother, hadn't wanted to embarrass her? She had seen her cringe with humiliation when Coryn's father had brought up some lapse of memory or some omitted errand. Or was it because she was afraid? Afraid her mother hadn't remembered buying and wrapping them? Afraid there might be something seriously wrong with her mother?

With a tiny clutch of fear she thrust that thought away. It was probably only a temporary condition, maybe something to do with menopause. Coryn didn't want to accept the fact that her always youthful, vibrant mother was getting older.

Besides, Coryn's thoughts and time were more and

more centered around Mark Emery. He had followed through on his promise to call. They had gone out several times after that. Mostly impromptu, casual dates. They'd met for lunch, gone to the movies and attended the opening of a new gallery in Old Town together. This appearance had occasioned introductions to some of Coryn's old friends. Cindy and her husband had also been there. Cindy had looked very curious when she saw who Coryn's escort was. She had phoned the next day for a report.

"So how long have you been seeing Mark Emery?" she asked. "I know a half-dozen people who have invited him to social events and he always turns them down. What's your secret?"

Coryn had laughed and tactfully dodged Cindy's probing.

"Just my charm and intelligence," she teased, then added, "We just have a lot in common."

"You do?" Cindy sounded doubtful. Then, "Well, if I decide to throw a dinner party or something will you bring him?"

"Sure, that is, if he'll come." Coryn agreed. "His work keeps him very busy and he has a little girl he spends a great deal of time with."

That seemed to satisfy Cindy for the moment. But after she put down the phone Coryn wondered if observers were already pegging them as a couple?

Besides these dates, on a couple of Sundays she had gone with Mark when he took Ginny to the park and the zoo. These times had been particularly enjoyable. Coryn had never been around children very much but she found Ginny a very sweet and endearing child.

Coryn realized that in a very short while she was spending substantial time with them and thinking about them. Mark's remark about Ginny's reluctance to wear her eye patch had stayed with Coryn. How to get her to do what was necessary and yet make it fun was the problem. Could she figure out a way to help them both? To make wearing the patch a happy experience and somehow make Ginny feel special?

Coryn wasn't exactly sure when she got the idea but once she did, she wasted no time starting the project. Why not make covers that would slip over the leather patch, pretty ones, colorful, fanciful to match some of Ginny's outfits?

Coryn went to the fabric store and bought squares of different colored fabric and felt, assorted ribbons and trim. At home, she cut out two for samples; one she made like a sunflower with brown center and bright yellow petals, the other she made a clown face.

When she finished them she had a few second thoughts. Would Ginny like them or think them silly? Would Mark think she was being too pushy, insinuating herself, her ideas into a private family matter. Well, the only thing to do was to find out.

Taking the two patches, she drove over to Mark's house. She'd never been there. She looked up the address and ventured over one weekday morning. She thought Mrs. Aguilar, the housekeeper, would be the best one to approach first. She was curious to meet this paragon, whose praises both Mark and Ginny sang unreservedly.

Mark's house was a sloping-roofed, brown shingle, the style known as California bungalow popular in the

1920s. There was a front porch and a huge holly tree, red with berries, on one side of the flagstone path leading up to the house.

She heard the old-fashioned doorbell echo inside the house and a few minutes later the door was opened by a plump, middle-aged woman, in a flowered apron. Her salt and pepper hair was braided in a coronet above a round face with very dark, shiny brown eyes.

"Yes?" she said as if Coryn might be selling something.

"Hi, I'm Coryn Dodge, a friend of Mark's. And Ginny's, too, of course. And you must be Mrs. Aguilar."

Did Mrs. Aguilar's expression change from caution to suspicion? Coryn wasn't sure but plunged on. This was a potential adversary that must be won. Without analyzing it, she realized she wanted the housekeeper to like her. It suddenly seemed important that she did.

"Mark told me he was having some trouble getting Ginny to wear her eye patch and I know it's really necessary that she does. So, I—" Coryn was watching Mrs. Aguilar closely as she pulled the two patch covers out of the bag she was carrying and held them up "—so I thought putting these on top might help."

A smile broke on Mrs. Aguilar's face.

"Why, if that isn't the cleverest thing! Well, if anything will help get the child to wear her patch these will. How kind of you to go to all that trouble." Mrs. Aguilar's voice was genuinely pleased and the sharp eyes had softened.

"I'm so glad you think so. I wanted to get your opinion. That's why I brought them by now when I knew Mark would be at work and Ginny at school. I thought you'd know best if this would work.''

''I don't see why it wouldn't! My, aren't they pretty?''

Coryn hesitated, then thought she'd come this far why not? She took a deep breath. ''I wondered if she had a favorite dress or an outfit that I could make a special one for her to wear with it?''

''Of course! Won't you come in and I'll show you Ginny's things. I've just been ironing and have some of them handy.''

She opened the door wider for Coryn to come inside and led her through the hall to a utility room behind the kitchen, where an ironing board was set up in front of a small portable TV set on the counter.

Mrs. Aguilar clicked it off and one by one held up a red and green plaid dress with ruffled collar, a bright blue jumper and striped blouse. ''And then her red parka she wears every day. Maybe you could make one for that.'' The housekeeper was really entering into the project enthusiastically.

Coryn jotted some quick notes in the small notebook she kept in her handbag.

''This is awfully kind of you, Miss Dodge,'' Mrs. Aguilar said. ''To take such an interest—'' her voice trailed off. She looked directly at Coryn, an unspoken question in her eyes. Coryn suddenly felt self-conscious and glanced away. Then Mrs. Aguilar continued, ''I worry about both of them. I do what I can but there's something missing in a house when there's no mother,'' Mrs. Aguilar said with concern then her manner turned cheerful again. "Won't you stay and have a cup of coffee or tea with me?"

Coryn felt she had passed some invisible test and smiled.

"Why, yes, thank you, that would be lovely."

Mrs. Aguilar busied herself with the kettle and getting out cups and saucers. She arranged some gingersnap cookies on a plate and set it on the table. Coryn had the feeling that the housekeeper was considering saying more. The tea brewed, the housekeeper brought the china teapot to the table, then sat down across from Coryn and held out the plate to offer her a cookie.

"As I say, I do my best," she said as she filled Coryn's cup with the steaming fragrant tea. "And Mr. Emery is certainly a fine man. A child couldn't ask for a better father. But nothing makes up for losing your mother. Especially for a girl, I think."

The housekeeper was definitely giving Coryn an opening. But Coryn felt too shy to take it. All she could manage was to say, "I'm awfully fond of both Mark and Ginny."

"I'm glad. Ginny's talked about you often." Mrs. Aguilar seemed satisfied. They chatted for another fifteen minutes or so then Coryn left, leaving the eye patch covers for Ginny. It was such a simple gesture, actually, yet as she drove away from the small, brown-shingled house, Coryn felt inextricably bound to it and its occupants. It was a sense of belonging that she had never quite experienced before. It had all sorts of happy possibilities.

That night Ginny, in pyjamas, robe and furry slippers, brought the tattered copy of her favorite book into the living room for Mark to read to her. Smelling sweetly of shampoo and talcum, she cuddled up in the crook of Mark's arm beside him in his armchair. "Now read," she directed, and he opened *The Velveteen Rabbit.*

He had read it a dozen times before, over and over, because it was usually Ginny's request. Sometimes he persuaded her to choose an alternate one but it was to this story that they returned the most often. Why, then, tonight, did the words he had spoken so many times in the past seem to ring true in his ears, as if he were hearing it for the first time? They seemed to have special meaning, as though they had been written especially for him to hear, to absorb.

Mark tucked Ginny in, kissed her good-night, received several hard hugs in return, turned on the nightlight and walked back into the living room. The book, with its worn edges, faded cover of the floppy-eared rabbit, was beside his chair. He picked it up and held it, looking at it thoughtfully. Love is what makes a person real. Genuine, authentic, truthful—vulnerable. As if he heard it spoken, this came through to him very clearly. Unless you allow yourself to be real, you'll never know love again.

Love requires sharing yourself with another person. Sharing your true feelings takes courage. Risk. Faith.

He remembered Shari once teasing him, saying, "If anything should happen to me, if I should die first, you better get married again quick. Otherwise you'll start getting too many picky bachelor habits—Mr. Neatnik."

He picked up one of the eye patch covers Coryn Dodge had made for Ginny, fingered it thoughtfully. She had acted spontaneously, out of compassion for a little girl's embarrassment about looking different and turned it into something that made her feel special. She had done it out of kindness and affection and caring. He felt touched and warmed by it. Ginny had been so happy. It was something he would never have thought to do. Even Mrs. Aguilar was impressed. Why would Coryn have bothered if she didn't feel something *real* for them? For him as well as Ginny. What was he so afraid of? Of being *real?* Of being *hurt?* What was it the book said, loving you run the risk of being hurt? But he wouldn't have missed loving Shari even knowing what had happened, even knowing the hurt that would be his after her accident. No one could have predicted that. If he and Coryn went on—if something *real* developed between them— So be it! Mark decided he was willing to risk it.

A few days later in her mail, Coryn received a laboriously printed note from Ginny extravagantly decorated with crayoned daisies, colorful stickers and an arched rainbow.

DEAR CORYN,
THANK YOU FOR THE PRETTY PATCHES.
THEY MADE ME HAPPY.
LOVE GINNY

The next week, after watching a foreign film at the University theater Coryn invited Mark in for coffee and homemade brownies. In the kitchen, Coryn let Ranger in from the utility room and he and Mark made friends. Mark sat on his heels stroking the Lab's head and looked up at Coryn as she measured out coffee. "Great dog."

"Yes. He's been my pal since sixth grade."

"Children and pets, go together. As I've been told!" he laughed. "Ginny wants one but I don't want to put another burden on Mrs. Aguilar. She has enough to do just looking after us."

Ranger took his place under the kitchen table when Coryn brought their cups and a plate of brownies.

Mark took one and bit into it, holding up his hand with his thumb and forefinger making a circle, indicating it was delicious.

"You know there's something familiar about all this," he said, then asked, "Did I ever tell you about the uncanny feeling I had when I first saw you in the San Francisco Airport—that I might have met you?"

Coryn shook her head.

"Well it was just a quick flash. Then I knew, of course, I hadn't," he paused, smiling. "I would have remembered." He went on, "But now it just seems so natural—I mean, like we've known each other for a long time, been friends."

"I feel that way, too. Not that first meeting, but now."

Mark looked around with satisfaction. "Kitchens are cozy places. The heart of a home. I think they say a lot about the people who live there, don't you?"

"I guess so, I just never thought about it."

"I remember my grandmother's kitchen. I loved going there when I was a kid. There was always this wonderful smell, something cooking or baking. It gave me a good, secure feeling.''

''Where did you grow up, Mark? I don't think you ever said.''

''A small mid-west town, in Ohio, a place you never heard of. I had the typical Norman Rockwell boyhood, little league, Scouts, swimming at the lake, going fishing with my dad—Sounds corny, huh?''

''No, it sounds wonderful!'' Coryn said. ''Ideal. The kind of childhood everyone wishes they had, the kind everyone wants for their own children.''

Mark reached across the table and took Coryn's hand.

''You, too, Coryn? You would opt for the vine-covered cottage with the white picket fence?'' His tone was half teasing, half serious.

''Of course! In a heartbeat!'' As soon as the words were out of her mouth Coryn's cheeks got warm.

''I would have thought that maybe you wanted something more sophisticated—'' He squeezed her hand, ''I'm glad I was wrong.''

Mark started to ask, *How about kids? Do they go with the picture? Even someone else's kid?* But he thought he might be pushing his luck. Or worse still, leading to subjects he wasn't quite ready to discuss and letting Coryn know just how serious he was beginning to feel about her, about them.

Any further discussion was sharply interrupted when Ranger, a husky growl deep in his throat, scrambled to his feet, his nails scratching on the vinyl floor, he skidded to the back door and began to bark.

Coryn rolled her eyes and got up, saying to Mark, "Chipmunks in the backyard. They drive him crazy. He used to have great fun chasing them away. Now all he can do is bark."

She gently tugged Ranger back by his collar, talking soothingly to him and patting him at the same time.

Mark rose. "I've got to be on my way." He leaned down to pat Ranger's head. "Too bad, ol' fella, but my car will probably do the job for you when I turn on the headlights."

As Coryn walked through the house to the front door with him, he held her hand. In the hall, their goodnight kiss was longer than usual.

# Chapter Twelve

It was one of those rare days that happen sometimes on the north coast in winter, a cloudless blue sky, bright sun, brisk wind. In the morning, Mark called.

"School's closed, county teachers' meeting. I'm playing hooky from the paper and taking Ginny to the beach. Want to come along?"

Without a moment's hesitation, Coryn said, "Yes."

"Good. How soon can you be ready?"

"Half an hour?"

"Great. We'll pick you up then." He rang off.

Coryn put down the phone, scrambled to change into a warm sweater, flannel-lined jeans. Even on a sunny day, north-coast beaches could be cold. When she came downstairs, she glanced out to look for Mark's station wagon then went into the kitchen to tell her mother where she was going.

"With Mark and Ginny? That will be fun. What a nice man and what a precious child. Would you like to take along something to drink, some snacks?"

"Good idea." Coryn kissed her mother's cheek. Coryn felt happy, Clare seemed so well, her old self, it was a glorious day and she was looking forward to spending it with Mark and Ginny. She helped pack a bag with snacks and small cans of juice.

"You and Mark will want coffee," her mother said, pouring steaming coffee into a thermos jug. Mark and Ginny arrived a few minutes later.

With an eye patch, and wearing a red knit cap with its dangling yarn pompom, Ginny looked like a rakish little elf.

They parked the station wagon on the bluff overlooking the beach and walked down the dunes to the beach. The salt-tinged wind was sharp. The sun and fine weather had brought others out, as well. One couple had two frisky little dogs who were yipping and running into the surf. As Ginny stood watching them, the woman handed her a small stick and told her to throw it to see if one of the dogs would fetch it. Ginny was into the game in a flash. The little dogs loved it, and they continued as long as Ginny would toss it.

Coryn and Mark followed, laughing and cheering Ginny on as the two small dogs played tirelessly. Coryn vividly remembered bringing Ranger out here. He would race, wheel, leap barking into the waves, chase the seagulls then come back. She'd toss a stick over and over. He'd run down the beach after it, head held high, come prancing back triumphantly to drop it at her feet.

"This is *so* fun!" exclaimed Ginny, running back to them, catching both their hands and swinging them. "Isn't it, Daddy?"

"You bet. Great fun."

Mark's laughing eyes met Coryn's over Ginny's head. Coryn felt a surge of happiness. The sense of freedom to *be* happy that she had somehow lost.

One of the little dogs came scampering up to Ginny with the stick in his mouth, circling and crouching, as if saying, "Come play some more!" Ginny dropped both their hands and was off again in another round of tossing and fetching.

As Ginny ran in front of them down the beach, Mark caught Coryn's hand in his. Her heart gave a small flip as his fingers closed around her hand, their palms touching. She glanced at him. He was looking at her. Her breath became shallow.

He stopped, turned her into his arms in a hug, then kissed her.

When the kiss ended, Coryn stepped back and they smiled at each other. Her arms slowly slid from his shoulders and moved down to clasp his, still holding her around the waist. For a few seconds they looked into each other's eyes. Then they started walking down the beach again together.

The morning sped by. Ginny made friends with two little girls, sisters, whose parents had brought them. She shared the graham crackers from the bag Coryn's mother had fixed, and the three of them had a great time building a sand fort. Mark and Coryn sat nearby on a weathered log watching them and talking. They seemed to have lots to say to each other, never running out of topics.

The sun moved high in the sky. Their watches told them it was past noon. They called to Ginny and climbed back up the dunes, clambered up on the stone jetty. The wind at their backs, they walked toward the Seascape, an old lighthouse converted into a restaurant.

The place was warm and crowded, filled with the sound of voices and laughter, the clatter of dishes. Fishermen sat up along the counter, swapping stories of weather and tall tales about the size and quantity of their day's catch. Savory smells emanated from the kitchen area, the swinging door constantly opening and closing. Waitresses brought out loaded trays, busily serving orders while flirting with and making snappy replies to the teasing patrons, most of whom seemed to be as comfortable here as in their own homes.

Mark and Coryn found a table with an ocean view. The surf was rough and high, dashing against the rocks.

A waitress with flaming henna hair and dangling earrings made of shells brought them each a glass of water, then poured two mugs of fresh coffee and placed them before Mark and Coryn, asking cheerfully, "What'll it be, folks?"

Coryn and Mark ordered chowder, a famous specialty of Seascape. Ginny chose fish and chips.

"Today was fun, wasn't it?" Ginny asked, lifting her glass of water carefully and taking a sip.

"It sure was," Coryn agreed.

"The dogs were really fun," Ginny said. "I liked throwing the sticks for them and saying fetch like their owner told me to."

She put down her glass and looked directly at

Coryn. "Did you have a pet when you were a little girl, Coryn?"

"Uh-oh, here we go," Mark said in a resigned voice.

"Did you?" Ginny persisted.

"Yes, a dog, Ranger. I still have him. He's getting pretty old now. He has arthritis."

"How old?"

"For a dog, very old."

"Did you take care of him yourself?"

"Well, sometimes I forgot, then..." Coryn started to say *my mother* did it for me. She darted a quick look at Mark but he was buttering his French bread and didn't meet her gaze. He was leaving her this round.

"*I* wouldn't forget," Ginny said. "Not if I had a little kitten."

The waitress returned with bowls of creamy clam chowder. As she set down Ginny's platter of fish sticks and French fries, she asked playfully, "Think you can manage all that, young lady?"

"Yes, thank you," Ginny said politely.

What a really lovely child she was, Coryn thought with a rush of tenderness as she watched her eat. Ginny's fingers, the little one curved daintily, dipped each of the fries into the small cup of catsup at the edge of her plate, taking small bites, then wiping her mouth with her napkin. Someone had taught her manners, all right. It amused Coryn that once they had been served, Ginny picked up the subject of pets again as if there had been no interruption.

"A kitty wouldn't be all that much trouble, would

it, Coryn?'' She glanced at Mark. ''I promise, Daddy, I'd do everything myself. You wouldn't have to remind me.''

''Even the litter box?'' Mark asked.

Ginny had just taken a bite of French fry so only nodded. When she finished chewing, she said to Coryn, ''I already have a name for one. Sunny. Isn't that a nice name for an orange kitty?''

Mark moaned. ''I give up! Subtlety, thy name is *not* woman!'' He laughed.

''Ready for dessert, folks?'' Their waitress was back. ''Homemade apple pie with cinnamon sauce or á la mode?'' she asked, giving her pencil a little twirl.

Coryn looked doubtful. ''I'm pretty full but... maybe, could we share one, Ginny?''

The little girl grinned. ''Yes, please.''

''Ice cream or sauce?''

''What shall it be, Ginny?'' asked Coryn.

''*You* choose.''

''Ice cream.''

''I would have choosed that, too.'' Ginny grinned happily.

They drove home singing several rollicking renditions of the sea chanty ''Blow the Man Down.'' They sung it over and over until Mark pleaded a change of tune. With lots of laughter and a couple of false starts, Ginny and Coryn sang some songs Ginny had learned at Brownies that Coryn remembered from her own Girl Scout days. Coryn felt a warm happiness spread all through her. It seemed as if the three of them had always been together. As though they were meant to be.

As they passed the Rockport city-limit sign, Mark asked, ''Mind if I make a quick stop at the grocery store. It's Mrs. Aguilar's day off. My night to be chef.''

Coryn pretended disbelief. She looked at Mark with mock astonishment. ''Is cooking one of your hidden talents?''

''Daddy's a good cook,'' piped up Ginny. ''Yummy hamburgers and French fries…mmm.'' She rolled her one visible eye.

''Obviously you have a fan,'' Coryn said to Mark.

''My cheering section. I think she likes the dessert on these nights best. Sara Lee to the rescue.'' He grinned.

'''Scuse me, Coryn,'' Ginny said, leaning over the back seat. ''I have to ask Daddy something and I need to whisper.''

''Is that really necessary, honey? Whispering is rude, remember?''

''I know but…''

''It's okay with me, Ginny. I won't listen,'' Coryn said.

In a stage whisper that was hard not to overhear, Ginny asked Mark, ''Can Coryn have supper with us?''

''I don't know whether she'd like to…but sure, of course,'' Mark told Ginny. To Coryn, he said, ''Would you? Willing to take a chance?'' He looked at her questioningly.

''Please, Coryn.'' Ginny tilted her head to one side. ''We don't get to have company very often.''

"Well, then, I'll be your company. Thank you very much."

"Goody!" Ginny clapped her hands.

"Drop me off at my house first. I'll get rid of some of the sand and stuff. I'll drive over later. What time?"

"About six. If that's not too early. Ginny has school tomorrow and I have to be at the paper at seven-thirty, so we have early evenings."

"That's fine. I'll bc there."

As Coryn got out of the car, Ginny giggled and called after her the old joke Mark had taught her on the way home. "See you later, alligator!"

"In a while, crocodile!" Coryn called back, laughing.

# *Chapter Thirteen*

Arriving at the Emerys' house, she rang the doorbell, then heard voices and running footsteps. The door opened and Ginny stood, shyly smiling.

Mark was not far behind.

"Hi, come in. We're getting things lined up. Mrs. Aguilar left us all sorts of instructions."

"She *always* does on Daddy's night in the kitchen!" chirped Ginny, then clapped her hand to her mouth, "Whoops, sorry!"

"Rumors." Mark grinned. "Here, let me take your jacket."

Coryn had changed into a plum colored tunic sweater and matching pants. She had tied her hair back with a velvet ribbon and wore silver and turquoise earrings. Mark's gaze moved over her appreciatively.

The first time Coryn had been here, the day she had come bringing Ginny's eye patch covers, Mrs. Aguilar had taken her right to the back of the house. Later, they had sat in the kitchen. She had not really seen the rest of the house.

From the center hall, Coryn saw two rooms. One was the living room, the other, from the glimpse she got through half-open glass doors, had probably originally been the dining room. It looked as though it had been turned into an office with a desk, computer and bookcases. It probably served as his study when Mark worked at home, she realized.

"Come in. I got a fire going, should take the chill off," Mark said. "Would you like something to drink? Soda, coffee? I've some apple cider simmering."

"That sounds good."

Mark rubbed his hands together. He seemed a little nervous. Ginny had told her that they didn't have company often. Did that include Mark entertaining ladies?

"Fine. Make yourself comfortable. Ginny, you want to help me?"

Ginny trotted off to the back of the house alongside him.

Coryn walked over to the fireplace, held out her hands to its glowing warmth, turned back, studied Mark's home.

On one side of the fireplace was a worn leather armchair and reading lamp. In front was a sofa, beside it a smaller armchair with matching, rather faded chintz covers. On both sides of the hearth were built-in bookcases crammed with books. There were lots of children's books on the lower shelves, easily accessible for Ginny.

Mark's domain was in sharp contrast to Jason's condo. Coryn remembered the first time she saw Jason's apartment. The address was a good one with an expensive view. The huge living room had glass doors leading out to a balcony overlooking the pool. Modern prints hung on the stark white walls. Furniture consisted of a contoured white sofa and a black-leather Eames chair. In front of the couch was a coffee table with a free-form glass top on which were neatly piled copies of *GQ* and *Fortune*. There was a gleaming black entertainment center with a twenty-four-inch television and CD cabinet. An exercise machine stood in one corner.

In Jason's black-and-white tile kitchen, the size of a boat galley, there was a chrome microwave and an automatic coffeemaker. It had struck her at the time that although he had lived there two years, the place looked like a high-priced motel room. As though Jason was just passing through, on the way to somewhere, on the way up. As it turned out, on the way out, out of her life.

The rattle of cups and spoons on a tray signaled Ginny's return. Holding the tray with both hands, Ginny approached with careful steps. Mark followed with a steaming server of apple cider.

Ginny put the tray down on the low coffee table, then stepped back, looked at Mark.

''That smells delicious,'' Coryn said.

''There are cinnamon sticks in each mug,'' Ginny told her, pointing. ''You stir them and they kind of melt into the cider. It tastes yummy.''

After they finished the cider, Ginny asked, ''Would you like to see my room, Coryn?''

Over Ginny's head Coryn met Mark's gaze. He gave an imperceptible nod and smiled.

"While you ladies take an inspection tour, I'll get the charcoal started."

Ginny was small and wiry. She had lost her baby fat and would soon be all arms and skinny legs. Her hair was short, cut with bangs. If it had a tendency to curl, Coryn couldn't tell. Perhaps this style had been decided upon because it was quick and easy, needed no dexterity for French braiding or some other kind of hairstyle a little girl might like.

"Mrs. Aguilar made the curtains," Ginny said, skipping over to the high windows. "They match the dust ruffle on my bed, see?"

Coryn admired them, then Ginny pointed out her small old-fashioned school desk. "We found it in a junk shop. Well, not really junk, sort of an antique shop." She put her head to one side and grinned impishly. "Daddy hates them but Mrs. Aguilar says, 'You just never know what you might find there.' And we found this."

There was a low bookshelf with books and games and a floor lamp beside a small rocking chair. Then Coryn saw the dollhouse. It was empty. No furniture, no little doll occupants.

"Is this new? Something you're working on?" she asked.

Ginny shook her head. "It's a kit. My gramma sent it for Daddy to put together. We were going to finish it—but we sort of..." She gave a little shrug. "A dollhouse family needs a daddy *and* a mommy."

It wasn't said sadly, just matter-of-factly. But the little girl's words made Coryn wince.

She thought of the elaborate dollhouse she had received the Christmas she was ten. Now she realized what a project it must have been for her parents. Especially her mother. The hours that had gone into the furnishing, the wallpaper, tiny curtains, coverlets for the beds. She also remembered the wonderful small china family that had come to live there, with a lace-capped grandmother and tweed-coated grandpa, even a small framed sampler cross-stitched "Home Sweet Home" that hung in the parlor.

Every little girl should have a dollhouse family. Coryn would have to ask Mark if she could give hers to Ginny.

"I guess we better go back. Daddy'll be wondering what's keeping us," Ginny said.

The evening passed with incredible speed and it was Ginny's bedtime before anyone realized. With one minor protest met with Mark's firm, "School tomorrow, honey, I'll be up in a few minutes, to hear your prayers and tuck you in."

Ginny made a reluctant start then asked, "You'll come again, won't you, Coryn?"

"Thank you, Ginny, I'd love to."

"We want her to, don't we, Daddy?" Ginny glanced at Mark.

"Sure thing," Mark answered. Ginny lingered a moment longer until Mark said with a grin, "Quit stalling, young lady."

"I'm not, Daddy, I just—" she hesitated. "Is it okay if I give Coryn a hug?"

"Of course you can!" Coryn said feeling a rush of pleasure, and holding out her arms. Ginny ran across the room and into them. Her body felt small and warm and incredibly dear against Coryn as she held her for a minute.

Ginny wiggled loose then said, "'Night, Coryn."

"'Night, honey," Coryn replied, her voice suddenly husky.

"Now, scoot," Mark said and with a mischievous grin Ginny skipped out of the room calling over her shoulder, "I'll call you when I'm ready, Daddy."

The two adults looked at each other and laughed softly. "She's a darling, Mark. You've done a great job bringing her up."

A shadow passed over his face before he answered. "I've tried. It's a big job. Mrs. Aguilar has been a tremendous help. I couldn't have done it without her."

Ginny's piping little voice called, "I'm ready, Daddy."

"Okay, hon. Coming." Mark unfolded himself from the deep chair. "Will you excuse me, Coryn? This may take a while. I don't like rushing bedtime. It's important to make a child feel safe, secure at nighttime."

"Of course," Coryn answered, thinking what a good father Mark was, patient, sensitive, understanding. She could see how hard he tried to make up for the loss of Ginny's mother.

After Mark left, Coryn got up. She wanted a closer look at some of the photographs she'd seen along the top bookshelf. There were lots of them. Pictures that could be captioned Happy Family.

Coryn picked up one of a gamine-faced young woman with wide dark eyes, a smiling mouth, short dark hair. Shari. There were pictures of her with Mark on a tennis court, each holding rackets, some photos of them sitting in beach chairs, palm trees in the background. Mexico? Hawaii? Honeymoon? Then Ginny began to appear in the shots, as a baby, a toddler. The photographs all seemed to stop when Ginny was about three.

On the lower shelf there was a picture of Shari against a snowy background, in ski togs, dark glasses pushed up on her head, smiling. Was that the weekend it had happened? The terrible accident Mark had told her about. Knowing the story, it broke Coryn's heart to look at the pictures. Why did Mark keep them on display? Coryn decided he probably wanted to keep Shari fresh in Ginny's memory, remind her that she had had a loving mother, that they had been a family.

When Mark came back after putting Ginny to bed, she asked, "All settled?"

"Yes. The last drink of water, the last hug, all settled." He grinned and sat down on the sofa beside her.

"She's a treasure, Mark."

"Yep, a great kid." He nodded. "By the way, I've made a decision. And you're responsible."

Coryn looked surprised. "Me? How?"

"I've decided to let Ginny have a pet. A kitten is what she wants."

"I really think it will be good for her, Mark."

"Will you go with us, help us pick one out?"

"Sure. I'd love to. The animal shelter always has

dozens of kittens available. They have their shots and everything. They're ready to take home."

"If I regret this, I'll know who to blame," he teased. "Ginny's not above using you to nag me, you know. 'Coryn had a dog when she was a little girl.'" Mark imitated Ginny's childish tone.

Coryn laughed. "I don't think you'll regret it, Mark. Making a child happy has to be the best possible thing to do."

"Yes, that's true," he agreed.

"You've done a great job, Mark. Ginny's a wonderful little girl," Coryn added.

"Thanks. She had a good start. Shari was a superb mother. I also have to give Mrs. Aguilar lots of credit. Ginny's like one of her own grandchildren to her."

"Don't sell yourself short, Mark. Girls have a special relationship with their fathers. I know. And Ginny absolutely adores you."

Mark put another log on the fire, then came to sit beside Coryn on the sofa. He didn't say anything for a minute, then sighed and said, "It still doesn't make up for not having a mother."

"Of course not, but—" Coryn started to suggest that maybe some day there would be someone else, not to take Shari's place, but to make up for that loss by creating another place in Ginny's life, an important but different place. But she stopped herself from saying that. It would seem too intrusive, too self-asserting. Besides, she asked herself, would I be ready to take all this on even if Mark was thinking of *me?*

Another silence fell between them. The flames of the new log flared brightly and the wood crackled as it burned. There was a certain intimacy simply sitting together in the firelight. Coryn was very conscious of Mark's nearness. A kind of inner tremor shot through her, an inner knowing. Mark was a man she could trust, someone she could fall in love with. That sudden conviction made her nervous and she shifted her position, moving a little away from him. At almost the same time, his arm went around her shoulder. Then he kissed her. There had been no anticipation that it would happen and yet no hesitation. It seemed as natural as breathing. It was a good kiss, a satisfying kiss without being demanding. A kiss that held a promise she found exciting.

Suddenly the bell chime of the marine clock in the hallway struck ten. Was it sounding a warning for her heart? She sat up, moving out of the circle of Mark's arm, "Time for me to go."

As he helped her on with her coat, she said, "It's been a wonderful day, Mark."

"There'll be others I hope, Coryn," he said in a low voice.

He turned her around and drew her close and kissed her again. The kiss was slow, very sweet. When it ended, she stepped back and they looked at each other smiling. As if acknowledging there would be other kisses just as there would be other times.

He walked her out to her car, opened the door so she could slide in the driver's seat.

Although she had not planned to, she put her arm around his neck, drew his head forward and very deliberately kissed him on the mouth. "Today was very special, Mark."

Driving home through the dark streets Coryn felt happy. It had been such a fantastic evening, so right, so natural to be with Mark and Ginny. As if somehow it was something they'd done before and might go on doing.

Cooking supper together had been fun. Ginny had made the hamburger patties, shaping the meat into flat circles with little hands, for Mark to grill. They all had made the salad, laughing as they took turns adding cut up carrots, celery, bits of broccoli to the bowl of torn lettuce, making jokes about a "tossed salad." It was a joy to hear Ginny laugh, to see the tender amusement in Mark's eyes observing her.

It had felt so cozy, like a family. Maybe that was dangerous thinking. After her experiences of dating in L.A. Coryn had almost given up on the idea that men of character and commitment were still around. A man like Mark Emery would be easy to fall in love with. What she wasn't ready for was to be hurt again. But then love sometimes just happened.

At the memory of Mark's kiss Coryn smiled as she turned into the driveway. Ready or not, maybe she had already fallen in love with Mark Emery.

Mark stood on the sidewalk watching Coryn's car make a boulevard stop, the taillight blinking as she made the turn, then he walked slowly back into the house.

He made himself a cup of coffee and brought it into the living room. He felt somewhat uneasy.

Today had been really wonderful. He'd felt happier than he had for a long time. Although he was undeniably attracted to Coryn Dodge, he wondered if getting seriously involved with anyone was the right thing to do. Sometimes he thought it would be best if he didn't get into a serious relationship with anyone until Ginny was older. Grown up even. Ginny had lost her mother and sometimes seeing her longing for that special presence in her life made his heart ache. But other times he thought it was best if some other woman didn't try to fill that empty place.

Yet he felt a deep-seated loneliness. The need, the longing, to share his life with someone was strong. But was Coryn Dodge the one? Was he getting in too deep, too fast with Coryn? He didn't want to make a mistake. It was too important a step. Maybe, he'd better slow down, be cautious.

# *Chapter Fourteen*

A week went by, then two. Mark hadn't called. Coryn was wracked with all kinds of doubts.

Why hadn't he called? Was he on assignment, out of town? Maybe Ginny was sick. Some childhood illness, like chicken pox or mumps? Still, he would have called, wouldn't he? He must have seen how fond she'd become of his little girl. She would have sent her a funny get-well card or a book or a game she could play in bed.

As each day passed, Coryn had to wonder if she'd handled things wrong again. With Mark, as she had with Jason. Come on too strong, seemed too eager? But with Mark, everything had felt so natural. So relaxed. So right. There'd been a spontaneous camaraderie, shared interests.

There was definite physical attraction, as well. She was sure of that. His kiss the evening they'd gone to the play, the kiss on the beach, the kiss that evening they'd spent together at his house. *That* had not been a *casual* kiss. It had awareness, excitement and passion. Passion held in check, but nevertheless, it had been there. What's more, Mark couldn't have mistaken *her* response to the kiss. Had she opened herself up too soon? Maybe that was it.

She'd thought a lot about relationships since Jason. She'd decided that Jason's rules of no strings, no commitment was shallow and wrong. Integrity, generosity, accountability was what she was looking for, what she wanted to give. Mark had too much character to play games.

By the end of the second week she hadn't heard from him, Coryn gave up making excuses. There could be any number of reasons. She wasn't going to allow herself to brood. She hated that she had regressed to listening for the phone, hoping Mark would call. Nonetheless, one afternoon when the phone rang she jumped to answer it.

"Hello." She sounded breathless, eager, even to herself. However, it was a woman friend of her mother's. Disappointment washed over her.

"Coryn? Is that you? It's Lucy Prentis. Is your mother on her way?" Her voice sounded extremely annoyed. "We've been waiting forty-five minutes."

"On her way?" Coryn repeated vaguely.

"Yes, of course." The irritation in Mrs. Prentis's voice increased. "This is our bridge day. The four of us have been playing bridge twice a month for nearly fifteen years. This is the second time your mother hasn't shown up."

Coryn felt a nervous flutter in her stomach. "She

isn't here, Mrs. Prentis. Maybe she had an appointment...I really don't know."

"An appointment? None of us ever make an appointment on our bridge day." The woman's tone was full of exasperation. "I simply don't understand it, Coryn. She could have at least called so we could have gotten a substitute. As it is...we've wasted another—"

"I'm sorry, Mrs. Prentis."

"Never mind. It's not your fault. I just wish if Clare has something else she'd rather do on these days, she would say so. Not ruin it for all of us."

Coryn didn't know what to say. Lucy Prentis and her mother had been close friends for as long as she could remember. It seemed odd that her mother would have forgotten a long-standing bridge date. Then she felt that elevator-drop feeling in the pit of her stomach. Or was it so odd? Not in light of the other puzzling incidents Clare had exhibited in the time Coryn had been home.

"I'm sorry, Mrs. Prentis," Coryn said. "I'll tell Mom you called."

The phone clicked. Coryn could imagine the expression on Lucy Prentis's face as she went back to the bridge table to inform the other two ladies that Clare had done it again.

Coryn put down the receiver. She felt a kind of sick jolt. She'd been so self-absorbed lately, preoccupied, she hadn't been aware that her mother might be having problems again. As she stood thinking about it, the back door opened and Clare walked in wearing an old sweater, jeans, gardening gloves. Her face had a smudge of dirt on one cheek and she had on a battered canvas hat. Her eyes were bright, her cheeks flushed. Seeing Coryn, she smiled. "I've been planting bulbs. They'll be gorgeous in the spring, grape hyacinths and jonquils."

Coryn started to tell her about Mrs. Prentis's irate call but something held her back. Her mother looked so happy she didn't have the heart. She would find out soon enough. Lucy Prentis wasn't known for tact.

Her mother seemed perfectly normal. Coryn was lulled into thinking that some of this might have to do with menopause. When she looked up symptoms for this what she learned felt rather reassuring. The severity of problems depended on the individual woman.

For the next ten days Coryn's attention focused on her mother. But even under this alerted observation Clare seemed normal. She went about the house doing the usual things. Perhaps she was a little quieter, a little distant, but on the whole herself.

Late one afternoon her mother tapped on Coryn's bedroom door, leaned in to say she was leaving to go to the grocery store. An hour later when Coryn went downstairs she found Clare sitting in the kitchen, staring blankly, her eyes confused, her expression troubled. Her car keys and grocery list were on the table in front of her.

When Coryn came in, her mother looked at her. "Darling, the craziest thing, I can't remember where the grocery store is. I've driven around, but I keep turning down the wrong streets, I just don't know…." Her voice trailed off and she shook her head helplessly.

Coryn felt a clutching sensation. She seemed to go

on automatic. Somehow her voice managed to sound steady as she asked, ''Do you still shop at Reddi-Rite?''

''Yes, of course. I always have. That's what makes this so insane.'' Her mother was genuinely baffled.

Gathering herself together quickly, Coryn asked, ''Well, don't worry, Mom. I'll drive you.'' She attempted a laugh. ''I think I remember how to get there.''

Clare still looked unconvinced. ''I just don't know what's gotten into me lately. I feel so foolish.'' She sounded exasperated, but she didn't protest Coryn's offer to take her.

The supermarket where they had shopped for groceries for as long as Coryn could remember was only a short distance away. It was, however, nearly five o'clock and the parking lot was crowded with late shoppers and people shopping after work. Coryn finally found a space, pulled in and turned off the engine.

Instead of immediately getting out of the car, Clare remained sitting there. ''Want me to go in and help you, Mom?'' Coryn said after a moment.

''Oh, honey, I don't know. Suddenly, I'm not feeling so well. Would you shop for me?''

Again Coryn felt a rush of anxiety. ''Sure, Mom. Give me your list. I'll make quick work of it.''

Her mother fumbled in her handbag and brought out a long slip of paper, and gave it to Coryn.

''Will you be okay? Would you like me to get a cola out of the soft-drink dispenser for you to sip while I shop?''

"I'll be fine, dear. I'll just roll down the window, get some fresh air."

Inside the store, Coryn looked at the list and had another shock. Her mother's handwriting was almost illegible. The scribbled items staggered crookedly down the page. It was hardly coherent. She'd just have to play it by ear, Coryn decided, pocketing the list. She grabbed a cart and started down the first aisle.

She felt breathless, disoriented. If only she had someone to talk to about her mother. Someone objective and not as involved in the situation as her father, someone with whom she could discuss her worry. But who? Mark's name came to her. If anyone, he would be the one compassionate enough, sensible enough. Mark would be the one, if she told anyone...

It was then that she saw two familiar figures just ahead of her, Mark and Ginny. She started to hurry to catch up with them then stopped herself. She felt awkward. It had been over three weeks since that evening at their home that had seemed so comfortable, so mutually enjoyable. She'd hoped—no, more than that, *expected* him to make another date. For just the two of them to go out to dinner, where they could talk. She had felt they were on the brink of something to be explored.

Suddenly Coryn was stricken with feelings of insecurity. Maybe she'd read too much into their being together. She had felt happy and hopeful. She loved Ginny, too. Had already begun to imagine how she could make the little girl's life happier...create a home that would be what Ginny had said wistfully a dollhouse family should be—with a daddy *and* a mommy.

As Coryn hesitated, Ginny turned around, saw her and waved. "Hi, Coryn." She tugged on Mark's sleeve. "Look, Daddy, there's Coryn. Oh, Coryn, I have something so exciting to tell you!"

Was it Coryn's imagination, or did Mark look embarrassed? He had too honest a face to hide what he was feeling. He *did* seem ill at ease. Why?

Then the blow struck. Ginny's little face was flushed, her eyes alive with excitement. "Oh, Coryn, I got my kitten! Orange, like I wanted, 'cept she has little white paws. And I called her Sunny just like I said."

It took all Coryn's effort to keep from looking at Mark. The *three* of them were *supposed* to have gone to the animal shelter to help Ginny select a kitten. It was something Mark had talked to her about. Something they had planned to do together. *She* was the one who had persuaded Mark to allow Ginny to have a pet.

Swallowing her hurt, Coryn said, "Oh, I'm so happy for you, Ginny. I bet she's precious."

"She's in the car in a box. We couldn't bring her into the store."

"Ginny, you were going to pick out the right kind of kitty food," Mark said.

Coryn glanced at him. He was definitely uncomfortable. Had he forgotten he had asked her to go with them? Or had he just thought better of the idea? Thought better about everything?

Stupidly, she felt like bursting into tears. Something like this shouldn't throw her. People forgot appointments, arrangements, plans...every day. Well, some people did. But not Mark, a small voice inside her head taunted.

When Ginny had gone happily down the aisle on her proud-pet-owner errand, it left the two of them standing awkwardly. A few inches apart. Worlds apart.

"I've been assigned a special feature series," he told her finally. "Lots of research into local stuff. Lots of interviews, that sort of thing. I've been swamped. Haven't had much free time."

Coryn stiffened. He didn't need to make excuses. She got the message. He'd had second thoughts about them. He wasn't planning to see her again anytime soon. And to think, she had almost…

"That should be interesting." She kept her voice even. "I've been busy, too, working on updating my résumé," she said briskly, smiling brightly. "Trying to make myself irresistible to a prospective employer." The minute she had said that, she could have bitten her tongue. "Well, *employable* anyway."

A cheerful voice came over the store's PA system. "Howdy, shoppers. Today's smart shopper's specials are on canned whole-kernel corn and hearty salsa in aisle four. Thanks for shopping Reddi-Rite."

Ironic, Coryn thought, my heart is breaking in the canned-foods department of the supermarket. She had to get away, yet she seemed rooted to the spot.

Coryn felt immensely thankful when Ginny came back with a large box of dry cat food and wedged it carefully beside the laundry detergent and cornflakes in Mark's cart.

"Well, I better get on with my shopping. Mother's waiting in the car for me," Coryn told Mark. "Bye,

Ginny,'' she said to the little girl. Swiftly she wheeled her shopping cart around Mark's and rushed down the aisle, not looking back.

Well, she didn't need things spelled out. It couldn't be any clearer. She could read between the lines. She'd had plenty of practice, hadn't she? With Jason. She was smarter now. At least she had *thought* she was. Of course, Mark hadn't tried to con her, use her the way Jason had. He was putting it right on the line.

Mindlessly she put food items in her cart. How on earth she would make a dinner out of any of this she could only guess. She knew she had not gotten half the things on the unreadable grocery list. But it didn't matter. All that mattered was getting out of there as quickly as possible. Out of the store. Away from Mark.

She stood at the checkout counter, biting her lower lip nervously, praying he didn't finish his shopping and join the same line or the one opposite hers. Her face felt stiff and stretched.

How many times did it have to happen to her before she saw the light? Showing your true feelings only made you a target. Being honest meant getting hurt. She thought she'd learned. But Mark seemed so different...Mark seemed—oh, how did she know? She wasn't good at reading people. Hadn't experience taught her that, if nothing else?

''We're all in this alone,'' comedian Lily Tomlin had quipped. Maybe that was true. You couldn't count on anyone. Trust anyone. How could she have forgotten that? Been crazy enough to hope?

Oh, why was the woman ahead of her being so slow? Coryn tapped her foot impatiently. The woman was carrying on a long explanation with the clerk about getting the wrong kind of dishwashing detergent. The clerk was sending the bag boy back down the store to exchange it for the right one. More delay. Coryn began to feel hot, choked. Exasperated. Desperate.

Out of the corner of her eye she thought she saw Mark and Ginny approach. She looked down into her cart, as though seeing if everything was there. Finally, the line moved. She unloaded her items onto the counter. The cash register was clicking. The clerk said something she didn't hear, she got out her wallet, hand poised to pull out the necessary bills. Thank goodness, at last. Her purchases were bagged, put back into the shopping cart and she rolled it toward the exit door.

Outside, the rush of cold air in her face revived her. Then she heard a voice behind her. "Miss, miss..."

She whirled around.

"Your change, miss." It was the bag boy. "You forgot your change."

"Oh, thank you," she said, thrusting the money into the pocket of her jacket. She stowed the groceries in the trunk of the car.

It was only when she was behind the wheel, fastening her seat belt that she realized her mother was no longer on the passenger side. Her heart literally stopped. She turned cold. Where in the world was she?

It was getting dark now and the shopping center was crowded with shoppers, cars. Coryn pulled the keys out of the ignition and got out of the car. Standing beside it she looked around frantically. Which way could Clare have gone? Breathing hard, Coryn walked back toward the Reddi-Rite entrance.

People in a hurry pushed loaded carts out through the automatic doors. No sign of her mother there. Should she go right or left? A number of smaller stores flanked the large grocery building. She couldn't have got too far, Coryn told herself. She'd only been in the store fifteen, twenty minutes.

Her heart hammered as she hurried down the sidewalk, checking the entryway into each store along the way. Then she saw her mother. She was standing in front of the display window of the variety store at the end of the block. Weak with relief, Coryn hurried toward her.

"Mom!" she said, grabbing her arm. "You scared me half to death. I didn't know where you were—"

Her mother turned to her with a wide-eyed stare. "Why, honey, I'm sorry...I just was doing a little window-shopping. Look at that dear little carousel. Isn't that sweet? Wouldn't that make a darling gift for Mark Emery's little girl?"

The mention of Ginny was like salt in an open wound. She was still smarting from the hurt of what had just happened. Her own pain caused her voice to be sharp. "I don't know, Mom." She tugged at her coat sleeve. "Come on. It's late and we better get home before Dad. He'll be worried." He'd be even more worried if he knew about today, Coryn thought. She put her hand through her mother's arm and led her back to the car.

Dear God, what next?

Coryn was taking deep breaths as she got back in

the car and slid behind the wheel. Her hand shook as she inserted her key into the ignition. Pulling out of her space, she went forward to make the turn into the highway, and saw Mark's station wagon. Foolish tears stung her eyes. She remembered an especially happy time they were all together. On their way home from the beach...singing.

It hurt, but then, she'd been hurt before. It was her own fault. Expecting too much, taking too much for granted.

Well, what had she expected? To dump on Mark right there in the middle of the canned section between sliced pineapple and cream of chicken soup? To tell him how worried she was about her mother? And even if she had and he had listened sympathetically because he liked her mother, what could he do? She would just have made him uncomfortable. People only listen to other people's troubles if they have to, or if they're paid to. That's all they can do, for fifteen minutes or an hour, at most. Then they go their own way, back to their own lives, feeling relieved that your problem, the one they've just heard about, isn't theirs. It's as if troubles or disasters were somehow contagious. If you get too close to one, you might contract it yourself.

Oh, I don't blame you, Mark, Coryn thought as she turned into the driveway. I wouldn't want to hear about this, either. If I had a choice. Which I don't.

"God help me," she prayed aloud as she got out of the car. Saying it, she knew only He could.

# *February*

# Chapter Fifteen

The next two days passed in an agony of indecision for Coryn. There was no use denying it any longer, there was something seriously wrong with her mother. She had to find out what. Dr. Roger Iverson had been their family physician as long as she could remember. Surely her mother had gone for a yearly physical checkup at least. Maybe she had told him about some of these memory lapses, the headaches, the lack of usual interest and energy. Certainly he could prescribe something that would help her. A mood elevator or maybe just some super vitamins.

The only way to find out was to make an appointment with him and talk to him herself. She planned to do it as soon as possible.

Coupled with this new worry was the disappointment about Mark Emery. The shattering of her brief hope for new happiness.

Both these things weighed heavily on Coryn's heart early that February morning when she came into the kitchen. Her father was alone. He put down the paper. "Good morning, hon. Your mother's sleeping in. Would you do a favor for me? Stop at the cleaners? Tonight's the banquet at the Highland Inn and they've got the suit I want to wear. Your mother was supposed to pick it up yesterday but evidently forgot."

"Sure, Dad," Coryn said quickly. Her father was frowning as if annoyed at another incident of her mother's memory slips.

Coryn again considered discussing her concerns about her mother with him. But he seemed so preoccupied and even a bit on edge this morning. He focused on the banquet, she realized.

The banquet was the annual fund-raising event for the benefit of the local heart association. Her father had reserved a table for them and some friends. Coryn had also forgotten about it. Even though it wasn't a blatantly political event, she knew by now that her father would be doing some networking there.

Later that morning, Coryn drove to the nearby small shopping mall where Wilson Dry Cleaners was located. The Dodges had been customers there for years. Both husband and wife worked in the establishment. When Coryn walked in, Mrs. Wilson was at the counter waiting on someone else.

After she finished with him, she turned to Coryn. "You've come to pick up your father's cleaning, right? It's been here over a week. I called and left a message for your mother but I guess she doesn't remember."

Mrs. Wilson cast a sympathetic glance at Coryn then went to the rotating clothes rack. After spinning it around a few times, examining tags, she took down two plastic bags and brought them back to the counter.

As she removed the sales slips and rang up the amount on the cash register, she said, "I'm glad you're back in Rockport, Coryn. I'm sure it's a comfort to your dad to have someone looking out for your mom these days."

She shook her head. "Such a pity." She glanced over both shoulders then leaned closer, lowered her voice. "Let me tell you, I know what it's like. I grew up with it. Both my parents were alcoholics, and it was tough."

Coryn pulled out her wallet and extracted two bills. Her ears rang. She couldn't believe what Mrs. Wilson had just said. What she was implying! Coryn felt her face flush hotly, then the blood drained from her head. Everything buzzed around her. The smell of the steam irons, the rhythmic slap of the mangles came from the back of the shop, Mrs. Wilson's flat voice merged into a droning hum. Coryn held out one icy hand for the change the woman was counting out, then turned and practically ran out of the store.

Back in the car, she sat very still for a long time. The old saying "It takes one to know one" sprang into Coryn's mind. Mrs. Wilson had somehow got the idea *her mother* was an alcoholic? That was idiotic. Her mother hardly ever touched liquor. To be identified as an alcoholic was outrageous. How had Mrs. Wilson ever got an idea like that?

The banquet room of the Highland Inn was filled with people. Elegantly gowned women chatted together. Men in dinner jackets streamed back and forth from the bar to their tables. The who's who of Rockport always turned out for this event. Dignitaries, aware of the importance of being seen at these community affairs, greeted people as they made their way to the head table; the mayor, members of the board of supervisors, directors of the Rockport Chamber of Commerce.

As Coryn entered with her parents, she saw Mark sitting at the press table. For a moment their glances locked. Coryn felt heat begin to rise into her face. She nodded. A brief smile touched her lips. These weeks of silence from Mark had renewed Coryn's resolve made after Jason, not to let herself be vulnerable to any man. Yet, she had let it happen again. Mark—and let's face it, Ginny—had become important to her. The hurt she now felt was doubly bitter.

As they made their way to their reserved table, her father was stopped several times by well-wishers. "Go for it, Neil!" and "Let me know when you decide. I want to help." These and other such remarks made Coryn realize her father was much more intent on running for the state assembly than she had assumed.

Coryn glanced at her mother. She looked lovely as usual, perfectly groomed except...before they left the house, Coryn had noticed that Clare was wearing two different-colored shoes. When she had called it to her attention, her mother had been embarrassed. Coryn had downplayed the incident and her father had not been aware of it. She was glad she'd made the appointment with Dr. Iverson. There must be a reason for all this.

When her father's conversation with someone

seemed to be dragging on, Coryn felt her mother's thin fingers clutch her arm and she turned to look at her. Clare's lips were pressed tightly together and her eyes were wide and frightened. She looked almost ill. Alarmed, Coryn asked, "Mom, are you okay?"

"Yes, dear, fine. Just a little dizzy for a moment." They had reached their table and Coryn helped her to a seat. With a shaky hand, her mother lifted the water glass and took a few sips. What had caused this—whatever it was—panic attack? Was it something someone had said? Didn't Clare want her husband to run for public office?

Under any other circumstances Coryn thought her mother would make the perfect politician's wife, beautiful, gracious, with all the social skills to charm constituents.

Feeling protective, Coryn took a seat beside Clare. Two other couples, old friends of the family, came to the table to join them. Immediately the conversation became general and lively. Neil came last. He was smiling broadly and seemed excited. Obviously he enjoyed all the attention. Knowing him as she did, Coryn knew her father considered the prospect of taking on the incumbent assemblyman a challenge, one he would assume with pleasure. But if her mother's problems were serious or got worse? The question hung unanswered in Coryn's mind.

Coryn glanced at Clare again. She seemed to have regained her composure. She and Lucy Prentis were discussing the Friends of the Library plans to fund the new reference room at the main library. For the moment she seemed all right. Relieved, Coryn sighed.

With conversations going at full tilt on either side of her, Coryn had a chance to look around the room. The press table was in her direct line of vision. It was disconcerting to realize that Mark was seated so he could observe her, which he was doing at the moment.

She felt uncomfortable. Conscious of Mark's regard, she lowered her eyes and looked down at the salad the waitress had just placed before her. Maybe she wouldn't feel so bad about it if she knew exactly why Mark had cooled.

A spattering of applause brought her back to the present. Don Moore, the president of the chamber of commerce was at the mike.

"Tonight I'd like to introduce some of our prominent citizens who are here supporting this project. These are people we all know and love because they are always there, ready to be counted on for whatever will help our county."

One by one he announced names, and people at various tables stood up to enthusiastic applause. Then Don Moore said, "Neil Dodge, who we hope is going to answer a groundswell of support to be our next north-coast assemblyman at the state legislature." Her father rose to his feet.

Everyone at their table began to clap loudly. There were exclamations from every corner of the room as her father smiled and waved his hand. The applause went on for a long time until Neil sat down. There was a buzz of congratulatory comment from all sides. Glancing at her mother, Coryn saw her face had turned deathly pale. A few minutes later, Clare murmured something and struggled to get up from her chair. She stumbled slightly, sat down again. Then, with great effort, she rose, steadied herself on the back of the chair and started toward the exit into the lobby.

Coryn's father, deep in conversation with the man to his left, did not see her mother leave. With growing concern, Coryn watched Clare's progress across the room. She was weaving visibly. A stab of fear pierced Coryn's heart. She put down her napkin and darted a quick look at her mother's place. Her wineglass was untouched. She looked back at Clare. She was definitely wobbling. Quickly, Coryn pushed back her chair and walked to her side.

Taking firm hold of her mother's arm, she whispered, "Lean on me, Mom."

Swaying slightly, Clare leaned against her. Slowly they moved forward. As they did, Mark Emery suddenly appeared on the other side of her. Holding her arm steadily, he walked with them out the door into the lobby. There they eased Clare into one of the velvet chairs.

She raised her hand and passed it wearily across her forehead, murmured, "Thank you." She closed her eyes for a few seconds. "I don't know what came over me. I felt so dizzy."

"It's terribly hot in there," Mark said quickly. "All that crowd and noise. I felt a little woozy myself."

Clare looked relieved, and Coryn shot him a grateful glance.

"Let me get you some water," Mark offered, then left to do so.

"Do you want me to take you home, Mom?" Coryn asked.

Alarmed, Clare said, "Oh, no, I'll have to go back. Your father will be upset if I don't."

"You don't have to, Mom. Not if you don't feel well."

"I'll be fine. Just give me a few minutes."

"You're sure?"

"Yes, dear. Honestly."

Mark came back with a glass of water, handed it to Clare.

She took it with her hand visibly shaking. "Thank you, Mr. Emery. You're very kind."

Mark stood there, an anxious frown on his face. He glanced at Coryn, thinking she looked especially lovely tonight. She was wearing the same deep blue dress she'd had on the day of the New Year's open house. She seemed unconscious of his presence. She was concentrating totally on her mother. He sensed her distress, longed to reach out, touch her, say something comforting.

Coryn felt Mark's gaze upon her and tensed. The situation could not have been more awkward. This was the first time they'd been in each other's presence since that awful day in the supermarket. Coryn felt embarrassed yet aware of his sensitivity, coming to their aid as he had. It was that very quality in him that had drawn her to him. It had caused her to let down her defenses, to dream, to hope. Almost tongue-tied with nervousness, Coryn murmured, "Yes, thank you."

Whatever Mark was feeling, he said, "Not at all. Gave me a chance to skip the rest of those boring speeches." He grinned. "I had to leave to go by the paper anyway."

He paused, then asked Coryn, "Is your father really planning to run for the assembly?"

"I guess he's thinking seriously about it." She glanced at her mother apprehensively. But she seemed her calm, poised self once more.

"I'd like to have an interview. That is, when he's ready."

"I'll tell him," Coryn replied.

"Well, I'll say good-night to you both. I hope you feel better, Mrs. Dodge."

"Oh, I'm fine now. Thank you again, Mr. Emery." Clare smiled her brilliant smile.

After Mark left, Coryn asked, "Ready?"

"Yes, darling, ready." Her mother seemed completely restored. "Ready to face the roaring lions in the den." She slipped her hand through Coryn's arm, pressed it slightly. "Don't mention my little spell to your dad. He'd worry. Unnecessarily. He's got so much on his mind just now."

They went back to their places at the table. Coryn glanced around. No one seemed to have missed them or noted their return. Coryn would have felt less at ease if she had known their table companions were purposely avoiding mentioning their sudden departure, that curious eyes had followed them as they had made their way to the lobby, and suspicious whispers on wagging tongues had spread malicious rumors from table to table.

# Chapter Sixteen

The day of Coryn's appointment with Dr. Iverson, she felt nervous. Now that she had arranged to see the doctor, she was afraid of what he would tell her. At least, maybe after talking with him, she'd be able to get some handle on what was wrong with her mother.

She hadn't wanted to go during his regular office hours. In order for the doctor to see a reasonable number of patients, the patient flow had to be kept moving. Conscious of the necessity of keeping each visit to twenty minutes, the nurse moved patients quickly from waiting room to examining room. To avoid this, Coryn requested an after-hours appointment. When the doctor's secretary had attempted to elicit the nature of the visit, Coryn had used her most assertive tone. "It's a personal matter. I'm sure if you give Dr. Iverson my name and tell him that I'll come at the most convenient time for him *after* his last appointment, he will see me."

She was put on hold, and a few minutes later the

secretary came back on the line. "If you can be here at five fifteen sharp, Dr. Iverson will see you."

Long before it was time for her to leave the house and drive downtown, Coryn was dressed and ready to go. Wondering how to fill up the time before she had to leave, she paced restlessly. Then the phone rang. She grabbed it on the second ring. In reply to her greeting she heard Mark's voice.

"Coryn?"

For him to call today, of all days was a shock. After all the days she had hoped and waited in vain for his call coming now was an anti-climax. That encounter in the supermarket had hurt badly. But she had already accepted that their brief romance was over. Regretted it, but had determined to recover. Instinctively, she steeled herself from letting her hopes be stirred up again.

"Coryn, I've been thinking about you, thought about calling several times, but—" he broke off, then, "What I'm calling about is that I'd like to see you. I *want* to see you. I feel—I mean I know I owe you an explanation—"

Coryn cut in. "Not at all, Mark," her voice sounding sharper than she intended. "You don't owe me anything."

"I feel I do," he said firmly, quietly. "Could we meet? I'd like a chance to talk."

She hesitated. Why was he starting this up again? Mixed feelings churned. Why *now* when she was just getting over him? She hesitated. His voice came again, "Please, Coryn, it's important."

"Well," she still hesitated. Why put herself through

another emotional scene? Yet, something within her wanted to hear what Mark had to say, what kind of explanation, excuse was he going to give. What harm was there in that? "I have an appointment downtown at five," she countered.

He jumped at that. "Great. Then we could meet at the little espresso place on the square."

She knew the one he was talking about. They'd met there before. It was right across from the newspaper. The Medical Arts building where Dr. Iverson's office was close by.

"All right. In about an hour?"

"I'll be there. Thanks," Mark said and hung up.

To her chagrin she arrived first. She found a table and sat down. Out the window she could see the front of the newspaper building. She could also see children playing around the fountain in the middle of the square, young mothers pushing strollers, couples walking hand in hand. Watching, she felt a thrust of nostalgia, a yearning to somehow trade places with any of them, a deep longing for something she had never had, possibly never would...

"Sorry to keep you waiting. Something came up just as I was leaving—"

Startled, she looked up. It was Mark. His hair was windblown, his tie askew, the collar of his corduroy jacket turned up.

"It's okay."

"I'll get our coffee," he said and walked over to the counter.

Coryn turned away, looked out the window again. The couple she had seen before were kissing. She felt a hard lump in her throat. Why had she come here? Why put herself through whatever Mark was going to say? Could she just get up and walk out? Leave before he came back to the table?

She heard the hiss of the espresso machine, smelled the warm scent of coffee, chocolate, cinnamon.

"Here we go." Mark was back, carefully placing the glass cup in its metal holder, containing the fragrant foamy brew, in front of her.

"Thanks for coming," he said in a low voice. "I really wanted to talk to you—needed to."

"It wasn't necessary, Mark, I told you on the phone."

"Look, Coryn, allow me this. It may not seem necessary to you but it is to me. I feel I've let you down and it wasn't fair because it had nothing to do with you. It was me. My fault." He paused, lowered his voice. "So that you understand, I have to go back to when Shari died. That first year afterward was rough going for both Ginny and me. I was so devastated, I wasn't much good for anything, mostly not for her as the parent she needed so desperately. When the shock started to wear off and I got myself together again, I decided to make her my priority in life. Concentrate on being a good father—being everything to her. We had a shaky start but finally we somehow got our life together. We moved up here and a kind of pattern was established. I began to think I had to stay the course, so to speak. To add another factor—a third person into our life wouldn't be a good idea." Mark's hands were clenched together on the table, so tightly the knuckles were pale. "That's why, when I found myself attracted to you, I got scared—asked myself was I ready? Was Ginny ready? Relationships take time, concentration, to build, develop—'' he sighed heavily, ''That's what I wanted to explain. It had nothing to do with you, actually. You've been wonderful. Ginny is crazy about you. She asks about you all the time. Then, when we saw you in the supermarket that day, I realized...I'd let you down. Hurt you without meaning to. And I'm sorry, Coryn. I'm truly...''

Coryn felt her heart throbbing in her throat. She couldn't take any more of this. It was too late for Mark to be telling her all this. Too late for his apologies, however heartfelt. She didn't need to hear them. Not now. She gathered up her purse and said, ''Mark, I have to go. I have an appointment—'' she got up and he put his hand on her arm.

''Wait, Coryn, do you understand what I'm saying?''

She shook her head. ''Mark, my life is very complicated right now. I'm sorry. I have to go.''

She rushed out of the café and outside the brisk wind was cold and she shivered. Her vision blurred by unshed tears, she walked quickly toward the Medical Arts building.

It was all just too much. There might have been a time, not too long ago when she could have listened, accepted what he was saying, but not now. She had enough to deal with.

She had to focus on her mother now and get to the bottom of this mystery. She pushed through the glass doors of the medical office building, she pushed aside all thoughts of Mark. She hurried through the lobby and caught an elevator before its doors were about to close.

When Coryn arrived at Dr. Iverson's office the waiting room was empty. She could see his office staff behind the glass enclosure turning off computers, putting folders into file cabinets, clearing off their desks. Nervously, Coryn sat down, automatically straightened some magazines on the low table in front of it.

Soon, the door opened and Dr. Iverson, wearing a white lab jacket, stuck his head in. ''Hello, Coryn, come on in.''

Roger Iverson was a tall, lean man with a deeply lined face, thick steel-gray hair, kind eyes behind rimless glasses. He held the door for her and she entered the hallway that led to his office at the end. Someone called his name, and he stopped to sign somcthing on a clipboard one of the nurses brought to him. ''Good night, Doctor,'' she said, and gave Coryn a curious glance before retracing her steps to the glass-enclosed space.

Dr. Iverson shut the office door and indicated the leather armchair opposite his desk. ''Sit down, Coryn. I'm glad you came. It's about your mother, isn't it?''

Coryn's heart gave a surprised little jump. She nodded as Dr. Iverson settled his tall frame in the swivel chair behind his desk. She watched as he reached for a manila folder, placed it in front of him and opened it. Then he clasped his hands together and looked over at her.

Coryn swallowed, her throat suddenly dry. Instinctively she knew that whatever he was about to say would change things forever.

So she began to talk, chatter really, as if to delay what eventually he was going to tell her. "Yes, Dr. Iverson. Since I've come home, I've noticed some changes in her that are puzzling, so unlike her. I mean, she seems confused, uncertain, forgetful. I think she's depressed, she's not herself at all. I just thought maybe you could give her something that might help—a prescription or—maybe she should see a psychiatrist..." Coryn's voice trailed off faintly as Dr. Iverson's gaze met hers steadily.

He shook his head slowly. "Your mother doesn't need a psychiatrist, Coryn. If it would help, I would have suggested it. Normally, I wouldn't disclose this kind of information without a patient's permission. But I've known your family for so long. And knowing the type of person your mother is, perhaps I should tell you everything."

"Tell me what, Doctor?" Coryn pressed him.

"I'm sorry to have to tell you this, but we've already made some tests. She came to me herself several months ago. She didn't want Neil to know but she was worried about herself. Although she tried to downplay the situation. You know how Clare is. She even made it sound slightly humorous...mentioning her forgetfulness, some incident or other that was funny—if it weren't so symptomatic of what her trouble is."

Coryn sat forward in her chair. "And that is?"

"Your mother is in the initial stages of Alzheimer's."

"Alzheimer's," Coryn repeated woodenly.

"You must have heard or read about it."

She had, of course. Alzheimer's. The disease of a

former president and a glamorous movie star of the fifties. But it was an old people's disease. Her mother was barely fifty. An image of vague eyes, tottering people on walkers or in wheelchairs, heads drooping, bodies slumped. The image had no connection with her beautiful mother.

While Coryn sat frozen, her hands clenched tightly in her lap, Dr. Iverson's voice went on as if coming from a long distance.

"Alzheimer's is a progressive disease. It is, so far, incurable. The patient deteriorates to the point of being helpless. Unable to remember places, events, people. Unable to even recognize family members, or dress or feed themselves." He hesitated, then said, "This is hard for me to tell you, Coryn. I tried to talk to Neil about it not long ago. But he is in denial. He doesn't want to hear this. No one could blame him. It isn't the kind of diagnosis a doctor wants to give to a family. Especially not to friends. I've known Clare as long as I've known you." Dr. Iverson shook his head. "He has to know, Coryn. He has to be told and he has to accept it. I guess it's up to you."

Her lips pressed close together, she nodded. "What can I do?"

"I suggest you learn as much as you can about this disease. That way you'll know what is ahead for you as your mother's condition worsens. At least it will prepare you for what to look for, what to expect. And you can help your father."

It was already dark when Coryn left Dr. Iverson's office. She drove slowly, but when she nearly turned twice into a one-way street, she knew she shouldn't be driving at all in her state of mind. She pulled to the side of the road and sat there for a few minutes taking deep breaths. It was all so unreal. And yet it was happening. She had to go home, somehow tell her father.

After a while she turned on the engine, started her car and drove the rest of the way home.

Coming into the house she saw the light in her father's den. The rest of the house was in darkness. She walked through the house turning on lamps as she went. At his den door she halted.

"Dad? Anything wrong?" the words were out of her mouth before she realized she'd said them. Momentarily she forgot *she* was the one with the bad news.

Her father lifted his head from his desk. His face was drawn, his eyes were circled with shadows, the lines around his mouth seemed to have deepened since she had seen him that morning.

"Hello, honey. You're late. Been shopping?" He tried a smile.

She shook her head. "Where's Mom?"

"Oh, she had a slight headache. Went up to bed."

Coryn felt she had to sit down. Her legs seemed suddenly to have lost their strength.

Her father looked at her, frowning. "What is it? You look—I don't know—worried."

"Dad, I have something to tell you. Something you have to know," she said. "I've just come from Dr. Iverson's office and—"

"You're not sick, are you?" her father asked, concerned.

"No, Dad, not me. It's Mother I went to see him

about. Surely you've noticed that there have been changes. Things you've mentioned yourself, like her leaving the stove burners on, that sort of thing. Well, she's sick, Dad. Very sick. Seriously sick."

He closed his eyes, looking pained.

"I know you don't want to hear this, Dad." Coryn's voice broke. "But it's something we can't deny any longer."

"I know." Her father spoke heavily. "I guess I've known for months, just didn't want to admit it was anything but maybe...a woman her age goes through changes."

"It's more than that, Dad. It's Alzheimer's. Dr. Iverson confirmed it. We can't ignore it."

Her father rubbed his hand across his forehead wearily and then, almost as if speaking to himself, he said, "One day a few months ago, before Thanksgiving, before you came home, she went out to do some errands...ordinary things, things she's always done, grocery shopping, taking clothes to the cleaners, getting gas for her car—" He halted, his expression was anguished. "Mike, at the service station, told me that not fifteen minutes after he'd filled her tank, checked the oil and tires, she came back. Evidently didn't remember she'd already been there. He made a joke of it. But I tell you, Coryn, it made my heart stop. She shouldn't be driving in her condition.

"Then, coming home one evening and finding her still in her bathrobe, sitting at the table in the kitchen staring out the window, the breakfast dishes still on the table. When she saw me, she was amazed...*what was I doing home?* She couldn't believe it was five o'clock. The whole day had passed and she wasn't even aware of it.

"I wrestled with that incident not knowing exactly what to think or do." He got up and started pacing. "I didn't want to alarm her. Every time something like that happened, she got so upset, apologetic...as though it were her fault, as if I were blaming her. I thought with you here, things would get better. That maybe she felt isolated, useless, lonely in this big house...you know, the empty-nest syndrome. Maybe, that she was depressed."

"I suggested that to Dr. Iverson," Coryn interrupted. "Asked him if seeing a psychiatrist might help, but he said—" Her father stopped pacing and looked directly at her. Hope seemed to leap into his eyes. Coryn shook her head slightly. "He told me a psychiatrist can't help Alzheimer's victims. It's a disease of the central nervous system. Not emotional, psychotic or neurotic." Coryn bit her lower lip, struggling to go on. "She won't get any better, she'll get steadily worse. She won't recognize us..."

Her father sat down again, put his head in his hands. "Oh, no dear God, no!" Then he mumbled, "Is Dr. Iverson sure?"

"Yes, Dad. There isn't any doubt."

Her father's face seemed to crumble, and he buried his head in his hands again. Hearing the wracking sobs, seeing the broad shoulders shake, Coryn watched helplessly. She had never heard a man cry before. Certainly not her father. It was heart-wrenching. It was something she would never forget.

Tears ran down her own cheeks. She reached out

her hand and placed it on his arm. "Dad, I'm so sorry, so very sorry."

He groped for her hand, clutched it. "I can't go through this alone, Coryn. I need you. Will you stay? Help me through this?"

"Yes, Dad, of course. I'll do whatever I can." Coryn tried to sound reassuring. She knew she was walking into a dark tunnel the end of which she couldn't see, even if there might be a light there.

They talked quietly for a half hour or so. Her father looked so drained, so weary, Coryn persuaded him he should go to bed, get some rest.

As he left, she gave him a hug, patted his shoulder. "Try not to worry too much, Dad. I'll be here for Mom—for both of you..."

"I know you will, sweetheart. I appreciate that."

Coryn watched him cross the hall to the foot of the stairway. His step was slow, his shoulders sagged visibly. She realized she was holding her breath.

She turned back into the room. The fire in the hearth sputtered, the logs crumbled to a blaze of glowing embers. Dr. Iverson had finally answered Coryn's questions about her mother's behavior. But it was not the answer she'd wanted to hear.

*"I can't go through this alone, Coryn,"* her father had said. But could she really help? *She* desperately needed someone to talk with about this awful thing that had attacked her mother, invaded their family life.

The thought of Mark came to her but just as quickly left. Not now. If things had worked out for them it might be different. He had known tragedy himself, would understand. Even as that possibility fleetingly came and went, the words of an old country song came into her mind. A plaintive ballad they all used to sing in the car on their way to go camping when she was a child. Her dad would put on a throbbing twang as he sang it. The lyrics spoke so poignantly about walking in a lonesome valley. Walking it by yourself.

Did everyone have to walk some lonesome valley by themselves in life? Was this hers?

# Chapter Seventeen

A week later, on a cold, rainy night, Coryn and her parents were just finishing dinner, when the phone rang. Neil answered it. "I see. In about twenty minutes? Sure, that will be fine." Her father put down the receiver and came back to the table with an odd expression on his face. "That was Mark Emery. He asked if he could come over this evening."

"I think he wants to interview you," Coryn said, feeling guilty she'd forgotten to mention that to her father. Since that painfully awkward incident at the supermarket and her meeting with Dr. Iverson, she'd had other things on her mind. "He said something about wanting to when we saw him at the inn the other evening." She glanced at her mother for confirmation. But she was rearranging the flowers in the centerpiece, not paying attention to this exchange between her husband and daughter. Her father frowned. "Maybe it's something Glenn set up."

Coryn knew one of her father's old friends, Glenn

Ackerman, was actively working on a grassroots organization to support her father for the assembly seat. She was sure her father had not yet given an official okay. *Was* he going ahead with this? Even now that he knew her mother's diagnosis? Coryn looked questioningly at him. He was looking at his wife, his frown deepening. What was he thinking? Was some part of him still in denial? Didn't he see the things Clare did? Hadn't he noticed the slippage? Clare was not quite so careful about her grooming, got her colors mixed up and sometimes did not have her usual carefully coordinated look. Then there were non sequiturs, the sentences that broke off in the middle, the random remarks that went nowhere, the tendency to stare off into space.

Tension gripped Coryn, tightening her stomach muscles. Her father seemed to have been totally unaware of what had happened at the banquet a week ago. Was he the only one who had not noticed Clare's shaky exit, her lack of balance? Mark had certainly noticed. There had been something in the look he had given her that made Coryn certain *he* knew...at least knew *something* was wrong.

Her mother's soft voice interjected itself into Coryn's uneasy thoughts. "I think I'll go up, if you two will excuse me. There's an old movie on TV, *Portrait of Jenny*—I loved it when I saw it as a teenager. I think I'll just curl up in bed and watch it."

"You don't want to wait and see Mark Emery?" Neil said.

"He just wants to talk politics with you, dear." She smiled at her husband. She got up, leaned over and kissed him, patted Coryn on the cheek as she passed her and floated out of the room.

The phone rang again and automatically her father picked it up. He was soon involved in a conversation. Coryn wondered if she should stay or not. Was her mother right? Was it just politics Mark wanted to discuss? Or was he coming for the interview he said he wanted? If so, she wondered why he hadn't arranged a meeting at her father's office.

Her father was still on the phone when the front doorbell chimed. Coryn would have to answer it. She rose from her chair and started walking toward the hall. Ranger, who had been drowsing in front of the fireplace, got stiffly to his feet and followed her.

Conscious of her inner nervousness, Coryn told herself, *Don't be silly.* Mark was coming to see her father, not her. She opened the door.

"Good evening, Coryn."

"Come in. My father's on the phone but he should be off in a few minutes."

Ranger wagged his tail and Mark bent to smooth the dog's head. "Hiyah, fella." He looked at Coryn. "Great dog."

"Yes, he is," she said. "Here, let me take your coat."

They went into the living room. Her father, having completed his conversation, joined them. He came forward, extending his hand to Mark. "Good to see you," he said heartily. "Can I offer you some coffee?"

"No, thank you, sir. This isn't a social visit exactly." Mark stood rubbing his hands together as if to warm them.

"An interview, then?"

"Not that, either—" Mark hesitated, as if uncertain how to proceed. He glanced at Coryn. For help? she wondered. "Maybe I should leave," she said.

"Not at all," Mark said. "I think you should stay. Hear what I've come to say to your father."

Suddenly the atmosphere in the room changed. This was something important. Something that couldn't be put off. Something they each needed to hear.

Coryn sat down on the edge of the sofa. Her father indicated Mark take one of the armchairs, and Neil sat down in the other. Mark leaned forward, clasped his hands in front of him.

Coryn had a good view of his face and as the moment lengthened before he began to speak, she had a chance to study it. She had seen it often at close range. It was a good face, an intelligent one of character and strength. She had seen how mobile it was. In it she had seen a number of expressions—tender and loving, as with Ginny, alert and intense when talking about something he believed in or cared deeply about. She had seen it briefly touched with sadness when he spoke of Shari, or alive with humor when he was amused.

"Mr. Dodge, I may be way out of line coming to you with this," Mark began. "I've given it a lot of thought and in the end, I had to. As a reporter in the community, I've watched you from a distance. I've also enjoyed the hospitality of your home and the company of your daughter. I don't think of myself as a close friend, but I do feel a responsibility to tell you what is being widely circulated and give you the option of addressing it."

"Well, go ahead, man. Whatever it is, say it."

"Of course, it is common knowledge you are seriously considering running for state office. You have plenty of support. But, much as I hate to say it, politics isn't lawn tennis, it's hardball. Anyone as visible and successful as you in any town has collected a few enemies as well as friends. I'm afraid your opponent is one of these, and his cronies are very adept at smear tactics and dirty tricks. Most politically ambitious people don't fully realize—some not until they're deep into it—that the family of the candidate is the easy target."

"What do you mean?" Neil demanded.

"I'm afraid there are some unfortunate rumors being circulated about—" Mark swallowed as if it was hard for him to speak "—about your wife, about Mrs. Dodge."

"What?" Coryn's father jumped up, anger reddening his face.

"Nothing about her character, sir. Anyone who knows her knows what a lovely—"

"Never mind. What are the rumors? What are people saying?"

"I'm sorry, sir. But they're saying she has a drinking problem, that she's an alcoholic."

Coryn's father muttered something under his breath. His hands clenched into fists. He paced the length of the living room and back two or three times before spinning around and facing Mark. "It's a lie. You know there isn't a shred of truth in it." He pounded one fist into his open palm. "She hardly ever has a sip of anything. Isn't that right, Coryn? Have you ever seen your mother even finish a glass of wine, for that matter? How dare they spread such a malicious falsehood!''

''I understand how you feel, Mr. Dodge. Some people will see it for what it is—an unscrupulous political tactic. But a lie told often enough begins to have a life of its own. One thing leads to another, something added here and there, and before you can stop it, it's too late. It's become a fact.''

Coryn felt like someone struck by lightning. Mrs. Wilson's remarks at the dry cleaners. The scene at the Highland Inn banquet flashed back into Coryn's mind. How many people had witnessed it? If they had already heard the rumor, that incident was the evidence they needed to confirm suspicion.

''Mr. Dodge, your political enemies will not only use this to discredit Mrs. Dodge and to weaken your position. Some people will do anything, use anyone, to gain power. Family values is the name of the game right now. If they can insinuate any kind of dysfunction, addiction. *Anything* to win, they will.'' He paused. ''I thought you ought to know. Then you can decide how to handle it.''

Her father was chalk-white. The veins in his forehead stood out. His mouth was pressed into a tight, straight line. Coryn did not think she had ever seen her father so upset. He fought his anger silently. It was a battle he was waging against his own ambition, the evil intent of others to wound and injure someone he loved.

Coryn held her breath, observing the inner struggle. Gradually, she saw a change come over her father's face. The tense lines relaxed. His eyes refocused on Mark. In a quiet voice, he said, ''I appreciate very much your coming here with this. It took courage to do so. Thank you.'' He waited a few minutes then asked, ''What do you suggest?''

Mark seemed a little taken aback by that. ''I hardly could advise you on that, Mr. Dodge, unless...''

''Unless what?''

''Unless I knew how much you wanted to run. How much it meant to you.''

''Nothing means as much to me as my family.'' His voice was steady.

''And you have given consideration to what kind of strain a political campaign puts on the family?''

''Maybe not enough. It's been an exciting idea. Running, that is. I've succeeded at anything I've set my mind on doing. I could always count on Clare to—'' He stopped abruptly. ''She hasn't been well lately but...'' He halted, glanced at Coryn.

''Dad,'' she remonstrated gently, reminding him of what Dr. Iverson had cautioned them both against. ''Alzheimer's is a slow, progressive disease, but don't fool yourself, it doesn't get any better—it irrevocably goes its course.''

Her father's whole body tensed dramatically. Coryn understood what this breach of family privacy cost him. Then he turned back to Mark. ''The truth is, Clare is in the early stages of Alzheimer's. That may account for some of the rumors. She is sometimes...not herself. There are symptoms. We may have grown used to them, but someone seeing her...unsteadiness, at times her confusion, her slurred speech, *might* think...'' He shook his head. "It wouldn't be good, wouldn't be fair to expose her to the limelight, the scrutiny of people. I guess I hadn't really thought this through."

His shoulders slumped. He sat back down.

"May I make a suggestion?" Mark ventured.

"Yes, sure. What is it?"

"I think if I were you...whatever your decision is...whether to run or not, I would make a public statement. Come right out with it. Tell people of Clare's illness. Just what it is, how it affects its victims. I'm sure there is hardly a family in this state who hasn't had someone, a parent, a relative, a spouse, afflicted with Alzheimer's. If you decide to run, your declaration would totally defeat any weapon the opponent had thought to use against you. If you decide not to, it would be a reasonable excuse to the people who wanted to support you. In either case, going public would gain you only sympathy and respect."

A thoughtful silence followed. Mark got to his feet.

Coryn's father stood, too, held out his hand, clasped Mark's. "Thank you for coming."

"Not at all, sir. I am very fond of Mrs. Dodge. She has been gracious to me and my daughter. I hope things turn out for the best for all of you." Mark hesitated a moment, then said, "Well, I'll be on my way."

Her father did not move. It was almost as if he couldn't.

Mark glanced at Coryn. Their gazes held a moment, then Mark said, "Would you see me to the door?"

Startled, Coryn felt jerked like a puppet, knowing she should have simply done that without being asked. "Of course." Together they walked to the front door.

"I want you to know how sorry I am," Mark said.

Her mind still on "pause," Coryn stared at him. Sorry? Sorry for what? For her mom? For not calling her in all these week? She did not know what to say to that. "Thank you very much" was all she could manage.

"I wish I could do something to help."

"You have. I think you said exactly what my father needed to hear. He's been in denial. Maybe we both have."

Mark stood there for another moment as though he wanted to say something else. Then apparently he decided there was nothing he *could* say. "Well, good night then." He opened the door, then hand on the knob, turned. "If there *is* anything I can do. Anything at all..."

Her throat felt swollen. She could hardly get out the words. "Thanks, it's very kind of you."

"Coryn..."

He spoke her name softly. She felt tears stinging at the back of her eyes. She wished he would go before she flung herself into his arms, sobbing.

The moment of uncertainty hovered, then Mark said, "Good night." This time he left.

She closed the front door and went slowly back into the living room. Her father was slumped in the armchair, one hand covered his eyes.

"Dad, I think Mark's right, don't you?" she asked gently.

"I *know* he's right. I don't know how I couldn't have seen it myself." He shook his head slowly. "Your poor mother. I've probably added to her problem. Couldn't see the forest for the trees. Or maybe I just didn't want to see. Mark Emery's right. I'll get a statement out tomorrow. I'll have him help me write it.''

He paused, then, ''He's a fine man. Not many people would have the guts to come right out and tell you something like this. I admire him a great deal.'' He pulled himself to his feet. ''I think I'll go up now, see how Clare's doing.''

He stood for a minute looking down at his daughter, then reached out and laid one hand on her head. ''Thanks, honey, for sticking around. We'll get through this—whatever it is—together.'' He sighed heavily then left the room.

Coryn felt drained. Limp. Unable to move. The fire had dwindled to a mass of glowing coals. When she was a youngster, she had tried to find pictures there, imagining all sort of shapes and forms. Tonight it was only Mark's face she saw. In it she had seen compassion, understanding, empathy. Her father, not known to be particularly discerning, had seen something fine in Mark, too.

Mark was a rare human being. A man who could be trusted, a man who could be loved without risk of betrayal.

Coryn wasn't sure how long she remained in the living room alone. Her thoughts were jumbled, flitting from one thing to another. There was so much to think about. Some time later, Coryn banked the fire, went upstairs. The door to her parents' bedroom was slightly ajar as she passed it on her way to her own. She heard the low murmur of voices and glanced in. She saw her mother, in a pink satin nightgown and robe, sitting on the side of the bed. Her head was turned toward the TV set so that only her profile was visible. Her hair was down and fell away from her slender neck onto her shoulders, making her look touchingly young.

Her father was on his knees beside her taking off her slippers. His hand was holding her delicate instep almost in a caress. Coryn drew in her breath. The scene was intimate, one of devotion that found no task too menial or ordinary to do for the beloved.

Coryn felt almost embarrassed at inadvertently seeing such a tender scene. Yet she was moved deeply by it. It was as if it had been given her as a gift. To witness the love her father was showing.

In that moment, Coryn realized her father would not run for office and she realized the sacrifice he was making. Putting aside his own ambitions, his own plans, his own goals—that this was what true marriage was all about. It was what had held her parents together all these years. Their vows taken so long ago, neither knowing what might lie ahead, what they might be called upon to do. Those promises to each other had perhaps been spoken without any real understanding, but they were now being met with courage and faith.

Coryn felt her heart twist with love and admiration for these two she loved so dearly. She moved quietly by, seeking the refuge of her own room. What she had glimpsed was truth. The truth of a long, enduring love that met whatever challenges lay upon the path they had chosen to walk together.

Would she ever know such a love, or be able to give

it? That kind of love was the key that opened a heart to pour out whatever was required. That was the kind of love she wanted, longed for, but that had so far eluded her.

# *March*

# Chapter Eighteen

Coryn's alarm clock buzzed persistently. Without opening her eyes, she reached out and shut it off. She lay there for a minute wondering why she had set it. Then slowly, like touching an aching tooth with her tongue, she remembered.

She dragged herself out of bed. She stumbled toward the bathroom to dash her face with water, brush her teeth, twist her hair up into a bun, secure it with an elastic ribbon. Dressing quickly in a sweater, pants, she tiptoed downstairs and out to her car.

It was still dark outside as Coryn drove to the community pool. She'd started going swimming every day, a therapy she'd discovered worked for her. She discovered the early morning gave her time before the rest of the day's duties faced her. She had taken on more and more of the jobs her mother used to handle so easily, so efficiently. It seemed to Coryn her mother was going steadily downhill. It frightened her, and swimming seemed to lessen the tension she felt.

She also used the time to pray. For strength, for courage, for whatever the next months held. In the last several weeks she had turned to prayer more than ever before in her life. They were not the quick, desperate prayers or the careless ones she had often prayed. These were different. She had felt more tuned in than ever before. They were a kind of listening prayer. Seeking strength, guidance. For the first time in her life she knew *she* had to be there for her parents the way they had always been there for her. It was a new role, one she hadn't expected, one she did not feel prepared for. The word *help* prayerfully said was often on her lips and in her mind and heart as she went through the day.

She parked her car, slung the bag containing her bathing suit, thongs, towel and toilette articles over her shoulder and went inside the pool building. At once the combined smells of chlorine, wet tile, canvas and plastic prickled her nostrils. She showed her pass card to be punched, got her locker key and went into the dressing room.

Earlier swimmers were already showering, using the hair dryers, chatting with one another. Coryn moved right to a locker, opened it, stowed her bag, started undressing. All around her women friends were discussing their weight, their diets, their husbands and children. She nodded to a few whom she recognized as regulars, but spoke to no one. The whole point of this self-prescribed therapy was her anonymity. She didn't want to speak to anyone or have anyone speak to her. She'd heard sharing burdens was helpful. She'd always heard that. But right now she knew that the only way she could bear this awful thing that was happening was not to talk about it. As if not talking about it made it not real.

She pulled on her tank suit, slipped her bare feet into thongs and moved like a robot into the prerequisite shower. Afterward she tossed her towel over her shoulder and walked down the green-painted corridor to the pool.

Aqua-tinted water shimmered from the painted bottom of the big, rectangular pool. Light from the gray day outside, filtered through the slanted windows, was augmented by glaring bulbs in aluminum fixtures set in the arched ceiling. A lifeguard sat at one end on a mounted place from where he could view the swimmers. Every sound was amplified in the enormous room. The ponging sound of the diving board's metal springs, the echoing splash as the diver hit the water. Coryn disliked the claustrophopic feeling of swimming indoors. She had always loved swimming in a mountain lake or in the ocean. Coryn bit her lip and struggled with the urge to leave. But she was here for a purpose. Necessary activity to combat stress-induced depression.

She shoved her hair into her bathing cap while looking for an empty lane. She went to the side of the pool. Suppressing the reluctance to get into the water, she sat down on the edge, dangled her feet in the water, shivering as the chill ripples swirled around her ankles. Finally, taking a deep breath, she pushed herself into the water.

There were two what she called ''serious swimmers'' in the lanes on either side of her. One was doing a vigorous backstroke, the other a butterfly crawl. Water spewed up in their wakes and Coryn quickly ducked her head and slid into a slow breaststroke down to the other end of the pool.

At first it took just grim determination to swim the length of the lane. She forced herself back and forth a half-dozen times, alternating from sidestroke to crawl then floating on her back, making her arms propel her.

Gradually some of the tension began to drift away as she concentrated on her swimming.

That was why she came here, to blank out the shock, sadness, grief she felt about her mother's illness. The unfairness of it all would gnaw, and the grinding pain would activate as she plowed through the resisting water. Slowly the tears would come and she would let them. No one saw or noticed. The marathon swimming went on on either side of her.

Kicking her feet, arms pulling strongly with each stroke, she fought back the terror of what they might be facing further along. Here she could let the tears she dared not cry at home in the presence of either parent flow. Running in rivulets down her cheeks and no one would see. She could swim under the surface of the water, come up, her face wet. Nobody paid any attention. Everyone was here for single-minded fitness goals, exercise, physical training.

She turned the panic into energy. The fear. She had to admit she was afraid. Afraid of what she might be called upon to do in the future. Her parents had always sheltered *her,* protected *her.* Shielded her as much as possible from disappointment, from hurt, from harm. She had lived most of her life in the cocoon of their love. Now it was her turn and she was afraid she wasn't up to it. *She had to be up to it. There was no other way. There was no one else.*

*"I can't go through this alone,"* her father had said. Neither can I! Coryn screamed silently.

Coryn felt the sobs coming, coming up through her tight chest, into her throat, choking her as she turned her head, gasping for air.

At the far end of the pool, she reached out with one hand, pulled herself against the side. The swimmers on both sides kept on swimming. She put her head down against the hands gripping the rail. Oh, God, I can't, I can't! *Yes you can, and you will.* She raised her head. Had someone spoken? *I will never leave you or forsake you.* Joshua 1:5. Those words from scripture learned a long time ago returned to her memory. She remembered she had received a medal in Sunday school for memorizing. She did not have to go it alone.

Strange, common thought was that it was in church you received inspiration, guidance, comfort. But isn't God everywhere? His spirit is not dependent on time or place or circumstance. He had given her this as a tool. Swimming as a coping skill. And it was working. She emerged from the pool, her body tingling from the exercise, knowing it had been worth the effort.

She pulled herself up, sat on the side of the pool, stripped off her cap, shook out her hair. She could go home now. Somehow comforted, strengthened, to face whatever there was to face.

She showered, changed into her sweatshirt, pulled on pants, sneakers, then went out into the damp morning. She drove through the quiet streets, past houses where people were just getting up, cooking breakfast, men dressing for work, children for school. She saw a boy on a bike delivering newspapers.

Then just a little ahead, on the left-hand side of the road, coming through the mist, she saw a figure, jogging. As she got closer, she could see who it was. Her hands tightened on the steering wheel. She saw his face, his intense expression. Hair dampened into waves fell on his broad forehead as he ran steadily forward. Mark. She passed him, not knowing whether he saw or recognized her. For a moment all the old feelings she had for him welled up within her. If only it could have been different…if they had met some other time…under other circumstances. It might have been different.…

# *Chapter Nineteen*

One morning after her swim, while waiting to turn in her locker key, Coryn happened to glance at the bulletin board. There, notices of various community events were posted. Her gaze caught an announcement.

CAREGIVERS HELD MONDAY
AFTERNOONS AT 3:00 P.M.

If you are or know someone who is a caregiver for a loved one, this is a group of concerned people who meet once a week to share their problems, receive help, advice, encouragement.

Coryn turned away, handed her key to the clerk behind the counter and started to leave the building. But something drew her back. Quickly she pulled out a small memo pad and pencil from her handbag, jotted down the address of the meeting.

Driving home, she wondered why she'd done that. She remembered Dr. Iverson's answer to her question,

*What can I do?* "Find out all you can about your mother's disease so you'll know what to expect, how to help your father." She hadn't really done that. All she'd done was watch helplessly as her mother became slower, more forgetful and vague. What she *had* done was take care of herself. Keep herself from falling to pieces. But that wasn't enough. More was going to be required of her. She needed just what that group seemed to offer—advice, encouragement. Maybe she should check it out. Go at least once. See what it was like.

It took all Coryn's inner strength to go to that first meeting. It was admitting something she didn't want to admit. That, as a family, they were in severe crisis. To acknowledge that they were facing something so dreadful, so frightening that she had almost become paralyzed. That first time Coryn had sat there in the circle of folding chairs, her arms crossed, not entering in, not sharing, not participating.

But something had happened there. She had seen people share their pain, their raw grief, pour out their deepest feelings, some of them negative ones. No one had criticized, no one had condemned or told them they shouldn't be feeling that way. All Coryn had seen was warmth, compassion, friendliness. There had even been some laughter.

She had gone back the next Monday and the next. Then one day a middle-aged man spoke about his wife. He was a good-looking man in his middle fifties, an executive type, solid and certainly not someone you would suspect of deep emotion or sensitivity.

"Alzheimer's is called the 'long goodbye.' It's not

like a stroke or a heart attack where a loved one goes suddenly, quickly. The family has to watch the person they know and love die by inches, lose them little by little. It's harder than most people realize. They desperately want to hold on to the former personality they knew, not accept this stranger that person has become.'' His voice cracked. ''I'm losing my dearest friend, the love of my life –''

At that point something inside Coryn broke. Tears welled up in her then poured out like an erupting dam. She put her head in her hands and sobbed heartbrokenly. She felt a stir around her, then arms hugging her, hands patting her, someone handing her a box of tissues. They just let her cry. When at last she came to a stop, she felt surrounded by love and understanding, sympathy of the deepest kind.

After that, Mondays were as much a part of her healing process as the daily swims. Coryn knew she was changing, that there was a new depth of feeling for others, for suffering of all kinds. She was growing and, as in all kinds of growth, there were growing pains.

Reading became another resource. Not the bestsellers and novels that she used to enjoy. Now she searched bookstore shelves, asked some of the members in the Monday group what books they had found helpful. She regularly went to bookstores and concentrated on the self-help and religion sections. She found C. S. Lewis's and Catherine Marshall's books particularly helpful.

Still, she felt she should do something more. She had the distinct feeling that more was expected of her.

What, she wasn't sure. She prayed that God would direct her path. Tell her what to do.

Every day when she drove to the pool, she passed Shady Nook Rest Home. She wasn't sure when she first began to notice the sign. However, after she did, she could not seem *not* to see it.

Coryn had a natural aversion for nursing homes. From TV she retained fleeting impressions of corridors filled with old people strapped into wheelchairs, others leaning on walkers. Wrinkled faces, with vacant expressions, bleary eyes, hollow cheeks and waddling chins. She suppressed a shudder just imagining what it must be like at Shady Nook. What it would be like to be confined there.

Day after day, an urgency grew within Coryn that she was supposed to do something. Take some kind of step. Although she recoiled from the idea, the conviction grew that it had something to do with Shady Nook Rest Home. It took root in her mind and heart. At last she could avoid it no longer.

One morning on her way back from swimming, something compelled her to swing into the Shady Nook parking lot. For a full minute, she stayed in the car, her hands clutching the steering wheel, not wanting to let go.

"I don't want to do this," she said aloud between clenched teeth.

It didn't matter. In another few seconds she was out of the car, walking up the steps and entering the lobby of the overheated building. Immediately the smells of disinfectant, cooking, plastic mingled, wrinkling Coryn's nose in distaste.

She forced herself to go up to the reception desk where a plump, gray-haired woman talked on the phone. Coryn felt the strong urge to turn and run. But she made herself stay until the woman was off the phone. She glanced at Coryn. "Yes?" she said. "Visiting hours are not until two."

"I didn't come to visit," Coryn said tightly. Then she heard herself ask, "I just wondered if you needed volunteers? Helpers of any kind."

The woman's eyebrows lifted alarmingly. She looked at Coryn skeptically, taking in her still-damp hair, her gray sweats, running shoes. "Do we need help? Volunteers? We certainly do. What do you have in mind?"

"What do you need doing?"

"Good heavens! Everything! Clerical. Setting up food trays. Feeding patients. Taking them to physical therapy. You name it, we need it," the woman declared. Then, as if in second thought, "Do you have any training?"

"No, not really. But I think I could do any of the things you just mentioned."

"Good girl!" The woman smiled broadly. "When can you start?"

It wasn't easy. It was very hard for Coryn. But she knew she was doing what she'd been directed to do.

Soon Coryn became a regular volunteer at Shady Nook Rest Home. In order to report to work the early shift, Coryn got her hair cut in a short style to minimize the drying time after her morning swim.

The overworked staff at Shady Nook Rest Home

welcomed her gratefully. She soon became one of their favorites.

She was dependable, reliable. She always showed up on time, never phoned in with excuses not to report, worked diligently at whatever task assigned.

It didn't take long for Coryn to realize she was the one who was benefiting most by coming. Every time she spooned soup into a mouth twisted by a stroke, wiped dribble from a chin, assisted some disabled elderly person from bed to chair, it was as if she heard an inner encouragement, "Assuredly, I say to you, inasmuch as you did it to one of the least of these My brethren, you did it to Me."

Coryn knew she was on training ground. One day, she didn't know when, or how soon, her own beloved mother might need this kind of care. God was preparing her for whatever was to come.

One afternoon as Coryn was stacking lunch trays into their rack in the kitchen area, Mrs. Dilworth the director of the nursing home spoke to her.

"Miss Dodge, I'd like to speak to you for a few minutes, if you would stop by my office before you leave today?"

"Yes, of course," Coryn replied, wondering what she had done or not done, why and about what the director wanted to talk to her. She finished her task then went on to spray the vinyl table tops in the dining room and wipe the chrome surfaces. Funny, how she took pride in doing even the menial tasks assigned. It was also a matter of pride, doing a job well. Better watch that, she reminded herself, remembering what

C. S. Lewis warned in *Mere Christianity.* Trying to be perfect at whatever you do had its traps.

Finishing up, Coryn took off her blue volunteer smock and hung it in her locker in the staff room. Then went down the hall to the director's office.

At her knock a pleasant voice invited her to come in. Coryn opened the door and entered. She had never been in here before and she was surprised to find it looked decidedly unbusinesslike. The walls were painted a warm coral, a flourishing philodendron in a basket hung in the window and on a desk was a blossoming African violet.

Mrs. Dilworth gave her a welcoming smile, "Do sit down, Miss Dodge. I've been wanting to talk to you but as you know this place keeps me extremely busy and the days go by...well, you understand."

Coryn took a seat in one of two velour upholstered chairs opposite the director's desk.

Mrs. Dilworth appeared to be in her mid-forties. She had a brisk, professional manner but twinkling eyes behind half glasses which hung from a chain around her neck. Her hair was a shade of auburn that perhaps was not its natural color but always perfectly coiffed.

"I particularly want to commend you on your performance as a volunteer. Ever since you started here I've had glowing reports from members of our staff as well as our residents."

"Thank you, that's very kind," Coryn murmured, pleased by the compliment.

"The reason I've asked you to come for this little chat today is, I wonder if you'd like to take on another kind of work here? You see, I've observed you, Miss

Dodge, and your natural rapport with the ladies you come in contact with as a volunteer. You seem to be able to make them feel that you're really interested in them as individuals, make them feel special."

"Well, I've come to be very fond of them."

"Yes, that's obvious, Miss Dodge." Mrs. Dilworth beamed. "That is why I'd like to suggest that you take over our Arts and Crafts program one day a week. The person who has been doing this is moving. Her husband is being transferred and we've been looking for someone who is creative and patient, *that* is almost equally important here. Some of our residents have various disabilities that make them unable to be very dextrous, as you very well know—but they enjoy the break in their schedule that this sort of change offers and they can try making simple things." She paused. "I've seen the little cards and things you put on the trays and I've been touched as well as impressed. It is the sort of extra effort we like our residents to receive but seldom have been able to supply it." Mrs. Dilworth tilted her head inquiringly. "Do you think you may want to take this on?"

"I've never thought of doing something like this. The things you mention, well, I just did them for fun, really. And the ladies *do* seem to enjoy and appreciate them."

"Exactly. That's just the sort of thing I mean." Mrs. Dilworth nodded her head. "Easy, simple crafts that most of them will be able to handle. And just have a good time trying."

The more she thought about it the more excited

Coryn became. All sorts of craft projects began forming in her mind.

The two women began exchanging various ideas Coryn could teach the ladies to make with a minimum of materials or skill.

"I see I had only to mention this and you're already way ahead of me." Mrs. Dilworth smiled. "We can get well-intentioned people, fine volunteers to help us with the practical tasks but people of creativity and artistic ability are not so readily available. It would be a great favor to us if you would agree to do this job."

It began as such a small thing but within weeks the afternoon Arts and Crafts session in the recreation room became the focal point of the week. Certainly for the residents and also for Coryn. She found she was always trying to think of new items to present to her eager participants each time. The best part of it was their enthusiasm. How the old eyes shone with anticipation when she arrived those afternoons, how even the ones whose hands were troubled with arthritis and couldn't handle a pair of scissors easily, still looked forward to the afternoon. Often the room rang with laughter, and quavery voices were raised happily as they worked and chatted.

One afternoon, Coryn was cleaning up after a hilarious session making Easter bunny baskets for centerpieces at each table in the dining room. She found Mrs. Dilworth standing at the entrance of the recreation room.

"Well, Miss Dodge, you seem to have had a successful afternoon. All the ladies seemed cheerful and lively."

"Yes, it was great fun," Coryn agreed.

Mrs. Dilworth's expression turned thoughtful, "You've really done a remarkable job in this program. I wonder, have you ever thought of it as a career? Occupational therapy? There's such a great need for it. Not only in places such as this, but in other institutions for victims recuperating from accidents and other traumas, for the physically and mentally challenged. People with that spark of creativity and the most important ingredient, compassion and understanding are rare."

"I've never even considered it. In fact, I don't think I ever considered there was a career possibility in work like this," Coryn answered.

"I suggest you should look into it. I believe the local college has a course. Classes you could take. Why don't you check it out?"

Mrs. Dilworth planted a small seed that day. One that began to grow in Coryn the more she thought about it. What she had been desperately searching for was a purpose for her life. Now a new direction had been pointed out to her. One for which she had a natural talent. A gift as Mrs. Dilworth had put it. Scripture said, "All good gifts come from above." Was this *her* gift?

Coryn was awed how it had come, by a seemingly circuitous route. Yet she was convinced nothing happened by chance. "God works in mysterious ways." Coryn had heard that phrase most of her life. Now she believed it.

When she investigated the courses the local college offered, she found there were two classes starting in the spring semester. She signed up for both. One was a psychology class, another in communications skills, both requisites for a degree as an occupational therapist. There were other courses she would have to take to earn enough credits to actually become a qualified therapist.

Coryn added school two evenings a week. For the first time in her life felt she was doing what she was supposed to be doing, that she had found her niche.

To have a goal for herself was the best therapy she could have found, she soon realized. Instead of groping just to maintain her own emotional balance in her increasingly difficult family situation, she now had a definite purpose, a potential new career, which offered her the fulfillment and satisfaction she'd been searching for.

# *April*

# *Chapter Twenty*

Recently, Mark had had trouble sleeping. He'd taken to watching late-night TV or reading until his eyelids grew heavy and he dropped off midsentence, the book fallen on his chest. He'd wake up sandy-eyed and sluggish, the bedside light still burning, the morning news programs coming on.

Since he'd stopped seeing Coryn he'd lost track of the passing of days, the weeks going by. He'd buried himself in work, laboring over his columns, writing at home in his study at his desk computer. Time didn't seem to have much meaning. It was just space to fill up.

Then one morning he was awakened by Ginny's small, round face close to his, bending over him. Tugging at his pajama sleeve, she said in an insistent voice, ''Wake up, Daddy.''

He blinked, struggling to get his eyes fully opened.

''Mrs. Aguilar is sick so you'll have to take me.''

He sat up on one elbow. ''Take you where?''

"To church, of course," she explained patiently.

"Church?" he echoed blankly.

The fuzziness in his brain began to clear and he also became aware that Mrs. Aguilar, bundled into a purple chenille bathrobe, smelling suspiciously of menthol, was standing in the bedroom doorway. A startling sight since Mark had never seen the housekeeper in anything but a flowered housedress, starched apron, her salt-and-pepper hair braided around her head in a neat coronet. Her face looked puffy and flushed, her eyes glazed.

"I'm sorry, Mr. Emery, I'm afraid I've got a flu bug," she croaked. She touched her gauze-swathed throat. Obviously it was a bad case. He had never known Mrs. Aguilar to have a day's sickness.

Still, he felt vaguely annoyed at the way both were staring at him. It wasn't enough that the one day a week he had to sleep in had been disturbed, they clearly expected something else. What it was hadn't yet sunk in. He managed to be reasonably sympathetic.

"That's too bad. You go back to bed. I'll manage breakfast." He reached for his bathrobe. "Have you taken anything?"

"Two aspirins and some tea with lemon," she replied.

"Daddy," Ginny began again, "you'll have to take me..."

"To church, Mr. Emery," Mrs. Aguilar said. "Maybe you've forgotten. Today is Easter Sunday and Ginny is in the program."

"*Easter?* What program?" he growled, knowing he sounded like a disgruntled bear.

"*Daddy!*" protested Ginny. "You *know*. I told you. It's the Flowering of the Cross. The kids bring flowers and put them on the cross. Mrs. Wiley, our Sunday school teacher, says it sym—sym—" Ginny's little face screwed up with the difficulty of pronouncing the word.

"Symbolizes," Mrs. Aguilar supplied.

"Symbolizes," Ginny repeated carefully. "Symbolizes the Resurrection," she finished proudly.

Mark was sitting up now, acutely conscious that Mrs. Aguilar had not budged. She was still standing in the doorway, arms crossed. "Well, now, look, honey, Daddy isn't much for..." He stopped, ashamed of making excuses before Ginny's solemn brown eyes, Mrs. Aguilar's accusatory stare. He swallowed and began again. "What I mean is, why don't we go somewhere for breakfast, say, the Pancake House? You'd like that, wouldn't you? Then, maybe this afternoon—"

Ginny shook her head vehemently. "No, Daddy. I *have* to go to church. It's *Easter*. Besides, they're counting on me for the program. We got the flowers yesterday, yellow daisies, bluebells." Her prim little voice turned suddenly hopeful. "Couldn't we go to the Pancake House *after* church?"

From the doorway, Mrs. Aguilar said pointedly, "These things mean a great deal to a child, Mr. Emery."

Mark sighed. He'd lost. They'd won.

"Okay, I'll grab a quick shower and shave. How much time have I got?"

Ginny twirled happily out of the room, calling back

over her shoulder, ''Service is at eleven, but *we* have to be there by ten-thirty!''

Mark hauled himself out of bed and into the bathroom. Under the needle spray of the showerhead, he came stingingly awake. He felt guilty. He'd only half listened to Ginny's regaling him with her Sunday-school class's plans. The truth was, he'd been preoccupied with thoughts of Coryn.

Had he done right breaking it off? So abruptly? There was so much at stake in making a commitment. Finding the right person for himself was one thing. Finding the right stepmother for Ginny was something else altogether. He hadn't been sure how Coryn felt about taking on a ready-made family. And was she really over that relationship in L.A.? She hadn't talked much about that, either. No question he had been physically attracted to Coryn. She was lovely to look at, but more than that superficial beauty was intelligence, humor. There was a special quality about her, a sensitivity that was definitely appealing. He had never really asked her how she felt about children. He didn't know. And someone else's child...an adopted one? But she had seemed to love Ginny and Ginny had taken to her right away.

Had he made things too complicated? Put up too many obstacles? Ones of his own making? Afraid of risking rejection? Had he messed up royally?

He was just toweling off when a sharp knock came at the bathroom door. ''Mr. Emery, it is ten o'clock,'' came Mrs. Aguilar's husky voice.

''Okay. I'm almost done.'' He lathered his face,

quickly started shaving. Next he heard Ginny's impatient, "Daddy, aren't you ready yet?"

"In a minute!" he snapped, then knowing he sounded cross, added, "Honey."

She was waiting, all dressed in a new ruffled dress, lace-trimmed white anklets, shiny black-patent Mary Janes. She looked adorable and Mark felt the familiar heart tug, wishing Shari could see her. *Maybe she can,* a strange voice seemed to say in his head.

"Here are her flowers, Mr. Emery." Mrs Aguilar handed him a fragrant small bouquet wrapped in moistened plastic wrap.

"Hurry, Daddy, I don't want to be late."

Mark exchanged an indulgent smile with Mrs. Aguilar.

"Okay, we're all set." And he held out his hand for Ginny to take.

Outside, a pale sun was pushing through the clouds in an overcast sky. North-coast weather, even on Easter, Mark thought as he put Ginny in the car. He helped her fasten her seat belt so her dress wouldn't be crushed. Then he lay the flowers carefully on the back seat, got in, started the engine and backed out of the driveway.

He walked with Ginny to the door of her Sunday-school class and left her there. She was smiling shyly and clutching her flowers. The teacher was at the door and seemed surprised to see him. He explained about the housekeeper, and Mrs. Wiley nodded sympathetically. "There's a lot of it going around. But it's nice to see *you,* Mr. Emery. I know Ginny is happy you came."

Mark felt the warmth rise into his face. He didn't need to be reminded he hadn't been to church since Shari's funeral. He couldn't explain why. It wasn't that he wasn't a believer. He *was*. He and Shari had gone to church regularly. It was just that after she was gone... Well, he didn't have to explain to anyone. God knew why. At least, the God Mark understood did.

There were clusters of people moving up the steps and into the church. Men in dark suits, women in pretty pastel dresses. After a whispered confrontation with an usher, Mark was escorted to one of the pews marked Parents. Luckily there was a seat on the aisle.

Above the altar was a magnificent stained-glass window depicting Christ as the Good Shepherd. Mark had always loved the Bible story of the one out of the ninety-nine that Jesus searched for until he found it and brought it back into the fold. Sunlight was beginning to stream in through the glass, illuminating and enhancing the colors. Mark sat in quiet contemplation of a favorite image, feeling a certain peace beginning to flow over him.

The organ began playing and white-surpliced choir members filed in and took their places, voices raised loudly, proclaiming, "This is the day that the Lord hath made, Let us rejoice and be glad in it."

There was a stirring and shuffling as the congregation stood, and with the rustling of the pages of the hymnals joined in the chorus. From the back of the church the children came down the aisle to the seats reserved for them in front. Ginny allowed herself one sidelong glance and a tiny smile of satisfaction as she passed and saw he was safely seated with the other parents.

With the close of the opening hymn, a youthful-looking minister accompanied by rosy-cheeked boys in red cassocks and starched surplices, entered from the sacristy. He mounted the pulpit and waited until, with great shifting and creaking, people settled into the wooden benches. A hushed expectancy filled the church.

In a surprisingly deep, resonant voice the minister declared, "Today we celebrate the glorious good news. 'I am the Resurrection and the Life. He that believeth in Me shall not die...'"

But Shari was dead, Mark mentally corrected. "*...but shall liveth forever in the place I have prepared for those who love Me.*" The phrase seemed to echo in Mark's mind. Shari had loved Jesus with all her heart. Her whole life had been a testimony, a witness. She had touched everyone she encountered. After her death, people Mark hadn't even known had written, sent condolence cards, messages. Shari couldn't ever be *really* gone, as long as people who loved her remembered.

Mark brought his attention back to what the young minister was saying so earnestly. He found himself leaning forward intently.

"Two of the hardest things in the world are to accept death and to accept life. To accept death only requires our faith. The great tragedy is not accepting the miracle of life. The gift God has given each of us with endless possibilities. Finding beauty in all the things around us, nature, creatures, weather, the people we know, the people we are yet to meet, who will bring us new evidences of God's caring. Life has many unexplained mysteries. We must accept them all as His gifts. The light, the shadow, the pain as well as the joyous times of happiness, and laughter. He wants us to meet it all with courage, serenity and hope."

The minister pointed to the bare cross at the foot of the altar. "The fact of death must be accepted but not with an unforgiving grief. Love that existed in life is real and lasts beyond death. What we have shared, what we have given and received on earth will remain forever."

Mark stirred uncomfortably. The words were hitting tender spots, wounded places. Somehow what the man was saying sounded vaguely familiar. Then he remembered he had been watching Bill Moyers's program "World of Ideas" on TV, and one of the guests had said, *"If you can accept death, you can affirm life."* This minister was saying practically the same thing.

"This is the day of our Lord's resurrection. Perhaps this is a day of a new beginning. We must look into our own hearts and see that here is the joy of expectation, the hope of our faith and the love that overcomes death."

The children, prompted by their hovering teachers, began to come forward. The older ones twined greenery around the cross made of florist's wire, then one by one the smaller children placed their flowers in the empty spaces until the outline of the symbol of death had become a bower of colorful blossoms and fragrance. Glory had replaced defeat.

The minister lifted his arms, inviting the congregation to join him in the triumphant declaration, "Let us say together, 'Christ has risen. Christ has risen, indeed.'"

Mark heard voices all around him ringing out in joyous affirmation, singing "Our God Reigns," a hymn he recalled from his own boyhood Sunday-school days. His throat was too tight to join in but he did so in his heart.

He watched as Ginny went back to her place with the other children. His heart twisted with love. Ginny deserved more than a distracted father, a man clinging to the past, not sure of the future. Things were going to change.

Love was worth the risk. He wouldn't not have had Shari even for the short time they had had together. Now he felt free to open his heart again. To Coryn? Maybe. If it wasn't too late.

Outside the church, after the service, Mark thought he caught a glimpse of Coryn and Mrs. Dodge But the courtyard was filled with people greeting each other and wishing "Happy Easter," parents exchanging compliments on their children's performance. The parking lot was crowded as well so he couldn't have got through to speak to them anyway. Besides, what would he say? He felt awkward. Embarrassed at the way he had handled the situation with Coryn. Had he let it go too long? Was there some way he could make amends? He should at least try.

Ginny left the group of little girls with whom she had been chatting, and ran up to Mark. "Wasn't it nice, Daddy? Didn't you like it?"

Mark felt his throat tighten. He smiled down at her. Held out his hand. "Yes, honey. It was very nice."

"Did I do good, Daddy?"

"You did wonderful!" He grinned, feeling something stinging at the back of his eyes.

"Now can we go to the Pançake House, Daddy?" she asked with a little skip.

"You bet." Mark grinned again. Now they could do a lot of things.

# Chapter Twenty-One

Mark couldn't sleep. Nothing new. He was finding it harder and harder to go to sleep at a decent hour. The techno thriller he'd read to get drowsy had only served the opposite purpose, leaving him wide-awake and tense with their near-life correspondence to the daily TV news.

He got up, got a glass of water and looked over the bookcase under the bedroom window for something to read that might be boring enough to induce sleep. For some reason, he pulled out Shari's well-thumbed copy of *The Road Less Traveled* by Scott Peck. Shari had bought paperback editions of bestsellers. She'd liked to highlight, underline and make notes in the margins of books she particularly liked. She'd tried to get him to read this one. Somehow he never had.

Mark went back to bed, thumped the pillows into a bunch behind his head and settled himself in his usual methodical way.

Mark's hands gripped the edges of the book as he

read page after page. This writer knew what he was talking about. It was as though he understood Mark's reluctance to follow his heart with Coryn Dodge. He was *afraid.* Afraid of being rejected, afraid of the pain that might be involved in getting to know someone, letting them know you.

Everything that makes living meaningful, rich, interesting requires putting yourself out there—being vulnerable, if you will, to whatever comes with loving. But, Peck maintained, "loving is worth the risk."

Mark lay there holding the book, stunned. It was almost as if he heard Shari's voice. She had liked to read aloud to him, paragraphs, excerpts from books she was excited about. Sometimes, caught up in his own book, he had only half listened. Tonight he listened.

He got up, and after a moment's hesitation, went to the phone and dialed the Dodges' number.

The phone rang and rang. There was no answer. Slowly Mark replaced the receiver. He realized he'd made a mistake cutting off his relationship with Coryn. Could he explain that somehow. Or was it too late? His determination strengthened. Better late than never. He'd try reaching her again tomorrow.

The phone echoed hollowly in the empty house.

Driving home through the rainy night from the airport where she had just put her parents on the plane, Coryn's thoughts were muddled.

The windshield wipers made a squeaky sound as they swept back and forth. It had been an unusually wet spring. It had been raining for what seemed weeks.

On the spur of the moment, her father had declared he had to go find some sunshine.

He had made reservations for Clare and him at the Silverado Country Club in the Napa Valley, and although invited to accompany them, Coryn had refused. She urged them to go without her. They would both feel better after a few long, lazy sun-drenched days in the valley.

The phone was ringing when she came inside the house. By the time she picked up the receiver, there was only the buzzing sound on the line that meant the party who had called had hung up.

The message machine wasn't turned on, she noticed. A clutching sensation in her stomach reminded her of recent events, of Dr. Iverson's warnings that things would grow gradually worse. Clare was always turning things off that should be left on, as well as doing the opposite. Coryn went around behind her mother, checking, righting these lapses of concentration. It was nerve-racking. Worse still was the realization that this was only the beginning of things getting worse.

An involuntary shudder shivered through her. It was happening, irrevocably. More missing pieces all the time. Coryn couldn't deny it, even though she wished she could.

She wished she had someone to confide in, someone who would understand, just by listening. She couldn't bring herself to go to one of her girlfriends. Their lives were full, happy, and they had their own problems. No one wanted to carry another's burden. Especially this kind. The kind that ended only in tragedy.

Who had called? Coryn wondered. Could it have

been Mark? It had been weeks since he had come on his sad "mission of mercy." He had seemed—what? As if he wanted to explain or apologize for not calling. That had made *her* feel embarrassed. She didn't want him to feel obligated. Yet there were so many unresolved things between them. She wondered about Ginny and the new kitten.

*Stop feeling sorry for yourself!* Face it. Whatever had almost happened between them had been abruptly cut off. His choice. Obviously. Maybe it was better this way. She had nearly fallen in love with him. Correction. She *had* fallen in love with him. And Ginny. She had truly loved the little girl, wanted to make life more—everything for her. For a few weeks, happiness had seemed possible for the three of them. She had sensed Mark felt that, too, but... Well, she had been wrong before.

Mark sat at his desk in the newsroom of the *Rockport Times.* His In box was overflowing, his Out box just as full. His computer was booted up, but the monitor was blank. He couldn't concentrate. He flipped through his notebook. He had dozens of scribbled pages of notes taken for the story he was working on. The feature the managing editor was waiting for. It looked like Chinese. He reached for the phone, dialed the number and waited. The buzz of a busy signal came. He put down the phone, waited a few minutes, tried again. The same irritating buzz.

How could it stay busy so long? He slammed down the receiver, frowning. He keyed in a header, typed "by Mark Emery." That's as far as he got. He reached for the phone again. This time he stayed with it even though it still gave off the busy signal. Forget it. Get to work. Maybe it wasn't such a good idea, after all, to try to reach Coryn. Maybe he'd burned his bridges with her. Maybe…

But maybe there was still a chance. He picked up the phone and dialed again. This time it rang!

Good! He tapped his pencil on the desktop, waiting. Waiting. There must be someone there. It had been busy only seconds ago. Why didn't someone answer? Frustrating.

Abruptly he replaced the receiver. Turned off the computer. Stood, grabbed his jacket, shrugged into it and walked through the room humming with other reporters' activity. Someone must be at home at 183 Chestnut Hills Drive. He'd take a chance it was Coryn.

There was something wrong with Ranger. For a few days he had hardly stirred from his pillowed basket in the utility room.

The morning after her parents left for Napa Valley, Coryn opened the door from the kitchen and looked in. Ranger lifted his head, his tail wagged feebly. At once she was kneeling on the floor beside him, stroking his head. "What's the matter, old fella?"

At the sound of her voice, he raised clouded eyes adoringly. She touched him gently and he struggled to move, but could not. Coryn let her hand smooth down over his body, his hind legs, to see if he was in pain anywhere. He did not seem to be. He simply could not get up.

Worried, Coryn refilled his water dish then brought

it back and placed it within easy reach. But he did not make any effort to drink. Should she call the vet? Or try to take him to the animal clinic? Hands shaking she looked up the number in the phone book and called.

When she explained her concern and described Ranger's condition, the vet's secretary said, "Well, our records show he *is* fifteen, Miss Dodge. That's quite an age for a dog."

Coryn felt instant resentment. What was that supposed to mean? The dog was *sick,* not *dying*...then she felt herself tremble, or *was* he?

"If you want to bring him in..." The crisp voice on the other end of the line sounded dubious, "We can schedule him in at three-thirty this afternoon."

Eight hours from now! Anything could happen before then. She hung up numbly and went back to Ranger. She sat down beside him, feeling helpless, infinitely sad. Ranger gave a long shuddering sigh that quivered the length of his body. Automatically she scratched behind his ears, smoothed his fur. After a while he shut his eyes and seemed to sleep. Coryn got up, tiptoed into the kitchen. She poured herself coffee, tried to swallow it over the hard lump in her throat.

She stood looking out the kitchen window. Ranger had been a large part of her life ever since the day her father had brought the silky black, wiggly Lab puppy home for her. They had run, romped together, he wheeling, jumping and barking when she used the swings in the backyard or threw balls into the basket over the garage door. He was always waiting for her at the gate when she got home from school. Her mother said when Ranger heard the school bus, his ears jerked up and he went to the door barking to be let out to run to meet her.

When she came home from college for vacations, he seemed ecstatic with happiness. He was always eager to go with her, walking or in the car…until this time. Coryn felt guilty that when she was in L.A. she had hardly thought about him. She had been too preoccupied with Jason….

She turned and went back where Ranger lay. His breath was coming in slow trembling sighs. He's going, Coryn thought. He's going to die. Oh, Ranger. She stifled a sob.

She heard the sound of wheels on the gravel driveway and hurried to the window in time to see the Sanders Landscape Service truck pull to a stop in front. Her parents employed Joe Sanders to take care of the lawn, to keep the hedges trimmed and the flower beds weeded. Her father didn't have time anymore. She saw Joe get out, pull his tools from the back of the truck.

It was comforting somehow to see Joe, the solid, steady strength of him out there while she kept her vigil inside. It wasn't long. When she went back to sit beside Ranger again, he had stopped breathing. He had died quietly. Coryn let the tears pour down her cheeks.

She covered him with an old soft blanket then went outside to where Joe was pruning the branches of the pyracantha bushes.

Her voice shook as she told him what had happened. ''I'm going to bury him up on the hillside behind the house,'' she said. ''But I'll need your help to lift him and get him up there.''

"Sure, Miss Dodge, be glad to. We can put him in the wheelbarrow, that'll make it easier." He put down his clippers and went to his truck. He wheeled close to the back door then followed Coryn inside. Together, they carried Ranger's body, wrapped in the blanket, outside and placed it carefully in the wheelbarrow.

"Would you want me to bury him for you, Miss Dodge?"

Fighting tears, Coryn shook her head. "No, thanks, Joe, he was my dog. I want to say goodbye to him by myself."

"Yep. I understand. That dog was sure enough *your* dog." Joe nodded. "But I can wheel him up there, can't I? It's pretty heavy."

"Thanks, Joe, that would be fine." Silently they made the journey. Coryn carrying the shovel Joe had handed her, he pushing the wheelbarrow.

He lifted the dog out of the barrow and placed him on the grass. He took off his duck-billed cap for a moment before replacing it then walked back down the hill.

Coryn began to dig. The earth was moist from the recent rains, but it was still hard work. She was breathing hard, and perspiration beaded her forehead and upper lip. Ranger was a big dog. She wanted his grave to be long and deep enough for him. She dug hard. Her heart was pounding, she was panting with the exertion. She wasn't sure how long she had been digging, when she heard movement behind her, her name spoken. "Coryn."

Her shovel midair, she spun around and saw Mark coming up on the crest of the hill. She let the shovel drop, leaned on the handle, slowing her deep breaths. Finally, she gasped, "Mark!" Then, "What are *you* doing here?"

"I've been trying to get you. Tried to call last night, but there was no answer. Then this morning, I called several times and the line was busy. I thought I'd just take a chance, come by this morning and see you."

Coryn stared at him, bewildered. Why had he been calling her? Trying to reach her? It didn't make sense. She glanced at Ranger's blanket-covered body then back at Mark.

He nodded. "Joe Sanders told me what happened. I'm sorry." He paused. "Really sorry."

At the sincere sympathy in his voice, tears rushed into her eyes again. She couldn't stop them, and a harsh sob thrust from her throat.

In a minute, he was beside her, arms around her, holding her close, his chin on her head. She leaned against him, sobbing. "I know, I know," she heard him whisper soothingly.

In a world of terrorist bombs, civil wars and upheaval all over the globe, to some it might have seemed almost shameful to cry over the death of an old dog. Mark had lost his wife! What must he think of this grief? But as he continued to hold her, gently stroking her hair, her cheek resting against his shoulder, Coryn had a revelation. Mark *knew* how she felt. By his knowing, he made it not seem foolish to grieve so for a dog. In fact, his empathy made it seem right to mourn for a dog you have loved.

After a while, her sobs had turned to long, drawn-out gasps. He handed her a clean handkerchief to wipe her eyes and blow her nose. Sniffling, she said, "I didn't mean to dump on you like that."

"Not at all. I'm glad I was here. I understand."

Coryn looked up at him and knew he did.

"Let me help," he said quietly. He took off his tan corduroy sport coat and laid it on the ground. Then he picked up the shovel she had let drop, and began lifting large shovelfuls of dirt.

She leaned back against a nearby tree, watching him work in a smooth, even swinging movement.

At last the hole was dug, long and wide enough to gently lift Ranger and place him on a pile of leaves Coryn had gathered to cushion him in the ground. They both stood looking down at him for a minute then Coryn felt Mark take her hand in his, press it. She felt he was joining her in a silent prayer. Her heart was so full she could not voice the words. But it was a prayer of thanksgiving to God for having had Ranger as long as she had. From the time he had been a shiny, black puppy, through all the years of loving companionship. A prayer for allowing her the privilege of seeing him out of life with dignity and affection.

After that quiet moment, slowly they took turns shoveling the dirt over him, packing it down. They both searched for stones to circle the spot where he lay.

"I think Dad will want to have some kind of marker made for him," Coryn said. "Thank you for coming, Mark. Your being here just now—well, it meant a great deal."

"I'm glad I was here," he said. "I want to be here for you, Coryn. That is, if you'll let me."

Coryn felt too worn-out, her heart too bruised to take in all that might mean. Maybe later, when she had had time to heal a little, she would remember and think about what was unspoken between them. Now it was enough to appreciate his sensitivity and compassion for what she was feeling.

Mark replaced the shovel in the wheelbarrow and together they walked back down the hill.

# *Chapter Twenty-Two*

The rain splashed noisily on the flagstone patio, played a staccato drum on the windows. Coryn was curled on the living-room sofa, reading. Earlier, her father had called from Silverado Country Club saying they were going to stay a few days longer.

"Your mother's really enjoying being here, looking tanned and rested. I think it's done her a world of good."

Coryn found herself puzzled by her father's confidence. Was her mother really doing that well? She had her good days and bad days and maybe that's what he was reporting. Today. It was just as well. To live each day as it came, praying for strength to get through whatever lay ahead. That's what she was trying to do.

Since Dr. Iverson had confirmed her mother's diagnosis, Coryn had read everything she could find about Alzheimer's. The Caregivers group had been immensely helpful. She had tried to persuade her father to come to one of the meetings. So far he hadn't. Was he still in denial in a way? What she had learned was that Alzheimer's disease was a treacherous one that affected the entire family. The unknown was the frightening part. It was, she thought, like those antique maps of the world where at the edge of the known world was printed the warning, *"Beyond this point lie sea dragons."* Coryn felt the more she learned the better she could anticipate these "dragons" and help her mother.

She had also bought inspirational tapes to listen to on her tape player earphones while out on her long walks. She knew she had to be strong and resourceful. It was necessary for at least one person in a family who had a member suffering from this illness to be as knowledgeable as possible.

Coryn had had to accept the harsh fact that as each day slipped by, more and more of her mother's world became blurred. Little by little the person Coryn had loved was becoming a stranger.

This acceptance had not come easily. It had come with anguish, weeping bitter tears long into many nights. In spite of her own pain, Coryn knew she had to be strong. She couldn't fall apart. Her father leaned on her. Most of all, she wanted to be able to see her mother safely home.

After she hung up from her father's call, she went back to the book she was reading. It was one she had found quite by chance. Or had it been? Coryn was beginning to find out that nothing in life was solely by chance. In this case, it had turned out to be exactly what she needed.

While browsing in a bookstore, she had discovered

C. S. Lewis books. In his works she had found a treasure trove of help. She had seen the movie *Shadowland* and been much moved by Lewis's love story with Joy Davidson. She hadn't realized he had written so many books, most of them spiritual. The title *A Grief Observed* seemed to leap out at her from among the others.

Although the content was profound, the writing style had such clarity it spoke to the very heart. Now she went back to what she was reading when the phone had rung.

In the poignant, poetic words the author warned that to love anything—even an animal—means risking heartbreak and pain. But the alternative, not to love at all, sealing your heart away in a coffin of selfishness, would change a feeling heart into something unbreakable, impenetrable. Even inhuman.

Coryn drew in her breath, put her finger in between the pages to mark her place, closed the book for a moment, letting the truth of those words sink in. That is exactly what she had been doing. Afraid of being hurt, she had withdrawn, closed herself off. Not even let herself feel the exquisite pain of Ranger's death fully. She had not allowed herself to love Ginny. She had never taken her the dollhouse family. What did it matter if Mark didn't feel romantically toward her, she still could be a friend to his little girl. And even to Mark. Certainly he had shown himself to be *her* friend and a friend to her family, when he had come to tell them the rumors about Clare, offer help.

He had surely been a friend the day she buried Ranger. Even before that...maybe. He said he'd been trying to get in touch with her, she had pulled back. Why? Wouldn't being friends with a person of Mark's caliber be a good thing? There were other kinds of love. Valuable kinds, enriching kinds. C. S. Lewis and Joy Davidson had started out being friends. Anything was possible if you allowed yourself to be open to it.

Just then the front doorbell sounded above the thundering downpour. She glanced at the mantel clock. It was after nine. Who could be coming by this late in the evening?

She turned on the porch light and looked through the peephole. She saw a man's figure, shoulders hunched against the wind and rain. She thought she recognized him. She unlocked and opened the door. A gust of rain-driven wind tugged at it, and she had to grip it with her other hand to keep it from blowing back upon her. It *was* Mark.

She became suddenly conscious of how she looked. She had on one of her dad's old flannel shirts, stirrup pants, fuzzy bedroom slippers. But she couldn't let Mark stand outside in the pouring rain.

"Coryn, I hope I'm not disturbing, interrupting anything?"

"No. Come in before you get soaked."

"Sure it's not a bad time? I came—on the spur of the moment. I was working late, or trying to, and was on my way home when—I think we need to talk… Is that okay?"

"Of course, come in." She ran her fingers through her hair self-consciously.

He stepped into the foyer, his raincoat was dripping. "I know I should have called but—actually, I drove around the block several times before stopping.'' He halted.

She was thinner than he remembered, looked as though she'd lost weight. Her eyes seemed larger than ever and her mouth, the mouth he had loved kissing, looked more vulnerable.

''Why don't you take off your coat, it's soaked.'' Coryn tried to sound normal. She felt tense, wondering what Mark had come to talk to her about. Whatever it was, it must be important. ''Come into the living room, I've got a fire going.''

He shrugged off his coat, handed it to her. She hung it up then he followed her into the living room.

''Are your parents here?'' he asked.

''No, they're still away.'' She gestured to the armchair on the other side of the fireplace and Mark sat down.

''How are things going? I mean, how is your mother?''

''At the moment, at least, Dad says she's doing fine. They're at the Silverado Country Club. Long, lazy days in the sun. He's playing a few rounds of golf. She's resting on the terrace.'' Coryn paused. ''There nothing's demanded of her. She doesn't have to perform even ordinary household tasks. So I think Dad feels she's improving.'' She sighed. ''Of course, we know that's impossible.''

''That's tough. I know you're going through some really hard times.''

''I guess no one escapes. Everyone has something in their lives...'' She paused, thinking of Mark's losing his wife just when everything seemed to be going so well for them.

"Yes, but when you're going through it, you can't help but ask why? Why me? Why us? But then you realize *why not me?*"

They were silent for a few moments, then Mark said, "You must be curious as to why I came by tonight. I hardly know where exactly to begin, but I think I owe you an apology."

Coryn held up one hand to halt him, shaking her head. "No, Mark, of course not—"

"But I think I do, Coryn. At least an explanation. I've been wrong about a lot of things and I'm afraid I hurt you. The last thing I ever wanted to do was that. Because, the truth is, I..." He stopped as if not knowing how to go on.

Coryn held her breath. Waiting. The only sound in the room was the slow ticking of the mantel clock, the hiss of the fire as a log broke apart. Her heart, however, had begun to beat loudly.

"The truth is, Coryn, I foolishly wrote you out of my life. Because I was afraid. Afraid it might not be real, but more than that, that it might be too painful. I wasn't willing to risk getting involved with anyone again. I felt I had all I could handle just bringing up Ginny, holding down my job. A relationship takes time to grow, and I wasn't willing to take a chance. It seemed too risky somehow."

"Mark, you don't have to tell me this. I think I understand. Right now my life is very complicated. My parents need me in a way they've never needed me before. I've a lot of growing to do myself to try to meet that need.'' She paused. ''A relationship can be absorbing and demanding and—''

''Yes, but that's where I was wrong, Coryn. Life doesn't get any smoother, any simpler. We both have difficulties, that's true. But this thing between us—the attraction I believe we both feel—if it is real, and I think it is, testing it will prove it. Sharing some of the burdens, as the saying goes, makes them lighter. And there are joys along the way, too. I don't regret having known the happy times with Shari. Not to have known her would have been far worse. A loss of another sort. Do you see what I mean?''

He reached over and took Coryn's hand, looked deeply into her eyes as if hoping to find what he was looking for there.

''Ginny misses you, Coryn. She's asked me several times when the three of us are going to do something together. Don't you think it would be worth it if we started spending time together again?''

Coryn gently pulled her hand away, stood up and moved over to the window. Rain pelted the windowpanes. She put her hands against the coolness of the glass then on her cheeks. They were flaming hot.

''Coryn.'' He spoke her name like a caress.

She felt shaky, her heart thrummed. Slowly she turned around from the window, faced him.

Mark rose, stood looking at her, waiting for her answer. Coryn's face was pale, there were smudges under her eyes as though she had not been sleeping much. But even without makeup, even in that shapeless baggy top, to him, she had never looked so appealing, so desirable. He said her name again, this time like a question. ''Coryn?''

She didn't remember taking a step toward him or him coming to her. She only knew that when Mark held out his arms she went into them and he was kissing her. There was a sweet tenderness in that kiss, as if time had lost all meaning.

When the kiss ended, Mark held her tight, then before loosening his hold, kissed her again. Slowly they drew apart. A marvelous feeling of warmth, gladness swept over her. She stepped back.

They gazed at each other with a new awareness, a kind of recognition of what had just happened. Mark's smile was wide, hopeful. Coryn's was wobbly.

''So, shall we give it another try?'' he asked.

Her breath quickened. ''Yes, let's,'' she whispered.

Later, sitting side by side on the sofa in front of the flickering fire, Mark's arm around her, they said all the things their hearts had longed to say to each other. They talked of the past, of Shari, of Ginny, of what they would do next and of the future.

''What it all comes down to is letting go, doesn't it?'' Mark asked. ''Letting go of old memories, old expectations, lovingly, without regret or bitterness. Remembering the happy times, hoping there will be others.

''No one has any guarantee of happiness, not for anyone. No matter what they try to gain or what they try to avoid. It's part of being human. None of us knows what lies ahead. Your parents didn't. Shari and I certainly didn't. But that didn't stop us from adopting Ginny and planning for a future with her.''

Coryn thought of all the time she had wasted looking back. Agonizing over the mistakes she had made with Jason. It all seemed a long time ago now, as if it had happened to somebody else.

She looked at Mark, and was caught up in the directness and honesty of his regard. He wasn't offering her protection, shelter from whatever storms there might be in this journey they would travel together. The journey to deeper understanding, of genuine friendship, of caring. He was asking her to risk loving him and Ginny.

Whatever "dragons" lay ahead, whatever was before her, with God's help and Mark beside her, she was ready to begin.

# *One Year Later*

# Epilogue

The couple and the child scrambled over the dunes onto a beach swept clean by the morning tide. A small golden retriever puppy, all paws and wagging tail, tumbled ahead of them, barking and sliding in the deeper sand.

The child, a little girl of about seven, turned, grinned widely, displaying two missing front teeth, laughed, shouted back to the man and woman following her, ‘‘Look, Goldie loves it!’’

Coryn met Mark’s eyes, and the glance between them was one of mutual awareness, amusement and affection.

They caught hands and swung them as they all walked down the beach. The waves rushed to shore in foamy curves. Above them, seagulls whirled, screeching, the sound mingling with Ginny’s happy cries to the rambunctious puppy.

Was it really possible to be this happy? Coryn asked herself.

The last five months had been the happiest of Coryn's life. They had been married in a small, private ceremony at the church they now attended. Coryn had wanted the wedding to take place before her mother had slipped too far from reality. Clare had looked beautiful in a blue lace gown, a wide-brimmed hat framing her still lovely face.

Coryn wanted Ginny to be part of the ceremony so she was the only attendant. Looking adorable in a smocked and ruffled dress and carrying a small bouquet of violets, she stood proud and happy at the altar with them, as they spoke their vows. It had been an unforgettable occasion.

Her mother's slow progress to oblivion was still taking its measured toll. Yet through it all, Coryn had found Mark and a love she had at one time thought out of her reach. Truly, God had been good. In every trial there was a triumph, in every loss gain.

Mark had taught her that grieving *is* the healing. To grieve the loss of a loved one is the path to healing. The length of time it takes is different for everyone. There is no set number of weeks, months, even years. It cannot be hastened. If the grieving is not suppressed, it does the healing. To be open to the grief and allow it to do its work is what is important. Help comes in all forms, understanding supportive friends, spiritual sources.

It had taken Mark more than three years to heal from Shari's death, to be ready, not to replace her, but to find another relationship was possible, to welcome the healing, to risk loving again.

Although her mother's death would not be the sudden death Shari's accident had been, but gradual, still Coryn had to learn to let her go, to allow the grieving to do its work.

Mark understood this and was there for Coryn as she slowly, painfully learned it, too. The puppy he had given her to mark their engagement, had been part of Mark's therapy to help her. Sensitively he had chosen a female *golden* retriever, not a black male one that might suppose she was meant to replace Ranger. Not to be afraid to love a dog again was another healing step for Coryn.

In the past months, Ginny had been an important part of that progress. There had been a touching bond between the little girl and Coryn's mother. They had spent time together in the sunny solarium of the Dodges' home where they had set up Ginny's dollhouse, now furnished and with its complete doll family. With some of Clare's favorite music playing in the background, Ginny had played happily in the quiet, dreamy presence of the older woman. Ginny had proven the center of a widening circle of love that included her and Mark.

After Coryn, Mark, and Ginny became a family certain changes were made. Mrs. Aguilar who had heartily approved of the marriage, offered to serve as caregiver of her mother the days Coryn went to the University pursuing her degree in occupational therapy. In the evenings, Neil Dodge took over, seeming to cherish the time spent with his beloved wife. He had mellowed in his acceptance of her illness and his devotion was unflagging. Their loving relationship was an inspiration to Mark and Coryn as they began their own life's journey together.

None of this was easy. But together they had traveled this difficult path, making the journey together. Together they had learned that "weeping may endure for the night but joy cometh in the morning."

Just then, sunshine broke through the clouds, tinting the bluffs behind them with gilded light. The wind off the ocean was crisp and smelled of brine. The surf swooped in with a roar, casting huge clumps of seaweed onto the sand. Down on the beach Ginny ran ahead, Goldie scampered along beside her.

Coryn looked over at Mark. He was looking at her. They stopped, threw their arms around each other and kissed. There was a taste of salt on his lips, but the kiss was sweet, long and infinitely tender.

*Yes!* It *was* possible to be this happy. Even walking in the shadow of death. In spite of everything! It would be wrong not to be happy on this beautiful day, not to appreciate it and the love that had been given her as a gift.

Coryn heard Goldie's bark, Ginny's happy laugh behind Mark's voice saying, "I love you."

* * * * *

Dear Reader,

Christmas is special to different people for different reasons. For me it is a time of cherished childhood memories—of creeping downstairs in the still-dark morning to see if the doll pointed out to the department store Santa was waiting for me under the tree. It is the excited anticipation, the joyful expectation remembered, that flood the spirit at Christmastime.

Why else do we search the TV schedules for re-runs of *Miracle on 34th Street* and *It's a Wonderful Life* if not to experience that longing to fulfill all our hopes and dreams? Maybe it is because we want to capture that sense of joy depicted in Charles Dickens's best known and best loved story, *A Christmas Carol*. To imagine the magical qualities he makes so real—the promise of snow, the gleam of glossy leaves and crimson holly berries, the sounds of carols, sleigh bells and church bells ringing out in the frosty air. Few of us will sit down to a festive old fashioned feast of roast goose and plum pudding, but, ideally, we will celebrate the warmth of family and friends. And beyond the mistletoe and the music, we will thoughtfully remember the real reason for it all.

Yes, Christmas is special, and as Dickens so aptly put it, "Let us keep Christmas in our hearts the year long" and say with Tiny Tim, "God bless us, every one."

Jane Peart

# HOME FOR THE HOLIDAYS

## Irene Hannon

To Tom—
my year-round blessing, who makes
every day feel like Christmas.

# Chapter One

Nick Sinclair felt his blood pressure begin to rise and his spirits crash. A few moments ago he'd been on a high, elated by the news that he'd won the commission to design a new headquarters building for the Midwest Regional Arts Center. It was a coup destined to move his architectural career into the limelight.

Then George Thompson dropped his bombshell. On behalf of the building committee, he had strongly suggested—more like mandated, Nick thought grimly—that the firm of Sinclair and Stevens use some unknown landscaping company to design the grounds.

"Taylor Landscaping?" Nick cleared his throat. "I don't believe I've heard of them," he said in a pleasant, conversational tone that betrayed none of his turmoil.

"You will," George replied with a decisive nod. "Great company. Small. Relatively new. But dynamic. Creative, yet practical. I like that." George always spoke in clipped sentences, a habit that Nick suddenly found irritating.

"How do you know about them?"

"Several of the board members have used them. Did the landscaping at my new house, in fact. Wonderful job! My wife said they were great to work with. Very professional. And stayed right on budget, too."

Nick struggled to keep his face impassive as a wave of panic washed over him. On his own, he knew he could assemble a team of contractors that would do the firm of Sinclair and Stevens proud. But one weak link was all it took to ruin an otherwise great job. Or, at the very least, to make his life miserable.

Nick carefully smoothed down his tie. Not that there was anything out of order in his appearance. His navy blue pin-striped suit, starched white cotton shirt and maroon-and-gray paisley tie sat well on his just-over-six-foot frame. Broad shouldered, with dark hair and even darker eyes, he didn't particularly care about clothes one way or the other, but he'd invested a good number of his thirty-six years to reach this point in his career, and he was smart enough to know that appearances *did* count. Today he looked every bit the part of a rising young architect, and nothing was amiss—including his tie. But that little maneuver bought him a few seconds of time—all he needed to recover from his surprise at George's suggestion and to rapidly formulate his response.

"Well, I'm sure they're very competent, but commercial landscaping is on an entirely different scale than residential," Nick said smoothly. "Now, I've worked with an established firm for several years that I think you'll find very—''

''Nick.'' George held up his hand, cutting the younger man off. ''Providing opportunities for young talent is in keeping with the philosophy of the Arts Center. And it's one of the reasons we chose *your* firm to design it. I think it's only fair that we at least give this company a chance, don't you?''

Nick looked at the man across from him in silence. Checkmate, he thought grudgingly. George Thompson's years as a respected trial attorney served him well in the business world. You couldn't raise an objection that he hadn't already considered.

And, Nick had to admit, he was right. The Arts Center board could have chosen a well-established architectural firm for this project. Instead, the board members—all of whom were influential business people in St. Louis—were giving him a shot at it. He couldn't argue the point that this Taylor Landscaping deserved a chance, too. It was just that he didn't relish the idea of some wet-behind-the-ears firm getting its chance at his expense. However, it looked as if he didn't have a choice.

''I see what you mean,'' he said, his even tone revealing nothing of his frustration.

''Good, good. Give them a look, get a bid…I think you'll be impressed.''

''I'll get in touch with them immediately,'' Nick promised. ''Now, about the schedule…''

By the time Nick left George's office, all of the details had been finalized. He should have been on top of the world. Instead, the sudden gust of cold March wind and the overcast, threatening sky that greeted him when he stepped through the glass doors better matched his mood, and he scowled at the dark clouds overhead.

There had to be a way around this, he reasoned as he climbed into a sleek red sports car parked in the visitors' lot. Obviously, the board wanted a first-class job. The Arts Center would be a St. Louis showpiece, and anything less than the best would reflect poorly on the city. Just as obviously, the board members were convinced this landscaping firm could handle the job. And maybe they were right. But *Nick* wasn't convinced. Not yet, anyway. And before he agreed to work with this company, he had to feel confident in its abilities. George *had* given him an out. A slim one, true, but it was there. And he intended to use it unless Taylor Landscaping did one terrific sell job on him.

Suddenly Nick found himself walking through the door of his office, with no recollection of the drive from downtown. For a man who prided himself on his alertness and attention to detail, it was an unsettling experience. Frowning, he nodded distractedly to the receptionist, glanced at the two part-time draftsmen at work in a large, airy room and stuck his head into his partner's office.

Jack Stevens glanced up from his drafting table and grinned hopefully, his short-cropped sandy hair giving him a fresh-faced, all-American-boy look. "Well?"

"Well what?"

"How'd it go?"

"Fine."

"You mean you got the job?"

''Yeah.''

Jack tilted his head quizzically. ''Well, try to contain your enthusiasm,'' he said dryly.

Nick shook his head impatiently and raked his fingers through his hair, jamming his other hand into the pocket of his slacks. ''There's a complication.''

''What?''

''Have you ever heard of Taylor Landscaping?''

Jack frowned thoughtfully. ''Taylor Landscaping… No, I don't think so. Why?''

''Because the board of the Arts Center *strongly* recommended them to do the landscape design.''

Jack leaned against the drafting table, propping his head on a fist. ''Is that bad? What do *you* know about Taylor Landscaping?''

''Nothing. That's the point. It's some new outfit that's probably fairly inexperienced.''

''Sort of like Sinclair and Stevens?'' Jack said with a mild grin.

Nick glared at him. ''Don't you start, too. That's exactly what George implied.''

Jack shrugged. ''Well, it's the truth. Why don't you keep cool until you check them out? Might be the proverbial diamond in the rough.''

''It also might be a lump of coal.''

''Maybe. Then again, maybe not.''

Nick gave him a disgusted look. He was in no mood for humoring, not with the commission of his career facing potential disaster at the hands of an inept landscape designer. ''Aren't you just a little worried about how this might affect the future of Sinclair and Stevens?'' he said tersely. ''Most people will only see the outside of the Arts Center, and a bad landscaping job could ruin the lines.''

''You're really worried about this, aren't you?''

''You better believe it.'' Nick walked restlessly over to the large window on one wall and stared out unseeingly for a long moment before he turned back to his colleague. ''You of all people know how hard we've worked to get this far. Fourteen-hour days for three long years, working in a cramped office with barely room for two drafting tables. It's beyond me where you ever found the time or energy to have two kids along the way! We've done okay, but you know as well as I do that we've been waiting for our real break, the one job that will move us into the big leagues. This is it, Jack. It may sound dramatic, but our future could depend on this commission. This is what will make or break our reputation with the people who count in this town. We blow it—we might as well close up shop because we'll never get another chance.''

Jack stared at his partner thoughtfully for a few minutes, his demeanor now just as serious as his friend's. ''I'm sorry, Nick. I didn't mean to make light of it. I realize how important this is. But if this landscaper doesn't cut it, we don't have to use them, do we? You said the board *recommended* them. So at least the door's open to other possibilities if they don't work out, isn't it?''

''Yeah. About half an inch.''

''Look, before we jump to any conclusions or panic unnecessarily, why don't you check out this Taylor Landscaping? I trust your judgment. If you're not satisfied with them, we just have to tell George. I'll back you up, but this project is really your baby, Nick. You went after it and you did the preliminary design that the committee selected. I know it's coming out of the Sinclair and Stevens shop and I'll help peripherally, but you're the one who needs to feel comfortable with this company because you're the one who'll have to work with them."

"Yeah, I know. And you're right. I need to check them out. I'm condemning without a trial, and that's really not fair." He glanced at his watch and gave an exasperated sigh. "Six o'clock! Where did the day go?" He shook his head. "It's too late to do anything today, but I'll follow up on this first thing in the morning."

At nine o'clock the next morning Nick punched in the number for Taylor Landscaping. He waited with an impatient frown as the phone rang once, twice, three times. By the sixth ring he was drumming his fingers on the desk. What kind of an outfit was this, anyway? Every business office he knew of was open by this hour. Hadn't anyone ever told this company that an unanswered phone meant lost business? Nick was just about to hang up when a slightly breathless voice answered.

"Taylor Landscaping."

"This is Nick Sinclair from Sinclair and Stevens. I'd like to speak with Mr. Taylor."

There was a long pause at the other end of the line. "Do you mean the owner?" There was a hint of amusement in the voice.

Nick bit back the sarcastic retort that sprang to his

lips, confining his response to a single, curt syllable. ''Yes.''

''Well, everyone's out at the job site right now.''

Nick debated. He could just leave a message. But it might not be a bad idea to see this outfit at work. ''All right. Just give me the address,'' he said in a clipped, authoritative tone.

''Well, I guess that would be okay.'' The voice sounded uncertain. ''Hang on a minute.'' A sound of papers being shuffled came over the line, and after several interminable minutes the information was relayed. Nick jotted it down. A residential job, in a nice area of large homes and expansive grounds. But not a commercial commission.

''Thanks,'' he said.

''My pleasure.'' The amused tone was back.

Nick frowned at the receiver, perplexed by the woman's attitude. But he wasn't about to waste time trying to figure it out. Instead, he glanced at his watch. If he hurried, there was time to pay a quick visit to Taylor Landscaping before his eleven o'clock meeting.

A half hour later Nick pulled up at the address provided by the woman on the phone. Four people, dressed in jeans and work shirts, were visible. Two wrestled with a large boulder. Next to them, a guy with a mustache fiddled with a jackhammer. Another slightly built worker, who appeared to be only a teenager, stood apart with a hose, watering some freshly planted azalea bushes.

Nick had no idea who the owner was, but the kid with the hose was closest to the street. Besides, he had no desire to approach the group with the jackhammer.

It was now in use, and the bone-jarring noise was already giving him a headache.

Nick stepped onto the lawn and took a moment to look over the grounds. It was a new house, built on a vacant lot in an already established neighborhood. The ground had been cleared during construction, and it was obvious that a complete landscaping job was under way. The work appeared to be just beginning, and it was difficult to tell whether a cohesive plan had been developed. But a well-maintained pickup truck bearing the name Taylor Landscaping stood parked in the circular driveway, and the crew seemed energetic.

The jackhammer stopped momentarily, and Nick opened his mouth to speak. But before he could make a sound the annoying noise started again. Shaking his head in irritation, he moved forward and tapped on the shoulder of the teenage boy who held the hose.

It happened so quickly Nick had no chance to step aside. The boy swung around in instinctive alarm, maintaining a death grip on the hose and drenching him in the most embarrassing possible place. Nick was stunned, but not too stunned to lunge for the hose and yank it in a different direction. He glanced down at his soggy gray wool slacks, and for the second time in less than twenty-four hours he felt his blood pressure edge up.

''Just what exactly were you trying to do?'' he demanded hotly. ''Of all the stupid antics...''

''I'm...I'm really sorry,'' the teenager stammered.

Nick removed his pocket handkerchief and tried to sop up the moisture, a task he quickly realized was futile. ''Yeah, well, that really solves everything, doesn't it?'' he said sarcastically. ''I have an important meeting in less than forty-five minutes. How do you suggest I explain this?''

The teenager stared at him blankly.

''You could say you had an accident,'' replied a mildly amused voice.

Nick glanced up. The worker who had offered the suggestion wore a baseball cap and dark sunglasses.

''Very funny,'' he said icily. ''Which one of you is Mr. Taylor?''

His question was met with silence, and he frowned in irritation. ''I'm looking for the owner,'' he said through gritted teeth.

''Well, why didn't you say so,'' the worker in sunglasses spoke again, the husky voice now even more amused. The baseball cap was flipped off, releasing a cascade of strawberry blond hair caught back in a ponytail. She removed the glasses to reveal two startlingly green eyes. ''You're looking at her.''

Nick stared at the woman across from him. Several moments passed while he tried to absorb this information. And in those few moments Laura Taylor quickly summed up the man across from her. Rude. Arrogant. Overbearing. No sense of humor. Probably a male chauvinist, judging by his reaction to her gender.

''Laura, I—I'm really sorry.''

Laura turned her attention to the young man holding the hose. He looked stricken, and she reached out and gripped his shoulder comfortingly. ''It's okay, Jimmy. No permanent damage was done. But those azaleas could use some more water. Why don't you finish up over there.'' She turned to the other two men. ''I'll be with you guys in a few minutes. Just do what you can in the meantime.''

They nodded and headed back to work, leaving Laura alone with the stranger. She tilted her head and looked up at him, realizing just how tall he was. At five-eight, she wasn't exactly petite, but this man made her feel...vulnerable. It was odd...and unsettling. And it was also ridiculous, she told herself sharply.

''What can I do for you?'' she asked, more curtly than she intended.

Nick stared down into the emerald green eyes that now held a hint of defiance. How had he failed to notice, even from a distance, that one of the workers was a woman? Sure, the glasses and the cap had effectively hidden two of her best features, but the lithe, willowy figure definitely did not belong to a man!

Laura saw the quick, discreet pass his eyes made over her body, and she resented it. She put her hands on her hips and glared at him. ''Look, mister, I don't have all day. I've got a lot of work to do.''

It suddenly occurred to Nick just what kind of work she was doing, and he frowned. ''You shouldn't be trying to move that boulder,'' he said. ''Why isn't he doing the heavy work?'' He gestured toward Jimmy, the young man with the hose.

The question took Laura by surprise, and she answered without even considering the appropriateness of the query. ''He's only sixteen. It's too much for him.''

''And it's not for you?''

''I'm used to this kind of work. He isn't.''

"How can you run this company if you're out in the field actually doing the manual labor?"

Her eyes narrowed. "Not that it's any of your business, but we happen to be one person short today."

"As a matter of fact, it does happen to be my business."

Laura frowned. "I'm not following you."

"I'm Nick Sinclair, of Sinclair and Stevens. We're designing the new Regional Arts Center, and you happen to own the firm of choice for the landscape portion, or so George Thompson tells me."

Now it was Laura's turn to be shocked into stunned silence. She stared at the man across from her, her initial elation at the news suddenly evaporating as her stomach dropped to her toes. What had she done? The Lord at last had answered her prayers, sending a dream commission her way, and she'd blown it by insulting the man who held the key to that dream. Why couldn't she have overlooked his bad manners long enough to find out his business?

Nick saw the conflicting emotions cross her face, debated the merits of trying to put her at ease and decided against it. Let her sweat it out. He certainly was. From what he'd seen so far, he wasn't impressed with Taylor Landscaping. Not by a long shot. He'd started the day off with the disorganized receptionist and then arrived on the scene to find that half of the crew consisted of a high school kid and a woman. Not a promising first impression.

Nick remained silent, his arms crossed. He noted the flush of color on her face, the look of despair in her eyes, the nervous way she bit her lower lip. His resolve began to waver. After all, he was the one who had appeared on the scene uninvited and disrupted what otherwise seemed to be a relatively smooth operation. And then he'd behaved arrogantly over a simple mistake. Not to mention his reaction to the discovery that a woman owned Taylor Landscaping. What had come over him? He wasn't a chauvinist. At least, he didn't think he was. But this woman sure must think so, and he couldn't blame her.

Nick had just decided that maybe an apology was in order when the woman across from him took a sudden deep breath, distractedly brushed a few stray wisps of hair back from her face and fixed those green eyes unflinchingly on his darker ones.

"Do you think it might be a good idea if we start over?"

"It couldn't hurt."

A quick look of relief crossed her face. She wiped her hand on her jeans and held it out. "Mr. Sinclair, I'm Laura Taylor. And as you've already discovered, I own Taylor Landscaping."

Nick took the hand that was offered, surprised by the firmness of the grip.

"Look, I'm sorry about that," she said, gesturing vaguely in the direction of the embarrassing water spot. "I guess Jimmy didn't hear you coming up behind him because of the jackhammer."

"Maybe not, but isn't sixteen a little young to be working in a crew like this?" he asked pointedly.

As if to say, can't you afford more experienced help, Laura thought.

She bit back her first reaction, then shrugged. "I

hired Jimmy through Christian Youth Outreach. Have you heard of it?''

''No, I don't think so.''

She sighed. ''Unfortunately, not enough people have. It's an organization that provides support for young people from troubled homes,'' she explained. ''A lot of the kids have been abused. Anyway, Jimmy is part of a work-study program sponsored by Outreach. He just works for me part-time, to earn money for college.'' She looked over at him, a frown marring her brow. ''He'll need all the help he can get. I'm just doing my bit.''

Nick felt embarrassed now by his question. He took a closer look at the woman across from him. She was older than he'd first thought. Early thirties, probably. A fan of barely perceptible lines radiated out from her eyes, and there were faint shadows under her lower lashes. Although she'd stopped frowning, slight creases remained. She seemed tense and serious, and he had a strong suspicion that she'd worked very hard to get where she was. Yet she still found time to help others. All of which was admirable. But it didn't alleviate his concerns about Taylor Landscaping's role in the Regional Arts Center. Hard work was important, but talent and creativity were the critical components. He still had no idea how her company would fare on that score, and he had to find out before he made any commitments.

''Ms. Taylor, I suggest that we defer our discussion about the Regional Arts Center to another time. You're obviously busy, and—'' he glanced at his watch with a frown "—I'm late for a meeting. How about tomorrow at one?"

"That would be fine."

He withdrew a business card from his pocket and handed it to her. "Sorry for the interruption today."

"And I'm sorry about that." Again she gestured vaguely toward his slacks.

"Well, as someone suggested, I'll just say I had an accident."

Laura caught the faint teasing tone in his voice and looked at him in confusion. Was this the same arrogant man who had been ranting at them less than ten minutes ago? It didn't seem possible.

Unsure how to respond, she chose not to. Instead, she reached back and twisted her hair up, securing it firmly under the baseball cap before once more settling the dark glasses on the bridge of her nose.

"I'll see you tomorrow, then."

Nick was taken aback by her abrupt goodbye, and watched for a moment as she strode back toward her crew. Despite the fact that she'd been unfailingly polite once the purpose of his visit had been revealed, she obviously didn't like him. His attempt to lighten the mood at their parting had been clearly rebuffed. As he turned toward his car, the jarring reverberations of the jackhammer started up again, and the headache he'd had earlier returned with a vengeance.

The partnership of Taylor Landscaping and Sinclair and Stevens was definitely off to a rocky start.

# *Chapter Two*

Nick turned sharply, swinging neatly into his reserved parking space. As he set the brake, he glanced at his watch with a frown. He was twenty minutes late for his meeting with Laura Taylor, and judging by the unfamiliar, older-model hatchback in the small parking lot, she was waiting for him.

For some odd reason, he still felt off balance from their meeting the previous day. From the moment he'd arrived at the job site, things had gone wrong. And being twenty minutes late for their meeting today wasn't going to help.

Nick strode into the reception area and stopped at the desk to pick up his messages.

''Laura Taylor is here,'' the woman behind the desk told him, confirming his assumption about the Toyota's owner. ''I was going to have her wait here, but when you weren't back at one Jack came out and got her. I think they're in his office.''

''Thanks, Connie. Did any of these sound urgent?''

he asked, waving the stack of pink message slips in his hand.

"No. I told everyone it would probably be late afternoon before you got back to them."

"Thanks. Would you handle my calls until Ms. Taylor leaves?"

"Sure."

Nick heard the sound of voices from Jack's office as he paused at his desk to deposit his briefcase. He couldn't make out the conversation, but Jack's sudden shout of laughter told him that his partner and Laura Taylor had hit it off. Good. Maybe if Jack had kept her entertained, she'd be less judgmental about his tardiness. He shrugged out of his jacket, rolled up the sleeves of his crisp white cotton shirt and loosened his tie, flexing the muscles in his shoulders. He wasn't in the mood for another encounter with Laura Taylor, not after the marathon lunch meeting he'd just attended with a difficult client, but he didn't have a choice.

As Nick approached Jack's office, the sounds of an animated conversation grew louder. Through the open door he could see half of Jack, who was leaning against his desk, ankles crossed and arms folded over his chest. But he gave his partner only a passing glance, directing his attention to Laura Taylor instead. She was sitting in one of the chairs by the desk, angled slightly away from him, legs crossed, her attention focused on Jack. Nick stopped walking, taking a moment to watch her unobserved. She was dressed the same as yesterday, in worn jeans and a blue cotton work shirt, her feet encased in heavy tan work boots. The baseball cap was missing, and her hair was once again caught back in a ponytail, the severe hairstyle emphasizing the fine bone structure of her face. Her full cotton shirt was neatly tucked in, a hemp belt encircling a waist that seemed no more than a hand span in circumference. The worn jeans molded themselves to her long, shapely legs like a second skin, he thought as his eyes leisurely traced their contours. It suddenly occurred to him that even in this workmanlike attire, Laura Taylor radiated more femininity than most of the women he knew, freshly manicured and dressed in designer clothes.

Manicures were obviously not part of Laura Taylor's life, he thought as his gaze moved to the hands that rested quietly on the arms of her chair. He remembered the strength of her handshake, and noted with surprise the long, slender fingers. Her nails were cut short and left unpolished, and her hands looked somewhat work worn. He thought again about her struggle with the boulder yesterday, and frowned. She was too fragile looking for that kind of work. He eyed her more critically, noting that despite her fabulous shape, she bordered on being too thin. The dark shadows under her eyes that he'd noticed yesterday were still there, speaking eloquently of tension and hard work and lack of rest. A powerful, unexpected twinge deep inside brought a frown to his face. Now what was that all about? he wondered, jamming a hand into the pocket of his slacks.

The sudden movement caught Laura's attention, and her gaze swung to the doorway. The image she saw was not comforting. Nick Sinclair stood frowning at her, and her stomach began to churn. She was painfully aware of the poor impression she'd made on him yesterday, but at least he'd agreed to meet with her today. She couldn't blow it. She couldn't! *Please, God, let him give me a chance with this project,* she prayed silently.

Nick's eyes locked on hers, and she returned the gaze unflinchingly, although it took all of her willpower. Based on his expression, it appeared that he might already have had second thoughts about using her company, she thought dispiritedly. He was an intimidating figure, even in shirtsleeves. The angular planes of his face and prominent cheekbones held a no-nonsense look, and his dark eyes seemed fathomless—and unreadable. At the same time, there was an almost tangible magnetism about him that seemed somehow…unsettling.

Jack, sensing the change in mood, leaned forward to look out the door.

"Nick! Come on in. Laura and I were just getting acquainted."

Nick tore his eyes away from the deep green ones locked on his. "Sorry about the delay. My lunch meeting took a lot longer than I expected. I hope the wait doesn't inconvenience you," he said, turning his attention back to Laura.

Laura struggled to present an outward facade of calm as questions and doubts raced through her mind. Had he changed his mind about giving her a chance? Was her behavior yesterday going to cause her to lose this job? Were his chauvinistic attitudes going to work against her? She struggled to control her inner turmoil, and when at last she spoke her voice sounded cool and composed.

"No. I've enjoyed chatting with Jack. I'm just going back to the job site when I finish here."

"Still one person short?"

"Yes."

He nodded curtly. "Then let's try to make this as brief as possible." He turned back to his partner. "Do you want to sit in, Jack?"

"I'd like to, but I have a two o'clock that I need to prepare for."

"Okay. Ms. Taylor, why don't we go into the conference room? There's more space to spread out the plans," Nick smoothly suggested.

"It's Mrs.," she corrected him, noting that his eyes automatically dropped to her left hand, which displayed no ring. "I'm ready whenever you are," she said, ignoring the question implicit in his look. She reached for the portfolio beside her chair and stood. "Jack, it was nice meeting you," she said, holding out her hand. Her voice was tinged with a husky warmth Nick had never heard before, and he noted that they were on a first-name basis.

"My pleasure."

Nick stepped aside for her to pass, catching Jack's eye as he did so. Jack grinned and gave a thumbs-up signal, but Nick just gave a slight shrug. Jack might have been impressed with Laura Taylor personally, but Nick was more interested in her abilities as a landscaper.

He followed her down the hall, conscious of a faint, pleasing fragrance that emanated from her hair. Again he felt a disturbing stirring deep within, which irritated him. ''Right here,'' he said, more sharply than he intended. She shot him a startled look. ''Go on in and I'll grab the plans from my office,'' he added, purposely gentling his tone.

She nodded and disappeared inside. He returned to his office, pausing to lean on his desk, palms down, and take a deep, steadying breath. For some reason, Laura Taylor had the oddest effect on him. She seemed so cool and composed, so strong and independent, yet she'd shown moments of touching vulnerability—yesterday when she'd found out who he was, and just now when he'd spoken to her in an unexpectedly harsh tone.

He couldn't quite get a handle on her. She was a small-business owner, apparently with enough smarts to weather the many pitfalls inherent in that situation. You had to be tough to survive, and he had seen the results of that struggle in many of the women he dated. He was inherently drawn to women who displayed independence, toughness, intelligence and drive. Women who were savvy and sophisticated in the business world, but who knew exactly what buttons to push to turn him on after hours. The only problem now was that these very qualities seemed to make his relationships mechanical, gratifying on a physical level but lacking some essential ingredient.

Lately his thoughts had been turning to a more serious involvement, to marriage and the kind of family Jack had. The only problem was that the women he'd been involved with put their careers first and relationships second. Like Clair. He was beginning to feel as if he was just one more appointment on her calendar. Their dates were always penciled in, and it was understood that if a business conflict arose, the personal commitment would be sacrificed. Nick understood that—he'd lived that way himself for the past ten years—but now he wanted—needed—something more. Once or twice he'd thought about suggesting marriage to Clair, but he'd never been able to bring himself to do it. Because, while he admired her and was physically attracted to her, he knew deep in his heart that she would never put her first priority on their relationship—as he intended to do with the woman he married. As a result, he saw her less and less. She was so busy with her own independent life that he sometimes wondered if she even noticed that he rarely called anymore.

Nick walked over to the window and ran his fingers through his hair, uncertain why his emotional dilemma had surfaced just now, in the midst of a business meeting. He supposed Laura Taylor had triggered it in some way, but he wasn't sure why. Maybe it was those intriguing glimpses of vulnerability, a surprising contrast to her usual businesslike demeanor. That vulnerability wasn't something he usually saw in the professional women of his acquaintance. Yet she obviously didn't let it get in the way of her business.

Impatiently Nick walked over to his desk and picked up the rolls of plans. An analysis of Laura Taylor's psyche was not on his agenda today, he told himself firmly.

Laura was grateful to have a few moments alone. It gave her a chance to compose herself and prepare for her next encounter with the unpredictable Nick Sinclair. She had no idea why he'd spoken to her so sharply just now. But she did know that this job was a once-in-a-lifetime opportunity, and she *had* to get it. *She* knew she could handle it—the question was, how could she convince the man in the next room?

As she often did when faced with a question or situation or decision that baffled her, Laura closed her eyes and opened her mind and heart to the One who had guided her so well in the past. Her faith had always been important to her, but only in the difficult years, when it had been put to the test, had she realized how powerful an anchor it could be. It had provided calm in the midst of turbulence, hope in the face of despair. She had learned to accept God's will without always understanding it, and she knew that whatever happened today was part of His plan for her. All she could do was her best and leave the rest in His hands.

Laura took a deep breath and opened her eyes. The panic was gone, and she felt ready to once more face the intimidating Nick Sinclair.

By the time Nick returned, Laura was bent over studying the model of the Regional Arts Center. She straightened up when she heard him enter, impressed despite herself by the clever integration of contemporary and classical features. "Very nice," she remarked.

"Thanks."

With an unconscious grace, she moved around the conference table and unzipped the portfolio that lay there, taking another deep, steadying breath before she spoke.

"I think it makes sense for us to be honest with

each other about the possibility of working together. I realize that you probably have no idea of the capabilities of Taylor Landscaping, and based on our encounter yesterday I have the distinct impression that our services are being—to put it bluntly—shoved down your throat. So I thought it might be helpful for you to see some examples of our work. I've brought some drawings and photographs of some of our jobs over the past two years. While there's nothing in here on the scale of the Regional Arts Center, I have every confidence that we can do an exceptional job for you. I've also brought a list of all of our jobs since the business began six years ago, as well as a review of my academic and professional credentials."

As she talked, Laura arranged the contents of her portfolio on the table, keeping her eyes averted from the man across from her. Last night, as she'd prepared for bed, she'd had a chance to think about their encounter yesterday. It had become clear to her that Nick Sinclair was probably extremely uncomfortable with the whole arrangement. If he was like most architects, he had established relationships with a group of proven, reliable contractors. Naturally, for a prestigious job like the Regional Arts Center he would have preferred to use one of those firms. Laura understood that. She also understood that he might still do so, providing he could justify it to George Thompson and the Arts Center board. So she had come prepared. This commission was vitally important to her business, and she wasn't about to let it slip away without a fight. She carefully finished arranging the contents of her portfolio on the table before she spoke again.

"Now, what would you like to see first?" she asked, looking up at last.

Nick Sinclair's attention was entirely focused upon her now. His grim expression made her feel uncomfortable, as if he was sure she'd never measure up. She dropped her eyes, a faint flush staining her cheeks.

Nick saw the look on her face and slowly settled himself on the edge of the conference table across from her. He opened his mouth to speak, then closed it. This project obviously meant as much to her as it did to him—maybe more, he thought, his jaw tightening as he once again pictured her struggling with the boulder.

"Let's look at some of the photos first," he suggested quietly.

Laura glanced up, their eyes locked and she saw nothing but sincerity. Maybe he'd give her a fair chance after all, she thought, pulling the photos toward her.

They worked their way through the photos and the designs, and then Nick quickly scanned the list of projects, spending more time on the sheet with her credentials. He was impressed by her background and by the quality of the jobs Taylor Landscaping had done, but he still wasn't honestly convinced that her firm could handle a job the magnitude of the Arts Center.

"What I've seen here looks very good," he said carefully, his eyes meeting hers as he handed back her list of credentials. "But most of what you've done is residential work, with the exception of a few small commercial jobs. Do you really think you're equipped to handle the Arts Center?"

"Yes," she said steadily. "I realize we'll have to

expand. I've been wanting to do that anyway, but I was waiting for the right commission to come along. And as for our ability to do the design itself, all I'm really asking for is a chance to give you some ideas. I won't even charge for spec time."

"No one is asking you to work for free."

"I'll do anything it takes to convince you that we can handle this job," she said steadily, her gaze locked on his.

She wants this assignment so much, Nick realized with a sharp pang of sympathy. He knew what it felt like to be in that position. But earnestness didn't guarantee talent or results, he reminded himself.

"Suppose we take a look at the plans," he suggested. "You've already seen the model, and I'll fill you in on the terrain."

"I've already been to the site," she informed him.

He looked at her in surprise. "You have?"

She nodded. "This morning. I knew where it was from all the articles in the paper, so I went over there early and walked around a bit. But I had no idea what you have in mind architecturally, or even what direction you want the building to face, so I need to see the plans before I can talk intelligently about the landscaping."

Nick nodded, impressed by her initiative. "Of course." He unrolled one of the elevations, and for the next two hours they worked their way through the plans. Laura's questions were astute, and the preliminary ideas she voiced were intelligent, appropriate and interesting. She took extensive notes as they talked, and Nick couldn't help notice the enthusiastic sparkle in her lovely green eyes.

When the last of the elevations had been rerolled, Laura leaned back in her chair. ''I'm impressed,'' she said honestly. ''It's a spectacular building, and I like the use of natural materials. This will lend itself beautifully to landscaping that features native plants and trees. I can just imagine the entrance in the spring if we do a design with dogwoods and azaleas and redbuds. And the reflecting pool in front could be flanked with gardens that feature seasonal flowers.'' She paused thoughtfully, and then looked over at Nick. ''Those are just preliminary thoughts, of course. I'd like to get some rough designs on paper and then meet with you again before you make a decision on your landscaper.''

Despite her calm, professional tone, Nick saw the strain around her mouth and eyes, and could sense the tenseness in her body as she waited for his answer. He had a totally illogical urge to reach over and smooth away the smudges under her lower lashes with his thumb, which he firmly stifled.

She's married, for heaven's sake, he chastised himself. Get a grip, pal. That's really not your style.

He cleared his throat and forced himself to glance away from those mesmerizing eyes. ''That would be fine,'' he said, gathering up the plans. ''I'll have a set of prints run for you. When would you like to get together again?''

''How about a week from today?''

He looked up in surprise. ''Will that give you enough time?''

She shrugged. ''Enough to do some preliminary work. It won't be detailed, but it should be sufficient for you to decide whether you want my firm for this job.''

''All right. Should we try one o'clock again?''

''That will be fine.''

''And next time I promise to be punctual,'' he said, his eyes twinkling.

She gave him a fleeting smile and then shrugged. ''I enjoyed chatting with Jack. He's a nice guy.''

''Give me a minute and I'll have those copies made for you.''

By the time he returned, Laura had gathered up all of her material. He handed her the copies and she slipped them inside the portfolio, zipping it before extending her hand.

''Thank you, Mr. Sinclair. I appreciate the chance you're giving me.''

''It's my pleasure. I do have one favor to ask, though.''

''Yes?'' she asked quizzically.

''Could we use first names? This Mr. and Mrs. business is too formal for me.''

She shrugged. ''Sure.''

He smiled. ''Good. Then I'll see you next week, Laura.''

Three nights later, the phone's persistent ringing finally penetrated Laura's awareness. She sat bent over the drawing board in a corner of her living room, working on the Regional Arts Center designs, and had no time for social calls. And it had to be a social call, she thought when a quick glance at her watch showed that it was after seven. So she ignored it and went back to work.

An hour and a half later, the doorbell rang. Laura looked up and sighed. She'd promised designs in a week with full knowledge that the commitment would appreciably lengthen her already long work days. But they were going to be even longer if she had too many interruptions.

The bell rang again, and this time the caller kept the button depressed. With a frown Laura slid off the stool where she'd been perched and, massaging her neck muscles with one hand, made her way to the door. Her eyes widened when she glanced through the peephole.

"Sam!" she said, swinging the door open. "This is a surprise! Come in."

The slim, fashionably dressed woman on the other side sauntered over the doorway and glanced around. "Have you had your phone fixed yet?"

"My phone?" Laura asked blankly, shutting and bolting the door.

"Well, it must be out of order. I keep calling, and it just keeps ringing. And you're obviously here."

"Oh." Laura's face flooded with color. "Sorry," she said apologetically. "I just didn't pick up. I'm on a deadline for what could be the commission that will finally put Taylor Landscaping on the map, and I just don't have time for anything else until next week."

"Including food?" Sam asked.

"I've been eating," she hedged.

"What did you have for dinner?"

"Well, I haven't had dinner yet," Laura admitted.

As Sam pointedly glanced at her watch, her shoulder-length red hair swung across her face. ''May I ask at just what hour you plan to dine?''

''When I get hungry.''

''You're not hungry yet? You must have had a big lunch,'' Sam persisted.

''Not exactly.'' Suddenly Laura realized she felt ravenous. She'd eaten only an apple for lunch, and that had been hours ago. As enticing smells emanated from the brown sack that Sam held Laura felt her empty stomach growl.

''You wouldn't want to share some Chinese with me, would you?'' Sam asked, waving the bag under Laura's nose.

Laura grinned. ''I could probably be persuaded. Why are you eating so late?''

''I was showing a house and my clients had to poke into every nook and cranny.''

''Well, I'm glad you decided to share your dinner with me,'' Laura admitted as Sam opened cartons and doled out Mongolian beef and cashew chicken, with healthy servings of rice. ''Although I never have understood this mothering complex you have,'' Laura teased. Sam certainly didn't look like the nurturing type, but she watched over Laura like a mother hen. ''Not that I'm complaining, you understand. But I really can take care of myself,'' Laura mumbled around a mouthful of food.

''Right,'' Sam said with mild sarcasm. ''That's why you don't eat right and work such long hours.''

''Getting a business off the ground isn't easy, Sam,'' Laura said, spearing a piece of green onion.

"Mmm, this is delicious," she said with a smile, closing her eyes. "Anyway, right now I don't care if I have to stay up every night until two in the morning for the next week. It will be worth it."

"Is that when you've been going to bed?" Sam asked. "How long can you keep up this pace?"

"As long as it takes. Sam, this could be it! You know the new Regional Arts Center that's going to be built?"

"Yeah, I've read about it in the paper."

"Well, I may get a shot at doing the landscaping!"

"No kidding!" Sam said, duly impressed. "How did this come about?"

Laura explained briefly, concluding with the day she'd met Nick Sinclair at the job site. "Although I haven't yet figured out how he knew where I was," she said with a frown.

"I think maybe I can enlighten you on that," Sam said slowly.

Laura looked at her in surprise. "You can?"

She nodded. "Uh-huh. When I stopped by your office the other morning to drop off the book you loaned me, the phone rang and I just answered it automatically. That was the guy's name—Nick Sinclair. He asked for *Mr.* Taylor and didn't seem to take my amusement too kindly. Anyway, your job schedule was right there, and I didn't think it would hurt to give him the address. You know," she said thoughtfully, "he was pretty heavy-handed, but he did have a really intriguing voice. What does he look like?"

Laura frowned. "I don't know," she said with a shrug. "He's attractive enough, I guess. Mid to late thirties, pretty tall, dark hair, high cheekbones, brown eyes. But to be honest, Sam, I've been so intimidated the two times we've met it's everything I can do to speak coherently let alone take inventory. After all, we didn't exactly get off to a good start,'' she said, a touch of irony in her voice.

''Hmm'' was all Sam said.

''What does that mean?'' Laura asked suspiciously.

Sam shrugged. ''Nothing. But do me a favor, kiddo. Next time, take inventory.''

''Why?''

''Why do you think?'' she asked with an exasperated sigh.

''Sam, for all I know the man is married! Besides, we've been over this before,'' Laura warned.

''Yes, and I still haven't changed my mind. After all, it's been nearly ten years, for Pete's sake! You could do with some male companionship.''

''I can do *without* it,'' she said emphatically.

Sam sighed dramatically. ''I wish you would at least make an effort. Is this guy nice?''

Laura frowned. ''He wasn't the first time we met. He was arrogant and rude, and when he found out I was the owner his shock was almost comical.''

''Well, after all, the man had just been doused with a hose,'' Sam reminded her.

''That's no excuse,'' Laura said.

''What about the second time you met?'' Sam persisted.

Laura shrugged. ''He seems to be a good architect. The plans for the Arts Center are very impressive.''

Sam rolled her eyes. "Why don't I just give up? Laura, was he nice?"

Laura remembered the way he'd patiently looked at all the material she'd brought, and then spent two hours explaining the plans, finally agreeing to let her have a shot at the job. But she also remembered the way she felt around him—intimidated and uncertain. "He makes me nervous," she said.

"Well, it's a start," Sam said optimistically.

Laura smiled and shook her head, reaching for a fortune cookie. "Don't get your hopes up," she said, breaking it open.

Sam watched her friend's face turn slightly pink as she read the slip of paper. "What does it say?" she asked curiously.

In reply, Laura crumpled the paper between her fingers. "These things are stupid," she said.

"What does it say?" Sam repeated.

Laura sighed. "If I tell you, will you promise not to make any comments?"

"Sure."

Laura looked at her friend skeptically, and then read, "His heart was yours from the moment you met."

Sam didn't say a word. She just smiled.

# Chapter Three

The harmonies of the string quartet could barely be heard above the voices of the crowd, driven under the large tent by a sudden June shower. Nick, alone for a moment, grimaced as he adjusted his bow tie. The late-afternoon air felt unusually muggy and warm, even for St. Louis, and his glass was almost empty. Not that he could stomach much more of the bubbly champagne being served, anyway. Maybe he could find something more thirst quenching if he made a search, he thought halfheartedly. But it didn't seem worth the effort of fighting his way through the dense crowd. Besides, he preferred to remain on the sidelines for the moment. The ground-breaking party for the Arts Center had brought out all of the "beautiful" people, the wealthy St. Louisans who could be counted on as patrons for anything arts related. He'd said hello to all the right people and smiled for the photographers, and now all he wanted to do was go home, shed his tux and relax. It had been a long week. Despite the festive surroundings, his spirits felt as flat as the residue of champagne in his glass.

It was odd, really, that he wasn't in a more upbeat mood. His plans had been given enthusiastic praise in the press, and the ground-breaking party today for the project he'd worked so hard to win should have left him filled with excitement and energy. Instead, he was suddenly bone weary.

Nick's gaze swept over the crowd once more and, with a sudden jolt, he realized that, unconsciously, he was doing what he'd been doing ever since he'd arrived—searching for Laura. That realization also revealed the surprising reason for his glum mood—he had needed her presence to make this party a success.

Nick frowned, honest enough to admit the truth but still taken aback by it. He readily acknowledged that he enjoyed Laura's company. Ever since he'd awarded Taylor Landscaping the job two months ago, he'd seen her regularly as she more fully developed her plans and brought them to the office for his approval. He had grown to look forward to their meetings, to respect her intensity and creativity, and to experience a sense of satisfaction every time he elicited one of her rare smiles.

And *rare* was an appropriate word, he thought grimly, shoving his free hand into the pocket of his slacks. She worked too hard. He'd suspected as much at their first encounter, and the suspicion had been confirmed at subsequent meetings. Not that she ever complained. It was more subtle than that. Like the time he'd asked if he could keep the designs and review them after his full day of meetings, and she'd assured him she could just stop by on her way home from the office that evening about eight to pick them up.

But why wasn't she here today? He knew she'd been invited, and she deserved a party after the work she'd put into this project. A chance to get out of her customary jeans and— Suddenly his thoughts were arrested by a startling possibility. Maybe she didn't have anything to wear to a black-tie occasion! He knew she operated on a shoestring, and it was conceivable that her budget was too tight to allow for frivolities like cocktail dresses. He still had no idea what her husband did for a living, although he obviously wasn't involved in the landscaping business. Maybe he was ill, or out of work, leaving Laura to carry the burden of support.

"Nick! Here you are! Just wanted to say congratulations again on an outstanding job. I've heard nothing but compliments from everyone who's looked at the model."

The familiar voice brought Nick back to reality, and he turned to smile at George Thompson. "Thank you. It's been a great party."

"All except for the weather. But it's brightening up now. Well, enjoy yourself. I'll see you soon, Nick."

The fickle weather had, indeed, changed once again. Rays of sun peeped through the clouds, and the guests began to make their way out of the tent. Nick breathed a sigh of relief as the crowd thinned and his eyes began to scan the gathering again, this time hoping to spot a waiter with a fresh tray of something other than champagne.

His eyes had completed only part of their circuit when they were arrested by a tantalizing view. A woman was seated in the far corner of the tent, angled sideways. Her body was blocked from his view by a tuxedoed figure, but her crossed legs were clearly revealed under a fashionably short black skirt. His appreciative gaze wandered leisurely up their shapely length, his thirst forgotten for the moment. This was the most enjoyable part of the event so far, he thought with a wry smile.

Suddenly the legs uncrossed and the woman rose. She now stood totally hidden from his view by the man in the tuxedo, and Nick shook his head ruefully. So much for that pleasant interlude, he thought.

He was just about to go in search of a drink when he saw the woman attempt to move out from behind the man, only to have him take her arm and forcibly restrain her, backing her even farther into the corner.

Nick frowned. He didn't fancy himself a Sir Galahad, and besides, most women today were quite capable of taking care of themselves in situations like this. His intrusion could only cause unpleasantness. The man was probably her husband or, even worse, someone very important who it would not be wise to offend. Yet he was unwilling to leave the woman unassisted if she actually needed help.

Nick hesitated uncertainly. He watched the woman make another attempt to walk away, moving to one side. The glimpse he caught of her face made the swallow of champagne catch in his throat, and he almost choked as he stared in disbelief. It was Laura!

No wonder he hadn't noticed her earlier, he thought. She wore a black crepe cocktail dress, with double spaghetti straps held in place by rhinestone clips on the straight-cut bodice. The dress gently hugged her figure, ending well above her knees. She was gorgeous, Nick thought, stunned. Loose and full, her hair fell in soft, shimmering waves against the creamy expanse of her exposed shoulders. Her subtle makeup enhanced her picture-perfect features and wide eyes. She looked chic and sophisticated and polished, and she seemed as comfortable here as she did on a construction site.

Nick's perusal was abruptly interrupted as Laura made yet another futile attempt to extricate herself from the man's grasp. His indecision evaporated and he surged forward, adeptly maneuvering his way through the crowd, his eyes never leaving her face. She looked pale, and though poised and obviously trying her best to be polite, he also saw that a trace of fear lurked in her eyes. His stomach tightened into a hard knot, and as a waiter passed, he removed two glasses of champagne from the tray, never stopping his advance.

"Laura! I've been looking everywhere for you. I finally found the champagne," he greeted her, forcing a pleasant, conversational tone into his voice.

Laura's eyes flew to his, and he could see the relief flood through them. "Thanks, Nick. I wondered where you went." Her voice sounded a bit unsteady, but she took his lead gamely. His hand brushed hers as he offered her the champagne, and he noted that her fingers felt icy as she took the glass, holding it with both hands.

The fortyish, balding man looked from Nick to Laura, his flushed face indicating that he'd had his share of the freely flowing champagne. "You two are together? Sorry. Why didn't you say so?" he mumbled, his hands dropping to his sides. Nick saw the red mark his grip had left on Laura's arm and his jaw tightened. "I think I'll go find some more champagne," the man said, glancing around fuzzily.

"Maybe you've had enough," Nick suggested curtly, but the man had already turned and disappeared into the crowd.

Laura carefully set her champagne glass down on the table next to her and took a deep breath. "Thank you," she said quietly.

"I didn't do much." He watched her closely, aware that she was deeply upset.

"Well, your timing was perfect," she replied, a forced lightness in her tone. She reached for her purse, unsnapped the clasp and retrieved a mirror. "I think I'm about to lose an earring," she said, buying herself some time while she regained her composure. She reached up and tightened the already secure rhinestone clip.

She was putting on a good show, Nick thought. But he wasn't fooled. He could hear the strain in her voice and he could see the unsteadiness of her hands. "Maybe you should drink this," he suggested quietly, picking up her glass of champagne.

She looked at it distastefully and shook her head. "No, thanks."

He glanced in the direction of her "admirer." "I guess I don't blame you."

She shrugged. "I don't have anything against moderate drinking," she said. "But I have no tolerance for abuse.'' Her eyes dropped to the silver filigreed mirror in her hands, and she played with it nervously before setting it on the table. She took a deep breath, and when she spoke again there was a husky uncertainty in her voice. ''I do appreciate your help, Nick. I—I'm not very good at handling those kinds of situations.''

''You shouldn't have to be,'' he said, with an edge to his voice that made her look up in surprise. ''No woman should.''

She was taken aback by the vehemence of his tone, given that she'd labeled him a male chauvinist. ''Yes, well, it sounds good in theory.'' She paused and took a deep breath. ''Look, Nick, I think I'm going to head home. It's been a long day.''

''Did you work all day?''

She nodded. ''Up until about three hours ago.''

''That hardly looks like your usual work attire,'' he said, hoping that the warmth of his smile would ease some of the tension he sensed in her body. ''If I may say so, you look stunning.''

''Well, you didn't expect me to come in my jeans, did you?'' she asked, unexpectedly pleased by his compliment. When he didn't reply, her eyes widened in disbelief. ''Or did you?''

''No, of course not,'' he said quickly. He didn't tell her that he thought she might have stayed away due to lack of appropriate attire rather than lack of taste. ''It's just that I've never seen you wear anything but work clothes.''

She tilted her chin up slightly, and there was a touch of defensiveness in her voice when she spoke. ''Jeans and overalls suit my job. This outfit would hardly be appropriate at a construction site. I don't have an office job, Nick. And I'm not afraid to get my hands dirty."

Nick frowned at her misinterpretation of his remark. "I realize that," he said quietly. "I didn't mean to offend you, Laura. My comment was meant as a compliment, not a criticism."

Laura looked at him, lost for a moment in the depth of his eyes. What else did he realize? she wondered. Did he realize that for some unaccountable reason her heart was hammering in her chest? Did he realize that her breathing had become slightly erratic? And did he realize that neither of those reactions was a result of her unpleasant encounter? Distractedly she pushed the hair back from her face. "I've really got to be going," she said, retrieving her purse from the chair at her side.

"Are you here alone?" Nick asked in surprise.

"Yes."

"Well, can I at least walk you to your car?"

"I'm fine, really. But thanks for the offer. Good night, Nick."

He hesitated, reluctant to let her leave alone, knowing he couldn't stop her. When Laura looked at him curiously, he found his voice. "Good night, Laura."

He watched her thread her way through the thinning crowd, frustrated by his inability to...to what? he wondered. He'd done all that was necessary by helping her out of an offensive situation. Yet he felt she'd needed something more, something he couldn't give. She'd seemed unaccountably shaken by the encounter, and he doubted whether she'd fully recovered. Certainly it had been unpleasant, but there'd been no real danger. Yet he'd caught the glimmer of fear in her eyes, of vulnerability. He wished she had at least let him walk her to her car. And where was her husband? he wondered, suddenly angry. She did have one. Or at least he assumed she did. Yet she always seemed so alone.

He continued to stare pensively into the crowd long after she'd disappeared from sight. Only when he realized that the majority of guests had departed did he rouse himself to do the same. It was time to call it a day.

Nick turned to set his glass on the table, and his eyes fell on Laura's silver mirror, obviously forgotten in her haste to depart. He picked it up and weighed it thoughtfully in his hand, turning it over to examine it more closely. It looked quite old, perhaps a family heirloom, he mused. He'd have to call Laura immediately and let her know it was safe. Hopefully he could reach her even before she realized it was missing. She'd had enough stress for one day, he thought, a muscle in his jaw tightening.

And then an idea slowly took form in his mind. Why not drop it off on his way home? That way he could assure himself that she had gotten home all right and, perhaps in the process, meet the elusive Mr. Taylor.

Nick slipped the mirror into the pocket of his jacket and turned to go, only to find a board member at his elbow. His patience was stretched to the breaking point by the time he could tactfully disengage himself from a discussion of the importance of art to the St. Louis community. Then it took another ten minutes to find a phone directory so he could look up Laura's address. With a frustrated sigh, he glanced at his watch. Seven o'clock. Laura was probably home by now. He *could* just call and let her know he had the mirror, he told himself. There was no urgency about returning it. But somehow that wasn't good enough. He *wanted* to go. And he wasn't going to waste time analyzing the reasons why.

Laura stirred the spaghetti sauce, raising the spoon to her lips for a taste. Perfect, she thought with a satisfied smile. But then, Grandmother's recipe never failed. It was one of those things you could always count on. And there weren't a lot of them in this world, she mused, her smile fading. There was her faith, of course. It had been her anchor in the difficult years of her marriage and the struggle for survival that followed. Her trust in the Lord was stable, sure and strong, and even in her darkest hours, it had offered her hope and comfort. The Lord had always stretched out his hand to steady her when she felt most shaky and lost. Yes, she could count on her faith.

She could also count on her family. And Sam. But certainly not men. Or at least not her judgment of them. How could she have been so wrong? she asked herself again, as she had countless times before. But the answer always eluded her.

As her mood started to darken, Laura fiercely took herself in hand. She refused to become melancholy over a stupid little incident that she'd blown out of all proportion, she told herself angrily. Okay, so the man's steel grip on her arm and the smell of liquor on his breath had brought back painful memories. So what? She wasn't the only one in the world with painful memories, and it was about time that she laid hers to rest.

At the same time, she had made progress, she consoled herself. She turned the spaghetti sauce down to simmer, removed her large white apron and headed for the bedroom to change clothes. Three or four years ago she probably would have been a basket case after that scene. She'd held up all right. Of course, if Nick hadn't come along…

Nick. Her arm froze as she reached around to unzip the black cocktail dress. Thoughts of him were almost as disturbing as thoughts of the unpleasant encounter. Both caused her breathing to quicken and her pulse rate to accelerate. Both made her stomach churn and her legs grow weak. Both made her nervous and uncertain.

But for very different reasons, she acknowledged honestly. Ever since Sam had planted the seed of romance in her head about Nick, Laura had reacted like a skittish colt whenever she was around him. And the explanation was simple. She felt attracted to him. Heaven help her, but she did. There was simply no way to honestly deny it, and Laura had learned through the years that being honest with herself was essential to her survival.

Slowly she unzipped the dress, stepped out of it and made her way toward the closet. When she passed the full-length mirror behind her door she hesitated, and then glanced at her reflection. It wasn't something she did often; for too many years she had disliked herself and her body so intensely that she avoided mirrors whenever possible. She was still much too thin, but at least her self-image had improved enough in the past few years that she could now look at herself without cringing.

One thing for sure, she thought with a wry smile, her job might be physically demanding, but it helped keep her in shape. Her body was that of a twenty-year-old—muscles toned, stomach flat, thighs firm. Joe had enjoyed her body once, she thought, allowing a moment of wistful recollection. At least he had until the problems started and she'd begun to lose weight. Then he'd started making fun of her thinness. And her looks. And her ambition. And her faith.

His loss of faith and belittlement of hers had been one of the most painful things to endure during those last difficult months. As their relationship had deteriorated, she'd turned more and more to her faith to sustain her, finding great comfort in the Bible. Joe, on the other hand, had found no solace there, had laughed when she suggested they spend some time each evening reading a few verses out loud. It was almost as if he was jealous of her faith, resenting the consolation she found there. She had tried to help, tried to share her faith with him, but he had resisted every attempt she'd made. In the end, his ridicule of all she had been raised to believe in had killed whatever love still survived in their relationship.

A lump formed in her throat, and she forced herself to swallow past it. The power of love—both constructive and destructive—never ceased to amaze her. Her faith had survived, but little else had, including her self-esteem. Even now, more than ten years later, she was still self-conscious about her body. "Bony," Joe had called her. She'd gained a little weight since then, but she was still probably too thin to be desirable. Not that she'd cared about that over the years. But for some reason Nick had activated hormones that she'd thought had died long ago. After Joe, Laura had been convinced that she would never be attracted to another man. With a shudder she recalled how the sweetness of their young love had gradually soured, how in the end lovemaking had become an ordeal, an act devoid of all tenderness, to be endured, not enjoyed. Even now the memories filled her with shame and disgust. It had taken her years to accept emotionally what she'd always known intellectually—that Joe's actions had been the result of his own sickness rather than anything she had done. She had dealt with the guilt—as much as she would ever be able to, knowing that some would always remain. And she had stopped asking the "what if?" questions ten times a day. But she had never recovered enough to risk another relationship.

Until she met Nick, Laura had been content to live the solitary life she'd created for herself, a life where no one made demands of her, no one belittled her, no one hurt her. It was a safe, if insulated, existence. Sam had been after her for years to reconsider her self-imposed physical and emotional celibacy, but, until Nick, Laura had never even been tempted. The idea of opening up again to any man had turned her off completely, and her passionate side was kept firmly under wraps.

So why were her hormones kicking in now? she wondered. Sure, Nick was a handsome man. And he seemed nice enough. After their initial confrontation, he'd proven to be a fair and considerate business associate. But until this afternoon she'd never related to him on anything but a professional level. Not that she should consider today's encounter very significant, she reminded herself. He had simply helped her out of an awkward situation, his action prompted more by good manners than personal interest. Yet the way he'd looked at her, as if he sensed the trauma of the situation for her and cared how she felt, had sent shock waves along her nerve endings and filled her with an almost forgotten warmth.

Laura took a deep breath and closed her eyes. What was wrong with her? Had she suppressed her needs for so long that even the slightest kindness and warmth from a man sent them clamoring for release?

Impatiently Laura pulled on a pair of shorts and a T-shirt. She had to get a grip on her emotions. Nick was a business associate. Period. Her reaction to him was just the result of long-suppressed physical needs. She would never again give herself to a man, now or in the future. It was simply too dangerous. No matter what Sam thought!

By the time Nick turned down Laura's street, it was nearly seven-thirty. He'd grown more uncertain with every mile he'd driven. Maybe her husband wouldn't appreciate his visit. And the last thing he wanted to do was cause Laura any further distress.

He still felt undecided when he pulled up in front of her apartment. He parked the car but remained behind the wheel, glancing around the neighborhood. Not the best part of town, he thought grimly. She lived in a four-family unit in the south part of the city, on a side street lined with similar brick flats. The buildings in this part of the city were probably at least seventy years old, and judging by the cars lining the street, it was not an affluent area. In fact, the longer he sat there, the more he began to realize that the surroundings were actually a little seedy. He frowned. He'd known money was tight, but she had a nice storefront office, albeit small, in one of the nicer suburbs, so he hadn't expected that she would live in such a run-down area.

He thought of his own West County condo, with its tennis courts and swimming pool and health club, and a surge of guilt washed over him. Nick was certain that Laura worked just as hard—if not harder—than he did, and she obviously had much less to show for it. Even in his leaner years, Nick's lifestyle had never been this impoverished.

He glanced at Laura's apartment building, still undecided. Why was he agonizing over a simple decision? he asked himself impatiently. After all, the worst that could happen would be that he would be treated as an unwelcome intruder. If so, he could make a hasty departure. It was no big deal.

Determinedly, Nick stepped out of his car, which was attracting interested glances from a few teenagers gathered on a neighboring porch. He felt them staring at the back of his tux as he bent to carefully lock the door, and he paused uncertainly, fiddling unnecessarily with the key. Was it wise to leave the car unattended? But he wouldn't be staying long, he assured himself. He strode inside, found that Laura lived on the top floor and took the steps two at a time.

Laura heard the doorbell and frowned, glancing at the clock. Sam was out of town until tomorrow, so it couldn't be her. Curiously she walked over to the door and peered through the peephole.

Her eyes widened, and with a muffled exclamation she stepped back from the door in alarm, her hand going to her throat. She began to take deep breaths, trying to steady the staccato beat of her heart. This wasn't good. This wasn't good at all. Not after the thoughts she'd just been having. Maybe she could just ignore him, she thought hopefully. Surely he'd go away if she didn't answer the door. But then logic took over. Why was he here? It must be something important for him to track her down at home. Was there a problem with the Arts Center, something he'd discovered after she'd left the party? That must be it, because he hadn't even bothered to change out of his tux. He'd come directly from the party. It had to be urgent.

Laura took another deep breath and stepped forward, sliding back the bolt and swinging the door open. "Nick! Is something wrong?" she asked without preamble.

Nick stared at the woman across from him. Her hair still swung loose and full, but she'd changed into shorts that snugly hugged her hips and revealed even more of her incredible legs than the cocktail dress had. A T-shirt clung softly to her upper body, the sea blue color complementing her hair and eyes. Suddenly aware that the silence was lengthening noticeably, he cleared his throat. "That's not the most enthusiastic welcome I've ever received," he said, flashing a quick, uncertain grin.

"Sorry," she said, flushing as she stepped aside. "Come in."

He hesitated. "I don't want to intrude…"

"I'm just making dinner."

"Well, only for a minute." He crossed the threshold into a tiny foyer and Laura shut the door behind him, sliding the bolt into place.

"Make yourself comfortable," she said, gesturing toward the living room, and Nick stepped into the softly lit room, which Laura had decorated in an English country style. Floral-patterned chintz covered the couches and chairs, and an old trunk served as a coffee table. Baskets of dried flowers and the soft yellow walls gave the room a warm, homey feel. A drafting table stood in one corner, with a wooden desk nearby, and lace curtains hung at the windows. There was a dining nook to one side, separated from the galley kitchen by a counter, and a glance down the hall revealed a bathroom door slightly ajar and a closed door that must be a bedroom.

"You've done a good job with this place," he said approvingly. "These older buildings are hard to decorate."

He regretted the words the moment he said them, thinking she might interpret his comment as criticism, but he was wrong.

"Thanks. It's amazing what a little paint, a needle and thread and some elbow grease can do."

She seemed skittish, not offended, and Nick wondered if her husband was in the bedroom or expected soon. He'd better do what he came to do and get out, he decided, withdrawing the mirror from his pocket and holding it out to her.

"I think you forgot this."

"Oh!" She gasped softly and reached for it.

"I thought you might be worried. It looks like it might be valuable."

She shrugged. "I have no idea about its monetary worth. But it has a lot of sentimental value." Her voice grew soft. "My grandfather gave this to my grandmother on their wedding day." She shook her head. "I can't believe I forgot it."

"Given the situation, I can. You were pretty upset."

She looked at him and took a deep breath. It seemed foolish to deny what had clearly been quite apparent. "Was it that obvious?" she asked quietly.

"Mmm-hmm."

"Like I said, I'm not very good at handling that sort of thing. Would you like to sit down for a minute?"

"The offer is tempting," he hedged, his eyes traveling around the room. "You've made this a very welcoming place." His eyes fell on the dining table and he noted with surprise that only one place was set. So Laura was here alone. But why? He decided to probe, knowing it was a gamble. "It's too bad your husband couldn't join you today," he said casually, strolling over to one of the overstuffed chairs. "That scene probably would have been avoided."

His back was to her when he spoke, and as he turned he caught the sudden look of pain in her eyes. Then they went flat, and she turned away. "My husband is dead," she said in a curiously unemotional voice.

"Will you excuse me for a minute? I need to check something in the kitchen."

Nick felt as if he'd been kicked in the stomach. He had wondered if she was divorced, although divorced women rarely asked to be called Mrs. anymore. Yet the idea that she might be a widow had never entered his mind. He'd satisfied his curiosity all right—at her expense, he thought, gritting his teeth. He jammed his hands into his pockets, his fists tightening in frustration at his lack of tact.

When Laura reappeared a few moments later, he turned to her, feeling that some comment was called for. "Laura, I'm sorry. I didn't know."

She looked at him, startled, as if surprised he'd reopened the subject. Then she shrugged. "No reason you should have. Please, sit down."

Nick hesitated for a moment, and then settled his large frame into a chair, noting that she perched nervously on the edge of the couch. Why was she so tense? Was it his presence that made her uncomfortable? And if so, why? He'd given her no reason to be nervous. In fact, since their first explosive encounter he'd gone out of his way to treat her with consideration.

"Laura, is there something wrong?" he asked quietly, knowing he was taking a chance but willing to accept the consequences.

The deep, mellow tone of his voice had a curiously soothing effect on Laura, and she looked down at the hands clasped tightly in her lap. At last she glanced up, aware that Nick's relaxed posture was at odds with the intensity of his eyes, which seemed to say "I care.'' And for just the briefest moment she felt tempted to pour her heart out to this man who was practically a stranger. But before the urge grew too strong to resist, she abruptly stood.

Nick seemed taken aback by her sudden movement, but he remained seated, waiting for her to speak.

Now that she was on her feet, Laura was at a loss. It was important that he leave, she knew that much. Never mind that she'd just invited him to sit down. Something intuitively told her that he represented danger. ''No, everything's fine,'' she lied. ''Except dinner I'm afraid it will burn if I don't get into the kitchen.'' Her voice was pitched above normal, and even to her ears it sounded strained.

Nick remained seated. ''It smells good,'' he said with a smile.

Dear Lord, why couldn't the man take the hint and just leave? Laura thought desperately. But she forced a bright smile to her lips. ''Thanks. It's an old family recipe. I really hadn't planned to fix dinner tonight, but I didn't get a chance to eat much at the party,'' she said, trying to talk away her nervousness.

''Me neither.''

Laura stared at him. Good grief, he was angling for a dinner invitation! This was great. Just great. She was trying to get rid of him and he wanted to stay. They were obviously not on the same wavelength. But how could she ignore the blatant hint without sounding ungracious? After all, he had come to her assistance today, and he'd gone out of his way to return the mirror.

Logic told her to ignore the prickling of her conscience. But good manners—and something else she refused to acknowledge—told her to listen. She sighed, capitulating.

"Would you like to stay for dinner?"

Nick smiled, the tense muscles in his abdomen relaxing. "As a matter of fact, yes." Then, suddenly, a shadow of doubt crept into his eyes, which narrowed as they swept over her too-thin form. "On second thought, maybe I won't. I don't want to take part of your dinner."

This was her out! All she had to say was "Maybe another time," and she'd be safe. But other words came out instead. "Oh, there's plenty. I made a whole batch of sauce and I was going to freeze what I didn't use. It's just a matter of cooking a bit more spaghetti."

Relief washed over his features, and he smiled. "In that case, I'll stay."

Laura smiled back. At least, she forced her lips to turn up into the semblance of a smile. But something told her she'd just made a big mistake.

# Chapter Four

"What can I do to help?" Nick asked, his engaging smile making her heart misbehave.

"There's really nothing," Laura said vaguely, still off balance by the unexpected turn of events. A visitor for dinner was the last thing she'd expected—especially this particular visitor.

Nick placed his fists on his hips, tilted his head and grinned at her. "Were you going to make a salad? I'm not too great on cooked stuff, but I can handle a head of lettuce."

Laura found herself responding to his lighthearted warmth, and a smile played at the corners of her mouth. "Well, I wasn't planning to. But since you offered…"

Nick gestured toward the kitchen. "Lead the way."

Laura was conscious of him close behind her as she walked toward the tiny kitchen, and she was even more conscious of him as they worked side by side in the cramped space, only a few inches apart. She suddenly felt all thumbs as she stirred the sauce and put the spaghetti into the boiling water. Nick, on the other hand, seemed totally relaxed. He was humming some nondescript tune under his breath as he worked, detouring occasionally to peer in her refrigerator and withdraw some other ingredient. So far she'd watched him chop lettuce, cut up tomatoes, slice red onion, sprinkle cheese and add croutons, all with a dexterity that surprised her. She had never expected him to be so at home in a kitchen.

"Voilà! A masterpiece!" he exclaimed finally, turning to her with a smile. "I just hope your spaghetti lives up to the standards of this creation," he said with an exaggerated French accent and an aristocratic sniff.

Laura found herself unexpectedly giggling at his comic antics, but her face quickly sobered when she saw an odd expression in his eyes. "What's wrong?" she asked uncertainly.

"Nothing. It's just that you should do that more often," he said quietly, suddenly serious.

She frowned in confusion. "What?"

"Laugh. It makes your face come alive."

Laura turned away, embarrassed, and stuck her head in the freezer on the pretense of looking for something. In reality, she hoped the cool air would take the flush from her cheeks. "Thanks, I think," she said over her shoulder, her voice muffled.

"You're welcome."

Her eyes fell on a package of garlic bread, and she reached for it gratefully. "I thought I had some of this left," she said glibly. "Should be perfect with our menu."

"Looks good," he agreed.

Suddenly the kitchen seemed even smaller than before. Nick leaned against the counter, his arms folded across his chest, one ankle crossed over the other. His cool confidence unnerved her, especially at this proximity. He was so close that if he wanted to he could simply reach over and pull her into his arms, she realized, quickly trying to stifle the unbidden thought. But it remained stubbornly in place, and her heart rate took a jump.

"Um, Nick, maybe you could set another place," she suggested. Anything to get him just a few feet farther away! she thought.

"Sure," he said easily, straightening up and walking around to the other side of the counter. "If you hand the stuff through, I'll take care of it."

Laura breathed a sigh of relief, feeling somehow safer now that they were separated by a counter. "Okay." She stood on tiptoe to open the overhead cabinet, unaware that when she reached up for the extra plate and glass, her T-shirt crept up to reveal a bare section of creamy white midriff and a perfectly formed navel.

Nick took a sharp, sudden deep breath and reached up to loosen his tie.

"Oh, you must be warm in that outfit," Laura said innocently as she handed the plate through. "I'm sorry I don't have the air on. I usually only run it during heat waves. Why don't you take off your tie and jacket?"

Nick swallowed with difficulty. "I think I will," he said, turning away, needing a minute to compose himself. Did Laura have any idea just how attractive she was? Even in shorts, her face now almost wiped free of makeup from the steamy kitchen, there was an appeal about her that he found strangely compelling.

He pulled off his tie and undid the top button of his shirt, slipping his arms out of the jacket and automatically rolling his sleeves to the elbows in his customary fashion. His hand hesitated for a fraction of a second on the cummerbund, and then he unsnapped it. He'd be a whole lot more comfortable without it.

Laura watched the cotton fabric of the shirt stretch across his broad shoulders as he went through these maneuvers, and a profound yearning surged through her. It had been so long, so very long…

With harsh determination she turned away and opened a cupboard to search for some cloth napkins. Her eye fell on an unopened bottle of red wine, a Christmas gift from a client. She'd been saving it for a special occasion. Thoughtfully, she reached for it, then hesitated. Was she asking for trouble? This wasn't a romantic tryst, after all. It was just a thank-you, and Laura didn't want Nick to read any more than that into this invitation. Still, wine would be a nice complement to the meal. With sudden decision, she grasped the bottle firmly and pulled it out. She was already flirting with danger merely by having him here. Why be cautious now?

Laura turned to find Nick in the doorway, and she paused, her eyes drawn to the V of springy, dark hair revealed at the open neck of his shirt. She clutched the bottle to her chest, suddenly at a loss for words, sorry now that she'd taken the wine out.

Nick glanced at the bottle curiously. ‘‘I’m surprised,’’ he commented. ‘‘After your encounter today, I wouldn’t think you’d be inclined to drink.’’

‘‘I told you, Nick. I have nothing against alcohol. Wine goes great with some food. But I can’t tolerate abuse. It freaks me out.’’

‘‘So I noticed,’’ he said, watching her closely, searching for a clue to the reason why.

Laura’s eyes flew to his, then skittered away at their intensity. ‘‘Well, shall we eat?’’ she asked a bit breathlessly.

He took the hint gracefully and dropped the subject, and Laura’s heart stopped hammering quite so painfully. Nevertheless, she was sure she wouldn’t be able to swallow a bite of food. Her stomach was churning, and even as he held her chair—an unexpected courtesy—she was fighting waves of panic. She was having a pleasant, intimate dinner with a man for the first time in more than a decade—never mind the circumstances. It would have been nerve-racking enough with any man. But it wasn’t just any man. It was Nick Sinclair, the man who only this afternoon had awakened her dormant hormones.

Nick sat down across from her and smiled. ‘‘Shall I pour?’’ he asked, picking up the bottle of wine.

‘‘Yes, please.’’

‘‘Everything smells delicious,’’ he commented, aware of her tension, struggling to put her at ease. ‘‘Your grandmother must have been some cook.’’

‘‘Yes, she was.’’

‘‘Was she Italian?’’

Laura found herself smiling. ‘‘Hardly. She just

loved to experiment with dishes from foreign lands. And in Jersey, Missouri, Italy is about as foreign as you can get.''

''Jersey,'' he mused. ''I don't think I've ever heard of it.''

''Not many people have. It's a tiny town in the southern part of the state.''

''Is that where you grew up?'' he asked.

''Mmm-hmm.''

''It must have been nice growing up in a small town. I've spent all of my life in big cities. I grew up in Denver.''

''Small-town life has some advantages,'' Laura said. ''But not many opportunities.''

''I suppose that's true. So how's the salad?''

Laura looked down in surprise at her half-empty plate. Nick's gentle, nonthreatening conversation had made her relax and she'd begun to eat without even realizing it. ''It's very good,'' she said.

''Well, you don't have to look so surprised,'' he said in mock chagrin.

She laughed. ''Sorry. You just don't look like the type of man who would spend much time in the kitchen,'' she admitted.

''As a bachelor, it's a matter of survival to learn some of the basics,'' he said.

As the meal progressed, Laura found that the tension was slowly ebbing from her body. She realized how much Nick's quiet, attentive, undemanding manner had calmed her. With a little prompting, she even found herself telling him about her work with Christian Youth Outreach and sharing her views about the importance of a Christian influence on young people and the difference it could make in troubled lives.

By the time the last crust of garlic bread had been eaten, Laura felt mellow and relaxed, and she smiled at Nick, no longer intimidated or frightened. He was easy to be with, she realized.

"I'm afraid I can't offer you dessert," she apologized. "I don't keep sweets in the house. It's just too much of a temptation."

"Well, I have a suggestion."

She looked at him curiously. "What?"

"How about Ted Drewes?"

Laura hadn't been to the South Side landmark in years, but the famous frozen custard was considered the ultimate summertime treat for many St. Louisans.

Nick watched her surprise turn to delight, and he grinned. "Why do I think this won't be a hard sell?"

She smiled back. "I must admit that I've always had a weakness for Ted Drewes," she confessed. "But it is getting late."

Nick glanced at his watch and let out a low whistle. "Is it actually ten o'clock?"

"I'm afraid so."

Nick looked up and saw the disappointment in her eyes. "Well, this is the peak time for Ted Drewes on a Friday night," he reminded her. "I'm game if you are."

"Nick...are you sure?" she asked uncertainly. "You've already gone to so much trouble for me today..."

He reached over and covered her hand with his, his

touch sending sparks along her nerve endings. "Laura, I'm doing this for *me,*" he said softly.

She looked into his eyes, trying to read his thoughts, but all she saw was a warmth and tenderness that made her breath catch in her throat. His hand still rested on hers, and she loved the protective feel of it. She'd almost forgotten that a touch could be so gentle.

"Well...in that case...okay," she said, her voice uneven.

"Good." He squeezed her hand and then released it. "I'm parked out in front."

"Let me just get my purse," she said, feeling as nervous as a teenager on her first date.

When Laura reached the sanctuary of her bedroom she groped in her purse for her lipstick and applied it with shaking hands. Then she ran a comb through her hair. All the while Nick's words kept replaying in her mind. *I'm doing this for me.* They made her feel good...and scared, all at the same time. But maybe that was okay, she thought. Maybe it was the Lord's way of reminding her to be cautious and move slowly.

When Laura returned to the living room Nick stood waiting, his jacket slung casually over his shoulder. He smiled as she walked toward him, and Laura felt nearly breathless. He really was a very handsome man. Maybe too handsome, she reflected.

"Ready?"

"Yes."

He opened the door for her and stepped aside as she carefully locked it, then followed her down the steps. When they reached the ground floor she found his hand at the small of her back as he guided her toward the red sports car, which was thankfully still in one piece, he noted.

Laura let him lead her to the car, enjoying his touch, impersonal though she knew it was. She sank into the cushions of the two-seater, the unaccustomed luxury making her smile.

"Nice car," she said, reverently running her hand over the leather cushions.

Nick flashed her a grin. "Thanks. It was a splurge, but we all deserve those now and then, don't you think?" He suddenly remembered her older-model hatchback and clenched his jaw, realizing that she probably had little discretionary income. He was afraid he might have offended her, but when she spoke her voice was friendly and conversational.

"Of course! What good is success if you can't enjoy the fruits of your labors?" she replied promptly. Her tone held no resentment, no envy, no self-pity that her own financial situation was not yet secure enough to allow for such luxuries. She was quite a woman, Nick thought—not for the first time that day.

As always, the lines at Ted Drewes stretched nearly into the street, and a good-natured crowd milled about. Families, couples young and old, teenagers in groups, all mingled. A stretch limo was even pulled up to the curb, but that was not an uncommon sight.

"This place never ceases to amaze me," she said with a smile, shaking her head as Nick jockeyed for a parking place.

"It's pretty incredible," he agreed, stopping by a spot that was being vacated. "We're in luck," he said triumphantly, skillfully pulling into the tight slot. By the time he turned off the ignition and started to come around to open Laura's door, he discovered that she'd already alighted, and he stopped in midstride.

Laura looked at him guiltily. It had been so long since she'd dated that she'd forgotten the niceties. Over the years she had grown accustomed to doing everything herself.

''Sorry,'' they said in unison.

Laura smiled. ''Why are you sorry?'' she asked.

He shrugged sheepishly. ''I thought maybe you were one of those women who felt offended by men opening doors and holding chairs. I've run into a few who let me know in no uncertain terms that they considered such behavior the height of chauvinism. But my mother did a good job training me, and now it's a habit. If I offended you, I'm sorry.''

''No, it's not that,'' Laura assured him quickly. ''As a matter of fact, I enjoy it. I just...'' Her voice trailed off. How could she tell him that it had been so long since she'd been with a man that she had simply forgotten the rules? ''I'm sorry,'' she finished lamely, seeing no way she could possibly explain her behavior without telling him things that were better left unsaid.

''No problem,'' Nick assured her with a smile. ''I just want to make sure we're on the same wavelength.''

After braving the long line at the order window they returned to Nick's car, leaning against the hood as they ate their chocolate chip concretes, so called because of their thick texture. As they enjoyed the frozen concoction Nick kept her amused with comments and outrageous speculations about various people in the crowd.

"See that guy over there? The one in the Bermuda shorts who looks like he's made too many visits here? He's a spy," he said solemnly.

"How do you figure that?" Laura asked, smiling up at him.

"It's elementary, my dear. Spies are picked to blend in with the crowd. Would *you* think he was a spy?"

"No," she admitted.

"Well, there you have it."

Laura giggled. "Nick Sinclair, you're crazy. Has anyone ever told you that?"

"I've been called a few things in my life," he admitted. "But 'crazy'...no, that's a new one. Should I be insulted?"

"No. You're crazy in the best sense of the word," she said, laughing.

"Well, it must not be so bad if it makes you laugh," he said softly, his voice suddenly serious.

Laura was thrown off balance by the change in mood, preferring the safe, easy banter of moments before. She shifted uncomfortably and focused on scraping the last bite of custard out of the bottom of her cup.

Nick sensed her withdrawal. For some reason, relationships with men made her uncomfortable, he realized. She seemed fine when the give and take was light and friendly, but introduce an element of seriousness or intimacy and she backed off, retreating behind a wall of caution. Why? He felt certain there was an explanation. And probably not a pleasant one. But he was equally sure that at this stage in their relationship she was not about to share it with him. He'd have to earn her trust first. And pushing or coming on too strong were not the right tactics, he warned himself. In fact, he instinctively knew that doing so would be the surest way to lose her.

"Well, I see you've managed to polish off that entire concrete," he said lightly, peering into her now empty container. His head was so close that Laura could smell the distinctive scent of his aftershave, could see the few flecks of silver in his full, incredibly soft-looking hair.

"Uh, yes, I did, didn't I? And on top of all that pasta, too." She groaned. "This was not a heart-healthy meal. And it wasn't so great for the waistline, either."

"You don't have to worry about that," he assured her.

Laura looked at him sharply. "What do you mean?"

Nick was taken aback by her prickly reaction. "It was a compliment, Laura. You don't have an extra ounce of fat on your entire body."

She looked down dejectedly, playing with her spoon. So Nick thought she looked scrawny, too. And scrawny was not attractive.

"Laura?" Nick's voice was uncertain. When she didn't look up, he reached over and gently cupped her chin in his hand, turning her head, forcing her to look at him. He gazed into her eyes, which suddenly looked miserable and lost, and felt an almost overwhelming desire to pull her into his arms. He resisted the urge with difficulty. "Laura?" he repeated questioningly, his voice now husky. "What is it?"

She couldn't lie, not when his eyes were locked on

hers with such intensity. "I'm just sort of paranoid about being skinny," she said softly. "It's not very...very—" she searched for the right word "—appealing," she finished.

Nick frowned. Good grief, did Laura think she was unattractive? It wasn't possible. No one could look like her and be unaware of her effect on the opposite sex. Or could they? he wondered incredulously. She didn't seem to hold a very high opinion of her physical attributes. Yes, she was on the thin side. But most models would kill to have her figure. And he personally preferred slender women. Voluptuous beauty had never appealed to him.

"Laura, you can't be serious," he said quietly, deciding that honesty was the only tactic. "You are a gorgeous woman! You knocked me off my feet today at the party in that slinky little black dress you had on." Usually he didn't lay his cards out on the table so early in the game, but her need for reassurance outweighed his need to protect his ego.

Laura's eyes reflected disbelief. "You're being very kind, Nick, but—"

"Laura, stop it," he said fiercely, cutting her off abruptly. Her look of shock made him soften his tone. "Look, I am not giving you empty compliments. I respect you too much for that. I'm telling you the truth. You are an extremely attractive woman, and if I wasn't looking into your eyes right now and reading the uncertainty, I'd think you were just fishing for compliments. It's almost beyond my comprehension that someone who looks like you should have any doubts about her attractiveness."

Laura swallowed past the lump in her throat and felt hot tears forming behind her eyes. She wanted to believe Nick. Wanted to desperately. But life had made her wary. And you didn't lose that wariness overnight, no matter how kind a person was.

"It's a long story, Nick," she said softly.

"I figured it might be." He casually draped an arm around her shoulders. "Sometimes it helps to talk," he offered.

"Sometimes," she agreed, conscious of the warmth of his fingers gently massaging her shoulder. His simple touch made her yearn for too much too soon.

"But not now?" he suggested.

"Not yet," she amended, knowing she was leaving the door open for the future.

"I'll settle for that," he said. "Ready to call it a night?" At her nod he stood and, extending a hand, drew her to her feet. He kept his hand familiarly in the small of her back as they walked around the car, releasing her only after he'd opened the door and she made a move to slip inside.

"Thank you," she said, suddenly shy.

"You're welcome."

The ride home was brief and quiet, but it was a companionable silence. Only when he pulled up in front of her apartment and came around to open her car door did he speak, glancing around as he did so.

"It's not very well lit here, is it?" he said.

"I've never thought about it," she replied truthfully.

"You don't wander around here at night, do you?" he asked worriedly.

"No. Nick, it's a safe neighborhood, if that's what you're asking," she assured him.

"If you say so," he replied, but he sounded unconvinced.

They walked up the dimly lit stairway to her second-floor apartment, and Nick silently took the key from her hand and fitted it into the lock.

Laura looked up at him, her eyes suddenly sad. She'd had a wonderful evening, an evening she'd never expected to have again. Now she felt a little like Cinderella at midnight as the chiming clock broke the magic spell, knowing that today had been a chance encounter that was unlikely to be repeated.

Nick saw the melancholy look steal over her eyes and reached up to brush a few stray strands of hair back from her face. Laura's breath caught in her throat at his intimate touch, and her heart began to pound.

"You look suddenly unhappy, Laura," he said, his voice edged with concern. "Didn't you have a good time tonight?"

"Oh, yes! I did! I'm just sorry it's over," she admitted. "It's the nicest evening I've had in a long time," she told him honestly. "I just hope I didn't disrupt any of your plans. This was so unexpected."

"Yes, it was. And yes, you did. But I'm not complaining," he said with a gentle smile that warmed her right down to her toes.

"Well..." Should she ask him to come in? she wondered. What was the protocol? Did an invitation to come in automatically include an invitation for more? She'd been out of the dating world too long to know. What she *did* know was that casual intimacy wasn't her style. It went against everything she believed as a Christian.

Nick, sensing her dilemma, solved the problem. He would have liked nothing better than to follow her through that door, to hold her in his arms until she melted against him, to leisurely taste her sweet kisses. But now was not the time, and he knew it.

"I'll see you soon, Laura," he said, his voice strangely husky. "Get a good night's sleep."

Nick hesitated. He knew she was scared. He didn't know why, but her fear was real. And he knew he couldn't push her. At the same time, he had to let her know that tonight's chance encounter had turned into a great deal more than that for him.

Carefully, so as not to frighten her, he lifted her hair back from her face, letting its silky strands slip through his fingers. He caressed her cheek with his thumb, his eyes locked on hers. He thought he detected desire, but if so, it was so tangled up with fear that the two were indistinguishable. Suddenly fearful himself, he slowly leaned down and gently pressed his lips to hers in a brief but tender kiss. He had followed his instinct, which told him to do that. But the same instinct told him to do no more. So with one last stroke of his thumb, exercising a degree of self-control that surprised him, he reluctantly stepped back.

"Good night, Laura," he said with a smile. "Pleasant dreams."

And then he disappeared down the dim stairway, leaving her filled with a deep, aching emptiness tempered only by the tender new buds of a frightening, uninvited hope.

# Chapter Five

"I haven't heard you mention our friend, Nick Sinclair, lately," Sam said, helping herself to another potato skin.

Laura glanced around the popular eatery, crowded on Saturday night with singles, and shook her head. "Why in the world did you pick this place?" she asked, the incessant din of high-pitched voices and laughter giving her a headache.

"It's a hot spot," Sam informed her.

"It's a meat market," Laura replied flatly.

Sam shrugged. "Same difference. So how's Nick?"

Laura sighed. "Sam, do you ever give up?"

"Nope," she replied without apology, taking a bite out of a potato skin and chewing it thoughtfully. "That's the problem with you, you know. You've given up."

"Given up?"

"Yeah. On men."

"How is it we always end up talking about men?"

"Because good friends should discuss important things. And men certainly fall into that category."

"Sam, you've been married—right?"

"Right."

"And it was a disaster, right?"

"Right."

"So how come you want to find another man and repeat the mistake?"

"Laura," Sam said patiently. "Just because we married two losers doesn't mean all men are bad. So, we got unlucky. There are plenty of good men out there who would love to meet a wholesome, hard-working woman like you and a straightforward, slightly kooky woman like me. And I bet if we found the right ones, they'd treat us like queens."

"Yeah?" Laura said skeptically. "Well, I'm not willing to take the chance. By the way, how did your date turn out last night? Who was it this week? The accountant?"

"Jay. The engineer. It was okay," Sam said with a shrug. "We went to a movie, stopped for a drink, had a few laughs. You know, the usual."

"No. I don't know," Laura replied.

"You could if you wanted to."

"Maybe," she said skeptically. "Anyway, that's not the point. I *don't* want to."

"That's precisely the point. This may not be your scene," Sam said, gesturing to the bar, "but there are other ways to meet men. I'm not saying you need to go out twice a week. But twice a month would be nice. Just for diversion. How about twice a year?" she teased her.

"I don't have time for diversions," Laura replied matter-of-factly. "But I must admit I'm in awe of your technique. How do you do it?"

"Do what?"

"Find all these men you go out with."

"I *look,* Laura. That's your problem, you know. You don't look. Even when there's a perfectly good specimen right under your nose, do you notice? No. Which reminds me ..what about Nick?" she prodded.

"What about him?"

"Do you see him much?"

"When necessary." And sometimes when not, she added silently, recalling the previous night's impromptu dinner and trip to Ted Drewes.

Sam gave a snort of disgust. "When necessary," she mimicked. "Laura, for Pete's sake, you've got to let a man know you're interested or you'll never get anywhere!"

"I don't want to get anywhere," she insisted firmly.

"Of course you do. You just don't know you do. So when did you see him last?"

"Sam." There was a warning note in her voice.

"What? Is it a state secret? I only asked a simple question."

"Okay, okay. Last night."

"Last *night?* As in after work?"

"Yes," Laura admitted. "The ground breaking for the Arts Center was yesterday, and I forgot my mirror there. You know, the one my grandmother gave me?" At Sam's impatient nod, Laura continued. "Well, anyway, he dropped it by the apartment after the party."

"And?"

"And what?"

"What happened?"

"Nothing."

"You mean he just handed you the mirror at the door and left?" Sam asked, disappointed.

"Well, not exactly. Neither of us ate at the party…and he…well, he smelled the spaghetti sauce and…I mean, he did go out of his way. I—I couldn't very well not ask him to stay," Laura stammered.

"Are you telling me you invited him to dinner?" Sam asked incredulously.

"Yes," Laura admitted reluctantly. "But don't jump to any conclusions," she warned quickly. "I felt like I owed him a favor. And besides, he practically invited himself."

"You don't have to justify it to me," Sam assured her. "I think it's great! So what happened then?"

"What do you mean?"

"Laura, it is like pulling teeth to get any information out of you," Sam said in frustration. "I mean, you ate, you talked…then what?"

"We went to Ted Drewes for dessert," Laura offered.

"Good. He extended the evening. Did you have a good time?"

"Yes. Well, sort of. Sam…" She took a deep breath. "I was really nervous," she admitted, playing with her glass.

"That's okay," Sam assured her. "It's perfectly natural. You haven't dated for a while."

"Try fourteen years," Laura said wryly.

"Well, there you go. You're just out of practice. Do you think he'll ask you out again?"

"What do you mean, 'again'? He didn't ask me out this time."

"Laura, you know what I mean."

Laura shrugged. "I don't know. I think he had a good time," she said cautiously.

"Is he attached?"

"I—I don't think so. Sam, he...he kissed me good-night," she said, her cheeks turning pink.

"And you let him?" Sam asked incredulously. "Well, hallelujah!"

"But, Sam, I'm not ready for this yet!" Laura protested.

"Laura, you're past ready. You're ripe," Sam said with her usual blunt, earthy honesty.

Laura smiled. Leave it to Sam to home right in on the problem. The woman across from her might be too outspoken for some, but she'd been a true friend and a real lifesaver to Laura during the rough times. Sam could always be counted on to remain steadfastly loyal and supportive.

"I'm not sure I'd go that far," Laura replied with a smile.

"Well, I would. So tell me, what does he look like? I assume you've taken inventory by now."

Laura flushed. "Sam, I'm not good at describing people."

"Well, does he look like anyone here?" Sam persisted.

Laura let her gaze roam over the room, first through the restaurant and then through the adjoining bar. "No.

I'm not good at seeing resemblances. I told you that… Oh, no!''

''Laura, what is it?'' Sam asked, alarmed by her friend's sudden pallor.

''I don't believe this,'' Laura muttered incredulously, sinking lower into the booth.

''What's wrong?'' Sam asked again.

''It's him!''

''Him?''

''Yes. Him!''

''*Him* him?'' Sam's head swiveled. ''Where?''

''Sam! Will you please turn around,'' she hissed. ''Maybe he won't see us,'' she said hopefully.

Nick leaned against the bar, swirling the ice in his drink, trying to figure a way to make his escape without looking rude. He fervently hoped that this was the last bachelor party he ever had to attend. They were so predictable and boring. He was tired of the singles scene, tired of going home alone every night, tired of wondering if he would ever find someone to spend his life with, as Jack had. He envied Jack and Peggy their satisfying existence. Sure, Jack complained good-naturedly about being nothing more than a Mr. Mom and a general handyman, but Nick knew he was deeply content. And that was the kind of life Nick wanted.

He let his eyes idly roam around the room, sipping his gin and tonic. His contacts were already drying out from the cigarette smoke that hung in the air, and he sighed wearily. At least there was a no-smoking area in the restaurant, he thought enviously, his gaze sweeping over the crowd. The faces were just a blur until his eye was caught by a redhead openly staring at him. She was attractive enough in a flamboyant sort of way, and he smiled lazily back. For a moment he thought she was alone, and then he realized there was another woman slumped in the booth beside her. Nick could only see the back of her head, but the unique strawberry blond hue caught his eye. Laura had hair that color, he thought. And then he frowned. Could it be her? he wondered. He tried to dismiss the possibility as too much of a coincidence, but he had a gut feeling that it really was her. Should he check it out? And what if he was wrong? Well, what if he was? he asked himself impatiently. He had nothing to lose. He could just make some innocuous remark to the redhead and beat a hasty retreat. It was worth a try.

"Sam," Laura hissed again, this time more urgently. "Will you please turn around? He's going to notice you if you keep staring."

"Too late," Sam replied. "He just smiled at me."

Laura moaned. "Well, will you at least stop encouraging him?" she pleaded.

"You didn't tell me he was such a hunk," her friend said accusingly, still looking over her shoulder. Suddenly she straightened up. "Hey! He's coming over!"

Laura gave her a panic-stricken look, and then searched wildly for an escape. But they were wedged in a corner booth, and the only way out would take her directly in Nick's path.

"Laura, chill out," Sam advised, aware that her friend was panicking. "You spent hours with him alone last night. This is no big deal."

"Maybe not to you," Laura replied tersely, her heart banging painfully against her rib cage. What was she going to say to him? she wondered. Would he mention last night? Oh, why hadn't Sam picked some other place!

"Hello, Laura. I thought it was you." Nick's deep, mellow voice intruded on her thoughts and she slowly raised her eyes. He smiled at her, looking utterly relaxed, dressed in a pair of khaki trousers and a striped cotton shirt. He held a drink in one hand and nonchalantly leaned on the corner of their booth. He looked fantastic, as always, and Laura suddenly wished she'd dressed in something more flattering than twill slacks and an oversize cotton sweater.

"Hello, Nick."

There was a moment's awkward pause while Nick waited for her to ask him to join them and Laura prayed he would go away.

Sam looked from one to the other, decided it was time to step in and salvage the situation and smiled brightly.

"I don't believe we've met. I'm Sam Reynolds," she said, extending her hand.

Nick took it, looking at her quizzically. "Are you sure we haven't met? Your voice sounds familiar."

"Not exactly," Sam said with an impudent grin. "But we have spoken before."

"We have?"

"Mmm-hmm. I've had a spare key to Laura's office ever since she locked herself out a couple of years ago, and I answered the phone the day you called looking for her."

Nick had the grace to flush. ''Then I think I owe you an apology. As I recall, my manners were somewhat lacking that day.''

''Well, I would hardly have described you as Mr. Congeniality,'' Sam agreed. ''But that's okay. I survived.''

''Well, maybe we can start over. After all, Laura gave me a second chance, and I was even more rotten to her,'' he said with an engaging grin.

''I don't know...'' Sam said, pretending to think it over. ''What do you think, Laura?''

Laura couldn't think, period. ''Sure. I guess so,'' she mumbled.

''All right. If Laura says it's okay, then I guess it is. Would you like to join us?''

Laura gave her a venomous look, which Sam ignored.

''As a matter of fact, yes. Thanks.'' Nick slid into the booth next to Laura, and she quickly tried to move over, only to find her progress blocked by Sam who had relinquished just a few measly inches of the seat. Nick didn't seem to mind the close proximity, but Laura was all too aware of his body whisper-close to hers.

''Help yourself to some potato skins,'' Sam offered.

''No, thanks. I've been eating bar food all night.''

''I hope we're not taking you away from your friends,'' Sam said.

''No. It's a bachelor party, and like they say, if you've seen one, you've seen them all. I was about to make my excuses, anyway.''

"Good. Then you can stay awhile. Isn't that great, Laura?"

Laura felt Sam's elbow in her ribs and realized that she hadn't taken any part in the conversation. "Oh. Yes, that's nice."

Nick casually draped his arm across the back of the booth, and the tips of his fingers rested on Laura's shoulder. She tried to move slightly away, but Sam had her wedged in.

"Can I buy you ladies a drink?" Nick asked.

"Thanks. I'll have a tonic water," Sam said.

"Laura?"

"Iced tea, please."

Nick signaled to the waitress and relayed the orders before resuming the conversation.

"So what brings you two to this mecca for swinging singles?" he asked.

"What do you think?" Sam said pertly. "We're looking for men. Are you available?"

Laura looked horrified, but after a moment of stunned silence, Nick chuckled. "Your friend here doesn't pull any punches, does she?" he said to Laura with a smile.

"Sam's pretty direct," Laura agreed. "But that's *not* why we're here. At least, *I'm* not. Sam picked this place."

"And I'm glad she did," Nick replied smoothly. "Otherwise there wouldn't have been anyone to rescue me from that bachelor party. And, Sam, to answer your question, yes, I am." He turned to look at the bar for a moment. "Would you excuse me for a minute? I think the group is leaving and I need to give the groom my best wishes.''

''Sure,'' Sam said. ''We'll still be here.''

''Will you?'' Nick asked quietly, directing his question to Laura. He was aware of her tension and he wouldn't put it past her to bolt the moment he was out of sight.

The thought had crossed her mind, and she flushed guiltily. It was almost as if he'd sensed her impulse to flee, and now he was asking for a promise to stay. But as long as Sam was here, what could be the harm? ''Yes.''

He smiled at her. ''Good. I'll be right back.''

The moment he was out of earshot Laura turned on Sam. ''Sam, how could you? First you invite him to join us, then you ask personal questions. I'm not only a nervous wreck, I'm embarrassed.''

''Why?'' Sam asked innocently. ''He didn't seem to mind. And you should thank me. Now you know for sure that he's available,'' she said smugly.

''So what? Available and interested are two different things.''

''Oh, he's interested,'' Sam said confidently.

''How do you know?''

''Because.''

''That tells me a lot,'' Laura retorted.

''Look, he came over here because he thought it was you. The man wasn't exactly trying to avoid an encounter—he arranged it. And when he talks to you there's a soft, gentle look in his eyes that makes me feel mushy inside,'' she said dreamily. ''Yeah, the man's interested.''

"Well, maybe the woman isn't."

"Oh, she's interested, too."

"What are you, a mind reader?"

"No. It doesn't take a sixth sense to pick up the vibrations between you two. Laura, you're scared, right?"

"Yes."

"And why do you think you're scared?"

"Because I haven't been around a man for a very long time."

"Nope. Wrong answer, kiddo. Not just any man could make you feel like this. It's Nick. Because you're attracted to him, too, and for the first time in years you sense a threat to that insulated existence you've created for yourself. You're not scared because he's a man. You're scared because he's Nick—a very special man. And by the way, I approve. He's not only a hunk, he's got a great personality and a good sense of humor."

Nick chose that moment to slip back into the booth, giving Laura no time to respond. She had been about to protest Sam's quick assessment, but in retrospect she had to admit that maybe Sam was right.

"Did you miss me?" Nick asked with a grin.

"Oh, were you gone?" Sam asked, feigning surprise.

"Well, that's a surefire way to deflate a man's ego," Nick replied good-naturedly.

Laura listened with envy to the exchange. Sam was so at ease with Nick, while she was a mass of vibrating nerves. She couldn't even think of any witty remarks to add to the repartee. Miserably she stirred her iced tea. The ice was slowly melting and diluting the color, washing it out to a pale image of its former self. Sort of like her, she thought. Sometimes, emotionally, she felt like an empty shell of the woman she used to be.

"...so I'll leave you two to carry on."

Laura's attention snapped back to the conversation and she realized that Sam was sliding out of the booth.

"Sam!" There was panic in her voice. "Where are you going?"

"I knew you were daydreaming," Sam declared. "I've got to go, kiddo. I have to show a house very early tomorrow morning and I want to be thinking clearly when I meet the client. He's only in town for the weekend, so it's now or never for the sale. Nick, it was nice meeting you." Sam extended her hand and Nick stood, taking it in a firm grip.

"Can I walk you to your car?" he offered.

"I'm parked right at the door," she assured him. "Besides, I just spotted someone at the bar that I know and I want to stop and say hi. But do me a favor, will you? Walk Laura to hers when she leaves, no matter what she says. She's at the far end of the lot."

"Done," he said with a smile.

Laura suddenly felt like an idiot child, being talked over instead of to. "Sam, I'm quite capable of taking care of myself," she said stiffly.

"Now don't get all huffy," Sam said. "If you're with a gentleman, let him act like one. Good night, Nick."

Nick watched Sam leave and then slid into the booth again next to Laura. "I like her," he said with a smile. "Her candor is very...charming."

"I can think of another word for it," Laura muttered.

Nick chuckled. "Come on, be nice. She's obviously a good friend. She's graciously bowed out, leaving you alone with me, and she's made sure you get to your car safely. What more could you ask?"

"That she butt out?" Laura suggested. "Look, Nick, you don't have to keep me company. Actually, I was thinking about heading home. This," she said, gesturing around the crowded, noisy room, "isn't my style, anyway."

"Mine, neither. And as for keeping you company, I wouldn't have come over here if I hadn't wanted to see you."

"That's what Sam said," Laura admitted, her eyes searching out her friend, who was now carrying on an animated conversation with an attractive man at the bar.

"Well, Sam is very insightful."

"But why?" Laura turned her attention back to Nick, truly bewildered by his interest.

Nick placed his elbows on the table and steepled his fingers, staring at her pensively. Then he shook his head. "You amaze me, Laura. I told you last night. You're an extremely attractive woman. I admire your determination. You are a great conversationalist and fun to be with when you're not totally stressed out, which you seem to be tonight. Is it me?"

Laura shifted uncomfortably. "I'm not stressed," she lied, avoiding his question.

In response Nick reached over and captured her fingers. "Your hands are trembling." His thumb moved to her wrist. ''Your pulse is rapid. With any other woman, Laura, I might attribute those symptoms to something else,'' he said bluntly. Then his voice gentled. ''But you're just plain scared, aren't you?''

Laura snatched her hand away and groped for her purse, making Nick realize he had pushed too hard.

''Laura, I'm sorry. Forget I asked, okay, and don't run off. Besides, there's something I want to ask you.''

Laura looked at him uncertainly. ''What is it?''

''Jack and his wife, Peggy, are giving a little party next weekend. Sort of a pre-Fourth-of-July barbecue. I wondered if you'd like to go.''

It took a moment for the invitation to register, and then Laura realized that Nick was actually asking her for a date. A real date, not an unexpected, spur-of-the-moment get-together.

''When is it?'' she asked.

''Saturday. About four.''

''I work on Saturdays, Nick.''

''All day?'' he asked with a frown.

''Sometimes.''

''Maybe that's one of the reasons you always look so tired,'' he said gently, reaching over with one finger to trace the shadow under one of her eyes. ''Everyone needs some fun in their life.''

Laura swallowed. ''I don't have time. I'm a one-person operation, Nick. Saturdays are a good time to get caught up on the books. Besides, I'm going home for a long weekend over Fourth of July, so I need to make up the time.''

''We could go to the party late,'' he offered.

"I don't want you to miss any of it because of me," she protested.

"Laura, to be perfectly honest, I'd rather be at *some* of the party with you than *all* of it alone," he replied with a smile.

"Well..." Nick was being completely accommodating, and there was no reason to refuse. Besides, she liked Jack. They would be in a crowd, so what could happen? Sam was always telling her to make an effort to improve her social life, and this was a good opportunity.

She looked toward the bar again, just in time to see her friend heading for the door on the arm of the man she'd been talking to. Sam never seemed at a loss for male companionship. Maybe there was a lesson to be learned here, Laura thought. Her best friend had more dates than she could handle and was always telling Laura to spice up her social life. Perhaps, Laura reasoned, the Lord had put her in this uncharacteristic setting tonight so that she and Nick would cross paths. It seemed like an awfully strange coincidence to have happened purely by chance. There must be a message here. And maybe it was simply that if Sam could go out with dozens of men, she could at least go out with one. Taking a deep breath, she turned back to Nick. "Okay," she agreed.

Laura was rewarded with an ecstatic grin. "Great! I'll call you this week to firm up the plans."

"All right." She withdrew her keys from her purse. "I really have to go, Nick. It's been a long day, and frankly the smoke in here is killing my eyes."

"Yeah, I know what you mean," he concurred. He

thought of suggesting a quieter lounge nearby, but decided against it. He'd already gotten more than he expected out of the evening when she'd agreed to go to Jack's party with him. He wasn't about to push his luck. ''I'll walk you to your car.''

''It's really not necessary. Sam's just overprotective.''

''A promise is a promise,'' Nick said firmly.

''Well, have it your way,'' she capitulated.

Nick signaled the waitress again and quickly settled the bill before sliding from the booth. He reached for her hand, and, short of rudely ignoring it, Laura was left with no option but to take it. Once on her feet, she assumed he'd release it, but Nick had other ideas, tucking it into the crook of his arm. Laura's heart went into fast-forward at the protective gesture. Calm down, she told herself sharply. Nick probably treats every woman he's with the same way. You're nothing special.

As they threaded their way through the crowd, Laura wasn't even aware of the glances directed her way from the bar. But Nick was. He looked down at her, noted that her eyes were focused straight ahead and realized that she was oblivious to the admiring glances. She was a woman with absolutely no conceit, he thought. Actually, she went the other direction in terms of self-image, which wasn't good, either. Why? he wondered for the hundredth time.

As they stepped into the warm night air, Laura drew a deep breath. ''I hate those kinds of places,'' she said vehemently.

''Then why come?''

"Sam likes them. She drags me along occasionally because she thinks it will enhance my social life," Laura joked, sorry immediately that she'd made such a revealing comment. She knew Nick was too attentive to let it pass unnoticed.

"If your social life is lacking, I can only believe it's by choice," he said.

Laura shrugged. "The business keeps me busy," she said noncommittally.

They had arrived at the corner of the parking lot, and Nick finally released her hand, making no comment. He leaned against the side of her car and folded his arms across his chest, apparently in no hurry to leave. Self-consciously, Laura fumbled for the right key and unlocked the door.

"Well…thank you for walking me to my car," she said breathily.

"No problem. I would have, even if Sam hadn't asked."

"I know." And she did. Nick's impeccable manners seemed inbred.

Nick gazed at her shadowed face and his throat tightened painfully. She always seemed so alone, so in need of loving. Without even stopping to think, tired of weighing the consequences of every action, he reached out and drew her toward him, looping his arms around her waist. Laura seemed stunned by this unexpected action and stared at him wide-eyed. Because he was leaning against the car, their eyes were on the same level, and his held hers compellingly, searchingly. At last he sighed. "Laura, what are you doing to me?" he muttered under his breath, shaking his head. He moved a hand up to cradle the back of her neck, rubbing his thumb gently over her skin as he spoke.

"Nick...I don't... You can't..." She drew in a sharp breath, tears of frustration hot behind her eyes. "Look, I'm scared, okay?" she choked, wanting to find a hole and crawl in.

Nick tightened his hold in a manner that was comforting, not threatening. "I know," he whispered hoarsely. "I just don't know why. I would never do anything to hurt you." He pulled her close, and she found herself pressed against the hard planes of his body as his hand guided her head to rest on his shoulder. He could feel her trembling, and gently he stroked her back, hoping she would relax in his arms. He felt as shaky as she did, and he forced himself to take deep, even breaths.

With her cheek pressed against the soft cotton of his shirt, her ear to his chest, Laura could hear the thudding of his heart, could feel his breath on her forehead. She knew she should pull away. Warning bells were clanging inside her head. But it felt so good to be held like this. So good. She would take this moment, take what was being offered, with no questions. A moment to enjoy being held in strong but gentle arms, that was all she asked.

Nick felt her relax slightly. Not much, but it was a start, he told himself. Whatever demons were in her past were powerful, and he'd have to be patient. If he wanted Laura, it would have to be on her own terms and in her own time.

As her trembling subsided, he eased her back, smiling at her with an achingly tender look in his eyes. "Laura, I'm going to kiss you good-night," he said softly. "I want you to know that this warning isn't part of my standard goodnight spiel," he admitted with a quirky smile, "but I don't want you to be scared. Okay?"

Laura hesitated, and then realized she was nodding. It had not been a conscious choice.

His eyes held hers for a moment longer, and then his lips gently closed over hers. Slowly, coaxingly, they began to explore, seeking a response. Her lips were stiff and uncertain at first, but when at last he felt them begin to yield, he intensified the kiss, pacing himself, allowing the embrace to progress only in small increments. Without intending to, without wanting to, she found herself responding to his touch as he fanned into life an ember of passion that had long lain dormant.

Laura didn't know how long they kissed. She just knew that the flame of passion Nick had ignited in her was more intense than any she had ever experienced. His caresses were knowing and sensitive, designed to draw the deepest possible response from her. Laura was not accustomed to such a tender touch. Joe had been her only lover, and she his. Together, through trial and error, they had learned about making love. But long before they had discovered all the things that made it so special, their marriage had started to turn sour.

Nick knew he might be pushing her too fast, and realized he had to stop, but her sweetly tender lips made the blood race through his veins. At the same time, he knew that if he kissed her any longer, tomorrow she might regret her ardent response and cut him off. It was a risk he wasn't willing to take.

With one last, lingering caress, Nick's lips broke contact with hers. Both of them were breathing raggedly, and Laura's hands were pressed flat against the front of his shirt. She stared at him, fear and wonder and uncertainty mingling in her eyes. Nick almost pulled her back into his arms, but forced himself to straighten up.

He opened her car door, and she silently slipped inside. When she rolled down the window, he leaned in and once more brushed his lips over hers.

''Until next week,'' he said quietly.

''Until next week,'' she agreed.

# *Chapter Six*

Laura was a little surprised to find a message from Sam on her answering machine when she arrived home, considering her friend had left the bar with an attractive man. But she might as well return the call tonight, she thought with a sigh. Sam would keep bugging her until she had a full report on the evening.

"I've been sitting by the phone waiting for you to call," Sam said eagerly before even one ring had been completed. "So, did my timely departure do the trick?"

"It was a little obvious," Laura said dryly.

"I'm sure Nick appreciated it," Sam replied smugly.

"Yeah, he did," Laura admitted. "He likes you."

"Great. I like him, too. But I'm more interested in how he feels about you. What happened after I left?"

"We didn't stay much longer," Laura said. "By the way, who was your friend?" she asked, more to buy time than out of any real curiosity. She'd long ago given up trying to keep track of Sam's male admirers. There seemed to be an ever-changing cast of thousands.

"Rick? Just a guy in my office. We've gone out a few times, had a few laughs. Nothing serious. He just walked me to my car. I have an early appointment tomorrow, remember? But why are *you* home so early?" Sam said worriedly. "Did you clam up or do something to discourage him?"

"I said I was tired and needed to get home."

"Oh, great," Sam said with disgust. "I should have hung around, after all. There would have been more action if I *had* stayed."

"No, I don't think so," Laura said slowly, playing with the phone cord.

"What does that mean?"

"Well, he asked me out next weekend."

"And you're going, I hope."

"Yes."

"All right! Now we're getting somewhere."

"He kissed me again, too."

"Well! This is definitely progress," Sam said enthusiastically.

"Sam..." Laura climbed onto a bar stool and propped her elbow on the counter, resting her chin in her hand. She frowned, unsure why she was having so much difficulty discussing this with the uninhibited Sam, who was never shocked by anything.

"Yes," Sam prompted.

"Um, Nick...he kisses...differently...than I've ever been kissed," she said awkwardly. "More...intimately, you know? And what's worse, I—I wanted him to...well, to kiss me even more. Oh, what's wrong with me?'' she moaned in despair.

''Absolutely nothing,'' Sam said flatly. ''You're a young, vibrant woman who's been living in an emotional cave for a decade. Frankly, I'm surprised those penned up hormones haven't revolted before now. Look, Laura, enjoy it. There's nothing wrong with physical affection. I understand your need to move forward slowly, and, believe it or not, I actually think it's wise. But at least move forward.''

As usual, Sam's straightforward advice sounded logical enough. But move forward...how far? Laura wondered. She had never made love to a man outside of marriage. Her morals and her faith just wouldn't allow it. A few kisses didn't seem that serious. But with Nick, she feared she'd be playing with fire.

''But, Sam, I—I just don't want to get hurt again,'' she admitted finally.

Sam knew how much that admission had cost Laura. Since the two had become friends nearly eleven years ago, Laura had never talked about the emotional scars of her first marriage. Sam knew they were breaking new ground, thanks to Nick. He'd gotten under her skin, opened some old wounds. She realized that it was painful for Laura, but at least now the wounds would have a chance to heal.

''Laura, not every relationship is built on hurt,'' Sam said, treading cautiously on what she knew was shaky turf. ''You've never said much about your marriage to Joe, but I could read between the lines. When I used to run into you at night school you always seemed so sad. And I saw what he did to you the night you left him,'' she said, her voice tightening. ''You did the right thing by walking away. Randy might have been a bum, but he never beat me.''

For a moment there was silence on the line, Sam wondering if Laura would deny the abuse, Laura lost in remembrance.

''Joe wasn't always like that, Sam,'' she said softly.

''I'm sure he wasn't,'' Sam said gently. ''But sometimes people change.''

''He just couldn't take the pressure,'' Laura said with a sigh. ''Something inside of him broke, and I didn't know how to help him fix it. He...he made me feel like his problems were my fault, and for a long time I bought into that,'' she said, a catch in her voice. ''But I finally realized that he was sick. I knew he needed help, but it infuriated him when I suggested it. And when he started expressing his anger with violence, I was too scared to push him. Maybe I should have.''

''You did the right thing,'' Sam said firmly. ''From what I saw, you might not be around if you'd pushed.''

''But what you said before, Sam, about people changing...that's what I'm afraid of. How do I know Nick won't do the same thing? I survived the last time, thanks to you and my family and my faith, but I'm not sure I would again.''

''Honey, I don't have the answers for you,'' Sam said with a sigh. ''Commitment means risk, that's for sure. Relationships don't come with a money-back guarantee or a lifetime warranty. All you can do is use your judgment and then take your best shot.''

''You know, despite my faith, I wouldn't have made

it through the last time if you hadn't stuck with me,'' Laura said quietly.

''Of course you would,'' Sam said briskly. ''You are one strong lady, Laura Taylor.''

''Lately I haven't been feeling all that strong.''

''You'll be fine. Like I said, don't rush things. Take it slowly, if that makes you more comfortable. But give it a chance, for your own sake.''

Laura lay awake a long time that night. She tried to push thoughts of Nick from her mind, but it was no use. She supposed she'd been attracted to him almost from the beginning, but her well-tuned defense mechanisms simply had not allowed her to admit it. Now that he had made his interest clear, she found that her defenses were not nearly as impenetrable as she'd assumed.

Laura thought back to her early years with Joe. She couldn't remember exactly when the disintegration of their marriage had begun. Joe's growing despondency had been the first sign, she supposed. Eventually he sought solace in liquor, which made him belligerent and abusive, both emotionally and physically. The deterioration had been a gradual thing that had slowly worsened until one day Laura realized that her life had become a living hell. In trying to appease him, to meet his unreasonable demands, she'd cut herself off from family and friends and lived in isolation, growing more desperate every day, trying to make it work, eventually realizing that she couldn't. It had taken a crisis to convince her that she couldn't go on that way anymore. She'd spent days in prayer and soul-searching, but in the end Joe's untimely death had taken the decision out of her hands. Somehow she'd pulled herself together and found the courage to start over alone, but the scars were deep.

With a strangled sob of frustration, Laura punched her pillow, letting the tears slide down her cheeks unchecked. Her stomach was curled into a tight knot, and the taste of salt was bitter on her lips. She had to let go of the past, like Sam said, and move forward—in her personal life as well as with her business. But she simply didn't know if she had the courage to take another chance on love.

By Friday, when she hadn't heard from Nick, Laura's nerves were stretched to the snapping point. He'd said he'd be in touch about Jack's party, but there'd been no call. What was he going to do, wait until nine o'clock tonight, leaving her dangling until the last minute? Or maybe he wasn't going to call at all, she thought in sudden panic.

Laura glanced at the sheet of paper in front of her. She'd been sitting at the drafting table in her office for the past hour, doodling instead of working, and she was disgusted with herself. *See what caring about a man does to you?* she chided herself angrily. *Your emotional state becomes dependent on his whims.* No way was she going to let that happen again, she told herself fiercely.

The sudden ring of the telephone at her elbow made her jump, and she snatched it up in irritation.

"Taylor Landscaping," she said shortly.

"Laura?" It was Nick's voice, hesitant and uncertain, and her heart jumped to her throat.

"Yes."

"Is everything all right?"

"Yes. Everything's fine," she said tersely.

"No, it's not. I can tell."

"Look, Nick, I said everything's fine. Let's drop it, okay?"

She heard him sigh. "I don't have the time or the energy to argue with you now, Laura. We'll talk when I see you," he said, and she realized that his voice sounded weary. "Unfortunately, that won't be until next week. That's why I'm calling."

He was canceling their date! Laura felt her heart dive to her shoes.

"Laura, are you still there?"

"Yes," she said in a small voice.

"I'm really sorry about tomorrow night. I talked to Jack, and you're still welcome to attend if you like."

"I'll probably pass," she said, her voice strained. "I have plenty of work to do."

"Laura, there isn't much in this world that would have made me break this date. But my dad had a heart attack Wednesday and I flew out to Denver on the red-eye Thursday morning. To be honest, I haven't really been thinking straight since then. I'm sorry for the last-minute notice."

Laura closed her eyes as a wave of guilt washed over her, and she gripped the phone tightly. "Nick, I'm so sorry," she said contritely. "How is he doing?"

"Okay. It turned out to be a fairly mild attack, but he had us all worried for a while."

"You sound tired," Laura ventured.

"Yeah. I am. I don't think I've had but five or six hours of sleep since Tuesday night."

"Well, don't worry about tomorrow," she said. "Obviously you need to be with your family. That takes priority."

"I hoped you'd understand. Can I call you when I get back?"

"Sure. I hope everything turns out well with your father," she said sincerely. "And get some sleep, Nick. You sound beat."

"I'll try. Talk to you soon, okay?"

"Okay."

The line went dead and Laura slowly hung up the receiver. She felt sorry for Nick and his family, but she had learned one thing. She was letting Nick become too important to her, so important that he could control her emotional state. And that was dangerous.

By the time Nick called Monday afternoon, Laura had convinced herself that, Sam's advice notwithstanding, it would be better if she didn't see him anymore except professionally. She just wasn't ready to trust a man again, it was as simple as that. Now all she had to do was tell Nick—which wasn't quite as simple.

"How's your dad doing?" she asked as soon as he said hello.

"Much better. They're pretty sure he'll make a full recovery."

"I'm really glad, Nick."

"Thanks."

"You sound more rested."

"I got in at a decent time last night and slept ten hours straight," he admitted.

''I have a feeling you needed it.''

''Yeah, I did. Jack tells me you didn't make the party.''

''No.'' She played with the phone cord, twisting and untwisting it.

''You would have enjoyed it, Laura. I'm sorry I couldn't take you.''

''It's okay.''

''Well, I feel like I should make it up to you. How about dinner Wednesday?''

Now was the time. She took a deep breath. ''Nick, I can't. I'm going home next weekend for Fourth of July and if I want to take off an extra day I really need to put in some longer hours this week.''

''But you have to eat,'' Nick stated practically. ''Can't you spare time for a quick dinner?'' he coaxed.

''Nick, I really can't.''

There was silence on the other end of the line for a moment, and Laura knew Nick was frowning.

''Maybe I'll stop by one night and we can make a late run to Ted Drewes.'' There was a note of caution in his voice now.

''I don't think I'll have time. But thank you.''

Nick stared at the wall in his office, thinking quickly. Laura was obviously giving him the brush-off. And he shouldn't be surprised, considering she'd admitted before that she was scared. It didn't take a genius to figure out what was going on here. She'd gotten cold feet, decided not to risk any sort of involvement. But he wasn't going to let her go this easily. She obviously wasn't in a receptive mood, so now was not the time to discuss it. Besides, he was sure he could be much more convincing in person. So he'd play dumb, ignore the message being sent, let her off the hook for this date, but renew the attack next week when she returned.

"I understand, Laura. I know how it is when you're trying to take a little vacation," he said sympathetically. "We'll try again next week. I'll call you soon."

"Nick, I—"

"Laura, it's okay," he cut her off. "You don't have to apologize for begging off. Duty calls. Believe me, I've been there. I'll talk to you soon. Take care, okay?"

"Yeah, I will."

Laura heard the click as the line went dead and stared at the receiver in her hand. Well, she'd certainly handled that well, she thought in disgust. Why hadn't she just come right out and said "Listen, Nick, this isn't going to work out. You're a nice guy, but I don't want any complications in my life." Period. That's all it would have taken. Instead, she'd tried the more subtle backdoor route. Unfortunately, he hadn't gotten the message. He was probably so used to women falling all over him that it had been beyond his comprehension that someone would actually not want to date him. Well, the next time he called she'd be more straightforward.

By Friday, when Nick still hadn't contacted her, Laura began to think that maybe he'd gotten the message, after all. But instead of feeling relieved, she was filled with despair. Which made no sense at all.

As Laura left her office Friday night, she was determined to put Nick out of her mind. She'd been looking forward to this rare long weekend at home for months, and she wasn't going to let anything ruin it. Once she got there, she wouldn't have time to think about him, anyway. The Anderson Fourth of July gathering was legendary, drawing family from far and wide for what had become an annual family reunion. Laura had missed several during her marriage to Joe, but none since.

She climbed into her car, depositing a portfolio on the seat beside her. Lately she'd been swamped, but she wasn't going to complain. The lean years were still too vivid in her memory. If she had to work a little more tonight at home before calling it a day, so be it. She'd have four glorious days of freedom after that.

Suddenly her stomach rumbled, and Laura grinned at the message. She'd worked through lunch, and now she was ravenous. With any luck she could have a simple meal on the table within an hour, she thought, placing her key in the ignition.

But luck was against her. When she turned the key, the engine sputtered but didn't catch. She tried again, with the same result. A third attempt was equally futile.

Laura stared at the dashboard in disbelief. Her little compact car might be old, but it had always been reliable. How could it pick tonight to act up? Without much hope, Laura climbed out of the car and lifted the hood. She had some rudimentary knowledge of mechanics, but nothing appeared to be out of order. Which meant that the car would have to be towed to the shop, she thought resignedly.

Two hours later, the mechanic emerged from the

garage, wiping his hands on a greasy rag. Larry had been working on her car for several years, mostly doing routine maintenance, and Laura trusted him implicitly. He'd gone out of his way for her more than once, including tonight, staying well beyond quitting time to help her out.

"Well?" she asked hopefully.

"Sorry, Laura," he said, shaking his head regretfully. "There's nothing I can do tonight. She's got a problem, all right, but it'll take me a while to figure it out. I'd come in tomorrow, but I'm taking the family down to Silver Dollar City for the holiday. We've had the reservations for months," he said apologetically.

Laura's spirits sank. "I understand, Larry."

"I'll work on it first thing Tuesday, though," he offered.

"I guess that's the best we can do," she said, suddenly weary.

"Can I give you a lift somewhere?" Larry asked.

"Well..." Laura hesitated, loath to put him to any more trouble. But she only lived a couple of miles from the garage. "If you're sure it's not a problem..."

"Not at all. Just let me turn off the lights."

By the time Larry dropped her off at her apartment, it was nearly eight o'clock. She let herself in, too tired now to even consider making dinner. Besides, she'd lost her appetite.

Dejectedly, Laura sank into one of her overstuffed chairs and weighed her options. Sam would have been the logical one to turn to for help. But Sam had left today for a week's vacation in Chicago. Besides, asking for a ride to the office was one thing. Asking for a ride halfway across the state was another. Even if Sam was here she doubted whether she could bring herself to impose to that extent.

On a holiday weekend like this one she'd never find a rental car—at least not one she could afford. She could take a bus, but with all the stops and time spent waiting for connections it hardly seemed worth the effort. Besides, long bus rides inevitably made her feel carsick.

The apartment gradually grew dark, but Laura made no move to turn on any lights. The gloom suited her mood. She'd been looking forward to this family weekend for so long. This just wasn't fair. But then, life wasn't, as she well knew.

Laura thought ahead to the weekend stretching emptily before her. She ought to call and let her mom know she wouldn't be coming. But she knew how disappointed her mother would be, and she couldn't bring herself to do it quite yet. Maybe her fairy godmother would appear with a coach, she fantasized. There were plenty of mice in this building to turn into footmen, she thought ruefully.

Laura rested her head against the back of the chair and closed her eyes. She desperately needed some R and R. There had to be a solution to this dilemma, but at the moment she was too tired to figure it out. So she put it in the hands of the Lord. *Please help me find a way to get home,* she prayed silently. *I need to be with my family this weekend. Please.*

She must have dozed slightly, because the sudden ringing of the phone jolted her upright. Sleepily she fumbled for the light, squinting against its sudden brightness, and made her way to the phone.

"Hello."

"Laura?"

"Nick!" She was suddenly awake. "Hi."

"Hi. You didn't sound like yourself for a minute there."

"I was half-asleep," she admitted.

"At nine-thirty? That doesn't fit your normal pattern. Are you sick?"

"No. Just tired."

"It's a good thing you're taking a few days off," he said. "You need a break."

"Yeah, well, it doesn't look like I'm going to get one, after all," she said tiredly.

"What do you mean?"

"My car gave out. It's in the shop, and they won't be able to get to it until Tuesday."

"Laura, I'm sorry." The deep, mellow tones of his voice stroked her soothingly. "I know how much you've been looking forward to this. Is there any other way for you to get there?"

"Actually, I was sitting around waiting for my fairy godmother to come and conjure up a coach," she said, trying to keep her voice light.

"What?" He sounded puzzled, and she had to laugh.

"Nothing. You obviously didn't read fairy tales when you were growing up."

"Oh." She heard the glimmer of understanding dawn in his voice. "Cinderella."

"Very good. The only problem is, my fairy godmother seems to have taken off for the weekend, too.'' There was silence on the other end of the line, and Laura frowned. ''Nick? Are you still there?''

''Yeah, I was just thinking. Listen, Laura, I may not be a fairy godmother, and my car may not be a coach, but why don't you let me give you a ride?''

There was a moment of silence while she absorbed this offer. ''Are you serious?'' she said at last, her voice incredulous.

''Absolutely.''

''But...that's really generous of you... My family lives three hours from here,'' she stumbled over her words, too taken aback by the offer to be coherent. ''And besides, I don't want to disrupt your plans for the holiday,'' she added more lucidly.

''You won't be. As a matter of fact, I was just going to go over to Jack's on the Fourth for a barbecue. I didn't have anything else scheduled. And, to be honest, I'd much rather spend the time with you.''

Laura bit her lip. The temptation to accept was strong, given her desperate desire to go south and the lack of any other options. But how could she accept his offer, knowing she was planning to end their relationship? It wouldn't be honest, or fair.

''Look, Laura, I'm not inviting myself to your party. There must be a motel in town, and I'll settle for whatever time you can spare during the holiday,'' he said quietly.

''Nick, it's too much to ask.''

''You didn't ask. I offered.''

''No,'' she said firmly. ''If you come, you come as my guest. There's always plenty of room at the house, even with all the relatives there. Mom loves company. It's no problem, and she'd never forgive me if I let you stay at the motel."

"I don't want to impose," he said firmly.

"I think you've got it backward. I'm the one who's imposing. Giving you a place to sleep is small compensation in return for the favor."

"Oh, there may be other compensations," he said lightly.

Laura stiffened. "Look, Nick. Your offer is generous. But I can't accept it if there are strings attached."

"You mean you won't even feed me?" he said disappointedly. "Man, I was hoping to at least get a good, home-cooked meal out of this."

"Oh." Laura was confused. Had she read too much into that last comment? Besides, what made her think he was that interested in her? Sure, they'd kissed a time or two. But that was probably the way he said good-night to every woman he dated. She took a deep breath. "Well, of course we'll feed you. Mom puts on quite a spread on the Fourth. In fact, it's sort of like a Norman Rockwell scene—long tables covered with checkered cloths and loaded down with every kind of all American food you can imagine."

"Now you're talking," he said enthusiastically. "What time do we leave?"

"Well, I have a Christian Youth Outreach board meeting at eight-thirty. It should be over by eleven. I could be ready by noon," she replied. Somehow the conversation had gotten out of hand. She didn't remember ever saying she'd go with him, and now they were making departure plans.

"Do you need a ride to the meeting?"

"No, but thank you," she said, touched by the offer. "There's another board member I can call."

"Okay. Then your coach will be there at twelve o'clock sharp, Cinderella. We'll grab some lunch on the way. Now go to bed and stop worrying. We're going to have a great weekend," he said confidently.

Laura replaced the receiver slowly, wishing she felt half as confident as Nick sounded. Being in his presence for four days was more apt to be nerve-racking and unsettling than relaxing, she thought. But as long as they stayed around the family she should be safe, she told herself. Besides, instead of focusing on the pitfalls, she should be grateful for his offer. Without Nick, she'd spend the holiday weekend sitting alone in her apartment. She'd asked the Lord for help, and He had come through for her. Okay, so it was a two-edged sword. She was going home, but she also had to deal with Nick. She'd just have to make sure they were never alone, she thought resolutely. Considering the size of the group, that wouldn't be too hard to arrange. Or would it? she wondered, suddenly sure that if Nick wanted to get her alone, he would find a way. And worse, she would let him.

# Chapter Seven

Laura was waiting when Nick arrived the next morning, still unsure how this had all come about, still uncertain about the wisdom of it. But Nick seemed to be on top of the world, reaching over to smooth away her frown lines with gentle fingers when he greeted her.

"What's this? Worried? Did you think your coach wouldn't materialize?" he teased.

"No, I knew you'd come. You're a pretty reliable guy."

"Thank you. Then why the frown?"

Laura crossed her arms over her chest in a self-protective hug. She'd wrestled with this problem all night. She knew she should have told him earlier in the week that she didn't want to see him socially anymore, and she should never have agreed to this arrangement. But she wanted to go home so badly, and the offer of a ride had been too tempting to refuse last night. Now she had second thoughts.

Taking a deep breath, she faced him. "Nick, I'm

just not sure this is right. I feel like I'm misleading you at best and using you at worst.''

''Why?''

''Because...because I...I really don't think that getting involved with each other is a good idea.''

Nick felt a knot forming in his stomach. He wasn't surprised. He'd sensed earlier in the week that she was backing off. But he hadn't expected to confront it now.

''No? Why not? Don't you like me?'' He grinned at her engagingly, his easy manner giving away nothing of his inner turmoil. He'd been planning to put off this discussion until after the holiday, but as long as he was going with her—and he *was* going with her, no matter what she said—they might as well get it out in the open now.

Laura found herself smiling at his teasing tone. ''Of course I like you.''

''Well, that's a start.''

''Nick,'' she said reprovingly. ''Will you be serious?''

''On a beautiful day like this? Mmm...that's asking a lot.''

''Well, could you try for just a minute?''

''Sure. I'll give it my best effort.'' He settled himself on the arm of her sofa. ''Shoot.''

Laura moved restlessly over to the window, double-checking the lock she knew was in place. Now that she had his attention, how could she explain her reluctance? ''Nick, you remember two weekends ago, in the parking lot?'' she asked tentatively.

''You better believe it. It's been on my mind all week.''

Laura gave him a startled look, then glanced away, nervously tucking a stray strand of hair behind her ear.

"Well, do you remember what I said about being scared?"

"Yes." Now his tone was more serious.

"I still am. Maybe more than ever. I'm just not ready for any kind of..." She stopped, fumbling for the right word, reluctant to make him think she was jumping to conclusions about his interest in her.

"Intimacy?"

She flushed. "Yes. And I have the feeling that's what you may be after."

"Guilty," he admitted readily.

She stared at him, taken aback at his unexpected honesty. The words she'd been about to say evaporated.

Nick stood and moved in front of her, placing his hands on her shoulders as his eyes locked on hers compellingly. "So now you know," he said quietly. "I like you a lot, Laura Taylor. I think something could develop here. I think you feel the same, and that's why you're scared. I've been completely honest about my feelings and my intentions, because some instinct tells me that you respect total honesty. No games. And I'm also being honest when I say that I realize you have some problems that prevent you from moving as quickly as I might want to. I also respect that. You can set the pace in this relationship."

Laura hadn't expected such a direct approach, and she was momentarily confused. Nick cared about her. He'd made that clear. Cared enough not to rush her. All he was asking her to do was give it a chance.

"Nick, I—I'm not sure what to say. You may be wasting your time. I can't make any promises."

"I'm not asking you to. I'm willing to take my chances. Who knows? Maybe my charms will win you over," he said with a grin, his tone suddenly lighter. "Now, is the serious discussion over for the day?" he asked, casually draping an arm around her shoulders.

"Yes, I guess so."

"Good. Then your coach awaits."

Laura still wasn't comfortable. She respected Nick's honesty, and she'd made her position clear, so the guilt was gone. But in its place was a knot of tension so real it made breathing difficult. Because now there was no question about Nick's interest. He wanted to date her; he wanted to see where their relationship might lead. Only God knew why, considering how messed up she was emotionally, but he did. And what was worse, she was beginning to want the same thing. Nick was a handsome, intelligent man with an engaging manner and an easy charm. But beyond that, he was also considerate and caring and gentle. Or at least he seemed to be. And there lay the problem. Laura no longer trusted her judgment when it came to men. She'd made one mistake, and the price had been high. More than she was willing to pay a second time. So where did that leave her with Nick?

Maybe, she thought, she should just take this one day at a time. And perhaps this weekend she should try to forget about heavy issues and just enjoy herself. After all, she'd been looking forward to this trip for weeks. Why ruin it by worrying about her relationship with Nick for the next few days? She needed to unwind, and that wasn't the way to do it.

Nick also seemed eager to relax, she thought as they headed south, through rolling wooded hills and farmland. He kept the conversation light, chatting about inconsequential things, and even made her laugh now and then. Without even realizing it, she began to relax, her pressures and worries slowly easing as they drove through the restful, green countryside.

"So...are you getting hungry?" he said, turning to her with a smile.

"As a matter of fact, I am," she admitted.

"Well, considering that I haven't spent a lot of time down in this area, Bennie's Burgers is about the extent of my suggestions," he said, nodding to a drive-though hamburger spot off the interstate.

She laughed. "Not exactly gourmet fare, I bet. Actually, there is one place I've been wanting to try. But it's a little out of our way," she said hesitantly.

"Are we on a schedule?"

"No."

"Then let's give it a shot. Where is it?"

"St. Genevieve. It's just a few miles off the interstate."

"Ah, St. Genevieve. The old French settlement," he said. "I was there a couple of times on class assignments when I was getting my degree."

"Isn't it charming?" she said enthusiastically. "My minister's sister opened a tea room there a year ago, and it's gotten some good press in St. Louis. I've been wanting to try it, but I just never seem to find the time to drive down there. Plus, I haven't seen her in a long time, and it would be nice to say hello. We all grew up together in Jersey,'' she explained.

''Sounds great to me,'' he said agreeably.

They found the restaurant with little trouble, right in the heart of the historic district. Laura's eyes roamed appreciatively over the charming country French decor as they were led to their table, and after they were seated she turned to the hostess, a slightly plump, white-haired woman with a pleasant round face. ''Is Rebecca here today?'' she asked.

The woman chuckled. ''Rebecca is *always* here,'' she said, her eyes twinkling. ''Would you like me to ask her to come out?''

''If you would. Tell her it's Laura Taylor.''

''Mmm, this all sounds great!'' Nick said, perusing the menu appreciatively. ''And very imaginative.''

''Rebecca studied at the Culinary Institute of America and did internships with a couple of the best restaurants in St. Louis,'' Laura told him, debating her own selection before finally settling on an unusual quiche.

Just as they finished placing their order, a slender, attractive woman appeared at the kitchen door. Her delicate facial structure and high cheekbones were accented by the simple but elegant French-twist style of her russet-colored hair. But her large, eloquent hazel eyes were her most striking feature. She scanned the room, and when her glance came to rest on Laura she smiled broadly and moved quickly in their direction.

Nick rose as she approached, and Laura stood up as well.

"Laura! It's so good to see you!" Rebecca said, giving the other woman a hug.

"Thanks, Becka," Laura said, reverting to her friend's childhood nickname. "I've been meaning to come down, but what with trying to get the business established..." Her voice trailed off apologetically.

The other woman smiled ruefully. "Tell me about it."

"Becka, this is Nick Sinclair. Nick, Rebecca Matthews."

Nick smiled and held out his hand. "It's a pleasure to meet you, Rebecca."

"Thanks. It's mutual," she said, returning his firm handshake. Then she turned to Laura. "I'm so glad you stopped in. May I join you for a minute?"

"Please," Nick said, retrieving a chair from an empty table nearby.

"What brings you to St. Genevieve?" Rebecca asked as she sat down.

"We're on our way to the Anderson Fourth of July reunion," Laura replied.

"Oh, yes. I should have remembered," Rebecca said with a smile. "Those gatherings are legendary in Jersey."

"See," Laura said, glancing at Nick with a smile. Then she turned her attention back to Rebecca. "So how is it going here? I've read about this place in the papers."

"The publicity has definitely helped," she admitted. "And it's going well. Just a lot of hard work and long hours. It doesn't leave much time for anything else. But it's very gratifying to see the business grow."

''I know what you mean,'' Laura concurred.

''Brad tells me you're doing well, too.''

''Brad's her brother—my minister,'' Laura informed Nick before responding to Rebecca. ''Yes. I can't complain. The Lord has been good to me. Hard work really does pay.''

''But too much work isn't a good thing, either,'' Nick interjected smoothly. ''Remember that old saying about all work and no play.'' He turned to Rebecca. ''Laura is a hard sell, but I'm trying.''

Rebecca smiled at Nick. ''Well, keep trying. I've known Laura all my life, and she's always pushed herself too hard.''

''Look who's talking,'' Laura chided teasingly.

Rebecca grinned and gave a rueful shrug. ''What can I say?''

''I'm sorry to interrupt, Rebecca.'' The white-haired woman paused at their table, her voice apologetic. ''But the repairman is here.''

''Thanks, Rose. I'll be right there.'' She turned back to Nick and Laura. ''Sorry to run. Although I suspect that three's a crowd anyway,'' she said, smiling as a flush rose to Laura's cheeks. She reached across and took her friend's hand. ''It was so good to see you,'' she said warmly. ''Stop by again, okay? And let me know in advance the next time. We do very romantic dinners here on Friday and Saturday nights,'' she said, directing her remark to Nick.

''I'll keep that in mind,'' he promised, rising to pull out her chair.

''It was nice meeting you,'' she said. ''And take care, Laura. Don't work too hard.''

"I'll try not to. But remember your own advice," she replied with a grin.

As Rebecca disappeared, Nick sat back down and turned to Laura with a smile. "She seems very nice."

"She's wonderful. Brad says she's making quite a go of it here. But he worries about her being alone. And about how hard she works."

"I feel that way about somebody myself," Nick said quietly.

Laura flushed and glanced down, playing with the edge of her napkin. The conversation was getting too serious—and too personal. Fortunately the timely arrival of their food kept Nick from pursuing the topic, and when the waitress left Laura deliberately turned the conversation to lighter subject matter. He followed her lead, and by the time a delicious and decadently rich chocolate torte arrived, compliments of the house, she was starting to relax again. Maybe this weekend would turn out all right after all, she thought hopefully, as they left the restaurant and resumed their drive.

Conversation flowed easily during the remainder of the trip, and as they approached her hometown, Nick turned to her with a smile. "How about a rundown on the agenda and the cast of characters?" he said.

"Okay," she agreed. "Let's start with the agenda. Today and tomorrow will be pretty low-key. We'll have dinner at Aunt Gladys's tomorrow. That's about the only real planned activity, but there will be lots of impromptu visiting going on. On the Fourth Mom has everyone over for a cookout, and then we play horseshoes or croquet and shoot off fireworks in the field after dark. Tuesday we can head back whenever we want. Now, as for the cast, there'll be my brother, John, and his family. They live in town. And my brother, Dennis, who lives in Memphis, will be up for the weekend and staying at the house. Aunt Gladys and Uncle George have five kids, most of whom are married, and a lot of them will come back for the Fourth.'' She paused and took a deep breath after her rapid-fire briefing. ''Those are the main players, but you'll find that a lot of other relatives show up, too,'' she added.

''Sounds like quite a gathering. What about your dad, Laura? You didn't mention him.''

Some of the brightness faded from her face and she turned to look out the window. ''He died eleven years ago,'' she said quietly.

''I'm sorry. You two were close, I take it.''

''Yes, very. I was the only girl in the family, and Dad spoiled me, I guess. He was a real special man, you know? Sometimes even now it's hard to believe he's gone. He died right after Fourth of July—one of the few I didn't spend with the family,'' she said, her voice edged with sadness and regret.

''How come you weren't here? I got the impression this was a sacred ritual.''

''It is now. But I missed a few years when I was married.''

''Why?''

Laura shrugged, and Nick could feel her closing down. ''Oh, you know how it is. Other things interfere.''

Like what? he wondered. But he knew better than to pursue a line of questioning that would alienate her and erase the lighthearted mood they'd established. So he changed the subject.

"You'll need to guide me from here," he said as he turned off the highway.

By the time he turned into the driveway leading to the modest white frame house on the outskirts of town, Laura's earlier mood was restored and her eyes were shining in anticipation. The crunching gravel announced their arrival, and before he even set the brake the front screen door opened and an older, slightly stout woman in a faded apron appeared.

She turned and called something over her shoulder before hurrying down the steps and throwing her arms around Laura.

"Oh, honey, it's so good to see you," she said.

"It's good to be home, Mom," Laura answered, and Nick heard the catch in her voice. He gave them a minute to themselves before climbing out of the car.

Laura's mother appeared instantly contrite. "Oh, goodness, I completely forgot about your young man." She stepped back and smoothed her hair.

"Mom, he's not my young man," Laura corrected her, flushing. "I told you about Nick last night on the phone."

"Of course you did. I hope you'll forgive me," Laura's mother said to Nick.

"I didn't mind in the least," he assured her.

Laura's mother looked pleased. "Well, good. Now, I assume you're Nick Sinclair," she said, holding out her hand. "Welcome to Jersey. I'm Laura's mother, Evelyn Anderson."

Nick returned her firm handshake with a smile, doing a rapid assessment. The years had clearly taken their toll on Laura's mother. Her face spoke of hard work, and the once-brown hair was now mostly gray. But her eyes sparkled and her smile was cheerful and warm. While life may have presented her with difficulties, Laura's mother seemed to have met them squarely and then moved on. Much like Laura herself, Nick thought.

"It's a pleasure to meet you, Mrs. Anderson. And thank you for inviting me. It was very generous of you."

"Not at all. We're glad to have you," she said. "Now let's go in and get you both settled and then you can have some dinner. Laura, I've put Nick in John's old room, if you'll take him up. I've got a pie in the oven that's just about done."

"Okay."

"Take your time unpacking. I didn't know when everyone would be arriving so I just put on a big pot of chili. It'll keep," she told them.

Laura followed Nick around to the back of the car and reached for her bag when he raised the lid of the trunk.

"I'll take care of it," he said, moving more quickly than she and effortlessly hoisting the strap of the small overnight case to his shoulder.

"You don't have to carry my luggage," she protested.

"Neither of us packed very heavily," he said with a crooked grin, holding up his duffel bag. "I think I can manage. You just lead the way and clear the path."

"Okay," she relented, walking ahead and opening the screen door. "Up the stairs, first door on your right," she instructed.

Nick made his way to the second floor and pushed the indicated door open with his shoulder. The room was simply furnished, with a navy blue bedspread on the full-size bed, an easy chair and an oak chest and desk. Rag rugs covered the polished plank floors, and woven curtains hung at the window. As Nick set his bag on the floor, Laura spoke at his elbow.

"I hope this will be okay," she said worriedly. She'd never really noticed before how plain the house was. It had always just been home to her—warm and inviting and welcoming. But to a stranger, it might appear old and worn. Not to mention hot. She noticed the beads of perspiration already forming on Nick's forehead. "Mom doesn't have air-conditioning," she said apologetically. "All the upstairs rooms have ceiling fans, though, so it stays pretty cool at night. During the day we don't spend a lot of time up here, anyway." She paused. "I guess I should have warned you."

"It wouldn't have made me change my mind about coming," he said with a smile.

"Are you sure the heat won't bother you?" she asked skeptically. "I'm used to it—this is how I grew up, and even now, I don't use my air all that much. But most people live in air-conditioning today. Especially in Missouri in July."

"Laura." He placed his hands on her shoulders. "I told you. This is fine. It's a small price to pay for a long weekend with you. Now, where do you want this?" he asked, nodding toward her overnight case.

"I'm right next door." She bent down to retrieve the bag, but he beat her to it. "Nick, it's just down the hall," she protested.

"Good. Then I won't have far to walk."

Laura shook her head. "You sure can be stubborn, do you know that?"

"Yep."

"Okay. I give up. Besides, it's too hot to argue."

Nick followed her down the hall. He could have let her take her own bag. It wasn't that heavy, and he'd seen evidence that she was stronger than she looked. No, his reasons were more selfish than chivalrous. He was curious about the room where Laura had spent her girlhood, and this might be his only chance to see it.

"You can just put it on the chair," Laura said, entering the room before him.

Nick took his time, glancing around as he strolled over to the white wicker chair with a floral cushion, which sat in one corner. The room was painted pale blue, with a delicate floral wallpaper border, and decorated with white wicker furniture and crisp organdy curtains. The floral spread on the twin bed matched the chair cushion, and a large print by one of the French Impressionists hung on one wall.

"Very nice," he said approvingly. "I particularly like this Matisse. Is it yours?"

"Yes."

"I'm surprised you didn't take it with you. It's a very fine print."

"Thanks. It was a high school graduation gift from Mom and Dad."

"And you left it?"

Laura turned away. "My husband wasn't a fan of impressionistic painting," she said with a shrug. "Besides, it would have left a blank spot on the wall here. I figured I could enjoy it whenever we came to visit."

"Which apparently wasn't often."

"Nick." Her eyes flew to his, and there was a note of warning in her voice. "Leave it alone."

He held up his hands. "Sorry."

She looked at him steadily for a moment, and then turned away. "I'm going to change into some shorts and freshen up. I'll meet you downstairs in about fifteen minutes for dinner, okay?"

"Sure."

Nick returned to his room and strolled restlessly over to the window, jamming his hands in his pockets, a frown marring his brow as he stared out over the distant fields. There was so much about Laura that he wanted to know. Needed to know. But she just wouldn't open up. What could possibly have happened to make her so gun-shy? He had no answers, but he did have three days ahead with Laura, in an environment where she seemed to feel safe. Maybe she would share some memories with him here. At least he could hope.

It didn't take Laura long to change. She was used to having too much to do in too little time, and she'd learned not to waste a moment. She slipped a pair of comfortable khaki shorts over her slim hips, tucking in a teal blue, short-sleeved cotton blouse and cinching the waist with a hemp belt. As she sat down on the bed to tie her canvas shoes, her eye fell on the Matisse, and she paused to look at it. The painting had always soothed her, and right now her nerves needed all the soothing they could get. Slowly she looked around the room that had been home for eighteen years, letting her gaze linger here and there. Everything was the same. The same blue walls. The same crystal dish on the dresser. The same worn spot on the rug. Everything was the same. Everything except her. So much had happened in the years since she had left this house as a bride. There had been so many hopes, heartaches and regrets....

Suddenly Laura's eyes grew misty. She wasn't prone to self-pity, so the tears took her off guard. It wasn't as if she had anything to complain about, she told herself. Yes, her life had turned out differently than she'd expected as a young bride. And some bad things had happened along the way. But the Lord had stood by her through the tough times, and her life now was very blessed. She had a successful business, a loving family, good friends and good health. The Lord always provided for her, even supplying a chauffeur for this weekend, she reminded herself.

Laura abruptly stood, brushing her tears aside. She wasn't going to give in to melancholy. Looking back did no good. She'd learned a long time ago that living in the past was a waste of time and an emotional drain. Live today, plan for tomorrow and trust in the Lord—that was her motto now.

Laura let herself out of her room, closing the door quietly behind her, and walked down the hall, her rubber-soled shoes noiseless on the hardwood floor. Nick's door was still closed, and her step faltered. Should she knock and let him know she was heading down? No, she could use a few minutes alone with the family.

Laura ran lightly down the steps and headed for the kitchen, sniffing appreciatively as she entered the bright, sunny room. John was sitting at the polished oak table unsuccessfully trying to convince eight-month-old Daniel to eat a spoon of strained peas, while Dana helped clear the remainder of three-year-old Susan's dinner off the table.

"Aunt Laura!" Susan squealed, catapulting herself toward Laura, who bent and swept her up.

"My goodness, what a big girl you are now!" Laura exclaimed, hugging the little body close to her. Susan tolerated the embrace for a few seconds, and then squirmed to be set loose.

John gave her a harried smile. "Hi, Sis. We'll clear out of here in just a minute so you can enjoy your dinner in peace."

"Don't rush on my account," Laura said, sitting down at the table and cupping her chin in her palm. Daniel chose that moment to spit out a particularly unappealing bite, and Laura laughed. "I'm enjoying this."

"You wouldn't want to take over, would you?" John asked hopefully.

"Oh, no, you're doing a masterful job. Hi, Dana. How'd you manage to get John to do the feeding chores?" she asked, turning toward her sister-in-law.

"Hi, Laura." Dana was a natural white blonde, and she wore her hair short and curled softly around her attractive, animated face. "We made a deal before we had the second one that feeding, diapering and bathing chores would be divided. And I must say, John's lived up to his side of the bargain really well.''

''Did I have a choice?'' he asked good-naturedly.

''No.''

He shrugged and grinned. ''Boy, has she gotten aggressive,'' he said to Laura.

''No, dear brother, the word is assertive. And good for you, Dana,'' Laura said with a smile.

''I should have figured you women would stick together,'' he lamented.

''Oh, get out the violins,'' Laura said, rolling her eyes.

John's grin softened to a smile. ''It's good to see you, Laura.''

''It's good to be home,'' she replied quietly, reaching over briefly to touch his shoulder. ''Is Dennis here yet?''

The screen door banged. ''Anybody home?'' a male voice bellowed.

John looked at Laura and grinned. ''Speak of the devil. We're in the kitchen,'' he called.

Dennis clomped down the hall and stood on the threshold, his hands on his hips. ''Who owns the sporty red number out front? Man, what a set of wheels!''

''Hello to you, too, brother,'' Laura said wryly.

''Oh. Sorry,'' he said sheepishly, engulfing her in a bear hug that left her breathless. ''Good to see you, Laura. So who owns the car?''

''The guy she brought down for the weekend,'' John said.

"Laura brought a guy down? No kidding! Where is he?"

"Look, you've all got it backward," Laura said, exasperation starting to wear down her patience. "*He* brought *me*. My car gave out, and he very graciously offered to drive me down. He was just being nice, so don't try to read any more into it."

"Just being nice? Give me a break! No guy with a car like that drives three hours to stay in an unairconditioned house in a town small enough to spit across just because he's nice," Dennis said.

Laura felt the color begin to rise in her face. "I knew this was a mistake," she muttered. "I just should have stayed home."

"Come on, you two. Leave your sister alone," Dana said sympathetically. "If she says this man is just a friend, then that's all he is."

"Oh, Laura! I didn't hear you come down," Mrs. Anderson said, bustling into the kitchen. "Are you and your young man ready for some chili?"

Laura looked at the grinning faces of her two brothers and dropped her head onto the table, burying her face in her crossed arms. "I give up," she said, her voice muffled.

Everyone started asking questions at once, and Laura ignored them all—until a sudden hush told her that Nick must have appeared in the doorway. She raised her eyes and his met hers quizzically. He didn't seem uncomfortable by the attention focused on him, just curious. Laura stood, glaring a warning over her shoulder and walked over to Nick.

"Nick, this is the family. My brothers John and

Dennis, and John's wife, Dana. And of course we can't forget Susan and Daniel. Daniel's the one with the green slime running down his chin and dripping onto John's shirt.''

''Oh, great!'' John muttered. He reached for a cloth and ineffectually wiped at the stain.

''Serves you right,'' Laura said sweetly, and John glared at her.

''Nice to meet you,'' Dennis said, sticking his hand out. ''Great car.''

''Thanks.''

''I'd shake hands, but I think it might be better if we just said hello,'' John said, still struggling with the peas.

''You look like you have your hands full,'' Nick commented with a chuckle.

''Yeah, you might say that,'' John replied, juggling Daniel on one knee while the suddenly shy Susan, a finger stuck in her mouth, watched the proceedings while clinging to his leg.

''Well, let's leave these two in peace to enjoy their food,'' Dana said as she came to John's rescue and hoisted Daniel onto her hip. ''Nick, it's nice to meet you. I'm sure we'll see a lot of you this weekend.''

''We'll be back later, Mom,'' John said, bending over to give her a peck on the cheek.

''Good. Drive safe, now. Dennis, you're just in time for some chili,'' she said, turning her attention to her younger son.

''Now that's what I call perfect timing,'' he said with a grin, turning a chair backward to the table and straddling it.

"Nick, go ahead and find a seat," Mrs. Anderson said as she set the table with quick efficiency.

Laura was glad Dennis had shown up in time for dinner. His boisterous chatter kept Nick occupied, giving Laura a chance to think. She should have expected her family's reaction, she supposed. She'd never brought a man home since…since Joe's death. In fact, she'd never brought anyone home except Joe. It was bound to cause a stir. She'd simply have to keep Nick at arm's length and convince everyone that he was just a friend. Except he wasn't helping.

She frowned at the dilemma and looked up, only to discover Nick's eyes on her. Dennis was at the sink refilling his water glass, and Nick's lazy smile and slow wink sent a sudden, sharp flash of heat jolting through her.

"Aren't you hungry?" he asked, his innocent words at odds with the inviting look in his eyes.

"Wh-what?" she stammered.

He nodded to her almost untouched chili, and she glanced down.

"Oh. Yes, I am. I guess I've been daydreaming. You look like you're doing okay, though," she said, trying to divert his attention.

"It's great." He turned to Laura's mother. "This is wonderful chili, Mrs. Anderson. Does Laura have this recipe?"

"Oh, my yes. She's quite a good cook when she has the time."

"I know," he said. His tone implied that he knew a lot more, and he turned to smile at Laura with that easy, heart-melting look of his.

Laura swallowed her mouthful of chili with difficulty and tried to think of some response, but she could barely remember her name, let alone formulate a snappy retort, when Nick looked at her like that. In desperation, she glanced toward her mother for assistance, but the older woman was watching them with an interested gleam in her eye. No ally there, she thought in disgust.

Dennis had returned and once again monopolized the conversation, so Laura focused on her chili, her mind racing. Her family was jumping to way too many conclusions, she thought. And Nick wasn't helping. If he kept looking at her in that intimate way, it wasn't going to be easy to convince everyone that friendship was all he had on his mind. Especially when she knew better. Or worse—depending on your point of view, she thought wryly.

# Chapter Eight

Laura was managing very nicely to keep Nick at bay, she thought late on Sunday, after everyone had over-indulged on Aunt Gladys's fried chicken. Nearly thirty people had shown up for the gathering, including the entire Anderson clan and assorted aunts, uncles, cousins, nieces and nephews. The lively exchanges during the meal had now given way to quiet satisfaction as everyone found a comfortable spot in the shade to relax. Except for a spirited game of horseshoes undertaken by the more energetic among the group, everyone else seemed content to do nothing more strenuous than chase away an occasional fly.

From his shady spot under a tree, Nick watched Laura help her mother and aunt clear away the remains of the meal. His offer of assistance had been promptly refused, so he had sought relief from the heat under the spreading branches of this oak, which also provided him with a good vantage point from which to observe Laura. She appeared more relaxed than he'd ever seen her, he noted through half-closed eyelids, his back propped against the trunk of the tree. With her hair pulled back into a ponytail, the trimness of her figure accentuated with shorts and a T-shirt and a good night's sleep behind her, she could pass for a teenager, at least from this distance. Even up close she seemed younger, almost carefree, the lines of tension around her mouth and eyes erased. She smiled more, and Nick began to glimpse the woman she had once been, before some demon from her past had stolen the laughter from her life.

He also knew that she was doing her best to make sure the two of them weren't alone. And he was just as sure that he had to get her alone. Here, in this relaxed, safe setting, she might open up a little, give him some insight to the fears she kept bottled inside. This was his best chance to discover more about Laura Taylor, and he wasn't about to let it pass. Because until he knew the secrets she kept hidden, the source of her fears, he would be at a distinct disadvantage. The only problem was figuring out a way to spirit her away from the group.

In the end, Laura's Aunt Gladys emerged as his unexpected ally. ''Land, it's a hot one,'' she said, fanning herself with part of a newspaper as the women came over to join him. Laura's aunt and mother opened up lawn chairs, and Laura dropped to the ground next to Nick. ''Does anyone want some iced tea or lemonade? Nick?''

''No, thank you. I'm still too full from dinner to even think about putting anything else in my stomach,'' he said with a lazy grin. ''That was one of the best meals I've had in a long time.''

''Well, I'm glad you liked it,'' Aunt Gladys said with a pleased grin. She glanced at Laura's mother before continuing, and Nick noted the conspiratorial look that passed between them. ''Laura, why don't you show Nick the spring?'' she suggested casually. ''It's a whole lot cooler down there.''

Laura had been halfheartedly watching the game of horseshoes, listening to the conversation only on a peripheral level, but now she gave it her full attention, turning startled eyes to Nick. He saw the panic in them, opened his mouth to politely decline, but caught himself in time. Instead, he idly reached for a blade of grass and twirled it silently between his fingers.

''Oh, Aunt Gladys, it's a pretty long walk. I'm sure Nick's too full to go hiking in this weather,'' she said breathlessly.

''It's not that far,'' Aunt Gladys replied. ''If I was as young as you two, I'd be heading there myself. I think Nick would enjoy it.''

''It sounds very interesting,'' he injected smoothly. ''And I'm all for finding a cooler spot, even if it does take a little effort to get there.'' Without waiting for a reply, he stood and extended his hand to Laura. ''Come on, Laura. You can be my tour guide,'' he coaxed, smiling down at her.

Laura stared up at him, her mind racing. How could she refuse without appearing rude? She looked to her aunt and mother for help, but they were smiling at her innocently. It was a conspiracy, she thought, realizing she was doomed. Nick wanted to get her alone, and her mother and aunt were clearly on his side. She might as well give up.

Nick saw the look of capitulation in her eyes and let out his breath slowly. He wouldn't have been surprised if she'd refused to go with him.

Laura put her hand in his, and in one lithe motion he drew her to her feet, tucking her arm in his. She saw the look of satisfaction Aunt Gladys and her mother exchanged and vowed to get even with them later.

"We'll be back soon," she said deliberately.

"Oh, take your time," her mother said. "You won't miss anything here."

Laura gave her a dirty look before turning to Nick. "It's down the road a bit and then through the woods," she said shortly.

"If we're not back by dark, send out a search party," Nick said to the two older women. Then he paused and looked down at Laura. "On second thought, never mind."

Laura's mother laughed. "I'm sure you'll take good care of her," she said. "Have fun, you two."

Laura knew she was blushing furiously, and she turned and began walking rapidly toward the road, practically dragging Nick with her.

"Hey, whoa! What's the rush?" he asked.

"I thought you wanted to see the spring."

"I do. But it's not going anywhere, is it?"

Reluctantly Laura slowed her gait. "No," she said glumly.

"That's what I like in a tour guide. Enthusiasm,"

Nick said, trying to elicit a smile and dispel some of the tension.

Laura looked up at him guiltily. He'd been a good sport about all the family activities over the past two days, blending right in with his easygoing manner and natural charm, and making no attempt to monopolize her time—until now. She supposed she owed him at least this much.

"Sorry," she apologized. "I just hate being railroaded into anything."

He stopped walking, and she looked up at him in surprise.

"If you'd rather not go, it's okay," he said, knowing he had to give her an out, hoping she wouldn't take it. If she wasn't a willing partner in this outing it was doomed to failure, anyway.

Laura seemed momentarily taken aback by his offer, and he saw the conflict in her eyes. He'd promised to let her set the pace, she recalled, and Nick had been a man of his word—so far. She knew that he hoped something romantic would develop when they were alone, but if she wasn't willing, she trusted him not to push. Maybe that was a mistake, but it was one she was suddenly willing to risk. "No. Let's go. It is cooler there, and you could probably use a break from all this family togetherness."

Relief flooded through him. "I like your family a lot, Laura. But some quiet time would be nice," he admitted with a smile.

"Well, it's quiet at the spring," she assured him.

They walked along a gravel road for a while, the late-afternoon sun relentless in its heat, and Laura looked up at Nick after a few minutes with a rueful smile. "Are you regretting this outing yet?" she asked.

He took a handkerchief from his pocket and mopped his forehead. "Well...that depends on how much farther it is," he said cautiously, the shadow of a grin making the corners of his mouth quirk up.

Laura pointed to a curve in the road about a hundred yards ahead. "The path is right up there. It cuts through the woods, so at least we'll be in the shade. The spring's about a ten-minute walk from the road."

"I can handle that."

They covered the remaining ground quickly and then paused a moment after turning onto the path, enjoying the welcome relief provided by the leafy canopy of trees.

"Whew! It's a lot hotter than it seemed back at your aunt's," Nick remarked, mopping his brow again.

"Yeah. It's got to be well over ninety."

"Is this a cold spring?"

"Very."

"Good. Lead me to it."

Fifteen minutes later, they sat side by side on a log, their feet immersed in a brook that was fed by the spring bubbling up a few yards away. Laura watched Nick close his eyes and smile. "This is heaven," he pronounced.

"It is nice," Laura agreed. "When we were kids we used to spend a lot of time playing here. It was a great place to grow up—fresh air, open spaces, pastures to run in, trees to climb, apples to pick..." Her voice trailed off.

"Sounds idyllic," Nick commented.

She nodded. "It was in a lot of ways. We didn't have much in the material sense, but we had more than our share of love. You may have noticed that this weekend."

"Mmm-hmm."

"I was very fortunate to have such a wonderful family," she continued softly. "We were sort of like the Waltons, you know? When that program was on TV I used to hear people say that no one really had a family like that. Well, we did. My parents taught us by example how to live our Christian faith and gave us an incredible foundation of love to build on. Those things are a priceless legacy." She drew up her legs and wrapped her arms around them, resting her chin on her knees. "That's one of the reasons I got involved with Christian Youth Outreach. Those poor kids have no idea what it's like to grow up in a warm, caring, supportive atmosphere. Outreach can't make up for that, but it does provide programs that help instill Christian values and give kids a sense of self-worth."

Nick looked over at her, the dappled sunlight playing across her face, and noted the faint shadows under her eyes. She worked too hard, always stretching herself to the limit. Yet she still found time to give to others, living her faith in a concrete way. She never ceased to amaze him.

"You know something, Laura Taylor? You're quite a woman," he said softly.

She looked at him in surprise, a delicate flush staining her cheeks, then turned away. "A lot of people do a lot more than me," she said with a dismissive shrug. She took a deep breath and closed her eyes. "This really is a great spot, isn't it? It brings back so many good memories,'' Laura said, a tender smile of recollection softening her features. Then it slowly faded. ''But things never stay the same, do they?''

''It must have been hard to leave here,'' Nick ventured, sensing a chance to find out more about her past.

She reached down and trailed her fingers through the cold water. ''In some ways, yes. But I was very much in love, and when you're in love nothing else matters,'' she said quietly. ''Besides, I had visions of recreating this lifestyle in the city. I figured there had to be someplace there with a small-town feel, and I found it pretty quickly. Webster Groves. When I was first married I used to love to drive through there and admire those wonderful, old Victorian houses. I always figured some day we'd have one.'' She paused and cupped her chin in her hand, resting her elbow on her knee, and the wistful smile on her face tightened Nick's throat. ''It would have had a big porch on three sides, with lots of gingerbread trim and cupolas, and fireplaces, and an arbor covered with morning glories that led to a rose garden. And children playing on a tire swing...'' She stopped abruptly and glanced at Nick self-consciously. ''Sorry. Coming home always makes me nostalgic,'' she apologized, a catch in her voice.

He was tempted to reach over and take her hand. But he held back, afraid that physical contact would break the mood. ''I didn't mind. I'm just sorry you never got your house.''

She shrugged. ''Oh, well. It wasn't in God's plan for me, I guess. At least my office is in Webster.

Sometimes, in the fall especially, I walk down Elm Street and let myself daydream even now,'' she confided.

''There's nothing wrong with dreaming, Laura.''

''There is when you have no way of making those dreams come true,'' she replied. ''If I've learned one thing in the past few years, it's to be realistic.''

''No more dreams?'' he asked gently.

She looked at him squarely. ''No. Dreams have a way of turning sour.''

''Not all dreams, Laura.''

''I know. My business is a good example. But it didn't happen by itself, Nick. It took a lot of hard work. Those kind of dreams, the ones you can control, where if you do certain things there's a predictable outcome, are fine.''

''Is that why you shy away from relationships? Because people are unpredictable and don't always do what you expect?'' He was afraid she'd tense up, resent his question, but the quiet of the woods, broken only by the call of an occasional bird and the splashing of the brook, seemed to have had a calming effect on her. She sighed.

''I suppose that's a fair question, Nick. You've told me how you feel, and I guess you have a right to know what your chances are with me. You were honest with me, so I'll be honest with you. I like you very much. Probably too much. But the odds aren't good.''

''Because you're scared?'' he asked quietly.

She hesitated, and then nodded slowly. ''Yes.''

''But, Laura...don't you ever get lonely?''

Laura swallowed past the lump in her throat and

looked away, afraid that the tears welling up in her eyes would spill out. ‘‘I have my family.’’

‘‘That’s not what I mean.’’

She knew exactly what he meant, but chose to ignore it. ‘‘I also have my faith, Nick. Believe it or not, that helps a lot to ease any loneliness I might feel. It’s a great source of strength.’’

Nick knew she was telling the truth. He had begun to realize just how important Laura’s faith was to her. He’d seen the worn and obviously much-read Bible at her apartment, knew she attended church every Sunday. He’d been struck by the peace in her eyes during the church service he’d attended with the Anderson clan that morning—a look of serenity and fullfilment he envied. Nick hadn’t attended church much since he was a teenager, and had almost made an excuse to skip the service that morning. But he had honestly enjoyed sharing the experience with Laura and even thought he might begin attending his own church more often after this weekend. But his comment had nothing to do with faith, and she knew it.

‘‘I do believe you, Laura,’’ he said quietly. ‘‘But even a strong faith doesn’t make up for the comfort of having a human person to share your life with, a hand to hold, someone to laugh with.’’

Laura debated her response. She could just ignore his remark, change the subject. But he was right, and she might as well admit it. With a sigh she conceded the point. ‘‘Yeah. I know. But I’ve learned to handle it.’’

Nick watched her closely. The subtle tilt of her chin told him she was struggling for control, and he wondered what could possibly have made her so fearful, so willing to live a life devoid of human tenderness and love.

''This fear you have of relationships is really strong, isn't it?''

''I guess so.''

''I assume there's a very good reason for it.''

She looked at him silently for a moment and then began pulling on her shoes, concentrating on the laces as she spoke. ''There is.''

He reached for his own shoes more slowly, sensing that the conversation was at an end, but wanting to ask so much more. Yet he knew that she'd said as much as she planned to for the moment. Maybe more.

They tied their shoes in silence, and then Laura stood, jamming her hands into the pockets of her shorts. ''We ought to start back,'' she said, glancing at her watch. ''We've been gone almost two hours.''

Nick rose reluctantly and leaned against a tree, crossing his arms. ''You don't mind if I keep trying, do you?''

She gave him a puzzled look. ''What do you mean?''

''To break down that wall you've built.''

She flushed and turned away. ''You're wasting your time, Nick.''

''I'm willing to take my chances.''

''Suit yourself,'' she said, wishing he'd just give up and find someone without emotional roadblocks, leaving her in peace, before his persistence eventually wore down her defenses.

Laura spoke very little as they made their way back

through the woods. She let Nick lead, and her eyes were drawn to the broad, powerful muscles of his shoulders, his trim waist, the corded tendons of his legs bare beneath his shorts. There was a magnetism about him that was almost tangible, and she found herself imagining what it would feel like to be enveloped in his strong arms, to feel his heartbeat mingling with hers. Lonely? he'd asked her. Oh, if he only knew! So many nights when she'd longed to be held, yearned for a tender touch, a whispered endearment. But always she went to bed alone. And lonely. Suddenly, watching Nick's strong back only inches from her, close enough to touch, a yearning surged through her so strong that she stumbled.

Nick turned instantly and reached out to steady her. "Are you okay, Laura?" he asked, studying her face with a worried frown. He noted the flush on her cheeks and the film of tears in her eyes, and his hands lingered on her shoulders.

"Yes, I'm fine," she said breathlessly, her heart hammering in her chest. "I just didn't see that rock." Her eyes lifted to his, making Nick's heart suddenly go into a staccato rhythm.

It took every ounce of his willpower not to immediately crush her to his chest, to imprison her in his arms and kiss her in ways that would leave her breathless and asking for more. He swallowed, and he realized that his hands were trembling as he struggled for control, trying to decide what to do next.

Laura stared at him, mesmerized by the play of emotions that crossed his face. With one word, one touch, she knew she could unleash the passion smoldering just beneath the surface. And she needed to be held so badly! Held by someone who cared about her, who would love her with a passion tempered by gentleness, who would soothe her with a touch that spoke of caring and commitment. Nick could give her that. Wanted to give her that. It was hers for the taking. She could see it in his eyes.

Without consciously making a decision, Laura slowly reached out a tentative hand. Nick grasped it, his eyes burning into hers, questioning, hoping, and when he pressed her palm to his lips, Laura closed her eyes and moaned softly, surrendering to the tide of emotion sweeping over her. She moved forward, inviting herself into his arms, waiting for the touch of his lips—

A sudden crashing of brush made her gasp, and, startled, she spun around as his arms protectively encircled her. A doe and fawn were hovering uncertainly only a few yards away, standing perfectly still, only their ears twitching. They remained motionless for a long moment, and then with one last, nervous look at the intruders, they bolted into the thicket.

Laura let her breath out slowly. She was shaking badly, not just because of the unexpected interruption, but because of what she'd almost done. She now knew why she'd been so reluctant to spend time alone with Nick. Just being in his presence awakened long-dormant impulses in her, impulses best left untouched. Another few minutes and she... She closed her eyes, refusing to allow her imagination any further rein. She didn't believe in casual intimacy. Never had. It went against every principle she held. But she'd never been so tempted in her life. She needed to be touched, to be held, to be loved, and the power of those compelling physical needs had stunned her. The Bible was right, she thought ruefully. The flesh really was weak. Maybe the sudden appearance of the deer had been God's way of giving her the time she needed to clear her head and make the right decision, difficult as it was.

Taking a deep breath she stepped away, and Nick's hands dropped from her shoulders. Immediately she missed his touch, missed the warmth of his hands that had penetrated her thin cotton blouse. The loss of contact was almost tangibly painful. But it was for the best, she told herself resolutely.

Turning to face him was one of the most difficult things Laura had ever done in her life. He was standing absolutely still, except for the unusually rapid rise and fall of his chest, and he looked shaken and grim. But he composed himself, running a hand through his hair and forcing his lips up into a semblance of a smile.

''Talk about bad timing,'' he said jokingly, his voice husky and uneven.

Laura brushed back a few tendrils of hair that had escaped from her ponytail. ''We'd better get back,'' she said choppily.

''Laura...''

He reached out a hand, but she ignored the gesture. ''Come on,'' she said simply. She brushed past him, walking with long determined strides toward the road.

Frustration and disappointment washed over him as he watched her retreating back. The moment was gone. But he had some consolation. The longing he'd seen in her eyes left him with hope. It wasn't much, but it was something. With a sigh he watched Laura disappear around a curve, and then forced himself to follow more slowly. At the rate she was going, she'd be back at the house before he even emerged from the woods.

He was surprised to find her waiting for him when he reached the road. "I can find my way back if you'd rather go on ahead," he said quietly.

"No. I'm sorry, Nick. That was rude of me. I'll walk with you."

She fell into step beside him, an introspective frown on her face, and though Nick tried a couple of times to lighten the mood, Laura was unresponsive and he finally gave up, lapsing into silence.

Once back, Laura's attempts to keep him at arm's length intensified. He wasn't able to say more than a few words to her in private the rest of the evening or the next morning. He realized she was running scared, frightened by what had almost happened in the woods, afraid to let that opportunity arise again. He resigned himself to the fact that the best he could hope for was to sit next to her at dinner.

By the time he filled his plate and made his way toward one of the long tables set up in the yard, however, Laura had already found a seat between her niece and her brother. As Nick surveyed the situation, juggling his plate in one hand and a lemonade in the other, John caught his eye. Nick quirked one eyebrow in Laura's direction, and John nodded imperceptibly.

"Susan, where's your fork?" John asked, leaning around Laura.

"Gone," she said, pointing under the table.

"I'll get her another one," Laura volunteered.

"Thanks, Sis."

As Laura headed for the buffet table, Nick made his move, slipping into Laura's seat. "I owe you one," he said quietly to John.

John grinned. "Laura needs a shove. She's a slow mover," he said.

"So I've noticed."

Laura was so busy talking to her aunt that she didn't realize her seat was occupied until she reached the table, whereupon she stopped short, glaring suspiciously at her brother when he turned.

"Oh, Laura. Nick was looking for a seat. We had plenty of room here." He scooted over, and Nick did likewise, leaving space for Laura to join them.

"I don't want to crowd you," she said crossly, reaching for her plate. "I'll go sit with Mom."

"We don't mind being crowded," Nick said, grasping her hand.

Laura looked around. They were beginning to attract attention, and the amused glances being sent her way made her cheeks flame. With a sigh, she squeezed in beside Nick.

"There. Now isn't this cozy?" John said brightly.

Laura gave him a withering glance. "Just whose side are you on?" she whispered between clenched teeth.

"Yours," he replied in a low voice.

She gave an unladylike snort and picked up her corn. She could feel Nick's eyes on her, but she refused to look at him. She knew she was acting like a coward, running away from a situation she was afraid of instead of facing it. Common sense told her she couldn't put off being alone with him forever. They'd be in the car together tomorrow for three hours, for goodness' sake. But at least while he was driving, his eyes and hands would be otherwise occupied, no matter what his inclinations, she thought dryly, slathering butter on her corn.

Suddenly a large bronzed hand entered her field of vision and removed the corn from her grasp. Startled, Laura turned to look at Nick, who had raised the corn to his lips.

Mesmerized, she watched as his strong white teeth took a bite of corn. Then he licked his lips and smiled with satisfaction.

"Wh-what are you doing?" she asked hoarsely, the sensuous dance of his tongue holding her spellbound.

"Nibbling your ear," he said softly, his words implying one thing, his eyes another. Her mouth suddenly went dry and she reached for her glass of lemonade and took a large swallow. He leaned closer. "This will have to do until the real thing becomes available," he added quietly.

Laura choked on the lemonade, which once more put her in the limelight. Curious gazes were directed her way, and then she felt Nick's arm go around her shoulder solicitously. Her face was flaming, and she dabbed at her mouth with a paper napkin.

"Are you okay, Laura?"

"Yes." She coughed. "I'm fine."

"You don't sound fine."

"I said I'm fine," she repeated grimly, shrugging off his arm.

"Okay. Do you want your corn back?"

"No. You keep it."

"Thanks."

Laura ate as fast as she could, bypassed dessert and left the table to join in a game of croquet. Nick watched her go and then sent John a despairing look.

"I'm beginning to wonder if she likes me," he said.

"Oh, she likes you. You make her as nervous as a cat in its ninth life. If she didn't like you, you wouldn't have any effect on her at all."

"You think so?" Nick asked doubtfully.

"Mmm-hmm. I know my sister."

"Has she always been like this around men?"

"Laura hasn't been around men much, Nick," John said, giving the other man a frank look. "Just Joe. He was her first and only beau, as far as I know."

"So you're attributing her skittishness to inexperience?"

"Partly," John hedged.

"It's the other part I wonder about," Nick said, directing a level gaze at John.

"I don't know much else myself, Nick," John said apologetically. "Laura's always been closemouthed about her private affairs."

"Yeah. So I've discovered." Nick sighed.

"Hang in there," John encouraged him. "You're making progress."

"Yeah?"

"She let you drive her down here, didn't she?"

"She was desperate," Nick said with a shrug.

"That's not the only reason. She wouldn't share her family with someone she didn't care about."

Nick thought about John's words later that night as he prepared for bed. The weekend hadn't gone exactly as he'd planned, but he had learned a lot about Laura's roots and her family. And if John was right, there was still hope for him.

Restlessly he strolled over to the window, trying to catch a breath of air. The second-floor bedroom was especially stuffy tonight, and the ceiling fan didn't seem to be helping at all. Even though it was eleven o'clock, the oppressive heat hadn't relented. He ought to go to bed. The house was quiet, so apparently everyone else had. But he knew sleep would be elusive. Maybe if he got some fresh air, cooled off a little, sleep would come more easily, he thought.

Nick stepped into the hall, quietly closing the door behind him, and made his way down the steps, cringing as the wood creaked. But it didn't seem to disturb anyone, he decided, pausing to listen for stirrings in the house, so he continued down and headed for the back porch, holding the screen door so it wouldn't bang. It *was* cooler out here, he thought, taking a deep breath of the night air.

''Hello, Nick.''

Startled, he turned to find Mrs. Anderson gently swaying in the porch swing.

''Did I scare you?'' she asked in apology. ''I'm sorry.''

''That's okay. I thought everyone was in bed,'' he said, walking closer. He leaned against the porch railing, crossing his ankles and resting his palms on the rail behind him.

''Sometimes on hot nights I like to come down and

swing for a while. Walter—Laura's father—and I used to do this, and I can't seem to break the habit. It's a bit lonelier now, though, so I'm glad to have some company,'' she said without a trace of self-pity.

''Laura speaks very warmly of her father.''

''Oh, they had a great relationship, those two. Course, as you may have noticed, we're a real close family. It was hard on all of us when Laura moved to St. Louis. We figured they'd come to visit pretty often, but it didn't work out that way.''

Laura's mother was being so open that Nick had the courage to do a little probing. ''Why not, Mrs. Anderson? I can see Laura loves being here with all of you.''

''I don't really know, Nick,'' she said honestly. ''Laura never did talk much about her life in St. Louis or about Joe, at least not after the first couple of years.'' She paused a moment, then continued more slowly. ''You know, Nick, you're the first man Laura's ever brought home, other than Joe. That's why you've gotten so many curious looks this weekend. I hope we didn't make you uncomfortable.''

''Not at all,'' he said, debating for a moment whether to probe further, quickly deciding he had nothing to lose. ''Joe must have been quite a guy, if Laura married him,'' he said, forcing a casual tone into his voice.

Laura's mother didn't respond immediately. ''He was nice enough,'' she said slowly, as if choosing her words carefully. ''But Walter and I didn't think he was right for Laura,'' she admitted. ''He was one of those people who always seems to have their head in the clouds, building castles in the air and never putting the foundation under them. Maybe even getting angry when things don't work out, you know what I mean? Laura's just the opposite. She plans for things and persists until she succeeds.'' She paused for a moment. ''Besides, they were so young when they got married. Too young, we thought. But there was no convincing them, so in the end we gave in. Like I said, Laura never did talk much about her life with Joe. Even when they separated, all she said was that they were having a few problems. She didn't offer any more of an explanation, and we didn't pry. Laura's always been a real private person. But she surely had a good reason. Laura isn't one to walk away from obligations or commitments, and she's a great believer in the sanctity of marriage. So for her to leave Joe—well, I can't even imagine what must have happened.''

Nick stared at Laura's mother, grateful for the darkness that hid the dumbfounded look on his face. Laura had left her husband? Why hadn't she told him? And what had broken up her marriage? She'd said earlier this weekend that she'd been in love with Joe, loved him enough to make leaving her hometown and the family she cherished bearable. Knowing she was a widow, he'd more or less begun to attribute her reluctance to get involved with him to fear of once again losing a man she loved. But now that explanation didn't seem as plausible. More likely she was afraid of making another mistake, and for that he couldn't blame her. But her fear and caution went beyond the normal bounds.

Mrs. Anderson held her watch toward the dim light.

"My, it's getting late! Time I went to bed." She stood and smiled at Nick. "Hope you didn't mind me bending your ear."

"Not at all," he replied, struggling for a casual tone.

"Well, I do worry about Laura. And it's nice to have someone who cares about her to share that with. Though I expect everything we talked about tonight is old news to you. You probably know much more about it than we do," she said good-naturedly.

Nick watched the screen door close behind her. *No,* he thought, *I know far less. Even less than I thought. But I'm learning.*

# Chapter Nine

Laura lay in bed sleepless for a long time Tuesday night, thinking about the past four days. Nick had been unusually quiet on the ride back from Jersey, and it was clear she need not have worried about being alone with him in the car. He was probably regretting that he'd ever made the offer to take her home, she thought miserably, punching her pillow. And if she was honest about it, she couldn't blame him. From his standpoint, the weekend had probably been a disaster. Forced to take part in a family gathering where the only person he knew avoided him like the plague was not conducive to a pleasant experience, she had to admit. He had obviously come to the same conclusion, silently carrying her bag upstairs when they'd arrived at her apartment and leaving her at the door, making his escape as quickly as possible.

Well, she'd wanted to discourage him, she told herself. The success of her plan should make her happy. So then why was she so miserable? And why did the loneliness she'd long ago learned to deal with now suddenly leave her feeling so empty and restless?

Laura tossed back the covers, the hot night air feeling much more oppressive here than it had in Jersey. She briefly considered turning on the air conditioner, but the older window unit was inefficient and one night's indulgence would probably boost her electric bill twenty dollars, she thought glumly. That was more than she was willing to spend. The heat would dissipate eventually, she told herself, and sleep would come.

Sleep did come, but not until nearly three, and when the alarm went off at five-thirty Laura moaned. So much for coming back from the weekend refreshed and rested, she thought dryly as she swung her legs to the floor and yawned.

By the time she was dressed, Ken, her foreman, had arrived per arrangement to take her to the office. He had also agreed to drop her at the garage tonight so she could pick up her car.

"Morning, Ken," she said sleepily, taking a last gulp of coffee from the mug cradled in her hands.

"Hi, Laura." He tilted his head and regarded her quizzically. "You look tired."

"Yeah, well, that's what happens when you only have two and a half hours' sleep," she said wryly.

"Did you get back late?"

"No. Just couldn't sleep." She grabbed her portfolio case and headed for the door. "Let's stop by the job sites first. How did things go yesterday?"

Laura now had two crews working, and Ken filled

her in as they drove, dropping her at the office by nine-thirty.

"I'll be back about four to give you a progress report, if that's okay," he said.

"Fine," she assured him. "I have plenty of paperwork to keep me busy. It sure will seem odd to spend a whole day in the office, though," she said.

He grinned. "Yeah, the crews won't know what to think."

"Well, I'll be back on the sites tomorrow," she said with a smile. "So don't let anybody slip up."

"Don't worry. I'll keep an eye on everything."

Laura watched Ken drive away, grateful again that she'd found someone of his caliber to fill the all-important foreman role. She'd done the job herself until the volume of work became too great, but she had to admit it was a relief to let someone else share part of the burden. Ken had only been with her for about six weeks, but he was a quick study and had proven to be reliable and trustworthy. She found herself delegating more and more to him as paperwork and new design projects demanded an increasing amount of her time. The Arts Center job had been the catalyst for growth, as she had hoped it would be, and Nick was also sending other commissions her way. She was beginning to feel that maybe, just maybe, she'd turned the corner. But her cautious nature wouldn't let her go quite that far, at least not yet. Still, business was certainly booming, and for that she was grateful. Soon she might even feel secure enough to allow herself the indulgence of air-conditioning at night, she thought with a grin.

It was nearly four before Laura stopped long enough to call the garage, and as soon as Larry answered she knew there was a problem.

"I was just getting ready to call you," he said. "I'm afraid the part hasn't come in yet. I kept thinking it might still show up this afternoon, but at this point I'm beginning to doubt it."

Laura frowned and rubbed her brow. "Well, it's not your fault, Larry," she said with a sigh. "Do you think it will be here tomorrow?"

"Oh, sure. I don't know what held it up today. It'll probably come first thing in the morning. I'll call you as soon as your car's ready."

"Okay."

"I'm sorry about this," he said apologetically. "I know it's an inconvenience."

"That's okay. I'll manage until tomorrow."

Laura hung up slowly, a resigned look on her face. So much for tonight's plans. The grocery store and laundromat would just have to wait until tomorrow. She rested her chin in her hand and looked over her cluttered desk with a sigh. There was so much to do, and now she had a whole empty evening stretching ahead of her. Too many hours alone to brood about Nick, she realized. She might as well work late tonight and then catch a bus home.

Ken arrived promptly at four, and after he quickly briefed her on the day's progress, Laura told him about the car.

"No problem," he assured her. "I can pick you up again tomorrow. Besides, the guys will have another day's reprieve from the slave driver,'' he said with a grin.

His good humor was infectious, and Laura smiled. ''Oh, yeah? Well, tell them I'll make up for it Friday.''

''I'll pass that along,'' he said, his grin broadening. ''Ready to leave?''

''Actually, I think I'll work for a while and catch a bus later.''

''Are you sure?''

''Yes. Go on home to that beautiful wife and darling new baby,'' she said, waving him out the door.

He grinned. ''You don't have to convince me. I'll see you tomorrow.''

It was hunger that finally made Laura set aside her work, that and aching shoulder muscles. She was used to heavy work, but hunching over a desk and drawing table all day must use entirely different muscles, she thought, gingerly massaging her neck. She glanced at her watch and was surprised to discover that it was already eight o'clock—definitely time to call it a day.

As Laura reached for her purse her gaze fell on the telephone, and she knew that the sudden hollow feeling in the pit of her stomach was symptomatic of more than hunger. She hadn't allowed herself to think of Nick all day, but subconsciously she knew that she had been hoping he would call. Each time the phone had rung her pulse had quickened, but it was never his deep, mellow voice that greeted her. He'd probably written her off for good, she thought, pulling the door shut and turning the key in the lock. And she had no one to blame but herself.

Laura made her way dejectedly to the bus stop, telling herself it had worked out for the best, that it was what she wanted, that her life would be much less complicated without Nick in it. The only problem was that it would also be much lonelier, she admitted.

Laura had to wait longer than she expected at the bus stop, and by the time she finally boarded and was on her way dusk had descended. She hadn't taken the bus in a long time, and apparently they ran much less frequently in the evening than she remembered.

That conclusion was borne out at the next stop, where she waited about twice as long as she expected for her connection. By the time she finally disembarked two blocks from her apartment, it was dark and she felt so bone tired that her walk home seemed to stretch out endlessly ahead of her. The lack of sleep was finally catching up with her, and all she wanted to do at the moment was stand under a warm shower, eat something and go to bed. She watched the bus disappear in a cloud of noxious fumes and, wrinkling her nose in distaste, turned wearily toward home.

Once off the main street, Laura was surprised to discover just how dark the neighborhood was at night. She didn't make a practice of wandering around once the sun set and had never noticed that the streets were so poorly lit. Since the side streets were not heavily traveled, the darkness wasn't even broken by car headlights. Nick had asked her once about the safety of the neighborhood and she had dismissed his concern, but now she looked at it with a fresh eye. It wasn't the best part of town, she'd always known that, but she'd never had any problems. So why was she suddenly nervous?

With an impatient shake of her head, she dismissed her sudden, unaccountable jitters. It was just the power of suggestion, intensified by her weariness, she told herself.

Laura had almost convinced herself that she was being silly when she felt a strange prickling at the back of her neck. It was an odd, unsettling sensation that sent a cold chill coursing through her body. Her step faltered, and she turned to look behind her. Nothing. Just shadows. Nevertheless, she picked up her pace, hugging her shoulder bag more tightly to her side.

Laura gave a sigh of relief when she at last turned the corner to her street and her apartment came into view. Now that home was in sight, her jitters eased. After all, there was only one more patch of darkness before she came to the entrance of her building.

Laura had very little warning before it happened. There was the sudden sound of running feet close behind her, and then she felt her purse being jerked away from her shoulder. Instinctively she tightened her grip. Dear God, she was being mugged! she thought incredulously.

The attacker was momentarily taken aback by Laura's resistance, and they both froze briefly, stunned. Laura noted that he had a hat pulled low over his eyes, but in the darkness she couldn't tell much else about him except that he was tall and broad shouldered. The freeze-frame lasted only a second, and as he moved back toward her fear coursed through her body. She responded with a well-placed knee, and his grunt told her that she'd hit pay dirt. Without pausing, she snatched the purse strap out of his hands and began to run, hoping her aggressive response would discourage him.

She heard a muttered oath of anger, but instead of abandoning the attack, the man pursued her. She didn't get more than a few steps before a hand closed on her arm. She stumbled, and then was jerked roughly around. She didn't even have time to scream before a powerful fist slammed into her face.

Laura's head snapped backward from the impact of the blow, and she staggered, then fell, the breath knocked completely out of her lungs. Her nose began to bleed profusely, and one eye was watering so badly she couldn't see. She gasped in pain as she once again felt the assailant relentlessly tugging on her purse.

"Let go," he muttered, "or you'll get more of the same."

Laura heard his words, but her fingers didn't relinquish their viselike grip on the purse.

"Okay, you asked for it," he muttered.

Laura looked up, just in time to realize his intention, but too late to do anything to protect herself. A second later the hard toe of his boot viciously connected with the tender skin over her ribs, and she gasped as a searing pain shot through her side. With a moan, she curled into a tight ball in a posture of self-protection and fought the waves of blackness that swept over her.

Hazily she realized that the assailant had once again gripped her purse, grabbing a handful of her blouse at the same time. The buttons gave way in response to his vicious yank, and Laura heard the fabric rip. She moaned softly, each breath now an agony of effort, and once more blackness descended.

Nick pulled to a stop in front of Laura's apartment, hoping for an impromptu trip to Ted Drewes. As he turned off the engine his eyes scanned the deserted neighborhood. It was obviously not a place where couples and families took evening strolls, he thought wryly.

Or was it? he wondered idly a moment later, his eyes caught by a movement in the shadows down the street. He grew instantly alert, however, when he realized that a struggle was taking place. One of the two figures was prone on the sidewalk while the other, clearly male, tried to grab something—a purse, he noted.

Nick sucked in a sharp breath and then reacted instinctively, his heart hammering as adrenaline pumped through his body. He flung open the door and sprinted toward the mugger, shouting furiously.

"Hey! You! Leave her alone!"

The mugger whirled around, saw Nick and, after one last, futile tug on the woman's purse, abandoned the attack and took off running in the opposite direction.

In a split second Nick decided it was more important to go to the woman's aid than chase the mugger. He turned to her, and it took only a second for sudden suspicion to turn into terrible certainty. Panicked, he dropped to his knees beside her, the mugger forgotten. Her blouse had been nearly torn off and blood covered her face. One eye had already swollen shut and she seemed barely conscious, her breathing labored. The color drained from his face and he felt his stomach turn over.

"Laura?" Dazed, he reached out a tentative hand,

feeling as if he were in a terrible nightmare. But her soft moan made it clear that the attack had been all too real.

"Laura, can you hear me?" he asked urgently, gripping her shoulders. Her only response was to curl into a tight ball, holding her side. Nick withdrew his handkerchief and held it against her nose, glancing around desperately for help. He couldn't leave her here and he was afraid to pick her up. He had no idea how severely she was injured.

Nick could barely remember the last time he prayed, but he suddenly found himself sending an urgent plea for assistance. *Dear Lord,* he pleaded silently, closing his eyes. *Please help us. Please!*

Suddenly, as if by miracle, Nick heard a siren, and his eyes flew open. A police car, its lights flashing, was turning the corner. His shoulders sagged in relief as he mouthed a silent thank-you, and he stood and waved. The car rolled to a stop and an officer got out.

"What happened?" the policeman asked, kneeling beside Laura.

"She was mugged."

"I'll call an ambulance," he said, rising.

Laura's eyes fluttered open, and though she had trouble focusing, her hearing was fine. An ambulance meant a hospital, and the last time she'd been to a hospital was the night she'd left Joe. She had no wish to return to a place of such unpleasant memories.

"No," she said hoarsely.

Nick took her hand. "Laura, sweetheart, you have to go to the hospital. You could be seriously injured," he said gently.

Laura's eyes turned to his. "Nick?" Her voice quavered, and he felt as if someone had kicked *him* in the gut.

"Yeah, honey, it's me."

"No hospital," she repeated stubbornly.

The police officer hesitated, and Nick looked up at him. "Call an ambulance," he said curtly. Then he turned his attention back to Laura. "Laura, I'll stay with you the whole time, okay? I won't leave you."

Laura looked up at him, and even in the dim light she could make out the lines of worry etched in his face. She tried to reach up and smooth them away, but the attempt brought a searing pain intense enough to make her realize that Nick was right.

"Okay," she said raspily.

"That's my girl," he said, squeezing her hand, making an effort to smile reassuringly.

Laura tried to smile in return, wanting to reassure him that she was okay, but the effort was beyond her. Instead, she closed her eyes, taking comfort in the warm clasp of his hand.

Nick saw her eyes close, wondered if she'd lost consciousness again and began to panic.

"So where's the ambulance?" he snapped when the officer rejoined them.

"It will be here any minute," the officer reassured him. He glanced down at Laura. "She looks pretty banged up," he said.

"Yeah."

"I take it you know her?"

"I was on my way to see her. She lives in an apartment over there," he replied, pointing out Laura's building. "I had just parked when I saw them. I don't know what would have happened if I hadn't..." His voice broke, and the officer reached out a hand to grip his shoulder.

"It was lucky for her," he agreed.

The faint echo of a siren was the most beautiful sound Nick had ever heard, and though he knew it must have taken only minutes to arrive, he felt as if he'd lived a lifetime. Laura's eyes flickered open as the two paramedics bent over her and Nick relinquished her hand.

"Nick?" Her voice was frightened.

"I'm right here, honey," he said.

The paramedics performed a quick examination and then went to retrieve the stretcher. Nick squatted beside Laura again. "I'll ride with you in the ambulance."

She nodded gratefully, her eyes clinging to his with a vulnerability that made his heart contract. He was filled with a sudden rage at the injustice of this, and at that moment he felt capable of murder.

As the paramedics bent to lift her to the stretcher, Laura moaned, and Nick saw the tears running down her cheeks.

"Can't you guys be a little more gentle?" he barked, wishing it was him on that stretcher instead of her.

The paramedics glanced at the policeman, who just inclined his head toward the ambulance. Then he turned his attention back to Nick. "I'll follow you to the hospital. I'll need a statement, since you were a witness, and hopefully the victim will be able to talk to me later.''

''Her name is Laura. Laura Taylor,'' Nick said, his voice tight. Then he strode toward the ambulance and climbed in beside her, noting how icy her hand felt when he took it in his.

''Her hands are cold,'' he said shortly as the ambulance pulled away from the curb.

''Shock,'' one of the paramedics replied.

Nick lapsed into silence, and Laura didn't open her eyes again until she was being wheeled into the emergency room. He stayed beside her, determined to honor his promise despite the nurse who was bearing down on him.

''Sir, you can wait over there,'' she said.

Nick glared at her. ''No way. I said I'd stay with her, and I intend to do just that. I'll keep out of your way.''

The woman took one look at the stubborn set of his jaw and nodded. ''I'll let the doctor know.''

''You do that,'' he said, his eyes never leaving Laura. As they rolled to a stop, he bent over her and stroked her forehead. ''Laura,'' he said gently, taking her hand. Her eyes flickered open. ''We're at the hospital. I've got to stand back so the doctor can take a look at you, but I'll only be a few steps away, close enough to talk to, if you want.'' Her eyes were frightened, but she nodded and he released her hand.

Nick moved to the side of the room while the nurse removed the tattered remnants of her blouse and eased the jeans down her hips. Nick swallowed and looked away, respecting her modesty, knowing she would be embarrassed by being so exposed before him. With an effort, he kept his eyes averted as the doctor did a cursory exam and spoke with the nurse in low tones. Not until she was wheeled to X ray did he leave her side, reassuring her that he'd be waiting.

Wearily he made his way toward the waiting room, where he found the policeman. After one look at Nick's face the officer disappeared into a side room, reappearing a moment later with a cup of coffee.

"You look like you could use this. Actually, you look like you could use something a lot stronger, but the closest thing they have in this place is rubbing alcohol."

Nick accepted it gratefully, noting in surprise that his hands were shaking. He took a long, scalding swallow, then he let his eyelids drop, forcing himself to take several deep breaths. It helped, but he still felt unsteady. When he opened his eyes, he met the policeman's sympathetic gaze.

"If I sounded a bit short-tempered before, I'm sorry," Nick said hoarsely. "I know you all were doing everything you could. And you sure showed up at the right time."

"A neighbor called and reported a disturbance," he explained. "And there's no need to apologize. I understand the strain you were under. Is she okay?"

Nick sighed and sank down into a plastic chair, the kind he always found so uncomfortable. Only tonight he didn't notice. "I don't know. She's in X ray."

"Can you tell me what happened?"

"Only what I saw. I think I must have come along toward the end," Nick explained.

The officer took notes as Nick spoke, looking up when he paused. ''Could you give me a description of the assailant?''

Ruefully, Nick shook his head. ''It was too dark. The guy took off before I got close enough to see anything, and he had a hat pulled low over his eyes. All I know for sure is that he was big—football-player type.''

The policeman nodded. ''Maybe Ms. Taylor will be able to add something to this,'' he said.

''I'm not sure she'll be up to talking to you tonight,'' Nick cautioned.

''If she's not, we'll do it another time,'' he said easily.

Nick's attention was suddenly distracted as he saw Laura being wheeled back into the examining room, and he was on his feet instantly. She had been left alone for the moment, and he moved close, alarmed by her pallor. Her face looked as white as the sheet drawn up barely high enough to cover her breasts. His eyes flickered across the expanse of skin, noting the long, angry bruise that marred the creamy flesh at her shoulder, apparently inflicted by the strap of her bag. He also noted something else—a three-inch-long scar of older vintage near the top of her right breast. He frowned, wondering about its origin. But before he could speculate, Laura called his name softly and his eyes flew to hers. Her hand reached for his through the bars of the gurney, and he gripped it tightly, reassuringly. His other hand smoothed the hair back from her face. The blood had been cleaned away, but her nose was puffy and one eye was purple and swollen nearly shut. His throat tightened painfully and he found it difficult to swallow.

"I guess I don't look so hot, huh?" she said, trying to smile.

"You look beautiful to me," he said hoarsely. Her eyes filled with tears, and he leaned closer, his breath warm on her cheek. "It's okay, sweetheart. It's okay to cry."

"I ne-never cry," she said, her words choppy as she fought for control.

"Well, maybe you should make an exception this once," he said softly.

The door swung open and, after one more worried look at Laura, Nick straightened up. The doctor glanced at him before his gaze came to rest on Laura. "Would you like him to stay while we discuss your condition?"

"Yes."

"All right." The doctor moved beside her. "You're a very lucky woman, Ms. Taylor. No broken bones, no internal injuries as far as we can determine. You've got quite a shiner, though, so I'd suggest an ice pack when you get home. The nose will be tender for a few days, but it will heal without any help. The ribs are another story. None are broken, but they're badly bruised. You'll need to take it easy for at least a week or so to give them a chance to start healing."

"A week?" she asked in alarm.

"At least," he confirmed.

"But, Doctor, I—"

"I'll see that she takes care of herself, Doctor," Nick interrupted, ignoring her protest.

Laura turned her head on the pillow and stared at him, but she remained silent.

The doctor looked from one to the other and gave a satisfied nod. "Good." Then he turned his attention to Laura. "There's a police officer here who would like to talk to you if you feel up to it."

Laura's hand reached for Nick's again. "I suppose I might as well get it over with."

"I'll send him in," the doctor said. "Then the nurse will help you dress and we'll give you something to relieve the pain so you can rest." He moved to the door and motioned to the officer.

Laura's details of the attack were even more vague than Nick's, and she looked at the policeman apologetically. "It happened so fast, and it was so dark... All I know is that he was big. And strong."

"Age? Race?" he prompted.

She shook her head slowly. "I'm sorry."

"Do you usually walk at that time of night?"

She shook her head. "No. I had taken the bus home, and—"

"Wait a minute," Nick interrupted. "What happened to your car? I thought you were picking it up tonight."

"It wasn't ready."

"Then why didn't you call me for a ride?" he demanded angrily.

"Mr. Sinclair." There was a warning note in the officer's voice.

Nick sighed and raked a hand through his hair. "Sorry."

"Go on, Ms. Taylor."

Laura finished her story and then looked at him resignedly. "I suppose there's not much chance of catching him, is there?"

"Honestly? None," he admitted frankly, closing his notebook. "He didn't get your purse, did he?"

"No. I had a pretty good grip on it."

"Let me leave you with one piece of advice, Ms. Taylor," the policeman said in a matter-of-fact tone. "I hope this never happens to you again. But if it should, forget your purse. Let it go. Your life is worth a lot more. That man could have had a gun or a knife. And I can guarantee you that if he had, you wouldn't be here right now. You'd be in the morgue," he said bluntly. Laura stared at him, tears welling up in her eyes. When he spoke again his voice was gentler. "I'll wait outside and give you folks a ride home whenever you're ready."

Nick could feel Laura trembling, and he stroked her head. "He's right, you know."

"But that guy was trying to take my purse," she said stubbornly.

"So let him have it! Good grief, Laura, was it worth this?"

"It's mine," she said, squeezing her eyelids shut. "I won't let anyone take what's mine. I won't be a victim again," she said fiercely, the tears spilling onto her cheeks. She opened her eyes and looked up at Nick. "Take me home, please," she pleaded.

He hesitated for a fraction of a second, still trying to figure out her last remark, and then reached down and smoothed the hair back from her face. "I'll get the nurse."

He waited outside while the woman helped Laura dress, and the doctor came over to speak to him. "I've given her a pretty strong sedative. She's had a bad shock, and the pain from her injuries will get worse before it gets better. This will knock her out for about twelve hours. By then her eye and nose should feel a little better. But those ribs are going to be sore, so she'll probably need this by tomorrow," he said, handing Nick a prescription. He paused for a moment before continuing. "She really shouldn't be left alone tonight."

"She won't be."

The doctor nodded. "That's what I thought."

The nurse appeared at the door, supporting Laura, who was walking hunched over, one hand pressed to her side. Her blouse, damaged beyond repair, had been replaced by an oversize surgical shirt that made her appear small and defenseless. Her face was gray with pain, and Nick moved to her side. "Maybe you should stay tonight," he said worriedly.

"No! I want to go home, Nick." Her eyes pleaded with him and, though it was against his better judgment, he relented.

"Okay. But not to your place. I'm not leaving you alone tonight. I want you close where I can keep an eye on you. You'll stay with me."

Laura looked up at him and opened her mouth to protest, but after one glance at his stony face she shut it. It was obvious that arguing would get her nowhere, and she wasn't up to it, anyway. She'd be perfectly all right alone, of course. But she had to admit that his concern had done more to relieve her pain than any drug the doctor could have offered.

# Chapter Ten

By the time they got back to Laura's apartment, the sedative she'd been given was making her feel strangely light-headed, She was grateful for Nick's steady arms as he eased her into the front seat of his sports car, then squatted down beside her.

"Laura, is there anything you absolutely have to have from your apartment tonight?" he asked slowly, enunciating each word.

She frowned, trying to concentrate, but her mind felt fuzzy. "No, I don't think so."

"Okay. Then we'll head over to my place. It won't take long," he said, giving her hand an encouraging squeeze before gently closing the door.

Laura dozed as they drove, rousing only when he stopped at a drugstore.

"I'll only be a minute, and I'll lock the doors," he said, turning to her. "Will you be all right?"

"Yes."

He studied her carefully, a frown on his face. "I

know you're hurting, sweetheart. But hang in there. We're almost home."

Oddly enough, she wasn't hurting. In fact, every bone in her body had gone limp and she felt as if she were floating. It was a pleasant sensation, and she let herself drift off again, hardly conscious of Nick's return and completely unaware of the worried frown he cast her way.

But reality came back with a vengeance when they arrived at Nick's condo and she tried to get out of the car. Even though he was helping her, a sharp, piercing pain shot through her rib cage, rudely assaulting her senses and leaving her gasping for breath.

Nick leaned in when she hesitated, took one look at her face and, without a word, put one arm under her knees and another around her shoulders, lifting her effortlessly out of the car. Even that hurt, though he'd been as gentle as possible, and tears stung her eyes. She bit her lip to keep from crying out, burying her face in his chest and clutching the soft cotton of his shirt as he cradled her in his arms.

Nick looked down at her bowed head, felt the tremor that ran through her body and wished he had some magical way of transporting her upstairs. But this was the best he could do. And the fact that she hadn't protested being carried told him more eloquently than words just how badly she was hurting.

Taking care to jostle her as little as possible, he pushed the door shut with his foot and strode to his condo, his step faltering only when he reached the door. He paused uncertainly and then leaned close to her ear, his breath comfortingly warm against her cheek as he spoke. ‘‘Laura, honey, I’ve got to put you down while I open the door. Can you stand on your own for a minute?’’

Laura wasn’t sure she could sit, let alone stand, but there was obviously no choice, so she nodded.

Carefully Nick lowered her legs to the ground, keeping one arm around her shoulders as he reached for the key. ‘‘Okay?’’ he asked gently.

She gave a barely perceptible nod, trying desperately to keep her knees from buckling.

From the way she clung to him, Nick knew that she was on shaky ground. The moment he had the door open he once again lifted her gently into his arms, and she nestled against him in a trusting way that made his throat constrict with the realization that, for the first time in this relationship, he felt truly needed. And surprisingly, for a man who’d studiously avoided the demands of a serious relationship, he found that it felt good. Amazingly good.

Laura shifted slightly in his arms, which effectively forced him to refocus his thoughts. Without bothering to turn on the lights downstairs, he quickly made his way through the dark living room and up the stairs to his bedroom, flicking on the light with his elbow as he entered. Laura felt herself being lowered to the bed, and when his arms released her she opened her eyes, took a deep breath and smiled at him shakily.

‘‘I’m impressed,’’ she said.

Nick was relieved that she was able to smile at all after what she’d been through, and he squatted down beside her. ‘‘What do you mean?’’

‘‘You must lift weights or something to be able to

lug me all the way from the parking lot to the condo and then up those stairs.''

''Well, I didn't want to tell you, but Superman was my cousin. Muscles run in our family,'' he teased gently. ''When you feel better, I'll show you my cape.'' He was rewarded by another smile. ''I'm going to fix an ice pack for that eye,'' Nick said, straightening up. ''Just lay there and rest until I get back.''

''Gladly.''

By the time he returned, Laura was dozing, and he paused in the doorway for a moment, his throat tightening as he studied her bruised face, his simmering rage once again threatening to erupt. If only he'd gotten to her a few moments sooner. She, who had always been so independent and strong, now seemed so fragile and vulnerable. He was surprised by the protective instinct she'd brought out in him, finding it a heady, but not unwelcome, feeling.

He moved beside her then, and her eyes fluttered open as he reached down and stroked her cheek. ''Laura, I've got the ice pack. But first you need to change into something more comfortable. Jeans are great—but not for sleeping.''

''I don't have anything,'' she said, her words slightly slurred.

''Well, I have a pajama top that might work.'' He moved to his dresser and rummaged in a drawer, looking for the rarely-used piece of clothing. The pajamas had been a gift from his mother, and he'd never worn them. In quick decision, he removed the bottoms as well as the top from the drawer before returning to her side.

"Laura, can you manage this?" he asked.

"I think so," she replied, looking at the pajama top he was holding.

"Okay. I'll wait outside. Let me know when you're ready."

Nick closed the door and leaned a shoulder against the wall, folding his arms against his chest. He took a deep, harsh breath and then expelled it slowly as a sudden, numbing weariness swept over him, the traumatic events of the past few hours finally extracting their toll. The sound of running water in the bathroom told him that at least Laura was able to move around a little, although what it cost her he couldn't imagine. Then he heard the water go off, and Nick waited expectantly for her to call to him. After several minutes, he frowned and knocked on the door. "Laura? Can I come in?"

There was a brief pause before she responded. "Yes."

He opened the door and found her still dressed, standing, one hand gripping the bedpost.

"Laura, honey, what's wrong?"

She looked at him, tears of pain and frustration in her eyes. "I can't get undressed," she said, her voice quavering. "It hurts too much."

"Then let me help you," he said without hesitation, quickly moving beside her. Noting the uncertainty in her eyes, he placed his hands on her shoulders and forced himself to smile. "Now, don't tell me you're worried about my intentions. I promise you I've never seduced a woman with a black eye."

Laura's lower lip trembled. She hated being so helpless, so dependent. But like it or not, she needed assistance tonight. Nick was available and willing, and if she had to rely on a man, there was no one else she would have chosen. "I guess I don't have a choice," she said with a sigh.

"Not tonight, I'm afraid. Now what exactly is the problem?"

"It hurts when I try to pull this thing over my head," she said, gesturing to the surgical top.

"Does it hurt when you lift your arms?"

"A little. But I can manage it."

"Okay, then just sit here," he said, easing her down on the side of the bed, "and lift your arms while I do the pulling. I'll stand behind you," he said easily. "It's okay if I look at your back, isn't it?" he asked with a grin.

She smiled shakily. "Yeah. I guess so."

He moved around to the other side of the bed, and she felt the mattress shift under his weight as he came up behind her. "Okay, sweetheart, let's give it a try."

Obediently she raised her arms, and Nick gently lifted the surgical top over her head. As it skimmed her sides he glanced down, his eyes arrested momentarily by the huge blackish-purple bruise stretching across her rib cage. He paused, a muscle tightening in his jaw, his stomach churning with anger and sympathy. She must be hurting—badly—yet she hadn't complained once.

"Nick?" Laura's voice was muffled, but he could hear the puzzled tone.

"We're doing great," he assured her, smoothly completing the maneuver. Then he turned to lay the garment aside, giving her a moment to slip her arms into the pajama top. By the time he came around to the other side of the bed, she was huddled miserably, her face once again pale and drawn. He dropped to one knee and took her hands between his, caressing the backs gently with his thumbs.

"I'm so sorry, Laura," he said, his voice laced with anguish. "I wish there was something I could do to help."

"You've done more than enough already. I'm sorry to have caused you all this trouble."

"It's no trouble. Believe me."

Laura looked into his eyes and believed. Unquestionably. Not knowing how to respond, unable in her present state to deal with complicated emotions, her gaze skittered away.

Sensing her discomfort, Nick rose and placed his hands on his hips. "What about the jeans?"

"I can get them down to my knees. I have trouble after that."

"Okay." He nodded, turning around. "Get them that far and I'll take care of the rest." He heard her stand, heard the zipper, heard the friction of the coarse denim fabric against her skin.

"All right, Nick."

When he turned back she was lying on the bed, the pajama top pulled down as far as possible but still revealing a long expanse of thigh and leg. He took a deep breath, forcing himself to focus on her pain. Any other thoughts were totally inappropriate at the moment, he told himself sternly. With an effort he drew his eyes away from the hem of the pajama top, and noted that the jeans were bunched around her knees. Silently he reached over and quickly eased them down her legs.

''Shoes,'' she said.

''What?'' he asked distractedly.

''Shoes,'' she repeated, pointing to the athletic shoes and socks she still wore. ''I don't think the jeans will go over them. And besides, I don't usually wear shoes to bed.''

Nick flashed her a grin and bent to remove them, quickly stripping off her socks, as well. ''Well, what's this?'' he asked in surprise, cradling her foot in his hand.

''What's what?'' she asked, puzzled. When he tapped one of her rosily polished toenails, she blushed. ''Oh. You've discovered my one concession to vanity,'' she admitted sheepishly. ''I've always envied women with beautiful nails, but unfortunately in my line of work that's not very practical. This is the next best thing. It's good for my ego, if nothing else.''

Nick smiled at this unexpected facet of her character. He would never have believed it if he hadn't seen it for himself. With her sensible nature, Laura just didn't seem the type who would indulge in something like polished toenails. But apparently even she had a frivolous side. Which was fine as far as he was concerned. He had begun to think she never did anything for herself. Painted toenails weren't much, admittedly, but they were a start.

''You think it's silly, don't you?'' she said, her cheeks still flushed.

''On the contrary. I think it's charming.''

She smiled shyly and closed her eyes as everything began to grow hazy again. ''I think I'll rest for a bit,'' she mumbled sleepily.

''Good idea. I'll hold this ice bag on your eye for a while, okay?'' She nodded, wincing when he first placed it against her skin, but then gradually drifting into welcome oblivion.

Nick stayed with her for another half hour, and when he was satisfied that her deep, even breathing indicated sleep, he pulled the sheet up and tenderly brushed his lips across her forehead before turning the light off.

Once in the hall, he wearily rubbed the back of his neck. Laura was docile tonight because she was hurting. But he knew when she woke up tomorrow she'd be hyper about her business, so diversionary tactics were needed. He frowned, trying to remember the name of her new foreman. Ken something. Nichols…Nolan…Nelson, that was it. With any luck, he'd be in the phone book.

Ten minutes later, after a satisfactory conversation with Ken, he headed back upstairs to the loft sitting area that overlooked the living room and opened up the sofa bed, glad now that he'd had the foresight to buy it. Although he'd never imagined that he'd be the first to use it, he thought ruefully.

By the time he took a quick shower downstairs and made up the bed, it was nearly two in the morning. But though he was bone tired, he still felt too keyed up emotionally to sleep. Rather than even try, he prowled around restlessly, verifying that he had breakfast food in the kitchen, going through his mail, looking over a few plans in the downstairs bedroom that he'd turned into an office, checking on Laura every few minutes. When at last his body revolted, he climbed into the sofa bed, yawned hugely and turned out the light.

Sleep came more quickly than he expected, a deep sleep that dulled his senses. So it took a long time for him to wake up, brought back to consciousness by something he couldn't immediately identify. Groggily he glanced at the illuminated dial of his watch and groaned. Three-thirty. His eyes flickered closed and he was beginning to drift back to sleep when Laura's soft sobs suddenly penetrated his sleep-fogged brain. Instantly alert, he swung his feet to the floor and moved quickly down the hall, pausing briefly on the threshold of her room, which was illuminated only by a dim night-light. In the shadows, he heard Laura thrashing fretfully around on the bed, mumbling incoherently, sobbing quietly. She must be having a nightmare, he thought, moving quietly beside her, and he wasn't surprised, not after what she'd been through. She'd probably be plagued with them for months, only the next time he wouldn't be there to comfort her, he thought, a muscle clenching in his jaw. He bent to gently touch her shoulder when suddenly Laura flung out an arm.

"No, Joe, don't! Please don't hurt me!" she cried.

Nick yanked his hand back at her impassioned plea, and his heart actually stopped, then lunged on, hammering painfully against his chest. She wasn't having a nightmare about tonight's attacker. She was having a nightmare about her husband! What had that bastard done to her? he wondered in sudden fury.

Laura's thrashing grew more intense, and Nick became alarmed, fearing that she would injure herself even further. He crouched beside the bed, reaching over to gently stroke her hair. "It's okay, sweetheart. It's okay," he murmured soothingly, aware that her whole body was trembling.

Her eyes flickered open, and she stared at his shadowy figure dazedly. "Nick?" Her voice was barely a whisper.

"It's me, honey," he said huskily. "Everything's okay. You just had a bad dream, that's all. Try to relax and go back to sleep."

"Could...could you stay with me for a little while?" she asked in a tremulous, little-girl voice that tore at his heart.

"Sure." He took her hand, and she grasped it with a steel grip that surprised him. "I'll be right here."

He continued to stroke her hair, murmuring soothing words, and slowly she relaxed. Her breathing grew more even and gradually her grip on his hand loosened as she slipped back into sleep.

When she seemed to be resting easily, Nick carefully extricated his hand and gingerly stood up, much to the relief of his protesting calf muscles. He frowned as he stared down at Laura, her face now at peace as she slumbered. He ought to go back to bed, he supposed. But he just couldn't leave her. Not yet, anyway. He wanted to be at her side if she awoke again in the grip of another nightmare.

Wearily he sank down in an overstuffed chair near the bed. It had been a very long day. And it looked like it was going to be a very long night.

Nick let his head drop onto the cushioned back and stared at the dark ceiling, torn by conflicting emotions that he didn't understand. He cared about Laura. Deeply. But what was he getting himself into? She was obviously troubled, clearly scarred emotionally, and he was no psychologist. He ought to get out of this relationship while he still could.

Only it was already too late, he acknowledged with a resigned sigh. He couldn't walk away, not now. Not after he'd seen the vulnerable look in her eyes tonight. And maybe not ever. But they couldn't go on as they had. He'd heard too much tonight, learned more from those few words spoken in sleep than he'd learned from all of their waking conversations. The time had come to demand some answers, to examine the reasons why she was so afraid of commitment. It wouldn't be easy for her. But psychologist or not, he knew with absolute certainty that until they confronted the demons from her past, they had no future together.

Laura awoke slowly, disoriented and sluggish. It was a struggle just to open her eyes. She raised her arm and stared at her watch, squinting as she tried to make out the time, but for some reason she had trouble focusing.

One thing did come suddenly—and clearly—into focus, however: her attire. She was wearing a man's pajama top! And just where exactly was she anyway? she wondered in sudden panic, her gaze sweeping over the unfamiliar surroundings. It jolted abruptly to a stop on Nick's sleeping figure, slumped uncomfortably in a chair near the bed, his leg slung over one of the arms.

Suddenly memories of the night before came rushing back—the horror, certainly, but even more prominently the care and tenderness of the wonderful man just a touch away. In sleep, his face had an endearing, boyish quality that she'd never seen before. His hair might be tousled, and he might look rumpled and unshaven, but as far as she was concerned he was the handsomest, most appealing man she'd ever seen.

Of course, the bare chest might have something to do with that perception, she admitted, her eyes drawn to the T pattern of dark, curly hair that rose and fell in time with his even breathing. Her own breathing was suddenly none too steady, and she had a sudden, compelling urge to reach over and lay her hand close to his heart, feel the rise and fall of his broad chest beneath her fingers.

At just that moment, as if sensing her gaze, Nick awoke—abruptly, immediately and fully. His gaze locked on hers, his stomach instinctively contracting at the purple, swollen eye and puffy nose, harshly spotlighted in the brightness of day. He rose stiffly from his uncomfortable position and then moved toward the bed in two long strides, squatting down beside her.

"Good morning, sweetheart," he said, his voice still husky from sleep. He reached over and stroked her hair, his eyes never leaving hers. "How do you feel?"

She frowned and gingerly touched her face, then her side, wincing at even the slightest pressure. "I'm a little sore," she said breathlessly, her voice unsteady.

"I have a feeling that's the understatement of the year," he replied with a frown, his lips compressing into a thin line.

"I'll be fine," she assured him. "But...did you sleep in that chair all night?" she asked, her eyes wide.

"What was left of it," he said with a wry grin.

"You must be exhausted! I'm so sorry to cause all this trouble," she apologized, her eyes filling with tears.

Nick reached over as one spilled out to trickle down her cheek, wiping it away with a gentle finger, his throat constricting painfully. "Laura, you were no trouble. Trust me," he said, his own voice uneven. She still looked unconvinced, and his instinct was to kiss away her doubts. But given her physical—and emotional—fragility at the moment, that was probably not wise. Mustering all of his self restraint, he tenderly touched her cheek and then stood up. "I'll run downstairs and get you a pill, okay?"

She nodded silently, still feeling off balance and uncharacteristically weepy.

His concerned eyes searched hers, and then he turned and rummaged in the closet for a shirt and slacks. "Just stay put till I get back," he said over his shoulder, sliding the door shut and making a quick exit.

When he reached the loft, he rapidly pulled on the cotton slacks and thrust his arms into the hastily retrieved shirt, distractedly rolling the sleeves to the elbows. Based on her pallor and lines of strain in her face, Laura needed a painkiller quickly. He took the steps two at a time, and returned in record time with the pill and a glass of water.

Laura was up, gripping her side and leaning against

the bedpost for support, when he entered the room. "I thought I told you to stay put," he said with a frown.

"Nick, do you know what time it is?" she asked, panic edging her voice.

He glanced at his watch. "Nine o'clock."

"I should have been at work an hour ago... Ken won't know what happened... He was supposed to pick me up at seven-thirty... My car's ready today," she said disjointedly.

"Relax, honey," he said, depositing the pill and water on the dresser and easing her back down to the bed. "I called Ken last night. Everything's under control. He'll fill in until you feel well enough to go back."

"But I have so much to do. I can't take another day off. I can at least go to the office. That won't be too taxing, and—"

"Forget it, Laura," he said flatly, cutting her off.

She stared at him. "Excuse me?"

He sighed, regretting the dictatorial approach. Maybe logic would work better. He sat down next to her and gently took her hand. "Look, Laura, you're in no shape to get out of bed, let alone go to the office. Do you honestly feel up to doing anything today?"

She stared at him, savoring the warm clasp of his hand on one level, thinking about his question on another. The truth was, she didn't. But that had never stopped her before. She hadn't been able to let it. It hadn't mattered how she'd felt; the job had to be done. But then again, she'd never felt quite this bad. Her ribs ached, she could barely see out of her left eye and her nose was almost too tender to touch. Besides, every muscle in her body felt as if it had been pulled taut.

But there was work to be done. "No, I don't," she admitted. "But I can't afford to lose a day," she said resolutely.

"For the sake of your health, you can't afford not to," he told her bluntly.

She looked at him in exasperation. "Nick, you just don't understand. I'm it. Taylor Landscaping is a one-person show at the management level. You have someone to fall back on. I don't. I can't take a day off."

Laura took a deep breath and stood, gripping the headboard to steady herself. Tears pricked her eyes and she forced them back, but she couldn't do anything about the trembling in her hands. And Nick wasn't blind.

He remained on the bed for a moment, looking up at her back, ramrod straight, and the defiant tilt of her head. She was probably going to hate him after this, he thought ruefully, but there was no way he was letting her set one foot outside this condo today. He wouldn't be surprised if her stubborn determination carried her through a day at the office. Laura wasn't a quitter, that was for sure. But by tonight she'd be a basket case. He steeled himself for her anger and stood, moving to face her, placing his hands on her shoulders.

"Laura, I'm sorry. No way. I've already called Ken, who sounds very competent, and he's handling everything. You're not leaving here until tomorrow."

"Tomorrow?" she stammered.

"Tomorrow," he declared.

"Nick, you can't do this!"

"I can and I am. I'm bigger than you are. And

you're in no shape to resist. I'll sit on you if I have to, but I hope it won't come to that.''

Nick saw the anger and defiance flash in her eyes and prepared to do battle. But then he watched in amazement as the flame of anger slowly flickered and went out. Her shoulders suddenly sagged and she carefully sat back on the bed, dropping her head to hide the tears that shimmered in her eyes. He squatted in front of her and took her hands in his, taken aback by her unexpected acquiescence. He'd expected a struggle; instead, she'd caved in. Had he pushed too hard, been too heavy-handed? He knew her emotions were tattered. ''Laura, I'm sorry for being so obstinate about this,'' he said gently. ''But I'm doing it for you.''

''I know,'' she said softly, struggling to keep the tears from spilling out of her eyes, but the tenderness in his voice just made it more difficult. It had been so long since she'd felt this cared for, this protected, this cherished. Her heart overflowed with gratitude...and something else she refused to acknowledge. Instead, she met his eyes and tried to smile, but didn't quite succeed. ''I'm very grateful. It's been a long time since...'' Her voice trailed off and she looked down at the strong, competent hands that held hers so comfortingly.

Nick didn't move. He just stared at her bowed head, struggling to regain his own composure. It wasn't easy, not when his emotions were pulling at him like a riptide, threatening to sweep him off balance, a protective instinct emerging on the one hand, a purely sensual one on the other. The latter instinct urged him to take her in his arms, to kiss away her tears, to love her as she deserved to be loved. She seemed so desperately in need of loving.

"Laura," he said at last, the unevenness of his voice making him stop and clear his throat before continuing. Her head remained bowed. "Laura," he repeated, squeezing her hands, this time forcing her to meet his eyes, which held hers with a compelling intensity. "You are very special to me. Special, and precious. When I think about what could have happened last night..." He closed his eyes for a moment and took a steadying breath, struggling for composure before fixing his intense gaze on her once again. "You're not in great shape," he said, reaching up to her eye with a whisper touch, "but you'll be okay. You'll be okay," he repeated more forcefully, as much to convince himself as to reassure her, touching her as he spoke—her arm, her cheek, her hair. "And I don't want you to ever be alone and frightened again."

She stared at him, swallowing with difficulty. "Is that why you slept in the chair last night?"

"Yeah. You had a nightmare," he said quietly. "I wanted to be close in case it happened again."

She studied his eyes—dark, intense and filled with integrity. He seemed too good to be real, and she reached over and tentatively touched the angled planes of his face. A muscle twitched in his jaw, and she watched as the smoldering sparks of passion in his eyes burst into flame. Alarmed, she tried to draw her hand away, not wanting to create false expectations. But he held her fast, his fingers tightening on her wrist.

"Laura?" his voice was gentle, his eyes probing. "What is it?"

"I—I'd really like it if you would just hold me," she said, so quietly he had to lean close to hear. "But that's not fair to you. I can see that…I mean, you want more and right now…I can't promise that."

He placed his fingers against her lips, and her eyes searched his. "Sweetheart, if being held is what you need now, that's what I'll give. Okay?"

Her head nodded jerkily, and he eased her back on the bed, then stretched out beside her, carefully gathering her soft, bruised body into his arms. It was some minutes before he felt her tension ease, and then he brushed his cheek against her hair. "Better?" he asked.

"Yes. But, Nick…I know this isn't enough for you."

"It's enough," he assured her. But then he added a qualification. "For now."

# Chapter Eleven

The persistent ringing of the phone slowly penetrated Laura's consciousness. Tenderly cradled in Nick's arms, feeling utterly safe and content, she had drifted off to sleep. When the ringing of the bedside phone continued, she opened her eyes and glanced up questioningly. "Nick?"

"Mmm-hmm."

"The phone's ringing."

"I know."

"Aren't you going to answer it?"

"I don't think so."

"But it might be something important."

"It's probably just the office."

The ringing stopped, and Laura's eyes grew wide. "The office! What are you doing home? Shouldn't you have been at work hours ago?"

"Normally, yes," he replied mildly.

"So?"

"The past eighteen hours haven't exactly been normal," he reminded her wryly.

"No, I suppose not," she conceded. "But I'll be okay here. You don't have to baby-sit."

"Work can wait," he insisted.

Suddenly the phone rang again, and Nick glanced at it in irritation. But Laura also saw the concern in his eyes, and she nudged him with her shoulder. "Go ahead. This will drive you crazy."

He sighed. "Yeah, I guess so." He reached over to pick up the receiver. "Jack? I told you this morning, we'll have to postpone it. I'm not leaving Laura today." Silence, while he absently continued to stroke her shoulder. "Yeah, yeah, I know, but you don't need me for the presentation." Silence again. "Look, just cover for me. Tell him...I don't know, tell him anything."

Laura frowned. Nick obviously had a commitment, apparently an important one. The thought that he was willing to forgo it on her behalf filled her with a warm glow, but at the same time, she'd struggled long enough herself to know that it was never wise to upset a client.

"Nick," she whispered.

He glanced down. "Jack, hang on a second." Depressing the mute button, he reached down to stroke her cheek, his brusque, businesslike tone of moments before suddenly gentled. "What is it, honey?"

"Go to your meeting. It sounds important."

"You're more important," he insisted.

She smiled her thanks, but shook her head. "I'll feel guilty if you don't go. There's no sense in both of us falling behind, and I'll be fine.'' She could see the flicker of indecision in his eyes, and with a determined smile she gently eased herself away from the warmth of his body and swung her feet to the floor, trying not to wince at the sudden pain in her side. Carefully she stood, and by the time she turned back to him her features were placid. ''Come on, you'll be late,'' she urged lightly.

Nick hesitated a fraction of a second longer and then released the mute button, glancing at his watch. ''Okay, Jack, I'll be there. But not until one-thirty. That will give us time to look over the presentation and make sure we're in sync before Andrews arrives... Yeah, I know.''

Nick replaced the receiver and stood, facing Laura across the bed. ''I hate to leave you,'' he said with simple honesty.

''I'll be fine,'' she assured him again. ''And you'll be back.''

''You can count on that. And as soon as possible,'' he said huskily. Laura felt the warmth creep up her cheeks at his tone and glanced down, tugging self-consciously at the brief hem of the pajama top she wore. Nick cleared his throat. ''Do you need anything from your apartment? I could stop by on the way back.''

''Other than my toothbrush, I think I'm okay for another day. Except...do you have an old shirt or something with buttons I could borrow? I'd rather not put that thing on again,'' she said, gesturing distastefully toward the discarded surgical top.

''I'm sure I can find something. And I may even

have a spare toothbrush.'' He returned triumphantly a few moments later with the latter item, still cellophane enclosed, and quickly riffled through his closet. ''Will this work?'' he asked, withdrawing a striped cotton shirt.

''Perfect. I'll just roll up the sleeves and it will be fine.''

''Can you get dressed on your own?''

''I think so. But I'd like to take a shower first.''

Nick nodded. ''I'll put some fresh towels out for you and come back in a few minutes.''

It took Laura a lot longer to shower than she expected. First, a glance in the mirror over the sink made her stop in midstride, alarmed at the extent of the damage. She looked terrible. Her nose wasn't too bad—just slightly puffy—but the purple-and-red eye, still half-swollen shut, made up for it. She wished she had some makeup, but she doubted whether anything would be able to disguise the discolored area. She'd barely come to grips with the appearance of her battered face when she'd been shocked by the huge, ugly blue-black swath of skin splayed over her ribs. It had made her momentarily queasy, and she'd forced herself to take a few deep breaths, telling herself that she was okay, that the bruise would eventually fade. But no wonder she hurt so much!

Carefully she stepped into the shower, adjusting the water temperature before turning on the spray. The sudden force of water against her ribs, however, made her gasp in pain, and she quickly angled away from the spray, shielding her side. Nick had been right about her going to work today, she admitted. She was in no shape to sit at a desk, let alone visit the job sites. Just the exertion of taking a shower had drained her. But the warm spray felt good, and she let it massage her body with its soothing caress.

At last, Laura reluctantly turned off the water and toweled herself dry, carefully avoiding the injured areas. She dressed slowly, easing the jeans over her legs, grimacing as she bent to pull them up. The voluminous shirt was easier, and as she slipped her arms into the sleeves she caught the unique scent that she had come to associate with Nick—warm, vibrant, slightly spicy…and very masculine. For a moment she buried her face in its folds, wistfully inhaling the essence. Then with a sigh she slipped it over her head.

Laura pulled a comb from her purse and carefully worked the tangles out of her wet, tousled hair. By the time she finished it was almost dry, hanging loose and long, with a few stray tendrils curling around her face.

"Laura, are you okay?" Nick's soft knock and worried voice came through the door.

"I'm fine. I'll be right out," she called. After neatly folding the wet towels and placing them on the edge of the tub, she picked up her purse and opened the door.

Nick's perceptive eyes swept over her. "How are you feeling?"

"Better. The shower helped."

He grinned and folded his arms, tilting his head as he looked at her. "You know, that shirt looks a whole lot better on you than it ever did on me," he said.

"It's a little big," she said, a smile hovering around the corners of her mouth.

"Big is in. It's a very attractive look."

Laura shrugged. "I don't feel very attractive," she admitted.

If any other woman had said that to him, Nick would have assumed she was angling for a compliment. With Laura, the remark had been artless and without pretense. He moved toward her and placed his hands on her shoulders. "Sweetheart, you are the most irresistible woman I've ever known," he said huskily. And then he lightened his tone. "Even with that shiner."

Laura looked up at him in surprise, suddenly realizing that he'd been using terms of endearment ever since last night. They seemed to come so naturally to him, and had sounded so natural to her, that it had taken all this time for the fact to register. Before she could evaluate its significance, however, he was leading her out the door.

"I'm afraid I'm not much of a cook, but you can't afford to skip any more meals and I didn't want you to have to fix anything yourself," he said over his shoulder. "I hope this is at least palatable."

He stepped aside when they reached the loft, where a tray rested on the coffee table in front of the now-made-up sofa sleeper. Laura's eyes grew wide. It wasn't so much the contents—scrambled eggs, toast, an orange that had been carefully peeled and separated into chunks, a steaming cup of coffee—but the thoughtfulness of the gesture that stirred her heart. Her throat constricted with emotion, and when she turned to Nick the warmth in her unguarded eyes made him catch his breath. "Nick, I… After all you've already done, this makes me feel so...'' She gestured helplessly.

He grinned, inordinately pleased by her response, and took her hand, steering her toward the sofa. ''Don't say anything else until you've tasted it,'' he warned teasingly. He settled her comfortably and then glanced at his watch. ''Do you mind if I get dressed while you eat?''

''No, of course not.''

By the time she'd finished the last bite of what she would always remember as one of the best meals of her life, Nick reappeared, dressed in a lightweight charcoal gray suit, crisp white shirt and paisley tie. He smiled when he saw the empty plate. ''Well, I guess it wasn't too bad. Or else you were starved.'' When she started to speak, he held up his hand. ''No, don't tell me which. I prefer to keep my illusions.''

Laura smiled. ''Thank you,'' she said simply.

His expression grew suddenly serious and he sat down beside her, grasping her hand as he studied her eyes. ''Laura, are you sure you'll be all right? I can still stay if you want me to.''

''I'll be fine,'' she assured him again. ''I took the pill you left on the tray, and I already feel very relaxed and sleepy. I'm just going to nap this afternoon, and it makes no sense for you to sit around and miss an important appointment while I sleep.''

Nick bowed to the logic of her argument. ''Okay. But I'll be back early—no later than five. Do you like Chinese food?''

''Love it.''

"I'll pick some up on the way home." He stood, taking the tray with him.

"Oh, Nick, let me take care of that," she protested.

"No way. You're not to lift a finger today. Promise me that, or I'm not leaving."

She shook her head. "You really do have a one-track mind."

"Promise?" he persisted.

"Promise," she agreed.

Laura's day went almost exactly as predicted. She took a few minutes to explore Nick's condo, admiring his spare but tasteful and obviously expensive furnishings. The cathedral-ceilinged living room, overlooked by the loft, featured a two-story wall of glass that offered a restful view of the wooded common ground. She peeked into his office, impressed by its neatness, and through the window she glimpsed what looked like a clubhouse and swimming pool. Compared to this, her apartment really was the pits, she thought. No wonder he had remarked on the neighborhood a few weeks ago. And rightly so, she thought wryly, wincing at the twinge in her side as she turned.

After a quick call to Sam, who was shocked by the mugging but clearly pleased by Nick's attentiveness and concern, Laura took another pill and lay down. Within minutes she was asleep.

The sound of Nick's voice calling from downstairs awakened her later in the afternoon, and by the time she had oriented herself and was struggling to sit up, he appeared in the doorway, his jacket already discarded, his face a mask of concern. He moved beside her immediately, his intense, dark eyes critically examining her. For a moment he hesitated, and then he reached over and touched his lips to her forehead. "I'd like to give you a better hello, but that's about the only spot I know of that isn't bruised," he said huskily, brushing her hair back from her face as he spoke.

Laura smiled hesitantly. "My lips are okay," she said softly.

Nick's momentary surprise was quickly followed by a pleased chuckle, and the deep, throaty sound of it sent a hot wave of desire crashing over her. "Are you saying you'd like to be kissed?" he asked with a smile.

She swallowed. "Only if it's what you want."

"Oh, I want," he said huskily, and the ardent light in his eyes left little doubt about his wants. "I just don't want to hurt you."

Laura's mouth went dry. Already her lips were throbbing in anticipation of his touch. "We'll be careful," she whispered.

Nick gave up the fight. He'd told himself she was in no shape, physically or emotionally, for intimacy right now. He'd told himself that he would keep his hands off until she was stronger. He'd told himself that she wasn't herself, that the trauma of the previous night could make her needy in ways she would later regret. But he was only human, after all. And the tender, welcoming look in her eyes was too much for him. With a soft groan he lowered his lips to hers, gently nipping at their pliant fullness, until her mouth stirred sweetly beneath his. He felt her shudder as he tasted the warm sweetness of her mouth, and her response nearly undid him. Gently he lowered her to the bed and stretched out beside her, cradling her head in his hands, his fingers lost in the thick fullness of her hair. How he'd waited for this moment, to have her close to him. His lips left hers, moving down to her neck, and she arched her throat for his touch, breathing heavily. Her arms clung to him, urging him closer. Nick let one hand travel downward until it rested lightly at her waist. Laura was so lost in the magic of his touch that it took her a moment to realize that his hand was gently but firmly tugging her shirt free.

Laura knew where this was leading, knew she was breaking every rule she'd ever made about allowing any man to get close to her again, knew that it went against everything she believed about casual intimacy. And yet she seemed powerless to stop what was happening. When Nick had appeared in the doorway tonight she'd had no plan to initiate this embrace. But he'd looked so wonderful standing there, so dear and so handsome and so very special. And she was very grateful for all he'd done for her. Yet she was honest enough to admit that gratitude wasn't the only explanation for her behavior. Last night had been like déjà vu, a bad dream come again to life, awakening old memories and old pain. Today she felt vulnerable, needy, scared—aching physically and emotionally. Nick, with his gentle touch and caring concern, could make her fears and pain disappear, at least for a little while. Her Christian faith put strict limits on intimacy outside of marriage, and she knew she was pushing those limits. Tomorrow she'd probably be sorry. But for now, she needed to be held, to be cared for and protected, to bask in the warmth of his caresses.

Laura felt her shirt being pulled free, felt his hand

hesitate briefly at her waist before sliding slowly up her back. The warmth of his fingers against her bare skin made her sigh. ''Oh, Nick,'' she breathed, her own fingers kneading his hard, muscled shoulders. He urged her closer, his lips once more capturing hers with an urgency that stole her breath away.

It was her sudden, sharp intake of breath that stilled his hands and made him draw back. Her face had gone white and tears glimmered in her eyes. ''Nick...I'm sorry,'' she said breathlessly. ''My side... I forgot...''

Her voice trailed off at the stricken look on Nick's face. ''Oh, sweetheart,'' he whispered, cradling her face in his hands, stroking her cheeks with his thumbs. ''I'm so sorry! Did I hurt you?''

''It's okay. It just...surprised me. It doesn't hurt now.'' She wanted to smooth out the deep creases that had appeared on his brow, ease the sudden tension in his jaw, erase the self-recrimination in his eyes.

''I told myself not to touch you. I knew better,'' he said angrily.

''Nick, it's my fault. I—I more or less asked you to.''

''Yeah, well, you're not thinking straight. You're probably half out of your mind in pain and you're doped up on those high-powered pills. Laura, let me take a look, okay? I promise not to hurt you. I just want to make sure I didn't do any more damage.''

Laura knew he needed to reassure himself, so she nodded silently. With utmost care he pulled up her shirttail, sucking in his breath at the bruise that extended from her breastbone to the bottom of her rib cage. ''Dear God, it looks worse than yesterday,'' he declared in dismay.

''Bruises usually do,'' she said lightly, easing the shirt back down. ''But it will fade, Nick.''

''No thanks to me.''

''Nick, I'm okay. And hungry. Where's that Chinese food you promised me?'' she asked, trying to divert his attention.

For the rest of the evening he treated her like spun glass, helping her up and down the steps, getting a cushion for the back of her chair while they ate, wrapping an afghan around her before they settled in to watch an old movie on video that he'd brought home.

When he tucked her in for the night, gently pressing a chaste kiss on her forehead, Laura smiled. ''You'd make a good mother,'' she joked gently.

''Laura, believe me, my feelings for you are anything but motherly,'' he said with an intensity that left no doubt about exactly what his feelings were. ''My restraint is the result of sheer terror. I never want to hurt you, sweetheart, and if touching you hurts at the moment, I won't touch. The important thing right now is for you to heal.''

Later, as Laura began to drift to sleep, she thought about Nick's parting words. She would heal—physically. It would just take time. It was the emotional healing that still troubled her. Today they'd been closer physically than ever before. Not because he'd pushed, as she'd feared all along, but because she'd pressed him. He'd responded readily, and she couldn't blame him; he'd long ago made his intentions clear. But they'd been heading for a level of intimacy that she believed should be reserved for a committed relationship. And even if he had suggested that, Laura knew she wasn't yet ready—just needy. And that wasn't enough. For either of them.

Nick didn't sleep well. His body was still vibrating with unrelieved tension, and his conscience was battering him for letting his emotions and physical needs cloud his sensitivity and judgment. It was the early hours of the morning before he finally fell into a restless sleep, and even then he only slept lightly, half expecting to again hear Laura's anguished cries, as he had the night before. But all was quiet.

It seemed he had just drifted off when he felt someone prodding his shoulder. "Come on, sleepyhead, wake up," an amused voice said.

Nick opened one eye and stared up at Laura, fully dressed, standing with her hands on her hips next to his bed. "What time is it?" he asked groggily.

"Seven-thirty."

He groaned and buried his head in his pillow.

"Nick Sinclair, even if you have time to loaf, I don't. I need to get to the office."

Nick sighed. It had been hard enough to hold Laura down for one day. He'd pretty much figured two days were out of the question. "Did anyone ever tell you that you're a hard taskmaster?" he growled.

She prodded him again. "Come on, Nick. Here, try this. Maybe it will help." She waved a fragrant-smelling cup of coffee under his nose.

He sniffed appreciatively and grasped the mug in both hands, taking a long swallow before he even opened his eyes. And this time he took a good look at her. Her nose seemed back to normal, her eye was slightly less swollen—though no less purple—and he could only speculate about her ribs. But her face had more color than yesterday, and she seemed to be in good spirits.

"How do you feel?" he asked, watching her over the rim of his cup as he took another swallow.

She shrugged. "Compared to what? Better than yesterday, worse than last weekend. It's all in your point of view. But I'll live."

She was her spunky self again, which meant that she really must be feeling better. Nick was glad, of course, but he felt a sudden, odd sense of loss. For the past thirty-six hours she'd needed him—really needed him—and though the circumstances had been less than ideal, the feeling had been good. Now, suddenly, he felt less needed, less important in her life. He took another sip of the coffee and, trying to throw off his melancholy mood, he glanced at his watch. "Okay, give me fifteen minutes and we can roll."

At her request, Nick dropped her off at the garage to pick up her car, coming around to open the door for her when they arrived. "Do you think you're up to driving?" he asked worriedly.

"Of course," she said with more confidence than she felt.

He sighed and raked his fingers through his hair. "Laura, will you promise me something? If you get tired, go home and rest. Don't force yourself to put in a full day."

"I'll be fine, Nick. Okay, okay." She held up her hands when he opened his mouth to protest. "I'll try not to push myself."

"Promise?"

"Promise."

''Okay. Now, what would you like for dinner tonight?''

''Tonight?'' she asked, startled.

''Mmm-hmm. Does pizza sound okay?''

''Well, sure. But, Nick, you don't have to feel obligated. I can manage.''

''Yeah, I know. I just hoped you might like to have dinner with me. Besides, you may feel perky now, but I have a feeling that you're going to fade by this afternoon, and I doubt whether you'll be in the mood to cook.'' More likely she'd just fall into bed without eating, he thought, and skipping meals was not something she could afford to do.

''Well...thank you. That would be great.''

''I'll see you about six,'' he said, walking around to the driver's side of his car and opening the door. ''And, Laura...?''

''Yes?''

''Will you take it easy today?''

''I'll try,'' she hedged.

Nick rolled his eyes and shook his head. ''You're stubborn, do you know that?''

She grinned. ''Yeah. But it takes one to know one.'' Then she grew more serious. ''Nick...I want to thank you for...well, for everything. You've been really great. I don't know how I would have managed without you. Knowing you were there—just having you with me—made all the difference.''

He looked at her for a long moment before speaking. ''Hold that thought,'' he said at last. Then he slipped into the low-slung car and was gone.

# Chapter Twelve

Nick called Laura several times during the day. Though she kept her voice determinedly cheerful, he could hear the underlying weariness that intensified with each call. She stuck it out most of the day, despite his urging to go home and take a nap, and by the time he arrived at her apartment with the pizza he wasn't sure what shape she'd be in.

Not good, he thought the moment she opened the door. Her face was as pale as it had been at the hospital two nights before, making the dark, ugly colors of her bruised eye stand out in stark relief.

Nick opened his mouth to tell her she had pushed too hard, took another look at her weary face and changed his mind. She'd clearly already had all she could take today. What she needed now was support, not criticism.

"Rough day," he said quietly. It was a statement, not a question.

"Is it that obvious?" she asked ruefully, shutting the door behind him.

"Mmm-hmm," he replied, aware that she was moving stiffly and slowly—and trying to hide it.

"You look tired," she said, studying his face.

He hadn't really thought it, but she was right. The strain and worry had taken their toll on him, too. "Yeah. I am."

"Why don't you sit down and I'll get you something to drink. I'm sorry about the heat. I turned on all the fans, but I know you're used to air-conditioning. At least you changed into something cooler before you came. Would you like some iced tea, or—"

"Laura." His quiet voice stilled her.

"Yes?"

"Would you please sit down before you fall down? You look half-dead. I did not come over here tonight to be waited on." He took her arm and guided her to the couch, and she went unprotestingly, the stream of adrenaline that had kept her on her feet all day suddenly running dry. All at once she was overcome with a numbing lethargy, and she sank down gratefully onto the soft, chintz-covered cushions of her couch.

"Would you like a cold drink?"

She gazed up at him, her eyes slightly dazed with fatigue. "Yes, I think I would. There's some soda in the fridge."

She heard the clatter of ice and then he was back beside her, a glass in each hand. "I put the pizza in the oven to warm for a few minutes."

She nodded, silently sipping the sweet liquid, fighting a losing battle to keep her eyelids open. When her head began to nod, Nick reached over and gently took the glass from her fingers, then he pulled her against him, carefully avoiding contact with her bruised ribs. She nestled into the crook of his arm, her cheek resting against the hard contours of his chest, and sighed.

"I'm not much company, am I?" she said apologetically.

"Don't worry about it. I didn't expect you to play hostess."

"I'm just so tired."

"I know." What Laura needed tonight was food and sleep, in that order and preferably as quickly as possible, he concluded. What he needed was beside the point, he thought longingly as her firm, supple body molded to his caused stirrings of emotion best held in check. This was not the time. "How about some pizza?" he asked, his chin resting on her hair.

Laura wasn't hungry. Just tired. But she knew she needed to eat, and Nick had gone to the trouble of bringing food, so she nodded.

She perked up a little as she munched on the spicy, rich pizza, enough to remember that she wanted to invite Nick to dinner the next night. He protested at first, suggesting instead that they go out so she wouldn't have to cook, but she insisted.

"I really want to, Nick. It's Saturday, so I can rest all day. And I like to cook. It's not exactly strenuous, and I find it relaxing. Besides, I want to thank you for everything you've done these past couple of days."

"You don't need to do that, Laura."

"I want to. Unless...that is...well, I understand if

you have other plans,'' she said, her voice suddenly sounding uncertain.

He reached across the table and took her hand, forcing her to meet his eyes. ''I don't have any other plans,'' he said firmly. ''I'll be here.'' He gave her fingers a gentle squeeze and then released them, standing to clear away the remnants of their meal. When she started to help, he placed a hand firmly on her shoulder. ''Just sit,'' he commanded.

''Can I at least move to the living room?'' she asked with a tired smile.

''Sure. I'll be right in.''

By the time he rejoined her, she was sitting in a corner of the couch, her legs tucked under her, her head resting against the back, her eyes closed. He thought she might have dozed off again, but when he quietly sat down next to her, her eyelids flickered open.

''Dinner was great. You're going to spoil me,'' she said with a smile.

''You could do with some spoiling.''

''Well, I'm not used to it, that's for sure.''

Nick reached over and took her hand, gently stroking the back with his thumb. ''Laura?''

''Mmm-hmm?''

''Will you be okay here tonight by yourself?''

''Of course,'' she lied. In reality, she was as nervous as the deer they'd spotted in the woods, but she wasn't about to admit that to Nick. He'd insist on spending the night on her couch and he looked wiped out. After the past couple of days, he deserved a decent night's sleep in his own bed.

"I could stay," he offered.

"No. You need to get some rest. I'll be fine."

"But what if you have another nightmare?"

"I won't. I was fine last night, wasn't I?"

"Yeah, but subconsciously you knew I was close by."

She couldn't argue with that. The simple fact was she *would* sleep better with Nick here. She was still spooked from the attack, and she knew that when quiet descended on the apartment after he left, every sound would seem magnified—and menacing. But she couldn't live the rest of her life afraid. "Nick, please...I've got to stay by myself eventually. It would just be postponing the inevitable," she said resolutely. "The memory of the attack will fade in time."

"That's true. But at the moment I'm more concerned about other memories."

She frowned. "What do you mean?"

"I mean the nightmare you had the other night wasn't about the attack," he said quietly.

"How do you know?"

"Because I heard what you said. Laura...it was about Joe."

A stricken look crossed her face, and she bit her lip. "Oh," she said in a small voice, turning away.

He reached over and stroked her arm, and then his hand strayed to the top of her right breast, his fingers resting lightly on the spot where he'd seen the scar two nights before. "Did he do this to you?" he asked, a sudden edge to his voice.

He felt her stiffen even before she pulled away. "What?"

"The scar. I saw it at the hospital."

She drew a deep, shaky breath. "Nick, what happened between Joe and me is in the past. Let's leave it there."

"I'd like to, because I know it's painful for you. But I can't. Because whatever happened between the two of you is coming between us, whether you want to face that or not. We've got to talk about it, Laura."

She wrapped her arms around her body and shook her head. "No."

With a muttered oath he stood abruptly and walked away from her, the rigid lines of his back speaking more eloquently than words of the strain of the past two days and his longer-term frustration. He was clearly a man on the edge, pushed to the limit of his patience, struggling to maintain control. Laura had never seen him this upset, and it frightened her. Not in terms of physical danger, the way such anger once might have frightened her, but in the knowledge that Nick could very well walk away—and with very good reason. He deserved to know more than she was willing—or able—to tell. She just didn't have the courage to dredge up her painful past for anyone—not even Nick.

It seemed as if an eternity passed before he at last turned and looked at her. When he spoke, she could hear the anger—and the underlying hurt—in his voice. "How long is it going to take for you to realize that you can trust me, Laura? Can't you see how much I care about you? Why won't you share your past with me?"

Laura huddled miserably on the couch, the sting of

tears hot behind her eyes. ''Nick, please. What happened with Joe is over.''

''No, it isn't! If he wasn't already dead I could kill him with my bare hands for what he's done to you! For what he's still doing to you,'' he said savagely.

She stared up at him, her face devoid of color. ''It wasn't like that,'' she whispered.

''No? Then explain to me why you're so terrified of commitment, so afraid to trust. Explain that,'' he said, pointing to the scar.

Laura blinked back tears. She felt hollow inside, and a deep emptiness echoed within the walls of her heart. ''If you need answers, Nick, I can't give them to you,'' she said wearily. ''I told you at the beginning it was a long shot with me.'' Her voice broke and she swallowed, struggling for control. ''Maybe you better just give it up.''

Nick looked at her for a long moment, and then he took a deep breath. ''Maybe I better,'' he said tiredly, his anger suddenly spent. ''Because I sure can't continue like this. When I saw what that mugger did to you, I felt like somebody had kicked me in the gut. It's tearing me up inside right now, wanting to share this with you, wanting to share everything with you, and watching you retreat behind your wall, knowing that the door is locked and I don't have a clue where to find the key.''

''I—I'm sorry, Nick.''

He sighed heavily. ''Yeah. Me, too.'' He jammed his hands into his pockets and walked over to the window, staring out into the darkness. The ticking of her clock echoed loudly in the oppressive stillness that had descended on the room. "What do you say we call it a night?" he said at last. "You need to get some rest."

"I am tired."

He nodded. "Lock the door behind me, okay?" She rose shakily and followed him to the door. He turned and looked at her for a long moment, one hand resting on the frame. "You've got to get out of this place, Laura. It's not safe."

She nodded. "I know. I was planning to move anyway when my lease is up."

"How long is left?"

"Seven months."

"Seven months! That's too long. You need to move now."

"I can't break the lease, Nick."

He sighed, recognizing the stubborn tilt of her chin. He hesitated, as if he wanted to say more, but in the end he didn't. "Good night, Laura."

"Good night," she whispered.

Then he turned and was gone.

Nick ran his finger down the phone listing. Ralph Reynolds. Robert Reynolds. Rudolph Reynolds. Samantha Reynolds. That was it. He quickly punched in the numbers, praying she'd be home. He'd had all night to think about his evening with Laura, and he knew he should never have started that discussion with her. The timing was lousy. If he hadn't been so tired, so stressed out, he would have realized that. She had been in no shape for a confrontation, for a true confessions session, and he had been wrong to press her.

But he had to have some answers, and Sam was his only hope.

Nick recognized the voice that greeted him and slowly let out his breath, relief washing over him. "Sam? This is Nick Sinclair."

"Nick?" The surprise in her voice quickly changed to alarm. "Is Laura okay?"

"Yes, she's fine," he assured her. "Or as fine as can be expected after what happened. Would you by any chance have time to meet me for lunch?"

There was a fractional hesitation, a question hovering palpably in the air, and Nick was grateful when Sam left it unasked. "Sure. I have to show houses at ten and two, so how about around eleven-thirty?"

"Fine. Just name the place."

Nick arrived early at the designated restaurant and was waiting in a quiet, secluded booth when Sam appeared in the doorway, her striking red hair announcing her arrival even before he caught a glimpse of her face. When she turned to scan the room he motioned to her, rising as she joined him.

"Nick, it's good to see you."

"Thanks for coming."

"It sounded important," she said as she slid into the booth.

"It is." A waiter appeared, and Nick glanced at Sam questioningly.

"Iced tea, please," she said.

"The same for me," Nick told the waiter, then turned his attention back to Sam. "I'm sure you're wondering why I asked you to meet me," he began.

"You might say that," she replied mildly.

He sighed. "The trouble is, I'm not sure myself. It's just that I don't know where else to turn." He paused as the waiter deposited their drinks and they gave their orders. Then he took a long swallow of his iced tea.

"You really do have a problem, don't you?" Sam said.

"Yeah. Laura."

"I figured as much."

He twirled the ice in his glass and stared broodingly into it. "Sam, I care about Laura. But she's running scared. It's like she puts up a No Trespassing sign on certain areas of her life."

Sam nodded. "I know. She's a very private person."

"I realize that. I also realize she's been burned. Badly. From what I can gather, her husband was not only a first-class jerk, but abusive."

"Did she tell you that?"

"No. I just put two and two together. Her mother casually mentioned the separation when we were there for the Fourth. Then I saw the scar above Laura's right breast at the hospital. And the night of the mugging, she had a nightmare. Not about the attack. About Joe. She was pleading for him not to hurt her." A muscle in his jaw twitched convulsively, and his lips compressed into a thin, white line.

"I knew it was bad, but it must have been even worse than I thought," Sam said in a subdued voice. "He really did a number on her, didn't he?"

"It sure looks that way." There was a moment of silence, and then Nick leaned forward intently. "Look, Sam. I don't want you to betray any confidences. But is there anything—anything at all—you can tell me about what happened to Laura in that relationship? I want to help, but my hands are tied. I don't know enough."

Sam toyed with her glass. "Don't you think this should come from Laura?"

He sighed and raked his fingers through his hair. "Yes. And I've tried to get her to open up. I pushed pretty hard last night, in fact. Probably too hard. All I succeeded in doing was upsetting her. I came to you because you're her best friend, and I thought..." He shook his head. "I don't know what I thought. I'm desperate. Because the truth is, I'm falling in love with her."

Sam quirked an eyebrow. "Have you told her that?"

"Are you kidding? She's frightened enough as it is, and love can be a very scary word."

Sam eyed him speculatively. "I see what you mean."

Their food arrived, and Sam stared down at her plate for a long moment, her brow furrowed. Nick waited, praying she'd trust him enough to tell him something. Anything. Finally she looked up. "Okay, Nick," she said in sudden decision, and he slowly expelled the breath he'd been holding. "It took me a long time to win Laura's trust, and I'm not about to jeopardize our friendship. But she does have blinders on when it comes to men, and I like you. I think the two of you could have something really special if she'd only give it a chance. So I'll tell you how we met, and I'll tell you what I know about the night she left Joe, because

I was involved. But that's it. And to be honest, I don't know much more, anyway. Laura has never talked much about her marriage, and even with my big mouth, I sometimes know when to keep it shut."

She speared a forkful of tuna salad and chewed thoughtfully. "Laura and I met when we were both in night school. In the ladies' room, of all places. Not exactly an auspicious beginning," she said dryly. "Anyway, I remember thinking that she looked like she could use a friend. We ran into each other a few more times, and something just clicked. I can't explain it, because we're obviously Mutt and Jeff. She's a lady through and through, discreet, polite, considerate. All that good stuff. I'm more the irreverent loudmouth, the class clown, the kid who was always getting in trouble. But despite our differences, we became friends.

"It hasn't been easy for Laura, that much I know," she said pensively. "Not that she's ever complained. That's not her style. You've seen her apartment? Well, that's a palace compared to where she and Joe lived. It was a dump," she said bluntly. "But it was all they could afford, and she refused to ask her family for help. To be honest, I doubt whether she's ever told them the real reason she left Joe. Anyway, she's had to fight every step of the way to get where she is, and she did it with sheer guts and determination."

"Tell me about when she left Joe," Nick prompted, when Sam paused.

She laid her fork down carefully. "That was a bad night," she said with a frown. "Laura called me from a pay phone at the corner of her street, hysterical and almost incoherent. When I got there, she was still in the phone booth, shaking like a leaf, not so much hysterical anymore as in shock. She was wearing a jacket, even though it was warm that night, which I thought was odd. After I got her into the car, I asked her what happened, and she said that Joe had gotten drunk again and that he'd hurt her. Then she opened the jacket and I saw the blood all over her blouse.''

Nick clenched his napkin into a tight ball, closed his eyes and swallowed convulsively.

''Nick?'' Sam paused, and with a worried frown reached over and touched his hand. ''Are you okay?''

He opened his eyes and expelled a long breath, then reached for his drink. ''Yeah. Go on.''

She hesitated briefly, then continued. ''Well, at first she wouldn't let me look, but I insisted. And I can be pretty pushy. It's a good thing I *was* pushy that night, because when I saw that cut I took off for the emergency room like a bat out of...well, you get the picture. The hospital took one look at her physical and emotional state, came to the obvious conclusion and called the cops. Laura wouldn't press charges, no matter how hard we tried to convince her to, but she did decide to leave Joe. That night. She insisted on going home to collect her things, so I drove her back to their apartment and waited at the door. Joe was sleeping it off by then, so there was no problem. I guess she left him a note. I never asked. Then I took her back to my place.''

There was a momentary pause as Nick stared into his glass, then he looked up at Sam. ''Did Joe try to get her to come back?''

''I think so. I know he called a lot. Fortunately I

answered one of the first calls and told him to keep his distance or I'd bring in the cops. I guess I was pretty convincing, because as far as I know he never actually came over."

"And Laura never went back?"

"No. But it was really hard on her, Nick. I'm sure you've discovered by now how strong her faith is. She really believes in the sanctity of marriage and she took those 'for better or worse' vows seriously. In case you haven't figured it out, she lives by the book—the good book, that is. She doesn't just talk about her Christian principles—she practices them. Anyway, I know she felt guilty about leaving Joe, despite what he did to her. She never once mentioned the word divorce and always acted as if their separation was only a temporary thing. I know she tried to get Joe into counseling for his problem. But he wouldn't go. She did tell me that she talked to her minister, who advised her to put her personal safety first, and I put my two cents in. But I think she might actually have gone back to him one day, if Joe hadn't been killed."

"What happened to him?"

"He was in a car accident two weeks after Laura left him."

There was silence for a long moment, and then Nick spoke quietly, the anger in his voice barely held in check. "How many times did he hurt her before the night she called you?"

"I have no idea."

He rested his elbows on the table and interlocked his fingers, his untouched lunch forgotten. "I guess I suspected all this. But I was hoping I was wrong. No wonder she's so petrified of intimacy!"

Sam nodded. "I've been talking to her like a Dutch uncle, but I'm afraid I haven't made much of a dent. Maybe you'll finally break through."

"I don't know, Sam. That's a pretty impenetrable fortress she's built around her heart."

"Hang in there, Nick," she said, touching his hand. Then she glanced at her watch. "Good grief! I've got to run," she said, gathering up her purse and jacket. "I'll tell you something, Nick," she said as she slid to the edge of the booth. "She's a fool if she lets someone like you get away. You don't happen to have any brothers, do you?"

He quirked his lips up into the semblance of a smile. "Afraid not."

Sam lifted one shoulder in resignation. "It figures."

She stood, and he rose and took her hand in a warm clasp. "Thank you."

She shrugged. "I didn't tell you much more than you'd already figured out. I know this isn't easy on you, but Laura's worth waiting for."

But for how long? he asked himself in despair as he watched Sam disappear in the crowd. And with what results?

# Chapter Thirteen

Laura had no idea if Nick intended to keep their dinner date, but she went ahead with preparations anyway, guilt pricking at her conscience as she worked, telling her that she wasn't treating Nick fairly. She took and took, but gave nothing back. Not even trust. And he deserved that at least.

Distractedly she rolled the chicken cordon bleu in bread crumbs, placed them in a pan and put them in the oven. Why was she so afraid to share her past? Was it pride? Embarrassment that she'd let herself be treated so badly? Concern that her bottled up anger and resentment would be destructive once released? Fear that the information would be used against her? Or the guilt she had never been able to fully put to rest?

Probably all of the above, she thought with a sigh as she laid a linen cloth on the table and set out crisply starched napkins and sparkling wineglasses, placing two long tapers in candlesticks.

Laura didn't know why she was so afraid. All she knew was that the fear was real. Why was Nick even bothering with her? she wondered in dismay as she riffled through her closet. There were probably thousands of women out there who would spill their guts to him and welcome him into their arms—and their hearts.

Laura's hand paused on her one good summer dress as she recalled the strength and comfort she had found in his embrace. And she'd found something more as well, she acknowledged. A tide of yearning, so strong it left her flushed and breathless, swept over her. No one had ever made her feel like this, not even…not even Joe, she forced herself to admit. With Nick it was different. Was it because she'd been so long without male companionship? Or was it more than that?

She slipped the teal green silk shirtwaist over her head, cinching the belt and leaving the bottom button open to reveal an enticing glimpse of leg. Then she turned her attention to her face, noting resignedly that the black eye hadn't faded one iota. No cosmetic magic was going to camouflage this shiner. She had to content herself with mascara on her good eye, lipstick and blush. Finally she brushed out her hair, leaving it loose and full. Usually it was too hot in the apartment to wear it down, but tonight she'd splurged and turned on the air-conditioning.

Should she tell Nick about her marriage? she wondered again as she distractedly fiddled with the buttons on her dress. Or maybe the more pressing question was whether she wanted to continue this relationship. Because if she did, this was the moment of truth. Nick had made that clear last night.

Restlessly she moved around her bedroom, tugging at the uneven hem of the comforter, straightening a picture, adjusting the blinds. The room was neat as a pin already, though, leaving her little to do. Her eyes did one more inspection, coming to rest on the nightstand where she'd left her Bible. Slowly she walked over and picked it up, paging through to the familiar twenty-third psalm as she sank down on the side of the bed. The Lord is my shepherd, there is nothing I shall want, she read silently, slowly working her way through the verse. As always, the lyrical beauty as well as the content refreshed her soul and brought her a sense of peace. Now if only she could decide whether to share her past with Nick!

Laura returned to the living room and inspected the small, carefully set dinette table, caught a glimpse of her meticulous appearance in the hall mirror as she passed, and smelled the aroma of the special, time-consuming dish she rarely prepared. And she realized with surprise that she'd already made her decision. She'd orchestrated the setting and ambience to show Nick she cared; now all she had to do was follow through with words. She closed her eyes. *Dear Lord, please stay beside me tonight,* she prayed silently. *Let me feel your presence and your strength. I don't know if Nick will even come, but if he does I owe him the truth. Give me the courage to share it with him.*

The sudden buzz of the doorbell startled her, and her eyes flew open, her heart soaring. He was here!

He'd come, after all! With shaking fingers she slid back the locks and pulled open the door.

At first all she could see was a huge bouquet of long-stemmed red roses and baby's breath. Then Nick's face appeared around the greenery, an uncertain smile hovering at the corners of his mouth. "Hi."

"Hi."

"I wasn't sure I'd be welcome."

"I wasn't sure you'd come."

"Laura, I'm sorry about last night. I was completely out of line. You were in no shape for a heavy discussion."

"Well, I feel better tonight," she said, stepping aside for him to enter. Then she reached over and touched one of the velvet-soft petals of a rose. "These are beautiful," she breathed softly.

"Not very original, though. I don't suppose flowers are anything special for someone in your business."

"These are," she said simply. "Thank you, Nick."

"It was my pleasure." As she took the vase from his hands, he sniffed appreciatively. "Hey, something smells great!"

"Dinner. It's ready, if you're hungry."

"I'm starved. I haven't eaten much today."

She placed the roses on the coffee table, and when she turned back she found Nick studying her. His eyes caught and held hers, and there was a warm light in their depths that made a bolt of heat shoot through her. "That's a lovely dress. And you look wonderful in it," he said quietly.

Laura felt a flush of pleasure creep onto her cheeks

at the compliment. "Even with a black eye?" she teased.

"Mmm-hmm."

"I think you need to have your vision checked."

"My taste buds are working," he said hopefully.

She laughed and shook her head. "Go ahead and sit down. I'll have dinner on the table in a minute."

She turned away, but he caught her hand and she looked back in surprise.

"How are you feeling?" he asked, scrutinizing her face.

She smiled. "I'll live." She tried to turn away again, but he didn't release her hand.

"Let me help."

She shook her head firmly. "Not tonight."

His eyes traced her face once more, and finally, with obvious reluctance, he let her go. He strolled over to the table, noting the linen, the crystal and the candles, and he glanced questioningly at Laura, who was hovering in the doorway. "You went to a lot of trouble."

"Not nearly as much as you went to for me," she said quietly.

Although Laura kept the conversation light as they ate the gourmet fare she'd prepared, he sensed an undercurrent of tension. By the time they settled on the couch after dessert, he knew something was up. She seemed distracted and preoccupied, and when he reached over and gently touched her arm, she jumped.

"Oh!" Her hand went to her throat and her startled eyes flew to his. "Sorry," she said with a shaky laugh.

"Laura, what's wrong?"

She stood and restlessly moved around the room,

touching the flowers, straightening a picture on the side table, adjusting a lampshade. Finally she sank down into a chair across the coffee table from Nick. He remained silent, guarded, a slight frown on his face and an unsettled feeling in the pit of his stomach.

"Nick...about what you said last night," she began hesitantly.

"I said a lot of things last night. Most of which I regret."

She shook her head. "No. You were right. You've been incredibly patient as it is. Why you're interested in someone with as many hang-ups as me..." She shook her head uncomprehendingly. "But the fact is you seem to be. You've never shown me anything but kindness and understanding, and you've shared your past with me. So I—I want to do the same with you."

Nick drew in his breath, not sure whether to believe his ears. It seemed too much to hope for, and he watched her silently.

When he didn't respond, she twisted her hands in her lap and looked down. "That is, if you still want to hear it," she said hesitantly. "It's a rather sordid tale." She tried to smile to lighten the mood, but didn't quite pull it off.

"I'd like to hear it. But I need to tell you something first." He took a deep breath, knowing that honesty was the only course. "I had lunch with Sam today."

Laura's head flew up in surprise. "Sam?"

He nodded and leaned forward earnestly, his forearms resting on his thighs, his hands clasped in front of him. "I didn't know where else to turn. I care about you, Laura, but you wouldn't let me get close. I thought maybe if I understood what happened to make you so afraid, I'd know how to address it.''

''What did Sam tell you?''

''Not much. She made it clear that she wasn't about to betray any confidences, and I didn't expect her to. She just told me how you two met, and about her role the night you left Joe.''

''She told you I left Joe?'' Nick could see the hurt in her eyes, the look of betrayal.

''No,'' he corrected her quickly. ''Actually, your mother told me.''

''My mother?'' she asked incredulously.

''In a roundabout way. The last night we were there I went out for some air and found her on the porch. In the course of conversation, she mentioned your separation. She assumed I knew.''

''Oh.''

''That's the extent of my knowledge, Laura. No one violated your confidence.''

She nodded, still assimilating what he'd just told her. ''You know a lot. More than I expected. Which may make this easier.'' She drew a shaky breath and stared off into a blank corner, carefully keeping her face expressionless and her tone factual. ''Joe and I were what romantics call childhood sweethearts,'' she began. ''I never went out with anyone else. We were always a pair, from the time we were children. When I was eighteen and he was twenty, we decided to get married. My parents never did think we were right for each other, but when they realized we were determined, they supported our decision.''

She leaned her head back against the chair and

transferred her gaze to the ceiling. ''Joe had an associate's degree in data processing, which made him well educated for Jersey, and he had great dreams. So we moved to St. Louis, with not much more than hope to sustain us. As it turned out, the competition here was a lot more fierce than Joe expected, and he just couldn't compete with four-year degrees and MBAs. He finally got a low-paying job, as a data entry clerk, and I worked in a department store to help make ends meet.

''As time went on, Joe began to lose heart. It was clear that his only hope of advancing was to get more education, but he had no interest in going back to school. I finally realized that if we were ever going to have a better life, it was up to me. So I went instead. I'd worked every summer in a greenhouse at home, so I got a job at a nursery and began to take classes in landscape design. I discovered I had a knack for it, and decided to go on for my degree.''

Her voice grew quieter. ''I don't exactly remember when it started to get really bad. It happened so gradually. I think Joe resented my ambition, for one thing. And I know he was frustrated. Anyway, he started to drink—heavily—and a side of him emerged that I'd never seen before. He'd get belligerent when he was drunk, and push me around physically. And he would belittle my efforts to get an education. Then he started making fun of the way I looked, especially my weight, which was dropping steadily. He…he even laughed at my faith. He began to lose jobs, one after another, and finally he just quit working. Our life grew more and more isolated, and I felt so cut off and alone. If I hadn't had school, and Sam, and my church, I doubt I would have made it. Those were the only normal things in my life—those, and my family,'' she said with a catch in her voice. She paused and took a deep breath.

''I told myself that he was sick, that what was happening wasn't my fault,'' she continued. ''But the guilt was there, anyway. I tried to convince him to get help, but whenever I brought it up he got angry. The last time I suggested it was the night I left. Believe it or not, it was our fourth anniversary.''

Nick didn't know when the tears had started. He just knew that suddenly they were there, twin rivers of grief running silently down her cheeks. The unnatural lack of sound unnerved him, and he sat there helplessly, silently cursing the man who had done this to Laura. He longed to reach for her, to hold her, to tell her that he'd never let anyone hurt her again. But he held back, knowing there was more, knowing that she needed to finish what she'd started. ''What did he do to you that night, Laura?'' he asked gently.

Her head swung around, and her startled eyes met his. It was almost as if she'd forgotten he was there. She swallowed with difficulty, and her eyes flitted away again. When she spoke, her words were choppy. ''It was late. I was asleep. A crash from the living room woke me up, and I ran in to see what had happened. There was a broken whiskey bottle on the floor, and I went over to help Joe clean it up. But he…he slapped me, and he started saying…terrible things.'' Her voice quavered, and she paused, struggling for control. ''I got scared and I backed away, pleading with him to get help, but he was yelling... I started to turn away, so I didn't even see it coming until it was too late.''

''See what, Laura?'' Nick prodded gently.

''The bottle. He threw the broken bottle at me. I had on a nightgown...my shoulders were bare... It hit me here.'' Her voice caught and she gestured toward her right breast.

Laura was close to losing it, she knew. Only superhuman control and the Lord's help had let her get this far without breaking down. That was why she'd physically removed herself from Nick. One touch from him, and she knew her fragile control would shatter.

Nick watched the struggle taking place on Laura's face. There was no way he could make this any easier for her. All he could do was let her finish and then be there to hold her, to stroke her, to love her.

''I guess I finally admitted then that things were probably over between us,'' she said unevenly. ''So I left. Sam took me in, bless her heart. Joe kept calling, begging me to come back. Sam told me I'd be a fool to give him another chance. So did my minister, in a more diplomatic way. But I still felt an obligation to try everything I could to straighten out our marriage. I was raised to believe that it was a sacred trust and something to be preserved at all costs. Except maybe physical danger,'' she admitted. ''I finally realized that the next time Joe got drunk I might not get off with only a three-inch scar. My safety was literally at stake. Besides, the love I'd once felt for Joe had just about died. All that was left was fear. So I finally made the decision that I wasn't going back unless he got some real help and we went into counseling together. I told him he had to truly change before I'd come back. He was so angry and upset the night I called to tell him…'' Her voice trailed off for a moment, and he saw her swallow convulsively. ''A few days later, he was killed in a drunk-driving accident.'' She paused and blinked rapidly. ''You want to hear something funny?'' she said, choking out a mirthless laugh. ''He wasn't the one who was drunk. All those nights I'd lain awake, terrified that he'd run down some innocent person…'' She fell silent, her mind clearly far away, but after a few seconds she resumed her story.

''After I pulled myself together, I got an apartment, applied for a grant, went to school full-time and worked a forty-hour week. Eighteen-hour days were the norm. Money was tight, and I lived on peanut-butter sandwiches and macaroni-and-cheese for years. But I made it. I finished school and I got a job with a landscaper. I had Joe's insurance money, which I'd saved, and that gave me the seed money to open my own place after I'd accumulated a little experience. That was six years ago, and I've poured every cent back into the business since then. Now, thanks to the Arts Center job, I think we've finally turned the corner.'' She paused and expelled a long breath, then turned to face Nick. ''So there you have my life story,'' she said, trying for a light tone and failing miserably, fighting to hold in the sobs that begged for release.

Nick moved for the first time since she'd started speaking. He stood and walked swiftly over to her, reaching down to draw her to her feet. Then he wrapped his arms around her and buried his face in her soft hair, holding her as tightly as he dared. Her whole body was trembling, and she was breathing erratically. Without releasing her, he reversed their positions and sat down, pulling her into his lap and cradling her in his arms.

"It's okay to cry, Laura," he said softly, stroking her hair.

She had struggled valiantly for control, but she finally surrendered, giving in to the deep, gut-wrenching sobs she'd held inside for so long. Her ribs ached, but once released, the tide of tears could not be stopped. She cried for so many things—for the lost illusions of youth; for the guilt she still carried over Joe's deterioration and death; for the lonely years with no hand to hold and no one with whom to share her life; and for her empty heart, and the fear that prevented her from giving love another chance.

Nick just held her, because there was nothing else he could do. His heart ached for the woman in his arms, and he was filled with a deep, seething anger at the injustice of the world.

When at last her sobs subsided, she spoke against his shirt. "How could I have been so wrong about someone I'd known all my life?" she asked in a small, sad voice.

"Not everyone reacts well to adversity and disappointment, Laura. You had no way of knowing what would happen when Joe was put to the test."

"All these years I've felt guilty," she admitted. "I keep wondering if there wasn't something I could have done or said that would have made a difference. Maybe he'd still be alive if I'd stayed.''

''And maybe you'd be dead,'' Nick said bluntly. Then his tone softened. ''What happened wasn't your fault, Laura. You stuck it out a lot longer than most people would have. Probably too long.''

She shifted in his arms and looked up at him. ''Nick?''

''Mmm-hmm.''

''After everything I've told you, do you still...I mean, I'd understand if you wanted to cut your losses and get as far away from me as you can.''

''Do you want me out of your life?''

''No,'' she said softly. ''But I'm still scared.''

Nick let his breath out slowly. Fear he could handle. Withdrawal was something else. But they'd just bridged that hurdle. ''I know, sweetheart,'' he said gently, running a finger down her tearstained cheek. ''But we'll work on it together, okay?''

Laura searched his eyes—tender, caring, filled with warmth and concern—and nodded, her throat constricting. ''Okay,'' she whispered. ''But I still need to move slowly.''

''Slow is fine,'' he said. ''Just as long as we're moving.''

Gradually, Laura began to forget what her life had been like before Nick. He became such an integral part of her existence that just as she once could not imagine life *with* him, now she could not imagine it *without* him. He became her wake-up call, making her smile as she sleepily reached for the phone each morning.

His was her last call of the day, the deep timbre of his voice lingering in her mind long after the connection had been severed. And in between, he was there—pulling her away for impromptu picnics, dropping by at night to take her to Ted Drewes, clipping funny articles he thought she'd enjoy. She grew to love his dependability, his gentleness, his enthusiasm, his ability to make her laugh, and slowly the lines of tension in her face eased and the shadows under her eyes disappeared. She gained a little weight, and the angular contours of her face softened and took on a new beauty. As her bruises healed, so, too, did her heart.

Nick watched the transformation with gratitude and pleasure. As her skittishness eased, he began to weave small, undemanding physical intimacies into their relationship. A welcoming kiss whenever they met; an arm casually draped around her shoulders at the movie theater; his hand holding hers when they walked. If she grew accustomed to the small intimacies, he reasoned, the bigger ones would come naturally in their own time. And he could wait. He'd promised to let her set the pace, and he intended to honor that vow. But he planned to set the direction.

Though it was slow going, Nick was not unhappy with the progress of their relationship. Laura was more relaxed than he'd ever seen her, laughing more readily, touching more naturally and easily. Her touches—initially tentative, as if she was afraid that they would be rejected—gradually grew bolder under his welcoming encouragement. She was learning to love all over again, cautiously, but with a restrained eagerness that delighted him and did more for his libido than any of the amorous ploys of the more sophisticated women of his acquaintance. As her confidence grew and she became more secure in their relationship, gradually she began to initiate physical contact on her own.

Nick had known from the beginning that physical closeness frightened her. She hadn't spoken about her intimate relationship with Joe, and Nick hadn't asked, but he imagined that making love had probably become a nightmare for Laura as the relationship deteriorated and the love had disappeared. And, given her background and her strong faith and Christian values, he also knew that she didn't take physical intimacy lightly. She was the kind of woman who equated making love with commitment, and she'd been avoiding that like the plague for years. He couldn't expect her to change overnight.

But slowly he guided her toward change, finding ways to touch her that were not threatening but that brought a flash of desire to her eyes. In time she grew to not only allow these touches, but to welcome them. He'd learned to keep his desires on a tight leash, though, and at her slightest hesitation he pulled back. He had come to realize that Laura's values were deeply entrenched and that she simply didn't believe in intimacy outside of marriage. He admired her for her beliefs and intended to respect them. But keeping his desires under control was hard, and getting harder every day.

Laura locked the office and glanced at her watch. She was due to meet Nick at one-thirty, and it was already one-twenty. Fortunately, the client's house was only a short distance from her office, she noted, consulting the address Nick had provided.

Laura rolled down the window as she drove, breathing deeply of the crisp October air. She loved fall, especially here in Webster, when the old, established maples put on their most colorful frocks. Her route took her through the heart of the small community, and she glanced admiringly at the wonderful turn-of-the-century houses.

When Laura reached her destination, she sat for a long moment in the car without moving, letting her eyes roam lovingly over the old frame Victorian. It was set far back from the street, on about an acre of ground, and was everything a Victorian should be. Painted a pale peach, it was embellished with white gingerbread accents, making it appear to be trimmed with lace. A wraparound porch hugged the house invitingly, and tall, stately maples stood on the front lawn. She saw Nick waiting for her on the front porch and waved as she climbed out of the car.

He watched her approach, his body stirring as it always did in her presence. She was dressed as she had been the day they'd met—jeans, work boots, a worn blue work shirt and sunglasses—and her hair was pulled back into a ponytail. But her greeting was certainly different. She ran lightly up the steps and reached on tiptoe, raising her face expectantly. Nick smiled and leaned down, grasping her shoulders and pulling her toward him hungrily for a lingering kiss.

"Mmm," she said dreamily, closing her eyes.

He chuckled, and the deep, seductive sound of it made her feel warm despite the slight chill in the air.

"Well, what do you think?" he asked, gesturing toward the house.

"It's wonderful!" she said.

"I thought you'd like it."

"I take it the new owner wants to make some changes?" she said, nodding toward the For Sale sign on the lawn.

"A few. I've already been over the inside, so we can skip that and just go around back. Unless, of course, you'd like to take a look?" He grinned and dangled the key enticingly in front of her.

"Are you kidding!" she exclaimed, her eyes shining. "I've been dying to get inside one of these houses ever since I moved to St. Louis."

Nick fitted the key in the lock and then stepped aside. "After you."

Laura stepped over the threshold—and into the house of her dreams. It was everything she had always imagined—tall ceilings, gleaming hardwood floors, private nooks and crannies and alcoves, fireplaces, a wonderful L-shaped stairway in the foyer that hugged the wall, a gorgeous art glass window and plenty of light and space. She examined it all rapturously, reverently running her hand over the fine wood moldings and marble mantels. When she'd explored every inch, she turned to Nick. "I don't know what the new owners have in mind, but I wouldn't change a thing. It's perfect."

"If all my clients were that satisfied with the status quo, I'd be out of business," he said with a grin.

"You aren't going to do anything to change the character, are you?" she asked worriedly.

"Nope. Just some minor updating. Ready to take a look at the grounds?"

"I suppose so," she said reluctantly, casting one more lingering, longing look at the foyer before stepping outside. "Can't you just imagine this house at Christmastime, Nick?" she said softly. "Snow on the ground, golden light shining from the windows, smoke curling above the chimneys, a wreath on the door... It's a perfect old-fashioned Christmas house. So warm and welcoming." She sighed. "What a wonderful place to call home."

"You make it sound very appealing," Nick said, locking the door and taking her arm as they strolled around the back.

"I don't have to try very hard. It's a very romantic house."

Laura pulled up short when they reached the backyard. It was heavily shrubbed on the edges, affording complete privacy, and several big trees were spaced over the lawn. Little had been done in the way of landscaping, but Laura could visualize the potential.

"Are your clients open to suggestions?" she asked.

"Yes."

"Well, my first thought is a gazebo—white lattice, of course. And a formal rose garden is a must. Somewhere there should be a trellis, overflowing with morning glories, that leads to a private area with a bench and a birdbath. And there's plenty of room for an English woodland country garden, sort of wild, yet controlled, you know? That's what gives them their charm. But we have to leave lots of open space for a croquet court. This is a perfect yard for that." She paused, and Nick heard her soft sigh. ''It could be so lovely here. I hope the client will let me do this right.''

There was a wistful note in her voice, and Nick squeezed her hand, then tugged her gently toward the back of the house. ''Let's sit for a minute, Laura.''

She followed, still scanning the grounds, visualizing the perfect backdrop for this house. It was the kind of home she'd always hoped to have, and even if that was never to be, perhaps she could create her dream for someone else to enjoy.

Nick pulled her down beside him on a small stone bench set under a tree near the house, and stroked the back of her hand with his thumb. ''Laura?''

''Hmm?'' With an effort she pulled her eyes away from the yard and forced her attention back to Nick.

''Laura, I...'' He stopped, as if he didn't know what to say next, and drew in a deep breath. He seemed at a loss for words, which was completely unlike him, and Laura stared at him curiously. ''About the client for this house...''

''Yes?'' she prompted, when his voice trailed off.

''Well...it's me.''

Her eyes widened in shock. ''What?''

''I've put an option on this house.''

''You? But, Nick—it's a wonderful house, don't get me wrong—it's just so big for just one person.''

''I know. I was hoping that you might share it with me.''

# *Chapter Fourteen*

Laura stared at him, her eyes wide with shock. "Nick…are you…are you asking me to marry you?" she stammered.

"I guess I'm not doing a very good job at it, am I?" He tried to grin, and then drew a deep breath, letting it out slowly. "Laura, the simple truth is I'm not getting any younger. The years have gone by a lot faster than I expected. I want a home, and a family, and a house with a white picket fence and a tree swing—the whole nine yards. And I want it before I'm too old to enjoy it." He stroked the back of her hand absently with his thumb, his eyes locked on hers. "I've been involved with my share of women over the years," he said honestly, struggling to find the right words because it was vitally important that she understand exactly how he felt. "But I've never really been 'involved,' not in the true sense of the word. In fact, I went to great lengths to *avoid* involvement, because I didn't want the complications and responsibilities that go with it. And then you came along, and suddenly everything was different. I *wanted* to share your life—and your responsibilities.'' He paused and searched her eyes. ''I guess that's what happens when you fall in love,'' he said quietly.

Laura tried to swallow past the lump in her throat. For the past few months she'd gone blithely along, relishing her developing relationship with Nick, refusing to think about the inevitable day of reckoning. Now it had come, and she wasn't ready. All the old fears, which had gradually subsided under Nick's gentle nurturing, resurfaced with alarming intensity. He was talking love and commitment and vows, and it scared her to death. There was no question that she loved Nick. But she'd loved Joe, too, and that had been a mistake, one that was still exacting a price.

Nick's eyes were locked on hers, trying to gauge her reaction to his proposal, watching the play of emotions cross her face. He'd known it was a risk to ask her to marry him, but it had been a calculated one. He knew Laura well enough to know that she was completely without guile or pretense. The affection she so willingly returned could be taken at face value as a true measure of her feelings. He'd hoped those feelings would be strong enough to overcome her fears, but now, searching her troubled eyes, he wasn't so sure.

''Nick, I—I don't know what to say.''

'''Yes' would be nice.'' When she didn't respond, he took a deep breath. ''Things have gone well between us, haven't they?'' he asked gently.

''Yes. But why can't we just leave them as they are?'' she pleaded.

"For how long?" His voice was sober, direct.

"I—I don't know," she replied helplessly. "It's such a big step. And I made a mistake once before."

"That was a long time ago, Laura. You were only eighteen years old—just a kid. And you had no way of knowing what would happen to Joe."

"But...but I'm so afraid it could happen again," she whispered.

Nick didn't say a word. He tried to understand, tried to remind himself that Laura's traumatic past was clouding her judgment, but he was still deeply hurt by her lack of trust. He'd done everything he could to prove that he was different than Joe, that he was trustworthy and dependable and even-tempered, that he cared about her and loved her unconditionally. And he had failed. Instead of the joy he had hoped to see in her eyes, there was only doubt and uncertainty. He glanced away, feeling as if his heart was being held in a vise, the life slowly being squeezed out of it. He gazed at the house he'd allowed himself to dream of sharing with the woman beside him, and felt something inside him begin to die. Finally he looked back at her.

"I don't know what else to do, Laura," he said wearily. "I'd hoped the fear had dimmed by now. But I'm beginning to think it never will."

Her eyes filled with tears, and she blinked them back. She wanted to tell him she loved him, but the words wouldn't come. Just saying them seemed too much of a risk. But she didn't want to lose him. Without Nick, her life would be empty, emptier even than before. She touched his arm and looked up at him desperately. ''Nick...maybe we could just... Lots of people live together nowadays,'' she said.

He gazed at her in surprise, completely taken aback. Yes, lots of people did live together. But Laura wasn't cut out to be one of them. It went against everything she'd been brought up to believe about love and commitment, flew in the face of her deeply held Christian principles. Her willingness to even consider compromising her values spoke more eloquently than words of the depths of her feelings for him. But it would impose a very heavy burden of guilt on her and, in the end, she would come to not only regret such a choice, but resent him for forcing her to make it. It just wouldn't work.

Nevertheless, Nick was tempted. He was losing her—she was slipping away even as he watched—and now she'd thrown out a lifeline. Maybe this was better than nothing, he thought, trying to convince himself. But how long would the arrangement last, even if she did go through with it, which he doubted? Would she ever feel secure enough to marry him? And if not, then what? What if she walked away, somewhere down the road?

As hard as it would be to let her go now, it would be even harder once they'd lived together intimately.

Slowly he shook his head. ''I'm sorry, Laura,'' he said, his voice filled with regret. ''I love you. I want to build a life with you—for always. It's got to be all or nothing.''

Laura began to feel physically ill. Her world was crumbling around her, and she felt powerless to stop it. The man she loved was about to walk away, taking all of the sunlight and warmth and tenderness out of her life. The tears that had welled up in her eyes slowly overflowed and trickled down her cheeks.

"Nick, I can't marry you," she said brokenly. "I'm not ready for that step and...and I don't know if I ever will be."

He took her hands, his gut twisting painfully at the shattered look in her eyes. She seemed so vulnerable and defenseless that he almost relented, just to ease her pain. Almost. But in the end, he shook his head.

"Laura, I love you," he repeated, his voice hoarse with emotion. "Part of me always will. I wish we could have made this work." Gently he released her hands and slowly stood.

Laura's heart was pounding in her chest, her eyes desperate. "Nick, I..." She tried again to say "I love you," but the words stuck in her throat. "I'll miss you," she said instead.

"I'll miss you, too." He bent down and placed his lips gently and lingeringly on hers, in a kiss as light as the wayward leaves that drifted down around them.

"Will I see you again?" she whispered.

"In the spring, I guess, when the landscaping starts for the Arts Center." He desperately hoped that by then the pain of this parting would have dulled. "Goodbye, Laura. And good luck. I hope someday you find someone who can bring you the happiness you deserve."

As the sun darted behind a cloud, she watched his back, ramrod straight and broad shouldered, disappear around the corner of the house. The air grew chilly, and so did her heart.

With Nick gone, there was an empty place in Laura's life that couldn't be filled. She tried working even longer hours, but that once reliable distraction barely eased the pain. She went back to doing more outdoor labor, but the physical tiredness couldn't mask her emotional fatigue and despair, nor did it help her sleep any better. Night after night she lay awake, thinking about what might have been, wondering if Nick missed her as much as she missed him, aching for the closeness she had grown to cherish. She had never felt more alone in her life.

Even her best friend seemed to desert her. Sam had always been the one she'd turned to for support during the difficult years after Joe died and through all the tough times when she'd been trying to establish her business. But Sam offered little sympathy. Laura knew her friend thought she was a fool for letting Nick walk away. She'd pretty much said so to her face, in her blunt, outspoken way.

Her family was too far away to be able to provide much consolation, even if she'd told them about her relationship with Nick, which she hadn't. All her mother knew was that they had been seeing each other, never that it had grown serious. As much as she loved her family, it had never been her custom to share the intimate details of her life.

Even in her darkest days she'd always found solace in talking over her problems with the Lord, but even He seemed distant. She just couldn't find the words to pray, beyond a desperate plea for help and guidance. But God worked in His own time, and no direction had yet been provided.

So Laura was left alone with her pain. She tried to tell herself that she'd done the right thing, that entering into a relationship when she wasn't ready would be wrong for everyone involved. At the same time, she couldn't blame Nick for walking out. She'd made it clear that marriage wasn't an option at the moment, maybe never would be. He wanted to share his life with someone on a permanent basis, to raise a family, to create a home, and she couldn't offer him that. Because Joe had left her with a legacy of fear that was debilitating and isolating, had shaken her confidence in her own judgment so badly that even now, ten years later, she was afraid to trust her heart. Nick had tried his best to convince her to risk loving again, and he'd failed. And if Nick—with his integrity and gentleness and love—couldn't succeed, she doubted whether anyone could.

Laura carried that depressing thought with her into December, through two long, lonely months without the sound of his voice each morning and night, without his impromptu visits, without the laughter he'd brought into her life. Her solitary existence, once carefully nurtured, now seemed oppressive.

Laura didn't even bother to put up a tree, a custom she'd never abandoned, even at the worst of times. But her heart wasn't in it this year. The Christmas decorations looked garish, the carols sounded flat and the weather was dismal. Her only concession to the holidays was the small crèche she always displayed on the mantel. As she placed the figure of baby Jesus in the manger she reminded herself that the Lord had never promised an easy road in this world. She accepted that.

She always had. But did it *always* have to be so hard? she cried in silent despair. Weren't there ever happy endings?

And then, with a jolt, she realized that the key to a potentially happy ending *had* been offered to her. She had refused—because she was afraid. And the simple fact was that despite the emptiness of the past two months, she still carried the same oppressive burden of fear.

Her loneliness only intensified as the holidays grew closer. Laura's mother had decided to visit her brother's family in California, and though Laura had been invited to spend Christmas with John and Dana and the kids, trying to look cheery for several days in front of her family seemed too much of an effort. Sam had gone to Chicago. Laura told everyone she was too busy to take time off anyway, but in reality business was slow. People typically didn't think about landscaping at Christmastime. They were too busy planning holiday gatherings and buying gifts for family and friends.

On Christmas Eve Laura closed the office at three o'clock, realizing as she slowly walked to her car that she had nowhere to go until the evening service at seven. Her cozy apartment, once a welcoming haven, now seemed empty and hollow. She tried strolling around a mall, but the laughing crowds, so at odds with her depressed mood, only made her feel worse.

In the end, even though the service wasn't scheduled to start for an hour and half, she just went to church. Maybe here, in the Lord's house, she could find some peace and solace.

Laura sat forlornly in the dim silence feeling more alone and lost than she had in a very long while. *Oh, Lord, show me what to do!* she pleaded. *I love Nick. And yet I let him walk away because I'm afraid. I need to move on with my life, find the courage to trust again. Please help me.* She closed her eyes and opened her heart, and slowly, as she poured out her fears and confusion to the Lord in an almost incoherent stream of consciousness, she began to feel a calmness steal over her.

The church was filling with people when she at last opened her eyes, and by the time the candles were lit and the service started, she had attained some measure of peace, though no insights. But she had faith that the Lord would offer those in His own time. If she was patient, He would show her the way.

As Brad Matthews stepped to the microphone, she forced herself to put her problems aside and focus on the words of her childhood friend. He was a wonderful minister, and he had offered her a sympathetic ear and sound advice during her darkest days. He was also an accomplished speaker, and she always found value in his thoughtfully prepared sermons.

Tonight was no exception. In fact, it almost seemed as if the end of his talk had been prepared especially for her, she thought in growing amazement as she listened to his words.

"And so tomorrow all of us will exchange gifts with the ones we love," he said in his rich, well-modulated voice. "They'll be brightly wrapped, in colorful paper and shiny bows. But let's not forget that those gifts are only meant to represent the true gift of this season—the gift of love. My friends, that is why we are here tonight. Because God so loved the world that he sent his only Son to save us. That gift of love is what makes this day so special. No one who knows the Lord is ever truly alone or unloved, because His love is never ending and He is always with us.

"God gave us the gift of perfect love when he sent us His Son. And that love is manifested here on earth in many ways, most beautifully in the love we have for each other. Love one another as I have loved you. That was His instruction.

"Well, all of us know that, as humans, we can never achieve the perfection of God's love. But it should stand as a shining example of what love is at its very best. It is unselfish. It is trusting. It is enduring. It is forgiving. It is limitless. And it is unconditional.

"On this Christmas Eve, let us all reflect on God's love and the gifts of human love with which we are blessed in this earthly life. And let us remember that God never promised us that love was easy. It isn't even easy to love the Lord. Christianity is a celebration, but it's also a cross. And it certainly isn't always easy to love each other. But love of the Lord, and the reflection of that love in our relationships with the people in our lives, is what sets us apart as Christians.

"So during this Christmas season, give yourself a special gift. It won't be as flashy as a new CD player or a computer, but I promise you it will be longer lasting. Because CD players and computers break. And love can, too. But the difference is that love can not only be mended, but strengthened. Sometimes all it takes is two simple words, spoken from the heart: I'm sorry. The power those two words contain is amazing.

"At this season of God's love, which manifested itself in the humble birth of a baby two thousand years, show the Lord that you've heard His voice. Mend a broken relationship. And I guarantee that the joy of Christmas will stay in your heart long after the gifts under your tree are just a memory.

"Now let us pray..."

As the service continued, Laura reflected on Brad's beautiful words, which deeply touched her heart. He was right. Love was a gift, both the divine and human forms. And both kinds of love required trust and a leap of faith to reach their full potential. Maybe that was what made love so unique and special.

A gentle snow was falling when she emerged from the church after the service, the soft flakes forming a delicate, transparent film of white on the ground. As she climbed into her car, an image of the cozy Victorian house Nick had so lovingly chosen for them suddenly flashed unbidden across her mind.

It was probably filled with laughter and music and love as the new owners enjoyed their first Christmas there, she thought wistfully. Without consciously making a decision, Laura put the car in gear and drove slowly toward the house that had come to represent Nick's love and the life he had offered her. Dusk descended, and the snow continued to fall, lightly dusting her windshield as she drove.

When she reached the street, Laura approached the house slowly, surprised to find the windows dark and the For Sale sign still on the lawn. Sam was always complaining that the real estate market was soft, but Laura found it surprising that a gem like this would still be unsold.

The street was lined with cars, so she had to drive a few houses away before she found a spot to park. Then, digging her hands into the pockets of her wool coat, she trudged up the sidewalk, stopping in front of the house. Her eyes filled with longing as they lovingly traced the contours of the structure. It was just as beautiful as she'd remembered it, but so empty and alone. Just like me, she thought, allowing herself a moment of self-pity. Both of us could have been filled with the magic of Nick's love, but instead we're cold and dark.

She walked up the pathway to the front door and slowly climbed the steps, running a hand over the banister, touching the brass knocker on the door. Then she sat down on the top step, folded her arms on her knees and rested her forehead on the scratchy wool of her sleeves. An aching sense of regret flooded through her as she faced the fact that something beautiful had been within her grasp and she'd allowed it to slip away. Brad had said that love required trust, and a leap of faith. And there were certainly no guarantees. She knew that. Life—and love—didn't come with warranties. But which was worse—to shun risk and spend her life alone and miserable, or to take a chance on love with the most wonderful man she'd ever met? Put that way, and in the context of the past two lonely months, the answer suddenly seemed obvious.

Brad had said that love could be mended, she reflected. But she had hurt Nick deeply. The look in his eyes when she'd admitted her fear was burnt into her memory forever. Because that fear also implied lack of trust. No wonder he'd walked away that day. Love without trust was just an empty shell, and he deserved better than that. If only she could retract her words!

But that was impossible, and it made no sense to yearn for impossible things, she thought bleakly. She just wished she could find a way to make him understand how deeply she loved him, to ask his forgiveness. All she really wanted, or could hope for, was a second chance.

Though her eyes were clouded with tears, Laura realized with a start that the toes of two boots had appeared in her field of vision. Probably a cop, about to cite her for trespassing, she thought dejectedly, quickly brushing a hand across her eyes before looking up.

"I'm sorry, I didn't mean..." The words died in her throat. Nick stood at the base of the steps, his hands in the pockets of a sheepskin-lined jacket, snow clinging to his dark hair, his eyes shadowed and unfathomable, with a fan spread of fine lines at the corners that hadn't been there two months before.

"Hello, Laura."

"Nick?" She took a great gulp of cold air.

"Fancy meeting you here," he said lightly, though his tone sounded forced.

"I—I thought it would look pretty in the snow," she stammered, still not trusting her eyes.

He nodded. "Yeah. Me, too." He glanced at the shuttered windows and placed one foot on the bottom step. "I remember the day we were here, how you said it would be beautiful at Christmastime, so I thought I'd take a look. I see it's still for sale."

A door opened nearby and the sound of carols and laughter drifted through the silent air.

"Yes, I noticed."

"I'm surprised you didn't go home for Christmas."

She shrugged. "I wasn't in the mood."

They fell silent, and Laura looked down, shuffling the toe of her shoe in the snow that was rapidly accumulating at the edge of the porch, trying to make some sense out of her chaotic thoughts. If Nick didn't still care about her, he wouldn't be here tonight, would he? Maybe, just maybe, it wasn't too late to salvage their relationship. She looked up and found that he was watching her. This was the second chance she'd wished for. *Please, God, don't let me blow it!* she prayed. *Help me find the words to make Nick understand how much I care and how sorry I am for hurting him.*

"Nick...I've missed you," she began tentatively.

"I've missed you, too," he said quietly.

"I've had a lot of time to think these past couple of months, and I was wondering... Is there... Do you still..." Her voice trailed off. She was making a mess of this!

"Do I still what, Laura?" Nick asked, his voice cautious.

She took a deep breath. There was no easy way to say it. "Do you still...do you still want me?" she asked artlessly.

He hesitated. "I've always wanted you," he replied, his voice guarded.

"No...I mean, do you still want to marry me?"

Instead of replying, Nick grabbed her hands and

pulled her to her feet. She gasped in surprise as he hauled her up onto the porch and over to a dim light by the door that offered only marginal illumination. Then he turned her to face him, his jaw tense, his hands gripping her shoulders almost painfully, his eyes burning into hers.

"Laura, what are you saying?" he asked tightly.

He wasn't going to make this easy for her, she thought. He wanted her to spell it out, and after her previous ambiguity, she couldn't blame him. She drew a deep breath and looked directly into his eyes, willing him to see the love, the sincerity, the apology, in her own. "Nick, I'm sorry for what I've put you through. I'm especially sorry for being afraid to commit to you, for not trusting you, when I've never met a more trustworthy person. But when I left Joe, I vowed never to get involved with anyone again. And I did pretty well, till you came along."

When she paused, he prodded. "Go on."

"These past two months have been miserable," she said, her voice breaking. "Maybe even harder emotionally than when I left Joe. Because when you left you took the sunshine with you. Oh, Nick," she cried, clinging to him. "I want the same things you want—the rose garden and the picket fence and the family. I realize I'm no bargain, that I still have a lot of problems to work through. But I'd like to work on them with you beside me. I'd still like a lifetime warranty, but I'll settle for an 'I'll do my best to make you happy.' And I'll do the same for you."

He studied her face, wanting to believe, but afraid that this was all an illusion, much as he'd thought *she* was an illusion when he'd first seen her slumped on the steps. Then, too, he realized, she hadn't yet said the three words that really counted.

Laura watched his face, saw a flicker of disappointment in his eyes and her stomach knotted into a tight ball. She panicked. He was going to tell her to forget it, that it was too late.

"I…have the feeling…that the offer is…no longer available," she said choppily. "I…know I hurt you, and I guess I can't blame you if…if you can't forgive me."

"It's not that, Laura." He released her and turned to walk over to the porch railing, leaning on it heavily with both hands, facing away from her. "I *was* hurt. Deeply. But I never really blamed you. If anyone ever had a reason to be wary, it was you. It was egotistical of me to think I could overcome years of debilitating fear in just a few months. In the end, I was just sad. For both of us. But there was nothing to forgive. You were a victim of your circumstances."

"Then what's wrong?" she pleaded.

"I still want to marry you, Laura, but…"

"But what?" she asked desperately.

"You say you're lonely, and God knows, I can relate to that," he said with a sigh. "But that's not reason enough to get married."

"But it's not just that. I want to be with you, Nick. For always."

"Why?"

"Why?" she parroted blankly. Then suddenly her taut nerves shattered. "Well, why do you think?" she snapped. ''Nick, I love you! What more do you want?''

He was beside her in one quick step, pulling her roughly against him, burying his face in her hair as he let out a long, shuddering sigh. ''That will be plenty,'' he said huskily.

''Then do you mind telling me what this was all about?'' she asked, still mildly annoyed, her voice muffled by his jacket.

He took her by the shoulders and backed up far enough to look down into her eyes. ''Laura Taylor, do you realize that this is the first time you've ever said, 'I love you'?''

She frowned. ''Yes, I guess it is. But I assumed you knew.''

''How could I know?''

''Well, by the way I acted. I tried to show you how I felt.''

''Showing isn't the same as telling.''

She smiled, a sudden, euphoric joy making her heart soar. She sent a silent, fervent prayer of thanks to the Lord for granting her a happy ending after all.

''Are you saying you'd rather have words than actions?'' she teased, tilting her head to one side and reaching up to run a finger down his cheek.

She heard his sharply indrawn breath and grinned.

''Well, action is good, too,'' he conceeded.

''I thought you'd agree.'' She slipped her hands inside his jacket and gazed up into his face, the ardent light in her eyes playing havoc with his metabolism.

''You can count on it,'' he said huskily, pulling her roughly against him, his mouth urgent and demanding on hers. Laura responded eagerly, tasting, teasing, touching.

"Excuse me...are you folks lost?"

Startled, they drew apart, their breath creating frosty clouds in the cold night air. An older man stood looking up at them from the sidewalk.

Nick put his arm around Laura and drew her close. "No. Not anymore," he said, smiling down at her. "We just came home." Then he turned back toward the street. "We're going to buy this house," he called, and the jubilant ring in his voice warmed Laura's heart.

The man chuckled softly. "Now that's what I call a Christmas present!"

# *Epilogue*

Nick brought the car to a stop and turned to Laura with an intimate smile that made her tingle all over. "Welcome home, Mrs. Sinclair," he said huskily.

Her throat constricted at the tenderness in his eyes, and she swallowed with difficulty. "I love you, Nick," she said softly, her voice catching as her own eyes suddenly grew misty.

"Believe me, the feeling is mutual," he replied, reaching over with a feather-light touch to leisurely trace a finger down her cheek, then across her lips. He drew an unsteady breath and smiled. "Shall we go in?"

She nodded mutely, not trusting her voice, and tried unsuccessfully to slow her rapid pulse as he came around and opened her door. He took her hand, drawing her to her feet in one smooth motion, then let his arm slip around her waist, pulling her close. She leaned against him with a contented sigh as they stood for a moment in the dark stillness to look at the old

Victorian house, its ornate gingerbread trim and huge wraparound porch silhouetted by the golden light spilling from the windows.

"It's beautiful, isn't it?" she said, her eyes glowing.

"Beautiful is a good word," he agreed.

She turned to find his eyes on *her*, not the house, and she blushed.

"You're even more beautiful when you do that," he said with a tender smile, touching her nose with the tip of his finger before taking her hand. As they climbed the steps to the porch he turned to her. "Are you sure you wouldn't have preferred the Ritz tonight?"

"This *is* my Ritz," she said softly, letting her free hand lovingly glide over the banister as they ascended.

"I agree," he replied with a tender smile. For both of them, the house had come to symbolize their love and the promise of a rich, full life together.

When they reached the door, he fitted the key in the lock, and before she realized his intention he swept her into his arms and lowered his lips to hers, drawing a sweet response from deep within her. Only when the kiss lengthened, then deepened, did Laura reluctantly pull away.

"Nick! The neighbors might see us!" she protested halfheartedly.

He grinned. "They're all in bed. Speaking of which..." He stepped across the threshold, pushed the door shut with his foot, and started up the curved staircase.

Laura didn't say a word as a wave of excitement and delicious anticipation swept over her. She just nestled against his chest, enjoying the feel of his strong arms as she listened to the rapid but steady beat of his heart against her ear.

When they reached the bedroom, he carefully set her on her feet and removed the light mohair wrap from around her shoulders. Soft, classical music was playing and the room was bathed in a gentle, subdued light.

"I want to show you something," Nick said, taking her hand and leading her to the antique oval mirror on a stand that stood in one corner of the room. He positioned her in front and then stood behind her, his hands on her shoulders. "What do you see?"

She gazed at their reflections, a tender smile on her face. She saw Nick, tall and incredibly handsome in his tux, the elegant formal attire enhancing his striking good looks and broad shoulders. And she saw herself, dressed in her wedding finery. Her peach-colored tea-length lace gown softly hugged her slender figure, and the sweetheart neckline and short, slightly gathered sleeves added an old-fashioned charm that perfectly complemented her femininity. Her hair hung loose and full, the way Nick liked it, and the soft waves were pulled back on one side with a small cluster of flowers and lacy ribbon, giving her a sweetly youthful appearance. But mostly what she saw was the two of them, together, for life.

"Well?" Nick prompted.

"I see a miracle," she replied softly, her eyes glowing with happiness.

"I'm inclined to agree with you on that," Nick concurred with a smile. Then his voice softened and his tone grew serious. "Do you know what I see? The most beautiful bride that ever lived and the most wonderful, desirable woman I've ever met.''

''Oh, Nick,'' she said, her eyes misting. ''I never thought I could be so happy!''

''Well, get used to it, Mrs. Sinclair. Because happiness is exactly what I have planned for you for the next sixty or seventy years,'' he said, turning her to face him, taking both her hands in his as he bent to trail his lips across her forehead. ''Now don't go away. I'll be right back,'' he said huskily, his breath warm against her face.

She closed her eyes, letting his touch work its magic. ''I'll be here,'' she whispered.

When Nick left, Laura turned slowly and let her gaze roam over the lovingly decorated room they'd created together—their first priority when they bought the house. The English country style suited the house, as did the canopy bed that was draped in a floral print of rose and forest green. The thick carpet was also rose-colored, and two comfortable chairs in complementary striped fabric stood close to the fireplace. Yes, this was far preferable to the Ritz, Laura thought with deep contentment. Tonight marked a new chapter in their relationship, and she wanted it to start here, in their own home.

Nick had clearly gone out of his way to make this night special, she thought with a soft smile, her eyes filled with tenderness at his thoughtfulness. Two champagne glasses rested on a low table, and the subdued lighting and soft music created the perfect ambience for their first night together.

Nick quietly reentered, pausing a moment to let his

eyes lovingly trace the contours of Laura's profile, bathed in the warm glow of the golden light. It was hard for him to even remember a time when she hadn't been the center of his world. She brought a joy and completeness to his life far beyond anything he could ever have imagined. Today, as they'd recited their vows, he'd felt as if he'd truly come home. Gazing at her now, he was overwhelmed with joy and gratitude for the gift of her love.

Quietly he came up behind her and nuzzled her neck. "Did you miss me?"

"Mmm. As a matter of fact, I did," she said, leaning back against him.

"I brought some champagne."

"I saw the glasses."

"Will you have some?"

"Mmm-hmm."

He popped the cork, poured the bubbly liquid into the two waiting glasses and bent to strike a match to the logs. They quickly flamed into life, sending shadows dancing on the walls. It was chilly for the first day of spring, and Laura moved closer to the welcome warmth.

"Cold?" Nick asked as he handed her a glass.

"A little," she admitted.

He gave her a lazy smile. "I think we can take care of that," he said, his eyes twinkling.

Laura flushed and looked down, a smile playing at the corners of her own mouth. "I was counting on it," she said softly.

"But first…I'd like to make a toast." Nick raised his glass, and Laura looked up at him, the love shining from her deep green eyes. ''To new beginnings—and a love that never ends,'' he said softly.

Laura raised her glass, and the bell-like tinkle as they clinked resonated in the room.

They both took a sip, and then Nick reached over and gently removed the glass from her trembling fingers. He set the two glasses side by side on the mantel, turned, held out his hand. And as she moved into his arms, Laura had one last coherent thought. The good book was right. To everything there was a season. And this, at last, was her time to love.

* * * * *

Dear Reader,

Ever since I could put pen to paper, I've enjoyed writing. It's a very special gift for which I am deeply grateful.

Love is a gift, too. A precious and beautiful gift that requires courage and faith and trust—and yes, even risk—to reach its full potential.

It is a great joy for me to write about people like Nick and Laura, who find love and romance without compromising their moral values. And given the success of Steeple Hill books, there are clearly many readers who enjoy stories that affirm the existence of character and honor and principles in today's world, despite media messages to the contrary.

I truly believe that good, old-fashioned romance lives even in this modern age. Virtues and values never go out of style. And heroes like Nick are out there, waitng to be found. I should know. I married one!

As the Christmas season approaches, I am delighted to be part of Steeple Hill's *Holiday Blessings* anthology. It seems especially appropriate to celebrate love at this time of year, for it was truly the gift of love that God bestowed on the world one starry night in Bethlehem two thousand years ago.

At this Christmas season, and throughout the year, may your life be filled with the blessings of faith, hope and—above all—love.

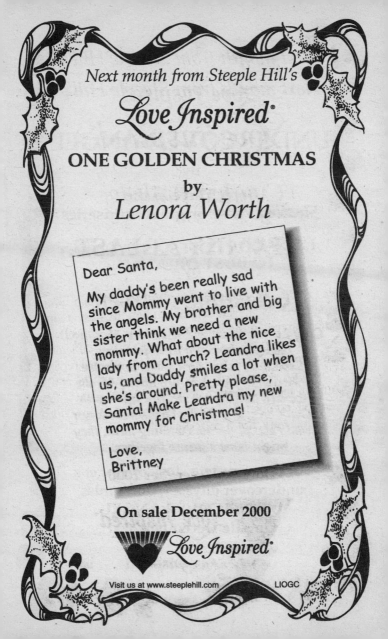

haired and plump, which led Caris to believe that the grange continued to prosper despite the plague. Because Norfolk was several days' journey away, the grange paid its dues to the priory in coins, rather than drive cattle or cart produce all that way, and Andrew brought the money in gold nobles, the new coin worth a third of a pound, with an image of King Edward standing on the deck of a ship. When Caris had counted the money and given it to Joan to stash in the new treasury, she said to Andrew: 'Why did Queen Isabella give us this grange twenty-two years ago, do you know?'

To her surprise, Andrew's pink face turned pale. He made several false starts at answering, then said: 'It's not for me to question her majesty's decisions.'

'No, indeed,' Caris said in a reassuring tone. 'I'm just curious about her motive.'

'She is a holy woman who has performed many pious acts.'

Like murdering her husband, Caris thought; but she said: 'However, there must be a reason she named Thomas.'

'He petitioned the queen for a favour, like hundreds of others, and she graciously granted it, as great ladies sometimes do.'

'Usually when they have some connection with the petitioner.'

'No, no, I'm sure there's no connection.'

His anxiety made Caris sure he was lying, and just as sure that he would not tell her the truth, so she dropped the subject, and sent Andrew off to have supper in the hospital.

Next morning she was accosted in the cloisters by Brother Thomas, the only monk left in the monastery. Looking angry, he said: 'Why did you interrogate Andrew Lynn?'

'Because I was curious,' she said, taken aback.

'What are you trying to do?'

'I'm not *trying* to do anything.' She was offended by his aggressive manner, but she did not want to quarrel with him. To ease the tension, she sat on the low wall around the edge of the arcade. A spring sun was shining bravely into the quadrangle. She spoke in a conversational tone. 'What's this all about?'

Thomas said stiffly: 'Why are you investigating me?'

'I'm not,' she said. 'Calm down. I'm going through all the

charters, listing them and having them copied. I came across one that puzzled me.'

'You're delving into matters that are none of your business.'

She bridled. 'I'm the prioress of Kingsbridge, and the acting prior – nothing here is secret from me.'

'Well, if you start digging up all that old stuff, you'll regret it, I promise you.'

It sounded like a threat, but she decided not to challenge him. She tried a different tack. 'Thomas, I thought we were friends. You have no right to forbid me to do anything, and I'm disappointed that you should even try. Don't you trust me?'

'You don't know what you're asking.'

'Then enlighten me. What does Queen Isabella have to do with you, me and Kingsbridge?'

'Nothing. She's an old woman now, living in retirement.'

'She's fifty-three. She's deposed one king, and she could probably depose another if she had a mind to. And she has some long-hidden connection with my priory which you are determined to keep from me.'

'For your own good.'

She ignored that. 'Twenty-two years ago someone was trying to kill you. Was it the same person who, having failed to do away with you, paid you off by getting you admitted to the monastery?'

'Andrew is going to go back to Lynn and tell Isabella that you've been asking these questions – do you realize that?'

'Why would she care? Why are people so afraid of you, Thomas?'

'Everything will be answered when I'm dead. None of it will matter then.' He turned round and walked away.

The bell rang for dinner. Caris went to the prior's palace, deep in thought. Godwyn's cat, Archbishop, was sitting on the doorstep. It glared at her and she shooed it away. She would not have it in the house.

She had got into the habit of dining every day with Merthin. Traditionally the prior regularly dined with the alderman, though to do so every day was unusual – but these were unusual times. That, at any rate, would have been her excuse, had anyone challenged her; but nobody did. Meanwhile they both looked out eagerly for another excuse to go on a trip so that they could again be alone together.

He came in muddy from his building site on Leper Island. He had stopped asking her to renounce her vows and leave the priory. He seemed content, at least for the moment, to see her every day and hope for future chances to be more intimate.

A priory employee brought them ham stewed with winter greens. When the servant had gone, Caris told Merthin about the charter and Thomas's reaction. 'He knows a secret that could damage the old queen if it got out.'

'I think that must be right,' Merthin said thoughtfully.

'On All Hallows' Day in 1327, after I ran away, he caught you, didn't he?'

'Yes. He made me help him bury a letter. I had to swear to keep it secret – until he dies, then I am to dig it up and give it to a priest.'

'He told me all my questions would be answered when he died.'

'I think the letter is the threat he holds over his enemies. They must know that its contents will be revealed when he dies. So they fear to kill him – in fact they have made sure he remains alive and well by helping him become a monk of Kingsbridge.'

'Can it matter, still?'

'Ten years after we buried the letter, I told him I hadn't ever let the secret out, and he said: "If you had, you'd be dead." That scared me more than the vow.'

'Mother Cecilia told me that Edward II did not die naturally.'

'How would she know a thing like that?'

'My uncle Anthony told her. So I presume the secret is that Queen Isabella had her husband murdered.'

'Half the country believes that anyway. But if there were proof ... Did Cecilia say how he was killed?'

Caris thought hard. 'No. Now that I think of it, what she said was: "The old king did not die of a fall." I asked her if he had been murdered – but she died without answering.'

'Still, why put out a false story about his death if not to cover up foul play?'

'And Thomas's letter must somehow prove that there was foul play, and that the queen was in on it.'

They finished their dinner in thoughtful silence. In the monastery day, the hour after dinner was for rest or reading. Caris and Merthin usually lingered for a while. Today, however, Merthin was anxious about the angles of the roof timbers being erected in the new tavern, the Bridge, that he was building on Leper Island. They kissed hungrily, but he tore himself away and hurried back to the site. Disappointed, Caris opened a book called *Ars Medica*, a Latin translation of a work by the ancient Greek physician Galen. It was the cornerstone of university medicine, and she was reading it to find out what priests learned at Oxford and Paris; though she had so far found little that would help her.

The maid came back and cleared the table. 'Ask Brother Thomas to come and see me, please,' Caris said. She wanted to make sure they were still friends despite their abrasive conversation.

Before Thomas arrived there was a commotion outside. She heard several horses, and the kind of shouting that indicated a nobleman wanting attention. A few moments later the door was flung open and in walked Sir Ralph Fitzgerald, lord of Tench.

He looked angry, but Caris pretended not to notice that. 'Hello, Ralph,' she said as amiably as she could. 'This is an unexpected pleasure. Welcome to Kingsbridge.'

'Never mind all that,' he said rudely. He walked up to where she sat and stood aggressively close. 'Do you realize you're ruining the peasantry of the entire county?'

Another figure followed him in and stood by the door, a big man with a small head, and Caris recognized his long-time sidekick, Alan Fernhill. Both were armed with swords and daggers. Caris was acutely aware that she was alone in the palace. She tried to defuse the scene. 'Would you like some ham, Ralph? I've just finished dinner.'

Ralph was not to be diverted. 'You've been stealing my peasants!'

'Peasants, or pheasants?'

Alan Fernhill burst out laughing.

Ralph reddened and looked more dangerous, and Caris

wished she had not made that joke. 'If you poke fun at me you'll be sorry,' he said.

Caris poured ale into a cup. 'I'm not laughing at you,' she said. 'Tell me exactly what's on your mind.' She offered him the ale.

Her shaking hand betrayed her fear, but he ignored the cup and wagged his finger at her. 'Labourers have been disappearing from my villages – and when I inquire after them, I find they have moved to villages belonging to you, where they get higher wages.'

Caris nodded. 'If you were selling a horse, and two men wanted to buy it, wouldn't you give it to the one who offered the higher price?'

'That's not the same.'

'I think it is. Have some ale.'

With a sudden sideswipe of his hand, he knocked the cup from her grasp. It fell to the floor, the ale spilling into the straw. 'They're *my* labourers.'

Her hand was bruised, but she tried to ignore the pain. She bent down, picked up the cup and set it on the sideboard. 'Not really,' she said. 'If they're labourers, that means you've never given them any land, so they have the right to go elsewhere.'

'I'm still their lord, damn it! And another thing. I offered a tenancy to a free man the other day and he refused it, saying he could get a better bargain from Kingsbridge Priory.'

'Same thing, Ralph. I need all the people I can get, so I give them what they want.'

'You're a woman, you don't think things through. You can't see that it will all end with everyone paying more for the same peasants.'

'Not necessarily. Higher wages might attract some of those who at present do no work at all – outlaws, for example, or those vagabonds who go around living off what they find in plague-emptied villages. And some who are now labourers might become tenants, and work harder because they're cultivating their own land.'

He banged the table with his fist, and she blinked at the sudden noise. 'You've no right to change the old ways!'

'I think I have.'

He grabbed the front of her robe. 'Well, I'm not putting up with it!'

'Take your hands off me, you clumsy oaf,' she said.

At that moment, Brother Thomas came in. 'You sent for me – what the devil is going on here?'

He stepped smartly across the room, and Ralph let go of Caris's robe as if it had suddenly caught fire. Thomas had no weapons and only one arm, but he had got the better of Ralph once before; and Ralph was scared of him.

Ralph took a step back, then realized he had revealed his fear, and looked ashamed. 'We're done here!' he said loudly, and turned to the door.

Caris said: 'What I'm doing in Outhenby and elsewhere is perfectly legitimate, Ralph.'

'It's interfering with the natural order!' he said.

'There's no law against it.'

Alan opened the door for his master.

'You wait and see,' said Ralph, and he went out.

# 67

In March that year, 1349, Gwenda and Wulfric went with Nathan Reeve to the midweek market at the small town of Northwood.

They were working for Sir Ralph now. Gwenda and Wulfric had escaped the plague, so far, but several of Ralph's labourers had died of it, so he needed help; and Nate, the bailiff of Wigleigh, had offered to take them on. He could afford to pay normal wages, whereas Perkin had been giving them nothing more than their food.

As soon as they announced they were going to work for Ralph, Perkin discovered that he could now afford to pay them normal wages – but he was too late.

On this day they took a cartload of logs from Ralph's forest to sell in Northwood, a town that had had a timber market since time immemorial. The boys, Sam and David, went with them: there was no one else to look after them. Gwenda did not trust her father, and her mother had died two years ago. Wulfric's parents were long dead.

Several other Wigleigh folk were at the market. Father Gaspard was buying seeds for his vegetable garden, and Gwenda's father, Joby, was selling freshly killed rabbits.

Nate, the bailiff, was a stunted man with a twisted back, and he could not lift logs. He dealt with customers while Wulfric and Gwenda did the lifting. At midday he gave them a penny to buy their dinner at the Old Oak, one of the taverns around the square. They got bacon boiled with leeks and shared it with the boys. David, at eight years of age, still had a child's appetite, but Sam was a fast-growing ten and perpetually hungry.

While they were eating, they overheard a conversation that caught Gwenda's attention.

There was a group of young men standing in a corner, drinking large tankards of ale. They were all poorly dressed, except one with a bushy blond beard who had the superior clothes of a prosperous peasant or a village craftsman: leather trousers, good boots and a new hat. The sentence that caused Gwenda to prick up her ears was: 'We pay two pence a day for labourers at Outhenby.'

She listened hard, trying to learn more, but caught only scattered words. She had heard that some employers were offering more than the traditional penny a day, because of the shortage of workers caused by the plague. She had hesitated to believe such stories, which sounded too good to be true.

She said nothing for the moment to Wulfric, who had not heard the magic words, but her heart beat faster. She and her family had endured so many years of poverty. Was it possible that life might get better for them?

She had to find out more.

When they had eaten, they sat on a bench outside, watching the boys and some other children running around the broad trunk of the tree that gave the tavern its name. 'Wulfric,' she said quietly. 'What if we could earn two pence a day – each?'

'How?'

'By going to Outhenby.' She told him what she had overheard. 'It could be the beginning of a new life for us,' she finished.

'Am I never to get back my father's lands, then?'

She could have hit him with a stick. Did he really still think that was going to happen? How foolish could he be?

She tried to make her voice as gentle as possible. 'It's twelve years since you were disinherited,' she said. 'In that time Ralph has become more and more powerful. And there's never been the least sign that he might mellow towards you. What do *you* think the chances are?'

He did not answer that question. 'Where would we live?'

'They must have houses in Outhenby.'

'But will Ralph let us go?'

'He can't stop us. We're labourers, not serfs. You know that.'

'But does Ralph know it?'

'Let's not give him the chance to object.'

'How could we manage that?'

'Well...' She had not thought this through, but now she saw that it would have to be done precipitately. 'We could leave today, from here.'

It was a scary thought. They had both lived their entire lives in Wigleigh. Wulfric had never even moved house. Now they were contemplating going to live in a village they had never seen without even going back to say goodbye.

But Wulfric was worrying about something else. He pointed at the hunchbacked bailiff, crossing the square to the chandler's shop. 'What would Nathan say?'

'We won't tell him what we're planning. We'll give him some story – say we want to stay here overnight, for some reason, and return home tomorrow. That way, nobody will know where we are. And we'll never go back to Wigleigh.'

'Never go back,' Wulfric said despondently.

Gwenda controlled her impatience. She knew her husband. Once Wulfric was set on a course he was unstoppable, but he took a long time to decide. He would come round to this idea eventually. He was not closed-minded, just cautious and deliberate. He hated to make decisions in a rush – whereas she thought it was the only way.

The young man with the blond beard came out of the Old Oak. Gwenda looked around: none of the Wigleigh folk was in sight. She stood up and accosted the man. 'Did I hear you say something about two pence a day for labourers?' she said.

'That's right, mistress,' he replied. 'In the vale of Outhenby, just half a day south-west of here. We need all we can get.'

'Who are you?'

'I'm the ploughman of Outhenby. My name is Harry.'

Outhenby must be a large and prosperous village to have a ploughman all of its own, Gwenda reasoned. Most ploughmen worked for a group of villages. 'And who is lord of the manor?'

'The prioress of Kingsbridge.'

'Caris!' That was wonderful news. Caris could be trusted. Gwenda's spirits lifted further.

'Yes, she is the current prioress,' Harry said. 'A very determined woman.'

'I know.'

'She wants her fields cultivated so that she can feed the sisters, and she's not listening to excuses.'

'Do you have houses at Outhenby for labourers to live in? With their families?'

'Plenty, unfortunately. We've lost many people to the plague.'

'You said it was south-west of here.'

'Take the southerly road to Badford, then follow the Outhen upstream.'

Caution returned to Gwenda. 'I'm not going,' she said quickly.

'Ah. Of course.' He did not believe her.

'I was really asking on behalf of a friend.' She turned away.

'Well, tell your friend to come as soon as he can – we've got spring ploughing and sowing to finish yet.'

'All right.'

She felt slightly dizzy, as if she had taken a draught of strong wine. Two pence a day – working for Caris – and miles away from Ralph, Perkin and flirty Annet! It was a dream.

She sat back down beside Wulfric. 'Did you hear all that?' she asked him.

'Yes,' he said. He pointed to a figure standing by the tavern door. 'And so did he.'

Gwenda looked. It was her father.

*

'PUT THAT HORSE in the traces,' Nate said to Wulfric around mid-afternoon. 'It's time to go home.'

Wulfric said: 'We'll be needing our wages for the week so far.'

'You'll be paid on Saturday as usual,' Nate said dismissively. 'Hitch that nag.'

Wulfric did not move towards the horse. 'I'll trouble you to pay me today,' he insisted. 'I know you've got the money, you've sold all that timber.'

Nate turned and looked directly at him. 'Why should you be paid early?' he said irritably.

'Because I shan't be returning to Wigleigh with you tonight.'

Nate was taken aback. 'Why not?'

Gwenda took over. 'We're going to Melcombe,' she said.

'What?' Nate was outraged. 'People like you have no business travelling to Melcombe!'

'We met a fisherman who needs crew for two pence a day.' Gwenda had worked out this story to throw any pursuit off the scent.

Wulfric added: 'Our respects to Sir Ralph, and may God be with him in the future.'

Gwenda added: 'But we don't expect to see him ever again.' She said it just to hear the sweet sound of it: never to see Ralph again.

Nathan said indignantly: 'He may not wish you to leave!'

'We're not serfs, we have no land. Ralph cannot forbid us.'

'You're the son of a serf,' Nathan said to Wulfric.

'But Ralph denied me my inheritance,' Wulfric replied. 'He cannot now demand my fealty.'

'It's a dangerous thing for a poor man to stand on his rights.'

'That's true,' Wulfric conceded. 'But I'm doing it, all the same.'

Nate was beaten. 'You shall hear more of this,' he said.

'Would you like me to put the horse to the cart?'

Nate scowled. He could not do it himself. Because of his back, he had difficulty with complicated physical tasks, and the horse was taller than he. 'Yes, of course,' he said.

'I'll be glad to. Would you kindly pay me first?'

Looking furious, Nate took out his purse and counted six silver pennies.

Gwenda took the money and Wulfric hitched up the horse. Nate drove away without another word.

'Well!' said Gwenda. 'That's done.' She looked at Wulfric. He was smiling broadly. She asked him: 'What is it?'

'I don't know,' he said. 'I feel as if I've been wearing a collar for years, and suddenly it's been taken off.'

'Good.' That was how she wanted him to feel. 'Now let's find a place to stay the night.'

The Old Oak was in a prime position in the market square, and charged top prices. They walked around the little town looking for somewhere cheaper. Eventually they went into the Gate House, where Gwenda negotiated accommodation for the four of them – supper, a mattress on the floor and breakfast – for a penny. The boys would need a decent night's sleep and some breakfast if they were to walk all morning.

She could hardly sleep for excitement. She was also worried. What was she taking her family to? She had only the word of one man, a stranger, for what they would find when they reached Outhenby. She really ought to have sought confirmation before committing herself.

But she and Wulfric had been stuck in a hole for ten years, and Harry Ploughman of Outhenby was the first person to offer them a way out of it.

The breakfast was meagre: thin porridge and watery cider. Gwenda bought a big loaf of new bread for them to eat on the road, and Wulfric filled his leather flask with cold water from a well. They passed through the city gate an hour after sunrise and set off on the road south.

As they walked, she thought about Joby, her father. As soon as he learned that she had not returned to Wigleigh, he would remember the conversation he had overheard, and he would guess she had gone to Outhenby. He would not be fooled by the story about Melcombe: he was an accomplished deceiver himself, too experienced to be taken in by a simple ruse. But would anyone think to ask him where she had gone? Everyone knew she never spoke to her father. And, if they did ask him, would he blurt out what he suspected? Or would some vestige of paternal feeling cause him to protect her?

There was nothing she could do about it, so she put him out of her mind.

It was good weather for travelling. The ground was soft with recent rain, and there was no dust; but today was a dry day with fitful sunshine, neither cold nor hot. The boys quickly grew tired, especially David, the younger, but Wulfric was good at distracting them with songs and rhymes, quizzing them about the names of trees and plants, playing number games and telling stories.

Gwenda could hardly believe what they had done. This time yesterday, it had looked as if their life would never change: hard work, poverty and frustrated aspirations would be their lot for ever. Now they were on the road to a new life.

She thought of the house where she had lived with Wulfric

for ten years. She had not left much behind: a few cooking pots, a stack of newly chopped firewood, half a ham and four blankets. She had no clothes other than what she was wearing, and neither did Wulfric or the boys; no jewellery, ribbons, gloves or combs. Ten years ago, Wulfric had had chickens and pigs in his yard, but they had gradually been eaten or sold during the years of penury. Their meagre possessions could be replaced with a week's wages at the promised Outhenby rates.

In accordance with Harry's directions they took the road south to a muddy ford across the Outhen, then turned west and followed the river upstream. As they progressed, the river narrowed, until the land funnelled between two ranges of hills. 'Good, fertile soil,' Wulfric said. 'It'll need the heavy plough, though.'

At noon they came to a large village with a stone church. They went to the door of a timber manor house next to the church. With trepidation, Gwenda knocked. Was she about to be told that Harry Ploughman did not know what he was talking about, and there was no work here? Had she made her family walk half a day for nothing? How humiliating it would be to have to return to Wigleigh and beg to be taken on again by Nate Reeve.

A grey-haired woman came to the door. She looked at Gwenda with the suspicious glare that villagers everywhere gave to strangers. 'Yes?'

'Good day, mistress,' Gwenda said. 'Is this Outhenby?'

'It is.'

'We're labourers looking for work. Harry Ploughman told us to come here.'

'Did he, now?'

Was there something wrong, Gwenda wondered, or was this woman just a grumpy old cow? She almost asked the question out loud. Stopping herself, she said: 'Does Harry live at this house?'

'Certainly not,' the woman replied. 'He's just a ploughman. This is the bailiff's house.'

Some conflict between bailiff and ploughman, Gwenda guessed. 'Perhaps we should see the bailiff, then.'

'He's not here.'

Patiently, Gwenda said: 'Would you be kind enough to tell us where we might find him?'

The woman pointed across the valley. 'North Field.'

Gwenda turned to look in the direction indicated. When she turned back, the woman had disappeared into the house.

Wulfric said: 'She didn't seem pleased to see us.'

'Old women hate change,' Gwenda commented. 'Let's find this bailiff.'

'The boys are tired.'

'They can rest soon.'

They set off across the fields. There was plenty of activity on the strips. Children were picking stones off ploughed land, women were sowing seeds and men were carting manure. Gwenda could see the ox team in the distance, eight mighty beasts patiently dragging the plough through the wet, heavy soil.

They came upon a group of men and women trying to move a horse-drawn harrow that had got stuck in a ditch. Gwenda and Wulfric joined in pushing it out. Wulfric's broad back made the difference, and the harrow was freed.

All the villagers turned and looked at Wulfric. A tall man with an old burn mark disfiguring one side of his face said amiably: 'You're a useful fellow – who are you?'

'I'm Wulfric, and my wife is Gwenda. We're labourers looking for work.'

'You're just what we need, Wulfric,' the man said. 'I'm Carl Shaftesbury.' He stuck out his hand to shake. 'Welcome to Outhenby.'

*

RALPH CAME eight days later.

Wulfric and Gwenda had moved into a small, well-built house with a stone chimney and an upstairs bedroom where they could sleep separately from the boys. They got a wary reception from the older, more conservative villagers – notably Will Bailiff and his wife, Vi, who had been so rude to them on the day they arrived. But Harry Ploughman and the younger set were excited by the changes and glad to have help in the fields.

They were paid two pence a day, as promised, and Gwenda looked forward eagerly to the end of their first full week, when they each got twelve pence – a shilling! – double the highest sum they had ever earned. What would they do with all that money?

Neither Wulfric nor Gwenda had worked anywhere but Wigleigh, and they were surprised to find that not all villages were the same. The ultimate authority here was the prioress of Kingsbridge, and that made a difference. Ralph's rule was personal and arbitrary: appealing to him was hazardous. By contrast, Outhenby folk seemed to know what the prioress would want in most situations, and they could settle disputes by figuring out what she would say if asked to adjudicate.

A mild disagreement of this kind was going on when Ralph came.

They were all walking home from the fields at sundown, the adults work-weary, the children running on ahead, and Harry Ploughman bringing up the rear with the unharnessed oxen. Carl Shaftesbury, the man with the burned face, who was a newcomer like Gwenda and Wulfric, had caught three eels at dawn for his family's supper, as it was Friday. The question was whether labourers had the same right as tenants to take fish from the Outhen river on fast days. Harry Ploughman said the privilege extended to all Outhenby residents. Vi Bailiff said that tenants owed customary dues to the landlord, which labourers did not, and those who had extra duties should have extra privileges.

Will Bailiff was called upon for a decision, and he ruled against his wife. 'I believe the Mother Prioress would say that if the church wishes people to eat fish, then fish must be provided for them to eat,' he said; and that was accepted by everyone.

Looking towards the village, Gwenda saw two horsemen.

A cold wind gusted suddenly.

The visitors were half a mile away across the fields, and heading for the houses at an angle to the path the villagers were taking. She could tell they were men-at-arms. They had big horses and their clothes looked bulky – men of violence generally wore heavily padded coats. She nudged Wulfric.

'I've seen them,' he said grimly.

Such men had no casual reason to come to a village. They

despised the people who grew the crops and cared for the livestock. They normally visited only to take from the peasants those things they were too proud to provide for themselves, bread and meat and drink. Their view of what they were entitled to, or how much they should pay, always differed from that of the peasants; so there was invariably trouble.

Within the next couple of minutes all the villagers saw them, and the group went quiet. Gwenda noticed that Harry turned the oxen slightly and headed for the far end of the village, though she could not immediately guess why.

Gwenda felt sure the two men had come to find runaway labourers. She found herself praying they would turn out to be the former employers of Carl Shaftesbury or one of the other newcomers. However, as the villagers came closer to the horsemen she recognized Ralph Fitzgerald and Alan Fernhill, and her heart sank.

This was the moment she had dreaded. She had known there was a chance Ralph would find out where they had gone: her father could make a good guess, and he could not be relied upon to keep his mouth shut. And although Ralph had no right to take them back, he was a knight and a nobleman, and such people generally did as they pleased.

It was too late to run. The group was walking along a path between broad ploughed fields: if some of them broke away and fled, Ralph and Alan would immediately see them and give chase; and then Gwenda and her family would lose whatever protection they might gain from being with other villagers. They were trapped in the open.

She called to her boys: 'Sam! David! Come here!'

They did not hear, or did not want to, and they ran on. Gwenda went after them, but they thought it was a game, and tried to outrun her. They were almost at the village now, and she found she was too tired to catch them. Almost in tears, she shouted: 'Come back!'

Wulfric took over. He ran past her and easily caught up with David. He scooped the boy up in his arms. But he was too late to catch Sam, who ran laughing in among the scattered houses.

The horsemen were reined in by the church. As Sam ran

towards them, Ralph nudged his horse forward, then leaned down from the saddle and picked the boy up by his shirt. Sam gave a shout of fright.

Gwenda screamed.

Ralph sat the boy on his horse's wither.

Wulfric, carrying David, came to a stop in front of Ralph.

Ralph said: 'Your son, I presume.'

Gwenda was appalled. She was afraid for her son. It would be beneath Ralph's dignity to attack a child, but there might be an accident. And there was another danger.

Seeing Ralph and Sam together, Wulfric might realize they were father and son.

Sam was still a little boy, of course, with a child's body and face, but he had Ralph's thick hair and dark eyes, and his bony shoulders were wide and square.

Gwenda looked at her husband. Wulfric's expression showed no sign that he had seen what was so obvious to her. She surveyed the faces of the other villagers. They seemed oblivious to the stark truth – except for Vi Bailiff, who was giving Gwenda a hard stare. That old battleaxe might have guessed. But no one else had – yet.

Will came forward and addressed the visitors. 'Good day to you, sirs. I'm Will, the bailiff of Outhenby. May I ask—'

'Shut your mouth, bailiff,' said Ralph. He pointed at Wulfric. 'What is he doing here?'

Gwenda sensed a slight easing of tension as the other villagers realized they were not the target of the lord's wrath.

Will replied: 'My lord, he's a labourer, hired on the authority of the prioress of Kingsbridge—'

'He's a runaway, and he's got to come home,' Ralph said.

Will fell silent, frightened.

Carl Shaftesbury said: 'And what authority do you claim for this demand?'

Ralph peered at Carl, as if memorizing his face. 'Watch your tongue, or I'll disfigure the other side of your face.'

Will said nervously: 'We don't want any bloodshed.'

'Very wise, bailiff,' said Ralph. 'Who is this insolent peasant?'

'Never you mind who I am, knight,' said Carl rudely. 'I know who you are. You're Ralph Fitzgerald, and I saw you convicted of rape and sentenced to death at Shiring court.'

'But I'm not dead, am I?' Ralph said.

'You should be, though. And you have no feudal rights over labourers. If you try to use force, you'll be taught a sharp lesson.'

Several people gasped. This was a reckless way to speak to an armed knight.

Wulfric said: 'Be quiet, Carl. I don't want you killed for my sake.'

'It's not for your sake,' Carl said. 'If this thug is allowed to drag you off, next week someone will come for me. We have to stick together. We're not helpless.'

Carl was a big man, taller than Wulfric and almost as broad, and Gwenda could see that he meant what he said. She was appalled. If they started fighting there would be terrible violence – and her Sam was still sitting on the horse with Ralph. 'We'll just go with Ralph,' she said frantically. 'It will be better.'

Carl said: 'No, it won't. I'm going to stop him taking you away, whether you want me to or not. It's for my own good.'

There was a murmur of assent. Gwenda looked around. Most of the men were holding shovels or hoes, and they looked ready to swing them, though they also looked scared.

Wulfric turned his back on Ralph and spoke in a low, urgent voice. 'You women, take the children into the church – quickly, now!'

Several women snatched up toddlers and grabbed youngsters by the arms. Gwenda stayed where she was, and so did several of the younger women. The villagers instinctively moved closer together, standing shoulder to shoulder.

Ralph and Alan looked disconcerted. They had not expected to face a crowd of fifty or more belligerent peasants. But they were on horseback, so they could get away any time they wanted.

Ralph said: 'Well, perhaps I'll just take this little boy to Wigleigh.'

Gwenda gasped with horror.

Ralph went on: 'Then, if his parents want him, they can come back where they belong.'

If anything, Merthin was understating. More than once he had seen a hysterical man or woman change, after just a few calming moments with Caris, into a sensible person capable of coping with whatever should happen.

Her inborn gift had been augmented, since the advent of the plague, by an almost supernatural reputation. Everyone for miles around knew that she and her nuns had carried on caring for the sick, despite the risk to themselves, even when the monks had fled. They thought she was a saint.

The atmosphere inside the castle compound was subdued. Those who had routine tasks were performing them: fetching firewood and water, feeding horses and sharpening weapons, baking bread and butchering meat. Many others – secretaries, men-at-arms, messengers – sat around doing nothing, waiting for news from the sick room.

The rooks cawed a sarcastic welcome as Merthin and Caris crossed the inner bridge to the keep. Merthin's father, Sir Gerald, always claimed to be directly descended from Jack and Aliena's son, Earl Thomas. As Merthin counted the steps to the great hall, placing his feet carefully in the smooth hollows worn by thousands of boots, he reflected that his ancestors had probably [illegible] just these old stones. To him, such notions were [illegible] Ralph was obsessed



Gwenda was beside herself. Ralph had Sam, and he could ride away at any moment. She fought down a hysterical scream. If he turned his horse, she decided, she would throw herself at him and try to drag him off the saddle. She moved a step closer.

Then, behind Ralph and Alan, she saw the oxen. Harry Ploughman was driving them through the village from the other end. Eight massive beasts lumbered up to the scene in front of the church, then stopped, looking around dumbly, not knowing which way to go. Harry stood behind them. Ralph and Alan found themselves in a triangular trap, hemmed in by the villagers, the oxen and the stone church.

Harry had planned this to stop Ralph riding away with Wulfric and herself, Gwenda guessed. But the tactic did just as well for this situation.

Carl said: 'Put the child down, Sir Ralph, and go in peace.'

The trouble was, Gwenda thought, it was now difficult for Ralph to back down without losing face. He was going to have to do something to avoid looking foolish, which was the ultimate horror for proud knights. They talked all the time about their honour, but that meant nothing – they were thoroughly dishonourable when it suited them. What they really prized was their dignity. They would rather die than be humiliated.

The tableau was frozen for several moments: the knight and the child on the horse, the mutinous villagers, and the dumb oxen.

Then Ralph lowered Sam to the ground.

Tears of relief came to Gwenda's eyes.

Sam ran to her, threw his arms around her waist and began to cry.

The villagers relaxed, the men lowering their shovels and hoes.

Ralph pulled on his horse's reins and shouted: 'Hup! Hup!' The horse reared. He dug in his spurs and rode straight at the crowd. They scattered. Alan rode behind him. The villagers desperately threw themselves out of the way, ending up in tangled heaps on the muddy ground. They were trampled by one another but not, miraculously, by the horses.

Ralph and Alan laughed loudly as they rode out of the village, as if the entire encounter had been nothing more than a huge joke.

But, in reality, Ralph had been shamed.

And that, Gwenda felt sure, meant that he would be back.



# 68

EARLSCASTLE HAD NOT CHANGED. Twelve years ago, Merthin recalled, he had been asked to demolish the old fortress and build a new, modern palace fit for an earl in a peaceful country. But he had refused, preferring to design the new bridge at Kingsbridge. Since then, it seemed, the project had languished, for here was the same figure-eight wall with two drawbridges, and the old-fashioned keep ensconced in the upper loop, where the family lived like frightened rabbits at the end of a burrow, unaware that there was no longer any danger from the fox. The place must have been much the same in the days of Lady Aliena and Jack Builder.

Merthin was with Caris, who had been summoned here by the countess, Lady Philippa. Earl William had fallen sick, and Philippa thought her husband had the plague. Caris had been dismayed. She had th likelihood was that the earl would now be dead, or nearly so. 'All I will be able to do is give him some poppy essence to ease the final agony,' Caris had said as they rode along.

'You do more than that,' Merthin had said. 'Your presence comforts people. You're calm and knowledgeable, and you talk about things they understand, swelling and confusion and pain – you don't try to impress them with jargon about humours, which just makes them feel more ignorant and powerless and frightened. When you're there, they feel that everything possible is being done; and that's what they want.'

'I hope you're right.'

trodden on just th…

intriguing but trivial. By contrast his broth…
with restoring the family to its former glory.

Caris was ahead of him, and the sway of her hips as she climbed the steps made his lips twitch in a smile. He was frustrated by not being able to sleep with her every night, but the rare occasions when they could be alone together were all the more thrilling. Yesterday they had spent a mild spring afternoon making love in a sunlit forest glade, while the horses grazed nearby, oblivious to their passion.

It was an odd relationship, but then she was an extraordinary woman: a prioress who doubted much of what the church taught; an acclaimed healer who rejected medicine as practised by physicians; and a nun who made enthusiastic love to her man whenever she could get away with it. If I wanted a normal relationship, Merthin told himself, I should have picked a normal girl.

er proud bosom. However, today her normally serene face was lotchy and her eyes were red. Her fashionably piled hairstyle was slightly awry, with stray locks of hair escaping from her headdress, adding to her air of glamorous distraction.

Merthin stood up and look at her expectantly.

She said: 'My husband has the plague, as I feared; and so do both my sons.'

The people around murmured in dismay.

It might turn out to be no more than the last remnants of the epidemic, of course; but it could just as easily be the start of a new outbreak – God forbid, Merthin thought.

He said: 'How is the earl feeling?'

Philippa sat on the bench next to him. 'Mother Caris has sed his pain. But she says he's near the end.'

Their knees were almost touching. He felt the magnetism of sexuality, even though she was drowning in grief and he was with love for Caris. 'And your sons?' he said.

he looked down at her lap, as if studying the pattern of gold lver threads woven into her blue gown. 'The same as their

thin said quietly: 'This is very hard for you, my lady, very

ave him a wary glance. 'You're not like your brother, are

knew that Ralph had been in love with Philippa, bsessive way, for many years. Did she realize that? not know. Ralph had chosen well, he thought. If g to have a hopeless love, you might as well pick ılar. 'Ralph and I are very different,' he said

you as youngsters. You were the cheeky one – uy a green silk to match my eyes. Then your ght.'

ink the younger of two brothers deliberately ite of the elder, just to differentiate himself.'

e of my two. Rollo is strong-willed and her and grandfather; and Rick has always

The hall was full of people. Some were working, laying dow fresh straw, building up the fire, preparing the table for dinner, and others were simply waiting. At the far end of the long room, sitting near the foot of the staircase that led up to the earl's private quarters, Merthin saw a well-dressed girl of about fifteen. She stood up and came towards them with a rather stately walk, and Merthin realized she must be Lady Philippa's daughter. Like her mother she was tall, with an hourglass figure. 'I am the Lad Odila,' she said with a touch of hauteur that was pure Phili Despite her composure, the skin around her young eyes wa and creased with crying. 'You must be Mother Caris. Tha for coming to attend my father.'

Merthin said: 'I'm the alderman of Kingsbridg Bridger. How is Earl William?'

'He is very ill, and both my brothers have Merthin recalled that the earl and countess h nineteen and twenty or thereabouts. 'My mo lady prioress should come to them immediat

Caris said: 'Of course.'

Odila went up the stairs. Caris took f linen cloth and fastened it over her followed.

Merthin sat on a bench to wait to infrequent sex, that did not st extra opportunities, and he sur eye, figuring out the sleeping house had a traditional lay would be where almost presumably led to a sola Modern castles had a guests, but there ap and Caris might lie hall, but they co causing a scand

After a wh down the st eyes were o posture only emp

been sweet-natured and obliging.' She began to cry. 'Oh, God, I'm going to lose them all.'

Merthin took her hand. 'You can't be sure what will happen,' he said gently. 'I caught the plague in Florence, and I survived. My daughter didn't catch it at all.'

She looked up at him. 'And your wife?'

Merthin looked down at their entwined hands. Philippa's was perceptibly more wrinkled than his, he saw, even though there was only four years' difference in their ages. He said: 'Silvia died.'

'I pray to God that I will catch it. If all my men die, I want to go too.'

'Surely not.'

'It's the fate of noblewomen to marry men they don't love – but I was lucky, you see, in William. He was chosen for me, but I loved him from the start.' Her voice began to fail her. 'I couldn't bear to have someone else . . .'

'You feel that way now, of course.' It was odd to be talking like this while her husband was still alive, Merthin thought. But she was so stricken by grief that she had little thought for niceties, and said just what was in her mind.

She collected herself with an effort. 'What about you?' she said. 'Have you remarried?'

'No.' He could hardly explain that he was having a love affair with the prioress of Kingsbridge. 'I think I could, though, if the right woman were ... willing. You might come to feel the same, eventually.'

'But you don't understand. As the widow of an earl with no heirs, I would have to marry someone King Edward chose for me. And the king would have no thought for my wishes. His only concern would be who should be the next earl of Shiring.'

'I see.' Merthin had not thought of that. He could imagine that an arranged marriage might be particularly loathsome to a widow who had truly loved her first husband.

'How dreadful of me to be speaking of another husband while my first is alive,' she said. 'I don't know what came over me.'

Merthin patted her hand sympathetically. 'It's understandable.'

The door at the top of the stairs opened and Caris came out, drying her hands on a cloth. Merthin suddenly felt uncomfortable about holding Philippa's hand. He was tempted to thrust it away from him, but realized how guilty that would look, and managed to resist the impulse. He smiled at Caris and said: 'How are your patients?'

Caris's eyes went to their linked hands, but she said nothing. She came down the stairs, untying her linen mask.

Philippa unhurriedly withdrew her hand.

Caris took off her mask and said: 'I'm very sorry to have to tell you, my lady, that Earl William is dead.'

*

'I NEED A new horse,' said Ralph Fitzgerald. His favourite mount, Griff, was getting old. The spirited bay palfrey had suffered a sprain in its left hind leg that had taken months to heal, and now it was lame again in the same leg. Ralph felt sad. Griff was the horse Earl Roland had given him when he was a young squire, and it had been with him ever since, even going to the French wars. It might serve him a few years longer for unhurried trips from village to village within his domain, but its hunting days were over.

'We could go to Shiring market tomorrow and buy another,' Alan Fernhill said.

They were in the stable, looking at Griff's fetlock. Ralph liked stables. He enjoyed the earthy smell, the strength and beauty of the horses, and the company of rough-handed men engrossed in physical tasks. It took him back to his youth, when the world had seemed a simple place.

He did not at first respond to Alan's suggestion. What Alan did not know was that Ralph did not have the money to buy a horse.

The plague had at first enriched him, through the inheritance tax: land that normally passed from father to son once in a generation had changed hands twice or more in a few months, and he got a payment every time – traditionally the best beast, but often a fixed sum in cash. But then land had started to fall into disuse for lack of people to farm it. At the same time, agricultural prices had dropped. The upshot was that Ralph's income, in money and produce, fell drastically.

Things were bad, he thought, when a knight could not afford a horse.

Then he remembered that Nate Reeve was due to come to Tench Hall today with the quarterly dues from Wigleigh. Every spring that village was obliged to provide its lord with twenty-four hoggets, year-old sheep. They could be driven to Shiring market and sold, and they should raise enough cash to pay for a palfrey, if not a hunter. 'All right,' Ralph said to Alan. 'Let's see if the bailiff of Wigleigh is here.'

They went into the hall. This was a feminine zone, and Ralph's spirits dropped immediately. Tilly was sitting by the fire, nursing their three-month-old son, Gerry. Mother and baby were in vigorous good health, despite Tilly's youth. Her slight, girlish body had changed drastically: she now had swollen breasts with large, leathery nipples at which the baby sucked greedily. Her belly sagged loosely like that of an old woman. Ralph had not lain with her for many months and he probably never would again.

Nearby sat the grandfather after whom the baby was named, Sir Gerald, with Lady Maud. Ralph's parents were now old and frail, but every morning they walked from their house in the village to the manor house to see their grandson. Maud said the baby looked like Ralph, but he could not see the resemblance.

Ralph was pleased to see that Nate was also in the hall.

The hunchbacked bailiff sprang up from his bench. 'Good day to you, Sir Ralph,' he said.

He had a hangdog look about him, Ralph observed. 'What's the matter with you, Nate?' he said. 'Have you brought my hoggets?'

'No, sir.'

'Why the devil not?'

'We've got none, sir. There are no sheep left in Wigleigh, except for a few old ewes.'

Ralph was shocked. 'Has someone stolen them?'

'No, but some have been given to you already, as heriot when their owners died, and then we couldn't find a tenant to take over Jack Shepherd's land, and many sheep died over the winter. Then there was no one to look to the early lambs this spring, so we lost most of those, and some of the mothers.'

'But this is impossible!' Ralph said angrily. 'How are noblemen to live if their serfs let the livestock perish?'

'We thought perhaps the plague was over, when it died down in January and February, but now it seems to be coming back.'

Ralph repressed a shudder of terror. Like everyone else, he had been thanking God that he had escaped the plague. Surely it could not return?

Nate went on: 'Perkin died this week, and his wife, Peg, and his son, Rob, and his son-in-law, Billy Howard. That's left Annet with all those acres to manage, which she can't possibly do.'

'Well, there must be a heriot due on that property, then.'

'There will be, when I can find a tenant to take it over.'

Parliament was in the process of passing new legislation to stop labourers flitting about the country demanding even higher wages. As soon as the ordinance became law, Ralph would enforce it and get his workers back. Even then, he now realized, he would be desperate to find tenants.

Nate said: 'I expect you've heard of the death of the earl.'

'No!' Ralph was shocked again.

'What's that?' Sir Gerald said. 'Earl William is dead?'

'Of the plague,' Nate explained.

Tilly said: 'Poor Uncle William!'

The baby sensed her mood and wailed.

Ralph spoke over the noise. 'When did this happen?'

'Only three days ago,' Nate replied.

Tilly gave the baby the nipple again, and he shut up.

'So William's elder son is the new earl,' Ralph mused. 'He can't be more than twenty.'

Nate shook his head. 'Rollo also died of the plague.'

'Then the younger son—'

'Dead too.'

'Both sons!' Ralph's heart leaped. It had always been his dream to become the earl of Shiring. Now the plague had given him the opportunity. And the plague had also improved his chances, for many likely candidates for the title had been wiped out.

He caught his father's eye. The same thought had occurred to Sir Gerald.

Tilly said: 'Rollo and Rick dead – it's so awful.' She began to cry.

Ralph ignored her and tried to think through the possibilities. 'Let's see, what surviving relatives are there?'

Gerald said to Nate: 'I presume the countess died too?'

'No, sir. Lady Philippa lives. So does her daughter, Odila.'

'Ah!' said Gerald. 'So, whoever the king chooses will have to marry Philippa in order to become earl.'

Ralph was thunderstruck. Since he was a lad he had dreamed of marrying Lady Philippa. Now there was an opportunity to achieve both his ambitions at one stroke.

But he was already married.

Gerald said: 'That's it, then.' He sat back in his chair, his excitement gone as quickly as it had come.

Ralph looked at Tilly, suckling their child and weeping at the same time. Fifteen years old and barely five feet tall, she stood like a castle wall between him and the future he had always yearned for.

He hated her.

*

EARL WILLIAM'S FUNERAL took place at Kingsbridge Cathedral. There were no monks except Brother Thomas, but Bishop Henri conducted the service and the nuns sang the hymns. Lady Philippa and Lady Odila, both heavily veiled, followed the coffin. Despite their dramatic black-clad presence, Ralph found the occasion lacked the momentous feeling that usually attended the funeral of a magnate, the sense of historical time passing by like the flow of a great river. Death was everywhere, every day, and even noble deaths were now commonplace.

He wondered whether someone in the congregation was infected, and was even now spreading the disease through his breath, or the invisible beams from his eyes. The thought made Ralph shaky. He had faced death many times, and learned to control his fear in battle; but this enemy could not be fought. The plague was an assassin who slid his long knife into people from behind then slipped away before he was spotted. Ralph shuddered and tried not to think about it.

Next to Ralph was the tall figure of Sir Gregory Longfellow, a lawyer who had been involved in suits concerning Kingsbridge in the past. Gregory was now a member of the king's council, an elite group of technical experts who advised the monarch – not on what he should do, for that was the job of Parliament, but on how he could do it.

Royal announcements were often made at church services, especially big ceremonies such as this. Today Bishop Henri took the opportunity to explain the new Ordinance of Labourers. Ralph guessed that Sir Gregory had brought the news and stayed to see how it was received.

Ralph listened attentively. He had never been summoned to Parliament, but he had talked about the labour crisis to Earl William, who had sat with the Lords, and to Sir Peter Jeffries, who represented Shiring in the Commons; so he knew what had been discussed.

'Every man must work for the lord of the village where he lives, and may not move to another village or work for another master, unless his lord should release him,' the bishop said.

Ralph rejoiced. He had known this was coming but he was delighted that at last it was official.

Before the plague there had never been a shortage of labourers. On the contrary, many villages had more than they knew what to do with. When landless men could find no paid work they sometimes threw themselves on the charity of the lord – which was an embarrassment to him, whether he helped them or not. So, if they wanted to move to another village, the lord was if anything relieved, and certainly had no need of legislation to keep them where they were. Now the labourers had the whip hand – a situation that obviously could not be allowed to continue.

There was a rumble of approval from the congregation at the

bishop's announcement. Kingsbridge folk themselves were not much affected, but those in the congregation who had come in from the countryside for the funeral were predominantly employers rather than employees. The new rules had been devised by and for them.

The bishop went on: 'It is now a crime to demand, to offer or to accept wages higher than those paid for similar work in 1347.'

Ralph nodded approval. Even labourers who stayed in the same village had been demanding more money. This would put a stop to that, he hoped.

Sir Gregory caught his eye. 'I see you nodding,' he said. 'Do you approve?'

'It's what we wanted,' Ralph said. 'I'll begin to enforce it in the next few days. There are a couple of runaways from my territory that I particularly want to bring home.'

'I'll come with you, if I may,' the lawyer said. 'I should like to see how things work out.'

# 69

THE PRIEST AT OUTHENBY HAD died of the plague, and there had been no services at the church since; so Gwenda was surprised when the bell began to toll on Sunday morning.

Wulfric went to investigate and came back to report that a visiting priest, Father Derek, had arrived; so Gwenda washed the boys' faces quickly and they all went out.

It was a fine spring morning, and the sun bathed the old grey stones of the little church in a clear light. All the villagers turned out, curious to view the newcomer.

Father Derek turned out to be a well-spoken city clergyman, too richly dressed for a village church. Gwenda wondered whether any special significance attached to his visit. Was there a reason why the church hierarchy had suddenly remembered the existence of this parish? She told herself that it was a bad habit always to imagine the worst, but all the same she felt something was wrong.

She stood in the nave with Wulfric and the boys, watching the priest go through the ritual, and her sense of doom grew stronger. A priest usually looked at the congregation while he was praying or singing, to emphasize that all this was for their benefit, not a private communication between himself and God; but Father Derek's gaze went over their heads.

She soon found out why. At the end of the service, he told them of a new law passed by the king and Parliament. 'Landless labourers must work for the lord in their village of origin, if required,' he said.

Gwenda was outraged. 'How can that be?' she shouted out. 'The lord is not obliged to help the labourer in hard times – I know, my father was a landless labourer, and when there was no work we went hungry. So how can the labourer owe loyalty to a lord who gives him nothing?'

A rumble of agreement broke out, and the priest had to raise his voice. 'This is what the king has decided, and the king is chosen by God to rule over us, so we must all do as he wishes.'

'Can the king change the custom of hundreds of years?' Gwenda persisted.

'These are difficult times. I know that many of you have come to Outhenby in the last few weeks—'

'Invited by the ploughman,' the voice of Carl Shaftesbury interrupted. His scarred face was livid with rage.

'Invited by all the villagers,' the priest acknowledged. 'And they were grateful to you for coming. But the king in his wisdom has ruled that this kind of thing must not go on.'

'And poor people must remain poor,' Carl said.

'God has ordained it so. Each man in his place.'

Harry Ploughman said: 'And has God ordained how we are to till our fields with no help? If all the newcomers leave, we will never finish the work.'

'Perhaps not all the newcomers will have to leave,' said Derek. 'The new law says only that they must go home if required.'

That quietened them. The immigrants were trying to figure out whether their lords would be able to track them down; the locals were wondering how many labourers would be left here. But Gwenda knew what her own future held. Sooner or later Ralph would come back for her and her family.

By then, she decided, they would be gone.

The priest retired and the congregation began to drift to the door. 'We've got to leave here,' Gwenda said to Wulfric in a low voice. 'Before Ralph comes back for us.'

'Where will we go?'

'I don't know – but perhaps that's better. If we don't know where we're going, no one else will.'

'But how will we live?'

'We'll find another village where they need labourers.'

'Are there many others, I wonder?'

He was always slower-thinking than she. 'There must be lots,' she said patiently. 'The king didn't pass this ordinance just for Outhenby.'

'Of course.'

'We should leave today,' she said decisively. 'It's Sunday, so we're not losing any work.' She glanced at the church windows, estimating the time of day. 'It's not yet noon – we could cover a good distance before nightfall. Who knows, we could be working in a new place tomorrow morning.'

'I agree,' Wulfric said. 'There's no telling how fast Ralph might move.'

'Say nothing to anyone. We'll go home, pick up whatever we want to take with us and just slip away.'

'All right.'

They reached the door and stepped outside into the sunshine, and Gwenda saw that it was already too late.

Six men on horseback were waiting outside the church: Ralph, his sidekick Alan, a tall man in London clothes, and three dirty, scarred, evil-looking ruffians of the kind that could be hired for a few pennies in any low tavern.

Ralph caught Gwenda's eye and smiled triumphantly.

Gwenda looked around desperately. A few days ago the men of the village had stood shoulder to shoulder against Ralph and Alan – but this was different. They were up against six men, not two. The villagers were unarmed, coming out of church, whereas previously they had been returning from the fields with tools in their hands. And, most important, on that first occasion they had believed they had right on their side, whereas today they were not so sure.

Several men met her eye and looked quickly away. That confirmed her suspicion. The villagers would not fight today.

Gwenda was so disappointed that she felt weak. Fearing that she might fall down, she leaned on the stonework of the church porch for support. Her heart had turned into something heavy and cold and damp, like a clod from a winter grave. A grim hopelessness possessed her completely.

For a few days they had been free. But it had just been a dream. And now the dream was over.

*

RALPH RODE SLOWLY through Wigleigh, leading Wulfric by a rope around his neck.

They arrived late in the afternoon. For speed, Ralph had let the two small boys ride, sharing the horses of the hired men. Gwenda was walking behind. Ralph had not bothered to tie her in any way. She could be relied upon to follow her children.

Because it was Sunday, most of the Wigleigh folk were outside their houses, enjoying the sun, as Ralph had anticipated. They all stared in horrified silence at the dismal procession. Ralph hoped the sight of Wulfric's humiliation might deter others from going in search of higher wages.

They reached the small manor house that had been Ralph's home before he moved to Tench Hall. He released Wulfric and sent him and his family off to their old home. He paid off the hired men, then took Alan and Sir Gregory into the manor house.

It was kept clean and ready for his visits. He ordered Vira to bring wine then prepare supper. It was too late now to go on to Tench: they could not get there before nightfall.

Gregory sat down and stretched out his long legs. He seemed like a man who could make himself comfortable anywhere. His straight dark hair was now tweeded with grey, but his long nose with its flared nostrils still gave him a supercilious look. 'How do you feel that went?' he said.

Ralph had been thinking about the new ordinance all the way home, and he had his answer ready. 'It's not going to work,' he said.

Gregory raised his eyebrows. 'Oh?'

Alan said. 'I agree with Sir Ralph.'

'Reasons?'

Ralph said: 'First of all, it's difficult to find out where the runaways have gone.'

Alan put in: 'It was only by luck that we traced Wulfric. Someone had overheard him and Gwenda planning where to go.'

'Second,' Ralph went on, 'recovering them is too troublesome.'

Gregory nodded. 'I suppose we have been all day at it.'

'And I had to hire those ruffians and get them horses. I can't spend my time and money chasing all over the countryside after runaway labourers.'

'I see that.'

'Third, what is to stop them running away again next week?'

Alan said: 'If they keep their mouths shut about where they're headed, we might never find them.'

'The only way it will work,' Ralph said, 'is if someone can go to a village, find out who the migrants are and punish them.'

Gregory said: 'You're talking about a sort of Commission of Labourers.'

'Exactly. Appoint a panel in each county, a dozen or so men who go from place to place ferreting out runaways.'

'You want someone else to do the work for you.'

It was a taunt, but Ralph was careful not to appear stung. 'Not necessarily – I'll be one of the commissioners, if you wish. It's just the way the job is to be done. You can't reap a field of grass one blade at a time.'

'Interesting,' said Gregory.

Vira brought a jug and some goblets, and poured wine for the three of them.

Gregory said: 'You're a shrewd man, Sir Ralph. You're not a Member of Parliament, are you?'

'No.'

'Pity. I think the king would find your counsel helpful.'

Ralph tried not to beam with pleasure. 'You're very kind.' He leaned forward. 'Now that Earl William is dead, there is of course a vacancy—' He saw the door open, and broke off.

Nate Reeve came in. 'Well done, Sir Ralph, if I may say so!' he said. 'Wulfric and Gwenda back in the fold, the two hardest-working people we've got.'

Ralph was annoyed with Nate for interrupting at such a crucial moment. He said irritably: 'I trust the village will now be able to pay more of its dues.'

'Yes, sir ... if they stay.'

Ralph frowned. Nate had immediately fastened on the weakness in his position. How was he going to keep Wulfric in Wigleigh? He could not chain a man to a plough all day and all night.

Gregory spoke to Nate. 'Tell me, bailiff, do you have a suggestion for your lord?'

'Yes, sir, I do.'

'I thought you might.'

Nate took that as an invitation. Addressing Ralph, he said: 'There is one thing you could do that would guarantee that Wulfric would stay here in Wigleigh until the day he dies.'

Ralph sensed a trick, but had to say: 'Go on.'

'Give him back the lands his father held.'

Ralph would have yelled at him, except that he did not want to give Gregory a bad impression. Controlling his anger, he said firmly: 'I don't think so.'

'I can't get a tenant for the land,' Nate persisted. 'Annet can't manage it, and she has no male relations living.'

'I don't care,' said Ralph. 'He can't have the land.'

Gregory said: 'Why not?'

Ralph did not want to admit that he still held a grudge against Wulfric because of a fight twelve years ago. Gregory had formed a good impression of Ralph, and Ralph did not want to spoil it. What would the king's counsellor think of a knight who acted against his own interests in pursuit of a boyhood squabble? He cast about for a plausible excuse. 'It would seem to be rewarding Wulfric for running away,' he said finally.

'Hardly,' said Gregory. 'From what Nate says, you'd be giving him something that no one else wants.'

'All the same, it sends the wrong signal to the other villagers.'

'I think you're being too scrupulous,' Gregory said. He was not the kind of man to keep his opinions tactfully to himself. 'Everyone must know you're desperate for tenants,' he went on. 'Most landlords are. The villagers will see that you're simply acting in your own interest, and consider that Wulfric is the lucky beneficiary.'

Nate added: 'Wulfric and Gwenda will work twice as hard if they've got their own land.'

Ralph felt cornered. He was desperate to look good in Gregory's eyes. He had started but not finished a discussion about the earldom. He could not put that at risk just because of Wulfric.

He had to give in.

'Perhaps you're right,' he said. He realized he was speaking through gritted teeth, and made an effort to be nonchalant. 'After all, he has been brought home and humiliated. That may be enough.'

'I'm sure it is.'

'All right, Nate,' Ralph said. For a moment words stuck in his throat, he hated so much to give Wulfric his heart's desire. But this was more important. 'Tell Wulfric he can have his father's lands back.'

'I'll do that before nightfall,' Nate said, and he left.

Gregory said: 'What were you saying about the earldom?'

Ralph picked his words carefully. 'After Earl Roland died at the battle of Crécy, I thought the king might have considered making me the earl of Shiring, especially as I had saved the life of the young prince of Wales.'

'But Roland had a perfectly good heir – who himself had two sons.'

'Exactly. And now all three are dead.'

'Hmm.' Gregory took a draught from his goblet. 'This is good wine.'

'Gascon,' said Ralph.

'I suppose it comes into Melcombe.'

'Yes.'

'Delicious.' Gregory drank some more. He seemed to be about to say something, so Ralph remained silent. Gregory took a long time choosing his words. At last he said: 'There is, somewhere in the neighbourhood of Kingsbridge, a letter that ... ought not to exist.'

Ralph was mystified. What was coming now?

Gregory went on: 'For many years, this document was in the hands of someone who could be relied upon, for various complicated reasons, to keep it safe. Lately, however, certain questions have been asked, suggesting to me that the secret may be in danger of getting out.'

All this was too enigmatic. Ralph said impatiently: 'I don't understand. Who has been asking embarrassing questions?'

'The prioress of Kingsbridge.'

'Oh.'

'It's possible she may have simply picked up some hint, and her questions may be harmless. But what the king's friends fear is that the letter may have got into her possession.'

'What is in the letter?'

Once again, Gregory chose his words warily, tiptoeing across a raging river on carefully placed stepping stones. 'Something touching the king's beloved mother.'

'Queen Isabella.' The old witch was still alive, living in splendour in her castle at Lynn, spending her days reading romances in her native French, so people said.

'In short,' said Gregory, 'I need to find out whether the prioress has this letter or not. But no one must know of my interest.'

Ralph said: 'Either you have to go to the priory and search through the nuns' documents … or the documents must come to you.'

'The second of those two.'

Ralph nodded. He was beginning to understand what Gregory wanted him to do.

Gregory said: 'I have made some very discreet inquiries, and discovered that no one knows exactly where the nuns' treasury is.'

'The nuns must know, or some of them.'

'But they won't say. However, I understand you're an expert in … persuading people to reveal secrets.'

So Gregory knew of the work Ralph had done in France. There was nothing spontaneous about this conversation, Ralph realized. Gregory must have planned it. In fact it was probably the real reason he had come to Kingsbridge. Ralph said: 'I may be able to help the king's friends solve this problem …'

'Good.'

'… if I were promised the earldom of Shiring as my reward.'

Gregory frowned. 'The new earl will have to marry the old countess.'

Ralph decided to hide his eagerness. Instinct told him that Gregory would have less respect for a man who was driven, even just partly, by lust for a woman. 'Lady Philippa is five years older than I am, but I have no objection to her.'

Gregory looked askance. 'She's a very beautiful woman,' he said. 'Whoever the king gives her to should think himself a lucky man.'

Ralph realized he had gone too far. 'I don't wish to appear indifferent,' he said hastily. 'She is indeed a beauty.'

'But I thought you were already married,' Gregory said. 'Have I made a mistake?'

Ralph caught Alan's eye, and saw that he was keenly curious to hear what Ralph would say next.

Ralph sighed. 'My wife is very ill,' he said. 'She hasn't long to live.'

*

GWENDA LIT the fire in the kitchen of the old house where Wulfric had lived since he was born. She found her cooking pots, filled one with water at the well and threw in some early onions, the first step in making a stew. Wulfric brought in more firewood. The boys happily went out to play with their old friends, unaware of the depth of the tragedy that had befallen their family.

Gwenda busied herself with household chores as the evening darkened outside. She was trying not to think. Everything that came into her mind just made her feel worse: the future, the past, her husband, herself. Wulfric sat and looked into the flames. Neither of them spoke.

Their neighbour, David Johns, appeared with a big jug of ale. His wife was dead of the plague, but his grown-up daughter, Joanna, followed him in. Gwenda was not happy to see them: she wanted to be miserable in private. But their intentions were kind, and it was impossible to spurn them. Gwenda glumly wiped the dust from some wooden cups, and David poured ale for everyone.

'We're sorry things worked out this way, but we're glad to see you,' he said as they drank.

Wulfric emptied his cup with one huge swallow and held it out for more.

A little later Aaron Appletree and his wife Ulla came in. She carried a basket of small loaves. 'I knew you wouldn't have any bread, so I made some,' she said. She handed them around and the house filled with the mouth-watering smell. David Johns poured them some ale, and they sat down. 'Where did you get the courage to run away?' Ulla asked admiringly. 'I would have died of fright!'

Gwenda began to tell the story of their adventures. Jack and Eli Fuller arrived from the mill, bringing a dish of pears baked in honey. Wulfric ate plenty and drank deep. The atmosphere lightened, and Gwenda's mood lifted a little. More neighbours came, each bringing a gift. When Gwenda told how the villagers of Outhenby with their spades and hoes had faced down Ralph and Alan, everyone rocked with delighted laughter.

Then she came to the events of today, and she descended into despair again. 'Everything was against us,' she said bitterly. 'Not just Ralph and his ruffians, but the king and the church. We had no chance.'

The neighbours nodded gloomily.

'And then, when he put a rope around my Wulfric's neck...' She was filled with bleak despair. Her voice cracked, and she could not go on. She took a gulp of ale and tried again. 'When he put a rope around Wulfric's neck – the strongest and bravest man I've ever known, any of us has ever known, led through the village like a beast, and that heartless, crass, bullying Ralph holding the rope – I just wanted the heavens to fall in and kill us all.'

These were strong words, but the others agreed. Of all the things the gentry could do to peasants – starve them, cheat them, assault them, rob them – the worst was to humiliate them. They never forgot it.

Suddenly Gwenda wanted the neighbours to leave. The sun had gone down and it was dusk outside. She needed to lie down and close her eyes and be alone with her thoughts. She did not want to talk even to Wulfric. She was about to ask everyone to go when Nate Reeve walked in.

The room went quiet.

'What do you want?' Gwenda said.

'I bring you good news,' he said brightly.

She made a sour face. 'There can be no good news for us today.'

'I disagree. You haven't heard it yet.'

'All right, what is it?'

'Sir Ralph says Wulfric is to have his father's lands back.'

Wulfric leaped to his feet. 'As a tenant?' he said. 'Not just to labour on?'

'As a tenant, on the same terms as your father,' said Nate

expansively, as if he were making the concession himself, rather than simply passing on a message.

Wulfric beamed with joy. 'That's wonderful!'

'Do you accept?' Nate said jovially, as if it were a mere formality.

Gwenda said: 'Wulfric! Don't accept!'

He looked at her, bewildered. As usual, he was slow to see beyond the immediate.

'Discuss the terms!' she urged him in a low voice. 'Don't be a serf like your father. Demand a free tenancy, with no feudal obligations. You'll never be in such a strong bargaining position again. Negotiate!'

'Negotiate?' he said. He wavered briefly, then gave in to the happiness of the occasion. 'This is the moment I've been hoping for for the last twelve years. I'm not going to negotiate.' He turned to Nate. 'I accept,' he said, and held up his cup.

They all cheered.

# 70

THE HOSPITAL WAS FULL AGAIN. The plague, which had seemed to retreat during the first three months of 1349, came back in April with redoubled virulence. On the day after Easter Sunday, Caris looked wearily at the rows of mattresses crammed together in a herringbone pattern, packed so tightly that the masked nuns had to step gingerly between them. Moving around was a little easier, however, because there were so few family members at the bedsides of the sick. Sitting with a dying relative was dangerous – you were likely to catch the plague yourself – and people had become ruthless. When the epidemic began, they had stayed with their loved ones regardless, mothers with children, husbands with wives, the middle-aged with their elderly parents, love overcoming fear. But that had changed. The most powerful of family ties had been viciously corroded by the acid of death. Nowadays the typical patient was brought in by a mother or father, a husband or wife, who then simply walked away, ignoring the piteous cries that followed them out. Only the nuns, with their face masks and their vinegar-washed hands, defied the disease.

Surprisingly, Caris was not short of help. The nunnery had enjoyed an influx of novices to replace the nuns who had died. This was partly because of Caris's saintly reputation. But the monastery was experiencing the same kind of revival, and Thomas now had a class of novice monks to train. They were all searching for order in a world gone mad.

This time the plague had struck some leading townspeople who had previously escaped. Caris was dismayed by the death of John Constable. She had never much liked his rough-and-ready approach to justice – which was to hit troublemakers over the head with a stick and ask questions afterwards – but it was going to be more difficult to maintain order without him. Fat Betty Baxter, baker of special buns for every town festivity, shrewd questioner at parish guild meetings, was dead, her business awkwardly shared out between four squabbling daughters. And Dick Brewer had died, the last of Caris's father's generation, a cohort of men who knew how to make money and how to enjoy it.

Caris and Merthin had been able to slow the spread of the disease by cancelling major public gatherings. There had been no big Easter procession in the cathedral, and there would be no Fleece Fair this Whitsun. The weekly market was held outside the city walls, in Lovers' Field, and most townspeople stayed away. Caris had wanted such measures when the plague first struck, but Godwyn and Elfric had opposed her. According to Merthin, some Italian cities had even closed their gates for a period of thirty or forty days, called a trentine or a quarantine. It was now too late to keep the disease out, but Caris still thought restrictions would save lives.

One problem she did not have was money. More and more people bequeathed their wealth to the nuns, having no surviving relatives, and many of the new novices brought with them lands, flocks, orchards and gold. The nunnery had never been so rich.

It was small consolation. For the first time in her life she felt tired – not just weary from hard work, but drained of energy, short of will power, enfeebled by adversity. The plague was worse than ever, killing two hundred people a week, and she did not know how she was going to carry on. Her muscles ached, her head hurt, and sometimes her vision seemed to blur. Where would it end, she wondered dismally. Would everyone die?

Two men staggered in through the door, both bleeding. Caris hurried forward. Before she got within touching distance she picked up the sweetly rotten smell of drink on them. They were both nearly helpless, although it was not yet dinner time. She groaned in frustration: this was all too common.

She knew the men vaguely: Barney and Lou, two strong youngsters employed in the abattoir owned by Edward Slaughterhouse. Barney had one arm hanging limp, possibly broken. Lou had a dreadful injury to his face: his nose was crushed and one eye was a ghastly pulp. Both seemed too drunk to feel pain. 'It was a fight,' Barney slurred, his words only just comprehensible. 'I didn't mean it. He's my best friend. I love him.'

Caris and Sister Nellie got the two drunks lying down on adjacent mattresses. Nellie examined Barney and said his arm was not broken but dislocated, and sent a novice to fetch Matthew Barber, the surgeon, who would try to relocate it. Caris bathed Lou's face. There was nothing she could do to save his eye: it had burst like a soft-boiled egg.

This kind of thing made her furious. The two men were not suffering from a disease or an accidental injury: they had harmed one another while drinking to excess. After the first wave of the plague, she had managed to galvanize the townspeople into restoring law and order; but the second wave had done something terrible to people's souls. When she called again for a return to civilized behaviour, the response had been apathetic. She did not know what to do next, and she felt so tired.

As she contemplated the two maimed men lying shoulder to shoulder on the floor, she heard a strange noise from outside. For an instant, she was transported back three years, to the battle of Crécy, and the terrifying booming sound made by King Edward's new machines that shot stone balls into the enemy ranks. A moment later the noise came again and she realized it was a drum – several drums, in fact, being struck in no particular rhythm. Then she heard pipes and bells whose notes failed to form any kind of tune; then hoarse cries, wailing, and shouts that might have indicated triumph or agony, or both. It was not unlike the noise of battle, but without the swish of deadly arrows or the screams of maimed horses. Frowning, she went outside.

A group of forty or so people had come on to the cathedral green, dancing a mad antic jig. Some played on musical instruments, or rather sounded them, for there was no melody or harmony to the noise. Their flimsy light-coloured clothes were ripped and stained, and some were half naked, carelessly exposing the intimate parts of their bodies. All those who did not have instruments were carrying whips. A crowd of townspeople followed, staring in curiosity and amazement.

The dancers were led by Friar Murdo, fatter than ever but

cavorting energetically, sweat pouring down his dirty face and dripping from his straggly beard. He led them to the great west door of the cathedral, where he turned to face them. 'We have all sinned!' he roared.

His followers cried out in response, inarticulate shrieks and groans.

'We are dirt!' he said thrillingly. 'We wallow in lasciviousness like pigs in filth. We yield, quivering with desire, to our fleshly lusts. We deserve the plague!'

'Yes!'

'What must we do?'

'Suffer!' they called. 'We must suffer!'

One of the followers dashed forward, flourishing a whip. It had three leather thongs, each of which appeared to have sharp stones attached to a knot. He threw himself at Murdo's feet and began to lash his own back. The whip tore the thin material of his robe and drew blood from the skin of his back. He cried out in pain, and the rest of Murdo's followers groaned in sympathy.

Then a woman came forward. She pulled her robe down to her waist and turned, exposing her bare breasts to the crowd; then lashed her bare back with a similar whip. The followers moaned again.

As they came forward in ones and twos, flogging themselves, Caris saw that many of them had bruises and half-healed cuts on their skin: they had done this before, some of them many times. Did they go from town to town repeating the performance? Given Murdo's involvement, she felt sure that sooner or later someone would start collecting money.

A woman in the watching crowd suddenly ran forward screaming: 'Me, too, I must suffer!' Caris was surprised to see that it was Mared, the browbeaten young wife of Marcel Chandler. Caris could not imagine that she had committed many sins, but perhaps she had at last seen a chance to make her life dramatic. She threw off her dress and stood stark naked before the friar. Her skin was unmarked, in fact she looked beautiful.

Murdo gazed at her for a long moment then said: 'Kiss my feet.'

She knelt in front of him, exposing her rear obscenely to the crowd, and lowered her face to his filthy feet.

He took a whip from another penitent and handed it to her. She lashed herself, then shrieked in pain, and red marks appeared instantly on her white skin.

Several more ran forward eagerly from the crowd, mostly men, and Murdo went through the same ritual with each. Soon there was an orgy. When they were not whipping themselves they were banging their drums and clanging their bells and dancing their fiendish jig.

Their actions had a mad abandon, but Caris's professional eye noted that the strokes of the whips, though dramatic and undoubtedly painful, did not appear to inflict permanent damage.

Merthin appeared beside Caris and said: 'What do you think of this?'

She frowned and said: 'Why does it make me feel indignant?'

'I don't know.'

'If people want to whip themselves, why should I object? Perhaps it makes them feel better.'

'I agree with you, though,' Merthin said. 'There's generally something fraudulent about anything Murdo is involved with.'

'That's not it.'

The mood here was not one of penitence, she decided. These dancers were not looking back contemplatively over their lives, feeling sorrow and regret for sins committed. People who genuinely repented tended to be quiet, thoughtful and undemonstrative. What Caris sensed in the air here was quite different. It was excitement.

'This is a debauch,' she said.

'Only instead of drink, they're overindulging in self-loathing.'

'And there's a kind of ecstasy in it.'

'But no sex.'

'Give them time.'

Murdo led the procession off again, heading out of the priory precincts. Caris noticed that some of the flagellants had produced bowls and were begging coins from the crowd. They would go through the principal streets of the town like this, she guessed.

They would probably finish up at one of the larger taverns, where people would buy them food and drink.

Merthin touched her arm. 'You look pale,' he said. 'How do you feel?'

'Just tired,' she said curtly. She had to soldier on regardless of how she felt, and it did not help her to be reminded of her tiredness. However, it was kind of him to notice, and she softened her tone to say: 'Come to the prior's house. It's almost dinner time.'

They walked across the green as the procession disappeared. They stepped inside the palace. As soon as they were alone, Caris put her arms around Merthin and kissed him. She suddenly felt very physical, and she thrust her tongue into his mouth, which she knew he liked. In response, he took both her breasts in his hands and squeezed gently. They had never kissed like this inside the palace, and Caris wondered vaguely whether something about Friar Murdo's bacchanal had weakened her normal inhibitions.

'Your skin is hot,' Merthin said in her ear.

She wanted Merthin to pull down her robe and put his mouth to her nipples. She felt she was losing control, and might find herself recklessly making love right here on the floor, where they might so easily be caught.

Then a girl's voice said: 'I didn't mean to spy.'

Caris was shocked. She sprang guiltily away from Merthin. She turned around, looking for the speaker. At the far end of the room, sitting on a bench, was a young woman holding a baby. It was Ralph Fitzgerald's wife. 'Tilly!' said Caris.

Tilly stood up. She looked exhausted and frightened. 'I'm so sorry to startle you,' she said.

Caris was relieved. Tilly had attended the nuns' school and lived at the nunnery for years, and she was fond of Caris. She could be trusted not to make a fuss about the kiss she had seen. But what was she doing here? 'Are you all right?' Caris said.

'I'm a bit tired,' Tilly said. She staggered, and Caris caught her arm.

The baby cried. Merthin took the child and rocked him expertly. 'There, there, my little nephew,' he said. The crying fell to a mild grizzle of discontent.

Caris said to Tilly: 'How did you get here?'

'I walked.'

'From Tench Hall? Carrying Gerry?' The baby was now six months old, and no easy burden.

'It took me three days.'

'My goodness. Has something happened?'

'I ran away.'

'Didn't Ralph come after you?'

'Yes, with Alan. I hid in the forest while they went by. Gerry was very good and didn't cry.'

The picture brought a lump to Caris's throat. 'But…' She swallowed. 'But why did you run away?'

'Because my husband wants to kill me,' Tilly said, and she burst into tears.

Caris sat her down and Merthin brought her a cup of wine. They let her sob. Caris sat on the bench beside her and put an arm around her shoulders while Merthin cradled baby Gerry. When at last Tilly had cried herself out, Caris said: 'What has Ralph done?'

Tilly shook her head. 'Nothing. It's just the way he looks at me. I know he wants to murder me.'

Merthin muttered: 'I wish I could say my brother is incapable of that.'

Caris said: 'But why would he want to do such a terrible thing?'

'I don't know,' Tilly said miserably. 'Ralph went to Uncle William's funeral. There was a lawyer from London there, Sir Gregory Longfellow.'

'I know him,' Caris said. 'A clever man, but I don't like him.'

'It started after that. I have a feeling it's all to do with Gregory.'

Caris said: 'You wouldn't have walked all this way, carrying a baby, because of something you just imagined.'

'I know it sounds fanciful, but he just sits and glares at me hatefully. How can a man look at his wife like that?'

'Well, you've come to the right place,' Caris said. 'You're safe here.'

'Can I stay?' she begged. 'You won't send me back, will you?'

'Certainly not,' said Caris. She caught Merthin's eye. She knew what he was thinking. It would be rash to give Tilly a guarantee. Fugitives might take refuge in churches, as a general principle, but it was very doubtful whether a nunnery had the right to shelter a knight's wife and keep her from him indefinitely. Moreover Ralph would certainly be entitled to make her give up the baby, his son and heir. All the same, Caris put as much confidence into her voice as she could and said: 'You can stay here just as long as you like.'

'Oh, thank you.'

Caris silently prayed that she would be able to keep her promise.

'You could live in one of the special guest rooms upstairs in the hospital,' she said.

Tilly looked troubled. 'But what if Ralph should come in?'

'He wouldn't dare. But if it makes you feel safer, you can have Mother Cecilia's old room, at the end of the nuns' dormitory.'

'Yes, please.'

A priory servant came in to lay the table for dinner. Caris said to Tilly: 'I'll take you to the refectory. You can have dinner with the nuns, then lie down in the dormitory and rest.' She stood up.

Suddenly she felt dizzy. She put a hand on the table to steady herself. Merthin, still holding baby Gerry, said anxiously: 'What's wrong?'

'I'll be fine in a moment,' Caris said. 'I'm just tired.'

Then she fell to the floor.

*

MERTHIN FELT a tidal wave of panic. For an instant, he was stunned. Caris had never been ill, never helpless – she was the one who took care of the sick. He could not think of her as a victim.

The moment passed like a blink. Fighting down his fear, he carefully handed the baby to Tilly.

The servant girl had stopped laying the table and stood staring in shock at the unconscious form of Caris on the floor. Merthin deliberately made his voice calm but urgent and said to her: 'Run to the hospital and tell them Mother Caris is ill. Bring Sister Oonagh. Go on, now, as quick as you can!' She hurried away.

Merthin knelt beside Caris. 'Can you hear me, my darling?' he said. He picked up her limp hand and patted it, then touched her cheek, then lifted an eyelid. She was out cold.

Tilly said: 'She's got the plague, hasn't she?'

'Oh, God.' Merthin took Caris in his arms. He was a slight man, but he had always been able to lift heavy objects, building stones and timber beams. He lifted her easily and stood upright, then laid her gently on the table. 'Don't die,' he whispered. 'Please don't die.'

He kissed her forehead. Her skin was hot. He had felt it when they embraced a few minutes ago, but he had been too excited to worry. Perhaps that was why she had been so passionate: fever could have that effect.

Sister Oonagh came in. Merthin was so grateful to see her that tears came to his eyes. She was a young nun, only a year or two out of her novitiate, but Caris thought highly of her nursing skill, and was grooming her to take responsibility for the hospital one day.

Oonagh wrapped a linen mask over her mouth and nose and tied it in a knot behind her neck. Then she touched Caris's forehead and cheek. 'Did she sneeze?' she said.

Merthin wiped his eyes. 'No,' he answered. He felt sure he would have noticed: a sneeze was an ominous sign.

Oonagh pulled down the front of Caris's robe. To Merthin she looked agonizingly vulnerable with her small breasts exposed. But he was glad to see there was no rash of purple-black spots on her chest. Oonagh covered her up again. She looked up Caris's nostrils. 'No bleeding,' she said. She felt Caris's pulse thoughtfully.

After a few moments she looked at Merthin. 'This may not be the plague, but it seems a serious illness. She's feverish, her pulse is rapid and her breathing is shallow. Carry her upstairs, lie her down and bathe her face with rose water. Anyone who attends her must wear a mask and wash their hands as if she had the plague. That includes you.' She gave him a linen strip.

Tears rolled down his face as he tied the mask. He carried

Caris upstairs, put her on the mattress in her room and straightened her clothing. The nuns brought rose water and vinegar. Merthin told them of Caris's instructions regarding Tilly, and they took the young mother and baby to the refectory. Merthin sat beside Caris, patting her forehead and cheeks with a rag damped with the fragrant liquid, praying for her to come round.

At last she did. She opened her eyes, frowned in puzzlement, then looked anxious and said: 'What happened?'

'You fainted,' he said.

She tried to sit up.

'Keep still,' he said. 'You're sick. It's probably not the plague, but you have a serious illness.'

She must have felt weak, for she lay back on the pillow without further protest. 'I'll just rest for an hour,' she said.

She was in bed for two weeks.

*

AFTER THREE DAYS the whites of her eyes turned the colour of mustard, and Sister Oonagh said she had the yellow jaundice. Oonagh prepared an infusion of herbs sweetened with honey, which Caris drank hot three times a day. The fever receded, but Caris remained weak. She inquired anxiously about Tilly every day, and Oonagh answered her questions, but refused to discuss any other aspect of life in the nunnery, in case it should tire Caris. Caris was too enfeebled to fight her.

Merthin did not leave the prior's palace. In the daytime he sat downstairs, close enough to hear her call, and his employees came to him for instructions about the various buildings they were putting up or tearing down. At night he lay on a mattress beside her and slept lightly, waking every time her breathing changed or she turned over in her bed. Lolla slept in the next room.

At the end of the first week, Ralph showed up.

'My wife has disappeared,' he said as he walked into the hall of the prior's palace.

Merthin looked up from a drawing he was making on a large slate. 'Hello, brother,' he said. Ralph looked shifty, he thought.

Clearly he had mixed feelings about Tilly's disappearance. He was not fond of her, but on the other hand no man likes his wife to run away.

Perhaps I have mixed feelings, too, Merthin thought guiltily. After all, I did help his wife to leave him.

Ralph sat on a bench. 'Have you got any wine? I'm parched.'

Merthin went to the sideboard and poured from a jug. It crossed his mind to say he had no idea where Tilly could be, but his instinct revolted from the idea of lying to his own brother, especially about something so important. Besides, Tilly's presence at the priory could not be kept secret: too many nuns, novices and employees had seen her here. It was always best to be honest, Merthin thought, except in dire emergency. Handing the cup to Ralph he said: 'Tilly is here, at the nunnery, with the baby.'

'I thought she might be.' Ralph lifted the cup in his left hand, showing the stumps of his three severed fingers. He took a long draught. 'What's the matter with her?'

'She ran away from you, Ralph.'

'You should have let me know.'

'I feel bad about that. But I couldn't betray her. She's frightened of you.'

'Why take sides with her against me? I'm your brother!'

'Because I know you. If she's scared, there's probably a reason.'

'This is outrageous.' Ralph was trying to appear indignant, but the act was unconvincing.

Merthin wondered what he really felt.

'We can't throw her out,' Merthin said. 'She's asked for sanctuary.'

'Gerry's my son and heir. You can't keep him from me.'

'Not indefinitely, no. If you start a legal action, I'm sure you'll win. But you wouldn't try to separate him from his mother, would you?'

'If he comes home, she will.'

That was probably true. Merthin was casting around for another way of persuading Ralph when Brother Thomas came in, bringing Alan Fernhill with him. With his one hand, Thomas was holding Alan's arm, as if to prevent him from running away. 'I found him snooping,' he said.

'I was just looking around,' Alan protested. 'I thought the monastery was empty.'

Merthin said: 'As you see, it's not. We've got one monk, six novices and a couple of dozen orphan boys.'

Thomas said: 'Anyway, he wasn't in the monastery, he was in the nuns' cloisters.'

Merthin frowned. He could hear a psalm being sung in the distance. Alan had timed his incursion well: all the nuns and novices were in the cathedral for the service of Sext. Most of the priory buildings were deserted at this hour. Alan had probably been walking around unhindered for some time.

This did not seem like idle curiosity.

Thomas added: 'Fortunately, a kitchen hand saw him and came to fetch me out of the church.'

Merthin wondered what Alan had been looking for. Tilly? Surely he would not have dared to snatch her from a nunnery in broad daylight. He turned to Ralph. 'What are you two plotting?'

Ralph batted the question off to Alan. 'What did you think you were doing?' he said wrathfully, though Merthin thought the anger was faked.

Alan shrugged. 'Just looking around while I waited for you.'

It was not plausible. Idle men-at-arms waited for their masters in stables and taverns, not cloisters.

Ralph said: 'Well ... don't do it again.'

Merthin realized that Ralph was going to stick with this story. I was honest with him, but he's not being honest with me, he thought sadly. He returned to the more important subject. 'Why don't you leave Tilly be for a while?' he said to Ralph. 'She'll be perfectly all right here. And perhaps, after a while, she'll realize you mean her no harm, and come back to you.'

'It's too shaming,' Ralph said.

'Not really. A noblewoman sometimes spends a few weeks at a monastery, if she feels the need to retire from the world for a while.'

'Usually when she's been widowed, or her husband has gone off to war.'

'Not always, though.'

'When there's no obvious reason, people always say she wants to get away from her husband.'

'How bad is that? You might like some time away from your wife.'

'Perhaps you're right,' Ralph said.

Merthin was startled by this response. He had not expected Ralph to be so easily persuaded. It took him a moment to get over the surprise. Then he said: 'That's it. Give her three months, then come back and talk to her.' Merthin had a feeling that Tilly would never relent, but at least this proposal would postpone the crisis.

'Three months,' said Ralph. 'All right.' He stood up to go.

Merthin shook his hand. 'How are Mother and Father? I haven't seen them for months.'

'Getting old. Father doesn't leave their house now.'

'I'll come and visit as soon as Caris is better. She's recovering from yellow jaundice.'

'Give her my best wishes.'

Merthin went to the door and watched Ralph and Alan ride away. He felt deeply disturbed. Ralph was up to something, and it was not simply getting Tilly back.

He returned to his drawing and sat staring at it without seeing it for a long time.

*

By the end of the second week it was clear that Caris was going to get better. Merthin was exhausted but happy. Feeling like a man reprieved, he put Lolla to bed early and went out for the first time.

It was a mild spring evening, and the sun and balmy air made him light-headed. His own tavern, the Bell, was closed for rebuilding, but the Holly Bush was doing brisk business, customers sitting on benches outside with their tankards. There were so many people out enjoying the weather that Merthin stopped and asked the drinkers if it was a holiday today, thinking he might have lost track of the date. 'Every day's a holiday now,' one said. 'What's the point in working, when we're all going to die of the plague? Have a cup of ale.'

'No, thanks.' Merthin walked on.

He noticed that many people wore very fancy clothes, elaborate headgear and embroidered tunics that they would not normally have been able to afford. He presumed they had inherited these garments, or perhaps just taken them from wealthy corpses. The effect was a bit nightmarish: velvet hats on filthy hair, gold threads and food stains, ragged hose and jewel-encrusted shoes.

He saw two men dressed all in women's clothing, floor-length gowns and wimples. They were walking along the main street arm in arm, like merchants' wives showing off their wealth – but they were unmistakably male, with big hands and feet and hair on their chins. Merthin began to feel disoriented, as if nothing could be relied on any more.

As the dusk thickened, he crossed the bridge to Leper Island. He had built a street of shops and taverns there, between the two parts of the bridge. The work was finished, but the buildings were untenanted, with boards nailed across their doors and windows to keep vagrants out. No one lived there but rabbits. The premises would remain empty until the plague died out and Kingsbridge returned to normal, Merthin supposed. If the plague never went away, they would never be occupied; but, in that eventuality, renting his property would be the least of his worries.

He returned to the old city just as the gate was closing. There seemed to be a huge party going on at the White Horse inn. The house was full of lights, and the crowd filled the road in front of the building. 'What's going on?' Merthin asked a drinker.

'Young Davey's got the plague, and he has no heirs to bequeath the inn to, so he's giving all the ale away,' the man said, grinning with delight. 'Drink as much as you can hold, it's free!'

He and many other people had clearly been working on the same principle, and dozens of them were reeling drunk. Merthin pushed his way into the crowd. Someone was banging a drum and others were dancing. He saw a circle of men and looked over their shoulders to see what they were hiding. A very drunk woman of about twenty years was bending over a table while a man entered her from behind. Several other men were clearly waiting their turn. Merthin turned away in distaste. At the side of the building, half concealed by empty barrels, his eye lit on Ozzie Ostler, a wealthy horse dealer, kneeling in front of a younger man and sucking his penis. That was against the law, in fact the penalty was death, but clearly no one cared. Ozzie, a married man who was on the parish guild, caught Merthin's eye but did not stop, in fact he continued with more enthusiasm, as if excited by being watched. Merthin shook his head, amazed. Just outside the tavern door was a table laden with partly eaten food: joints of roasted meat, smoked fish, puddings and cheese. A dog was standing on the table tearing at a ham. A man was throwing up into a bowl of stew. Beside the tavern door Davey Whitehorse sat in a big wooden chair with a huge cup of wine. He was sneezing and sweating, and the characteristic trickle of blood came from his nose, but he was looking around and cheering the revellers on. He seemed to want to kill himself with drink before the plague finished him off.

Merthin felt nauseated. He left the scene and hurried back to the priory.

To his surprise, he found Caris up and dressed. 'I'm better,' she said. 'I'm going to return to my usual work tomorrow.' Seeing his sceptical look, she added: 'Sister Oonagh said I could.'

'If you're taking orders from someone else, you can't be back to normal,' he said; and she laughed. The sight brought tears to his eyes. She had not laughed for two weeks, and there had been moments when he had wondered whether he would ever hear the sound again.

'Where have you been?' she asked.

He told her about his walk around the town, and the disturbing sights he had seen. 'None of it was very wicked,' he said. 'I just wonder what they'll do next. When all their inhibitions have gone, will they start to kill one another?'

A kitchen hand brought a tureen of soup for their supper. Caris sipped warily. For a long time, all food had made her feel sick. However, she seemed to find the leek soup palatable, and drank a bowlful.

When the maid had cleared away, Caris said: 'While I was ill, I thought a lot about dying.'

'You didn't ask for a priest.'

'Whether I've been good or bad, I don't think God will be fooled by a last-minute change of heart.'

'What, then?'

'I asked myself if there was anything I really regretted.'

'And was there?'

'Lots of things. I'm bad friends with my sister. I haven't any children. I lost that scarlet cloak my father gave my mother on the day she died.'

'How did you lose it?'

'I wasn't allowed to bring it with me when I entered the nunnery. I don't know what happened to it.'

'What was your biggest regret?'

'There were two. I haven't built my hospital; and I've spent too little time in bed with you.'

He raised his eyebrows. 'Well, the second one is easily rectified.'

'I know.'

'What about the nuns?'

'Nobody cares any more. You saw what it was like in the town. Here in the nunnery, we're too busy dealing with the dying to fuss about the old rules. Joan and Oonagh sleep together every night in one of the upstairs rooms of the hospital. It doesn't matter.'

Merthin frowned. 'It's odd that they do that, and still go to church services in the middle of the night. How do they reconcile the two things?'

'Listen. St Luke's Gospel says: "He that hath two coats, let him impart to him that hath none." How do you think the bishop of Shiring reconciles that with his chest full of robes? Everybody takes what they like from the teachings of the church, and ignores the parts that don't suit them.'

'And you?'

'I do the same, but I'm honest about it. So I'm going to live with you, as your wife, and if anyone questions me I shall say that these are strange times.' She got up, went to the door and barred it. 'You've been sleeping here for two weeks. Don't move out.'

'You don't have to lock me in,' he said with a laugh. 'I'll stay voluntarily.' He put his arms around her.

She said: 'We started something a few minutes before I fainted. Tilly interrupted us.'

'You were feverish.'

'In that way, I still am.'

'Perhaps we should pick up where we left off.'

'We could go to bed first.'

'All right.'

Holding hands, they went up the stairs.

# 71

Ralph and his men hid in the forest north of Kingsbridge, waiting. It was May, and the evenings were long. When night fell Ralph encouraged the others to take a nap while he sat up, watching.

With him were Alan Fernhill and four hired men, soldiers demobilized from the king's army, fighters who had failed to find their niche in peacetime. Alan had hired them at the Red Lion in Gloucester. They did not know who Ralph was and had never seen him in daylight. They would do as they were told, take their money, and ask no questions.

Ralph stayed awake, noting the passing of time automatically, as he had when with the king in France. He had found that, if he tried too hard to figure out how many hours had gone by, he became doubtful; but, if he simply guessed, what came into his head was always right. Monks used a burning candle, marked with rings for the hours, or an hourglass with sand or water trickling through a narrow funnel; but Ralph had a better measure in his head.

He sat very still, with his back to a tree, staring into the low fire they had built. He could hear the rustle of small animals in the undergrowth and the occasional hoot of a predatory owl. He never felt so calm as in the waiting hours before action. There was quiet, and darkness, and time to think. The knowledge of danger to come, which made most men jumpy, actually soothed him.

The main risk tonight did not in fact come from the hazards of fighting. There would be some hand-to-hand combat, but the enemy would consist of fat townsmen or soft-skinned monks. The real peril was that Ralph might be recognized. What he was about to do was shocking. It would be talked of with outrage in every church in the land, perhaps in Europe. Gregory Longfellow, for whom Ralph was doing this, would be the loudest in condemning it. If the fact ever got out that Ralph was the villain, he would be hanged.

But if he succeeded, he would be the earl of Shiring.

When he judged it was two hours past midnight, he roused the others.

They left their tethered horses and walked out of the woodland and along the road to the city. Alan was carrying the equipment, as he always had when they fought in France. He had a short ladder, a coil of rope, and a grappling iron they had used when attacking city walls in Normandy. In his belt were a mason's chisel and a hammer. They might not need these tools, but they had learned that it was best to be prepared.

Alan also had several large sacks, rolled up tightly and tied with string in a bundle.

When they came within sight of the city, Ralph gave out hoods with holes for the eyes and mouth, and they all put them on. Ralph also wore a mitten on his left hand, to conceal the telltale stumps of his three missing fingers. He was completely unrecognizable – unless, of course, he should be captured.

They all pulled felt bags over their boots, tying them to their knees, to muffle their footsteps.

It was hundreds of years since Kingsbridge had been attacked by an army, and security was slack, especially since the advent of the plague. Nevertheless, the southern entrance to the town was firmly closed. At the townward end of Merthin's great bridge was a stone gatehouse barred with a mighty wooden door. But the river defended the town only on the east and south sides. To the north and west no bridge was needed, and the town was protected by a wall that was in poor repair. That was why Ralph was approaching from the north.

Mean houses huddled outside the walls like dogs at the back of a butcher's shop. Alan had scouted the route several days ago, when the two of them had come to Kingsbridge and inquired about Tilly. Now Ralph and the hired men followed Alan, padding between the hovels as quietly as possible. Even paupers in the suburbs could raise the alarm if awakened. A dog barked, and Ralph tensed, but someone cursed the animal and it fell silent. In another moment they came to a place where the wall was broken down and they could easily clamber over the fallen stones.

They found themselves in a narrow alley behind some warehouses. It came out just inside the north gate of the city. At the gate, Ralph knew, was a sentry in a booth. The six men approached silently. Although they were now within the walls, a sentry would question them if he saw them, and shout for help if he was not satisfied with their answers. But, to Ralph's relief, the man was fast asleep, sitting on a stool and leaning against the side of his box, a stub of candle guttering on a shelf beside him.

All the same, Ralph decided not to risk the man's waking up. He tiptoed close, leaned into the booth, and slit the sentry's throat with a long knife. The man woke up and tried to scream with pain, but all that came out of his mouth was blood. As he slumped, Ralph caught him and held him for the few moments it took him to lose consciousness. Then he propped the body back up against the wall of the booth.

He wiped his bloody blade on the dead man's tunic and sheathed the knife.

The large double door that stopped the gateway had within it a smaller, man-sized doorway. Ralph unbarred this little door, ready for a quick getaway later.

The six men walked silently along the street that led to the priory.

There was no moon – Ralph had chosen tonight for that reason – but they were faintly lit by starlight. He looked anxiously at the upstairs windows of the houses on either side. If sleepless people happened to look out, they would see the unmistakably sinister sight of six masked men. Fortunately it was not quite warm enough to leave windows open at night, and all the shutters were closed. Just the same, Ralph pulled up the hood of his cloak and dragged it forward as far as it would go, in the hope of shadowing his face and concealing the mask; then he signed to the others to do the same.

This was the city where he had spent his adolescence, and the streets were familiar. His brother Merthin still lived here, although Ralph was not sure exactly where.

They went down the main street, past the Holly Bush, closed

for the night and locked up hours ago. They turned into the cathedral close. The entrance had tall ironbound timber gates, but they stood open, not having been closed for years, their hinges rusted and seized up.

The priory was dark except for a dim light in the windows of the hospital. Ralph reckoned this would be the time when the monks and nuns were sleeping most deeply. In an hour or so they would be wakened for the service of Matins, which started and finished before dawn.

Alan, who had reconnoitred the priory, led the team around the north side of the church. They walked silently through the graveyard and past the prior's palace, then turned along the narrow strip of land that divided the east end of the cathedral from the river bank. Alan propped his short ladder up against a blank wall and whispered: 'Nuns' cloisters. Follow me.'

He went up the wall and over the roof. His feet made little noise on the slates. Happily, he did not need to use the grappling iron, which might have made an alarming clang.

The others followed, Ralph last.

On the inside, they dropped from the roof and landed with soft thumps on the turf of the quadrangle. Once there, Ralph looked warily at the regular stone columns of the cloisters around him. The arches seemed to stare at him like watchmen, but nothing stirred. It was a good thing monks and nuns were not allowed to have pet dogs.

Alan led them around the deep-shadowed walkway and through a heavy door. 'Kitchen,' he whispered. The room was dimly lit by the embers of a big fire. 'Move slowly so that you don't knock over any pots.'

Ralph waited, letting his eyes adjust. Soon he could make out the outlines of a big table, several barrels and a stack of cooking vessels. 'Find somewhere to sit or lie down, and try to make yourselves comfortable,' he said to them. 'We stay here until they all get up and go into the church.'

*

PEERING OUT OF the kitchen an hour later, Ralph counted the nuns and novices shuffling out of the dormitory and heading through the cloisters towards the cathedral, some carrying lamps that threw antic shadows on the vaulted ceiling. 'Twenty-five,' he whispered to Alan. As he had expected, Tilly was not among them. Visiting noblewomen were not expected to attend services in the middle of the night.

When they had all disappeared, he moved. The others remained behind.

There were only two places where Tilly might be sleeping: the hospital, and the nuns' dormitory. Ralph had guessed she would feel safer in the dormitory, and headed there first.

He went softly up the stone steps, his boots still muffled by felt overshoes. He peeped into the dorm. It was lit by a single candle. He was hoping that all the nuns would be in the church, for he did not want miscellaneous people confusing the situation. He was afraid one or two might have stayed behind, because of illness or laziness. But the room was empty – not even Tilly was there. He was about to retreat when he saw a door at the far end.

He padded the length of the dormitory, picking up the candle, and went through the door silently. The unsteady light revealed the young head of his wife on a pillow, her hair in disarray around her face. She looked so innocent and pretty that Ralph felt a stab of remorse, and had to remind himself of how much he hated her for standing in the way of his advancement.

The baby, his son Gerry, lay in a crib next to her, eyes closed, mouth open, sleeping peacefully.

Ralph crept closer and, with a swift movement, clamped his right hand hard over Tilly's mouth, waking her and at the same time stopping her making any noise.

Tilly opened her eyes wide and stared at him in dread.

He put the candle down. In his pocket he had an assortment of useful odds and ends, including rags and leather thongs. He stuffed a rag into Tilly's mouth to keep her quiet. Despite his mask and glove, he had a feeling she recognized him, even though he had not spoken. Perhaps she could smell him, like a dog. It did not matter. She was not going to tell anyone.

He tied her hands and feet with leather thongs. She was not struggling now, but she would later. He checked that her gag was secure. Then he settled down to wait.

He could hear the singing from the church: a strong choir of females, and a ragged few male voices trying to match them. Tilly kept staring at him with big, pleading eyes. He turned her over so that he could not see her face.

She had guessed he was going to kill her. She had read his mind. She must be a witch. Perhaps all women were witches. Anyway, she had known his intention almost as soon as he had formed it. She had started to watch him, especially in the evenings, her fearful eyes following him around the room, no matter what he did. She had lain stiff and alert beside him at night while he fell asleep, and in the mornings when he awoke she was invariably up already. Then, after a few days of this, she had disappeared. Ralph and Alan had searched for her without success, then he had heard a rumour that she had taken refuge in Kingsbridge Priory.

Which happened to fit in with his plans very neatly.

The baby snuffled in his sleep, and it occurred to Ralph that he might cry. What if the nuns came back just then? He thought it through. One or two would probably come in here to see if Tilly needed help. He would just kill them, he decided. It would not be the first time. He had killed nuns in France.

At last he heard them shuffling back into the dormitory.

Alan would be watching from the kitchen, counting them as they returned. When they were all safely inside the room, Alan and the other four men would draw their swords and make their move.

Ralph lifted Tilly to her feet. Her face was streaked with tears. He turned her so that her back was to him, then put an arm around her waist and lifted her, hoisting her on to his hip. She was as light as a child.

He drew his long dagger.

From outside, he heard a man say: 'Silence, or you die!' It was Alan, he knew, although the hood muffled the voice.

This was a crucial moment. There were other people on the premises – nuns and patients in the hospital, monks in their own quarters – and Ralph did not want them to appear and complicate matters.

Despite Alan's warning, there were several shouts of shock

and shrieks of fear – but, Ralph thought, not too loud. So far, so good.

He threw open the door and stepped into the dormitory carrying Tilly on his hip.

He could see by the light of the nuns' lamps. At the far end of the room, Alan had a woman in his grasp, his knife to her throat, in the same pose as Ralph with Tilly. Two more men stood behind Alan. The other two hirelings would be on guard at the foot of the stairs.

'Listen to me,' Ralph said.

When he spoke, Tilly jerked convulsively. She had recognized his voice. But that did not matter so long as no one else did.

There was a terrified silence.

Ralph said: 'Which of you is treasurer?'

No one spoke.

Ralph touched the edge of his blade to the skin of Tilly's throat. She began to struggle, but she was too small, and he held her easily. Now, he thought, now is the time to kill her; but he hesitated. He had killed many people, women as well as men, but suddenly it seemed terrible to stick a knife into the warm body of someone he had embraced and kissed and slept with, the woman who had borne his child.

Also, he told himself, the effect on the nuns would be more shocking if one of their own died.

He nodded to Alan.

With one strong cut, Alan slit the throat of the nun he was holding. Blood gushed out of her neck on to the floor.

Someone screamed.

It was not merely a cry or a shriek, but a fortissimo yell of pure terror that might have awakened the dead, and it went on until one of the hired men hit the screamer a mighty blow over her head with his club and she fell unconscious to the floor, blood trickling down her cheek.

Ralph said again: 'Which of you is treasurer?'

*

MERTHIN HAD WOKEN UP briefly when the bell rang for Matins and Caris slipped out of bed. As usual, he turned over and fell into a light doze, so that when she returned it seemed as if she had been away only for a minute or two. She was cold when she got back into bed, and he drew her to him and wrapped his arms around her. They often stayed awake for a while, talking, and usually made love before going to sleep. It was Merthin's favourite time.

She pressed up against him, her breasts squashed comfortably against his chest. He kissed her forehead. When she had warmed up, he reached between her legs and gently stroked the soft hair there.

But she was feeling talkative. 'Did you hear yesterday's rumour? Outlaws in the woods north of town.'

'It seems a bit unlikely,' he said.

'I don't know. The walls are decrepit on that side.'

'But what are they going to steal? Anything they want is theirs for the taking. If they need meat, there are thousands of sheep and cattle unguarded in the fields, with no one to claim ownership.'

'That's what makes it strange.'

'These days, stealing is like leaning over the fence to breathe your neighbour's air.'

She sighed. 'Three months ago I thought this terrible plague was over.'

'How many more people have we lost?'

'We've buried a thousand since Easter.'

That seemed about right to Merthin. 'I hear that other towns are similar.'

He felt her hair move against his shoulder as she nodded in the dark. She said: 'I believe something like a quarter of the population of England is gone already.'

'And more than half the priests.'

'That's because they make contact with so many people every time they hold a service. They can hardly escape.'

'So half the churches are closed.'

'A good thing, if you ask me. I'm sure crowds spread the plague faster than anything.'

'Anyway, most people have lost respect for religion.'

To Caris, that was no great tragedy. She said: 'Perhaps they'll stop believing in mumbo-jumbo medicine, and start thinking about what treatments actually make a difference.'

'You say that, but it's hard for ordinary people to know what is a genuine cure and what a false remedy.'

'I'll give you four rules.'

He smiled in the dark. She always had a list. 'All right.'

'One: If there are dozens of different remedies for a complaint, you can be sure none of them works.'

'Why?'

'Because if one worked, people would forget the rest.'

'Logical.'

'Two: Just because a remedy is unpleasant doesn't mean it's any good. Raw larks' brains do nothing for a sore throat, even though they make you heave; whereas a nice cup of hot water and honey will soothe you.'

'That's good to know.'

'Three: Human and animal dung never does anyone any good. It usually makes them worse.'

'I'm relieved to hear it.'

'Four: If the remedy looks like the disease – the spotted feathers of a thrush for the pox, say, or sheep's urine for yellow jaundice – it's probably imaginative rubbish.'

'You should write a book about this.'

She made a scornful noise. 'Universities prefer ancient Greek texts.'

'Not a book for university students. One for people like you – nuns and midwives and barbers and wise women.'

'Wise women and midwives can't read.'

'Some can, and others have people who can read for them.'

'I suppose people might like a little book that tells them what to do about the plague.'

She was thoughtful for a few moments.

In the silence, there was a scream.

'What was that?' Merthin said.

'It sounded like a shrew being caught by an owl,' she said.

'No, it didn't,' he said, and he got up.

*

One of the nuns stepped forward and addressed Ralph. She was young – they were nearly all young – with black hair and blue eyes. 'Please don't hurt Tilly,' she begged. 'I'm Sister Joan, the treasurer. We'll give you anything you want. Please don't do any more violence.'

'I am Tam Hiding,' Ralph said. 'Where are the keys to the nuns' treasury?'

'I have them here on my belt.'

'Take me there.'

Joan hesitated. Perhaps she sensed that Ralph did not know where the treasury was. On their reconnaissance trip, Alan had been able to scout the nunnery quite thoroughly before he was caught. He had plotted their way in, identified the kitchen as a good hiding place, and located the nuns' dormitory; but he had not been able to find the treasury. Clearly Joan did not want to reveal its location.

Ralph had no time to lose. He did not know who might have heard that scream. He pressed the point of his knife into Tilly's throat until it drew blood. 'I want to go to the treasury,' he said.

'All right, just don't hurt Tilly! I'll show you the way.'

'I thought you would,' Ralph said.

He left two of the hired men in the dormitory to keep the nuns quiet. He and Alan followed Joan down the steps to the cloisters, taking Tilly.

At the foot of the stairs, the other two hired men were detaining at knife point three more nuns. Ralph guessed that those on duty in the hospital had come to investigate the scream. He was pleased: another threat had been neutralized. But where were the monks?

He sent the extra nuns up into the dormitory. He left one hired man on guard at the foot of the stairs and took the other with him.

Joan led them into the refectory, which was at ground level directly under the dorm. Her flickering lamp revealed trestle tables, benches, a lectern and a wall painting of Jesus at a wedding feast.

At the far end of the room Joan moved a table to reveal a trapdoor in the floor. It had a keyhole just like a normal upright door. She turned a key in the lock and lifted the trapdoor. It gave on to a narrow spiral of stone steps. She descended the stairs. Ralph left the hired man on guard and went down, awkwardly carrying Tilly, and Alan followed him.

Ralph reached the bottom of the staircase and looked around him with a satisfied air. This was the holy of holies, the nuns' secret treasury. It was a cramped underground room like a dungeon, but better built: the walls were of ashlar, smoothly squared-off stones as used in the cathedral, and the floor was paved with closely set flagstones. The air felt cool and dry. Ralph put Tilly, trussed like a chicken, on the floor.

Most of the room was taken up by a huge lidded box, like a coffin for a giant, chained to a ring in the wall. There was not much else: two stools, a writing desk, and a shelf bearing a stack of parchment rolls, presumably the nunnery's account books. On a hook on the wall hung two heavy wool coats, and Ralph guessed they were for the treasurer and her assistant to wear when working down here in the coldest months of the winter.

The box was far too large to have come down the staircase. It must have been brought here in pieces and assembled in situ. Ralph pointed to the clasp, and Joan unlocked it with another of the keys on her belt.

Ralph looked inside. There were scores more parchment rolls, obviously all the charters and title deeds that proved the nunnery's ownership of its property and rights; a pile of leather and wool bags that undoubtedly held jewelled ornaments; and another, smaller chest that probably contained money.

At this point he had to be subtle. His object was those charters, but he did not want that to be apparent. He had to steal them, but appear not to have done so.

He ordered Joan to open the small chest. It contained a few gold coins. Ralph was puzzled by how little money there was. Perhaps more was hidden somewhere in this room, possibly behind stones in the wall. However, he did not stop to ponder: he was only pretending to be interested in the money. He poured the coins into the purse at his belt. Meanwhile, Alan unrolled a capacious sack and began filling it with cathedral ornaments.

Having let Joan see that, Ralph ordered her back up the stairs.

Tilly was still here, watching with wide, terrified eyes, but it did not matter what she saw. She would never have a chance to tell.

Ralph unrolled another sack and began loading the parchment rolls into it as fast as he could.

When they had bagged everything, Ralph told Alan to break up the wooden chests with his hammer and chisel. He took the wool coats from the hook, bundled them up, and held the tip of his candle flame to the bundle. The wool caught fire immediately. He piled wood from the chests on top of the burning wool. Soon there was a merry bonfire, and the smoke caught in his throat.

He looked at Tilly, lying helpless on the floor. He drew his knife. Then, once again, he hesitated.

*

FROM THE PRIOR'S palace, a small door led directly into the chapter house, which itself communicated with the north transept of the cathedral. Merthin and Caris took this route in their search for the source of the scream. The chapter house was empty, and they went into the church. Their single candle was too dim to illuminate the vast interior, but they stood in the centre of the crossing and listened hard.

They heard the click of a latch.

Merthin said: 'Who's there?' and was ashamed of the fear that made his voice tremble.

'Brother Thomas,' they heard.

The voice came from the south transept. A moment later Thomas moved into the light of their candle. 'I thought I heard someone scream,' he said.

'So did we. But there's no one here in the church.'

'Let's look around.'

'What about the novices, and the boys?'

'I told them to go back to sleep.'

They passed through the south transept into the monks' cloisters. Once again they saw no one and heard nothing. From here, they followed a passage through the kitchen stores to the hospital. The patients lay in their beds as normal, some sleeping and some moving and groaning in pain – but, Merthin realized after a moment, there were no nuns in the room.

'This is strange,' said Caris.

The scream might have come from here, but there was no sign of emergency, or of any kind of disturbance.

They went into the kitchen, which was deserted, as they would have expected.

Thomas sniffed deeply, as if trying to pick up a scent.

Merthin said: 'What is it?' He found himself whispering.

'Monks are clean,' Thomas murmured in reply. 'Someone dirty has been here.'

Merthin could not smell anything unusual.

Thomas picked up a cleaver, the kind a cook would use to chop through meat and bones.

They went to the kitchen door. Thomas held up the stump of his left arm in a warning gesture and they halted. There was a faint light in the nuns' cloisters. It seemed to be coming from the recess at the near end. It was the reflected gleam of a distant candle, Merthin guessed. It might be coming from the nuns' refectory, or from the flight of stone steps that led up to their dormitory; or both.

Thomas stepped out of his sandals and went forward, his bare feet making no sound on the flagstones. He melted into the shadows of the cloister. Merthin could just about make him out as he edged towards the recess.

A faint but pungent aroma came to Merthin's nose. It was not the smell of dirty bodies that Thomas had detected in the kitchen, but something quite different and new. A moment later Merthin identified it as smoke.

Thomas must have picked it up too, for he froze in place up against the wall.

Someone unseen gave a grunt of surprise, then a figure stepped out from the recess into the cloister walk, faintly but clearly visible, the weak light outlining the silhouette of a man with some kind of hood covering his entire head and face. The man turned towards the refectory door.

Thomas struck.

The cleaver glinted briefly in the dark, then there was a sickening thud as it sank into the man's body. He gave a shout of terror and pain. As he fell Thomas swung again, and the man's cry turned into a sickening gurgle, then stopped. He hit the stone pavement with a lifeless thump.

Beside Merthin, Caris gasped with horror.

Merthin ran forward. 'What's going on?' he cried.

Thomas turned to him, making go-back motions with the cleaver. 'Quiet!' he hissed.

The light changed in a heartbeat. Suddenly the cloisters were illuminated with the bright glow of a flame.

Someone came running out of the refectory with a heavy tread. It was a big man carrying a sack in one hand and a blazing torch in the other. He looked like a ghost, until Merthin realized he was wearing a crude hood with holes for the eyes and mouth.

Thomas stepped in front of the running man and raised his cleaver. But he was a moment too late. Before he could strike, the man cannoned into him, sending him flying.

Thomas crashed into a pillar, and there was a crack that sounded like his head hitting the stone. He slumped to the ground, out cold. The running man lost his balance and fell to his knees.

Caris pushed past Merthin and knelt beside Thomas.

Several more men appeared, all hooded, some carrying torches. It seemed to Merthin that some emerged from the refectory and others came down the stairs from the dorm. At the same time he heard the sound of women screaming and wailing. For a moment the scene was chaos.

Merthin rushed to Caris's side and tried to protect her, with his body, from the stampede.

The intruders saw their fallen comrade and they all paused in their rush, suddenly shocked into stillness. By the light of their torches they could see that he was unquestionably dead, his neck sliced almost all the way through, his blood spilled copiously over the stone floor of the cloisters. They looked around, moving their heads from side to side, peering through the holes in their hoods, looking like fish in a stream.

One of them spotted Thomas's cleaver, red with blood, lying

on the ground next to Thomas and Caris, and pointed at it to show the others. With a grunt of anger, he drew a sword.

Merthin was terrified for Caris. He stepped forward, attracting the swordsman's attention. The man moved towards Merthin and raised his weapon. Merthin retreated, drawing the man away from Caris. As the danger to her receded he felt more frightened for himself. Walking backwards, shaking with fear, he slipped on the dead man's blood. His feet flew from under him and he fell flat on his back.

The swordsman stood over him, weapon raised high to kill him.

Then one of the others intervened. He was the tallest of the intruders, and moved with surprising speed. With his left hand, he grabbed the upraised arm of Merthin's assailant. He must have had authority, for without speaking he simply shook his hooded head from side to side in negation, and the swordsman lowered his weapon obediently.

Merthin noticed that his saviour wore a mitten on his left hand, but nothing on the right.

The interaction lasted only as long as it might take a man to count to ten, and ended as suddenly as it had begun. One of the hooded men turned towards the kitchen and broke into a run, and the others followed. They must have planned to escape that way, Merthin realized: the kitchen had a door that gave on to the cathedral green, and that was the quickest way out. They disappeared, and without the blaze of their torches the cloisters went dark.

Merthin stood still, unsure what to do. Should he run after the intruders, go up to the dormitory and find out why the nuns were screaming, or find out where the fire was?

He knelt beside Caris. 'Is Thomas alive?' he said.

'I think he's banged his head, and he's unconscious, but he's breathing, and there's no blood.'

Behind him, Merthin heard the familiar voice of Sister Joan. 'Help me, please!' He turned. She stood in the doorway of the refectory, her face lit up grotesquely by the candle lamp in her hand, her head wreathed in smoke like a fashionable hat. 'For God's sake, come quickly!'

He stood up. Joan disappeared back into the refectory, and Merthin ran after her.

Her lamp threw confusing shadows, but he managed to avoid falling over the furniture as he followed her to the end of the room. Smoke was pouring from a hole in the floor. Merthin saw immediately that the hole was the work of a careful builder: it was perfectly square, with neat edges and a well-made trapdoor. He guessed this was the nuns' hidden treasury, built in secrecy by Jeremiah. But tonight's thieves had found it.

He got a lungful of smoke, and coughed. He wondered what was burning down there, and why, but he had no intention of finding out – it looked too dangerous.

Then Joan screamed at him: 'Tilly is in there!'

'Dear God,' Merthin said despairingly; and he went down the steps.

He had to hold his breath. He peered through the smoke. Despite his fear, his builder's eye noticed that the spiral stone staircase was well made, each step exactly the same size and shape, and each set at precisely the same angle to the next; so that he was able to go down with confidence even when he could not see what was underfoot.

In a second he reached the underground chamber. He could see flames near the middle of the room. The heat was intense, and he knew he would not be able to stand it for more than a few instants. The smoke was thick. He was still holding his breath, but now his eyes began to water, and his vision blurred. He wiped his eyes with his sleeve and peered into the murk. Where was Tilly? He could not see the floor.

He dropped to his knees. Visibility improved slightly: the smoke was less dense lower down. He moved around on all fours, staring into the corners of the room, sweeping with his hands where he could not see. 'Tilly!' he shouted. 'Tilly, where are you?' The smoke caught in his throat and he suffered a coughing fit that would have drowned any reply she made.

He could not last any longer. He was coughing convulsively, but every breath seemed to choke him with more smoke. His eyes watered copiously and he was nearly blind. In desperation, he went so close to the fire that the flames began to singe his sleeve. If he collapsed and lost consciousness, he would die for certain.

Then his hand touched flesh.

He grabbed. It was a human leg, a small leg, a girl's leg. He pulled her towards him. Her clothes were smouldering. He could hardly see her face and could not tell whether she was conscious, but she was tied hand and foot with leather thongs, so she could not move of her own accord. Striving to stop coughing, he got his arms under her and picked her up.

As soon as he stood upright the smoke became blindingly thick. Suddenly he could not remember which way the stairs were. He staggered away from the flames and crashed into the wall, almost dropping Tilly. Left or right? He went left and came to a corner. Changing his mind, he retraced his steps.

He felt as if he was drowning. His strength gone, he dropped to his knees. That saved him. Once again he found he could see better close to the floor, and a stone step appeared, like a vision from heaven, right in front of him.

Desperately holding on to the limp form of Tilly, he moved forward on his knees and made it to the staircase. With a last effort, he got to his feet. He put one foot on the lowest step and hauled himself up; then he managed the next step. Coughing uncontrollably, he forced himself upward until there were no more steps. He staggered, fell to his knees, dropped Tilly and collapsed on the refectory floor.

Someone bent over him. He spluttered: 'Close the trapdoor – stop the fire!' A moment later he heard a bang as the wooden door slammed shut.

He was grabbed under the arms. He opened his eyes for a moment and saw Caris's face, upside down; then his vision blurred. She dragged him across the floor. The smoke thinned and he began to suck air into his lungs. He sensed the transition from indoors to out, and tasted clean night air. Caris put him down and he heard her footsteps run back inside.

He gasped, coughed, gasped and coughed. Slowly he began to breathe more normally. His eyes stopped watering, and he saw that dawn was breaking. The faint light showed him a crowd of nuns standing around him.

He sat upright. Caris and another nun dragged Tilly out of the refectory and put her beside him. Caris bent over her. Merthin tried to speak, coughed, and tried again. 'How is she?'

'She's been stabbed through the heart,' Caris said. She began to cry. 'She was dead before you got to her.'

# 72

MERTHIN OPENED HIS EYES to bright daylight. He had slept late: the angle of the sun's rays shining through the bedroom window told him it was the middle of the morning. He recalled the events of the previous night like a bad dream, and for a moment he cherished the thought that they might not really have happened. But his chest hurt when he breathed, and the skin of his face was painfully scorched. The horror of Tilly's murder came back to him. And Sister Nellie, too – both innocent young women. How could God permit such things to happen?

He realized what had awakened him when his eye lit on Caris, putting a tray down on the small table near the bed. Her back was to him but he could tell, by the hunch of her shoulders and the set of her head, that she was angry. It was not surprising. She was grieving for Tilly, and enraged that the sanctity and safety of the nunnery had been violated.

Merthin got up. Caris pulled two stools to the table and they both sat down. He studied her face fondly. There were lines of strain around her eyes. He wondered if she had slept. There was a smear of ash on her left cheek, so he licked his thumb and gently wiped it off.

She had brought new bread with fresh butter and a jug of cider. Merthin found he was hungry and thirsty, and he tucked in. Caris, bottling up fury, ate nothing.

Through a mouthful of bread Merthin said: 'How is Thomas this morning?'

'He's lying down in the hospital. His head hurts, but he can talk coherently and answer questions, so there's probably no permanent damage to his brain.'

'Good. There will have to be an inquest on Tilly and Nellie.'

'I've sent a message to the sheriff of Shiring.'

'They will probably blame it on Tam Hiding.'

'Tam Hiding is dead.'

He nodded. He knew what was coming. His spirits had been lifted by the breakfast, but now they sank again. He swallowed and pushed away his plate.

Caris went on: 'Whoever it was that came here last night, he wanted to conceal his identity, so he told a lie – not knowing that Tam died in my hospital three months ago.'

'Who do you think it could have been?'

'Someone we know – hence the masks.'

'Perhaps.'

'Outlaws don't wear masks.'

It was true. Living outside the law, they did not care who knew about them and the crimes they committed. Last night's intruders were different. The masks strongly suggested they were respected citizens who were afraid of being recognized.

Caris went on with merciless logic. 'They killed Nellie to make Joan open up the treasury – but they had no need to kill Tilly: they were already inside the treasury by then. They wanted her dead for some other reason. And they were not content to leave her to be suffocated by smoke and burned to death: they also stabbed her fatally. For some reason, they had to be sure she was dead.'

'What does that tell you?'

Caris did not answer the question. 'Tilly thought Ralph wanted to kill her.'

'I know.'

'One of the hooded men was about to do away with you, at one point.' Her voice caught in her throat, and she had to stop. She took a sip of Merthin's cider, composing herself; then she went on. 'But the leader stopped him. Why would he do that? They had already murdered a nun and a noblewoman – why scruple to kill a mere builder?'

'You think it was Ralph.'

'Don't you?'

'Yes.' Merthin sighed heavily. 'Did you see his mitten?'

'I noticed he was wearing gloves.'

Merthin shook his head. 'Only one. On his left hand. Not a glove with fingers, but a mitten.'

'To hide his injury.'

'I can't be sure, and we certainly couldn't prove anything, but I have a dreadful conviction about it.'

Caris stood up. 'Let's inspect the damage.'

They went to the nuns' cloisters. The novices and the orphans were cleaning the treasury, bringing sacks of charred wood and ashes up the spiral staircase, giving anything not completely destroyed to Sister Joan and carrying the detritus out to the dunghill.

Laid out on a refectory table Merthin saw the cathedral ornaments: gold and silver candlesticks, crucifixes and vessels, all finely wrought and studded with precious stones. He was surprised. 'Didn't they take these?' he said.

'Yes – but they seem to have had second thoughts, and dumped them in a ditch outside town. A peasant on his way in with eggs to sell found them this morning. Luckily he was honest.'

Merthin picked up a gold aquamanile, a jug for washing the hands, made in the shape of a cockerel, the feathers of its neck beautifully chased. 'It's hard to sell something like this. Only a few people could afford to buy it, and most of those would guess it had been stolen.'

'The thieves could have melted it down and sold the gold.'

'Obviously they decided that was too much trouble.'

'Perhaps.'

She was not convinced. Nor was Merthin: his own explanation did not quite fit. The robbery had been carefully planned, that was evident. So why would the thieves not have made up their minds in advance about the ornaments? Either to take them or leave them behind?

Caris and Merthin went down the steps and into the chamber, Merthin's stomach clenching in fear as he was grimly reminded of last night's ordeal. More novices were cleaning the walls and floor with mops and buckets.

Caris sent the novices away to take a break. When she and

Merthin were alone, she picked up a length of wood from a shelf and used it to prise up one of the flagstones underfoot. Merthin had not previously noticed that the stone was not fitted as tightly as most, having a narrow gap all around it. Now he saw that underneath was a spacious vault containing a wooden box. Caris reached into the hole and pulled out the box. She opened it with a key from her belt. It was full of gold coins.

Merthin was surprised. 'They missed that!'

'There are three more concealed vaults,' Caris told him. 'Another in the floor and two in the walls. They missed them all.'

'They can't have looked very hard. Most treasuries have hiding places. People know that.'

'Especially robbers.'

'So maybe the cash wasn't their first priority.'

'Exactly.' Caris locked the chest and put it back in its vault.

'If they didn't want the ornaments, and they weren't sufficiently interested in cash to search the treasury thoroughly for hidden vaults, why did they come here at all?'

'To kill Tilly. The robbery was a cover.'

Merthin thought about that. 'They didn't need an elaborate cover story,' he said after a pause. 'If all they wanted was to kill Tilly, they could have done it in the dormitory and been far away from here by the time the nuns got back from Matins. If they had done it carefully – suffocated her with a feather pillow, say – we would not even have been sure she had been murdered. It would have looked as if she had died in her sleep.'

'Then there's no explanation for the attack. They ended up with next to nothing – a few gold coins.'

Merthin looked around the underground chamber. 'Where are the charters?' he said.

'They must have burned. It doesn't much matter. I've got copies of everything.'

'Parchment doesn't burn very well.'

'I've never tried to light it.'

'It smoulders, shrinks and distorts, but it doesn't catch fire.'

'Perhaps the charters have been retrieved from the debris.'

'Let's check.'

They climbed back up the steps and left the vault. Outside in the cloisters, Caris asked Joan: 'Have you found any parchment among the ashes?'

She shook her head. 'Nothing at all.'

'Could you have missed it?'

'I don't think so – not unless it has burned to cinders.'

'Merthin says it doesn't burn.' She turned to him. 'Who would want our charters? They're no use to anyone else.'

Merthin followed the thread of his own logic, just to see where it might lead. 'Suppose there's a document that you've got – or you *might* have, or they *think* you might have – and they want it.'

'What could it be?'

Merthin frowned. 'Documents are intended to be public. The whole point of writing something down is so that people can look at it in the future. A secret document is a strange thing...' Then he thought of something.

He drew Caris away from Joan, and walked casually around the cloisters with her until he was sure they could not be overheard. Then he said: 'But, of course, we do know of one secret document.'

'The letter Thomas buried in the forest.'

'Yes.'

'But why would anyone imagine it might be in the nunnery's treasury?'

'Well, think. Has anything happened lately that might arouse such a suspicion?'

A look of dismay came over Caris's face. 'Oh, my soul,' she exclaimed.

'There is something.'

'I told you about Lynn Grange being given to us by Queen Isabella for accepting Thomas, all those years ago.'

'Did you speak to anyone else about it?'

'Yes – the bailiff of Lynn. And Thomas was angry that I had done so, and said there would be dire consequences.'

'So someone is afraid you might have got hold of Thomas's secret letter.'

'Ralph?'

'I don't think Ralph is aware of the letter. I was the only one of us children who saw Thomas burying it. He's certainly never mentioned it. Ralph must be acting on behalf of someone else.'

Caris looked scared. 'Queen Isabella?'

'Or the king himself.'

'Is it possible that the king ordered Ralph to invade a nunnery?'

'Not personally, no. He would have used an intermediary, someone loyal, ambitious, and with absolutely no scruples. I came across such men in Florence, hanging around the Doge's palace. They're the scum of the earth.'

'I wonder who it was?'

'I think I can guess,' said Merthin.

*

GREGORY LONGFELLOW MET Ralph and Alan two days later at Wigleigh, in the small timber manor house. Wigleigh was more discreet than Tench. At Tench Hall there were too many people watching Ralph's every move: servants, followers, his parents. Here in Wigleigh the peasants had their own backbreaking business to do, and no one would question Ralph about the contents of the sack Alan was carrying.

'I gather it went off as planned,' Gregory said. News of the invasion of the nunnery had spread all over the county in no time.

'No great difficulty,' Ralph said. He was a bit let down by Gregory's muted reaction. After all the trouble that had been taken to get the charters, Gregory might have shown some elation.

'The sheriff has announced an inquest, of course,' Gregory said dourly.

'They'll blame it on outlaws.'

'You were not recognized?'

'We wore hoods.'

Gregory looked at Ralph strangely. 'I did not know that your wife was at the nunnery.'

'A useful coincidence,' Ralph said. 'It enabled me to kill two birds with one stone.'

The strange look intensified. What was the lawyer thinking?

Was he going to pretend to be shocked that Ralph had killed his wife? If so, Ralph was ready to point out that Gregory was complicit in everything that had happened at the nunnery – he had been the instigator. He had no right to judge. Ralph waited for Gregory to speak. But, after a long pause, all he said was: 'Let's have a look at these charters.'

They sent the housekeeper, Vira, on a lengthy errand, and Ralph made Alan stand at the door to keep out casual callers. Then Gregory tipped the charters out of the sack on to the table. He made himself comfortable and began to examine them. Some were rolled and tied with string, others bundled flat, a few sewn together in booklets. He opened one, read a few lines in the strong sunlight coming through the open windows, then threw the charter back into the sack and picked up another.

Ralph had no idea what Gregory was looking for. He had only said that it might embarrass the king. Ralph could not imagine what kind of document Caris might possess that would embarrass a king.

He got bored watching Gregory read, but he was not going to leave. He had delivered what Gregory wanted, and he was going to sit here until Gregory confirmed his half of the deal.

The tall lawyer worked his way patiently through the documents. One caught his attention, and he read it all the way through, but then he threw it in the sack with the others.

Ralph and Alan had spent most of the last week in Bristol. It was not likely that they would be asked to account for their movements, but they had taken precautions anyway. They had caroused at taverns every evening except the night they went to Kingsbridge. Their companions would remember the free drinks, but probably would not recall that on one night of the week Ralph and Alan had been absent – or, if they did, they certainly would not know whether it was the fourth Wednesday after Easter or the Thursday but two before Whitsun.

At last the table was clear and the sack was full again. Ralph said: 'Did you not find what you were looking for?'

Gregory did not answer the question. 'You brought everything?'

'Everything.'

'Good.'

'So you haven't found it?'

Gregory chose his words carefully, as always. 'The specific item is not here. However, I did come across a deed that may explain why this … issue … has arisen in recent months.'

'So you're satisfied,' Ralph persisted.

'Yes.'

'And the king need no longer be anxious.'

Gregory looked impatient. 'You should not concern yourself with the king's anxieties. I'll do that.'

'Then I can expect my reward immediately.'

'Oh, yes,' said Gregory. 'You shall be the earl of Shiring by harvest time.'

Ralph felt a glow of satisfaction. The earl of Shiring – at last. He had won the prize he had always longed for, and his father was still alive to hear the news. 'Thank you,' he said.

'If I were you,' said Gregory, 'I should go and woo Lady Philippa.'

'Woo her?' Ralph was astonished.

Gregory shrugged. 'She has no real choice in the matter, of course. But still, the formalities should be observed. Tell her that the king has given you permission to ask for her hand in marriage, and say you hope she will learn to love you as much as you love her.'

'Oh,' said Ralph. 'All right.'

'Take her a present,' said Gregory.

# 73

ON THE MORNING OF Tilly's burial, Caris and Merthin met on the roof of the cathedral at dawn.

The roof was a world apart. Calculating the acreage of slates was a perennial geometry exercise in the advanced mathematics class at the priory school. Workmen needed constant access for repairs and maintenance, so a network of walkways and ladders linked the slopes and ridges, corners and gulleys, turrets and pinnacles, gutters and gargoyles. The crossing tower had not yet been rebuilt, but the view from the top of the west façade was impressive.

The priory was already busy. This would be a big funeral. Tilly had been a nobody in life, but now she was the victim of a notorious murder, a noblewoman killed in a nunnery, and she would be mourned by people who had never spoken three words to her. Caris would have liked to discourage mourners, because of the risk of spreading the plague, but there was nothing she could do.

The bishop was already here, in the best room of the prior's palace – which was why Caris and Merthin had spent the night apart, she in the nuns' dormitory and he and Lolla at the Holly Bush. The grieving widower, Ralph, was in a private room upstairs at the hospital. His baby, Gerry, was being taken care of by the nuns. Lady Philippa and her daughter Odila, the only other surviving relatives of the dead girl, were also staying at the hospital.

Neither Merthin nor Caris had spoken to Ralph when he arrived yesterday. There was nothing they could do, no way to get justice for Tilly, for they could prove nothing; but all the same they knew the truth. So far they had told no one what they believed: there was no point. During today's obsequies they would have to pretend something like normalcy with Ralph. It was going to be difficult.

While the important personages slept, the nuns and the priory employees were hard at work preparing the funeral dinner. Smoke was rising from the bakery, where dozens of long four-pound loaves of wheat bread were already in the oven. Two men were rolling a new barrel of wine across to the prior's house. Several novice nuns were setting up benches and a trestle table on the green for the common mourners.

As the sun rose beyond the river, throwing a slanting yellow light on the rooftops of Kingsbridge, Caris studied the marks made on the town by nine months of plague. From this height she could see gaps in the rows of houses, like bad teeth. Timber buildings collapsed all the time, of course – because of fire, rain damage, incompetent construction or just old age. What was different now was that no one bothered to repair them. If your house fell down you just moved into one of the empty homes in the same street. The only person building anything was Merthin, and he was seen as a mad optimist with too much money.

Across the river, the gravediggers were already at work in another newly consecrated cemetery. The plague showed no signs of relenting. Where would it end? Would the houses just continue to fall down, one at a time, until there was nothing left, and the town was a wasteland of broken tiles and scorched timbers, with a deserted cathedral in the middle and a hundred-acre graveyard at its edge?

'I'm not going to let this happen,' she said.

Merthin did not at first understand. 'The funeral?' he said, frowning.

Caris made a sweeping gesture to take in the city and the world beyond it. 'Everything. Drunks maiming one another. Parents abandoning their sick children on the doorstep of my hospital. Men queuing to fuck a drunken woman on a table outside the White Horse. Livestock dying in the pastures. Half-naked penitents whipping themselves then collecting pennies from bystanders. And, most of all, a young mother brutally murdered here in my nunnery. I don't care if we are all going to die of the plague. As long as we're still alive, I'm not going to let our world fall apart.'

'What are you going to do?'

She smiled gratefully at Merthin. Most people would have told her she was powerless to fight the situation, but he was always ready to believe in her. She looked at the stone angels carved on a pinnacle, their faces blurred by two hundred years of wind and rain, and she thought of the spirit that had moved the cathedral builders. 'We're going to re-establish order and routine here. We're going to force Kingsbridge people to return to normal, whether they like it or not. We're going to rebuild this town and its life, despite the plague.'

'All right,' he said.

'This is the moment to do it.'

'Because everyone is so angry about Tilly?'

'And because they're frightened at the thought that armed men can come into the town at night and murder whomever they will. They think no one's safe.'

'What will you do?'

'I'm going to tell them it must never happen again.'

*

'THIS MUST NEVER happen again!' she cried, and her voice rang out across the graveyard and echoed off the ancient walls of the cathedral.

A woman could never speak out as part of a service in church, but the graveside ceremony was a grey area, a solemn moment that took place outside the church, a time when lay people such as the family of the deceased would sometimes make speeches or pray aloud.

All the same, Caris was sticking her neck out. Bishop Henri was officiating, backed up by Archdeacon Lloyd and Canon Claude. Lloyd had been diocesan clerk for decades, and Claude was a colleague of Henri's from France. In such distinguished clerical company, it was audacious for a nun to make an unscheduled speech.

Such considerations had never meant much to Caris, of course.

She spoke just as the small coffin was being lowered into the grave. Several of the congregation had begun to cry. The crowd was at least five hundred strong, but they fell silent at the sound of her voice.

'Armed men have come into our town at night and killed a young woman in the nunnery – and I will not stand for it,' she said.

There was a rumble of assent from the crowd.

She raised her voice. 'The priory will not stand for it – the bishop will not stand for it – and the men and women of Kingsbridge will not stand for it!'

The support became louder, the crowd shouting: 'No!' and 'Amen!'

'People say the plague is sent by God. I say that when God sends rain we take shelter. When God sends winter, we build up the fire. When God sends weeds, we pull them up by the roots. We must defend ourselves!'

She glanced at Bishop Henri. He was looking bemused. He had had no warning of this sermon, and if he had been asked for his permission he would have refused it; but he could tell that Caris had the people on her side, and he did not have the nerve to intervene.

'What can we do?'

She looked around. All faces were turned to her expectantly. They had no idea what to do, but they wanted a solution from her. They would cheer at anything she said, if only it gave them hope.

'We must rebuild the city wall!' she cried.

They roared their approval.

'A new wall that is taller, and stronger, and longer than the broken down old one.' She caught the eye of Ralph. 'A wall that will keep murderers out!'

The crowd shouted: 'Yes!' Ralph looked away.

'And we must elect a new constable, and a force of deputies and sentries, to uphold the law and enforce good behaviour.'

'Yes!'

'There will be a meeting of the parish guild tonight to work out the practical details, and the guild's decisions will be announced in church next Sunday. Thank you and God bless you all.'

*

AT THE FUNERAL BANQUET, in the grand dining hall of the prior's palace, Bishop Henri sat at the head of the table. On his right was Lady Philippa, the widowed countess of Shiring. Next to her was seated the chief mourner, Tilly's widower, Sir Ralph Fitzgerald.

Ralph was delighted to be next to Philippa. He could stare at her breasts while she concentrated on her food, and every time she leaned forward he could peek down the square neckline of her light summer dress. She did not know it yet, but the time was not far away when he would command her to take off her clothes and stand naked in front of him, and he would see those magnificent breasts in their entirety.

The dinner provided by Caris was ample but not extravagant, he noted. There were no gilded swans or towers of sugar, but there was plenty of roasted meat, boiled fish, new bread, beans and spring berries. He helped Philippa to some soup made of minced chicken with almond milk.

She said to him gravely: 'This is a terrible tragedy. You have my most profound sympathy.'

People had been so compassionate that sometimes, for a few moments, Ralph thought of himself as the pitiable victim of a dreadful bereavement, and forgot that he was the one who had slid the knife into Tilly's young heart. 'Thank you,' he said solemnly. 'Tilly was so young. But we soldiers get used to sudden death. One day a man will save your life, and swear eternal friendship and loyalty; and the next day he is struck down by a crossbow bolt through the heart, and you forget him.'

She gave him an odd look that reminded him of the way Sir Gregory had regarded him, with a mixture of curiosity and distaste, and he wondered what it was about his attitude to Tilly's death that provoked this reaction.

Philippa said: 'You have a baby boy.'

'Gerry. The nuns are looking after him today, but I'll take him home to Tench Hall tomorrow. I've found a wet nurse.' He saw an opportunity to drop a hint. 'Of course, he needs someone to mother him properly.'

'Yes.'

He recalled her own bereavement. 'But you know what it is to lose your spouse.'

'I was fortunate to have my beloved William for twenty-one years.'

'You must be lonely.' This might not be the moment to propose, but he thought to edge the conversation towards the subject.

'Indeed. I lost my three men – William and our two sons. The castle seems so empty.'

'But not for long, perhaps.'

She stared at him as if she could not believe her ears, and he realized he had said something offensive. She turned away and spoke to Bishop Henri on her other side.

On Ralph's right was Philippa's daughter, Odila. 'Would you like some of this pasty?' he said to her. 'It's made with peacocks and hares.' She nodded, and he cut her a slice. 'How old are you?' he asked.

'I'll be fifteen this year.'

She was tall, and had her mother's figure already, a full bosom and wide, womanly hips. 'You seem older,' he said, looking at her breasts.

He intended it as a compliment – young people generally wanted to seem older – but she blushed and looked away.

Ralph looked down at his trencher and speared a chunk of pork cooked with ginger. He ate it moodily. He was not very good at what Gregory called wooing.

*

Caris was seated on the left of Bishop Henri, with Merthin, as alderman, on her other side. Next to Merthin was Sir Gregory Longfellow, who had come for the funeral of Earl William three months ago and had not yet left the neighbourhood. Caris had to suppress her disgust at being at a table with the murdering Ralph and the man who had, almost certainly, put him up to it. But she had work to do at this dinner. She had a plan for the revival of the town. Rebuilding the walls was only the first part. For the second, she had to get Bishop Henri on her side.

She poured the bishop a goblet of clear red Gascon wine, and he took a long draught. He wiped his mouth and said: 'You preach a good sermon.'

'Thank you,' she said, noting the ironic reproof that underlay his compliment. 'Life in this town is degenerating into disorder and debauchery, and if we're to put it right we need to inspire the townspeople. I'm sure you agree.'

'It's a little late to ask whether I agree with you. However, I do.' Henri was a pragmatist who did not re-fight lost battles. She had been counting on that.

She served herself some heron roasted with pepper and cloves, but did not begin to eat: she had too much to say. 'There's more to my plan than the walls and the constabulary.'

'I thought there might be.'

'I believe that you, as the bishop of Kingsbridge, should have the tallest cathedral in England.'

He raised his eyebrows. 'I wasn't expecting that.'

'Two hundred years ago this was one of England's most important priories. It should be so again. A new church tower would symbolize the revival – and your eminence among bishops.'

He smiled wryly, but he was pleased. He knew he was being flattered, and he liked it.

Caris said: 'The tower would also serve the town. Being visible from a distance, it would help pilgrims and traders find their way here.'

'How would you pay for it?'

'The priory is wealthy.'

He was surprised again. 'Prior Godwyn complained of money problems.'

'He was a hopeless manager.'

'He struck me as rather competent.'

'He struck a lot of people that way, but he made all the wrong decisions. Right at the start he refused to repair the fulling mill, which would have brought him an income; but he spent money on this palace, which returned him nothing.'

'And how have things changed?'

'I've sacked most of the bailiffs and replaced them with younger men who are willing to make changes. I've converted about half the land to grazing, which is easier to manage in these times of labour shortage. The rest I've leased for cash rents with no customary obligations. And we've all benefited from inheritance taxes and from the legacies of people who died without heirs because of the plague. The monastery is now as rich as the nunnery.'

'So all the tenants are free?'

'Most. Instead of working one day a week on the demesne farm, and carting the landlord's hay, and folding their sheep on the landlord's field, and all those complicated services, they just pay money. They like it better and it certainly makes our life simpler.'

'A lot of landlords – abbots especially – revile that type of tenancy. They say it ruins the peasantry.'

Caris shrugged. 'What have we lost? The power to impose petty variations, favouring some serfs and persecuting others, keeping them all subservient. Monks and nuns have no business tyrannizing peasants. Farmers know what crops to sow and what they can sell at market. They work better left to themselves.'

The bishop looked suspicious. 'So you feel the priory can pay for a new tower?'

He had been expecting her to ask him for money, she guessed. 'Yes – with some assistance from the town's merchants. And that's where you can help us.'

'I thought there must be something.'

'I'm not asking you for money. What I want from you is worth more than money.'

'I'm intrigued.'

'I want to apply to the king for a borough charter.' As she said the words, Caris felt her hands begin to shake. She was taken back to the battle she had fought with Godwyn, ten years ago, that had ended in her being accused of witchcraft. The issue then had been the borough charter, and she had nearly died fighting for it. Circumstances now were completely different, but the charter was no less important. She put down her eating knife and clasped her hands together in her lap to keep them still.

'I see,' said Henri noncommittally.

Caris swallowed hard and went on. 'It's essential for the regeneration of the town's commercial life. For a long time Kingsbridge has been held back by the dead hand of priory rule. Priors are cautious and conservative, and instinctively say no to any change or innovation. Merchants live by change – they're always looking for new ways to make money, or at least the good ones are. If we want the men of Kingsbridge to help pay for our new tower, we must give them the freedom they need to prosper.'

'A borough charter.'

'The town would have its own court, set its own regulations, and be ruled by a proper guild, rather than the parish guild we have now, which has no real power.'

'But would the king grant it?'

'Kings like boroughs, which pay lots of taxes. But, in the past, the prior of Kingsbridge has always opposed a charter.'

'You think priors are too conservative.'

'Timid.'

'Well,' said the bishop with a laugh, 'timidity is a thing you'll never be accused of.'

Caris pressed her point. 'I think a charter is essential if we're to build the new tower.'

'Yes, I can see that.'

'So, do you agree?'

'To the tower, or the charter?'

'They go together.'

Henri seemed amused. 'Are you making a deal with me, Mother Caris?'

'If you're willing.'

'All right. Build me a tower, and I'll help you get a charter.'

'No. It has to be the other way around. We need the charter first.'

'So I must trust you.'

'Is that difficult?'

'To be honest, no.'

'Good. Then we're agreed.'

'Yes.'

Caris leaned forward and looked past Merthin. 'Sir Gregory?'

'Yes, Mother Caris?'

She forced herself to be polite to him. 'Have you tried this rabbit in sugar gravy? I recommend it.'

Gregory accepted the bowl and took some. 'Thank you.'

Caris said to him: 'You will recall that Kingsbridge is not a borough.'

'I certainly do.' Gregory had used that fact, more than a decade ago, to outmanoeuvre Caris in the royal court in the dispute over the fulling mill.

'The bishop thinks it's time for us to ask the king for a charter.'

Gregory nodded. 'I believe the king might look favourably on such a plea – especially if it were presented to him in the right way.'

Hoping that her distaste was not showing on her face, she said: 'Perhaps you would be kind enough to advise us.'

'May we discuss this in more detail later?'

Gregory would require a bribe, of course, though he would undoubtedly call it a lawyer's fee. 'By all means,' she said, repressing a shudder.

The servants began clearing away the food. Caris looked down at her trencher. She had not eaten anything.

*

'OUR FAMILIES are related,' Ralph was saying to Lady Philippa. 'Not closely, of course,' he added hastily. 'But my father is descended from that earl of Shiring who was the son of Lady Aliena and Jack Builder.' He looked across the table at his brother Merthin, the alderman. 'I think I inherited the blood of the earls, and my brother that of the builders.'

He looked at Philippa's face to see how she took that. She did not seem impressed.

'I was brought up in the household of your late father-in-law, Earl Roland,' he went on.

'I remember you as a squire.'

'I served under the earl in the king's army in France. At the battle of Crécy, I saved the life of the prince of Wales.'

'My goodness, how splendid,' she said politely.

He was trying to get her to see him as an equal, so that it would seem more natural when he told her that she was to be his wife. But he did not appear to be getting through to her. She just looked bored and a bit puzzled by the direction of his conversation.

The dessert was served: sugared strawberries, honey wafers, dates and raisins, and spiced wine. Ralph drained a cup of wine and poured more, hoping that the drink would help him relax with Philippa. He was not sure why he found it difficult to talk to her. Because this was his wife's funeral? Because Philippa was a countess? Or because he had been hopelessly in love with her for years, and could not believe that now, at last, she really was to be his wife?

'When you leave here, will you go back to Earlscastle?' he asked her.

'Yes. We depart tomorrow.'

'Will you stay there long?'

'Where else would I go?' She frowned. 'Why do you ask?'

'I will come and visit you there, if I may.'

Her response was frosty. 'To what end?'

'I want to discuss with you a subject that it would not be appropriate to raise here and now.'

'What on earth do you mean?'

'I'll come and see you in the next few days.'

She looked agitated. In a raised voice she said: 'What could you possibly have to say to me?'

'As I said, it wouldn't be appropriate to speak of it today.'

'Because this is your wife's funeral?'

He nodded.

She went pale. 'Oh, my God,' she said. 'You can't mean to suggest…'

'I told you, I don't want to discuss it now.'

'But I must know!' she cried. 'Are you planning to propose marriage to me?'

He hesitated, shrugged, and then nodded.

'But on what grounds?' she said. 'Surely you need the king's permission!'

He looked at her and raised his eyebrows briefly.

She stood up suddenly. 'No!' she said. Everyone around the table looked at her. She stared at Gregory. 'Is this true?' she said. 'Is the king going to marry me to *him*?' She jerked a thumb contemptuously at Ralph.

Ralph felt stabbed. He had not expected her to display such revulsion. Was he so repellent?

Gregory looked reproachfully at Ralph. 'This was not the moment to raise the matter.'

Philippa cried: 'So it's true! God save me!'

Ralph caught Odila's eye. She was staring at him in horror. What had he ever done to earn her dislike?

Philippa said: 'I can't bear it.'

'Why?' Ralph said. 'What is so wrong? What right have *you* to look down on me and my family?' He looked around at the company: his brother, his ally Gregory, the bishop, the prioress, minor noblemen and leading citizens. They were all silent, shocked and intrigued by Philippa's outburst.

Philippa ignored his question. Addressing Gregory, she said: 'I will not do it! I will not, do you hear me?' She was white with rage, but tears ran down her cheeks. Ralph thought how beautiful she was, even while she was rejecting and humiliating him so painfully.

Gregory said coolly: 'It is not your decision, Lady Philippa, and it certainly is not mine. The king will do as he pleases.'

'You may force me into a wedding dress, and you may march me up the aisle,' Philippa raged. She pointed at Bishop Henri. 'But when the bishop asks me if I take Ralph Fitzgerald to be my husband I will not say yes! I will not! Never, never, never!'

She stormed out of the room, and Odila followed.

*

WHEN THE BANQUET was over, the townspeople returned to their homes, and the important guests went to their rooms to sleep off the feast. Caris supervised the clearing up. She felt sorry for Philippa, profoundly sorry, knowing – as Philippa did not – that Ralph had killed his first wife. But she was concerned about the fate of an entire town, not just one person. Her mind was on her scheme for Kingsbridge. Things had gone better than she imagined. The townspeople had cheered her, and the bishop had agreed to everything she proposed. Perhaps civilization would return to Kingsbridge, despite the plague.

Outside the back door, where there was a pile of meat bones and crusts of bread, she saw Godwyn's cat, Archbishop, delicately picking at the carcase of a duck. She shooed it away. It scampered a few yards then slowed to a stiff walk, its white-tipped tail arrogantly upstanding.

Deep in thought, she went up the stairs of the palace, thinking of how she would begin implementing the changes agreed to by Henri. Without pausing, she opened the door of the bedroom she shared with Merthin and stepped inside.

For a moment she was disoriented. Two men stood in the middle of the room, and she thought: I *must be in the wrong house*, and then: I *must be in the wrong room*, before she remembered that her room, being the best bedroom, had naturally been given to the bishop.

The two men were Henri and his assistant, Canon Claude. It took Caris a moment to realize that they were both naked, with their arms around one another, kissing.

She stared at them in shock. 'Oh!' she said.

They had not heard the door. Until she spoke, they did not realize they were observed. When they heard her gasp of surprise they both turned towards her. A look of horrified guilt came over Henri's face, and his mouth fell open.

'I'm sorry!' Caris said.

The men sprang apart, as if hoping they might be able to deny what was going on; then they remembered they were naked. Henri was plump, with a round belly and fat arms and legs, and grey hair on his chest. Claude was younger and slimmer, with very little body hair except for a blaze of chestnut at his groin. Caris had never before looked at two erect penises at the same time.

'I beg your pardon!' she said, mortified with embarrassment. 'My mistake. I forgot.' She realized that she was babbling and they were dumbstruck. It did not matter: nothing that anyone could say would make the situation any better.

Coming to her senses, she backed out of the room and slammed the door.

*

MERTHIN WALKED AWAY from the banquet with Madge Webber. He was fond of this small, chunky woman, with her chin jutting out in front and her bottom jutting out behind. He admired the way she had carried on after her husband and children had died of the plague. She had continued the enterprise, weaving cloth and dyeing it red according to Caris's recipe. She said to him: 'Good for Caris. She's right, as usual. We can't go on like this.'

'You've continued normally, despite everything,' he said.

'My only problem is finding the people to do the work.'

'Everyone is the same. I can't get builders.'

'Raw wool is cheap, but rich people will still pay high prices for good scarlet cloth,' Madge said. 'I could sell more if I could produce more.'

Merthin said thoughtfully: 'You know, I saw a faster type of loom in Florence – a treadle loom.'

'Oh?' She looked at him with alert curiosity. 'I never heard of that.'

He wondered how to explain. 'In any loom, you stretch a number of threads over the frame to form what you call the warp, then you weave another thread crossways through the warp, under one thread and over the next, under and over, from one side to the other and back again, to form the weft.'

'That's how simple looms work, yes. Ours are better.'

'I know. To make the process quicker, you attach every second warp thread to a movable bar, called a heddle, so that when you shift the heddle, half the threads are lifted away from the rest. Then, instead of going over and under, over and under, you can simply pass the weft thread straight through the gap in one easy movement. Then you drop the heddle below the warp for the return pass.'

'Yes. By the way, the weft thread is wound on a bobbin.'

'Each time you pass the bobbin through the warp from left to right, you have to put it down, then use both hands to move the heddle, then pick up the bobbin again and bring it back from right to left.'

'Exactly.'

'In a treadle loom, you move the heddle with your feet. So you never have to put the bobbin down.'

'Really? My soul!'

'That would make a difference, wouldn't it?'

'A huge difference. You could weave twice as much – more!'

'That's what I thought. Shall I build one for you to try?'

'Yes, please!'

'I don't remember exactly how it was constructed. I think the treadle operated a system of pulleys and levers...' He frowned, thinking. 'Anyway, I'm sure I can figure it out.'

*

LATE IN THE afternoon, as Caris was passing the library, she met Canon Claude coming out, carrying a small book. He caught her eye and stopped. They both immediately thought of the scene Caris had stumbled upon an hour ago. At first Claude looked embarrassed, but then a grin lifted the corners of his mouth. His put his hand to his face to cover it, obviously feeling it was wrong to be amused. Caris remembered how startled the two naked men had been and she, too, felt inappropriate laughter bubbling up inside her. On impulse, she said what was in her mind: 'The two of you did look funny!' Claude giggled despite himself, and Caris could not help chuckling too, and they made each other worse, until they fell into one another's arms, tears streaming down their cheeks, helpless with laughter.

*

THAT EVENING, CARIS took Merthin to the south-west corner of the priory grounds, where the vegetable garden grew alongside the river. The air was mild, and the moist earth gave up a fragrance of new growth. Caris could see spring onions and radishes. 'So, your brother is to be the earl of Shiring,' she said.

'Not if Lady Philippa has anything to do with it.'

'A countess has to do what she is told by the king, doesn't she?'

'All women should be subservient to men, in theory,' Merthin said with a grin. 'Some defy convention, though.'

'I can't think who you mean.'

Merthin's mood changed abruptly. 'What a world,' he said. 'A man murders his wife, and the king elevates him to the highest rank of the nobility.'

'We know these things happen,' she said. 'But it's shocking when it's your own family. Poor Tilly.'

Merthin rubbed his eyes as if to erase visions. 'Why have you brought me here?'

'To talk about the final element in my plan: the new hospital.'

'Ah. I was wondering...'

'Could you build it here?'

Merthin looked around. 'I don't see why not. It's a sloping site, but the entire priory is built on a slope, and we're not talking about putting up another cathedral. One storey or two?'

'One. But I want the building divided into medium-sized rooms, each containing just four or six beds, so that diseases don't spread so quickly from one patient to everyone else in the place. It must have its own pharmacy – a large, well-lit room – for the preparation of medicines, with a herb garden outside. And a spacious, airy latrine with piped water, very easy to keep clean. In fact the whole building must have lots of light and space. But, most importantly, it has to be at least a hundred yards from the rest of the priory. We have to separate the sick from the well. That's the key feature.'

'I'll do some drawings in the morning.'

She glanced around and, seeing that they were not observed, she kissed him. 'This is going to be the culmination of my life's work, do you realize that?'

'You're thirty-two – isn't it a little early to be talking about the culmination of your life's work?'

'It hasn't happened yet.'

'It won't take long. I'll start on it while I'm digging the foundations for the new tower. Then, as soon as the hospital is built, I can switch my masons to work on the cathedral.'

They started to walk back. She could tell that his real enthusiasm was for the tower. 'How tall will it be?'

'Four hundred and five feet.'

'How high is Salisbury?'

'Four hundred and four.'

'So it *will* be the highest building in England.'

'Until someone builds a higher one, yes.'

So he would achieve his ambition too, she thought. She put her arm through his as they walked to the prior's palace. She felt happy. That was strange, wasn't it? Thousands of Kingsbridge people had died of the plague, and Tilly had been murdered, but Caris felt hopeful. It was because she had a plan, of course. She always felt better when she had a plan. The new walls, the constabulary, the tower, the borough charter, and most of all the new hospital: how would she find time to organize it all?

Arm in arm with Merthin, she walked into the prior's house. Bishop Henri and Sir Gregory were there, deep in conversation with a third man who had his back to Caris. There was something unpleasantly familiar about the newcomer, even from behind, and Caris felt a tremor of unease. Then he turned around and she saw his face: sardonic, triumphant, sneering, and full of malice.

It was Philemon.

# 74

Bishop Henri and the other guests left Kingsbridge the next morning. Caris, who had been sleeping in the nuns' dormitory, returned to the prior's palace after breakfast and went upstairs to her room.

She found Philemon there.

It was the second time in two days that she had been startled by men in her bedroom. However, Philemon was alone and fully dressed, standing by the window looking at a book. Seeing him in profile, she realized that the trials of the last six months had left him thinner.

She said: 'What are you doing here?'

He pretended to be surprised by the question. 'This is the prior's house. Why should I not be here?'

'Because it's not your room!'

'I am the sub-prior of Kingsbridge. I have never been dismissed from that post. The prior is dead. Who else should live here?'

'Me, of course.'

'You're not even a monk.'

'Bishop Henri made me acting prior – and last night, despite your return, he did not dismiss me from this post. I am your superior, and you must obey me.'

'But you're a nun, and you must live with the nuns, not with the monks.'

'I've been living here for months.'

'Alone?'

Suddenly Caris saw that she was on shaky ground. Philemon knew that she and Merthin had been living more or less as man and wife. They had been discreet, not flaunting their relationship, but people guessed these things, and Philemon had a wild beast's instinct for weakness.

She considered. She could insist on Philemon's leaving the building immediately. If necessary, she could have him thrown out: Thomas and the novices would obey her, not Philemon. But what then? Philemon would do all he could to call attention to what Merthin and she were up to in the palace. He would create a controversy, and leading townspeople would take sides. Most would support Caris, almost whatever she did, such was her reputation; but there would be some who would censure her behaviour. The conflict would weaken her authority and undermine everything else she wanted to do. It would be better to admit defeat.

'You may have the bedroom,' she said. 'But not the hall. I use that for meetings with leading townspeople and visiting dignitaries. When you're not attending services in the church, you will be in the cloisters, not here. A sub-prior does not have a palace.' She left without giving him a chance to argue. She had saved face, but he had won.

She had been reminded last night of how wily Philemon was. Questioned by Bishop Henri, he seemed to have a plausible explanation for everything dishonourable that he had done. How did he justify deserting his post at the priory and running away to St-John-in-the-Forest? The monastery had been in danger of extinction, and the only way to save it had been to flee, in accordance with the saying: 'Leave early, go far and stay long.' It was still, by general consent, the only sure way to avoid the plague. Their sole mistake had been to remain too long in Kingsbridge. Why, then, had no one informed the bishop of this plan? Philemon was sorry, but he and the other monks were only obeying the orders of Prior Godwyn. Then why had he run away from St John when the plague caught up with them there? He had been called by God to minister to the people of Monmouth, and Godwyn had given him permission to leave. How come Brother Thomas did not know about this permission, in fact denied firmly that it had ever been given? The other monks had not been told of Godwyn's decision for fear it would cause jealousy. Why, then, had Philemon left Monmouth? He had met Friar Murdo, who had told him that Kingsbridge Priory needed him, and he regarded this as a further message from God.

Caris concluded that Philemon had run from the plague until he had realized he must be one of those fortunate people who were not prone to catch it. Then he had learned from Murdo that Caris was sleeping with Merthin in the prior's palace, and he had immediately seen how he could exploit that situation to restore his own fortunes. God had nothing to do with it.

But Bishop Henri had believed Philemon's tale. Philemon was careful to appear humble to the point of obsequiousness. Henri did not know the man, and failed to see beneath the surface.

She left Philemon in the palace and walked to the cathedral. She climbed the long, narrow spiral staircase in the north-west tower and found Merthin in the mason's loft, drawing designs on the tracing floor in the light from the tall north-facing windows.

She looked with interest at what he had done. It was always difficult to read plans, she found. The thin lines scratched in the mortar had to be transformed, in the viewer's imagination, into thick walls of stone with windows and doors.

Merthin regarded her expectantly as she studied his work. He was obviously anticipating a big reaction.

At first she was baffled by the drawing. It looked nothing like a hospital. She said: 'But you've drawn ... a cloister!'

'Exactly,' he said. 'Why should a hospital be a long narrow room like the nave of a church? You want the place to be light and airy. So, instead of cramming the rooms together, I've set them around a quadrangle.'

She visualized it: the square of grass, the building around, the doors leading to rooms of four or six beds, the nuns moving from room to room in the shelter of the covered arcade. 'It's inspired!' she said. 'I would never have thought of it, but it will be perfect.'

'You can grow herbs in the quadrangle, where the plants will have sunshine but be sheltered from the wind. There will be a fountain in the middle of the garden, for fresh water, and it can drain through the latrine wing to the south and into the river.'

She kissed him exuberantly. 'You're so clever!' Then she recalled the news she had to tell him.

He must have seen her face fall, for he said: 'What's the matter?'

'We have to move out of the palace,' she said. She told him

about her conversation with Philemon, and why she had given in. 'I foresee major conflicts with Philemon – I don't want this to be the one on which I make my stand.'

'That makes sense,' he said. His tone of voice was reasonable, but she knew by his face that he was angry. He stared at his drawing, though he was not really thinking about it.

'And there's something else,' she said. 'We're telling everyone they have to live as normally as possible – order in the streets, a return to real family life, no more drunken orgies. We ought to set an example.'

He nodded. 'A prioress living with her lover is about as abnormal as could be, I suppose,' he said. Once again his equable tone was contradicted by his furious expression.

'I'm very sorry,' she said.

'So am I.'

'But we don't want to risk everything we both want – your tower, my hospital, the future of the town.'

'No. But we're sacrificing our life together.'

'Not entirely. We'll have to sleep separately, which is painful, but we'll have plenty of opportunities to be together.'

'Where?'

She shrugged. 'Here, for example.' An imp of mischief possessed her. She walked away from him across the room, slowly lifting the skirt of her robe, and went to the doorway at the top of the stairs. 'I don't see anyone coming,' she said as she raised her dress to her waist.

'You can hear them, anyway,' he said. 'The door at the foot of the stairs makes a noise.'

She bent over, pretending to look down the staircase. 'Can you see anything unusual, from where you are?'

He chuckled. She could usually pull him out of an angry mood by being playful. 'I can see something winking at me,' he laughed.

She walked back towards him, still holding her robe up around her waist, smiling triumphantly. 'You see, we don't have to give up everything.'

He sat on a stool and pulled her towards him. She straddled

his thighs and lowered herself on to his lap. 'You'd better get a straw mattress up here,' she said, her voice thick with desire.

He nuzzled her breasts. 'How would I explain the need for a bed in a mason's loft?' he murmured.

'Just say that masons need somewhere soft to put their tools.'

*

A WEEK LATER Caris and Thomas Langley went to inspect the rebuilding of the city wall. It was a big job but simple and, once the line had been agreed, the actual stonework could be done by inexperienced young masons and apprentices. Caris was glad the project had begun so promptly. It was necessary that the town be able to defend itself in troubled times – but she had a more important motive. Getting the townspeople to guard against disruption from outside would lead naturally, she hoped, to a new awareness of the need for order and good behaviour among themselves.

She found it deeply ironic that fate had cast her in this role. She had never been a rule keeper. She had always despised orthodoxy and flouted convention. She felt she had the right to make her own rules. Now here she was clamping down on merrymakers. It was a miracle that no one had yet called her a hypocrite.

The truth was that some people flourished in an atmosphere of anarchy, and others did not. Merthin was one of those who were better off without constraints. She recalled the carving he had made of the wise and foolish virgins. It was different from anything anyone had seen before – so Elfric had made that his excuse for destroying it. Regulation only served to handicap Merthin. But men such as Barney and Lou, the slaughterhouse workers, had to have laws to stop them maiming one another in drunken fights.

All the same, her position was shaky. When you were trying to enforce law and order, it was difficult to explain that the rules did not actually apply to you personally.

She was mulling over this as she returned with Thomas to the priory. Outside the cathedral she found Sister Joan pacing up and down in a state of agitation. 'I'm so angry with Philemon,' she said. 'He claims you have stolen his money, and I must give it back!'

'Just calm down,' Caris said. She led Joan into the porch of the church, and they sat on a stone bench. 'Take a deep breath and tell me what happened.'

'Philemon came up to me after Terce and said he needed ten shillings to buy candles for the shrine of St Adolphus. I said I would have to ask you.'

'Quite right.'

'He became very angry and shouted that it was the monks' money, and I had no right to refuse him. He demanded my keys, and I think he would have tried to snatch them from me, but I pointed out that they would be no use to him, as he didn't know where the treasury was.'

'What a good idea it was to keep that secret,' Caris said.

Thomas was standing beside them, listening. He said: 'I notice he picked a time when I was off the premises – the coward.'

Caris said: 'Joan, you did absolutely right to refuse him, and I'm sorry he tried to bully you. Thomas, go and find him and bring him to me at the palace.'

She left them and walked through the graveyard, deep in thought. Clearly, Philemon was set on making trouble. But he was not the kind of blustering bully whom she could have overpowered with ease. He was a wily opponent, and she must watch her step.

When she opened the door of the prior's house, Philemon was there in the hall, sitting at the head of the long table.

She stopped in the doorway. 'You shouldn't be here,' she said. 'I specifically told you—'

'I was looking for you,' he said.

She realized she would have to lock the building. Otherwise he would always find a pretext for flouting her orders. She controlled her anger. 'You looked for me in the wrong place,' she said.

'I've found you now, though, haven't I?'

She studied him. He had shaved and cut his hair since his arrival, and he wore a new robe. He was every inch the priory official, calm and authoritative. She said: 'I've been speaking to Sister Joan. She's very upset.'

'So am I.'

She realized he was sitting in the big chair, and she was standing in front of him, as if he were in charge and she a supplicant. How clever he was at manipulating these things. She said: 'If you need money, you must ask me.'

'I'm the sub-prior!'

'And I'm the acting prior, which makes me your superior.' She raised her voice. 'So the first thing you must do is stand up when you're speaking to me!'

He started, shocked by her tone; then he controlled himself. With insulting slowness he pulled himself out of the chair.

Caris sat down in his place and let him stand.

He seemed unabashed. 'I understand you're using monastery money to pay for the new tower.'

'By order of the bishop, yes.'

A flash of annoyance crossed his face. He had hoped to ingratiate himself and make the bishop his ally against Caris. Even as a child he had toadied unendingly to people in authority. That was how he had gained admission to the monastery.

He said: 'I must have access to the monastery's money. It's my right. The monks' assets should be in my charge.'

'The last time you were in charge of the monks' assets, you stole them.'

He went pale: that arrow had struck the bull's eye. 'Ridiculous,' he blustered, trying to cover his embarrassment. 'Prior Godwyn took them for safekeeping.'

'Well, nobody is going to take them for "safekeeping" while I'm acting prior.'

'You should at least give me the ornaments. They are sacred jewels, to be handled by priests, not women.'

'Thomas has been dealing with them quite adequately, taking them out for services and restoring them to our treasury afterwards.'

'It's not satisfactory—'

Caris remembered something, and interrupted him. 'Besides, you haven't yet returned all that you took.'

'The money—'

'The ornaments. There's a gold candlestick missing, a gift from the chandlers' guild. What happened to that?'

His reaction surprised her. She was expecting another blustering denial. But he looked embarrassed and said: 'That was always kept in the prior's room.'

She frowned. 'And . . . ?'

'I kept it separate from the other ornaments.'

She was astonished. 'Are you telling me that *you* have had the candlestick all this time?'

'Godwyn asked me to look after it.'

'And so you took it with you on your travels to Monmouth and elsewhere?'

'That was his wish.'

This was a wildly implausible tale, and Philemon knew it. The fact was that he had stolen the candlestick. 'Do you still have it?'

He nodded uncomfortably.

At that moment, Thomas came in. 'There you are!' he said to Philemon.

Caris said: 'Thomas, go upstairs and search Philemon's room.'

'What am I looking for?'

'The lost gold candlestick.'

Philemon said: 'No need to search. You'll see it on the prie-dieu.'

Thomas went upstairs and came down again carrying the candlestick. He handed it to Caris. It was heavy. She looked at it curiously. The base was engraved with the names of the twelve members of the chandlers' guild in tiny letters. Why had Philemon wanted it? Not to sell or melt down, obviously: he had had plenty of time to get rid of it but he had not done so. It seemed he had just wanted to have his own gold candlestick. Did he gaze at it and touch it when he was alone in his room?

She looked at him and saw tears in his eyes.

He said: 'Are you going to take it from me?'

It was a stupid question. 'Of course,' she replied. 'It belongs in the cathedral, not in your bedroom. The chandlers gave it for the glory of God and the beautification of church services, not the private pleasure of one monk.'

He did not argue. He looked bereft, but not penitent. He did not understand that he had done wrong. His grief was not remorse for wrongdoing, but regret for what had been taken from him. He had no sense of shame, she realized.

'I think that ends our discussion about your access to the priory's valuables,' she said to Philemon. 'Now you may go.' He went out.

She handed the candlestick back to Thomas. 'Take it to Sister Joan and tell her to put it away,' she said. 'We'll inform the chandlers that it has been found, and use it next Sunday.'

Thomas went off.

Caris stayed where she was, thinking. Philemon hated her. She wasted no time wondering why: he made enemies faster than a tinker made friends. But he was an implacable foe and completely without scruples. Clearly he was determined to make trouble for her at every opportunity. Things would never get better. Each time she overcame him in one of these little skirmishes, his malice would burn hotter. But if she let him win he would only be encouraged in his insubordination.

It was going to be a bloody battle, and she could not see how it would end.

*

THE FLAGELLANTS came back on a Saturday evening in June.

Caris was in the scriptorium, writing her book. She had decided to begin with the plague and how to deal with it, then go on to lesser ailments. She was describing the linen face masks she had introduced in the Kingsbridge hospital. It was hard to explain that the masks were effective but did not offer total immunity. The only certain safeguard was to leave town before the plague arrived and stay away until it had gone, but that was never going to be an option for the majority of people. Partial protection was a difficult concept for people who believed in miracle cures. The truth was that some masked nuns still caught the plague, but not as many as would otherwise have been expected. She decided to compare the masks to shields. A shield did not guarantee that a man would survive attack, but it certainly gave him valuable protection, and no knight would go into battle without one. She was writing this down, on a pristine sheet of blank parchment, when she heard the flagellants, and groaned in dismay.

The drums sounded like drunken footsteps, the bagpipes like a wild creature in pain and the bells like a parody of a funeral. She went outside just as the procession entered the precincts. There were more of them this time, seventy or eighty, and they seemed wilder than before: their hair long and matted, their clothing a few shreds, their shrieks more lunatic. They had already been around the town and gathered a long tail of followers, some looking on in amusement, others joining in, tearing their clothes and lashing themselves.

She had not expected to see them again. The pope, Clement VI, had condemned flagellants. But he was a long way away, at Avignon, and it was up to others to enforce his rulings.

Friar Murdo led them, as before. When he approached the west front of the cathedral, Caris saw to her astonishment that the great doors were open wide. She had not authorized that. Thomas would not have done it without asking her. Philemon must be responsible. She recalled that Philemon on his travels had met up with Murdo. She guessed that Murdo had forewarned Philemon of this visit and they had conspired together to get the flagellants into the church. No doubt Philemon would argue that he was the only ordained priest in the priory, therefore he had the right to decide what kind of services were conducted.

But what was Philemon's motive? Why did he care about Murdo and the flagellants?

Murdo led the procession through the tall central doorway and into the nave. The townspeople crowded in afterwards. Caris hesitated to join in such a display, but she felt the need to know what was going on, so she reluctantly followed the crowd inside.

Philemon was at the altar. Friar Murdo joined him. Philemon raised his hands for quiet, then said: 'We come here today to confess our wickedness, repent our sins and do penance in propitiation.'

Philemon was no preacher, and his words drew a muted reaction; but the charismatic Murdo immediately took over. 'We confess that our thoughts are lascivious and our deeds are filthy!' he cried, and they shouted their approval.

The proceedings took the same form as before. Worked into a frenzy by Murdo's preaching, people came to the front, cried out that they were sinners and flogged themselves. The townspeople looked on, mesmerized by the violence and nudity. It was a performance, but the lashes were real, and Caris shuddered to see the weals and cuts on the backs of the penitents. Some of them had done this many times before, and were scarred. Others had recent wounds that were reopened by the fresh whipping.

Townspeople soon joined in. As they came forward, Philemon held out a collection bowl, and Caris realized that his motivation was money. Nobody got to confess and kiss Murdo's feet until they put a coin in Philemon's bowl. Murdo was keeping an eye on the takings, and Caris assumed the two men would share out the coins afterwards.

There was a crescendo of drumming and piping as more and more townspeople came forward. Philemon's bowl filled up rapidly. Those who had been 'forgiven' danced ecstatically to the mad music.

Eventually all the penitents were dancing and no more were coming forward. The music built to a climax and stopped suddenly, whereupon Caris noticed that Murdo and Philemon had disappeared. She assumed they had slipped out through the south transept to count their takings in the monks' cloisters.

The spectacle was over. The dancers lay down, exhausted. The spectators began to disperse, drifting out through the open doors into the clean air of the summer evening. Soon Murdo's followers found the strength to leave the church, and Caris did the same. She saw that most of the flagellants were heading for the Holly Bush.

She returned with relief to the cool hush of the nunnery. As dusk gathered in the cloisters, the nuns attended Evensong and ate their supper. Before going to bed, Caris went to check on the hospital. The place was still full: the plague raged unabated.

She found little to criticize. Sister Oonagh followed Caris's principles: face masks, no bloodletting, fanatical cleanliness. Caris was about to go to bed when one of the flagellants was brought in.

It was a man who had fainted in the Holly Bush and cracked his head on a bench. His back was still bleeding, and Caris guessed that loss of blood was as much responsible as the blow to his head for the loss of consciousness.

Oonagh bathed his wounds with salt water while he was unconscious. To bring him round, she set fire to the antler of a deer and wafted the pungent smoke under his nose. Then she made him drink two pints of water mixed with cinnamon and sugar, to replace the fluid his body had lost.

But he was only the first. Several more men and women were brought in suffering from some combination of loss of blood, excess of strong drink and injuries received in accidents or fights. The orgy of flagellation increased the number of Saturday-night patients tenfold. There was also a man who had flogged himself so many times that his back was putrid. Finally, after midnight, a woman was brought in after having been tied up, flogged and raped.

Fury stoked up in Caris as she worked with the other nuns to tend these patients. All their injuries arose from the perverted notions of religion put about by men such as Murdo. They said the plague was God's punishment for sin, but people could avoid the plague by punishing themselves another way. It was as if God were a vengeful monster playing a game with insane rules. Caris believed that God's sense of justice must be more sophisticated than that of the twelve-year-old leader of a boys' gang.

She worked until Matins on Sunday morning, then went to sleep for a couple of hours. When she got up, she went to see Merthin.

He was now living in the grandest of the houses he had built on Leper Island. It was on the south shore, and stood in a broad garden newly planted with apple and pear trees. He had hired a middle-aged couple to take care of Lolla and maintain the place. Their names were Arnaud and Emily, but they called one another Arn and Em. Caris found Em in the kitchen, and was directed to the garden.

Merthin was showing Lolla how her name was written, using a pointed stick to form the letters in a patch of bare earth, and he made her laugh by drawing a face in the 'o'. She was four years old, a pretty girl with olive skin and brown eyes.

Watching them, Caris suffered a pang of regret. She had been sleeping with Merthin for almost half a year. She did not want to have a baby, for it would mean the end of all her ambitions; yet a part of her was sorry that she had not become pregnant. She was torn, which was probably why she had taken the risk. But it had not happened. She wondered whether she had lost the ability to conceive. Perhaps the potion Mattie Wise had given her to abort her pregnancy a decade ago had harmed her womb in some way. As always, she wished she knew more about the body and its ills.

Merthin kissed her and they walked around the grounds, with Lolla running in front of them, playing in her imagination an elaborate and impenetrable game that involved talking to each tree. The garden looked raw, all the plants new, the soil carted in from elsewhere to enrich the island's stony ground. 'I've come to talk to you about the flagellants,' Caris said, and she told him about last night at the hospital. 'I want to ban them from Kingsbridge,' she finished.

'Good idea,' Merthin said. 'The whole performance is just another money-maker for Murdo.'

'And Philemon. He was holding the bowl. Will you talk to the parish guild?'

'Of course.'

As acting prior, Caris was in the position of lord of the manor, and she could theoretically have banned the flagellants herself, without asking anyone else. However, her application for a borough charter was before the king, and she expected soon to hand over the government of the town to the guild, so she treated the current situation as a transition. Besides, it was always smarter to win support before trying to enforce a rule.

She said: 'I'd like to have the constable escort Murdo and his followers out of town before the midday service.'

'Philemon will be furious.'

'He shouldn't have opened the church to them without consulting anyone.' Caris knew there would be trouble, but she could not allow fear of Philemon's reaction to prevent her doing the right thing for the town. 'We've got the pope on our side. If we handle this discreetly and move fast, we can solve the problem before Philemon's had breakfast.'

'All right,' said Merthin. 'I'll try to get the guildsmen together at the Holly Bush.'

'I'll meet you there in an hour.'

The parish guild was badly depleted, like every other organization in town, but a handful of leading merchants had survived the plague, including Madge Webber, Jake Chepstow and Edward Slaughterhouse. The new constable, John's son Mungo, attended, and his deputies waited outside for their instructions.

The discussion did not last long. None of the leading citizens had taken part in the orgy, and they all disapproved of such public displays. The pope's ruling clinched the matter. Formally, Caris as prior promulgated a by-law forbidding whipping in the streets and public nudity, with violators to be expelled from the town by the constable on the instructions of any three guildsmen. The guild then passed a resolution supporting the new law.

Then Mungo went upstairs and roused Friar Murdo from his bed.

Murdo did not go quietly. Coming down the stairs he raved, he wept, he prayed and he cursed. Two of Mungo's deputies took him by the arms and half carried him out of the tavern. In the street he became louder. Mungo led the way, and the guildsmen followed. Some of Murdo's adherents came to protest and were themselves put under escort. A few townspeople tagged along as the group headed down the main street towards Merthin's bridge. None of the citizens objected to what was being done, and Philemon did not appear. Even some who had flogged themselves yesterday said nothing today, looking a bit shamefaced about it all.

The crowd fell away as the group crossed the bridge. With a reduced audience, Murdo became quieter. His righteous indignation was replaced by smouldering malevolence. Released at the far end of the double bridge, he stumped away through the suburbs without looking back. A handful of disciples trailed after him uncertainly.

Caris had a feeling she would not see him again.

She thanked Mungo and his men, then returned to the nunnery.

In the hospital, Oonagh was releasing the overnight accident cases to make room for new plague victims. Caris worked in the hospital until midday, then left gratefully and led the procession into the church for the main Sunday service. She found she was looking forward to an hour or two of psalms and prayers and a boring sermon: it would seem restful.

Philemon had a thunderous look when he led Thomas and the novice monks in. He had obviously heard about the expulsion of Murdo. No doubt he had seen the flagellants as a source of income for himself independent of Caris. That hope had been dashed, and he was livid.

For a moment, Caris wondered what he would do in his anger. Then she thought: Let him do what he likes. If it were not this, it would be something else. Whatever she did, sooner or later Philemon would be angry with her. There was no point in worrying about it.

She nodded off during the prayers and woke up when he began to preach. The pulpit seemed to heighten his charmlessness, and his sermons were poorly received, in general. However, today he grabbed the attention of his audience at the start by announcing that his subject would be fornication.

He took as his text a verse from St Paul's first letter to the early Christians at Corinth. He read it in Latin, then translated it in ringing tones: 'Now I have written to you not to keep company with anyone who is a fornicator!'

He elaborated tediously on the meaning of keeping company. 'Don't eat with them, don't drink with them, don't live with them, don't talk to them.' But Caris was wondering anxiously where he was going with this. Surely he would not dare to attack her directly from the pulpit? She glanced across the choir to Thomas, on the other side with the novice monks, and caught a worried look from him.

She looked again at Philemon's face, dark with resentment, and realized he was capable of anything.

'Who does this refer to?' he asked rhetorically. 'Not to

outsiders, the saint specifically writes. It is for God to judge them. But, he says, you are judges within the fellowship.' He pointed at the congregation. 'You!' He looked down again at the book and read: 'Put away from among yourselves that wicked person!'

The congregation was quiet. They sensed that this was not the usual generalized exhortation to better behaviour. Philemon had a message.

'We must look around ourselves,' he said. 'In our town – in our church – in our priory! Are there any fornicators? If so, they must be put out!'

There was no doubt now in Caris's mind that he was referring to her. And the more astute townspeople would have come to the same conclusion. But what could she do? She could hardly get up and contradict him. She could not even walk out of the church, for that would underline his point and make it obvious, to the stupidest member of the congregation, that she was the target of his tirade.

So she listened, mortified. Philemon was speaking well for the first time ever. He did not hesitate or stumble, he enunciated clearly and projected his voice, and he managed to vary his usual dull monotone. For him, hatred was inspirational.

No one was going to put her out of the priory, of course. Even if she had been an incompetent prioress the bishop would have kept her on, simply because the scarcity of clergy was chronic. Churches and monasteries all over the country were closing because there was no one to hold services or sing psalms. Bishops were desperate to appoint more priests, monks and nuns, not sack them. Anyway, the townspeople would have revolted against any bishop who tried to get rid of Caris.

All the same, Philemon's sermon was damaging. It would now be more difficult for the town's leaders to turn a blind eye to Caris's liaison with Merthin. This kind of thing undermined people's respect. They would forgive a man for a sexual peccadillo more readily than a woman. And, as she was painfully aware, her position invited the accusation of hypocrisy.

She sat grinding her teeth through the peroration, which was the same message shouted louder, and the remainder of the service. As soon as the nuns and monks had processed out of the church, she went to her pharmacy and sat down to compose a letter to Bishop Henri, asking him to move Philemon to another monastery.

*

INSTEAD, HENRI promoted him.

It was two weeks after the expulsion of Friar Murdo. They were in the north transept of the cathedral. The summer day was hot, but the interior of the church was always cool. The bishop sat on a carved wooden chair, and the others on benches: Philemon, Caris, Archdeacon Lloyd and Canon Claude.

'I'm appointing you prior of Kingsbridge,' Henri said to Philemon.

Philemon smirked with delight and shot a triumphant look at Caris.

She was appalled. Two weeks ago she had given Henri a long list of sound reasons why Philemon could not be permitted to continue in a responsible position here – starting with his theft of a gold candlestick. But it seemed her letter had had the opposite effect.

She opened her mouth to protest, but Henri glared at her and
his hand, and she decided to remain silent and find out
he had to say. He continued to address Philemon. 'I'm
despite, not because of, your behaviour since you
You've been a malicious troublemaker, and if the
desperate for people I wouldn't promote you in

Caris wondered.
rior, and it simply is not satisfactory
despite her undoubted ability.'
him to appoint Thomas. But
y. He had been scarred by
d Prior Anthony, twelve
to get involved in a
well have spoken to
arned this.
ced about with provisos,'
will not be confirmed in the

role until Kingsbridge has obtained its borough charter. You are not capable of running the town and I won't put you in that position. In the interim, therefore, Mother Caris will continue as acting prior, and you will live in the monks' dormitory. The palace will be locked up. If you misbehave in the waiting period, I will rescind the appointment.'

Philemon looked angry and wounded by this, but he kept his mouth shut tight. He knew he had won and he was not going to argue about the conditions.

'Secondly, you will have your own treasury, but Brother Thomas is to be the treasurer, and no money will be spent nor precious objects removed without his knowledge and consent. Furthermore, I have ordered the building of a new tower, and I have authorized payments according to a schedule prepared by Merthin Bridger. The priory will make these payments from the monks' funds, and neither Philemon nor anyone else shall have the power to alter this arrangement. I don't want half a tower.'

Merthin would get his wish, at least, Caris thought gratefully.

Henri turned to Caris. 'I have one more command to issue, and it is for you, Mother Prioress.'

Now what? she thought.

'There has been an accusation of fornication.'

Caris stared at the bishop, thinking about the time she had surprised him and Claude naked. How did he dare to raise thi subject?

He went on: 'I say nothing about the past. But for the futu it is not possible that the prioress of Kingsbridge should ha relationship with a man.'

She wanted to say: But you live with your lover! Ho she suddenly noticed the expression on Henri's face. I pleading look. He was begging her not to make the a that, he well knew, would show him up as a hypocrite that what he was doing was unjust, she realized, bu choice. Philemon had forced him into this position.

She was tempted, all the same, to sting him But she restrained herself. It would do no good. H to the wall and he was doing his best. Caris cla shut.

Henri said: 'May I have your assurance, Mother Prioress, that from this moment on there will be absolutely no grounds for the accusation?'

Caris looked at the floor. She had been here before. Once again her choice was to give up everything she had worked for – the hospital, the borough charter, the tower – or to part with Merthin. And, once again, she chose her work.

She raised her head and looked him in the eye. 'Yes, my lord bishop,' she said. 'You have my word.'

*

SHE SPOKE TO Merthin in the hospital, surrounded by other people. She was trembling and close to tears, but she could not see him in private. She knew that if they were alone her resolve would weaken, and she would throw her arms around him and tell him that she loved him, and promise to leave the nunnery and marry him. So she sent a message, and greeted him at the door of the hospital, then spoke to him in a matter-of-fact voice, her arms folded tightly across her chest so that she would not be tempted to reach out with a fond gesture and touch the body she loved so much.

When she had finished telling him about the bishop's ultimatum and her decision, he looked at her as if he could kill her. 'This is the last time,' he said.

'What do you mean?'

'If you do this, it's permanent. I'm not going to wait around any more, hoping that one day you will be my wife.'

She felt as if he had hit her.

He went on, delivering another blow with each sentence. 'If you mean what you're saying, I'm going to try to forget you now. I'm thirty-three years old. I don't have for ever – my father is dying at the age of fifty-eight. I'll marry someone else and have more children and be happy in my garden.'

The picture he painted tortured her. She bit her lip, trying to control her grief, but hot tears ran down her face.

He was remorseless. 'I'm not going to waste my life loving you,' he said, and she felt as if he had stabbed her. 'Leave the nunnery now, or stay there for ever.'

She tried to look steadily at him. 'I won't forget you. I will always love you.'

'But not enough.'

She was silent for a long moment. It wasn't like that, she knew. Her love was not weak or inadequate. It just presented her with impossible choices. But there seemed no point in arguing. 'Is that what you really believe?' she said.

'It seems obvious.'

She nodded, though she did not really agree. 'I'm sorry,' she said. 'More sorry than I have ever been in my whole life.'

'So am I,' he said, and he turned away and walked out of the building.

# 75

Sir Gregory Longfellow at last went back to London, but he returned surprisingly quickly, as if he had bounced off the wall of that great city like a football. He showed up at Tench Hall at supper time looking harassed, breathing hard through his flared nostrils, his long grey hair matted with perspiration. He walked in with something less than his usual air of being in command of all men and beasts that crossed his path. Ralph and Alan were standing by a window, looking at a new broad-bladed style of dagger called a basilard. Without speaking, Gregory threw his tall figure into Ralph's big carved chair: whatever might have happened, he was still too grand to wait for an invitation to sit.

Ralph and Alan stared at him expectantly. Ralph's mother sniffed censoriously: she disliked bad manners.

Finally Gregory said: 'The king does not like to be disobeyed.'

That scared Ralph.

He looked anxiously at Gregory, and asked himself what he had done that could possibly be interpreted as disobedient by the king. He could think of nothing. Nervously he said: 'I'm sorry his majesty is displeased – I hope it's not with me.'

'You're involved,' Gregory said with annoying vagueness. 'And so am I. The king feels that when his wishes are frustrated it sets a bad precedent.'

'I quite agree.'

'That is why you and I are going to leave here tomorrow, ride to Earlscastle, see the Lady Philippa, and *make* her marry you.'

So that was it. Ralph was mainly relieved. He could not be held responsible for Philippa's recalcitrance, in all fairness – not that fairness made much difference to kings. But, reading between the lines, he guessed that the person taking the blame was

Gregory, and so Gregory was now determined to rescue the king's plan and redeem himself.

There was fury and malice in Gregory's expression. He said: 'By the time I have finished with her, I promise you, she will beg you to marry her.'

Ralph could not imagine how this was to be achieved. As Philippa herself had pointed out, you could lead a woman up the aisle but you could not force her to say 'I do'. He said to Gregory: 'Someone told me that a widow's right to refuse remarriage is actually guaranteed by Magna Carta.'

Gregory gave him a malevolent look. 'Don't remind me. I made the mistake of mentioning that to his majesty.'

Ralph wondered, in that case, what threats or promises Gregory planned to use to bend Philippa to his will. Himself, he could think of no way to marry her short of abducting her by force, and carrying her off to some isolated church where a generously bribed priest would turn a deaf ear to her cries of 'No, never!'

They set off early next morning with a small entourage. It was harvest time and, in the North Field, the men were reaping tall stalks of rye while the women followed behind, binding the sheaves.

Lately Ralph had spent more time worrying about the harvest than about Philippa. This was not because of the weather, which was fine, but the plague. He had too few tenants and almost no labourers. Many had been stolen from him by unscrupulous landlords such as Prioress Caris, who seduced other lords' men by offering high wages and attractive tenancies. In desperation, Ralph had given some of his serfs free tenancies, which meant they had no obligation to work on his land – an arrangement that left Ralph denuded of labour at harvest time. In consequence, it was likely that some of his crops would rot in the fields.

However, he felt his troubles would be over if he could marry Philippa. He would have ten times the land he now controlled, plus income from a dozen other sources including courts, forests, markets and mills. And his family would be restored to its rightful place in the nobility. Sir Gerald would be the father of an earl before he died.

He wondered again what Gregory had in mind. Philippa had set herself a challenging task, in defying the formidable will and powerful connections of Gregory. Ralph would not have wished to be standing in her beaded silk shoes.

They arrived at Earlscastle shortly before noon. The sound of the rooks quarrelling on the battlements always reminded Ralph of the time he had spent here as a squire in the service of Earl Roland – the happiest days of his life, he sometimes thought. But the place was very quiet now, without an earl. There were no squires playing violent games in the lower compound, no warhorses snorting and stamping as they were groomed and exercised outside the stables, no men-at-arms throwing dice on the steps of the keep.

Philippa was in the old-fashioned hall with Odila and a handful of female attendants. Mother and daughter were working on a tapestry together, sitting side by side on a bench in front of the loom. The picture looked as if it would show a forest scene, when finished. Philippa was weaving brown thread for the tree trunks and Odila bright green for the leaves.

'Very nice, but it needs more life,' Ralph said, making his voice cheerful and friendly. 'A few birds and rabbits, and maybe some dogs chasing a deer.'

Philippa was as immune to his charm as ever. She stood up and stepped back, away from him. The girl did the same. Ralph noticed that mother and daughter were equal in height. Philippa said: 'Why have you come here?'

Have it your way, Ralph thought resentfully. He half turned away from her. 'Sir Gregory here has something to say to you,' he said, and he went to a window and looked out, as if bored.

Gregory greeted the two women formally, and said he hoped he was not intruding on them. It was rubbish – he did not give a hoot for their privacy – but the courtesy seemed to mollify Philippa, who invited him to sit down. Then he said: 'The king is annoyed with you, countess.'

Philippa bowed her head. 'I am very sorry indeed to have displeased his majesty.'

'He wishes to reward his loyal servant, Sir Ralph, by making him earl of Shiring. At the same time, he will be providing a young, vigorous husband for you, and a good stepfather for your daughter.' Philippa shuddered, but Gregory ignored that. 'He is mystified by your stubborn defiance.'

Philippa looked scared, as well she might. Things would have been different if she had had a brother or an uncle to stick up for her, but the plague had wiped out her family. As a woman without male relations, she had no one to defend her from the king's wrath. 'What will he do?' she said apprehensively.

'He has not mentioned the word "treason" ... yet.'

Ralph was not sure Philippa could legally be accused of treason, but all the same the threat caused her to turn pale.

Gregory went on: 'He has asked me, in the first instance, to reason with you.'

Philippa said: 'Of course, the king sees marriage as a political matter—'

'It *is* political,' Gregory interrupted. 'If your beautiful daughter, here, were to fancy herself in love with the charming son of a scullery maid, you would say to her, as I say to you, that noblewomen may not marry whomever they fancy; and you would lock her in her room and have the boy flogged outside her window until he renounced her for ever.'

Philippa looked affronted. She did not like being lectured on the duties of her station by a mere lawyer. 'I understand the obligations of an aristocratic widow,' she said haughtily. 'I am a countess, my grandmother was a countess, and my sister was a countess until she died of the plague. But marriage is not *just* politics. It is also a matter of the heart. We women throw ourselves on the mercy of the men who are our lords and masters, and who have the duty of wisely deciding our fate; and we beg that what we feel in our hearts be not entirely ignored. Such pleas are usually heard.'

She was upset, Ralph could see, but still in control, still full of contempt. That word 'wisely' had a sarcastic sting.

'In normal times, perhaps you would be right, but these are strange days,' Gregory replied. 'Usually, when the king looks around him for someone worthy of an earldom, he sees a dozen wise, strong, vigorous men, loyal to him and keen to serve him in any way they can, any of whom he could appoint to the title with confidence. But now that so many of the best men have been struck down by the plague, the king is like a housewife who goes to the fishmonger at the end of the afternoon – forced to take whatever is left on the slab.'

Ralph saw the force of the argument, but also felt insulted. However, he pretended not to notice.

Philippa changed her tack. She waved a servant over and said: 'Bring us a jug of the best Gascon wine, please. And Sir Gregory will be having dinner here, so let's have some of this season's lamb, cooked with garlic and rosemary.'

'Yes, my lady.'

Gregory said: 'You're most kind, countess.'

Philippa was incapable of coquetry. To pretend that she was simply being hospitable, with no ulterior motive, was beyond her. She returned straight to the subject. 'Sir Gregory, I have to tell you that my heart, my soul and my entire being revolt against the prospect of marrying Sir Ralph Fitzgerald.'

'But why?' said Gregory. 'He's a man like any other.'

'No, he's not,' she said.

They were speaking about Ralph as if he were not there, in a way that he found deeply offensive. But Philippa was desperate, and would say anything; and he was curious to know just what it was about him that she disliked so much.

She paused, collecting her thoughts. 'If I say rapist, torturer, murderer ... the words just seem too abstract.'

Ralph was taken aback. He did not think of himself that way. Of course, he had tortured people in the king's service, and he had raped Annet, and he had murdered several men, women and children in his days as an outlaw ... At least, he consoled himself, Philippa did not appear to have guessed that he was the hooded figure who had killed Tilly, his own wife.

Philippa went on: 'Human beings have within them something that prevents them from doing such things. It is the ability ... no, the compulsion to feel another's pain. We can't help it. You, Sir Gregory, could not rape a woman, because you would feel her grief and agony, you would suffer with her, and this would compel you to relent. You could not torture or murder for the same reason. One who lacks the faculty to feel another's pain is not a man, even though he may walk on two legs and speak English.' She leaned forward, lowering her voice, but even so Ralph heard her clearly. 'And I will not lie in bed with an *animal*.'

Ralph burst out: 'I am not an animal!'

He expected Gregory to back him up. Instead, Gregory seemed to give in. 'Is that your final word, Lady Philippa?'

Ralph was astonished. Was Gregory going to let that pass, as if it might be even half true?

Philippa said to Gregory: 'I need you to go back to the king and tell him that I am his loyal and obedient subject, and that I long to win his favour, but that I could not marry Ralph if the Archangel Gabriel commanded me.'

'I see.' Gregory stood up. 'We will not stay to dinner.'

Was that all? Ralph had been waiting for Gregory to produce his surprise, a secret weapon, some irresistible bribe or threat. Did the clever court lawyer really have nothing up his costly brocade sleeve?

Philippa seemed equally startled to find the argument so suddenly terminated.

Gregory went to the door, and Ralph had no choice but to follow. Philippa and Odila stared at the two of them, unsure what to make of this cool walkout. The ladies-in-waiting fell silent.

Philippa said: 'Please, beg the king to be merciful.'

'He will be, my lady,' said Gregory. 'He has authorized me to tell you that, in the light of your obstinacy, he will not force you to marry a man you loathe.'

'Thank you!' she said. 'You have saved my life.'

Ralph opened his mouth to protest. He had been promised! He had committed sacrilege and murder for this reward. Surely it could not be taken from him now?

But Gregory spoke first. 'Instead,' he said, 'it is the king's command that Ralph will marry your daughter.' He paused, and pointed at the tall fifteen-year-old girl standing beside her mother. 'Odila,' he said, as if there were any need to emphasize who he was talking about.

Philippa gasped and Odila screamed.

Gregory bowed. 'Good day to you both.'

Philippa cried: 'Wait!'

Gregory took no notice, and went out.

Stunned, Ralph followed.

*

GWENDA WAS WEARY when she woke up. It was harvest time, and she was spending every hour of the long August days in the fields. Wulfric would swing the scythe tirelessly from sunrise to nightfall, mowing down the corn. Gwenda's job was to bundle the sheaves. All day long she bent down and scooped up the mown stalks, bent and scooped, bent and scooped until her back seemed to burn with pain. When it was too dark to see, she staggered home and fell into bed, leaving the family to feed themselves with whatever they could find in the cupboard.

Wulfric woke at dawn, and his movements penetrated Gwenda's deep slumber. She struggled to her feet. They all needed a good breakfast, and she put cold mutton, bread, butter and strong beer on the table. Sam, the ten-year-old, got up, but Davy, who was only eight, had to be shaken awake and pulled to his feet.

'This holding was never farmed by one man and his wife,' Gwenda said grumpily as they ate.

Wulfric was irritatingly positive. 'You and I got the harvest in on our own, the year the bridge collapsed,' he said cheerfully.

'I was twelve years younger then.'

'But you're more beautiful now.'

She was in no mood for gallantry. 'Even when your father and brother were alive, you took on hired labour at harvest time.'

'Never mind. It's our land, and we planted the crops, so we'll benefit from the harvest, instead of earning just a penny a day wages. The more we work, the more we get. That's what you always wanted, isn't it?'

'I always wanted to be independent and self-sufficient, if that's what you mean.' She went to the door. 'A west wind, and a few clouds in the sky.'

Wulfric looked worried. 'We need the rain to hold off for another two or three days.'

'I think it will. Come on, boys, time to go to the field. You can eat walking along.' She was bundling the bread and meat into a sack for their dinner when Nate Reeve hobbled in through the door. 'Oh, no!' she said. 'Not today – we've almost got our harvest in!'

'The lord has a harvest to get in, too,' said the bailiff.

Nate was followed in by his ten-year-old son, Jonathan, known as Jonno, who immediately started making faces at Sam.

Gwenda said: 'Give us three more days on our own land.'

'Don't bother to dispute with me about this,' Nate said. 'You owe the lord one day a week, and two days at harvest time. Today and tomorrow you will reap his barley in Brookfield.'

'The second day is normally forgiven. That's been the practice for a long time.'

'It was, in times of plentiful labour. The lord is desperate now. So many people have negotiated free tenancies that he has hardly anyone to bring in his harvest.'

'So those who negotiated with you, and demanded to be freed of their customary duties, are rewarded, while people like us, who accepted the old terms, are punished with twice as much work on the lord's land.' She looked accusingly at Wulfric, remembering how he had ignored her when she told him to argue terms with Nate.

'Something like that,' Nate said carelessly.

'Hell,' Gwenda said.

'Don't curse,' said Nate. 'You'll get a free dinner. There will be wheat bread and a new barrel of ale. Isn't that something to look forward to?'

'Sir Ralph feeds oats to the horses he means to ride hard.'

'Don't be long, now!' Nate went out.

His son, Jonno, poked out his tongue at Sam. Sam made a grab for him, but Jonno slipped out of his grasp and ran after his father.

Wearily, Gwenda and her family trudged across the fields to where Ralph's barley stood waving in the breeze. They got down to work. Wulfric reaped and Gwenda bundled. Sam followed behind, picking up the stray stalks she missed, gathering them until he had enough for a sheaf, then passing them to her to be tied. David had small, nimble fingers, and he plaited straws into tough cords for tying the sheaves. Those other families still working under old-style tenancies laboured alongside them, while the cleverer serfs reaped their own crops.

When the sun was at its highest, Nate drove up in a cart with a barrel on the back. True to his word, he provided each family with a big loaf of delicious new wheat bread. Everyone ate their fill, then the adults lay down in the shade to rest while the children played.

Gwenda was dozing off when she heard an outbreak of childish screaming. She knew immediately, from the voice, that neither of her boys was making the noise, but all the same she leaped to her feet. She saw her son Sam fighting with Jonno Reeve. Although they were roughly the same age and size, Sam had Jonno on the ground and was punching and kicking him mercilessly. Gwenda moved towards the boys, but Wulfric was quicker, and he grabbed Sam with one hand and hauled him off.

Gwenda looked at Jonno in dismay. The boy was bleeding from his nose and mouth, and his face around one eye was inflamed and already beginning to swell. He was holding his stomach, moaning and crying. Gwenda had seen plenty of scraps between boys, but this was different. Jonno had been beaten up.

Gwenda stared at her ten-year-old son. His face was unmarked: it looked as if Jonno had not landed a single blow. Sam showed no sign of remorse at what he had done. Rather, he looked smugly triumphant. It was a vaguely familiar expression, and Gwenda searched her memory for its likeness. She did not take long to recall who she had seen looking like that after giving someone a beating.

She had seen the same expression on the face of Ralph Fitzgerald, Sam's real father.

*

Two days after Ralph and Gregory visited Earlscastle, Lady Philippa came to Tench Hall.

Ralph had been considering the prospect of marrying Odila. She was a beautiful young girl, but you could buy beautiful young girls for a few pennies in London. Ralph had already had the experience of being married to someone who was little more than a child. After the initial excitement wore off, he had been bored and irritated by her.

He wondered for a while whether he might marry Odila and get Philippa too. The idea of marrying the daughter and keeping the mother as his mistress intrigued him. He might even have them together. He had once had sex with a mother-daughter pair of prostitutes in Calais, and the element of incest had created an exciting sense of depravity.

But, on reflection, he knew that was not going to happen. Philippa would never consent to such an arrangement. He might look for ways to coerce her, but she was not easily bullied. 'I don't want to marry Odila,' he had said to Gregory as they rode home from Earlscastle.

'You won't have to,' Gregory had said, but he refused to elaborate.

Philippa arrived with a lady-in-waiting and a bodyguard but without Odila. As she entered Tench Hall, for once she did not look proud. She did not even look beautiful, Ralph thought: clearly she had not slept for two nights.

They had just sat down to dinner: Ralph, Alan, Gregory, a handful of squires and a bailiff. Philippa was the only woman in the room.

She walked up to Gregory.

The courtesy he had shown her previously was forgotten. He did not stand, but rudely looked her up and down, as if she were a servant girl with a grievance. 'Well?' he said at last.

'I will marry Ralph.'

'Oh!' he said in mock surprise. 'Will you, now?'

'Yes. Rather than sacrifice my daughter to him, I will marry him myself.'

'My lady,' he said sarcastically, 'you seem to think that the king has led you to a table laden with dishes, and asked you to choose which you like best. You are mistaken. The king does not ask what is your pleasure. He commands. You disobeyed one command, so he issued another. He did not give you a choice.'

She looked down. 'I am very sorry for my behaviour. Please spare my daughter.'

'If it were up to me, I would decline your request, as punishment for your intransigence. But perhaps you should plead with Sir Ralph.'

She looked at Ralph. He saw rage and despair in her eyes. He felt excited. She was the most haughty woman he had ever met, and he had broken her pride. He wanted to lie with her now, right away.

But it was not yet over.

He said: 'You have something to say to me?'

'I apologize.'

'Come here.' Ralph was sitting at the head of the table, and she approached and stood by him. He caressed the head of a lion carved into the arm of his chair. 'Go on,' he said.

'I am sorry that I spurned you before. I would like to withdraw everything I said. I accept your proposal. I will marry you.'

'But I have not renewed my proposal. The king orders me to marry Odila.'

'If you ask the king to revert to his original plan, surely he will grant your plea.'

'And that is what you are asking me to do.'

'Yes.' She looked him in the eye and swallowed her final humiliation. 'I am asking you ... I am begging you. Please, Sir Ralph, make me your wife.'

Ralph stood up, pushing his chair back. 'Kiss me, then.'

She closed her eyes.

He put his left arm around her shoulders and pulled her to him. He kissed her lips. She submitted unresponsively. With his right hand, he squeezed her breast. It was as firm and heavy as he had always imagined. He ran his hand down her body and between her legs. She flinched, but remained unresistingly in his embrace, and he pressed his palm against the fork of her thighs. He grasped her mound, cupping its triangular fatness in his hand.

Then, holding that position, he broke the kiss and looked around the room at his friends.

# 76

At the same time as Ralph was created earl of Shiring, a young man called David Caerleon became earl of Monmouth. He was only seventeen, and related rather distantly to the dead man, but all nearer heirs to the title had been wiped out by the plague.

A few days before Christmas that year, Bishop Henri held a service in Kingsbridge Cathedral to bless the two new earls. Afterwards David and Ralph were guests of honour at a banquet given by Merthin in the guild hall. The merchants were also celebrating the granting of a borough charter to Kingsbridge.

Ralph considered David to have been extraordinarily lucky. The boy had never been outside the kingdom, nor had he ever fought in battle, yet he was an earl at seventeen. Ralph had marched all through Normandy with King Edward, risked his life in battle after battle, lost three fingers, and committed countless sins in the king's service, yet he had had to wait until the age of thirty-two.

However, he had made it at last, and sat next to Bishop Henri at the table, wearing a costly brocade coat woven with gold and silver threads. People who knew him pointed him out to strangers, wealthy merchants made way for him and bowed their heads respectfully as he passed, and the maidservant's hand shook with nervousness as she poured wine into his cup. His father, Sir Gerald, confined to bed now but hanging on tenaciously to life, had said: 'I'm the descendant of an earl, and the father of an earl. I'm satisfied.' It was all profoundly gratifying.

Ralph was keen to talk to David about the problem of labourers. It had eased temporarily now that the harvest was in and the autumn ploughing was finished: at this time of year the days were short and the weather was cold, so not much work could be done in the fields. Unfortunately, as soon as the spring ploughing began and the ground was soft enough for the serfs to sow seeds, the trouble would start again: labourers would recommence agitating for higher wages, and if refused would illegally run off to more extravagant employers.

The only way to stop this was for the nobility collectively to stand firm, resist demands for higher pay and refuse to hire runaways. This was what Ralph wanted to say to David.

However, the new earl of Monmouth showed no inclination to talk to Ralph. He was more interested in Ralph's stepdaughter, Odila, who was near his own age. They had met before, Ralph gathered: Philippa and her first husband, William, had often been guests at the castle when David had been a squire in the service of the old earl. Whatever their history, they were friends now: David was talking animatedly and Odila was hanging on every word – agreeing with his opinions, gasping at his stories and laughing at his jokes.

Ralph had always envied men who could fascinate women. His brother had the ability, and consequently was able to attract the most beautiful women, despite being a short, plain man with red hair.

All the same, Ralph felt sorry for Merthin. Ever since the day that Earl Roland had made Ralph a squire and condemned Merthin to be a carpenter's apprentice, Merthin had been doomed. Even though he was the elder, it was Ralph who was destined to become the earl. Merthin, now sitting on the other side of Earl David, had to console himself with being a mere alderman – and having charm.

Ralph could not even charm his own wife. She hardly spoke to him. She had more to say to his dog.

How was it possible, Ralph asked himself, for a man to want something as badly as he had wanted Philippa, and then to be so dissatisfied when he got it? He had yearned for her since he was a squire of nineteen. Now, after three months of marriage, he wished with all his heart that he could get rid of her.

Yet it was hard for him to complain. Philippa did everything a wife was obliged to do. She ran the castle efficiently, as she had been doing ever since her first husband had been made earl after the battle of Crécy. Supplies were ordered, bills were paid, clothes were sewn, fires were lit, and food and wine arrived on the table unfailingly. And she submitted to Ralph's sexual attentions. He could do anything he liked: tear her clothes, thrust his fingers ungently inside her, take her standing up or from behind – she never complained.

But she did not reciprocate his caresses. Her lips never moved against his, her tongue never slipped into his mouth, she never stroked his skin. She kept a vial of almond oil handy, and lubricated her unresponsive body with it whenever he wanted sex. She lay as still as a corpse while he grunted on top of her. The moment he rolled off, she went to wash herself.

The only good thing about the marriage was that Odila was fond of little Gerry. The baby brought out her nascent maternal instinct. She loved to talk to him, sing him songs and rock him to sleep. She gave him the kind of affectionate mothering he would never really get from a paid nurse.

All the same, Ralph was regretful. Philippa's voluptuous body, which he had stared at with longing for so many years, was now revolting to him. He had not touched her for weeks, and he probably never would again. He looked at her heavy breasts and round hips, and wished for the slender limbs and girlish skin of Tilly. Tilly, whom he had stabbed with a long, sharp knife that went up under her ribs and into her beating heart. That was a sin he did not dare to confess. How long, he wondered wretchedly, would he suffer for it in purgatory?

The bishop and his colleagues were staying in the prior's palace, and the Monmouth entourage filled the priory's guest rooms, so Ralph and Philippa and their servants were lodging at an inn. Ralph had chosen the Bell, the rebuilt tavern owned by his brother. It was the only three-storey house in Kingsbridge, with a big open room at ground level, male and female dormitories above, and a top floor with six expensive individual guest rooms. When the banquet was over, Ralph and his men removed to the tavern, where they installed themselves in front of the fire, called for more wine and began to play at dice. Philippa remained behind, talking to Caris and chaperoning Odila with Earl David.

Ralph and his companions attracted a crowd of admiring

young men and women such as always gathered around free-spending noblemen. Ralph gradually forgot his troubles in the euphoria of drink and the thrill of gambling.

He noticed a young fair-haired woman watching him with a yearning expression as he cheerfully lost stacks of silver pennies on the throw of the dice. He beckoned her to sit beside him on the bench, and she told him her name was Ella. At moments of tension she grabbed his thigh, as if captured by the suspense, though she probably knew exactly what she was doing – women usually did.

He gradually lost interest in the game and transferred his attention to her. His men carried on betting while he got to know Ella. She was everything Philippa was not: happy, sexy, and fascinated by Ralph. She touched him and herself a lot – she would push her hair off her face, then pat his arm, then hold her hand to her throat, then push his shoulder playfully. She seemed very interested in his experiences in France.

To Ralph's annoyance, Merthin came into the tavern and sat down with him. Merthin was not running the Bell himself – he had rented it to the youngest daughter of Betty Baxter – but he was keen that the tenant should make a success of it, and he asked Ralph if everything was to his satisfaction. Ralph introduced his companion, and Merthin said: 'Yes, I know Ella,' in a dismissive tone that was uncharacteristically discourteous.

Today was only the third or fourth time the two brothers had met since the death of Tilly. On previous occasions, such as Ralph's wedding to Philippa, there had hardly been time to talk. All the same Ralph knew, from the way his brother looked at him, that Merthin suspected him of being Tilly's killer. The unspoken thought was a looming presence, never addressed but impossible to ignore, like the cow in the cramped one-room hovel of a poor peasant. If it was mentioned, Ralph felt that would be the last time they ever spoke.

So tonight, as if by mutual consent, they once again exchanged a few meaningless platitudes, then Merthin left, saying he had work to do. Ralph wondered briefly what work he was going to do at dusk on a December evening. He really had no idea how Merthin spent his time. He did not hunt, or hold court, or attend on the king. Was it possible to spend all day, every day, making drawings and supervising builders? Such a life would have driven Ralph mad. And he was baffled by how much money Merthin seemed to make from his enterprises. Ralph himself had been short of money even when he had been lord of Tench. Merthin never seemed to lack it.

Ralph turned his attention back to Ella. 'My brother's a bit grumpy,' he said apologetically.

'It's because he hasn't had a woman for half a year.' She giggled. 'He used to shag the prioress, but she had to throw him out after Philemon came back.'

Ralph pretended to be shocked. 'Nuns aren't supposed to be shagged.'

'Mother Caris is a wonderful woman – but she's got the itch, you can tell by the way she walks.'

Ralph was aroused by such frank talk from a woman. 'It's very bad for a man,' he said, playing along. 'To go for so long without a woman.'

'I think so too.'

'It leads to ... swelling.'

She put her head on one side and raised her eyebrows. He glanced down at his own lap. She followed his gaze. 'Oh, dear,' she said. 'That looks uncomfortable.' She put her hand on his erect penis.

At that moment, Philippa appeared

Ralph froze. He felt guilty and scared, and at the same time he was furious with himself for caring whether Philippa saw what he was doing or not.

She said: 'I'm going upstairs – oh.'

Ella did not release her hold. In fact she squeezed Ralph's penis gently, while looking up at Philippa and smiling triumphantly.

Philippa flushed red, her face registering shame and distaste.

Ralph opened his mouth to speak, then did not know what to say. He was not willing to apologize to his virago of a wife, feeling that she had brought this humiliation on herself. But he also felt somewhat foolish, sitting there with a tavern tart holding his prick while his wife, the countess, stood in front of them looking embarrassed.

The tableau lasted only a moment. Ralph made a strangled sound, Ella giggled, and Philippa said 'Oh!' in a tone of exasperation and disgust. Then Philippa turned and walked away, head held unnaturally high. She approached the broad staircase and went up, as graceful as a deer on a hillside, and disappeared without looking back.

Ralph felt both angry and ashamed, though he reasoned that he had no need to feel either. However, his interest in Ella diminished visibly, and he took her hand away.

'Have some more wine,' she said, pouring from the jug on the table, but Ralph felt the onset of a headache and pushed the wooden cup away.

Ella put a restraining hand on his arm and said in a low, warm voice: 'Don't leave me in the lurch now that you've got me all, you know, excited.'

He shook her off and stood up.

Her face hardened and she said: 'Well, you'd better give me something by way of compensation.'

He dipped into his purse and took out a handful of silver pennies. Without looking at Ella, he dumped the money on the table, not caring whether it was too much or too little.

She began to scoop up the coins hastily.

Ralph left her and went upstairs.

Philippa was on the bed, sitting upright with her back against the headboard. She had taken off her shoes but was otherwise fully dressed. She stared accusingly at Ralph as he walked in.

He said: 'You have no right to be angry with me!'

'I'm not angry,' she said. 'But you are.'

She could always twist words around so that she was in the right and he in the wrong.

Before he could think of a reply, she said: 'Wouldn't you like me to leave you?'

He stared at her, astonished. This was the last thing he had expected. 'Where would you go?'

'Here,' she said. 'I won't become a nun, but I could live in the convent nevertheless. I would bring just a few servants: a maid, a clerk and my confessor. I've already spoken to Mother Caris, and she is willing.'

'My last wife did that. What will people think?'

'A lot of noblewomen retire to nunneries, either temporarily or permanently, at some point in their lives. People will think you've rejected me because I'm past the age for conceiving children – which I probably am. Anyway, do you care what people say?'

The thought briefly flashed across his mind that he would be sorry to see Gerry lose Odila. But the prospect of being free of Philippa's proud, disapproving presence was irresistible. 'All right, what's stopping you? Tilly never asked permission.'

'I want to see Odila married first.'

'Who to?'

She looked at him as if he were stupid.

'Oh,' he said. 'Young David, I suppose.'

'He is in love with her, and I think they would be well suited.'

'He's under age – he'll have to ask the king.'

'That's why I've raised it with you. Will you go with him to see the king, and speak in support of the marriage? If you do this for me, I swear I will never ask you for anything ever again. I will leave you in peace.'

She was not asking him to make any sacrifices. An alliance with Monmouth could do Ralph nothing but good. 'And you'll leave Earlscastle, and move into the nunnery?'

'Yes, as soon as Odila is married.'

It was the end of a dream, Ralph realized, but a dream that had turned into a sour, bleak reality. He might as well acknowledge the failure and start again.

'All right,' he said, feeling regret mingled with liberation. 'It's a bargain.'

# 77

Easter came early in the year 1350, and there was a big fire blazing in Merthin's hearth on the evening of Good Friday. The table was laid with a cold supper: smoked fish, soft cheese, new bread, pears and a flagon of Rhenish wine. Merthin was wearing clean underclothes and a new yellow robe. The house had been swept, and there were daffodils in a jug on the sideboard.

Merthin was alone. Lolla was with his servants, Arn and Em. Their cottage was at the end of the garden but Lolla, who was five, loved to stay there overnight. She called it going on pilgrimage, and took a travelling bag containing her hair brush and a favourite doll.

Merthin opened a window and looked out. A cold breeze blew across the river from the meadow on the south side. The last of the evening was fading, the light seeming to fall out of the sky and sink into the water, where it disappeared in the blackness.

He visualized a hooded figure emerging from the nunnery. He saw it tread a worn diagonal across the cathedral green, hurry past the lights of the Bell and descend the muddy main street, the face shadowed, speaking to no one. He imagined it reaching the foreshore. Did it glance sideways into the cold black river, and remember a moment of despair so great as to give rise to thoughts of self-destruction? If so, the recollection was quickly dismissed, and it stepped forward on to the cobbled roadbed of his bridge. It crossed the span and made landfall again on Leper Island. There it diverted from the main road and passed through low shrubbery, across scrubby grass cropped by rabbits, and around the ruins of the old lazar house until it came to the south-west shore. Then it tapped on Merthin's door.

He closed the window and waited. No tap came. He was wishfully a little ahead of schedule.

He was tempted to drink some wine, but he did not: a ritual had developed, and he did not want to change the order of events.

The knock came a few moments later. He opened the door. She stepped inside, threw back her hood and dropped the heavy grey cloak from her shoulders.

She was taller than he by an inch or more, and a few years older. Her face was proud, and could be haughty, although now her smile radiated warmth like the sun. She wore a robe of bright Kingsbridge Scarlet. He put his arms around her, pressing her voluptuous body to his own, and kissed her wide mouth. 'My darling,' he said. 'Philippa.'

They made love immediately, there on the floor, hardly undressing. He was hungry for her, and she was if anything more eager. He spread her cloak on the straw, and she lifted the skirt of her robe and lay down. She clung to him like one drowning, her legs wrapped around his, her arms crushing him to her soft body, her face buried in his neck.

She had told him that, after she left Ralph and moved into the priory, she had thought no one would ever touch her again until the nuns laid out her cold body for burial. The thought almost made Merthin cry.

For his part, he had loved Caris so much that he felt no other woman would ever arouse his affection. For him as well as Philippa, this love had come as an unexpected gift, a spring of cold water bubbling up in a baking-hot desert, and they both drank from it as if they were dying of thirst.

Afterwards they lay entwined by the fire, panting, and he recalled the first time. Soon after she moved to the priory she had taken an interest in the building of the new tower. A practical woman, she had trouble filling the long hours that were supposed to be spent in prayer and meditation. She enjoyed the library but could not read all day. She came to see him in the mason's loft, and he showed her the plans. She quickly got into the habit of visiting every day, talking to him while he worked. He had always admired her intelligence and strength, and in the intimacy of the loft he came to know the warm, generous spirit beneath her stately manner. He discovered that she had a lively sense of humour, and he learned how to make her laugh. She responded with a rich, throaty chuckle that, somehow, led him to think of making love to her. One day she had paid him a compliment. 'You're a kind man,' she had said. 'There aren't enough of them.' Her sincerity had touched him, and he had kissed her hand. It was a gesture of affection, but one she could reject, if she wished, without drama: she simply had to withdraw her hand and take a step back, and he would have known he had gone a little too far. But she had not rejected it. On the contrary, she had held his hand and looked at him with something like love in her eyes, and he had wrapped his arms around her and kissed her lips.

They had made love on the mattress in the loft, and he had not remembered until afterwards that Caris had encouraged him to put the mattress there, with a joke about masons needing a soft place for their tools.

Caris did not know about him and Philippa. No one did except Philippa's maid and Arn and Em. She went to bed in her private room on the upper floor of the hospital soon after nightfall, at the same time as the nuns retired to their dormitory. She slipped out while they were asleep, using the outside steps that permitted important guests to come and go without passing through the common people's quarters. She returned by the same route before dawn, while the nuns were singing Matins, and appeared at breakfast as if she had been in her room all night.

He was surprised to find that he could love another woman less than a year after Caris had left him for the final time. He certainly had not forgotten Caris. On the contrary, he thought about her every day. He felt the urge to tell her about something amusing that had happened, or he wanted her opinion on a knotty problem, or he found himself performing some task the way she would want it done, such as carefully bathing Lolla's grazed knee with warm wine. And then he saw her most days. The new hospital was almost finished, but the cathedral tower was barely begun, and Caris kept a close eye on both building projects. The priory had lost its power to control the town merchants, but nevertheless Caris took an interest in the work Merthin and the guild were doing to create all the institutions of a borough – establishing new courts, planning a wool exchange and encouraging the craft guilds to codify standards and measures. But his thoughts about her always had an unpleasant aftertaste, like the bitterness left at the back of the throat by sour beer. He had loved her totally, and she had, in the end, rejected him. It was like remembering a happy day that had ended with a fight.

'Do you think I'm peculiarly attracted to women who aren't free?' he said idly to Philippa.

'No, why?'

'It does seem odd that after twelve years of loving a nun, and nine months of celibacy, I should fall for my brother's wife.'

'Don't call me that,' she said quickly. 'It was no marriage. I was wedded against my will, I shared his bed for no more than a few days, and he will be happy if he never sees me again.'

He patted her shoulder apologetically. 'But still, we have to be secretive, just as I did with Caris.' What he was not saying was that a man was entitled, by law, to kill his wife if he caught her committing adultery. Merthin had never known it happen, certainly among the nobility, but Ralph's pride was a terrible thing. Merthin knew, and had told Philippa, that Ralph had killed his first wife, Tilly.

She said: 'Your father loved your mother hopelessly for a long time, didn't he?'

'So he did!' Merthin had almost forgotten that old story.

'And you fell for a nun.'

'And my brother spent years pining for you, the happily married wife of a nobleman. As the priests say, the sins of the fathers are visited upon the sons. But enough of this. Do you want some supper?'

'In a moment.'

'There's something you want to do first?'

'You know.'

He did know. He knelt between her legs and kissed her belly and her thighs. It was a peculiarity of hers that she always wanted to come twice. He began to tease her with his tongue. She groaned, and pressed the back of his head. 'Yes,' she said. 'You know how I like that, especially when I'm full of your seed.'

He lifted his head. 'I do,' he said. Then he bent again to his task.

*

THE SPRING BROUGHT a respite in the plague. People were still dying, but fewer were falling ill. On Easter Sunday, Bishop Henri announced that the Fleece Fair would take place as usual this year.

At the same service, six novices took their vows and so became full-fledged monks. They had all had an extraordinarily short novitiate, but Henri was keen to raise the number of monks at Kingsbridge, and he said the same thing was going on all over the country. In addition five priests were ordained – they, too, benefiting from an accelerated training programme – and sent to replace plague victims in the surrounding countryside. And two Kingsbridge monks came down from university, having received their degrees as physicians in three years instead of the usual five or seven.

The new doctors were Austin and Sime. Caris remembered both of them rather vaguely: she had been guest master when they left, three years ago, to go to Kingsbridge College in Oxford. On the afternoon of Easter Monday she showed them around the almost completed new hospital. No builders were at work as it was a holiday.

Both had the bumptious self-confidence that the university seemed to instil in its graduates along with medical theories and a taste for Gascon wine. However, years of dealing with patients had given Caris a confidence of her own, and she described the hospital's facilities and the way she planned to run it with brisk assurance.

Austin was a slim, intense young man with thinning fair hair. He was impressed with the innovative new cloister-like layout of the rooms. Sime, a little older and round-faced, did not seem eager to learn from Caris's experience: she noticed that he always looked away when she was talking.

'I believe a hospital should always be clean,' she said.

'On what grounds?' Sime inquired in a condescending tone, as if asking a little girl why Dolly had to be spanked.

'Cleanliness is a virtue.'

'Ah. So it has nothing to do with the balance of humours in the body.'

'I have no idea. We don't pay too much attention to the humours. That approach has failed spectacularly against the plague.'

'And sweeping the floor has succeeded?'

'At a minimum, a clean room lifts patients' spirits.'

Austin put in: 'You must admit, Sime, that some of the masters at Oxford share the Mother Prioress's new ideas.'

'A small group of the heterodox.'

Caris said: 'The main point is to take patients suffering from the type of illnesses that are transmitted from the sick to the well and isolate them from the rest.'

'To what end?' said Sime.

'To restrict the spread of such diseases.'

'And how is it that they are transmitted?'

'No one knows.'

A little smile of triumph twitched Sime's mouth. 'Then how do you know by what means to restrict their spread, may I ask?'

He thought he had trumped her in argument – it was the main thing they learned at Oxford – but she knew better. 'From experience,' she said. 'A shepherd doesn't understand the miracle by which lambs grow in the womb of a ewe, but he knows it won't happen if he keeps the ram out of the field.'

'Hm.'

Caris disliked the way he said: 'Hm.' He was clever, she thought, but his cleverness never touched the world. She was struck by the contrast between this kind of intellectual and Merthin's kind. Merthin's learning was wide, and the power of his mind to grasp complexities was remarkable – but his wisdom never strayed far from the realities of the material world, for he knew that if he went wrong his buildings would fall down. Her father, Edmund, had been like that, clever but practical. Sime, like Godwyn and Anthony, would cling to his faith in the humours of the body regardless of whether his patients lived or died.

Austin was smiling broadly. 'She's got you there, Sime,' he

said, evidently amused that his smug friend had failed to overwhelm this uneducated woman. 'We may not know exactly how illnesses spread, but it can't do any harm to separate the sick from the well.'

Sister Joan, the nuns' treasurer, interrupted their conversation. 'The bailiff of Outhenby is asking for you, Mother Caris.'

'Did he bring a herd of calves?' Outhenby was obliged to supply the nuns with twelve one-year-old calves every Easter.

'Yes.'

'Pen the beasts and ask the bailiff to come here, please.'

Sime and Austin took their leave and Caris went to inspect the tiled floor in the latrines. The bailiff found her there. It was Harry Ploughman. She had sacked the old bailiff, who was too slow to respond to change, and she had promoted the brightest young man in the village.

He shook her hand, which was over familiar of him, but Caris liked him and did not mind.

She said: 'It must be a nuisance, your having to drive a herd all the way here, especially when the spring ploughing is under way.'

'It is that,' he said. Like most ploughmen, he was broad-shouldered and strong-armed. Strength as well as skill was required for driving the communal eight-ox team as they pulled the heavy plough through wet clay soil. He seemed to carry with him the air of the healthy outdoors.

'Wouldn't you rather make a money payment?' Caris said. 'Most manorial dues are paid in cash these days.'

'It would be more convenient.' His eyes narrowed with peasant shrewdness. 'But how much?'

'A year-old calf normally fetches ten to twelve shillings at market, though prices are down this season.'

'They are – by half. You can buy twelve calves for three pounds.'

'Or six pounds in a good year.'

He grinned, enjoying the negotiation. 'There's your problem.'

'But you would prefer to pay cash.'

'If we can agree the amount.'

'Make it eight shillings.'

'But then, if the price of a calf is only five shillings, where do we villagers get the extra money?'

'I tell you what. In future, Outhenby can pay the nunnery either five pounds or twelve calves – the choice is yours.'

Harry considered that, looking for snags, but could find none. 'All right,' he said. 'Shall we seal the bargain?'

'How should we do that?'

To her surprise, he kissed her.

He held her slender shoulders in his rough hands, bent his head, and pressed his lips to hers. If Brother Sime had done this she would have recoiled. But Harry was different, and perhaps she had been titillated by his air of vigorous masculinity. Whatever the reason, she submitted to the kiss, letting him pull her unresisting body to his own, and moving her lips against his bearded mouth. He pressed up against her so that she could feel his erection. She realized that he would cheerfully take her here on the newly laid tiles of the latrine floor, and that thought brought her to her senses. She broke the kiss and pushed him away. 'Stop!' she said. 'What do you think you're doing?'

He was unabashed. 'Kissing you, my dear,' he said.

She realized that she had a problem. No doubt gossip about her and Merthin was widespread: they were probably the two best-known people in Shiring. While Harry surely did not know the truth, the rumours had been enough to embolden him. This kind of thing could undermine her authority. She must squash it now. 'You must never do anything like that again,' she said as severely as she could.

'You seemed to like it!'

'Then your sin is all the greater, for you have tempted a weak woman to perjure her holy vows.'

'But I love you.'

It was true, she realized, and she could guess why. She had swept into his village, reorganized everything and bent the peasants to her will. She had recognized Harry's potential and elevated him above his fellows. He must think of her as a goddess. It was not surprising that he had fallen in love with her. He had better fall out of love as soon as possible. 'If you ever speak to me like that again, I'll have to get another bailiff in Outhenby.'

'Oh,' he said. That stopped him short more effectively than the accusation of sin.

'Now, go home.'

'Very well, Mother Caris.'

'And find yourself another woman – preferably one who has not taken a vow of chastity.'

'Never,' he said, but she did not believe him.

He left, but she stayed where she was. She felt restless and lustful. If she could have felt sure of being alone for a while she would have touched herself. This was the first time in nine months that she had been bothered by physical desire. After finally splitting up with Merthin she had fallen into a kind of neutered state, in which she did not think about sex. Her relationships with other nuns gave her warmth and affection: she was fond of both Joan and Oonagh, though neither loved her in the physical way Mair had. Her heart beat with other passions: the new hospital, the tower, and the rebirth of the town.

Thinking of the tower, she left the hospital and walked across the green to the cathedral. Merthin had dug four enormous holes, the deepest anyone had ever seen, outside the church around the foundations of the old tower. He had built great cranes to lift the earth out. Throughout the wet autumn months, ox-carts had lumbered all day long down the main street and across the first span of the bridge to dump the mud on rocky Leper Island. There they had picked up building stones from Merthin's wharf, then climbed the street again, to stack the stones around the grounds of the church in ever-growing piles.

As soon as the winter frost was over, his masons had begun laying the foundations. Caris went to the north side of the cathedral and looked into the hole in the angle formed by the outside wall of the nave and the outside wall of the north transept. It was dizzyingly deep. The bottom was already covered with neat masonry, the squared-off stones laid in straight lines and joined by thin layers of mortar. Because the old foundations were inadequate, the tower was being built on its own new, independent foundations. It would rise outside the existing walls of the church, so no demolition would be needed over and above what Elfric had already done in taking down the upper levels of the old tower. Only when it was finished would Merthin remove the temporary roof Elfric had built over the crossing. It was a typical Merthin design: simple yet radical, a brilliant solution to the unique problems of the site.

As at the hospital, no builders were at work on Easter Monday, but she saw movement in the hole and realized someone was walking around on the foundations. A moment later she recognized Merthin. She went to one of the surprisingly flimsy rope-and-branch ladders the masons used, and clambered shakily down.

She was glad to reach the bottom. Merthin helped her off the ladder, smiling. 'You look a little pale,' he said.

'It's a long way down. How are you getting on?'

'Fine. It will take many years.'

'Why? The hospital seems more complicated, and that's finished.'

'Two reasons. The higher we go, the fewer masons will be able to work on it. Right now I've got twelve men laying the foundations. But as it rises it will get narrower, and there just won't be room for them all. The other reason is that mortar takes so long to set. We have to let it harden over a winter before we put too much weight on it.'

She was hardly listening. Watching his face, she was remembering making love to him in the prior's palace, between Matins and Lauds, with the first gleam of daylight coming in through the open window and falling over their naked bodies like a blessing.

She patted his arm. 'Well, the hospital isn't taking so long.'

'You should be able to move in by Whitsun.'

'I'm glad. Although we're having a slight respite from the plague: fewer people are dying.'

'Thank God,' he said fervently. 'Perhaps it may be coming to an end.'

She shook her head bleakly. 'We thought it was over once

before, remember? About this time last year. Then it came back worse.'

'Heaven forbid.'

She touched his cheek with her palm, feeling his wiry beard. 'At least you're safe.'

He looked faintly displeased. 'As soon as the hospital is finished we can start on the wool exchange.'

'I hope you're right to think that business must pick up soon.'

'If it doesn't, we'll all be dead anyway.'

'Don't say that.' She kissed his cheek.

'We have to act on the assumption that we're going to live.' He said it irritably, as if she had annoyed him. 'But the truth is that we don't know.'

'Let's not think about the worst.' She put her arms around his waist and hugged him, pressing her breasts against his thin body, feeling his hard bones against her yielding flesh.

He pushed her away violently. She stumbled backwards and almost fell. 'Don't do that!' he shouted.

She was as shocked as if he had slapped her. 'What's the matter?'

'Stop touching me!'

'I only . . .'

'Just don't do it! You ended our relationship nine months ago. I said it was the last time, and I meant it.'

She could not understand his anger. 'But I only hugged you.'

'Well, don't. I'm not your lover. You have no right.'

'I have no right to touch you?'

'No!'

'I didn't think I needed some kind of permission.'

'Of course you knew. You don't let people touch you.'

'You're not *people*. We're not strangers.' But as she said these things she knew she was wrong and he was right. She had rejected him, but she had not accepted the consequences. The encounter with Harry from Outhenby had fired her lust, and she had come to Merthin looking for release. She had told herself she was touching him in affectionate friendship, but that was a lie. She had treated him as if he were still available to her, as a rich and idle lady might put down a book and pick it up again. Having denied him the right to touch her all this time, it was wrong of her to try to reinstate the privilege just because a muscular young ploughman had kissed her.

All the same, she would have expected Merthin to point this out in a gentle and affectionate way. But he had been hostile and brutal. Had she thrown away his friendship as well as his love? Tears came to her eyes. She turned away from him and went back to the ladder.

She found it hard to climb up. It was tiring, and she seemed to have lost her energy. She stopped for a rest, and looked down. Merthin was standing on the bottom of the ladder, steadying it with his weight.

When she was almost at the top, she looked down again. He was still there. It occurred to her that her unhappiness would be over if she fell. It was a long drop to those unforgiving stones. She would die instantly.

Merthin seemed to sense what she was thinking, for he gave an impatient wave, indicating that she should hurry up and get off the ladder. She thought of how devastated he would be if she killed herself, and for a moment she enjoyed imagining his misery and guilt. She felt sure God would not punish her in the afterlife, if there was an afterlife.

Then she climbed the last few rungs and stood on solid ground. How foolish she had been, just for a moment. She was not going to end her life. She had too much to do.

She returned to the nunnery. It was time for Evensong, and she led the procession into the cathedral. As a young novice she had resented the time wasted in services. In fact Mother Cecilia had taken care to give her work that permitted her to be excused for much of the time. Now she welcomed the chance to rest and reflect.

This afternoon had been a low moment, she decided, but she would recover. All the same she found herself fighting back tears as she sang the psalms.

For supper the nuns had smoked eel. Chewy and strongly flavoured, it was not Caris's favourite dish. Tonight she was not hungry, anyway. She ate some bread.

After the meal she retired to her pharmacy. Two novices were there, copying out Caris's book. She had finished it soon after Christmas. Many people had asked for copies: apothecaries, prioresses, barbers, even one or two physicians. Copying the book had become part of the training of nuns who wanted to work in the hospital. The copies were cheap – the book was short, and there were no elaborate drawings or costly inks – and the demand seemed never-ending.

Three people made the room feel crowded. Caris was looking forward to the space and light of the pharmacy in the new hospital.

She wanted to be alone, so she sent the novices away. However, she was not destined to get her wish. A few moments later Lady Philippa came in.

Caris had never warmed to the reserved countess, but sympathized with her plight, and was glad to give sanctuary to any woman fleeing from a husband such as Ralph. Philippa was an easy guest, making few demands, spending a lot of time in her room. She had only a limited interest in sharing the nuns' life of prayer and self-denial – but Caris of all people could understand that.

Caris invited her to sit on a stool at the bench.

Philippa was a remarkably direct woman, despite her courtly manners. Without preamble, she said: 'I want you to leave Merthin alone.'

'What?' Caris was astonished and offended.

'Of course you have to talk to him, but you should not kiss or touch him.'

'How dare you?' What did Philippa know – and why did she care?

'He's not your lover any more. Stop bothering him.'

Merthin must have told her about their quarrel this afternoon. 'But why would he tell you . . . ?' Before the question was out of her mouth, she guessed the answer.

Philippa confirmed it with her next utterance. 'He's not yours, now – he's mine.'

'Oh, my soul!' Caris was flabbergasted. 'You and Merthin?'

'Yes.'

'Are you ... have you actually ...'

'Yes.'

'I had no idea!' She felt betrayed, though she knew she had no right. When had this happened? 'But how ... where ... ?'

'You don't need to know the details.'

'Of course not.' At his house on Leper Island, she supposed. At night, probably. 'How long ... ?'

'It doesn't matter.'

Caris could work it out. Philippa had been here less than a month. 'You moved fast.'

It was an unworthy jibe, and Philippa had the grace to ignore it. 'He would have done anything to keep you. But you threw him over. Now let him go. It's been difficult for him to love anyone else, after you – but he has managed it. Don't you dare interfere.'

Caris wanted to rebuff her furiously, tell her angrily that she had no right to give orders and make moral demands – but the trouble was that Philippa was in the right. Caris had to let Merthin go, for ever.

She did not want to show her heartbreak in front of Philippa. 'Would you leave me now, please?' she said with an attempt at Philippa's style of dignity. 'I would like to be alone.'

Philippa was not easily pushed around. 'Will you do as I say?' she persisted.

Caris did not like to be cornered, but she had no spirit left. 'Yes, of course,' she said.

'Thank you.' Philippa left.

When she was sure Philippa was out of earshot, Caris began to cry.

# 78

PHILEMON AS PRIOR was no better than Godwyn. He was overwhelmed by the challenge of managing the assets of the priory. Caris had made a list, during her spell as acting prior, of the monks' main sources of income:

1. *Rents*
2. *A share of profits from commerce and industry (tithing)*
3. *Agricultural profits on land not rented out*
4. *Profits from grain mills and other, industrial mills*
5. *Waterway tolls and a share of all fish landed*
6. *Stallage in markets*
7. *Proceeds of justice – fees and fines from courts*
8. *Pious gifts from pilgrims and others*
9. *Sale of books, holy water, candles, etc.*

She had given the list to Philemon, and he had thrown it back at her as if insulted. Godwyn, better than Philemon only in that he had a certain superficial charm, would have thanked her and quietly ignored her list.

In the nunnery, she had introduced a new method of keeping accounts, one she had learned from Buonaventura Caroli when she was working for her father. The old method was simply to write in a parchment roll a short note of every transaction, so that you could always go back and check. The Italian system was to record income on the left-hand side and expenditure on the right, and add them up at the foot of the page. The difference between the two totals showed whether the institution was gaining or losing money. Sister Joan had taken this up with enthusiasm, but when she offered to explain it to Philemon he refused curtly. He regarded offers of help as insults to his competence.

He had only one talent, and it was the same as Godwyn's: a flair for manipulating people. He had shrewdly weeded the new intake of monks, sending the modern-minded physician, Brother Austin, and two other bright young men to St-John-in-the-Forest, where they would be too far away to challenge his authority.

But Philemon was the bishop's problem now. Henri had appointed him and Henri would have to deal with him. The town was independent, and Caris had her new hospital.

The hospital was to be consecrated by the bishop on Whit Sunday, which was always seven weeks after Easter. A few days beforehand, Caris moved her equipment and supplies into the new pharmacy. There was plenty of room for two people to work at the bench, preparing medicines, and a third to sit at a writing desk.

Caris was preparing an emetic, Oonagh was grinding dried herbs, and a novice, Greta, was copying out Caris's book, when a novice monk came in with a small wooden chest. It was Josiah, a teenage boy usually called Joshie. He was embarrassed to be in the presence of three women. 'Where shall I put this?' he said.

Caris looked at him. 'What is it?'

'A chest.'

'I can see that,' she said patiently. The fact that someone was capable of learning to read and write did not, unfortunately, make him intelligent. 'What does the chest contain?'

'Books.'

'And why have you brought me a chest of books?'

'I was told to.' Realizing, after a moment, that this answer was insufficiently informative, he added: 'By Brother Sime.'

Caris raised her eyebrows. 'Is Sime making me a gift of books?' She opened the chest.

Joshie made his escape without answering the question.

The books were medical texts, all in Latin. Caris looked through them. They were the classics: Avicenna's Poem on Medicine, Hippocrates' Diet and Hygiene, Galen's On the Parts of Medicine, and De Urinis by Isaac Judaeus. All had been written more than three hundred years ago.

Joshie reappeared with another chest.

'What now?' said Caris.

'Medical instruments. Brother Sime says you are not to touch them. He will come and put them in their proper places.'

Caris was dismayed. 'Sime wants to keep his books and instruments here? Is he planning to work here?'

Joshie did not know anything about Sime's intentions, of course.

Before Caris could say any more, Sime appeared, accompanied by Philemon. Sime looked around the room then, without explanation, began unpacking his things. He moved some of Caris's vessels from a shelf and replaced them with his books. He took out sharp knives for opening veins, and the teardrop-shaped glass flasks used for examining urine samples.

Caris said neutrally: 'Are you planning to spend a great deal of time here in the hospital, Brother Sime?'

Philemon answered for him, clearly having anticipated the question with relish. 'Where else?' he said. His tone was indignant, as if Caris had challenged him already. 'This is the hospital, is it not? And Sime is the only physician in the priory. How shall people be treated, if not by him?'

Suddenly the pharmacy did not seem so spacious any more.

Before Caris could say anything a stranger appeared. 'Brother Thomas told me to come here,' he said. 'I am Jonas Powderer, from London.'

The visitor was a man of about fifty dressed in an embroidered coat and a fur hat. Caris noted his ready smile and affable manner, and guessed that he made his living by selling things. He shook hands, then looked around the room, nodding with apparent approval at Caris's neat rows of labelled jars and vials. 'Remarkable,' he said. 'I have never seen such a sophisticated pharmacy outside London.'

'Are you a physician, sir?' Philemon asked. His tone was cautious: he was not sure of Jonas's status.

'Apothecary. I have a shop in Smithfield, next to St Bartholomew's hospital. I shouldn't boast, but it is the largest such business in the city.'

Philemon relaxed. An apothecary was a mere merchant, well

below a prior in the pecking order. With a hint of a sneer he said: 'And what brings the biggest apothecary in London all the way down here?'

'I was hoping to acquire a copy of the Kingsbridge Panacea.'

'The what?'

Jonas smiled knowingly. 'You cultivate humility, Father Prior, but I see this novice nun making a copy right here in your pharmacy.'

Caris said: 'The book? It's not called a panacea.'

'Yet it contains cures for all ills.'

There was a certain logic to that, she realized. 'But how do you know of it?'

'I travel a good deal, searching for rare herbs and other ingredients, while my sons take care of the shop. I met a nun of Southampton who showed me a copy. She called it a panacea, and told me it was written in Kingsbridge.'

'Was the nun Sister Claudia?'

'Yes. I begged her to lend me the book just long enough to make a copy, but she would not be parted from it.'

'I remember her.' Claudia had made a pilgrimage to Kingsbridge, stayed in the nunnery and nursed plague victims with no thought for her own safety. Caris had given her the book in thanks.

'A remarkable work,' Jonas said warmly. 'And in English!'

'It's for healers who aren't priests, and therefore don't speak much Latin.'

'There is no other book of its kind in *any* language.'

'Is it so unusual?'

'The arrangement of subjects!' Jonas enthused. 'Instead of the humours of the body, or the classes of illness, the chapters refer to the pains of the patient. So, whether the customer's complaint is stomach ache, or bleeding, or fever, or diarrhoea, or sneezing, you can just go to the relevant page!'

Philemon said impatiently: 'Suitable enough for apothecaries and their *customers*, I am sure.'

Jonas appeared not to hear the note of derision. 'I assume, Father Prior, that you are the author of this invaluable book.'

'Certainly not!' he said.

'Then who . . . ?'

'I wrote it,' Caris said.

'A woman!' Jonas marvelled. 'But where did you get all the information? Virtually none of it appears in other texts.'

'The old texts have never proved very useful to me, Jonas. I was first taught how to make medicines by a wise woman of Kingsbridge, called Mattie, who sadly left town for fear of being persecuted as a witch. I learned more from Mother Cecilia, who was prioress here before me. But gathering the recipes and treatments is not difficult. Everyone knows a hundred of them. The difficulty is to identify the few effective ones in all the dross. What I did was to keep a diary, over the years, of the effects of every cure I tried. In my book, I included only those I have seen working, with my own eyes, time after time.'

'I am awestruck to be speaking to you in person.'

'Well, you shall have a copy of my book. I'm flattered that someone should come such a long way for it!' She opened a cupboard. 'This was intended for our priory of St-John-in-the-Forest, but they can wait for another copy.'

Jonas handled it as if it were a holy object. 'I am most grateful.' He produced a bag of soft leather and gave it to Caris. 'And, in token of my gratitude, accept a modest gift from my family to the nuns of Kingsbridge.'

Caris opened the bag and took out a small object swathed in wool. When she unwrapped the material she found a gold crucifix embedded with precious stones.

Philemon's eyes glittered with greed.

Caris was startled. 'This is a costly present!' she exclaimed. That was less than charming, she realized. She added. 'Extraordinarily generous of your family, Jonas.'

He made a deprecatory gesture. 'We are prosperous, thanks be to God.'

Philemon said enviously: 'That – for a book of old women's nostrums!'

Jonas said: 'Ah, Father Prior, you are above such things, of course. We do not aspire to your intellectual heights. We do not try to understand the body's humours. Just as a child sucks on a cut finger because that eases the pain, so we administer cures only because they work. As to why and how these things happen, we leave that to greater minds than ours. God's creation is too mysterious for the likes of us to comprehend.'

Caris thought Jonas was speaking with barely concealed irony. She saw Oonagh smother a grin. Sime, too, picked up the undertone of mockery, and his eyes flashed anger. But Philemon did not notice, and he seemed mollified by the flattery. A sly look came over his face, and Caris guessed he was wondering how he could share in the credit for the book – and get some jewelled crucifixes for himself.

*

THE FLEECE FAIR opened on Whit Sunday, as always. It was traditionally a busy day for the hospital, and this year was no exception. Elderly folk fell ill after making a long journey to the fair; babies and children got diarrhoea from strange food and foreign water; men and women drank too much in the taverns and injured themselves and each other.

For the first time, Caris was able to separate the patients into two categories. The rapidly diminishing number of plague victims, and others who had catching illnesses such as stomach upsets and poxes, went into the new building, which was officially blessed by the bishop early in the day. Victims of accidents and fights were treated in the old hospital, safe from the risk of infection. Gone were the days when someone would come into the priory with a dislocated thumb and die there of pneumonia.

The crisis came on Whit Monday.

Early in the afternoon Caris happened to be at the fair, taking a stroll after dinner, looking around. It was quiet by comparison with the old days, when hundreds of visitors and thousands of townspeople thronged not just the cathedral green but all the principal streets. Nevertheless, this year's fair was better than expected after last year's cancellation. Caris figured that people had noticed how the grip of the plague seemed to be weakening. Those who had survived so far thought they must be invulnerable – and some were, though others were not, for it continued to kill people.

Madge Webber's cloth was the talking point of the fair. The

new looms designed by Merthin were not just faster – they also made it easier to produce complex patterns in the weave. She had sold half her stock already.

Caris was talking to Madge when the fight started. Madge was embarrassing her by saying, as she had often said before, that without Caris she would still be a penniless weaver. Caris was about to give her customary denial when they heard shouts.

Caris recognized immediately the deep-chested sound of aggressive young men. It came from the neighbourhood of an ale barrel thirty yards away. The shouts increased rapidly, and a young woman screamed. Caris hurried over to the place, hoping to stop the fight before it got out of control.

She was a little too late.

The fracas was well under way. Four of the town's young tearaways were fighting fiercely with a group of peasants, identifiable as such by their rustic clothing, and probably all from the same village. A pretty girl, no doubt the one who had screamed, was struggling to separate two men who were punching one another mercilessly. One of the town boys had drawn a knife, and the peasants had heavy wooden shovels. As Caris arrived, more people were joining in on both sides.

She turned to Madge, who had followed her. 'Send someone to fetch Mungo Constable, quick as you can. He's probably in the basement of the guild hall.' Madge hurried off.

The fight was getting nastier. Several town boys had knives out. A peasant lad was lying on the ground bleeding copiously from his arm, and another was fighting on despite a gash in his face. As Caris watched, two more townies started kicking the peasant on the ground.

Caris hesitated another moment, then stepped forward. She grabbed the nearest fighter by the shirt. 'Willie Bakerson, stop this right now!' she shouted in her most authoritative voice.

It almost worked.

Willie stepped back from his opponent, startled, and looked at Caris guiltily. She opened her mouth to speak again, but at that instant a shovel struck her a violent blow on the head that had surely been intended for Willie.

It hurt like hell. Her vision blurred, she lost her balance, and the next thing she knew she hit the ground. She lay there dazed, trying to recover her wits, while the world seemed to sway around her. Then someone grabbed her under the arms and dragged her away.

'Are you hurt, Mother Caris?' The voice was familiar, though she could not place it.

Her head cleared at last, and she struggled to her feet with the help of her rescuer, whom she now identified as the muscular corn merchant Megg Robbins. 'I'm just a bit stunned,' Caris said. 'We have to stop these boys killing each other.'

'Here come the constables. Let's leave it to them.'

Sure enough, Mungo and six or seven deputies appeared, all wielding clubs. They waded into the fight, cracking heads indiscriminately. They were doing as much damage as the original fighters, but their presence confused the battleground. The boys looked bewildered, and some ran off. In a remarkably few moments the fight was over.

Caris said: 'Megg, run to the nunnery and fetch Sister Oonagh, and tell her to bring bandages.'

Megg hurried away.

The walking wounded quickly disappeared. Caris began to examine those who were left. A peasant boy who had been knifed in the stomach was trying to hold his guts in: there was little hope for him. The one with the gashed arm would live if Caris could stop the bleeding. She took off his belt, wound it around his upper arm and tightened it until the flow of blood slowed to a trickle. 'Hold that there,' she told him, and moved on to a town boy who seemed to have broken some bones in his hand. Her head was still hurting but she ignored it.

Oonagh and several more nuns appeared. A moment later, Matthew Barber arrived with his bag. Between them they patched up the wounded. Under Caris's instructions, volunteers picked up the worst victims and carried them to the nunnery. 'Take them to the old hospital, not the new one,' she said.

She stood up from a kneeling position and felt dizzy. She grabbed Oonagh to steady herself. 'What's the matter?' said Oonagh.

'I'll be all right. We'd better get to the hospital.'

They threaded their way through the market stalls to the old hospital. When they went in they saw immediately that none of the wounded were here. Caris cursed. 'The fools have taken them all to the wrong place,' she said. It was going to take a while for people to learn the importance of the difference, she concluded.

She and Oonagh went to the new building. The cloister was entered through a wide archway. As they went in, they met the volunteers coming out. 'You brought them to the wrong place!' Caris said crossly.

One said: 'But, Mother Caris—'

'Don't argue, there's no time,' she said impatiently. 'Just carry them to the old hospital.'

Stepping into the cloisters, she saw the boy with the gashed arm being carried into a room where, she knew, there were five plague victims. She rushed across the quadrangle. 'Stop!' she yelled furiously. 'What do you think you're doing?'

A man's voice said: 'They are carrying out my instructions.'

Caris stopped and looked around. It was Brother Sime. 'Don't be a fool,' she said. 'He's got a knife wound – do you want him to die of the plague?'

His round face turned pink. 'I don't propose to submit my decision to you for approval, Mother Caris.'

That was stupid and she ignored it. 'All these injured boys must be kept away from plague victims, or they'll catch it!'

'I think you're overwrought. I suggest you go and lie down.'

'Lie down?' She was outraged. 'I've just patched up all these men – now I've got to look at them properly. But not here!'

'Thank you for your emergency work, mother. You can now leave me to examine the patients thoroughly.'

'You idiot, you'll kill them!'

'Please leave the hospital until you have calmed down.'

'You can't throw me out of here, you stupid boy! I built this hospital with the nuns' money. I'm in charge here.'

'Are you?' he said coolly.

Caris realized that, although she had not anticipated this moment, he almost certainly had. He was flushed but he had his feelings under control. He was a man with a plan. She paused, thinking fast. Looking around, she saw that the nuns and volunteers were all watching, waiting to see how this would turn out.

'We have to attend to these boys,' she said. 'While we're standing here arguing, they're bleeding to death. We'll compromise, for now.' She raised her voice. 'Put every one down exactly where they are, please.' The weather was warm, there was no need for the patients to be indoors. 'We'll see to their needs first, then decide later where they are to be bedded.'

The volunteers and nuns knew and respected Caris, whereas Sime was new to them; and they obeyed her with alacrity.

Sime saw that he was beaten, and a look of utter fury came over his face. 'I cannot treat patients in these circumstances,' he said, and he stalked out.

Caris was shocked. She had tried to save his pride with her compromise, and she had not thought he would walk away from sick people in a fit of petulance.

She quickly put him out of her mind as she began to look again at the injured.

For the next couple of hours she was busy bathing wounds, sewing up gashes and administering soothing herbs and comforting drinks. Matthew Barber worked alongside her, setting broken bones and fixing dislocated joints. Matthew was in his fifties, now, but his son Luke assisted him with equal skill.

The afternoon was cooling into evening when they finished. They sat on the cloister wall to rest. Sister Joan brought them tankards of cool cider. Caris still had a headache. She had been able to ignore it while she was busy but now it bothered her. She would go to bed early, she decided.

While they were drinking their cider, young Joshie appeared. 'The lord bishop asks you to attend on him in the prior's palace at your convenience, Mother Prioress.'

She grunted irritably. No doubt Sime had complained. This was the last thing she needed. 'Tell him I'll come immediately,' she said. In a lower voice she added: 'Might as well get it over with.' She drained her tankard and left.

Wearily she walked across the green. The stallholders were packing up for the night, covering their goods and locking their boxes. She passed through the graveyard and entered the palace.

Bishop Henri sat at the head of the table. Canon Claude and Archdeacon Lloyd were with him. Philemon and Sime were also there. Godwyn's cat, Archbishop, was sitting on Henri's lap, looking smug. The bishop said: 'Please sit down.'

She sat beside Claude. He said kindly: 'You look tired, Mother Caris.'

'I've spent the afternoon patching up stupid boys who got into a big fight. Also, I got a bang on the head myself.'

'We heard about the fight.'

Henri added: 'And about the argument in the new hospital.'

'I assume that's why I'm here.'

'Yes.'

'The whole idea of the new place is to separate patients with infectious illnesses—'

'I know what the argument is about,' Henri interrupted. He addressed the group. 'Caris ordered that those injured in the fight be taken to the old hospital. Sime countermanded her orders. They had an unseemly row in front of everyone.'

Sime said: 'I apologize for that, my lord bishop.'

Henri ignored that. 'Before we go any farther, I want to get something clear.' He looked from Sime to Caris and back again. 'I am your bishop and, *ex officio*, the abbot of Kingsbridge Priory. I have the right and power to command you all, and it is your duty to obey me. Do you accept that, Brother Sime?'

Sime bowed his head. 'I do.'

Henri turned to Caris. 'Do you, Mother Prioress?'

There was no argument, of course. Henri was completely in the right. 'Yes,' she said. She felt confident that Henri was not stupid enough to force injured hooligans to catch the plague.

Henri said: 'Allow me to state the arguments. The new hospital was built with the nuns' money, to the specifications of Mother Caris. She intended it to provide a place for plague victims and others whose illnesses may, according to her, be spread from the sick to the well. She believes it is essential to compartmentalize the two types of patient. She feels she is entitled, in all the circumstances, to insist that her plan be carried out. Is that fair, mother?'

'Yes.'

'Brother Sime was not here when Caris conceived her plan, so he could not be consulted. However, he has spent three years studying medicine at the university, and has been awarded a degree. He points out that Caris has no training and, apart from what she has picked up by practical experience, little understanding of the nature of disease. He is a qualified physician and, more than that, he is the only one in the priory, or indeed in Kingsbridge.'

'Exactly,' said Sime.

'How can you say I have no training?' Caris burst out. 'After all the years I've cared for patients—'

'Be quiet, please,' Henri said, hardly raising his voice; and something in his quiet tone caused Caris to shut up. 'I was about to mention your history of service. Your work here has been invaluable. You are known far and wide for your dedication during the plague that is still with us. Your experience and practical knowledge are priceless.'

'Thank you, bishop.'

'On the other hand, Sime is a priest, a university graduate ... and a man. The learning he brings with him is essential to the proper running of a priory hospital. We do not want to lose him.'

Caris said: 'Some of the masters at the university agree with my methods – ask Brother Austin.'

Philemon said: 'Brother Austin has been sent to St-John-in-the-Forest.'

'And now we know why,' Caris said.

The bishop said: 'I have to make this decision, not Austin nor the masters at the university.'

Caris realized that she had not prepared for this showdown. She was exhausted, she had a headache, and she could hardly think straight. She was in the middle of a power struggle, and she had no strategy. If she had been fully alert she would not have come when the bishop called. She would have gone to bed and got over her bad head and woken up refreshed in the morning, and she would not have met with Henri until she had worked out her battle plan.

Was it yet too late for that?

She said: 'Bishop, I don't feel adequate to this discussion tonight. Perhaps we could postpone it until tomorrow, when I'm feeling better.'

'No need,' said Henri. 'I've heard Sime's complaint, and I know your views. Besides, I will be leaving at sunrise.'

He had made up his mind, Caris realized. Nothing she said would make any difference. But what had he decided? Which way would he jump? She really had no idea. And she was too tired to do anything but sit and listen to her fate.

'Humankind is weak,' Henri said. 'We see, as the apostle Paul puts it, as through a glass, darkly. We err, we go astray, we reason poorly. We need help. That is why God gave us His church, and the pope, and the priesthood – to guide us, because our own resources are fallible and inadequate. If we follow our own way of thinking, we will fail. We must consult the authorities.'

It looked as if he was going to back Sime, Caris concluded. How could he be so stupid?

But he was. 'Brother Sime has studied the ancient texts of medical literature, under the supervision of the masters at the university. His course of study is endorsed by the church. We must accept its authority, and therefore his. His judgement cannot be subordinated to that of an uneducated person, no matter how brave and admirable she may be. His decisions must prevail.'

Caris felt so weary and ill that she was almost glad the interview was over. Sime had won; she had lost; and all she wanted to do was sleep. She stood up.

Henri said: 'I'm sorry to disappoint you, Mother Caris . . .'

His voice tailed off as she walked away.

She heard Philemon say: 'Insolent behaviour.'

Henri said quietly. 'Let her go.'

She reached the door and went out without turning back.

The full meaning of what had happened became clear to her as she walked slowly through the graveyard. Sime was in charge of the hospital. She would have to follow his orders. There would be no separation of different categories of patient. There would be no face masks or hand washing in vinegar. Weak people would be made weaker by bleeding; starved people would be made thinner by purging; wounds would be covered with poultices made of animal dung to encourage the body to produce pus. No one would care about cleanliness or fresh air.

She spoke to nobody as she walked across the cloisters, up the stairs, and through the dormitory to her own room. She lay face down on her bed, her head pounding.

She had lost Merthin, she had lost her hospital, she had lost everything.

Head injuries could be fatal, she knew. Perhaps she would go to sleep now and never wake up.

Perhaps that would be for the best.

# 79

Merthin's orchard had been planted in the spring of 1349. A year later most of the trees were established, and came out in a scatter of brave leaves. Two or three were struggling, and only one was inarguably dead. He did not expect any of them to bear fruit yet but, by July, to his surprise, one precocious sapling had a dozen or so tiny dark-green pears, small as yet and as hard as stones, but promising ripeness in the autumn.

One Sunday afternoon he showed them to Lolla, who refused to believe that they would grow into the tangy, juicy fruits she loved. She thought – or pretended to think – that he was playing one of his teasing games. When he asked her where she imagined ripe pears came from, she looked at him reproachfully and said: 'The market, silly!'

She, too, would ripen one day, he thought, although it was hard to imagine her bony body rounding out into the soft shape of a woman. He wondered whether she would bear him grandchildren. She was five years old, so that day might be only a decade or so away.

His thoughts were on ripeness when he saw Philippa coming towards him through the garden, and it struck him how round and full her breasts were. It was unusual for her to visit him in daylight, and he wondered what had brought her here. In case they were observed, he greeted her with only a chaste kiss on the cheek, such as a brother-in-law might give without arousing comment.

She looked troubled, and he realized that for a few days now she had been more reserved and thoughtful than usual. As she sat beside him on the grass he said: 'Something on your mind?'

'I've never been good at breaking news gently,' she said. 'I'm pregnant.'

'Good God!' He was too shocked to hold back his reaction. 'I'm surprised because you told me…'

'I know. I was sure I was too old. For a couple of years my monthly cycle was irregular, and then it stopped altogether – I thought. But I've been vomiting in the morning, and my nipples hurt.'

'I noticed your breasts as you came into the garden. But can you be sure?'

'I've been pregnant six times previously – three children and three miscarriages – and I know the feeling. There's really no doubt.'

He smiled. 'Well, we're going to have a child.'

She did not return the smile. 'Don't look pleased. You haven't thought through the implications. I'm the wife of the earl of Shiring. I haven't slept with him since October, haven't lived with him since February, yet in July I'm two or at most three months pregnant. He and the whole world will know that the baby is not his, and that the countess of Shiring has committed adultery.'

'But he wouldn't…'

'Kill me? He killed Tilly, didn't he?'

'Oh, my God. Yes, he did. But…'

'And if he killed me, he might kill my baby, too.'

Merthin wanted to say it was not possible, that Ralph would not do such a thing – but he knew otherwise.

'I have to decide what to do,' said Philippa.

'I don't think you should try to end the pregnancy with potions – it's too dangerous.'

'I won't do that.'

'So you'll have the baby.'

'Yes. But then what?'

'Suppose you stayed in the nunnery, and kept the baby secret? The place is full of children orphaned by the plague.'

'But what couldn't be kept secret is a mother's love. Everyone would know that the child was my particular care. And then Ralph would find out.'

'You're right.'

'I could go away – vanish. London, York, Paris, Avignon. Not tell anyone where I was going, so that Ralph could never come after me.'

'And I could go with you.'

'But then you wouldn't finish your tower.'

'And you would miss Odila.'

Philippa's daughter had been married to Earl David for six months. Merthin could imagine how hard it would be for Philippa to leave her. And the truth was that he would find it agony to abandon his tower. All his adult life he had wanted to build the tallest building in England. Now that he had at last begun, it would break his heart to abandon the project.

Thinking of the tower brought Caris to mind. He knew, intuitively, that she would be devastated by this news. He had not seen her for weeks: she had been ill in bed after suffering a blow on the head at the Fleece Fair, and now, though she was completely recovered, she rarely emerged from the priory. He guessed that she had lost some kind of power struggle, for the hospital was being run by Brother Sime. Philippa's pregnancy would be another shattering blow for Caris.

Philippa added: 'And Odila, too, is pregnant.'

'So soon! That's good news. But even more reason why you can't go into exile and never see her, or your grandchild.'

'I can't run, and I can't hide. But, if I do nothing, Ralph will kill me.'

'There must be a way out of this,' Merthin said.

'I can think of only one answer.'

He looked at her. She had thought this out already, he realized. She had not told him about the problem until she had the solution. But she had been careful to show him that all the obvious answers were wrong. That meant he was not going to like the plan she had settled on.

'Tell me,' he said.

'We have to make Ralph think the baby is his.'

'But then you'd have to . . .'

'Yes.'

'I see.'

The thought of Philippa sleeping with Ralph was loathsome

to Merthin. This was not so much jealousy, though that was a factor. What weighed most with him was how terrible she would feel about it. She had a physical and emotional revulsion from Ralph. Merthin understood the revulsion, though he did not share it. He had lived with Ralph's brutishness all his life, and the brute was his brother, and somehow that fact remained no matter what Ralph did. All the same, it made him sick to think that Philippa would have to force herself to have sex with the man she hated most in the world.

'I wish I could think of a better way,' he said.

'So do I.'

He looked hard at her. 'You've already decided.'

'Yes.'

'I'm very sorry.'

'So am I.'

'But will it even work? Can you ... seduce him?'

'I don't know,' she said. 'I'll just have to try.'

*

THE CATHEDRAL WAS symmetrical. The mason's loft was at the west end in the low north tower, overlooking the north porch. In the matching south-west tower was a room of similar size and shape that looked over the cloisters. It was used to store items of small value that were used only rarely. All the costumes and symbolic objects employed in the mystery plays were there, together with an assortment of not-quite-useless things: wooden candlesticks, rusty chains, cracked pots, and a book whose vellum pages had rotted with age so that the words penned so painstakingly were no longer legible.

Merthin went there to check how upright the wall was, by dangling a lead pointer on a long string from the window; and while there he made a discovery.

There were cracks in the wall. Cracks were not necessarily a sign of weakness: their meaning had to be interpreted by an experienced eye. All buildings moved, and cracks might simply show how a structure was adjusting to accommodate change. Merthin judged that most of the cracks in the wall of this storeroom were benign. But there was one that puzzled him by its shape. It did not look normal. A second glance told him that someone had taken advantage of a natural crack to loosen a small stone. He removed the stone.

He realized immediately that he had found someone's secret hiding place. The space behind the stone was a thief's stash. He took the objects out one by one. There was a woman's brooch with a large green stone; a silver buckle; a silk shawl; and a scroll with a psalm written on it. Right at the back he found the object that gave him the clue to the identity of the thief. It was the only thing in the hole that had no monetary value. A simple piece of polished wood, it had letters carved into its surface that read: M:Phmn:AMAT.

M was just an initial. Amat was the Latin for 'loves'. And Phmn was surely Philemon.

Someone whose name began with M, boy or girl, had once loved Philemon and given him this; and he had hidden it with his stolen treasures.

Since childhood Philemon had been rumoured to be light-fingered. Around him, things went missing. It seemed that this was where he hid them. Merthin imagined him coming up here alone, perhaps at night, to pull out the stone and gloat over his loot. No doubt it was a kind of sickness.

There had never been any rumours about Philemon having lovers. Like his mentor Godwyn, he seemed to be one of that small minority of men in whom the need for sexual love was weak. But someone had fallen for him, at some time, and he cherished the memory.

Merthin replaced the objects, putting them back exactly the way he had found them – he had a good memory for that sort of thing. He replaced the loose stone. Then, thoughtfully, he left the room and went back down the spiral staircase.

*

Ralph was surprised when Philippa came home.

It was a rare fine day in a wet summer, and he would have liked to be out hawking, but to his anger he was not able to go. The harvest was about to begin, and most of the twenty or thirty stewards, bailiffs and reeves in the earldom needed to see him urgently. They all had the same problem: crops ripening in the fields and insufficient men and women to harvest them.

He could do nothing to help. He had taken every opportunity to prosecute labourers who defied the ordinance by leaving their villages in search of higher wages – but those few who could be caught just paid the fine out of their earnings and ran off again. So his bailiffs had to make do. However, they all wanted to explain their difficulties to him, and he had no choice but to listen and give his approval to their makeshift plans.

The hall was full of people: bailiffs, knights and men-at-arms, a couple of priests, and a dozen or more loitering servants. When they all went quiet, Ralph suddenly heard the rooks outside, their harsh call sounding like a warning. He looked up and saw Philippa in the doorway.

She spoke first to the servants. 'Martha! This table is still dirty from dinner. Fetch hot water and scrub it, now. Dickie – I've just seen the earl's favourite courser covered with what looks like yesterday's mud, and you're here whittling a stick. Get back to the stables where you belong and clean up that horse. You, boy, put that puppy outside, it's just pissed on the floor. The only dog allowed in the hall is the earl's mastiff, you know that.' The servants were galvanized into action, even those to whom she had not spoken suddenly finding work to do.

Ralph did not mind Philippa issuing orders to the domestic servants. They got lazy without a mistress to harry them.

She came up to him and made a deep curtsey, as was only appropriate after a long absence. She did not offer to kiss him.

He said neutrally: 'This is ... unexpected.'

Philippa said irritably: 'I shouldn't have had to make the journey at all.'

Ralph groaned inwardly. 'What brings you here?' he said. Whatever it was, there would be trouble, he felt sure.

'My manor of Ingsby.'

Philippa had a small number of properties of her own, a few villages in Gloucestershire that paid tribute to her rather than to the earl. Since she had gone to live at the nunnery, the bailiffs from these villages had been visiting her at Kingsbridge Priory,

Ralph knew, and accounting to her directly for their dues. But Ingsby was an awkward exception. The manor paid tribute to him and he passed it on to her – which he had forgotten to do since she left. 'Damn,' he said. 'It slipped my mind.'

'That's all right,' she said. 'You've got a lot to think about.'

That was surprisingly conciliatory.

She went upstairs to the private chamber, and he returned to his work. Half a year of separation had improved her a little, he thought as another bailiff enumerated the fields of ripening corn and bemoaned the shortage of reapers. Still, he hoped she did not plan to stay long. Lying beside her at night was like sleeping with a dead cow.

She reappeared at supper time. She sat next to Ralph and spoke politely to several visiting knights during the meal. She was as cool and reserved as ever – there was no affection, not even any humour – but he saw no sign of the implacable, icy hatred she had shown after their wedding. It was gone, or at least deeply hidden. When the meal was over she retired again, leaving him to drink with the knights.

He considered the possibility that she was planning to come back permanently, but in the end he dismissed the idea. She would never love him or even like him. It was just that a long absence had blunted the edge of her resentment. The underlying feeling would probably never leave her.

He assumed she would be asleep when he went upstairs but, to his surprise, she was at the writing desk, in an ivory-coloured linen nightgown, a single candle throwing a soft light over her proud features and thick dark hair. In front of her was a long letter in a girlish hand, which he guessed was from Odila, now the countess of Monmouth. Philippa was penning a reply. Like most aristocrats, she dictated business letters to a clerk, but wrote personal ones herself.

He stepped into the garderobe, then came out and took off his outer clothing. It was summer, and he normally slept in his underdrawers.

Philippa finished her letter, stood up – and knocked over the jar of ink on the desk. She jumped back, too late. Somehow it fell towards her, disfiguring her white nightdress with a broad black stain. She cursed. He was mildly amused: she was so prissily particular that it was funny to see her splashed with ink.

She hesitated for a moment, then pulled the nightdress off over her head.

He was startled. She was not normally quick to take off her clothes. She had been disconcerted by the ink, he realized. He stared at her naked body. She had put on a little weight at the nunnery: her breasts seemed larger and rounder than before, her belly had a slight but discernible bulge, and her hips had an attractive swelling curve. To his surprise, he felt aroused.

She bent down to mop the ink off the tiled floor with her bundled-up nightgown. Her breasts swayed as she rubbed the tiles. She turned, and he got a full view of her generous behind. If he had not known her better, he would have suspected her of trying to inflame him. But Philippa had never tried to inflame anyone, let alone him. She was just awkward and embarrassed. And that made it even more stimulating to stare at her exposed nakedness while she wiped the floor.

It was several weeks since he had been with a woman, and the last one had been a very unsatisfactory whore in Salisbury.

By the time Philippa stood up, he had an erection.

She saw him staring. 'Don't look at me,' she said. 'Go to bed.' She threw the soiled garment into the laundry hamper.

She went to the clothes press and lifted its lid. She had left most of her clothes here when she went to Kingsbridge: it was not considered seemly to dress richly when living in a nunnery, even for noble guests. She found another nightdress. Ralph raked her with his eyes as she lifted it out. He stared at her uplifted breasts, and the mound of her sex with its dark hair, and his mouth went dry.

She caught his look. 'Don't you touch me,' she said.

If she had not said that, he would probably have lain down and gone to sleep. But her swift rejection stung him. 'I'm the earl of Shiring and you're my wife,' he said. 'I'll touch you any time I like.'

'You wouldn't dare,' she said, and she turned away to put on the gown.

That angered him. As she lifted the garment to put it on over her head, he slapped her bottom. It was a hard slap on bare skin, and he could tell that it hurt her. She jumped and cried out. 'So much for not daring,' he said. She turned to him, a protest on her lips, and on impulse he punched her in the mouth. She was knocked back and fell to the floor. Her hands flew to her mouth, and blood seeped through her fingers. But she was on her back, naked, with her legs spread, and he could see the triangle of hair at the fork of her thighs, with its cleft slightly parted in what looked like an invitation.

He fell on her.

She wriggled furiously, but he was bigger than she, and strong. He overcame her resistance effortlessly. A moment later he was inside her. She was dry, but somehow that excited him.

It was all over quite quickly. He rolled off her, panting. After a few moments he looked at her. There was blood on her mouth. She did not look back at him: her eyes were closed. Yet it seemed to him that there was a curious expression on her face. He thought about it for a while until he worked it out; then he was even more puzzled than before.

She looked triumphant.

*

MERTHIN KNEW THAT Philippa had returned to Kingsbridge, because he saw her maid in the Bell. He expected his lover to come to his house that night, and was disappointed when she did not. No doubt she felt awkward, he thought. No lady would be comfortable with what she had done, even though the reasons were compelling, even though the man she loved knew and understood.

Another night went by without her appearing, then it was Sunday and he felt sure he would see her in church. But she did not come to the service. It was almost unheard-of for the nobility to miss Sunday mass. What had kept her away?

After the service he sent Lolla home with Arn and Em, then went across the green to the old hospital. On the upper floor were three rooms for important guests. He took the outside staircase.

In the corridor he came face to face with Caris.

She did not bother to ask what he was doing here. 'The countess doesn't want you to see her, but you probably should,' she said.

Merthin noted the odd turn of phrase: Not 'The countess doesn't want to see you,' but 'The countess doesn't want *you* to see *her*.' He looked at the bowl Caris was carrying. It contained a bloodstained rag. Fear struck his heart. 'What's wrong?'

'Nothing too serious,' Caris said. 'The baby is unharmed.'

'Thank God.'

'You're the father, of course?'

'Please don't ever let anyone hear you say that.'

She looked sad. 'All the years you and I were together, and I only conceived that one time.'

He looked away. 'Which room is she in?'

'Sorry to talk about myself. I'm the last thing you're interested in. Lady Philippa is in the middle room.'

He caught the poorly suppressed grief in her voice and paused, despite his anxiety for Philippa. He touched Caris's arm. 'Please don't believe I'm not interested in you,' he said. 'I'll always care what happens to you, and whether you're happy.'

She nodded, and tears came to her eyes. 'I know,' she said. 'I'm being selfish. Go and see Philippa.'

He left Caris and entered the middle room. Philippa was kneeling on the prie-dieu with her back to him. He interrupted her prayers. 'Are you all right?'

She stood up and turned to him. Her face was a mess. Her lips were swollen to three times their normal size, and badly scabbed.

He guessed that Caris had been bathing the wound – hence the bloody rag. 'What happened?' he said. 'Can you speak?'

She nodded. 'I sound queer, but I can talk.' Her voice was a mumble, but comprehensible.

'How badly are you hurt?'

'My face looks awful, but it's not serious. Other than that, I'm fine.'

He put his arms around her. She laid her head on his shoulder. He waited, holding her. After a while, she began to cry.

He stroked her hair and her back while she shook with sobs. He said: 'There, there,' and kissed her forehead, but he did not try to silence her.

Slowly, her weeping subsided.

He said: 'Can I kiss your lips?'

She nodded. 'Gently.'

He brushed them with his own. He tasted almonds: Caris had smeared the cuts with oil. 'Tell me what happened,' he said.

'It worked. He was fooled. He will be sure it's his baby.'

He touched her mouth with his fingertip. 'And he did this?'

'Don't be angry. I tried to provoke him, and succeeded. Be glad he hit me.'

'Glad! Why?'

'Because he thinks he had to force me. He believes I would not have submitted without violence. He has no inkling that I intended to seduce him. He will never suspect the truth. Which means I'm safe – and so is our baby.'

He put his hand on her belly. 'But why didn't you come and see me?'

'Looking like this?'

'I want to be with you even more when you're hurt.' He moved his hand to her breast. 'Besides, I've missed you.'

She took his hand away. 'I can't go from one to the other like a whore.'

'Oh.' He had not thought of it that way.

'Do you understand?'

'I think so.' He could see that a woman would feel cheap – although a man might be proud of doing exactly the same thing. 'But how long . . . ?'

She sighed, and moved away. 'It's not how long.'

'What do you mean?'

'We've agreed to tell the world that this is Ralph's baby, and I've made sure he'll believe that. Now he's going to want to raise it.'

Merthin was dismayed. 'I hadn't thought about the details, but I imagined you would continue to live in the priory.'

'Ralph won't allow his child to be raised in a nunnery, especially if it's a boy.'

'So what will you do, go back to Earlscastle?'

'Yes.'

The child was nothing yet, of course; not a person, not even a baby, just a swelling in Philippa's belly. But all the same Merthin felt a stab of grief. Lolla had become the great joy of his life, and he had been looking forward eagerly to another child.

But at least he had Philippa for a little while longer. 'When will you go?' he asked.

'Immediately,' she said. She saw the look on his face, and tears came to her eyes. 'I can't tell you how sorry I am – but I would just feel wrong, making love to you and planning to return to Ralph. It would be the same with any two men. The fact that you're brothers just makes it uglier.'

His eyes blurred with tears. 'So it's over with us already? Now?'

She nodded. 'And there's another thing I have to tell you, one more reason why we can never be lovers again. I've confessed my adultery.'

Merthin knew that Philippa had her own personal confessor, as was appropriate for a high-ranking noblewoman. Since she came to Kingsbridge, he had been living with the monks, a welcome addition to their thinned ranks. So now she had told him of her affair. Merthin hoped he could keep the secrets of the confessional.

Philippa said: 'I have received absolution, but I must not continue the sin.'

Merthin nodded. She was right. They had both sinned. She had betrayed her husband, and he had betrayed his brother. She had an excuse: she had been forced into the marriage. He had none. A beautiful woman had fallen in love with him and he had loved her back, even though he had no right. The yearning ache of grief and loss he was feeling now was the natural consequence of such behaviour.

He looked at her – the cool grey-green eyes, the smashed mouth, the ripe body – and realized that he had lost her. Perhaps he had never really had her. In any case it had always been wrong, and now it was over. He tried to speak, to say goodbye, but his throat seemed to seize up, and nothing came out. He could hardly see for crying. He turned away, fumbled for the door, and somehow got out of the room.

A nun was coming along the corridor carrying a jug. He could not see who it was, but he recognized Caris's voice when she said: 'Merthin? Are you all right?'

He made no reply. He went in the opposite direction and passed through the door and down the outside staircase. Weeping openly, not caring who saw, he walked across the cathedral green, down the main street and across the bridge to his island.

# 80

SEPTEMBER 1350 WAS cold and wet, but all the same there was a sense of euphoria. As damp sheaves of wheat were gathered in the surrounding countryside, only one person died of the plague in Kingsbridge: Marge Taylor, a dressmaker sixty years old. No one caught the disease in October, November or December. It seemed to have vanished, Merthin thought gratefully – at least for the time being.

The age-old migration of enterprising, restless people from countryside to town had been reversed during the plague, but now it recommenced. They came to Kingsbridge, moved into empty houses, fixed them up and paid rent to the priory. Some started new businesses – bakeries, breweries, candle manufactories – to replace the old ones that had disappeared when the owners and all their heirs died off. Merthin, as alderman, had made it easier to open a shop or a market stall, sweeping away the lengthy process of obtaining permission that had been imposed by the priory. The weekly market grew busier.

One by one Merthin rented out the shops, houses and taverns he had built on Leper Island, his tenants either enterprising newcomers or existing tradesmen who wanted a better location. The road across the island, between the two bridges, had become an extension of the main street, and therefore prime commercial property – as Merthin had foreseen, twelve years ago, when people had thought he was mad to take the barren rock as payment for his work on the bridge.

Winter drew in, and once again the smoke from thousands of fires hung over the town in a low brown cloud; but the people still worked and shopped, ate and drank, played dice in taverns and went to church on Sundays. The guild hall saw the first Christmas Eve banquet since the parish guild had become a borough guild.

Merthin invited the prior and prioress. They no longer had power to overrule the merchants, but they were still among the most important people in town. Philemon came, but Caris declined the invitation: she had become worryingly withdrawn.

Merthin sat next to Madge Webber. She was now the richest merchant and the largest employer in Kingsbridge, perhaps in the whole county. She was deputy alderman, and probably should have been alderman but that it was unusual to have a woman in that position.

Among Merthin's many enterprises was a workshop turning out the treadle looms that had improved the quality of Kingsbridge Scarlet. Madge bought more than half his production, but enterprising merchants came from as far away as London to place orders for the rest. The looms were complex pieces of machinery that had to be made accurately and assembled with precision, so Merthin had to employ the best carpenters available; but he priced the finished product at more than double what it cost him to make, and still people could hardly wait to give him the money.

Several people had hinted that he should marry Madge, but the idea did not tempt him or her. She had never been able to find a man to match Mark, who had had the physique of a giant and the disposition of a saint. She had always been chunky, but these days she was quite fat. Now in her forties, she was growing into one of those women who looked like barrels, almost the same width all the way from shoulders to bottom. Eating and drinking well were now her chief pleasures, Merthin thought as he watched her tuck into gingered ham with a sauce made of apples and cloves. That and making money.

At the end of the meal they had a mulled wine called hippocras. Madge took a long draught, belched, and moved closer to Merthin on the bench. 'We have to do something about the hospital,' she said.

'Oh?' He was not aware of a problem. 'Now that the plague has ended, I would have thought people didn't have much need of a hospital.'

'Of course they do,' she said briskly. 'They still get fevers and bellyache and cancer. Women want to get pregnant and can't, or they suffer complications giving birth. Children burn themselves and fall out of trees. Men are thrown by their horses or knifed by their enemies or have their heads broken by angry wives—'

'Yes, I get the picture,' Merthin said, amused by her garrulousness. 'What's the problem?'

'Nobody will go to the hospital any more. They don't like Brother Sime and, more importantly, they don't trust his learning. While we were all coping with the plague, he was at Oxford reading ancient textbooks, and he still prescribes remedies such as bleeding and cupping that no one believes in any more. They want Caris – but she never appears.'

'What do people do when they're sick, if they don't go to the hospital?'

'They see Matthew Barber, or Silas Pothecary, or a newcomer called Marla Wisdom, who specializes in women's problems.'

'So what's worrying you?'

'They're starting to mutter about the priory. If they don't get help from the monks and nuns, they say, why should they pay towards building the tower?'

'Oh.' The tower was a huge project. No individual could possibly finance it. A combination of monastery, nunnery and city funds was the only way to pay for it. If the town defaulted, the project could be threatened. 'Yes, I see,' said Merthin worriedly. 'That is a problem.'

*

IT HAD BEEN a good year for most people, Caris thought as she sat through the Christmas Day service. People were adjusting to the devastation of the plague with astonishing speed. As well as bringing terrible suffering and a near-breakdown of civilized life, the disease had provided the opportunity for a shake-up. Almost half the population had died, by her calculations; but one effect was that her remaining peasants were farming only the most fertile soils, so each man produced more. Despite the Ordinance of Labourers, and the efforts of noblemen such as Earl Ralph to enforce it, she was gratified to see that people continued to move to where the pay was highest, which was usually where the land was most productive. Grain was plentiful and herds of cattle and sheep were growing again. The nunnery was thriving and, because Caris had reorganized the monks' affairs as well as the nuns' after the flight of Godwyn, the monastery was now more prosperous than it had been for a hundred years. Wealth created wealth, and good times in the countryside brought more business to the towns, so Kingsbridge craftsmen and shopkeepers were beginning to return to their former affluence.

As the nuns left the church at the end of the service, Prior Philemon spoke to her. 'I need to talk to you, Mother Prioress. Would you come to my house?'

There had been a time when she would have politely acceded to such a request without hesitation, but those days were over. 'No,' she said. 'I don't think so.'

He reddened immediately. 'You can't refuse to speak to me!'

'I didn't. I refused to go to your palace. I decline to be summoned before you like a subordinate. What do you want to talk about?'

'The hospital. There have been complaints.'

'Speak to Brother Sime – he's in charge of it, as you well know.'

'Is there no reasoning with you?' he said exasperatedly. 'If Sime could solve the problem I would be talking to him, not you.'

By now they were in the monks' cloisters. Caris sat on the low wall around the quadrangle. The stone was cold. 'We can talk here. What do you have to say to me?'

Philemon was annoyed, but he gave in. He stood in front of her, and now he was the one who seemed like a subordinate. He said: 'The townspeople are unhappy about the hospital.'

'I'm not surprised.'

'Merthin complained to me at the guild's Christmas dinner. They don't come here any more, but see charlatans like Silas Pothecary.'

'He's no more of a charlatan than Sime.'

Philemon realized that several novices were standing nearby, listening to the argument. 'Go away, all of you,' he said. 'Get to your studies.'

They scurried off.

Philemon said to Caris: 'The townspeople think you ought to be at the hospital.'

'So do I. But I won't follow Sime's methods. At best, his cures have no effect. Much of the time they make patients worse. That's why people no longer come here when they're ill.'

'Your new hospital has so few patients that we're using it as a guest house. Doesn't that bother you?'

That jibe went home. Caris swallowed and looked away. 'It breaks my heart,' she said quietly.

'Then come back. Figure out a compromise with Sime. You worked under monk-physicians in the early days, when you first came here. Brother Joseph was the senior doctor then. He had the same training as Sime.'

'You're right. In those days, we felt that the monks sometimes did more harm than good, but we could work with them. Most of the time we didn't call them in at all, we just did what we thought best. When they did attend, we didn't always follow their instructions exactly.'

'You can't believe they were always wrong.'

'No. Sometimes they cured people. I remember Joseph opening a man's skull and draining accumulated fluid that had been causing unbearable headaches – it was very impressive.'

'So do the same now.'

'It's no longer possible. Sime put an end to that, didn't he? He moved his books and equipment into the pharmacy and took charge of the hospital. And I'm sure he did so with your encouragement. In fact it was probably your idea.' She could tell from Philemon's expression that she was right. 'You and he plotted to push me out. You succeeded – and now you're suffering the consequences.'

'We could go back to the old system. I'll make Sime move out.'

She shook her head. 'There have been other changes. I've learned a lot from the plague. I'm surer than ever that the physicians' methods can be fatal. I won't kill people for the sake of a compromise with you.'

'You don't realize how much is at stake.' He had a faintly smug look.

So, there was something else. She had been wondering why he had brought this up. It was not like him to fret about the hospital: he had never cared much for the work of healing. He was interested only in what would raise his status and defend his fragile pride. 'All right,' she said. 'What have you got up your sleeve?'

'The townspeople are talking about cutting off funds for the new tower. Why should they pay extra to the cathedral, they say, when they're not getting what they want from us? And now that the town is a borough, I as prior can no longer enforce the payment.'

'And if they don't pay . . . ?'

'Your beloved Merthin will have to abandon his pet project,' Philemon said triumphantly.

Caris could see that he thought this was his trump card. And, indeed, there had been a time when the revelation would have jolted her. But no longer. 'Merthin isn't my beloved any more, is he?' she said. 'You put a stop to that, too.'

A look of panic crossed his face. 'But the bishop has set his heart on this tower – you can't put that at risk!'

Caris stood up. 'Can't I?' she said. 'Why not?' She turned away, heading for the nunnery.

He was flabbergasted. He called after her: 'How can you be so reckless?'

She was going to ignore him, then she changed her mind and decided to explain. She turned back. 'You see, all that I ever held dear has been taken from me,' she said in a matter-of-fact tone. 'And when you've lost everything—' Her façade began to crumble, and her voice broke, but she made herself carry on. 'When you've lost everything, you've got nothing to lose.'

*

THE FIRST SNOW fell in January. It formed a thick blanket on the roof of the cathedral, smoothed out the delicate carving of the spires, and masked the faces of the angels and saints sculpted over the west door. The new masonry of the tower foundations had been covered with straw to insulate the new mortar against winter frost, and now the snow overlaid the straw.

There were few fireplaces in a priory. The kitchen had fires, of course, which was why work in kitchens was always popular with novices. But there was no fire in the cathedral, where the monks and nuns spent seven or eight hours every day. When churches burned down, it was usually because some desperate monk had brought a charcoal brazier into the building, and a spark had flown from the fire to the timber ceiling. When not in church or labouring, the monks and nuns were supposed to walk and read in the cloisters, which were out of doors. The only concession to their comfort was the warming room, a small chamber off the cloisters where a fire was lit in the most severe weather. They were allowed to come into the warming room from the cloisters for short periods.

As usual, Caris ignored rules and traditions, and permitted nuns to wear woollen hose in the winter. She did not believe that God needed his servants to get chilblains.

Bishop Henri was so worried about the hospital – or rather, about the threat to his tower – that he drove from Shiring to Kingsbridge through the snow. He came in a charette, a heavy wooden cart with a waxed canvas cover and cushioned seats. Canon Claude and Archdeacon Lloyd came with him. They paused at the prior's palace only long enough to dry their clothes and drink a warming cup of wine before summoning a crisis meeting with Philemon, Sime, Caris, Oonagh, Merthin and Madge.

Caris knew it would be a waste of time but she went anyway: it was easier than refusing, which would have required her to sit in the nunnery and deal with endless messages begging, commanding and threatening her.

She looked at the snowflakes falling past the glazed windows as the bishop drearily summarized a quarrel in which she really had no interest. 'This crisis has been brought about by the disloyal and disobedient attitude of Mother Caris,' Henri said.

That stung her into a response. 'I worked in the hospital here for ten years,' she said. 'My work, and the work of Mother Cecilia before me, are what made it so popular with the townspeople.' She pointed a rude finger at the bishop. 'You changed it. Don't try to blame others. You sat in that chair and announced that Brother Sime would henceforth be in charge. Now you should take responsibility for the consequences of your foolish decision.'

'You must obey me!' he said, his voice rising to a screech in frustration. 'You are a nun – you have taken a vow.' The grating sound disturbed the cat, Archbishop, and it stood up and walked out of the room.

'I realize that,' Caris said. 'It puts me in an intolerable position.' She spoke without forethought, but as the words came out she realized they were not really ill-considered. In fact they were the fruit of months of brooding. 'I can no longer serve God in this way,' she went on, her voice calm but her heart pounding. 'That is why I have decided to renounce my vows and leave the nunnery.'

Henri actually stood up. 'You will not!' he shouted. 'I will not release you from your holy vows.'

'I expect God will, though,' she said, scarcely disguising her contempt.

That made him angrier. 'This notion that individuals can deal with God is wicked heresy. There has been too much of such loose talk since the plague.'

'Do you think that might have happened because, when people approached the church for help during the plague, they so often found that its priest and monks –' here she looked at Philemon '– had fled like cowards?'

Henri held up a hand to stifle Philemon's indignant response. 'We may be fallible but, all the same, it is only through the church and its priests that men and women may approach God.'

'You would think that, of course,' Caris said. 'But that doesn't make it right.'

'You're a devil!'

Canon Claude intervened. 'All things considered, my lord bishop, a public quarrel between yourself and Caris would not be helpful.' He gave her a friendly smile. He had been well disposed towards her ever since the day she had caught him and the bishop kissing and had said nothing about it. 'Her present noncooperation must be set against many years of dedicated, sometimes heroic service. And the people love her.'

Henri said: 'But what if we do release her from her vows? How would that solve the problem?'

At this point, Merthin spoke for the first time. 'I have a suggestion,' he said.

Everyone looked at him.

He said: 'Let the town build a new hospital. I will donate a large site on Leper Island. Let it be staffed by a convent of nuns quite separate from the priory, a new group. They will be under the spiritual authority of the bishop of Shiring, of course, but have no connection with the prior of Kingsbridge or any of the physicians at the monastery. Let the new hospital have a lay patron, who would be a leading citizen of the town, chosen by the guild, and would appoint the prioress.'

They were all quiet for a long moment, letting this radical proposal sink in. Caris was thunderstruck. A new hospital ... on Leper Island ... paid for by the townspeople ... staffed by a new order of nuns ... having no connection with the priory ...

She looked around the group. Philemon and Sime clearly hated the idea. Henri, Claude and Lloyd just looked bemused.

At last the bishop said: 'The patron will be very powerful – representing the townspeople, paying the bills and appointing the prioress. Whoever plays that role will control the hospital.'

'Yes,' said Merthin.

'If I authorize a new hospital, will the townspeople be willing to resume paying for the tower?'

Madge Webber spoke for the first time. 'If the right patron is appointed, yes.'

'And who should it be?' said Henri.

Caris realized that everyone was looking at her.

*

A FEW HOURS LATER, Caris and Merthin wrapped themselves in heavy cloaks, put on boots and walked through the snow to the island, where he showed her the site he had in mind. It was on the west side, not far from his house, overlooking the river.

She was still dizzy from the sudden change in her life. She

was to be released from her vows as a nun. She would become a normal citizen again, after almost twelve years. She found she could contemplate leaving the priory without anguish. The people she had loved were all dead: Mother Cecilia, Old Julie, Mair, Tilly. She liked Sister Joan and Sister Oonagh well enough, but it was not the same.

And she would still be in charge of a hospital. Having the right to appoint and dismiss the prioress of the new institution, she would be able to run the place according to the new thinking that had grown out of the plague. The bishop had agreed to everything.

'I think we should use the cloister layout again,' Merthin said. 'It seemed to work really well for the short time you were in charge.'

She stared at the sheet of unmarked snow and marvelled at his ability to imagine walls and rooms where she could see only whiteness. 'The entrance arch was used almost like a hall,' she said. 'It was the place where people waited, and where the nuns first examined the patients before deciding what to do with them.'

'You would like it larger?'

'I think it should be a real reception hall.'

'All right.'

She was bemused. 'This is hard to believe. Everything has turned out just as I would have wanted it.'

He nodded. 'That's how I worked it out.'

'Really?'

'I asked myself what you would wish for, then I figured out how to achieve it.'

She stared at him. He had said it lightly, as if merely explaining the reasoning process that had led him to his conclusions. He seemed to have no idea how momentous it was to her that he should be thinking about her wishes and how to achieve them.

She said: 'Has Philippa had the baby yet?'

'Yes, a week ago.'

'What did she have?'

'A boy.'

'Congratulations. Have you seen him?'

'No. As far as the world is concerned, I'm only his uncle. But Ralph sent me a letter.'

'Have they named him?'

'Roland, after the old earl.'

Caris changed the subject. 'The river water isn't very pure this far downstream. A hospital really needs clean water.'

'I'll lay a pipe to bring you water from farther upstream.'

The snowfall eased and then stopped, and they had a clear view of the island.

She smiled at him. 'You have the answer to everything.'

He shook his head. 'These are the easy questions: clean water, airy rooms, a reception hall.'

'And what are the difficult ones?'

He turned to face her. There were snowflakes in his red beard. He said: 'Questions like: Does she still love me?'

They stared at one another for a long moment.

Caris was happy.

# Part Seven

*March to November, 1361*

# 81

WULFRIC AT FORTY WAS STILL the handsomest man Gwenda had ever seen. There were threads of silver now in his tawny hair, but they just made him look wise as well as strong. When he was young his broad shoulders had tapered dramatically to a narrow waist, whereas nowadays the taper was not so sharp nor the waist so slim – but he could still do the work of two men. And he would always be two years younger than she.

She thought she had changed less. She had the kind of dark hair that did not go grey until late in life. She was no heavier than she had been twenty years ago, although since having the children her breasts and belly were not quite as taut as formerly.

It was only when she looked at her son Davey, at his smooth skin and the restless spring in his step, that she felt her years. Now twenty, he looked like a male version of herself at that age. She, too, had had a face with no lines, and she had walked with a jaunty stride. A lifetime of working in the fields in all weathers had wrinkled her hands, and given her cheeks a raw redness just beneath the skin, and taught her to walk slowly and conserve her strength.

Davey was small like her, and shrewd, and secretive: since he was little she had never been sure what he was thinking. Sam was the opposite: big and strong, not clever enough to be deceitful, but with a mean streak that Gwenda blamed on his real father, Ralph Fitzgerald.

For several years now the two boys had been working alongside Wulfric in the fields – until two weeks ago, when Sam had vanished.

They knew why he had gone. All winter long he had been talking about leaving Wigleigh and moving to a village where he could earn higher wages. He had disappeared the moment the spring ploughing began.

Gwenda knew he was right about the wages. It was a crime to leave your village, or to accept pay higher than the levels of 1347, but all over the country restless young men were flouting the law, and desperate farmers were hiring them. Landlords such as Earl Ralph could do little more than gnash their teeth.

Sam had not said where he would go, and he had given no warning of his departure. If Davey had done the same, Gwenda would have known he had thought things out carefully and decided this was the best way. But she felt sure Sam had just followed an impulse. Someone had mentioned the name of a village, and he had woken up early the next morning and decided to go there immediately.

She told herself not to worry. He was twenty-two years old, big and strong. No one was going to exploit him or ill-treat him. But she was his mother, and her heart ached.

If she could not find him, no one else could, she figured, and that was good. All the same she yearned to know where he was living, and if he was working for a decent master, and whether the people were kind to him.

That winter, Wulfric had made a new light plough for the sandier acres of his holding, and one day in spring Gwenda and he went to Northwood to buy an iron ploughshare, the one part they could not make for themselves. As usual, a small group of Wigleigh folk travelled together to the market. Jack and Eli, who operated the fulling mill for Madge Webber, were stocking up on supplies: they had no land of their own so they bought all their food. Annet and her eighteen-year-old daughter, Amabel, had a dozen hens in a crate, to sell at the market. The bailiff, Nathan, came too, with his grown son Jonno, the childhood enemy of Sam.

Annet still flirted with every good-looking man who crossed her path, and most of them grinned foolishly and flirted back. On the journey to Northwood she chatted with Davey. Although he was less than half her age, she simpered and tossed her head and smacked his arm in mock reproach, just as if she were twenty-two rather than forty-two. She was not a girl any more, but she did not seem to know it, Gwenda thought sourly. Annet's daughter, Amabel, who was as pretty as Annet had once been, walked a little apart, and seemed embarrassed by her mother.

They reached Northwood at mid-morning. After Wulfric and Gwenda had made their purchase, they went to get their dinner at the Old Oak tavern.

For as long as Gwenda could remember there had been a venerable oak outside the inn, a thick squat tree with malformed branches that looked like a bent old man in winter and cast a welcome deep shade in summer. Her sons had chased one another around it as little boys. But it must have died or become unstable, for it had been chopped down, and now there was a stump, as wide across as Wulfric was tall, used by the customers as a chair, a table, and – for one exhausted carter – a bed.

Sitting on its edge, drinking ale from a huge tankard, was Harry Ploughman, the bailiff of Outhenby.

Gwenda was taken back twelve years in a blink. What came to her mind, so forcefully that it brought tears to her eyes, was the hope that had lifted her heart as she and her family had set out, that morning in Northwood, to walk through the forest to Outhenby and a new life. The hope had been crushed, in less than a fortnight, and Wulfric had been taken back to Wigleigh – the memory still made her burn with rage – with a rope around his neck.

But Ralph had not had things all his own way since then. Circumstances had forced him to give Wulfric back the lands his father had held, which for Gwenda had been a savagely satisfying outcome, even though Wulfric had not been smart enough to win a free tenancy, unlike some of his neighbours. Gwenda was glad they were now tenants rather than labourers, and Wulfric had achieved his life's ambition; but she still longed for more independence – a tenancy free of feudal obligations, with a cash rent to pay, the whole agreement written down in the manorial records so that no lord could go back on it. It was what most serfs wanted, and more of them were getting it since the plague.

Harry greeted them effusively and insisted on buying them ale. Soon after Wulfric and Gwenda's brief stay at Outhenby, Harry had been made bailiff by Mother Caris, and he still held that position, though Caris had long ago renounced her vows, and Mother Joan was now prioress. Outhenby continued prosperous, to judge by Harry's double chin and alehouse belly.

As they were preparing to leave with the rest of the Wigleigh folk, Harry spoke to Gwenda in a low voice. 'I've got a young man called Sam labouring for me.'

Gwenda's heart leaped. 'My Sam?'

'Can't possibly be, no.'

She was bewildered. Why mention him, in that case?

But Harry tapped his wine-red nose, and Gwenda realized he was being enigmatic. 'This Sam assures me that his lord is a Hampshire knight I've never heard of, who has given him permission to leave his village and work elsewhere, whereas your Sam's lord is Earl Ralph, who never lets his labourers go. Obviously I couldn't employ your Sam.'

Gwenda understood. That would be Harry's story if official questions were asked. 'So, he's in Outhenby.'

'Oldchurch, one of the smaller villages in the valley.'

'Is he well?' she asked eagerly.

'Thriving.'

'Thank God.'

'A strong boy and a good worker, though he can be quarrelsome.'

She knew that. 'Is he living in a warm house?'

'Lodging with a good-hearted older couple whose own son has gone to Kingsbridge to be apprenticed to a tanner.'

Gwenda had a dozen questions, but suddenly she noticed the bent figure of Nathan Reeve leaning on the doorpost of the tavern entrance, staring at her. She suppressed a curse. There was so much she wanted to know, but she was terrified of giving Nate even a clue to Sam's whereabouts. She needed to be content with what she had. And she was thrilled that at least she knew where he could be found.

She turned away from Harry, trying to give the impression of casually ending an unimportant conversation. Out of the corner of her mouth she said: 'Don't let him get into fights.'

'I'll do what I can.'

She waved perfunctorily and went after Wulfric.

Walking home with the others, Wulfric carried the heavy ploughshare on his shoulder with no apparent effort. Gwenda was bursting to tell him the news, but she had to wait until the group straggled out along the road, and she and her husband were separated from the others by a few yards. Then she repeated the conversation, speaking quietly.

Wulfric was relieved. 'At least we know where the lad has got to,' he said, breathing easily despite his load.

'I want to go to Outhenby,' Gwenda said.

Wulfric nodded. 'I thought you might.' He rarely challenged her, but now he expressed a misgiving. 'Dangerous, though. You'll have to make sure no one finds out where you've gone.'

'Exactly. Nate mustn't know.'

'How will you manage that?'

'He's sure to notice that I'm not in the village for a couple of days. We'll have to think of a story.'

'We can say you're sick.'

'Too risky. He'll probably come to the house to check.'

'We could say you're at your father's place.'

'Nate won't believe that. He knows I never stay there longer than I have to.' She gnawed at a hangnail, racking her brains. In the ghost stories and fairy tales that people told around the fire on long winter evenings, the characters generally believed one another's lies without question; but real people were less easily duped. 'We could say I've gone to Kingsbridge,' she said at last.

'What for?'

'To buy laying hens at the market, perhaps.'

'You could buy hens from Annet.'

'I wouldn't buy anything from that bitch, and people know it.'

'True.'

'And Nate knows I've always been a friend of Caris, so he'll believe I could be staying with her.'

'All right.'

It was not much of a story, but she could not think of anything better. And she was desperate to see her son.

She left the next morning.

She slipped out of the house before dawn, wrapped in a heavy cloak against the cold March wind. She walked softly through the village in pitch darkness, finding her way by touch and memory. She did not want to be seen and questioned before she had even left the neighbourhood. But no one was up yet. Nathan Reeve's dog growled quietly then recognized her tread, and she heard a soft thump as he wagged his tail against the side of his wooden kennel.

She left the village and followed the road through the fields. When dawn broke she was a mile away. She looked at the road behind her. It was empty. No one had followed her.

She chewed a crust of stale bread for breakfast, then stopped at mid-morning at a tavern where the Wigleigh-to-Kingsbridge road crossed the Northwood-to-Outhenby road. She recognized no one at the inn. She watched the door nervously as she ate a bowl of salt-fish stew and drank a pint of cider. Every time someone came in she got ready to hide her face, but it was always a stranger, and no one took any notice of her. She left quickly, and set off on the road to Outhenby.

She reached the valley around mid-afternoon. It was twelve years since she had been here, but the place had not changed much. It had recovered from the plague remarkably quickly. Apart from some small children playing near the houses, most of the villagers were at work, ploughing and sowing, or looking after new lambs. They stared at her across the fields, knowing she was a stranger, wondering about her identity. Some of them would recognize her close up. She had been here for only ten days, but those had been dramatic times, and they would remember. Villagers did not often see such excitement.

She followed the river Outhen as it meandered along the flat plain between two ranges of hills. She went from the main village through smaller settlements that she knew, from the time she had spent here, as Ham, Shortacre and Longwater, to the smallest and most remote, Oldchurch.

Her excitement grew as she approached, and she even forgot her sore feet. Oldchurch was a hamlet, with thirty hovels, none big enough to be a manor house or even a bailiff's home. However, in accordance with the name there was an old church. It was several hundred years of age, Gwenda guessed. It had a squat tower and a short nave, all built of crude masonry, with tiny square windows placed apparently at random in the thick walls.

She walked to the fields beyond. She ignored a group of shepherds in a distant pasture: shrewd Harry Ploughman would not waste big Sam on such light work. He would be harrowing, or clearing a ditch, or helping to manage the eight-ox plough team. Searching the three fields methodically, she looked for a crowd of mostly men, with warm hats and muddy boots and big voices to call to one another across the acres; and a young man a head taller than the others. When she did not at first see her son, she suffered renewed apprehension. Had he already been recaptured? Had he moved to another village?

She found him in a line of men digging manure into a newly ploughed strip. He had his coat off, despite the cold, and he was hefting an oak spade, the muscles of his back and arms bunching and shifting under his old linen shirt. Her heart filled with pride to see him, and to think that such a man had come from her diminutive body.

They all looked up as she approached. The men stared at her in curiosity: Who was she and what was she doing here? She walked straight up to Sam and embraced him, even though he stank of horse dung. 'Hello, Mother,' he said, and all the other men laughed.

She was puzzled by their hilarity.

A wiry man with one empty eye socket said: 'There, there, Sam, you'll be all right now,' and they laughed again.

Gwenda realized they thought it funny that a big man such as Sam should have his little mother come and check on him as if he were a wayward boy.

'How did you find me?' Sam said.

'I met Harry Ploughman at Northwood Market.'

'I hope no one tracked you here.'

'I left before it was light. Your father was to tell people I went to Kingsbridge. No one followed me.'

They talked for a few minutes, then he said he had to get back to work, or the other men would resent his leaving it all to them. 'Go back to the village and find old Liza,' he said. 'She lives opposite the church. Tell her who you are and she'll give you some refreshment. I'll be there at dusk.'

Gwenda glanced up at the sky. It was a dark afternoon, and the men would be forced to stop work in an hour or so. She kissed Sam's cheek and left him.

She found Liza in a house slightly larger than most – it had two rooms rather than one. The woman introduced her husband, Rob, who was blind. As Sam had promised, Liza was hospitable: she put bread and pottage on the table and poured a cup of ale.

Gwenda asked about their son, and it was like turning on a tap. Liza talked unstoppably about him, from babyhood to apprenticeship, until the old man interrupted her harshly with one word: 'Horse.'

They fell silent, and Gwenda heard the rhythmic thud of a trotting horse.

'Smallish mount,' blind Rob said. 'A palfrey, or a pony. Too little for a nobleman or a knight, though it might be carrying a lady.'

Gwenda felt a shiver of fear.

'Two visitors within an hour,' Rob observed. 'Must be connected.'

That was what Gwenda was afraid of.

She got up and looked out of the door. A sturdy black pony was trotting along the path between the houses. She recognized the rider immediately, and her heart sank: it was Jonno Reeve, the son of the bailiff of Wigleigh.

How had he found her?

She tried to duck quickly back into the house, but he had seen her. 'Gwenda!' he shouted, and reined in his horse.

'You devil,' she said.

'I wonder what you're doing here?' he said mockingly.

'How did you get here? No one was following me.'

'My father sent me to Kingsbridge, to see what mischief you might be making there, but on the way I stopped at the Cross Roads tavern, and they remembered you taking the road to Outhenby.'

She wondered whether she could outwit this shrewd young man. 'And why should I not visit my old friends here?'

'No reason,' he said. 'Where's your runaway son?'

'Not here, though I hoped he might be.'

He looked momentarily uncertain, as if he thought she might be telling the truth. Then he said: 'Perhaps he's hiding. I'll look around.' He kicked his horse on.

Gwenda watched him go. She had not fooled him, but perhaps she had planted a doubt in his mind. If she could get to Sam first she might be able to conceal him.

She walked quickly through the little house, with a hasty word to Liza and Rob, and left by the back door. She headed across the field, staying close to the hedge. Looking back towards the village, she could see a man on horseback moving out at an angle to her direction. The day was dimming, and she thought her own small figure might be indistinguishable against the dark background of the hedge.

She met Sam and the others coming back, their spades over their shoulders, their boots thick with muck. From a distance, at first sight, Sam could have been Ralph: the figure was the same, and the confident stride, and the set of the handsome head on the strong neck. But as he talked she could see Wulfric in him too: he had a way of turning his head, a shy smile and a deprecating gesture of the hand that exactly imitated his foster father.

The men spotted her. They had been tickled by her arrival earlier, and now the one-eyed man called out: 'Hello, Mother!' and they all laughed.

She took Sam aside and said: 'Jonno Reeve is here.'

'Hell!'

'I'm sorry.'

'You said you weren't followed!'

'I didn't see him, but he picked up my trail.'

'Damn. Now what do I do? I'm not going back to Wigleigh!'

'He's looking for you, but he left the village heading east.' She scanned the darkening landscape but could not see much. 'If we hurry back to Oldchurch we could hide you – in the church, perhaps.'

'All right.'

They picked up their pace. Gwenda said over her shoulder: 'If you men come across a bailiff called Jonno ... you haven't seen Sam from Wigleigh.'

'Never heard of him, Mother,' said one, and the others concurred. Serfs were generally ready to help one another outwit the bailiff.

Gwenda and Sam reached the settlement without seeing Jonno. They headed for the church. Gwenda thought they could probably get in: country churches were usually empty and bare inside, and generally left open. But if this one should turn out to be an exception, she was not sure what they would do.

They threaded through the houses and came within sight of the church. As they passed Liza's front door, Gwenda saw a black pony. She groaned. Jonno must have doubled back under cover of the dusk. He had gambled that Gwenda would find Sam and bring him to the village, and he had been right. He had his father Nate's low cunning.

She took Sam's arm to hurry him across the road and into the church – then Jonno stepped out from Liza's house.

'Sam,' he said. 'I thought you'd be here.'

Gwenda and Sam stopped and turned.

Sam leaned on his wooden spade. 'What are you going to do about it?'

Jonno was grinning triumphantly. 'Take you back to Wigleigh.'

'I'd like to see you try.'

A group of peasants, mostly women, appeared from the west side of the village and stopped to watch the confrontation.

Jonno reached into his pony's saddlebag and brought out some kind of metal device with a chain. 'I'm going to put a leg iron on you,' he said. 'And if you've got any sense you won't resist.'

Gwenda was surprised by Jonno's nerve. Did he really expect to arrest Sam all on his own? He was a beefy lad, but not as big as Sam. Did he hope the villagers would help him? He had the law on his side, but few peasants would think his cause just. Typical young man, he had no sense of his own limitations.

Sam said: 'I used to beat the shit out of you when we were boys, and I'll do the same today.'

Gwenda did not want them to fight. Whoever won, Sam would be wrong in the eyes of the law. He was a runaway. She said: 'It's too late to go anywhere now. Why don't we discuss this in the morning?'

Jonno gave a disparaging laugh. 'And let Sam slip away before dawn, the way you sneaked out of Wigleigh? Certainly not. He sleeps in irons tonight.'

The men Sam had been working with appeared, and stopped to see what was going on. Jonno said: 'All law-abiding men have a duty to help me arrest this runaway, and anyone who hinders me will be subject to the punishment of the law.'

'You can rely on me,' said the one-eyed man. 'I'll hold your horse.' The others chuckled. There was little sympathy for Jonno. On the other hand, no villager spoke in Sam's defence.

Jonno moved suddenly. With the leg iron in both hands, he stepped towards Sam and bent down, trying to snap the device on to Sam's leg in one surprise move.

It might have worked on a slow-moving older man, but Sam reacted quickly. He stepped back then kicked out, landing one muddy boot on Jonno's outstretched left arm.

Jonno gave a grunt of pain and anger. Straightening up, he drew back his right arm and swung the iron, intending to hit Sam over the head with it. Gwenda heard a frightened scream and realized it came from herself. Sam darted back another step, out of range.

Jonno saw that his blow was going to miss, and let go of the iron at the last moment.

It flew through the air. Sam flinched away, turning and ducking, but he could not dodge it. The iron hit his ear and the chain whipped across his face. Gwenda cried out as if she herself had been hurt. The onlookers gasped. Sam staggered, and the iron fell to the ground. There was a moment of suspense. Blood came from Sam's ear and nose. Gwenda took a step towards him, stretching out her arms.

Then Sam recovered from the shock.

He turned back to Jonno and swung his heavy wooden spade in one graceful movement. Jonno had not quite recovered his balance after the effort of his throw, and he was unable to dodge.

The edge of the spade caught him on the side of the head. Sam was strong, and the sound of wood on bone rang out across the village street.

Jonno was still reeling when Sam hit him again. Now the spade came straight down from above. Swung by both Sam's arms, it landed on top of Jonno's head, edge first, with tremendous force. This time the impact did not ring out, but sounded more like a dull thud, and Gwenda feared Jonno's skull had cracked.

As Jonno slumped to his knees, Sam hit him a third time, another full-force blow with the oak blade, this one across his victim's forehead. An iron sword could hardly have been more damaging, Gwenda thought despairingly. She stepped forward to restrain Sam, but the village men had had the same idea a moment earlier, and got there before her. They pulled Sam away, two of them holding each arm.

Jonno lay on the ground, his head in a pool of blood. Gwenda was sickened by the sight, and could not help thinking of the boy's father, Nate, and how grieved he would be by his son's injuries. Jonno's mother had died of the plague, so at least she was in a place where grief could not afflict her.

Gwenda could see that Sam was not badly hurt. He was bleeding, but still struggling with his captors, trying to get free so that he could attack again. Gwenda bent over Jonno. His eyes were closed and he was not moving. She put a hand on his heart and felt nothing. She tried for a pulse, the way Caris had shown her, but there was none. Jonno did not seem to be breathing.

The implications of what had happened dawned on her, and she began to weep.

Jonno was dead, and Sam was a murderer.

# 82

On Easter Sunday that year, 1361, Caris and Merthin had been married ten years.

Standing in the cathedral, watching the Easter procession, Caris recalled their wedding. Because they had been lovers, off and on, for so long, they had seen the ceremony as no more than confirmation of a long-established fact, and they had foolishly envisaged a small, quiet event: a low-key service in St Mark's church and a modest dinner for a few people afterwards at the Bell. But Father Joffroi had informed them, the day before, that by his calculation at least two thousand people were planning to attend the wedding, and they had been forced to move it to the cathedral. Then it turned out that, without their knowledge, Madge Webber had organized a banquet in the guild hall for leading citizens and a picnic in Lovers' Field for everyone else in Kingsbridge. So, in the end, it had been the wedding of the year.

Caris smiled at the recollection. She had worn a new robe of Kingsbridge Scarlet, a colour the bishop probably thought appropriate for such a woman. Merthin had dressed in a richly patterned Italian coat, chestnut brown with gold threads, and had seemed to glow with happiness. They both had realized, belatedly, that their drawn-out love affair, which they had imagined to be a private drama, had been entertaining the citizens of Kingsbridge for years, and everyone wanted to celebrate its happy ending.

Her pleasant memories evaporated as her old enemy Philemon mounted the pulpit. In the decade since the wedding he had grown quite fat. His monkish tonsure and shaved face revealed a ring of blubber around his neck, and the priestly robes billowed like a tent.

He preached a sermon against dissection.

Dead bodies belonged to God, he said. Christians were

instructed to bury them in a carefully specified ritual; the saved in consecrated ground, the unforgiven elsewhere. To do anything else with corpses was against God's will. To cut them up was sacrilege, he said with uncharacteristic passion. There was even a tremor in his voice as he asked the congregation to imagine the horrible scene of a body being opened, its parts separated and sliced and pored over by so-called medical researchers. True Christians knew there was no excuse for these ghoulish men and women.

The phrase 'men and women' was not often heard from Philemon's mouth, Caris thought, and could not be without significance. She glanced at her husband, standing next to her in the nave, and he raised his eyebrows in an expression of concern.

The prohibition against examining corpses was standard dogma, propounded by the church since before Caris could remember, but it had been relaxed since the plague. Progressive younger clergymen were vividly aware of how badly the church had failed its people then, and they were keen to change the way medicine was taught and practised by priests. However, conservative senior clergy clung to the old ways and blocked any change in policy. The upshot was that dissection was banned in principle and tolerated in practice.

Caris had been performing dissections at her new hospital from the start. She never talked about it outside the building: there was no point in upsetting the superstitious. But she did it every chance she got.

In recent years she had usually been joined by one or two younger monk-physicians. Many trained doctors never saw inside the body except when treating very bad wounds. Traditionally, the only carcases they were allowed to open were those of pigs, thought to be the animals most like humans in their anatomy.

Caris was puzzled as well as worried by Philemon's attack. He had always hated her, she knew, though she had never been sure why. But since the great standoff in the snowfall of 1351 he had ignored her. As if in compensation for his loss of power over the town, he had furnished his palace with precious objects: tapestries, carpets, silver tableware, stained-glass windows, illuminated manuscripts. He had become ever more grand, demanding elaborate deference from his monks and novices, wearing gorgeous robes for services, and travelling, when he had to go to other towns, in a charette that was furnished like a duchess's boudoir.

There were several important visiting clergymen in the choir for the service – Bishop Henri of Shiring, Archbishop Piers of Monmouth and Archdeacon Reginald of York – and presumably Philemon was hoping to impress them with this outburst of doctrinal conservatism. But to what end? Was he looking for promotion? The archbishop was ill – he had been carried into the church – but surely Philemon could not aspire to that post? It was something of a miracle that the son of Joby from Wigleigh should have risen to be prior of Kingsbridge. Besides, elevation from prior to archbishop would be an unusually big jump, a bit like going from knight to duke without becoming a baron or an earl in between. Only a special favourite could hope for such a rapid rise.

However, there was no limit to Philemon's ambition. It was not that he felt himself to be superbly well qualified, Caris thought. That had been Godwyn's attitude, arrogant self-confidence. Godwyn had assumed that God made him prior because he was the cleverest man in town. Philemon was at the opposite extreme: in his heart he believed he was a nobody. His life was a campaign to convince himself that he was not completely worthless. He was so sensitive to rejection that he could not bear to consider himself undeserving of any post, no matter how lofty.

She thought of speaking to Bishop Henri after the service. She might remind him of the ten-year-old agreement that the prior of Kingsbridge had no jurisdiction over the hospital of St Elizabeth on Leper Island, which came under the bishop's direct control; so that any attack on the hospital was an attack on the rights and privileges of Henri himself. But, on further reflection, she realized that such a protest would confirm to the bishop that she was conducting dissections, and turn what might now be only a vague suspicion, easily ignored, into a known fact that must be dealt with. So she decided to remain silent.

Standing beside her were Merthin's two nephews, the sons of

Earl Ralph: Gerry, age thirteen, and Roley, ten. Both boys were enrolled in the monks' school. They lived in the priory but spent much of their free time with Merthin and Caris at their house on the island. Merthin had his hand resting casually on the shoulder of Roley. Only three people in the world knew that Roley was not his nephew but his son. They were Merthin himself, Caris, and the boy's mother, Philippa. Merthin tried not to show special favour to Roley, but found it hard to disguise his true feelings, and was especially delighted when Roley learned something new or did well at school.

Caris often thought about the child she had conceived with Merthin and then aborted. She always imagined it to have been a girl. She would be a woman now, Caris mused, twenty-three years old, probably married with children of her own. The thought was like the ache of an old wound, painful but too familiar to be distressing.

When the service was over they all left together. The boys were invited to Sunday dinner, as always. Outside the cathedral, Merthin turned to look back at the tower that now soared high over the middle of the church.

As he examined his almost-finished work, frowning at some detail visible only to him, Caris studied him fondly. She had known him since he was eleven years old, and had loved him almost as long. He was forty-five now. His red hair was receding from his brow, and stood up around his head like a curly halo. He had carried his left arm stiffly ever since a small carved stone corbel, dropped from the scaffolding by a careless mason, had fallen on his shoulder. But he still had the expression of boyish eagerness that had drawn the ten-year-old Caris to him on All Hallows' Day a third of a century ago.

She turned to share his view. The tower appeared to stand neatly on the four sides of the crossing, and to be exactly two bays square, even though in fact its weight was held up by massive buttresses built into the exterior corners of the transepts, which themselves rested on new foundations separate from the old original ones. The tower looked light and airy, with slender columns and multiple window openings through which you could see blue sky in fine weather. Above the square top of the tower, a web of scaffolding was rising for the final stage, the spire.

When Caris brought her gaze back down to ground level she saw her sister approaching. Alice was only a year older at forty-five, but Caris felt she was from another generation. Her husband, Elfric, had died in the plague, but she had not remarried, becoming frumpy, as if she thought that was how a widow should be. Caris had quarrelled with Alice, many years ago, over Elfric's treatment of Merthin. The passage of time had blunted the edge of their mutual hostility, but there was still a resentful tilt to Alice's head when she said hello.

With her was Griselda, her stepdaughter, though only a year younger than Alice. Griselda's son, known as Merthin Bastard, stood beside her, towering over her, a big man with superficial charm – just like his father, the long-gone Thurstan, and about as different from Merthin Bridger as could be. Also with her was her sixteen-year-old daughter, Petranilla.

Griselda's husband, Harold Mason, had taken over the business after Elfric died. He was not much of a builder, according to Merthin, but he was doing all right, although he did not have the monopoly of priory repairs and extensions that had made Elfric rich. He stood next to Merthin now and said: 'People think you're going to build the spire with no formwork.'

Caris understood. Formwork, or centering, was the wooden frame that held the masonry in place until the mortar dried.

Merthin said: 'Not much room for formwork inside that narrow spire. And how would it be supported?' His tone was polite, but Caris could tell from its briskness that he did not like Harold.

'I could believe it if the spire was going to be round.'

Caris understood this, too. A round spire could be built by placing one circle of stones on top of another, each a little narrower than the last. No formwork was needed because the circle was self-supporting: the stones could not fall inwards because they pressed on one another. The same was not true of any shape with corners.

'You've seen the drawings,' Merthin said. 'It's an octagon.'

The corner turrets on the top of the square tower faced diagonally outwards, easing the eye as it progressed upwards to the different shape of the narrower spire. Merthin had copied this feature from Chartres. But it made sense only if the tower was octagonal.

Harold said: 'But how can you build an octagonal tower without formwork?'

'Wait and see,' said Merthin, and he moved away.

As they walked down the main street Caris said: 'Why won't you tell people how you're going to do it?'

'So that they can't fire me,' he replied. 'When I was building the bridge, as soon as I'd done the hard part they got rid of me, and hired someone cheaper.'

'I remember.'

'They can't do that now, because no one else can build the spire.'

'You were a youngster then. Now you're alderman. No one would dare sack you.'

'Perhaps not. But it's nice to feel they can't.'

At the bottom of the main street, where the old bridge had stood, there was a disreputable tavern called the White Horse. Caris saw Merthin's sixteen-year-old daughter, Lolla, leaning on the wall outside, with a group of older friends. Lolla was an attractive girl, with olive skin and lustrous dark hair, a generous mouth and sultry brown eyes. The group was crowded around a dice game, and they were all drinking ale from large tankards. Caris was sorry, though not surprised, to see her stepdaughter carousing on the street at midday.

Merthin was angry. He went up to Lolla and took her arm. 'You'd better come home for your dinner,' he said in a tight voice.

She tossed her head, shaking her thick hair in a gesture that was undoubtedly meant for the eyes of someone other than her father. 'I don't want to go home, I'm happy here,' she said.

'I didn't ask what you wanted,' Merthin replied, and he jerked her away from the others.

A good-looking boy of about twenty detached himself from the crowd. He had curly hair and a mocking smile, and he was picking his teeth with a twig. Caris recognized Jake Riley, a lad of no particular profession who nevertheless always seemed to have money to spend. He sauntered over. 'What's going on?' he said. He spoke with the twig sticking out of his mouth like an insult.

'None of your damn business,' Merthin said.

Jake stood in his way. 'The girl doesn't want to leave.'

'You'd better get out of my way, son, unless you want to spend the rest of the day in the town stocks.'

Caris froze with anxiety. Merthin was in the right: he was entitled to discipline Lolla, who was still five years short of adulthood. But Jake was the kind of boy who might punch him anyway, and take the consequences. However, Caris did not intervene, knowing it might make Merthin angry with her instead of with Jake.

Jake said: 'I suppose you're her father.'

'You know perfectly well who I am, and you can call me Alderman, and speak respectfully to me, or suffer the consequences.'

Jake stared insolently at Merthin a moment longer then turned aside, casually saying: 'Yes, all right.'

Caris was relieved that the confrontation had not turned into fisticuffs. Merthin never got into fights, but Lolla was capable of driving him to distraction.

They walked on towards the bridge. Lolla shook herself free of her father's grasp and walked on ahead, arms folded under her breasts, head down, frowning and muttering to herself in a full-dress sulk.

This was not the first time Lolla had been seen in bad company. Merthin was horrified and enraged that his little girl should be so determined to seek out such people. 'Why does she do it?' he said to Caris as they followed Lolla across the bridge to Leper Island.

'God knows.' Caris had observed that this kind of behaviour was more common in youngsters who had suffered the loss of a parent. After Silvia died, Lolla had been mothered by Bessie Bell, Lady Philippa, Merthin's housekeeper Em, and of course Caris herself. Perhaps she was confused about who she should obey.

But Caris did not voice this thought, as it might seem to suggest that Merthin had somehow failed as a parent. 'I had terrible fights with Aunt Petranilla when I was that age.'

'What about?'

'Similar things. She didn't like me spending time with Mattie Wise.'

'That's completely different. You didn't go to low taverns with rogues.'

'Petranilla thought Mattie was bad company.'

'It's not the same.'

'I suppose not.'

'You learned a lot from Mattie.'

Lolla was undoubtedly learning a lot from handsome Jake Riley, but Caris kept that inflammatory thought to herself – Merthin was furious enough already.

The island was entirely built up now, and an integral part of the city. It even had its own parish church. Where once they had wandered across waste ground, they now followed a footpath that ran straight between houses and turned sharp corners. The rabbits had long gone. The hospital occupied most of the western end. Although Caris went there every day, she still felt a glow of pride when she looked at the clean grey stonework, the large windows in regular rows and the chimneys lined up like soldiers.

They passed through a gate into Merthin's grounds. The orchard was mature, and blossom covered the apple trees like snow.

As always, they went in through the kitchen door. The house had a grand entrance on the river side which no one ever used. Even a brilliant architect can make a mistake, Caris thought with amusement; but, once again, she decided to give the thought no voice today.

Lolla stamped upstairs to her room.

From the front room a woman called: 'Hello, everyone!' The two boys rushed into the parlour with glad cries. It was their mother, Philippa. Merthin and Caris greeted her warmly.

Caris and Philippa had become sisters-in-law when Caris married Merthin, but their past rivalry had continued to make Caris feel awkward in Philippa's presence for some years.

Eventually the boys had brought them together. When first Gerry then Roley enrolled at the priory school, it was natural for Merthin to look after his nephews, and then it became normal for Philippa to call at Merthin's house whenever she was in Kingsbridge.

At first, Caris had felt jealous of Philippa for having attracted Merthin sexually. Merthin had never tried to pretend that his love for Philippa had been merely superficial. He clearly still cared about her. But Philippa nowadays cut a sad figure. She was forty-nine and looked older, her hair grey and her face lined with disappointment. She lived now for her children. She was a frequent guest of her daughter, Odila, the countess of Monmouth; and when she was not there she often visited Kingsbridge Priory to be close to her sons. She managed to spend very little time at Earlscastle with her husband Ralph.

'I've got to take the boys to Shiring,' she said, explaining her presence here. 'Ralph wants them to attend the county court with him. He says it's a necessary part of their education.'

'He's right,' Caris said. Gerry would be the earl, if he lived long enough; and if he did not Roley would inherit the title. So they both needed to be familiar with courts.

Philippa added: 'I intended to be in the cathedral for the Easter service, but my charette broke a wheel and I made an overnight stop.'

'Well, now that you're here, let's have dinner,' Caris said.

They went into the dining hall. Caris opened the windows that looked on to the river. Cool fresh air came in. She wondered what Merthin would do about Lolla. He said nothing, leaving her to stew upstairs, to Caris's relief: a brooding adolescent at the dinner table could bring down everyone's spirits.

They ate mutton boiled with leeks. Merthin poured red wine, and Philippa drank thirstily. She had become fond of wine. Perhaps it was her consolation.

While they were eating, Em came in looking anxious. 'There's somebody at the kitchen door to see the mistress,' she said.

Merthin said impatiently: 'Well, who is it?'

'He wouldn't mention his name, but he said the mistress would know him.'

'What kind of person?'

'A young man. By his clothes a peasant, not a town dweller.' Em had a snobbish dislike of villagers.

'Well, he sounds harmless. Let him come in.'

A moment later, in walked a tall figure with a hood pulled forward to cover most of his face. When he drew it back, Caris recognized Gwenda's elder son, Sam.

Caris had known him all his life. She had seen him born, had watched his slimy head emerge from the small body of his mother. She had observed him as he grew and changed and became a man. She saw Wulfric in him now, in the way he walked and stood and raised a hand slightly as he was about to speak. She had always suspected that Wulfric was not in fact his father – but, close as she was to Gwenda, she had never mentioned her doubt. Some questions were better left unasked. However, the suspicion had inevitably returned when she heard that Sam was wanted for the murder of Jonno Reeve. For Sam when born had had a look of Ralph.

Now he came up to Caris, lifted his hand in that gesture of Wulfric's, hesitated, then went down on one knee. 'Save me, please,' he said.

Caris was horrified. 'How can I save you?'

'Hide me. I've been on the run for days. I left Oldchurch in the dark and walked through the night and I've hardly rested since. Just now I tried to buy something to eat in a tavern and someone recognized me, and I had to run.'

He looked so desperate that she felt a surge of compassion. Nevertheless, she said: 'But you can't hide here, you're wanted for murder!'

'It was no murder, it was a fight. Jonno struck first. He hit me with a leg iron – look.' Sam touched his face in two places, ear and nose, to indicate two scabbed gashes.

The physician in Caris could not help noting that the injuries were about five days old, and the nose was healing well enough though the ear really needed a stitch. But her main thought was that Sam should not be here. 'You have to face justice,' she said.

'They'll take Jonno's side, they're sure to. I ran away from

Wigleigh, for higher wages in Outhenby. Jonno was trying to take me back. They'll say he was entitled to chain a runaway.'

'You should have thought of that before you hit him.'

He said accusingly: 'You employed runaways at Outhenby, when you were prioress.'

She was stung. 'Runaways, yes – killers, no.'

'They will hang me.'

Caris was torn. How could she turn him away?

Merthin spoke. 'There are two reasons why you can't hide here, Sam. One is that it's a crime to conceal a fugitive, and I'm not willing to put myself on the wrong side of the law for your sake, fond though I am of your mother. But the second reason is that everyone knows your mother is an old friend of Caris's, and if the Kingsbridge constables are searching for you this is the first place they will look.'

'Is it?' Sam said.

He was not very bright, Caris knew – his brother Davey had all the brains.

Merthin said: 'You could hardly think of a worse place than this to hide.' He softened. 'Drink a cup of wine, and take a loaf of bread with you, and get out of town,' he said more kindly. 'I'll have to find Mungo Constable and report that you were here, but I can walk slowly.' He poured wine into a wooden cup.

'Thank you.'

'Your only hope is to go far away where you aren't known and start a new life. You're a strong boy, you'll always find work. Go to London and join a ship. And don't get into fights.'

Philippa said suddenly: 'I remember your mother ... Gwenda?'

Sam nodded.

Philippa turned to Caris. 'I met her at Casterham, when William was alive. She came to me about that girl in Wigleigh who had been raped by Ralph.'

'Annet.'

'Yes.' Philippa turned back to Sam. 'You must be the baby she had in her arms at the time. Your mother is a good woman. I'm sorry for her sake that you're in trouble.'

There was a moment of quiet. Sam drained the cup. Caris was

thinking, as no doubt Philippa and Merthin were too, about the passage of time, and how it can change an innocent, beloved baby into a man who commits murder.

In the silence, they heard voices.

It sounded like several men at the kitchen door.

Sam looked around him like a trapped bear. One door led to the kitchen, the other outside to the front of the house. He dashed to the front door, flung it open and ran out. Without pausing he headed down towards the river.

A moment later Em opened the door from the kitchen, and Mungo Constable came into the dining hall, with four deputies crowding behind him, all carrying wooden clubs.

Merthin pointed at the front door. 'He just left.'

'After him, lads,' said Mungo, and they all ran through the room and out of the door.

Caris stood up and hurried outside, and the others followed her.

The house was built on a low, rocky bluff only three or four feet high. The river flowed rapidly past the foot of the little cliff. To the left, Merthin's graceful bridge spanned the water; to the right was a muddy beach. Across the river, trees were coming into leaf in the old plague graveyard. Pokey little suburban hovels had grown up like weeds either side of the cemetery.

Sam could have turned left or right, and Caris saw with a feeling of despair that he had made the wrong choice. He had gone right, which led nowhere. She saw him running along the foreshore, his boots leaving big impressions in the mud. The constables were chasing him like dogs after a hare. She felt sorry for Sam, as she always felt sorry for the hare. It was nothing to do with justice, merely that he was the quarry.

Seeing he had nowhere to go, he waded into the water.

Mungo had stayed on the paved footpath at the front of the house, and now he turned in the opposite direction, to the left, and ran towards the bridge.

Two of the deputies dropped their clubs, pulled off their boots, got out of their coats and jumped into the water in their undershirts. The other two stood on the shoreline, presumably unable to swim, or perhaps unwilling to jump into the water on a cold day. The two swimmers struck out after Sam.

Sam was strong, but his heavy winter coat was now sodden and dragging him down. Caris watched with horrid fascination as the deputies gained on him.

There was a shout from the other direction. Mungo had reached the bridge and was running across, and he had stopped to beckon the two non-swimming deputies to follow him. They acknowledged his signal and ran after him. He continued across the bridge.

Sam reached the far shore just before the swimmers caught up with him. He gained his footing and staggered through the shallows, shaking his head, water running from his clothing. He turned and saw a deputy almost on him. The man stumbled, bending forward inadvertently, and Sam swiftly kicked him in the face with a heavy waterlogged boot. The deputy cried out and fell back.

The second deputy was more cautious. He approached Sam then stopped, still out of reach. Sam turned and ran forward, coming out of the water on to the turf of the plague graveyard; but the deputy followed him. Sam stopped again, and the deputy stopped. Sam realized he was being toyed with. He gave a roar of anger and rushed at his tormentor. The deputy ran back, but he had the river behind him. He ran into the shallows, but the water slowed him, and Sam was able to catch him.

Sam grabbed the man by the shoulders, turned him and headbutted him. On the far side of the river, Caris heard a crack as the poor man's nose broke. Sam tossed him aside and he fell, spurting blood into the river water.

Sam turned again for the shore – but Mungo was waiting for him. Now Sam was lower down the slope of the foreshore and hampered by the water. Mungo rushed at him, stopped, let him come forward, then raised his heavy wooden club. He feinted, Sam dodged, then Mungo struck, hitting Sam on the top of his head.

It looked a dreadful blow, and Caris herself gasped with shock as if she had been hit. Sam roared with pain and reflexively put his hands over his head. Mungo, experienced in fighting with strong young men, hit him again with the club, this time in his unprotected ribs. Sam fell into the water. The two deputies who had run across the bridge now arrived on the scene. Both jumped on Sam, holding him down in the shallows. The two he had wounded took their revenge, kicking and punching him savagely while their colleagues held him down. When there was no fight left in him they at last let up and dragged him out of the water.

Mungo swiftly tied Sam's hands behind his back. Then the constables marched the fugitive back towards the town.

'How awful,' said Caris. 'Poor Gwenda.'

# 83

The town of Shiring had a carnival air during sessions of the county court. All the inns around the square were busy, their parlours crowded with men and women dressed in their best clothes, all shouting for drinks and food. The town naturally took the opportunity to hold a market, and the square itself was so closely packed with stalls that it took half an hour to move a couple of hundred yards. As well as the legitimate stallholders there were dozens of strolling entrepreneurs: bakers with trays of buns, a busking fiddle player, maimed and blind beggars, prostitutes showing their breasts, a dancing bear, a preaching friar.

Earl Ralph was one of the few people who could cross the square quickly. He rode with three knights ahead of him and a handful of servants behind, and his entourage went through the melee like a ploughshare, turning the crowd aside by the force of their momentum and their carelessness for the safety of people in their way.

They rode on up the hill to the sheriff's castle. In the courtyard they wheeled with a flourish and dismounted. The servants immediately began shouting for ostlers and porters. Ralph liked people to know he had arrived.

He was tense. The son of his old enemy was about to be tried for murder. He was on the brink of the sweetest revenge imaginable, but some part of him feared it might not happen. He was so on edge that he felt slightly ashamed: he would not have wanted his knights to know how much this meant to him. He was careful to conceal, even from Alan Fernhill, how eager he was that Sam should hang. He was afraid something would go wrong at the last minute. No one knew better than he how the machinery of justice could fail: after all, he himself had escaped hanging twice.

He would sit on the judge's bench during the trial, as was his right, and do his best to make sure there was no upset.

He handed his reins to a groom and looked around. The castle was not a military fortification. It was more like a tavern with a courtyard, though strongly built and well guarded. The sheriff of Shiring could live here safe from the vengeful relatives of the people he arrested. There were basement dungeons in which to keep prisoners, and guest apartments where visiting judges could stay unmolested.

Sheriff Bernard showed Ralph to his room. The sheriff was the king's representative in the county, responsible for collecting taxes as well as administering justice. The post was lucrative, the salary usefully supplemented by gifts, bribes, and percentages skimmed off the top of fines and forfeited bail money. The relationship between earl and sheriff could be fractious: the earl ranked higher, but the sheriff's judicial power was independent. Bernard, a rich wool merchant of about Ralph's age, treated Ralph with an uneasy mixture of camaraderie and deference.

Philippa was waiting for Ralph in the apartment set aside for them. Her long grey hair was tied up in an elaborate headdress, and she wore an expensive coat in drab shades of grey and brown. Her haughty manner had once made her a proud beauty, but now she just looked like a grumpy old woman. She might have been his mother.

He greeted his sons, Gerry and Roley. He was not sure how to deal with children, and he had never seen much of his own: as babies they had been cared for by women, of course, and now they were at the monks' school. He addressed them somewhat as if they were squires in his service, giving them orders at one moment and joshing them in a friendly way the next. He would find them easier to talk to when they were older. It did not seem to matter: they regarded him as a hero whatever he did.

'Tomorrow you shall sit on the judge's bench in the court room,' he said. 'I want you to see how justice is done.'

Gerry, the elder, said: 'Can we look around the market this afternoon?'

'Yes – get Dickie to go with you.' Dickie was one of the

Earlscastle servants. 'Here, take some money to spend.' He gave them each a handful of silver pennies.

The boys went out. Ralph sat down across the room from Philippa. He never touched her, and tried always to keep his distance so that it would not happen by accident. He felt sure that she dressed and acted like an old woman to make sure he was not attracted to her. She also went to church every day.

It was a strange relationship for two people who had once conceived a child together, but they had been stuck in it for years and it would never change. At least it left him free to fondle servant girls and tumble tavern wenches.

However, they had to talk about the children. Philippa had strong views and, over the years, Ralph had realized it was easier to discuss things with her, rather than make unilateral decisions and then have a fight when she disagreed.

Now Ralph said: 'Gerald is old enough to be a squire.'

Philippa said: 'I agree.'

'Good!' said Ralph, surprised – he had expected an argument.

'I've already spoken to David Monmouth about him,' she added.

That explained her willingness. She was one jump ahead. 'I see,' he said, playing for time.

'David agrees, and suggests we send him as soon as he is fourteen.'

Gerry was only just thirteen. Philippa was in fact postponing Gerry's departure by almost a year. But this was not Ralph's main worry. David, earl of Monmouth, was married to Philippa's daughter, Odila. 'Being a squire is supposed to turn a boy into a man,' Ralph said. 'But Gerry will get too easy a ride with David. His stepsister is fond of him – she'll probably protect him. He could have it too soft.' After a moment's reflection, he added: 'I expect that's why you want him to go there.'

She did not deny it, but said: 'I thought you would be glad to strengthen your alliance with the earl of Monmouth.'

She had a point. David was Ralph's most important ally in the nobility. Placing Gerry in the Monmouth household would create another bond between the two earls. David might become fond of the boy. In later years, perhaps David's sons would be squires at Earlscastle. Such family connections were priceless. 'Will you undertake to make sure the boy isn't mollycoddled there?' Ralph said.

'Of course.'

'Well, all right then.'

'Good. I'm glad that's settled.' Philippa stood up.

But Ralph was not finished. 'Now what about Roley? He could go too, so that they would be together.'

Philippa did not like this idea at all, Ralph could tell, but she was too clever to contradict him flatly. 'Roley's a bit young,' she said, as if thinking it over. 'And he hasn't properly learned his letters yet.'

'Letters aren't as important to a nobleman as learning to fight. After all, he is second in line to the earldom. If anything should happen to Gerry . . .'

'Which God forbid.'

'Amen.'

'All the same, I think he should wait until he's fourteen.'

'I don't know. Roley's always been a bit womanish. Sometimes he reminds me of my brother, Merthin.' He saw a flash of fear in her eyes. She was afraid of letting her baby go, he guessed. He was tempted to insist, just to torture her. But ten was young for a squire. 'We'll see,' he said noncommittally. 'He'll have to be toughened up sooner or later.'

'All in good time,' said Philippa.

*

THE JUDGE, Sir Lewis Abingdon, was not a local man, but a London lawyer from the king's court, sent on tour to try serious cases in county courts. He was a beefy type with a pink face and a fair beard. He was also ten years younger than Ralph.

Ralph told himself he should not be surprised. He was now forty-four. Half his own generation had been wiped out by the plague. Nevertheless, he continued to be startled by distinguished and powerful men who were younger than he.

They waited, with Gerry and Roley, in a side chamber at the Courthouse inn, while the jury assembled and the prisoners were brought down from the castle. It turned out that Sir Lewis had been at Crécy, as a young squire, though Ralph did not recall him. He treated Ralph with wary courtesy.

Ralph tried subtly to probe the judge and find out how tough he was. 'The Statute of Labourers is difficult to enforce, we find,' he said. 'When peasants see a way to make money, they lose all respect for the law.'

'For every runaway who is working for an illegal wage, there is an employer who is paying it,' the judge said.

'Exactly! The nuns of Kingsbridge Priory have never obeyed the statute.'

'Difficult to prosecute nuns.'

'I don't see why.'

Sir Lewis changed the subject. 'You have a special interest in this morning's proceedings?' he asked. He had probably been told that it was unusual for Ralph to exercise his right to sit beside the judge.

'The murderer is a serf of mine,' Ralph admitted. 'But the main reason I'm here is to give these boys a look at how justice works. One of them is likely to be the earl when I give up the ghost. They can watch the hangings tomorrow, too. The sooner they get used to seeing men die, the better.'

Lewis nodded agreement. 'The sons of the nobility cannot afford to be soft-hearted.'

They heard the clerk of the court bang his gavel, and the hubbub from the next room died down. Ralph's anxiety was not allayed: Sir Lewis's conversation had not told him much. Perhaps that in itself was revealing: it might mean he was not easily influenced.

The judge opened the door and stood aside for the earl to go first.

At the near end of the room, two large wooden chairs were set on a dais. Next to them was a low bench. A murmur of interest arose from the crowd as Gerry and Roley sat on the bench. The people were always fascinated to see the children who would grow into their overlords. But more than that, Ralph thought, there was a look of innocence about the two prepubescent boys that was strikingly out of place in a court whose business was violence, theft and dishonesty. They looked like lambs in a pigpen.

Ralph sat in one of the two chairs and thought of the day, twenty-two years ago, when he had stood in this very courtroom as a criminal accused of rape – a ludicrous charge to bring against a lord when the so-called victim was one of his own serfs. Philippa had been behind that malicious prosecution. Well, he had made her suffer for it.

At that trial, Ralph had fought his way out of the room as soon as the jury pronounced him guilty, and then had been pardoned when he joined the king's army and went to France. Sam was not going to escape: he had no weapon, and his ankles were chained. And the French wars seemed to have petered out, so there were no more free pardons.

Ralph studied Sam as the indictment was read. He had Wulfric's build, not Gwenda's: he was a tall lad, broad across the shoulders. He might have made a useful man-at-arms if he had been more nobly born. He did not really look like Wulfric, though something about the cast of his features rang a bell. Like so many accused men, he wore an expression of superficial defiance overlaying fear. That's just how I felt, Ralph thought.

Nathan Reeve was the first witness. He was the father of the dead man but, more importantly, he testified that Sam was a serf of Earl Ralph's and had not been given leave to go to Oldchurch. He said he had sent his son Jonno to follow Gwenda in the hope of tracking down the runaway. He was not likeable, but his grief was clearly genuine. Ralph was pleased: it was damning testimony.

Sam's mother was standing next to him, the top of her head level with her son's shoulder. Gwenda was not beautiful: her dark eyes were set close to a beaky nose, and her forehead and chin both receded sharply, giving her the look of a determined rodent. Yet there was something strongly sexual about her, even in middle age. It was more than twenty years since Ralph had lain with her, but he remembered her as if it were yesterday. They had done it in a room at the Bell in Kingsbridge, and he had made her kneel up on the bed. He could picture it now, and the memory of her compact body excited him. She had a lot of dark hair, he recollected.

Suddenly she met his eye. She held his gaze and seemed to sense what he was thinking. On that bed she had been indifferent and motionless, to begin with, accepting his thrusts passively because he had coerced her; but, at the end, something strange had come over her, and almost against her own will she had moved in rhythm with him. She must have remembered the same thing, for an expression of shame came over her plain face, and she looked quickly away.

Next to her was another young man, presumably the second son. This one was more like her, small and wiry, with a crafty look about him. He met Ralph's gaze with a stare of intense concentration, as if he was curious what went on in the mind of an earl; and thought he might find the answer in Ralph's face.

But Ralph was most interested in the father. He had hated Wulfric since their fight at the Fleece Fair of 1337. He touched his broken nose reflexively. Several other men had wounded him in later years, but none had hurt his pride so badly. However, Ralph's revenge on Wulfric had been terrible. I deprived him of his birthright for a decade, Ralph thought. I lay with his wife. I gave him that scar across his cheek when he tried to stop me escaping from this very courtroom. I dragged him home when he tried to run away. And now I'm going to hang his son.

Wulfric was heavier than he used to be, but he carried it well. He had a salt-and-pepper beard that did not grow over the long scar of the sword wound Ralph had given him. His face was lined and weatherbeaten. Where Gwenda looked angry, Wulfric was grief stricken. As the peasants of Oldchurch testified that Sam had killed Jonno with an oak spade, Gwenda's eyes flashed defiance, whereas Wulfric's broad forehead creased in anguish.

The foreman of the jury asked whether Sam had been in fear for his life.

Ralph was displeased. The question implied an excuse for the killer.

A thin peasant with one eye responded. 'He wasn't in fear of the bailiff, no. I think he was scared of his mother, though.' The crowd tittered.

The foreman asked whether Jonno had provoked the attack, another question that bothered Ralph by indicating sympathy for Sam.

'Provoked?' said the one-eyed man. 'Only by hitting him across the face with a leg iron, if you call that provoking.' They laughed loudly.

Wulfric looked bewildered. How can people be amused, his expression said, when my son's life is at stake?

Ralph was feeling more anxious. The foreman seemed unsound.

Sam was called to testify, and Ralph noticed that the young man resembled Wulfric more when he spoke. There was a tilt of the head and a gesture of the hand that immediately brought Wulfric to mind. Sam told how he had offered to meet Jonno the following morning, and Jonno had responded by trying to put an iron on his leg.

Ralph spoke to the judge in an undertone. 'None of this makes any difference,' he said with suppressed indignation. 'Whether he was in fear, whether he was provoked, whether he offered to meet the following day.'

Sir Lewis said nothing.

Ralph said: 'The bare fact is that he's a runaway and he killed the man who came to fetch him.'

'He certainly did that,' said Sir Lewis guardedly, giving Ralph no satisfaction.

Ralph looked at the spectators while the jury questioned Sam. Merthin was in the crowd, with his wife. Before becoming a nun Caris had enjoyed dressing fashionably, and after renouncing her vows she had reverted to type. Today she wore a gown made of two contrasting fabrics, one blue and the other green, with a fur-trimmed cloak of Kingsbridge Scarlet and a little round hat. Ralph remembered that Caris had been a childhood friend of Gwenda's, in fact she had been there the day they all saw Thomas Langley kill two men-at-arms in the woods. Merthin and Caris would be hoping, for Gwenda's sake, that Sam would be treated mercifully. Not if I have anything to do with it, Ralph thought.

Caris's successor as prioress, Mother Joan, was in court, presumably because the nunnery owned the vale of Outhenby and was therefore the illegal employer of Sam. Joan ought to be in the dock with the accused, Ralph thought; but when he caught her eye she gave him an accusing glance, as if she thought the murder was his fault more than hers.

The prior of Kingsbridge had not shown up. Sam was Prior Philemon's nephew, but Philemon would not want to draw attention to the fact that he was the uncle of a murderer. Philemon had once had a protective affection for his younger sister, Ralph recalled; but perhaps that had faded with the years.

Sam's grandfather, the disreputable Joby, was present, a white-haired old man now, bent and toothless. Why was he here? He had been at odds with Gwenda for years, and was not likely to have much affection for his grandson. He had probably come to steal coins from people's purses while they were absorbed in the trial.

Sam stood down and Sir Lewis spoke briefly. His summing-up pleased Ralph. 'Was Sam Wigleigh a runaway?' he asked. 'Did Jonno Reeve have the right to arrest him? And did Sam kill Jonno with his spade? If the answer to all three questions is yes, then Sam is guilty of murder.'

Ralph was surprised and relieved. There was no nonsense about whether Sam was provoked. The judge was sound after all.

'What is your verdict?' the judge asked.

Ralph looked at Wulfric. The man was stricken. This is what happens to those who defy me, Ralph thought, and he wished he could say it out loud.

Wulfric caught his eye. Ralph held his gaze, trying to read Wulfric's mind. What emotion was there? Ralph saw that it was fear. Wulfric had never shown fear to Ralph before, but now he crumbled. His son was going to die, and that had weakened him fatally. A profound satisfaction filled Ralph's being as he stared into Wulfric's frightened eyes. I have crushed you at last, he thought, after twenty-four years. Finally, you're scared.

The jury conferred. The foreman seemed to be arguing with the others. Ralph watched them impatiently. Surely they could not be in doubt, after what the judge had said? But there was no certainty with juries. It can't all go wrong at this stage, Ralph thought, can it?

They seemed to come to a resolution, though he could not guess who had prevailed. The foreman stood up.

'We find Sam Wigleigh guilty of murder,' he said.

Ralph kept his eyes fixed on his old enemy. Wulfric looked as if he had been stabbed. His face went pale and he closed his eyes as if in pain. Ralph tried not to smile in triumph.

Sir Lewis turned to Ralph, and Ralph tore his gaze away from Wulfric. 'What are your thoughts about the sentence?' said the judge.

'There's only one choice, as far as I'm concerned.'

Sir Lewis nodded. 'The jury has made no recommendation for mercy.'

'They don't want a runaway to get away with murdering his bailiff.'

'The ultimate penalty, then?'

'Of course!'

The judge turned back to the court. Ralph locked his gaze on Wulfric again. Everyone else looked at Sir Lewis. The judge said: 'Sam Wigleigh, you have murdered the son of your bailiff, and you are sentenced to death. You shall be hanged in Shiring market square tomorrow at dawn, and may God have mercy on your soul.'

Wulfric staggered. The younger son grabbed his father's arm and held him upright, otherwise he might have fallen to the floor. Let him drop, Ralph wanted to say; he's finished.

Ralph looked at Gwenda. She was holding Sam's hand, but she was looking at Ralph. Her expression surprised him. He expected grief, tears, screams, hysterics. But she stared back at him steadily. There was hatred in her eyes, and something else: defiance. Unlike her husband, she did not look crushed. She did not believe the case was over.

She looked, Ralph thought with dismay, as if she had something up her sleeve.

# 84

Caris was in tears as Sam was taken away, but Merthin could not pretend to be grief-stricken. It was a tragedy for Gwenda, and he felt desperately sorry for Wulfric. However, it was no bad thing, for the rest of the world, that Sam should be hanged. Jonno Reeve had been carrying out the law. It might well be a bad law, an unjust law, an oppressive law – but that did not give Sam the right to kill Jonno. After all, Nate Reeve was also bereaved. The fact that nobody liked Nate made no difference.

A thief was brought up before the bench, and Merthin and Caris left the courtroom and went into the parlour of the tavern. Merthin got some wine and poured a cup for Caris. A moment later, Gwenda came up to where they sat. 'It's noon,' she said. 'We have eighteen hours to save Sam.'

Merthin looked up at her in surprise. 'What do you propose?' he said.

'We must get Ralph to ask the king to pardon him.'

That seemed highly unlikely. 'How would you persuade him to do that?'

'I can't, obviously,' Gwenda said. 'But you can.'

Merthin felt trapped. He did not believe Sam deserved a pardon. On the other hand, it was hard to refuse a pleading mother. He said: 'I intervened with my brother on your behalf once before – do you remember?'

'Of course,' Gwenda said. 'Over Wulfric not inheriting his father's land.'

'He turned me down flat.'

'I know,' she said. 'But you have to try.'

'I'm not sure I'm the best person.'

'Who else would he even listen to?'

That was right. Merthin had little chance of success, but no one else had any.

Caris could see that he was reluctant, and she threw her weight in on Gwenda's side. 'Please, Merthin,' she said. 'Think how you would feel if it was Lolla.'

He was about to say that girls don't get into fights, then he realized that in Lolla's case it was all too likely. He sighed. 'I think this is a doomed enterprise,' he said. He looked at Caris. 'But, for your sake, I'll try.'

Gwenda said: 'Why don't you go now?'

'Because Ralph is still in court.'

'It's almost dinner time. They'll be finished soon. You could wait in the private chamber.'

He had to admire her resolve. 'All right,' he said.

He left the parlour and walked around to the back of the tavern. A guard was standing outside the judge's private room. 'I'm the earl's brother,' Merthin said to the sentry. 'Alderman Merthin of Kingsbridge.'

'Yes, alderman, I know you,' the guard said. 'I'm sure it will be all right for you to wait inside.'

Merthin went into the little room and sat down. He felt uncomfortable asking his brother for a favour. The two of them had not been close for decades. Ralph had long ago turned into something Merthin did not recognize. Merthin did not know the man who could rape Annet and murder Tilly. It seemed impossible that such a one could have grown from the boy Merthin had called his brother. Since their parents had died, they had not met except on formal occasions, and even then they spoke little. It was presumptuous of him to use their relationship as justification for asking for a privilege. He would not have done it for Gwenda. But for Caris, he had to.

He did not wait long. After a few minutes the judge and the earl came in. Merthin noticed that his brother's limp – the result of a wound suffered in the French wars – was getting worse as he aged.

Sir Lewis recognized Merthin and shook hands. Ralph did the same and said ironically: 'A visit from my brother is a rare pleasure.'

It was not an unfair jibe, and Merthin acknowledged it with a nod. 'On the other hand,' he said, 'I suppose that if anyone is entitled to plead with you for mercy, I am.'

'What need do you have of mercy? Did you kill someone?'

'Not yet.'

Sir Lewis chuckled.

Ralph said: 'What, then?'

'You and I have known Gwenda since we were all children together.'

Ralph nodded. 'I shot her dog with that bow you made.'

Merthin had forgotten that incident. It was an early sign of how Ralph was going to turn out, he realized with hindsight. 'Perhaps you owe her mercy on that account.'

'I think Nate Reeve's son is worth more than a damn dog, don't you?'

'I didn't mean to suggest otherwise. Just that you might balance cruelty then with kindness now.'

'Balance?' Ralph said, with anger rising in his voice, and Merthin knew then that his cause was lost. 'Balance?' He tapped his broken nose. 'What should I balance against this?' He pointed a finger aggressively at Merthin. 'I'll tell you why I won't give Sam a pardon. Because I looked at Wulfric's face in the courtroom today, as his son was declared guilty of murder, and do you know what I saw there? Fear. That insolent peasant is afraid of me, at last. He has been tamed.'

'He means so much to you?'

'I'd hang six men to see that look.'

Merthin was ready to give up, then he thought of Gwenda's grief, and he tried once more. 'If you've conquered him, your work is done, isn't it?' he argued. 'So let the boy go. Ask the king for a pardon.'

'No. I want to keep Wulfric the way he is.'

Merthin wished he had not come. Putting pressure on Ralph only brought out the worst in him. Merthin was appalled by his vengefulness and malice. He never wanted to speak to his brother again. The feeling was familiar: he had been through this with Ralph before. Somehow it always came as a shock to be reminded of what he was really like.

Merthin turned away. 'Well, I had to try,' he said. 'Goodbye.'

Ralph became cheery. 'Come up to the castle for dinner,' he said. 'The sheriff lays a good table. Bring Caris. We'll have a real talk. Philippa's with me – you like her, don't you?'

Merthin had no intention of going. 'Let me speak to Caris,' he said. Caris would rather have dinner with Lucifer, he knew.

'I may see you later, then.'

Merthin made his escape.

He returned to the parlour. Caris and Gwenda looked expectantly at him as he crossed the room. He shook his head. 'I did my best,' he said. 'I'm sorry.'

*

GWENDA HAD EXPECTED this. She was disappointed but not surprised. She had felt she had to try through Merthin. The other remedy she had at her disposal was so much more drastic.

She thanked Merthin perfunctorily and left the inn, heading for the castle on the hill. Wulfric and Davey had gone to a cheap tavern in the suburbs where they could get a filling dinner for a farthing. Wulfric was no good at this sort of thing anyway. His strength and honesty were useless in negotiations with Ralph and his kind.

Besides, Wulfric could not be allowed even to know about how she hoped to persuade Ralph.

As she was walking up the hill she heard horses behind her. She stopped and turned. It was Ralph and his entourage with the judge. She stood still and looked hard at Ralph, making sure he caught her eye as he passed. He would guess she was coming to see him.

A few minutes later she entered the courtyard of the castle, but access to the sheriff's house was barred. She made her way to the porch of the main building and spoke to the marshal of the hall. 'My name is Gwenda from Wigleigh,' she said. 'Please tell Earl Ralph I need to see him in private.'

'Yes, yes,' said the marshal. 'Look around you: all these people need to see the earl, the judge or the sheriff.'

There were twenty or thirty people standing around the courtyard, some clutching rolls of parchment.

Gwenda was prepared to take a terrible risk to save her son from hanging – but she would not get the opportunity unless she succeeded in speaking to Ralph before dawn.

'How much?' she said to the marshal.

He looked at her with a little less disrespect. 'I can't promise he'll see you.'

'You can give him my name.'

'Two shillings. Twenty-four silver pennies.'

It was a lot of money, but Gwenda had all their savings in her purse. However, she was not yet ready to hand over the money. 'What is my name?' she said.

'I don't know.'

'I just told you. How can you give Earl Ralph my name if you can't remember it?'

He shrugged. 'Tell me again.'

'Gwenda from Wigleigh.'

'All right, I'll mention it to him.'

Gwenda slipped her hand into her purse, brought out a handful of little silver coins and counted twenty-four. It was four weeks' wages for a labourer. She thought of the backbreaking work she had done to earn the money. Now this idle, supercilious doorkeeper was going to get it for doing next to nothing.

The marshal held out his hand.

She said: 'What's my name?'

'Gwenda.'

'Gwenda from where?'

'Wigleigh.' He added: 'That's where this morning's murderer came from, isn't it?'

She gave him the money. 'The earl will want to see me,' she said as forcefully as she could.

The marshal pocketed the coins.

Gwenda retreated into the courtyard, not knowing whether she had wasted her money.

A moment later she saw a familiar figure with a small head on wide shoulders: Alan Fernhill. That was a piece of luck. He was crossing from the stables to the hall. The other petitioners did not recognize him. Gwenda stood in his way. 'Hello, Alan,' she said.

'It's Sir Alan now.'

'Congratulations. Will you tell Ralph that I want to see him?'

'I don't need to ask you what it's about.'

'Say I want to meet him in private.'

Alan raised an eyebrow. 'No offence, but you were a girl last time. You're twenty years older today.'

'Do you think perhaps we should let him decide?'

'Of course.' He grinned insultingly. 'I know he remembers that afternoon at the Bell.'

Alan had been there, of course. He had watched Gwenda take off her dress, and stared at her naked body. He had seen her walk to the bed and kneel on the mattress, facing away. He had laughed coarsely when Ralph said she was better looking from behind.

She hid her revulsion and shame. 'I was hoping he would remember,' she said as neutrally as she could.

The other petitioners realized Alan must be someone important. They began to crowd around, speaking to him, begging and pleading. He pushed them aside and went into the hall.

Gwenda settled down to wait.

After an hour it was clear Ralph was not going to see her before dinner. She found a patch of ground that was not too muddy and sat with her back to a stone wall, but she never took her eyes off the entrance to the hall.

A second hour passed, and a third. Noblemen's dinners often went on all afternoon. Gwenda wondered how they could keep on eating and drinking for such a long time. Why did they not burst?

She had eaten nothing all day, but she was too tense to feel hungry.

It was grey April weather, and the sky began to darken early. Gwenda shivered on the cold ground, but she stayed where she was. This was her only chance.

Servants came out and lit torches around the courtyard. Lights appeared behind the shutters in some of the windows. Night fell, and Gwenda realized there were about twelve hours left until dawn. She thought of Sam, sitting on the floor in one of the underground chambers beneath the castle, and wondered if he was cold. She fought back tears.

It's not over yet, she told herself; but her courage was weakening.

A tall figure blocked the light from the nearest torch. She looked up to see Alan. Her heart leaped.

'Come with me,' he said.

She jumped to her feet and moved towards the hall door.

'Not that way.'

She looked inquiringly at him.

'You said privately, didn't you?' Alan said. 'He's not going to see you in the chamber he shares with the countess. Come this way.'

She followed him through a small door near the stables. He led her through several rooms and up a staircase. He opened a door to a narrow bedchamber. She stepped inside. Alan did not follow her in, but closed the door from the outside.

It was a low room almost completely filled by a bedstead. Ralph stood by the window in his undershirt. His boots and outer clothing were piled on the floor. His face was flushed with drink, but his speech was clear and steady. 'Take off your dress,' he said with a smile of anticipation.

Gwenda said: 'No.'

He looked startled.

'I'm not taking my clothes off,' she said.

'Why did you tell Alan you wanted to see me in private?'

'So that you would think I was willing to have sex with you.'

'But if not ... why are you here?'

'To beg you to ask the king for a pardon.'

'But you're not offering yourself to me?'

'Why would I? I did that once before, and you broke your word. You reneged on the deal. I gave you my body, but you didn't give my husband his land.' She allowed the contempt she felt to be heard in her tone of voice. 'You would do the same again. Your honour is nothing. You remind me of my father.'

Ralph coloured. It was an insult to tell an earl that he could not be trusted, and even more offensive to compare him with a landless labourer who trapped squirrels in the woods. Angrily he said: 'Do you imagine this is the way to persuade me?'

'No. But you're going get that pardon.'

'Why?'

'Because Sam is your son.'

Ralph stared at her for a moment. 'Hah,' he said contemptuously. 'As if I would believe that.'

'He is your son,' she repeated.

'You can't prove that.'

'No, I can't,' she said. 'But you know that I lay with you at the Bell in Kingsbridge nine months before Sam was born. True, I lay with Wulfric, too. So which of you is his father? Look at the boy! He has some of Wulfric's mannerisms, yes – he has learned those, in twenty-two years. But look at his features.'

She saw a thoughtful expression appear on Ralph's face, and knew that something she had said had hit the mark.

'Most of all, think about his character,' she said, pressing home. 'You heard the evidence at the trial. Sam didn't just fight Jonno off, as Wulfric would have done. He didn't knock him down then help him up again, which would have been Wulfric's way. Wulfric is strong, and quick to anger, but he's tender-hearted. Sam is not. Sam hit Jonno with a spade, a blow that would have knocked any man senseless; then, before Jonno fell, Sam hit him again, even harder, although he was already helpless; and then, before Jonno's limp form reached the ground, Sam hit him a third time. If the Oldchurch peasants hadn't jumped on Sam and restrained him, he would have continued to lash out with that bloody spade until Jonno's head was smashed to a pulp. He wanted to kill!' She realized she was crying, and wiped the tears away with her sleeve.

Ralph was staring at her with a horrified look.

'Where does the killer instinct come from, Ralph?' she said. 'Look in your own black heart. Sam is your son. And, God forgive me, he's mine.'

*

WHEN GWENDA had gone, Ralph sat on the bed in the little chamber, staring at the flame of the candle. Was it possible? Gwenda would lie, if it suited her, of course; there was no question of trusting her. But Sam could be Ralph's son as easily as Wulfric's. They had both lain with Gwenda at the crucial time. The truth might never be known for sure.

Even the possibility that Sam might be his child was enough to fill Ralph's heart with dread. Was he about to hang his own son? The dreadful punishment he had devised for Wulfric might be inflicted on himself.

It was already night. The hanging would take place at dawn. Ralph did not have long to decide.

He picked up the candle and left the little room. He had intended to satisfy a carnal desire there. Instead he had been given the shock of his life.

He went outside and crossed the courtyard to the cell block. On the ground floor of the building were offices for the sheriff's deputies. He went inside and spoke to the man on guard duty. 'I want to see the murderer, Sam Wigleigh.'

'Very good, my lord,' the jailer said. 'I'll show you the way.' He led Ralph into the next room, carrying a lamp.

There was a grating set in the floor, and a bad smell. Ralph looked down through the grating. The cell was nine or ten feet deep with stone walls and a dirt floor. There was no furniture: Sam sat on the floor with his back against the wall. Beside him was a wooden jug, presumably containing water. A small hole in the floor appeared to be the toilet. Sam glanced up, then looked away indifferently.

'Open up,' said Ralph.

The jailer unlocked the grating with a key. It swung up on a hinge.

'I want to go down.'

The jailer was surprised, but did not dare argue with an earl. He picked up a ladder that was leaning against the wall and slid it into the cell. 'Take care, please, my lord,' he said nervously. 'Remember, the villain has nothing to lose.'

Ralph climbed down, carrying his candle. The smell was disgusting, but he hardly cared. He reached the foot of the ladder and turned.

Sam looked up at him resentfully and said: 'What do you want?'

Ralph stared at him. He crouched down and held the candle

close to Sam's face, studying his features, trying to compare them with the face he saw when he looked into a mirror.

'What is it?' Sam said, spooked by Ralph's intense stare.

Ralph did not answer. Was this his own child? It could be, he thought. It could easily be. Sam was a good-looking boy, and Ralph had been called handsome in his youth, before his nose got broken. In court earlier, Ralph had thought that something about Sam's face rang a bell, and now he concentrated, searching his memory, trying to think who Sam reminded him of. That straight nose, the dark-eyed gaze, the head of thick hair that girls would envy...

Then he got it.

Sam looked like Ralph's mother, the late Lady Maud.

'Dear God,' he said, and it came out as a whisper.

'What?' said Sam, his voice betraying fear. 'What is this?'

Ralph had to say something. 'Your mother...' he began, then he trailed off. His throat was constricted with emotion, making it difficult for him to get words out. He tried again. 'Your mother has pleaded for you ... most eloquently.'

Sam looked wary and said nothing. He thought Ralph had come here to mock him.

'Tell me,' Ralph said. 'When you hit Jonno with that spade ... did you mean to kill him? You can be honest, you have nothing more to fear.'

'Of course I meant to kill him,' Sam said. 'He was trying to take me in.'

Ralph nodded. 'I would have felt the same,' he said. He paused, staring at Sam, then said it again. 'I would have felt the same.'

He stood up, turned to the ladder, hesitated, then turned back and put the candle on the ground next to Sam. Then he climbed up.

The jailer replaced the grating and locked it.

Ralph said to him: 'There will be no hanging. The prisoner will be pardoned. I will speak to the sheriff immediately.'

As he left the room, the jailer sneezed.

# 85

WHEN MERTHIN AND CARIS returned from Shiring to Kingsbridge, they found that Lolla had gone missing.

Their long-standing house servants, Arn and Em, were waiting at the garden gate and looked as if they had been stationed there all day. Em began to speak but burst into incoherent sobs, and Arn had to break the news. 'We can't find Lolla,' he said, distraught. 'We don't know where she is.'

At first Merthin misunderstood. 'She'll be here by supper time,' he said. 'Don't upset yourself, Em.'

'But she didn't come home last night, nor the night before,' Arn said.

Merthin realized then what they meant. She had run away. A blast of fear like a winter wind chilled his skin and gripped his heart. She was only sixteen. For a moment he could not think rationally. He just pictured her, half way between child and adult, with the intense dark-brown eyes and sensual mouth of her mother, and an expression of blithe false confidence.

When rationality returned to him, he asked himself what had gone wrong. He had been leaving Lolla in the care of Arn and Em for a few days at a time ever since she was five years old, and she had never come to any harm. Had something changed?

He realized that he had hardly spoken to her since Easter Sunday, two weeks ago, when he had taken her by the arm and pulled her away from her disreputable friends outside the White Horse. She had sulked upstairs while the family ate dinner, and had not emerged even when Sam was arrested. She had still been in a snit a few days later, when Merthin and Caris had kissed her goodbye and set out for Shiring.

Guilt stabbed him. He had treated her harshly, and driven

her away. Was Silvia's ghost watching, and despising him for his failure to care for their daughter?

The thought of Lolla's disreputable friends came back to him. 'That fellow Jake Riley is behind this,' he said. 'Have you spoken to him, Arn?'

'No, master.'

'I'd better do that right away. Do you know where he lives?'

'He lodges next to the fishmonger's behind St Paul's church.'

Caris said to Merthin: 'I'll go with you.'

They crossed the bridge back into the city and headed west. The parish of St Paul took in the industrial premises along the waterfront: abattoirs, leather tanners, sawmills, manufactories, and the dyers that had sprung up like September mushrooms since the invention of Kingsbridge Scarlet. Merthin headed for the squat tower of St Paul's church, visible over the low roofs of the houses. He found the fish shop by smell, and knocked at a large, run-down house next door.

It was opened by Sal Sawyers, poor widow of a jobbing carpenter who had died in the plague. 'Jake comes and goes, alderman,' she said. 'I haven't seen him for a week. He can do as he pleases, so long as he pays the rent.'

Caris said: 'When he left, was Lolla with him?'

Sal warily looked sideways at Merthin. 'I don't like to criticize,' she said.

Merthin said: 'Please just tell me what you know. I won't be offended.'

'She's usually with him. She does anything Jake wants, I'll say no more than that. If you look for him, you'll find her.'

'Do you know where he might have gone?'

'He never says.'

'Can you think of anyone who might know?'

'He doesn't bring his friends here, except for her. But I believe his pals are usually to be found at the White Horse.'

Merthin nodded. 'We'll try there. Thank you, Sal.'

'She'll be all right,' Sal said. 'She's just going through a wild phase.'

'I hope you're right.'

Merthin and Caris retraced their steps until they came to

the White Horse, on the riverside near the bridge. Merthin recalled the orgy he had witnessed here at the height of the plague, when the dying Davey Whitehorse had given away all his ale. The place had stood empty for several years afterwards, but now it was once again a busy tavern. Merthin often wondered why it was popular. The rooms were cramped and dirty, and there were frequent fights. About once a year someone was killed there.

They went into a smoky parlour. It was mid-afternoon, but there were a dozen or so desultory drinkers sitting on benches. A small group was clustered around a backgammon board, and several small piles of silver pennies on the table indicated that money was being wagered on the outcome. A red-cheeked prostitute called Joy looked up hopefully at the newcomers, then saw who they were and relapsed into bored indolence. In a corner, a man was showing a woman an expensive-looking coat, apparently offering it for sale; but when he saw Merthin he folded the garment quickly and put it out of sight, and Merthin guessed it was stolen property.

The landlord, Evan, was eating a late dinner of fried bacon. He stood up, wiping his hands on his tunic, and said nervously: 'Good day to you, alderman – an honour to have you in the house. May I draw you a pot of ale?'

'I'm looking for my daughter, Lolla,' Merthin said briskly.

'I haven't seen her for a week,' said Evan.

Sal had said exactly the same about Jake, Merthin recalled. He said to Evan: 'She may be with Jake Riley.'

'Yes, I've noticed that they're friendly,' Evan said tactfully. 'He's been gone about the same length of time.'

'Do you know where he went?'

'He's a close-lipped type, is Jake,' said Evan. 'If you asked him how far it was to Shiring, he'd shake his head and frown and say it was none of his business to know such things.'

The whore, Joy, had been listening to the conversation, and now she chipped in. 'He's open-handed, though,' she said. 'Fair's fair.'

Merthin gave her a hard look. 'And where does his money come from?'

'Horses,' she said. 'He goes around the villages buying foals from peasants, and sells them in the towns.'

He probably stole horses from unwary travellers, too, Merthin thought sourly. 'Is that what he's doing now – buying horses?'

Evan said: 'Very likely. The big fair season is coming up. He could be acquiring his stock-in-trade.'

'And perhaps Lolla went with him.'

'Not wishing to give offence, alderman, but it's quite likely.'

'It's not you who has given offence,' Merthin said. He nodded a curt farewell and left the tavern, with Caris following.

'That's what she's done,' he said angrily. 'She's gone off with Jake. She probably thinks it's a great adventure.'

'I'm afraid I think you're right,' Caris said. 'I hope she doesn't become pregnant.'

'I wish that was the worst I feared.'

They headed automatically for home. Crossing the bridge, Merthin stopped at the highest point and looked out over the suburban rooftops to the forest beyond. His little girl was somewhere out there with a shady horse dealer. She was in danger, and there was nothing he could do to protect her.

*

WHEN MERTHIN WENT to the cathedral the next morning, to check on the new tower, he found that all work had stopped. 'Prior's orders,' said Brother Thomas when Merthin questioned him. Thomas was almost sixty years old, and showing his age. His soldierly physique was bent and he shuffled around the precincts unsteadily. 'There's been a collapse in the south aisle,' he added.

Merthin glanced at Bartelmy French, a gnarled old mason from Normandy, who was sitting outside the lodge sharpening a chisel. Bartelmy shook his head in silent negation.

'That collapse was twenty-four years ago, Brother Thomas,' Merthin said.

'Ah, yes, you're right,' said Thomas. 'My memory's not as good as it used to be, you know.'

Merthin patted his shoulder. 'We're all getting older.'

Bartelmy said: 'The prior is up the tower, if you want to see him.'

Merthin certainly did. He went into the north transept, stepped through a small archway, and climbed a narrow spiral stair within the wall. As he passed from the old crossing into the new tower, the colour of the stones changed from the dark grey of storm clouds to the light pearl of the morning sky. It was a long climb: the tower was already more than three hundred feet high. However, he was used to it. Almost every day for eleven years he had climbed a stair that was higher each time. It occurred to him that Philemon, who was quite fat nowadays, must have had a compelling reason to drag his bulk up all these steps.

Near the top, Merthin passed through a chamber that housed the great wheel, a wooden winding mechanism twice as high as a man, used for hoisting stones, mortar and timber up to where they were needed. When the spire was finished the wheel would be left here permanently, to be used for repair work by future generations of builders, until the trumpets sounded on the Day of Judgement.

He emerged on top of the tower. A stiff, cold breeze was blowing, though none had been noticeable at ground level. A leaded walkway ran around the inside of the tower's summit. Scaffolding stood around an octagonal hole, ready for the masons who would build the spire. Dressed stones were piled nearby, and a heap of mortar was drying up wastefully on a wooden board.

There were no workmen here. Prior Philemon stood on the far side with Harold Mason. They were deep in conversation, but stopped guiltily when Merthin came into view. He had to shout into the wind to make himself heard. 'Why have you stopped the building?'

Philemon had his answer ready. 'There's a problem with your design.'

Merthin looked at Harold. 'You mean some people can't understand it.'

'Experienced people say it can't be built,' Philemon said defiantly.

'Experienced people?' Merthin repeated scornfully. 'Who in Kingsbridge is experienced? Who has built a bridge? Who has worked with the great architects of Florence? Who has seen

Rome, Avignon, Paris, Rouen? Certainly not Harold here. No offence, Harold, but you've never even been to London.'

Harold said: 'I'm not the only one who thinks it's impossible to build an octagonal tower with no formwork.'

Merthin was about to say something sarcastic, but stopped himself. Philemon must have more than this, he realized. The prior had deliberately chosen to fight this battle. Therefore he must have weapons more formidable than the mere opinion of Harold Mason. He had presumably won some support among members of the guild – but how? Other builders who were prepared to say that Merthin's spire was impossible must have been offered some incentive. That probably meant construction work for them. 'What is it?' he said to Philemon. 'What are you hoping to build?'

'I don't know what you mean,' Philemon blustered.

'You've got an alternative project, and you've offered Harold and his friends a piece of it. What's the building?'

'You don't know what you're talking about.'

'A bigger palace for yourself? A new chapter house? It can't be a hospital, we've already got three. Come on, you might as well tell me. Unless you're ashamed of it.'

Philemon was stung into a response. 'The monks wish to build a Lady chapel.'

'Ah.' That made sense. The cult of the Virgin was increasingly popular. The church hierarchy approved because the wave of piety associated with Mary counterbalanced the scepticism and heresy that had afflicted congregations since the plague. Numerous cathedrals and churches were adding a special small chapel at the east end – the holiest part of the building – dedicated to the Mother of God. Merthin did not like the architecture: on most churches, a Lady chapel looked like an afterthought, which of course it was.

What was Philemon's motive? He was always trying to ingratiate himself with someone – that was his modus operandi. A Lady chapel at Kingsbridge would undoubtedly please conservative senior clergy.

This was the second move Philemon had made in that

direction. On Easter Sunday, from the pulpit of the cathedral, he had condemned dissection of corpses. He was mounting a campaign, Merthin realized. But what was its purpose?

Merthin decided to do nothing more until he had figured out what Philemon was up to. Without saying anything further, he left the roof and started down the series of staircases and ladders to the ground.

Merthin arrived home at the dinner hour, and Caris came in from the hospital a few minutes later. 'Brother Thomas is getting worse,' he said to Caris. 'Is there anything that can be done for him?'

She shook her head. 'There's no cure for senility.'

'He told me the south aisle had collapsed as if it had happened yesterday.'

'That's typical. He remembers the distant past but doesn't know what's going on today. Poor Thomas. He'll probably deteriorate quite fast. But at least he's in a familiar place. Monasteries don't change much over the decades. His daily routine is probably the same as it has always been. That will help.'

As they sat down to mutton stew with leeks and mint, Merthin explained the morning's developments. The two of them had been battling Kingsbridge priors for decades: first Anthony, then Godwyn, and now Philemon. They had thought that the granting of the borough charter would put an end to the constant jockeying. It had certainly improved matters, but it seemed Philemon had not given up yet.

'I'm not really worried about the spire,' Merthin said. 'Bishop Henri will overrule Philemon, and order the building restarted, just as soon as he hears. Henri wants to be bishop of the tallest cathedral in England.'

'Philemon must know that,' Caris said thoughtfully.

'Perhaps he simply wants to make the gesture towards a Lady chapel, and get the credit for trying, while blaming his failure on someone else.'

'Perhaps,' Caris said doubtfully.

In Merthin's mind there was a more important question. 'But what is he really after?'

'Everything Philemon does is driven by the need to make himself feel important,' Caris said confidently. 'My guess is he's after a promotion.'

'What job could he have in mind? The archbishop of Monmouth seems to be dying, but surely Philemon can't hope for that position?'

'He must know something we don't.'

Before they could say any more, Lolla walked in.

Merthin's first reaction was a feeling of relief so powerful that it brought tears to his eyes. She was back, and she was safe. He looked her up and down. She had no apparent injuries, she walked with a spring in her step, and her face showed only the usual expression of moody discontent.

Caris spoke first. 'You're back!' she said. 'I'm so glad!'

'Are you?' Lolla said. She often pretended to believe that Caris did not like her. Merthin was not fooled, but Caris could be thrown into doubt, for she was sensitive about not being Lolla's mother.

'We're both glad,' Merthin said. 'You gave us a scare.'

'Why?' said Lolla. She hung her cloak on a hook and sat at the table. 'I was perfectly all right.'

'But we didn't know that, so we were terribly worried.'

'You shouldn't be,' Lolla said. 'I can take care of myself.'

Merthin suppressed an angry retort. 'I'm not sure you can,' he said as mildly as possible.

Caris stepped in to try to lower the temperature. 'Where did you go?' she asked. 'You've been away for two weeks.'

'Different places.'

Merthin said tightly: 'Can you give us one or two examples?'

'Mudeford Crossing. Casterham. Outhenby.'

'And what have you been doing?'

'Is this the catechism?' she said petulantly. 'Do I have to answer all these questions?'

Caris put a restraining hand on Merthin's arm and said to Lolla: 'We just want to know that you haven't been in danger.'

Merthin said: 'I'd also like to know who you've been travelling with.'

'Nobody special.'

'Does that mean Jake Riley?'

She shrugged and looked embarrassed. 'Yes,' she said, as if it were a trivial detail.

Merthin had been ready to forgive and embrace her, but she was making that difficult. Trying to keep his voice neutral, he said: 'What sleeping arrangements did you and Jake have?'

'That's my business!' she cried.

'No, it's not!' he shouted back. 'It's mine, too, and your stepmother's. If you're pregnant, who will care for your baby? Are you confident that Jake is ready to settle down and be a husband and father? Have you talked to him about that?'

'Don't speak to me!' she yelled. Then she burst into tears and stomped up the stairs.

Merthin said: 'Sometimes I wish we lived in one room – then she wouldn't be able to pull that trick.'

'You weren't very gentle with her,' Caris said with mild disapproval.

'What am I supposed to do?' Merthin said. 'She talks as if she's done nothing wrong!'

'She knows the truth, though. That's why she's crying.'

'Oh, hell,' he said.

There was a knock, and a novice monk put his head around the door. 'Pardon me for disturbing you, alderman,' he said. 'Sir Gregory Longfellow is at the priory, and would be grateful for a word with you, as soon as is convenient.'

'Damn,' said Merthin. 'Tell him I'll be there in a few minutes.'

'Thank you,' the novice said, and left.

Merthin said to Caris: 'Perhaps it's just as well to give her time to cool off.'

'You, too,' Caris said

'You're not taking her side, are you?' he said with a touch of irritation.

She smiled and touched his arm. 'I'm on your side, always,' she said. 'But I remember what it was like to be a sixteen-year-old girl. She's as worried as you are about her relationship with Jake. But she's not admitting it, even to herself, because that would wound her pride. So she resents you for speaking the truth. She has constructed a fragile defence around her self-esteem, and you just tear it down.'

'What should I do?'

'Help her build a better fence.'

'I don't know what that means.'

'You'll figure it out.'

'I'd better go and see Sir Gregory.' Merthin stood up.

Caris put her arms around him and kissed him on the lips. 'You're a good man doing your best, and I love you with all my heart,' she said.

That took the edge off his frustration, and he felt himself calm down as he strode across the bridge and up the main street to the priory. He did not like Gregory. The man was sly and unprincipled, willing to do anything for his master the king, just as Philemon had been when he served Godwyn as prior. Merthin wondered uneasily what Gregory wanted to discuss with him. It was probably taxes – always the king's worry.

Merthin went first to the prior's palace where Philemon, looking pleased with himself, told him that Sir Gregory was to be found in the monks' cloisters to the south of the cathedral. Merthin wondered what Gregory had done to win himself the privilege of holding audience there.

The lawyer was getting old. His hair was white, and his tall figure was stooped. Deep lines had appeared like brackets either side of that sneering nose, and one of the blue eyes was cloudy. But the other eye saw sharply enough, and he recognized Merthin instantly, though they had not met for ten years. 'Alderman,' he said. 'The archbishop of Monmouth is dead.'

'Rest his soul,' Merthin said automatically.

'Amen. The king asked me, as I was passing through his borough of Kingsbridge, to give you his greetings, and tell you this important news.'

'I'm grateful. The death is not unexpected. The archbishop has been ill.' The king certainly had not asked Gregory to meet with Merthin purely to give him interesting information, he thought suspiciously.

'You're an intriguing man, if you don't mind my saying so,'

Gregory said expansively. 'I first met your wife more than twenty years ago. Since then I've seen the two of you slowly but surely take control of this town. And you've got everything you set your hearts on: the bridge, the hospital, the borough charter, and each other. You're determined, and you're patient.'

It was condescending, but Merthin was surprised to detect a grain of respect in Gregory's flattery. He told himself to remain mistrustful: men such as Gregory praised only for a purpose.

'I'm on my way to see the monks of Abergavenny, who must vote for a new archbishop.' Gregory leaned back in his chair. 'When Christianity first came to England, hundreds of years ago, monks elected their own superiors.' Explaining was an old man's habit, Merthin reflected: the young Gregory would not have bothered. 'Nowadays, of course, bishops and archbishops are too important and powerful to be chosen by small groups of pious idealists living detached from the world. The king makes his choice, and his holiness the pope ratifies the royal decision.'

Even I know it's not that simple, Merthin thought. There's usually some kind of power struggle. But he said nothing.

Gregory continued: 'However, the ritual of the monks' election still goes on, and it is easier to control it than to abolish it. Hence my journey.'

'So you're going to tell the monks whom to elect,' Merthin said.

'To put it bluntly, yes.'

'And what name will you give them?'

'Didn't I say? It's your bishop, Henri of Mons. Excellent man: loyal, trustworthy, never makes trouble.'

'Oh, dear.'

'You're not pleased?' Gregory's relaxed air evaporated, and he became keenly attentive.

Merthin realized that this was what Gregory had come for: to find out how the people of Kingsbridge – as represented by Merthin – would feel about what he was planning, and whether they would oppose him. He collected his thoughts. The prospect of a new bishop threatened the spire and the hospital. 'Henri is the key to the balance of power in this town,' he said. 'Ten years ago, a kind of armistice was agreed between the merchants, the monks and the hospital. As a result, all three have prospered mightily.' Appealing to Gregory's interest – and the king's – he added: 'That prosperity is of course what enables us to pay such high taxes.'

Gregory acknowledged this with a dip of his head.

'The departure of Henri obviously puts into question the stability of our relationships.'

'It depends on who replaces him, I should have thought.'

'Indeed,' said Merthin. Now we come to the crux, he thought. He said: 'Have you got anyone in mind?'

'The obvious candidate is Prior Philemon.'

'No!' Merthin was aghast. 'Philemon! Why?'

'He's a sound conservative, which is important to the church hierarchy in these times of scepticism and heresy.'

'Of course. Now I understand why he preached a sermon against dissection. And why he wants to build a Lady chapel.' I should have foreseen this, Merthin thought.

'And he has let it be known that he has no problem with taxation of the clergy – a constant source of friction between the king and some of his bishops.'

'Philemon has been planning this for some time.' Merthin was angry with himself for letting it sneak up on him.

'Since the archbishop fell ill, I imagine.'

'This is a catastrophe.'

'Why do you say that?'

'Philemon is quarrelsome and vengeful. If he becomes bishop he will create constant strife in Kingsbridge. We have to prevent him.' He looked Gregory in the eye. 'Why did you come here to forewarn me?' As soon as he had asked the question, the answer came to him. 'You don't want Philemon either. You didn't need me to tell you what a troublemaker he is – you knew already. But you can't just veto him, because he has already won support among senior clergy.' Gregory just smiled enigmatically – which Merthin took to mean he was right. 'So what do you want me to do?'

'If I were you,' Gregory said, 'I'd start by finding another candidate to put up as the alternative to Philemon.'

So that was it. Merthin nodded pensively. 'I'll have to think about this,' he said.

'Please do.' Gregory stood up, and Merthin realized the meeting was over. 'And let me know what you decide,' Gregory added.

Merthin left the priory and walked back to Leper Island, musing. Who could he propose as bishop of Kingsbridge? The townspeople had always got on well with Archdeacon Lloyd, but he was too old – they might succeed in getting him elected only to have to do the whole thing again in a year's time.

He had not thought of anyone by the time he got home. He found Caris in the parlour and was about to ask her when she pre-empted him. Standing up, with a pale face and a frightened expression, she said: 'Lolla's gone again.'

# 86

THE PRIESTS SAID SUNDAY was a day of rest, but it had never been so for Gwenda. Today, after church in the morning and then dinner, she was working with Wulfric in the garden behind their house. It was a good garden, half an acre with a hen house, a pear tree and a barn. In the vegetable patch at the far end, Wulfric was digging furrows and Gwenda sowing peas.

The boys had gone to another village for a football game, their usual recreation on Sundays. Football was the peasant equivalent of the nobility's tournaments: a mock battle in which the injuries were sometimes real. Gwenda just prayed her sons would come home intact.

Today Sam returned early. 'The ball burst,' he said grumpily.

'Where's Davey?' Gwenda asked.

'He wasn't there.'

'I thought he was with you.'

'No, he quite often goes off on his own.'

'I didn't know that.' Gwenda frowned. 'Where does he go?'

Sam shrugged. 'He doesn't tell me.'

Perhaps he was seeing a girl, Gwenda thought. Davey was close about all sorts of things. If it was a girl, who was she? There were not many eligible girls in Wigleigh. The survivors of the plague had remarried quickly, as if eager to repopulate the land; and those born since were too young. Perhaps he was meeting someone from the next village, at a rendezvous in the forest. Such assignations were as common as heartache.

When Davey came home, a couple of hours later, Gwenda confronted him. He made no attempt to deny that he had been sneaking off. 'I'll show you what I've been doing, if you like,' he said. 'I can't keep it secret for ever. Come with me.'

They all went, Gwenda, Wulfric and Sam. The Sabbath was

observed to the extent that no one worked in the fields, and the Hundredacre was deserted as the four of them walked across it in a blustery spring breeze. A few strips looked neglected: there were still villagers who had more land than they could cope with. Annet was one such – she had only her eighteen-year-old daughter Amabel to help her, unless she could hire labour, which was still difficult. Her strip of oats was getting weedy.

Davey led them half a mile into the forest and stopped at a clearing off the beaten track. 'This is it,' he said.

For a moment Gwenda did not know what he was talking about. She was standing on the edge of a nondescript patch of ground with low bushes growing between the trees. Then she looked again at the bushes. They were a species she had never seen before. It had a squarish stem with pointed leaves growing in clusters of four. The way it had covered the ground made her think it was a creeping plant. A pile of uprooted vegetation at one side showed that Davey had been weeding. 'What is it?' she said.

'It's called madder. I bought the seeds from a sailor that time we went to Melcombe.'

'Melcombe?' Gwenda said. 'That was three years ago.'

'That's how long it's taken.' Davey smiled. 'At first I was afraid it wouldn't grow at all. He told me it needed sandy soil and would tolerate light shade. I dug over the clearing and planted the seeds, but the first year I got only three or four feeble plants. I thought I'd wasted my money. Then, the second year, the roots spread underground and sent up shoots, and this year it's all over the place.'

Gwenda was astonished that her child could have kept this from her for so long. 'But what use is madder?' she said. 'Does it taste good?'

Davey laughed. 'No, it's not edible. You dig up the roots, dry them and grind them to a powder that makes a red dye. It's very costly. Madge Webber in Kingsbridge pays seven shillings for a gallon.'

That was an astonishing price, Gwenda reflected. Wheat, the most expensive grain, sold for about seven shillings a quarter, and a quarter was sixty-four gallons. 'This is sixty-four times as precious as wheat!' she said.

Davey smiled. 'That's why I planted it.'

'Why you planted what?' said a new voice. They all turned to see Nathan Reeve, standing beside a hawthorn tree as bent and twisted as he was. He wore a triumphant grin: he had caught them red-handed.

Davey was quick with an answer. 'This is a medicinal herb called ... hagwort,' he said. Gwenda could tell he was improvising, but Nate would not be sure. 'It's good for my mother's wheezy chest.'

Nate looked at Gwenda. 'I didn't know she had a wheezy chest.'

'In the winter,' Gwenda said.

'A herb?' Nate said sceptically. 'There's enough here to dose all Kingsbridge. And you've been weeding it, to get more.'

'I like to do things properly,' Davey said.

It was a feeble response, and Nate ignored it. 'This is an unauthorized crop,' he said. 'First of all, serfs need permission for what they plant – they can't go raising anything they like. That would lead to total chaos. Secondly, they can't cultivate the lord's forest, even by planting herbs.'

None of them had any answer to that. Those were the rules. It was frustrating: often peasants knew they could make money by growing non-standard crops that were in demand and fetched high prices: hemp for rope, flax for expensive underclothing, or cherries to delight rich ladies. But many lords and their bailiffs refused permission, out of instinctive conservatism.

Nate's expression was venomous. 'One son a runaway and a murderer,' he said. 'The other defies his lord. What a family.'

He was entitled to feel angry, Gwenda thought. Sam had killed Jonno and got away with it. Nate would undoubtedly hate her family to his dying day.

Nate bent down and roughly pulled a plant out of the ground. 'This will come before the manor court,' he said with satisfaction; and he turned and limped away through the trees.

Gwenda and her family followed. Davey was undaunted. 'Nate will impose a fine, and I'll pay it,' he said. 'I'll still make money.'

'What if he orders the crop destroyed?' Gwenda said.

'How?'

'It could be burned, or trampled.'

Wulfric put in: 'Nate wouldn't do that. The village wouldn't stand for it. A fine is the traditional way to deal with this.'

Gwenda said: 'I just worry about what Earl Ralph will say.'

Davey made a deprecatory gesture with his hand. 'No reason why the earl should find out about a little thing like this.'

'Ralph takes a special interest in our family.'

'Yes, he does,' Davey said thoughtfully. 'I still don't understand what made him pardon Sam.'

The boy was not stupid. Gwenda said: 'Perhaps Lady Philippa persuaded him.'

Sam said: 'She remembers you, mother. She told me that when I was at Merthin's house.'

'I must have done something to endear myself to her,' Gwenda said, extemporizing. 'Or it could be that she just felt compassion, one mother for another.' It was not much of a story, but Gwenda did not have a better one.

In the days since Sam had been released they had had several conversations about what might account for Ralph's pardon. Gwenda just pretended to be as perplexed as everyone else. Fortunately Wulfric had never been the suspicious type.

They reached their house. Wulfric looked at the sky, said there was another good hour of light left and went into the garden to finish sowing peas. Sam volunteered to help him. Gwenda sat down to mend a rip in Wulfric's hose. Davey sat opposite Gwenda and said: 'I've got another secret to tell you.'

She smiled. She did not mind him having a secret if he told his mother. 'Go on.'

'I have fallen in love.'

'That's wonderful!' She leaned forward and kissed his cheek. 'I'm very happy for you. What's she like?'

'She's beautiful.'

Gwenda had been speculating, before she found out about the madder, that Davey might be meeting a girl from another village. Her intuition had been right. 'I had a feeling about this,' she said.

'Did you?' He seemed anxious.

'Don't worry, there's nothing wrong. It just occurred to me that you might be meeting someone.'

'We go to the clearing where I'm growing the madder. That's sort of where it started.'

'And how long has this been going on?'

'More than a year.'

'It's serious, then.'

'I want to marry her.'

'I'm so pleased.' She looked fondly at him. 'You're still only twenty, but that's old enough if you've found the right person.'

'I'm glad you think so.'

'What village is she from?'

'This one, Wigleigh.'

'Oh?' Gwenda was surprised. She had not been able to think of a likely girl here. 'Who is she?'

'Mother, it's Amabel.'

'No!'

'Don't shout.'

'Not Annet's daughter!'

'You're not to be angry.'

'Not to be angry!' Gwenda struggled to calm herself. She was as shocked as if she had been slapped. She took several deep breaths. 'Listen to me,' she said. 'We have been at odds with that family for more than twenty years. That cow Annet broke your father's heart and never left him alone afterwards.'

'I'm sorry, but that's all in the past.'

'It's not – Annet still flirts with your father every chance she gets!'

'That's your problem, not ours.'

Gwenda stood up, her sewing falling from her lap. 'How can you do this to me? That bitch would be part of our family! My grandchildren would be her grandchildren. She'd be in and out of this house all the time, making a fool of your father with her coquettish ways and then laughing at me.'

'I'm not going to marry Annet.'

'Amabel will be just as bad. Look at her – she's just like her mother!'

'She's not, actually—'

'You can't do this! I absolutely forbid it!'

'You can't forbid it, Mother.'

'Oh, yes I can – you're too young.'

'That won't last for ever.'

Wulfric's voice came from the doorway. 'What's all the shouting?'

'Davey says he wants to marry Annet's daughter – but I won't permit it.' Gwenda's voice rose to a shriek. 'Never! Never! Never!'

*

EARL RALPH SURPRISED Nathan Reeve when he said he wanted to look at Davey's strange crop. Nate mentioned the matter in passing, on a routine visit to Earlscastle. A bit of unlicensed cultivation in the forest was a trivial breach of the rules, regularly dealt with by a fine. Nate was a shallow man, interested in bribes and commissions, and he had little conception of the depth of Ralph's obsession with Gwenda's family: his hatred of Wulfric, his lust for Gwenda, and now the likelihood that he was Sam's real father. So Nate was startled when Ralph said he would inspect the crop next time he was in the neighbourhood.

Ralph rode with Alan Fernhill from Earlscastle to Wigleigh on a fine day between Easter and Whitsun. When they reached the small timber manor house, there was the old housekeeper, Vira, bent and grey now but still hanging on. They ordered her to prepare their dinner, then found Nate and followed him into the forest.

Ralph recognized the plant. He was no farmer, but he knew the difference between one bush and another, and on his travels with the army he had observed many crops that did not grow naturally in England. He leaned down from his saddle and pulled up a handful. 'This is called madder,' he said. 'I've seen it in Flanders. It's grown for the red dye that has the same name.'

Nate said: 'He told me it was a herb called hagwort, used to cure a wheezy chest.'

'I believe it does have medicinal properties, but that's not why people cultivate it. What will his fine be?'

'A shilling would be the usual amount.'

'It's not enough.'

Nate looked nervous. 'So much trouble is caused, lord, when these customs are flouted. I would rather not—'

'Never mind,' Ralph said. He kicked his horse and trotted through the middle of the clearing, trampling the bushes. 'Come on, Alan,' he said. Alan imitated him, and the two of them cantered around in tight circles, flattening the growth. After a few minutes all the shrubs were destroyed.

Ralph could see that Nate was shocked by the waste, even though the planting was illegal. Peasants never liked to see crops despoiled. Ralph had learned in France that the best way of demoralizing the population was to burn the harvest in the fields.

'That will do,' he said, quickly getting bored. He was irritated by Davey's insolence in planting this crop, but that was not the main reason he had come to Wigleigh. The truth was that he wanted to see Sam again.

As they rode back to the village he scanned the fields, looking for a tall young man with thick dark hair. Sam would stand out, because of his height, among these stunted serfs hunched over their spades. He saw him, at a distance, in Brookfield. He reined in and peered across the windy landscape at the twenty-two-year-old son he had never known.

Sam and the man he thought was his father – Wulfric – were ploughing with a horse-drawn light plough. Something was wrong, for they kept stopping and adjusting the harness. When they were together it was easy to see the differences between them. Wulfric's hair was tawny, Sam's dark; Wulfric was barrel-chested, ox-like, where Sam was broad-shouldered but lean, like a horse; Wulfric's movements were slow and careful, but Sam was quick and graceful.

It was the oddest feeling to look at a stranger and think: my son. Ralph believed himself immune to womanish emotions. If he had been subject to feelings of compassion or regret he could not have lived as he had. But the discovery of Sam threatened to unman him.

He tore himself away, and cantered back to the village; then he succumbed again to curiosity and sentiment, and sent Nate to find Sam and bring him to the manor house.

He was not sure what he intended to do with the boy: talk to him, tease him, invite him to join them for dinner, or what. He might have foreseen that Gwenda would not leave him free to choose. She showed up with Nate and Sam, and Wulfric and Davey followed them in. 'What do you want with my son?' she demanded, speaking to Ralph as if he were an equal rather than her overlord.

Ralph spoke without forethought. 'Sam was not born to be a serf tilling the fields,' he said. He saw Alan Fernhill look at him in surprise.

Gwenda looked puzzled. 'Only God knows what we are born for,' she said, playing for time.

'When I want to know about God, I'll ask a priest, not you,' Ralph said to her. 'Your son has something of the mettle of a fighting man. I don't need to pray to see that – it's obvious to me, as it would be to any veteran of the wars.'

'Well, he's not a fighting man, he's a peasant, and the son of a peasant, and his destiny is to grow crops and raise livestock like his father.'

'Never mind his father.' Ralph remembered what Gwenda had said to him in the sheriff's castle at Shiring, when she had persuaded him to pardon Sam. 'Sam has the killer instinct,' he said. 'It's dangerous in a peasant, but priceless in a soldier.'

Gwenda looked scared as she began to divine Ralph's purpose. 'What are you getting at?'

Ralph realized where this chain of logic was leading him. 'Let Sam be useful, rather than dangerous. Let him learn the arts of war.'

'Ridiculous, he's too old.'

'He's twenty-two. It's late, but he's fit and strong. He can do it.'

'I don't see how.'

Gwenda was pretending to find practical objections, but he could see through her simulation, and knew that she hated the idea with all her heart. That made him all the more determined. With a smile of triumph he said: 'Easily enough. He can be a squire. He can come and live at Earlscastle.'

Gwenda looked as if she had been stabbed. Her eyes closed for a moment, and her olive-skinned face paled. She mouthed the word 'No' but no sound came out.

'He's been with you for twenty-two years,' Ralph said. 'That's long enough.' Now it's my turn, he thought, but instead he said: 'Now he's a man.'

Because Gwenda was temporarily silent, Wulfric spoke up. 'We won't permit it,' he said. 'We are his parents, and we do not consent to this.'

'I didn't ask for your consent,' Ralph said contemptuously. 'I'm your earl, and you are my serfs. I don't request, I command.'

Nate Reeve put in: 'Besides, Sam is over the age of twenty-one, so the decision is his, not his father's.'

Suddenly they all turned and looked at Sam.

Ralph was not sure what to expect. Becoming a squire was something many young men of all classes dreamed about, but he did not know whether Sam was one of them. Life in the castle was luxurious and exciting, by comparison with breaking your back in the fields; but, on the other hand, men-at-arms died young, or – worse than that – came home crippled, to live the rest of their miserable days begging outside taverns.

However, as soon as Ralph saw Sam's face he knew the truth. Sam was smiling broadly, and his eyes gleamed with eagerness. He could hardly wait to go.

Gwenda found her voice. 'Don't do it, Sam!' she said. 'Don't be tempted. Don't let your mother see you blinded by an arrow, or mutilated by the swords of French knights, or crippled by the hooves of their warhorses!'

Wulfric said: 'Don't go, son. Stay in Wigleigh and live a long life.'

Sam began to look doubtful.

Ralph said: 'All right, lad. You've listened to your mother, and to the peasant father who raised you. But the decision is yours. What will you do? Live out your life here in Wigleigh, tilling the fields alongside your brother? Or escape?'

Sam paused only for a moment. He looked guiltily at Wulfric and Gwenda, then turned to Ralph. 'I'll do it,' he said. 'I'll be a squire, and thank you, my lord!'

'Good lad,' Ralph said.

Gwenda began to cry. Wulfric put his arm around her. Looking up at Ralph, he said: 'When shall he go?'

'Today,' Ralph said. 'He can ride back to Earlscastle with me and Alan after dinner.'

'Not so soon!' Gwenda cried.

No one took any notice of her.

Ralph said to Sam: 'Go home and fetch anything you want to bring with you. Have dinner with your mother. Come back and wait for me in the stables. Meanwhile, Nate can requisition a mount to carry you to Earlscastle.' He turned away, having finished with Sam and his family. 'Now, where's my dinner?'

Wulfric and Gwenda went out with Sam, but Davey stayed behind. Had he already found out that his crop had been trampled? Or was it something else? 'What do you want?' Ralph said.

'Lord, I have a boon to ask.'

This was almost too good to be true. The insolent peasant who had planted madder in the woods without permission was now a supplicant. What a satisfying day this was turning out to be. 'You can't be a squire, you've got your mother's build,' Ralph told him, and Alan laughed.

'I want to marry Amabel, the daughter of Annet,' said the young man.

'That won't please your mother.'

'I will be of age in less than a year.'

Ralph knew all about Annet, of course. He had nearly been hanged for her sake. His history was entwined with hers almost as much as with Gwenda's. He recalled that all her family had died in the plague. 'Annet still has some of the lands her father held.'

'Yes, lord, and she is willing for them to be transferred to me when I marry her daughter.'

Such a request would not normally have been refused, although all lords would charge a tax, called an entry fee, on the transfer. However, there was no obligation on a lord to consent. The right of lords to refuse such requests on a whim, and blight the course of a serf's life, was one of the peasants' greatest gripes. But it provided the ruler with a means of discipline that could be extraordinarily effective.

'No,' said Ralph. 'I will not transfer the land to you.' He grinned. 'You and your bride can eat madder.'

# 87

Caris had to prevent Philemon becoming bishop. This was his boldest move yet, but he had made his preparations carefully, and he had a chance. If he succeeded, he would have control of the hospital again, giving him the power to destroy her life's work. But he could do worse than that. He would revive the blind orthodoxy of the past. He would appoint hard-hearted priests like himself in the villages, close schools for girls and preach sermons against dancing.

She had no say in the choice of a bishop, but there were ways to exert pressure.

She began with Bishop Henri.

She and Merthin travelled to Shiring to see the bishop in his palace. On the way, Merthin stared at every dark-haired girl that came into view, and when there was no one he scanned the woods at the side of the road. He was looking for Lolla, but they reached Shiring without seeing any sign of her.

The bishop's palace was on the main square, opposite the church and beside the Wool Exchange. It was not a market day, so the square was clear but for the scaffold that stood there permanently, a stark warning to villains of what the people of the county did to those who broke the law.

The palace was an unpretentious stone building with a hall and chapel on the ground floor and a series of offices and private apartments upstairs. Bishop Henri had imposed upon the place a style that Caris thought was probably French. Each room looked like a painting. The place was not decorated extravagantly, like Philemon's palace in Kingsbridge, where the profusion of rugs and jewels suggested a robber's cave. However, there was something pleasantly artful about everything in Henri's house: a silver candlestick placed to catch the light from a window; the polished gleam of an ancient oak table; spring flowers in the cold fireplace; a small tapestry of David and Jonathan on the wall.

Bishop Henri was not an enemy, but he was not quite an ally either, Caris thought nervously as they waited for him in the hall. He would probably say that he tried to rise above Kingsbridge quarrels. She, more cynically, thought that whatever decision he had to make, he remained unshakeably focused on his own interests. He disliked Philemon, but he might not allow that to affect his judgement.

Henri came in followed, as always, by Canon Claude. The two of them did not seem to age. Henri was a little older than Caris, and Claude perhaps ten years younger, but they both looked like boys. Caris had noticed that clergy often aged well, better than aristocrats. She suspected it was because most priests – with some notorious exceptions – led lives of moderation. Their regime of fasting obliged them to eat fish and vegetables on Fridays and saints' days and all through Lent, and in theory they were never allowed to get drunk. By contrast, noblemen and their wives indulged in orgies of meat-eating and heroic wine-drinking. That might be why their faces became lined, their skin flaky and their bodies bent, while clerics stayed fit and spry later into their quiet, austere lives.

Merthin congratulated Henri on having been nominated archbishop of Monmouth, then got straight to the point. 'Prior Philemon has stopped work on the tower.'

Henri said with studied neutrality: 'Any reason?'

'There's a pretext, and a reason,' Merthin said. 'The pretext is a fault in the design.'

'And what is the alleged fault?'

'He says an octagonal spire can't be built without formwork. It is generally true, but I've found a way around it.'

'Which is . . . ?'

'Rather simple. I will build a round spire, which will need no formwork, then give its exterior a cladding of thin stones and mortar in the shape of an octagon. Visually, it will be an octagonal spire, but structurally it will be a cone.'

'Have you told Philemon this?'

'No. If I do, he'll find another pretext.'

'What is his real reason?'

'He wants to build a Lady chapel instead.'

'Ah.'

'It's part of a campaign to ingratiate himself with senior clergy. He preached a sermon against dissection when Archdeacon Reginald was there. And he has told the king's advisers that he will not campaign against taxation of the clergy.'

'What is he up to?'

'He wants to be bishop of Shiring.'

Henri raised his eyebrows. 'Philemon always had nerve, I'll give him that.'

Claude spoke for the first time. 'How do you know?'

'Gregory Longfellow told me.'

Claude looked at Henri and said: 'Gregory would know if anyone does.'

Caris could tell that Henri and Claude had not anticipated that Philemon would be so ambitious. To make sure they did not overlook the significance of the revelation, she said: 'If Philemon gets his wish, you as archbishop of Monmouth will have endless work adjudicating disputes between Bishop Philemon and the townspeople of Kingsbridge. You know how much friction there has been in the past.'

Claude said: 'We certainly do.'

'I'm glad we're in agreement,' Merthin said.

Thinking aloud, Claude said: 'We must put forward an alternative candidate.'

That was what Caris had hoped he would say. 'We have someone in mind,' she said.

Claude said: 'Who?'

'You.'

There was a silence. Caris could tell that Claude liked the idea. She guessed he might be quietly envious of Henri's promotion, and wondering whether it was his destiny always to be a kind of assistant to Henri. He could easily cope with the post of bishop. He knew the diocese well and handled most of the practical administration already.

However, both men were now surely thinking about their personal lives. She had no doubt they were all but husband and wife: she had seen them kissing. But they were decades past the first flush of romance, and her intuition told her they could tolerate a part-time separation.

She said: 'You would still be working together a good deal.'

Claude said: 'The archbishop will have many reasons to visit Kingsbridge and Shiring.'

Henri said: 'And the bishop of Kingsbridge will need to come to Monmouth often.'

Claude said: 'It would be a great honour to be bishop.' With a twinkle in his eye he added: 'Especially under you, archbishop.'

Henri looked away, pretending not to notice the double meaning. 'I think it's a splendid idea,' he said.

Merthin said: 'The Kingsbridge guild will back Claude – I can guarantee that. But you, Archbishop Henri, will have to put the suggestion to the king.'

'Of course.'

Caris said: 'If I may make one suggestion?'

'Please.'

'Find another post for Philemon. Propose him as, I don't know, archdeacon of Lincoln. Something he would like, but that would take him many miles from here.'

'That's a sound idea,' Henri said. 'If he's up for two posts, it weakens his case for either one. I'll keep my ear to the ground.'

Claude stood up. 'This is all very exciting,' he said. 'Will you have dinner with us?'

A servant came in and addressed Caris. 'There's someone asking for you, mistress,' the man said. 'It's only a boy, but he seems distressed.'

Henri said: 'Let him come in.'

A boy of about thirteen appeared. He was dirty, but his clothes were not cheap, and Caris guessed he came from a family that was comfortably off but suffering some kind of crisis. 'Will you come to my house, Mother Caris?'

'I'm not a nun any more, child, but what's the problem?'

The boy spoke fast. 'My father and mother are ill and so is my brother, and my mother heard someone say you were at the bishop's palace and said to fetch you, and she knows you help the poor but she can pay, but will you please come, please?'

This type of request was not unusual, and Caris carried a leather case of medical supplies with her wherever she went. 'Of course I'll come, lad,' she said. 'What's your name?'

'Giles Spicers, mother, and I'm to wait and bring you.'

'All right.' Caris turned to the bishop. 'Go ahead with your dinner, please. I'll join you as soon as I can.' She picked up her case and followed the boy out.

Shiring owed its existence to the sheriff's castle on the hill, just as Kingsbridge did to the priory. Near the market square were the grand houses of the leading citizens, the wool merchants and sheriff's deputies and royal officials such as the coroner. A little farther out were the homes of moderately prosperous traders and craftsmen, goldsmiths and tailors and apothecaries. Giles's father was a dealer in spices, as his name indicated, and Giles led Caris to a street in this neighbourhood. Like most houses of this class, it had a stone-built ground floor that served as warehouse and shop, and flimsier timber living quarters above. Today the shop was closed and locked. Giles led Caris up the outside staircase.

She smelled the familiar odour of sickness as soon as she walked in. Then she hesitated. There was something special about the smell, something that struck a chord in her memory that for some reason made her feel very frightened.

Rather than ponder it, she walked through the living room into the bedroom, and there she found the dreadful answer.

Three people lay on mattresses around the room: a woman of her own age, a slightly older man and an adolescent boy. The man was farthest gone in sickness. He lay moaning and sweating in a fever. The open neck of his shirt showed that he had a rash of purple-black spots on his chest and throat. There was blood on his lips and nostrils.

He had the plague.

'It's come back,' said Caris. 'God help me.'

For a moment fear paralysed her. She stood motionless, staring at the scene, feeling powerless. She had always known, in theory, that the plague might return – that was half the reason she had written her book – but even so she was not prepared for the shock of once again seeing that rash, that fever, that nosebleed.

The woman lifted herself on one elbow. She was not so far gone: she had the rash and the fever, but did not appear to be bleeding. 'Give me something to drink, for the love of God,' she said.

Giles picked up a jug of wine, and at last Caris's mind started to work and her body unfroze. 'Don't give her wine – it will make her thirstier,' she said. 'I saw a barrel of ale in the other room – draw her a cup of that.'

The woman focused on Caris. 'You're the prioress, aren't you?' she said. Caris did not correct her. 'People say you're a saint. Can you make my family well?'

'I'll try, but I'm not a saint, just a woman who has observed people in sickness and health.' Caris took from her bag a strip of linen and tied it over her mouth and nose. She had not seen a case of the plague for ten years, but she had got into the habit of taking this precaution whenever she dealt with patients whose illness might be catching. She moistened a clean rag with rose water and bathed the woman's face. As always, the action soothed the patient.

Giles came back with a cup of ale, and the woman drank. Caris said to him: 'Let them have as much to drink as they want, but give them ale or watered wine.'

She moved to the father, who did not have long to live. He was not speaking coherently and his eyes failed to focus on Caris. She bathed his face, cleaning the dried blood from around his nose and mouth. Finally she attended to Giles's elder brother. He had only recently succumbed, and was still sneezing, but he was old enough to realize how seriously ill he was, and he looked terrified.

When she had finished she said to Giles: 'Try to keep them comfortable and give them drinks. There's nothing else you can do. Do you have any relations? Uncles or cousins?'

'They're all in Wales.'

She made a mental note to warn Bishop Henri that he might need to make arrangements for an orphan boy.

'Mother said to pay you,' the boy said.

'I haven't done much for you,' Caris said. 'You can pay me sixpence.'

There was a leather purse beside his mother's bed. He took out six silver pennies.

The woman raised herself again. Speaking more calmly now, she said: 'What's wrong with us?'

'I'm sorry,' said Caris. 'It's the plague.'

The woman nodded fatalistically. 'That's what I was afraid of.'

'Don't you recognize the symptoms from last time?'

'We were living in a small town in Wales – we escaped it. Are we all going to die?'

Caris did not believe in deceiving people about such important questions. 'A few people survive it,' she said. 'Not many, though.'

'May God have mercy on us, then,' said the woman.

Caris said: 'Amen.'

*

ALL THE WAY back to Kingsbridge, Caris brooded on the plague. It would spread, of course, just as fast as last time. It would kill thousands. The prospect filled her with rage. It was like the senseless carnage of war, except that war was caused by men, and the plague was not. What was she going to do? She could not sit back and watch as the events of thirteen years ago were cruelly repeated.

There was no cure for the plague, but she had discovered ways to slow its murderous progress. As her horse jogged the well-worn road through the forest, she thought over what she knew about the illness and how to combat it. Merthin was quiet, recognizing her mood, probably guessing accurately what she was thinking about.

When they got home, she explained to him what she wanted to do. 'There will be opposition,' he warned. 'Your plan is drastic. Those who did not lose family and friends last time may imagine they are invulnerable, and say you're overreacting.'

'That's where you can help me,' she said.

'In that case, I recommend we divide up the potential objectors and deal with them separately.'

'All right.'

'You have three groups to win over: the guild, the monks and the nuns. Let's start with the guild. I'll call a meeting – and I won't invite Philemon.'

Nowadays the guild met in the Cloth Exchange, a large new stone building on the main street. It enabled traders to do business even in bad weather. It had been paid for by profits from Kingsbridge Scarlet.

But before the guild convened, Caris and Merthin met individually with the leading members, to win their support in advance, a technique Merthin had developed long ago. His motto was: 'Never call a meeting until the result is a foregone conclusion.'

Caris herself went to see Madge Webber.

Madge had married again. Much to everyone's amusement, she had enchanted a villager as handsome as her first husband and fifteen years her junior. His name was Anselm, and he seemed to adore her, though she was as plump as ever and covered her grey hair with a selection of exotic caps. Even more surprising, in her forties she had conceived again and given birth to a healthy baby girl, Selma, now eight years old and attending the nuns' school. Motherhood had never kept Madge from doing business, and she continued to dominate the market in Kingsbridge Scarlet, with Anselm as her lieutenant.

Her home was still the large house on the main street that she and Mark had moved into when she first began to profit from weaving and dyeing. Caris found her and Anselm taking delivery of a consignment of red cloth, trying to find room for it in the overcrowded storeroom on the ground floor. 'I'm stocking up for the Fleece Fair,' Madge explained.

Caris waited while she checked the delivery, then they went upstairs, leaving Anselm in charge of the shop. As Caris entered the living room she was vividly reminded of the day, thirteen years ago, when she had been summoned here to see Mark – the first Kingsbridge victim of the plague. She suddenly felt depressed.

Madge noticed her expression. 'What is it?' she said.

You could not hide things from women the way you could

from men. 'I walked in here thirteen years ago because Mark was ill,' Caris said.

Madge nodded. 'That was the beginning of the worst time of my life,' she said in her matter-of-fact voice. 'That day, I had a wonderful husband and four healthy children. Three months later I was a childless widow with nothing to live for.'

'Days of grief,' Caris said.

Madge went to the sideboard, where there were cups and a jug, but instead of offering Caris a drink she stood staring at the wall. 'Shall I tell you something strange?' she said. 'After they died, I couldn't say Amen to the paternoster.' She swallowed, and her voice went quieter. 'I know what the Latin means, you see. My father taught me. "Fiat voluntas tua: Thy will be done." I couldn't say that. God had taken my family, and that was sufficient torture – I would not acquiesce in it.' Tears came to her eyes as she remembered. 'I didn't want God's will to prevail, I wanted my children back. "Thy will be done." I knew I'd go to hell, but still I couldn't say Amen.'

Caris said. 'The plague has come back.'

Madge staggered, and clutched the sideboard for support. Her solid figure suddenly looked frail, and as the confidence went from her face she appeared old. 'No,' she said.

Caris pulled a bench forward and held Madge's arm while she sat on it. 'I'm sorry to shock you,' she said.

'No,' Madge said again. 'It can't come back. I can't lose Anselm and Selma. I can't bear it. I can't bear it.' She looked so white and drawn that Caris began to fear she might suffer some kind of attack.

Caris poured wine from the jug into a cup. She gave it to Madge, who drank it automatically. A little of her colour came back.

'We understand it better now,' Caris said. 'Perhaps we can fight it.'

'Fight it? How can we do that?'

'That's what I've come to tell you. Are you feeling a little better?'

Madge met Caris's eye at last. 'Fight it,' she said. 'Of course that's what we must do. Tell me how.'

'We have to close the city. Shut the gates, man the walls, prevent anyone coming in.'

'But the city has to eat.'

'People will bring supplies to Leper Island. Merthin will act as middleman, and pay them – he contracted the plague last time and survived, and no one has ever got it twice. Traders will leave their goods on the bridge. Then, when they have gone, people will come out from the city and get the food.'

'Could people leave the city?'

'Yes, but they couldn't come back.'

'What about the Fleece Fair?'

'That may be the hardest part,' Caris said. 'It must be cancelled.'

'But Kingsbridge merchants will lose hundreds of pounds!'

'It's better than dying.'

'If we do as you say, will we avoid the plague? Will my family survive?'

Caris hesitated, resisting the temptation to tell a reassuring lie. 'I can't promise,' she said. 'The plague may already have reached us. There may be someone right now dying alone in a hovel near the waterfront, with nobody to get help. So I fear we may not escape entirely. But I believe my plan gives you the best chance of still having Anselm and Selma by your side at Christmas.'

'Then we'll do it,' Madge said decisively.

'Your support is crucial,' Caris said. 'Frankly, you will lose more money than anyone else from the cancellation of the fair. For that reason, people are more likely to believe you. I need you to say how serious it is.'

'Don't worry,' said Madge. 'I'll tell them.'

*

'A VERY SOUND IDEA,' said Prior Philemon.

Merthin was surprised. He could not remember a time when Philemon had agreed readily with a proposal of the guild's. 'Then you will support it,' he said, to make sure he had heard aright.

'Yes, indeed,' said the prior. He was eating a bowl of raisins, stuffing handfuls into his mouth as fast as he could chew them.

He did not offer Merthin any. 'Of course,' he said, 'it wouldn't apply to monks.'

Merthin sighed. He might have known better. 'On the contrary, it applies to everyone,' he said.

'No, no,' said Philemon, in the tone of one who instructs a child. 'The guild has no power to restrict the movements of monks.'

Merthin noticed a cat at Philemon's feet. It was fat, like him, with a mean face. It looked just like Godwyn's cat, Archbishop, though that creature must be long dead. Perhaps it was a descendant. Merthin said: 'The guild has the power to close the city gates.'

'But we have the right to come and go as we please. We're not subject to the authority of the guild – that would be ridiculous.'

'All the same, the guild controls the city, and we have decided that no one can enter while the plague is rife.'

'You cannot make rules for the priory.'

'But I can for the city, and the priory happens to be in the city.'

'Are you telling me that if I leave Kingsbridge today, you will refuse me admission tomorrow?'

Merthin was not sure. It would be highly embarrassing, at a minimum, to have the prior of Kingsbridge standing outside the gate demanding admission. He had been hoping to persuade Philemon to accept the restriction. He did not want to put the resolve of the guild to the test quite so dramatically. However, he tried to make his answer sound confident. 'Absolutely.'

'I shall complain to the bishop.'

'Tell him he can't enter Kingsbridge.'

*

THE PERSONNEL OF the nunnery had hardly changed in ten years, Caris realized. Nunneries were like that, of course: you were supposed to stay for ever. Mother Joan was still prioress, and Sister Oonagh ran the hospital under the supervision of Brother Sime. Few people came here for medical care, now: most preferred Caris's hospital on the island. Those patients Sime did have, devoutly religious for the most part, were cared for in the old hospital, next to the kitchens, while the new building was used for guests.

Caris sat down with Joan, Oonagh and Sime in the old pharmacy, now used as the prioress's private office, and explained her plan. 'People outside the walls of the old city who fall victim to the plague will be admitted to my hospital on the island,' she said. 'While the plague lasts, the nuns and I will stay within the building night and day. Nobody will leave, except those lucky few who recover.'

Joan asked: 'What about here in the old city?'

'If the plague gets into the city despite our precautions, there may be too many victims for the accommodation you have. The guild has ruled that plague victims and their families will be confined to their homes. The rule applies to anyone who lives in a house struck by plague: parents, children, grandparents, servants, apprentices. Anyone caught leaving such a house will be hanged.'

'It's very harsh,' Joan said. 'But if it prevents the awful slaughter of the last plague, it's worth while.'

'I knew you'd see that.'

Sime was saying nothing. The news of the plague seemed to have deflated his arrogance.

Oonagh said: 'How will the victims eat, if they're imprisoned in their homes?'

'Neighbours can leave food on the doorstep. No one may go in – except monk-physicians and nuns. They will visit the sick, but they must have no contact with the healthy. They will go from the priory to the home, and from the home back to the priory, without entering any other building or even speaking to anyone on the street. They should wear masks at all times, and wash their hands in vinegar each time they touch a patient.'

Sime was looking terrified. 'Will that protect us?' he said.

'To some degree,' Caris said. 'Not completely.'

'But then it will be highly dangerous for us to attend the sick!'

Oonagh answered him. 'We have no fear,' she said. 'We look forward to death. For us, it is the longed-for reunion with Christ.'

'Yes, of course,' said Sime.

The next day, all the monks left Kingsbridge.

# 88

Gwenda felt murderously angry when she saw what Ralph had done to Davey's madder plants. Wanton destruction of crops was a sin. There should be a special place in hell for noblemen who despoiled what peasants had sweated to grow.

But Davey was not dismayed. 'I don't think it matters,' he said. 'The value is in the roots, and he hasn't touched them.'

'That would have been too much like work,' Gwenda said sourly, but she cheered up.

In fact the shrubs recovered remarkably quickly. Ralph probably did not know that madder propagated underground. Throughout May and June, as reports began to reach Wigleigh of an outbreak of the plague, the roots sent up new shoots and, at the beginning of July, Davey decided it was time to harvest the crop. One Sunday Gwenda, Wulfric and Davey spent the afternoon digging up the roots. They would first loosen the soil around the plant, then pull it out of the ground, then strip its foliage, leaving the root attached to a short stem. It was back-aching work of the kind Gwenda had done all her life.

They left half the plantation untouched, in the hope that it would regenerate itself next year.

They pulled a handcart piled with madder roots back through the woods to Wigleigh, then unloaded the roots into the barn and spread them in the hayloft to dry.

Davey did not know when he would be able to sell his crop. Kingsbridge was a closed city. The people still bought supplies, of course, but only through brokers. Davey was doing something new, and he would need to explain the situation to his buyer. It would be awkward to do that through an intermediary. But perhaps he would have to try. He had to dry the roots first, then grind them to a powder, and that would take time anyway.

Davey had said no more about Amabel, but Gwenda felt sure he was still seeing the girl. He pretended to be cheerfully resigned to his fate. If he had really given her up, he would have moped resentfully.

All Gwenda could do was hope he would get over her before he was old enough to marry without permission. She still could hardly bear even to think of her family being joined to Annet's. Annet had never ceased to humiliate her by flirting with Wulfric, who continued to grin foolishly at every stupid coquettish remark. Now that Annet was in her forties, with broken veins in her rosy cheeks and grey streaks among her fair ringlets, her behaviour was not just embarrassing but grotesque; yet Wulfric reacted as if she were still a girl.

And now, Gwenda thought, my son has fallen into the same trap. It made her want to spit. Amabel looked just like Annet twenty-five years ago, a pretty face with flyaway curls, a long neck and narrow white shoulders, and small breasts like the eggs that mother and daughter sold at markets. She had the same way of tossing her hair, the same trick of looking at a man with mock reproach and hitting his chest with the back of her hand in a gesture that pretended to be a smack but was in fact a caress.

However, Davey was at least physically safe and well. Gwenda was more worried about Sam, living now with Earl Ralph at the castle, learning to be a fighting man. In church she prayed he would not be injured hunting, or learning to use a sword, or fighting in a tournament. She had seen him every day for twenty-two years, then suddenly he had been taken from her. It's hard to be a woman, she thought. You love your baby with all your heart and soul, and then one day he just leaves.

For several weeks she looked for an excuse to travel to Earlscastle and check on Sam. Then she heard that the plague had struck there, and that decided her. She would go before the harvest got under way. Wulfric would not go with her: he had too much to do on the land. Anyway, she had no fear of travelling alone. 'Too poor to be robbed, too old to be raped,' she joked. The truth was that she was too tough for either. And she carried a long knife.

She walked across the drawbridge at Earlscastle on a hot July day. On the battlements of the gatehouse a rook stood like a sentry, the sun glinting off his glossy black feathers. He cawed a warning at her. It sounded like: 'Go, go!' She had escaped the plague once, of course; but that might have been luck: she was risking her life by coming here.

The scene in the lower compound was normal, if a little quiet. A woodcutter was unloading a cart full of firewood outside the bakehouse, and a groom was unsaddling a dusty horse in front of the stables, but there was no great bustle of activity. She noticed a small group of men and women outside the west entrance of the little church, and crossed the baked-earth ground to investigate. 'Plague victims inside,' a maidservant said in answer to her inquiry.

She stepped through the door, feeling dread like a cold lump in her heart.

Ten or twelve straw mattresses were lined up on the floor so that the occupants could face the altar, just as in a hospital. About half the patients seemed to be children. There were three grown men. Gwenda scanned their faces fearfully.

None of them was Sam.

She knelt down and said a prayer of thanks.

Outside, she approached the woman she had spoken to earlier. 'I'm looking for Sam from Wigleigh,' she said. 'He's a new squire.'

The woman pointed to the bridge leading to the inner compound. 'Try the keep.'

Gwenda took the route indicated. A sentry at the bridge ignored her. She climbed the steps to the keep.

The great hall was dark and cool. A big dog slept on the cold stones of the fireplace. There were benches around the walls and a pair of large armchairs at the far end of the room. Gwenda noticed that there were no cushions, no upholstered seats and no wall hangings. She deduced that Lady Philippa spent little time here and took no interest in the furnishings.

Sam was sitting near a window with three younger men. The parts of a suit of armour were laid out on the floor in front of them, arranged in order from faceplate to greaves. Each of the men was cleaning a piece. Sam was rubbing the breastplate with a smooth pebble, trying to remove rust.

She stood watching him for a moment. He wore new clothes in the red-and-black livery of the earl of Shiring. The colours suited his dark good looks. He seemed to be at ease, talking in a desultory way with the others while they all worked. He appeared healthy and well fed. It was what Gwenda had hoped for, but all the same she suffered a perverse pang of disappointment that he was doing so well without her.

He glanced up and saw her. His face registered surprise, then pleasure, then amusement. 'Lads,' he said, 'I am the oldest among you, and you may think I'm capable of looking after myself, but it's not so. My mother follows me everywhere to make sure I'm all right.'

They saw her and laughed. Sam put down his work and came over. Mother and son sat on a bench in a corner near the staircase that led to the upstairs rooms. 'I'm having a wonderful time,' Sam said. 'Everyone plays games here most days. We go hunting and hawking, we have wrestling matches and contests of horsemanship, and we play football. I've learned so much! It's a bit embarrassing to be grouped with these adolescents all the time, but I can put up with that. I just have to master the skill of using a sword and shield while riding a horse at the same time.'

He was already speaking differently, she noticed. He was losing the slow rhythms of village speech. And he used French words for 'hawking' and 'horsemanship'. He was becoming assimilated into the life of the nobility.

'What about the work?' she said. 'It can't be all play.'

'Yes, there's plenty of work.' He gestured at the others cleaning the armour. 'But it's easy by comparison with ploughing and harrowing.'

He asked about his brother, and she told him all the news from home: Davey's madder had regenerated, they had dug up the roots, Davey was still involved with Amabel, no one had fallen sick of the plague yet. While they were talking, she began to feel that she was being watched, and she knew her feeling was not fanciful. After a moment, she looked over her shoulder.

Earl Ralph was standing at the top of the staircase in front of an open door, evidently having stepped out of his room. She wondered how long he had been looking at her. She met his gaze. His stare was intense, but she could not read it, did not understand what it meant. She began to feel the look was uncomfortably intimate, and she glanced away.

When she looked back, he had gone.

*

THE NEXT DAY, when she was on the road and half way home, a horseman came up behind her, riding fast, then slowed down and stopped.

Her hand went to the long dagger in her belt.

The rider was Sir Alan Fernhill. 'The earl wants to see you,' he said.

'Then he had better come himself, instead of sending you,' she replied.

'You've always got a smart answer, haven't you? Do you imagine it endears you to your superiors?'

He had a point. She was taken aback, perhaps because in all the years he had been Ralph's sidekick she had never known Alan to say anything intelligent. If she was really smart she would suck up to people such as Alan, not poke fun at them. 'All right,' she said wearily. 'The earl bids me to him. Must I walk all the way back to the castle?'

'No. He has a lodge in the forest, not far from here, where he sometimes stops for refreshment during a hunt. He's there now.' He pointed into the woods beside the road.

Gwenda did not much like this but, as a serf, she had no right to decline a summons from her earl. Anyway, if she did refuse she felt sure Alan would knock her down and tie her up and carry her there. 'Very well,' she said.

'Jump up on the saddle in front of me, if you like.'

'No, thanks, I'd rather walk.'

At this time of year the undergrowth was thick. Gwenda followed the horse into the woods, taking advantage of the path it trampled through the nettles and ferns. The road behind them swiftly disappeared into the greenery. Gwenda wondered nervously what whim had caused Ralph to arrange this forest meeting. It could not be good news for her or her family, she felt.

They walked a quarter of a mile and came to a low building with a thatched roof. Gwenda would have assumed it to be a verderer's cottage. Alan looped his reins around a sapling and led the way inside.

The place had about it the same bare utilitarian look Gwenda had noted at Earlscastle. The floor was beaten earth, the walls unfinished wattle-and-daub, the ceiling nothing more than the underside of the thatch. The furniture was minimal: a table, some benches and a plain wooden bedstead with a straw mattress. A door at the back stood half open on a small kitchen where, presumably, Ralph's servants prepared food and drink for him and his fellow huntsmen.

Ralph was sitting at the table with a cup of wine. Gwenda stood in front of him, waiting. Alan leaned against the wall behind her. 'So, Alan found you,' Ralph said.

'Is there no one else here?' Gwenda said nervously.

'Just you, me and Alan.'

Gwenda's anxiety went up a notch. 'Why do you want to see me?'

'To talk about Sam, of course.'

'You've taken him from me. What else is there to say?'

'He's a good boy, you know ... our son.'

'Don't call him that.' She looked at Alan. He showed no surprise: clearly he had been let in on the secret. She was dismayed. Wulfric must never find out. 'Don't call him our son,' she said. 'You've never been a father to him. Wulfric raised him.'

'How could I raise him? I didn't even know he was mine! But I'm making up for lost time. He's doing well, did he tell you?'

'Does he get into fights?'

'Of course. Squires are supposed to fight. It's practice for when they go to war. You should have asked whether he wins.'

'It's not the life I wanted for him.'

'It's the life he was made for.'

'Did you bring me here to gloat?'

'Why don't you sit down?'

Reluctantly, she sat opposite him at the table. He poured wine into a cup and pushed it towards her. She ignored it.

He said: 'Now that I know we have a son together, I think we should be more intimate.'

'No, thank you.'

'You're such a killjoy.'

'Don't you talk to me about joy. You've been a blight on my life. With all my heart I wish I had never set eyes on you. I don't want to be intimate with you, I want to get away from you. If you went to Jerusalem it wouldn't be far enough.'

His face darkened with anger, and she regretted the extravagance of her words. She recalled Alan's rebuke. She wished she could say no simply and calmly, without stinging witticisms. But Ralph aroused her ire like no one else.

'Can't you see?' she said, trying to be reasonable. 'You have hated my husband for, what, a quarter of a century? He broke your nose and you slashed his cheek open. You disinherited him, then you were forced to give him back his family's lands. You raped the woman he once loved. He ran away and you dragged him back with a rope around his neck. After all that, even having a son together cannot make you and me friends.'

'I disagree,' he said. 'I think we can be not just friends, but lovers.'

'No!' It was what she had feared, in the back of her mind, ever since Alan had reined in on the road in front of her.

Ralph smiled. 'Why don't you take off your dress?'

She tensed.

Alan leaned over her from behind and slipped the long dagger out of her belt with a smooth motion. He had obviously premeditated the move, and it happened too quickly for her to react.

But Ralph said: 'No, Alan – that won't be necessary. She'll do it willingly.'

'I will not!' she said.

'Give her back the dagger, Alan.'

Reluctantly, Alan reversed the knife, holding it by the blade, and offered it to her.

She snatched it and leaped to her feet. 'You may kill me but I'll take one of you with me, by God,' she said.

She backed away, holding the knife at arm's length, ready to fight.

Alan stepped towards the door, moving to cut her off.

'Leave her be,' Ralph said. 'She's not going anywhere.'

She had no idea why Ralph was so confident, but he was dead wrong. She was getting out of this hut and then she was going to run away as fast as she could, and she would not stop until she dropped.

Alan stayed where he was.

Gwenda got to the door, reached behind her and lifted the simple wooden latch.

Ralph said: 'Wulfric doesn't know, does he?'

Gwenda froze. 'Doesn't know what?'

'He doesn't know that I'm Sam's father.'

Gwenda's voice fell to a whisper. 'No, he doesn't.'

'I wonder how he would feel if he found out.'

'It would kill him,' she said.

'That's what I thought.'

'Please don't tell him,' she begged.

'I won't ... so long as you do as I say.'

What could she do? She knew Ralph was drawn to her sexually. She had used that knowledge, in desperation, to get in to see him at the sheriff's castle. Their encounter at the Bell all those years ago, a vile memory to her, had lived in his recollection as a golden moment, probably much enhanced by the passage of time. And she had put into his head the idea of reliving that moment.

This was her own fault.

Could she somehow disabuse him? 'We aren't the same people we were all those years ago,' she said. 'I will never be an innocent young girl again. You should go back to your serving wenches.'

'I don't want serving girls, I want you.'

'No,' she said. 'Please.' She fought back tears.

He was implacable. 'Take off your dress.'

She sheathed her knife and unbuckled her belt.

# 89

THE MOMENT MERTHIN woke up, he thought of Lolla.

She had been missing now for three months. He had sent messages to the city authorities in Gloucester, Monmouth, Shaftesbury, Exeter, Winchester and Salisbury. Letters from him, as alderman of one of the great cities of the land, were treated seriously, and he had received careful replies to them all. Only the mayor of London had been unhelpful, saying in effect that half the girls in the city had run away from their fathers, and it was no business of the mayor's to send them home.

Merthin had made personal inquiries in Shiring, Bristol and Melcombe. He had spoken to the landlord of every tavern, giving them a description of Lolla. They had all seen plenty of dark-haired young women, often in the company of handsome rogues called Jake, or Jack, or Jock; but none could say for sure that they had seen Merthin's daughter, or heard the name Lolla.

Some of Jake's friends had also vanished, along with a girlfriend or two, the other missing women all some years older than Lolla.

Lolla might be dead – Merthin knew that – but he refused to give up hope. It was unlikely she had caught the plague. The new outbreak was ravaging towns and villages, and taking away most of the children under ten. But survivors of the first wave, such as Lolla and himself, must have been people who for some reason had the strength to resist the illness, or – in a very few cases, such as his own – to recover from it; and they were not falling sick this time. However, the plague was only one of the hazards to a sixteen-year-old girl running away from home, and Merthin's fertile imagination tortured him, in the small hours of the night, with thoughts of what might have happened to her.

One town not ravaged by the plague was Kingsbridge. The

illness had affected about one house in a hundred in the old town, as far as Merthin could tell from the conversations he held, shouted across the city gate, with Madge Webber, who was acting as alderman inside the city walls while Merthin managed affairs outside. The Kingsbridge suburbs, and other towns, were seeing something like one in five afflicted. But had Caris's methods overcome the plague, or merely delayed it? Would the illness persist, and eventually overcome the barriers she had put up? Would the devastation be as bad as last time in the end? They would not know until the outbreak had run its course – which might be months or years.

He sighed and got up out of his lonely bed. He had not seen Caris since the city was closed. She was living at the hospital, a few yards from Merthin's house, but she could not leave the building. People could go in but not come out. Caris had decided she would have no credibility unless she worked side by side with her nuns, so she was stuck.

Merthin had spent half his life separated from her, it seemed. But it did not get any easier. In fact he ached for her more now, in middle age, than he had as a youngster.

His housekeeper, Em, was up before him, and he found her in the kitchen, skinning rabbits. He ate a piece of bread and drank some weak beer, then went outside.

The main road across the island was already crowded with peasants and their carts bringing supplies. Merthin and a team of helpers spoke to each of them. Those bringing standard products with agreed prices were the simplest: Merthin sent them across the inner bridge to deposit their goods at the locked door of the gatehouse, then paid them when they came back empty. With those bringing seasonal produce such as fruits and vegetables he negotiated a price before allowing them to deliver. For some special consignments, a deal had been made days earlier, when he placed the order: hides for the leather trade; stones for the masons, who had recommenced building the spire under Bishop Henri's orders; silver for the jewellers; iron, steel, hemp and timber for the city's manufacturers, who had to continue working even though they were temporarily cut off from most of their customers. Finally there were the one-off cargoes, for which

Merthin would need to take instructions from someone in the city. Today brought a vendor of Italian brocade who wanted to sell it to one of the city's tailors; a year-old ox for the slaughterhouse; and Davey from Wigleigh.

Merthin listened to Davey's story with amazement and pleasure. He admired the lad for his enterprise in buying madder seeds and cultivating them to produce the costly dye. He was not surprised to learn that Ralph had tried to scuttle the project: Ralph was like most noblemen in his contempt for anything connected with manufacture or trade. But Davey had nerve as well as brains, and he had persisted. He had even paid a miller to grind the dried roots into powder.

'When the miller washed the grindstone afterwards, his dog drank some of the water that ran off,' Davey told Merthin. 'The dog pissed red for a week, so we know the dye works!'

Now he was here with a handcart loaded with old four-gallon flour sacks full of what he believed to be precious madder dye.

Merthin told him to pick up one of the sacks and bring it to the gate. When they got there, he called out to the sentry on the other side. The man climbed to the battlements and looked down. 'This sack is for Madge Webber,' Merthin shouted up. 'Make sure she gets it personally, would you, sentry?'

'Very good, alderman,' said the sentry.

As always, a few plague victims from the villages were brought to the island by their relatives. Most people now knew there was no cure for the plague and simply let their loved ones die, but a few were ignorant or optimistic enough to hope that Caris could work a miracle. The sick were left outside the hospital doors, like supplies at the city gate. The nuns came out for them at night when the relatives had gone. Now and again a lucky survivor emerged in good health, but most patients went out through the back door and were buried in a new graveyard on the far side of the hospital building.

At midday Merthin invited Davey to dinner. Over rabbit pie and new peas, Davey confessed he was in love with the daughter of his mother's old enemy. 'I don't know why Ma hates Annet, but it's all so long in the past, and it's nothing to do with me or Amabel,' he said, with the indignation of youth against the irrationality of parents. When Merthin nodded sympathetically, Davey asked: 'Did your parents stand in your way like this?'

Merthin thought for a moment. 'Yes,' he said. 'I wanted to be a squire and spend my life as a knight fighting for the king. I was heartbroken when they apprenticed me to a carpenter. However, in my case it worked out quite well.'

Davey was not pleased by this anecdote.

In the afternoon access to the inner bridge was closed off at the island end, and the gates of the city were opened. Teams of porters came out and picked up everything that had been left, and carried the supplies to their destinations in the city.

There was no message from Madge about the dye.

Merthin had a second visitor that day. Towards the end of the afternoon, as trading petered out, Canon Claude arrived.

Claude's friend and patron, Bishop Henri, was now installed as archbishop of Monmouth. However, his replacement as bishop of Kingsbridge had not been chosen. Claude wanted the position, and had been to London to see Sir Gregory Longfellow. He was on his way back to Monmouth, where he would continue to work as Henri's right-hand man for the moment.

'The king likes Philemon's line on taxation of the clergy,' he said over cold rabbit pie and a goblet of Merthin's best Gascon wine. 'And the senior clergy liked the sermon against dissection and the plan to build a Lady chapel. On the other hand, Gregory dislikes Philemon – says he can't be trusted. The upshot is, the king has postponed a decision by ruling that the monks of Kingsbridge cannot hold an election while they are in exile at St-John in the Forest.'

Merthin said: 'I assume the king sees little point in selecting a bishop while the plague rages and the city is closed.'

Claude nodded agreement. 'I did achieve something, albeit small,' he went on. 'There is a vacancy for an English ambassador to the pope. The appointee has to live in Avignon. I suggested Philemon. Gregory seemed intrigued by the idea. At least, he didn't rule it out.'

'Good!' The thought of Philemon being sent so far away lifted Merthin's spirits. He wished there were something he could do to weigh in on Claude's side; but he had already written to

Gregory pledging the support of the guild, and that was the limit of his influence.

'One more piece of news – sad news, in fact,' Claude said. 'On my way to London, I went to St-John-in-the-Forest. Henri is still abbot, technically, and he sent me to reprimand Philemon for decamping without permission. Waste of time, really. Anyway, Philemon has adopted Caris's precautions, and would not let me in, but we talked through the door. So far, the monks have escaped the plague. But your old friend Brother Thomas has died of old age. I'm sorry.'

'God rest his soul,' Merthin said sadly. 'He was very frail towards the end. His mind was going, too.'

'The move to St John probably didn't help him.'

'Thomas encouraged me when I was a young builder.'

'Strange how God sometimes takes the good men from us and leaves the bad.'

Claude left early the next morning.

As Merthin was going through his daily routine, one of the carters came back from the city gate with a message. Madge Webber was on the battlements and wanted to talk to Merthin and Davey.

'Do you think she'll buy my madder?' Davey said as they walked across the inner bridge.

Merthin had no idea. 'I hope so,' he said.

They stood side by side in front of the closed gate and looked up. Madge leaned over the wall and shouted down: 'Where did this stuff come from?'

'I grew it,' Davey said.

'And who are you?'

'Davey from Wigleigh, son of Wulfric.'

'Oh – Gwenda's boy?'

'Yes, the younger one.'

'Well, I've tested your dye.'

'It works, doesn't it?' Davey said eagerly.

'It's very weak. Did you grind the roots whole?'

'Yes – what else would I have done?'

'You're supposed to remove the hulls before grinding.'

'I didn't know that.' Davey was crestfallen. 'Is the powder no good?'

'As I said, it's weak. I can't pay the price of pure dye.'

Davey looked so dismayed that Merthin's heart went out to him.

Madge said: 'How much have you got?'

'Nine more four-gallon sacks like the one you have,' Davey said despondently.

'I'll give you half the usual price – three shillings and sixpence a gallon. That's fourteen shillings a sack, so exactly seven pounds for ten sacks.'

Davey's face was a picture of delight. Merthin wished Caris were with him just to share it. 'Seven pounds!' Davey repeated.

Thinking he was disappointed, Madge said: 'I can't do better than that – the dye just isn't strong enough.'

But seven pounds was a fortune to Davey. It was several years' wages for a labourer, even at today's rates. He looked at Merthin. 'I'm rich!' he said.

Merthin laughed and said: 'Don't spend it all at once.'

The next day was Sunday. Merthin went to the morning service at the island's own little church of St Elizabeth of Hungary, patron saint of healers. Then he went home and got a stout oak spade from his gardener's hut. With the spade over his shoulder, he walked across the outer bridge, through the suburbs and into his past.

He tried hard to remember the route he had taken through the forest thirty-four years ago with Caris, Ralph and Gwenda. It seemed impossible. There were no pathways other than deer runs. Saplings had become mature trees, and mighty oaks had been felled by the king's woodcutters. Nevertheless, to his surprise there were still recognizable landmarks: a spring gurgling up out of the ground where he remembered the ten-year-old Caris kneeling to drink; a huge rock that she said looked as if it must have fallen from heaven; a steep-sided little valley with a boggy bottom where she had got mud in her boots.

As he walked, his recollection of that day of childhood became more vivid. He remembered how the dog, Hop, had followed them, and Gwenda had followed her dog. He felt again the pleasure of having Caris understand his joke. His face reddened at the recollection of how incompetent he had been, in front of Caris, with the bow he had made – and how easily his younger brother had mastered the weapon.

Most of all, he remembered Caris as a girl. They had been pre-adolescent, but nevertheless he had been bewitched by her quick wits, her daring, and the effortless way she had assumed command of the little group. It was not love, but it was a kind of fascination that was not unlike love.

Remembrance distracted him from pathfinding, and he lost his bearings. He began to feel as if he was in completely unfamiliar territory – then, suddenly, he emerged into a clearing and knew he was in the right place. The bushes were more extensive; the trunk of the oak tree was even broader; and the clearing in between was gay with a scatter of summer flowers, as it had not been on that November day in 1327. But he was in no doubt: it was like a face he had not seen for years, changed but unmistakable.

A shorter and skinnier Merthin had crawled under that bush to hide from the big man crashing through the undergrowth. He remembered how the exhausted, panting Thomas had stood with his back to that oak tree and drawn his sword and dagger.

He saw in his imagination the events of that day played out again. Two men in yellow-and-green livery had caught up with Thomas and asked him for a letter. Thomas had distracted the men by telling them they were being observed by someone hiding in a bush. Merthin had felt sure he and the other children would be murdered – then Ralph, just ten years old, had killed one of the men-at-arms, showing the quick and deadly reflexes that had served him so well, years later, in the French wars. Thomas had despatched the other man, though not before receiving the wound that had ended in his losing his left arm – despite, or perhaps because of, the treatment given him in the hospital at Kingsbridge Priory. Then Merthin had helped Thomas bury the letter.

'Just here,' Thomas had said. 'Right in front of the oak tree.'

There was a secret in the letter, Merthin knew now; a secret so potent that high-ranking people were frightened of it. The secret had given Thomas protection, though he had nevertheless sought sanctuary in a monastery and spent his life there.

'If you hear that I've died,' Thomas had said to the boy Merthin, 'I'd like you to dig up this letter and give it to a priest.'

Merthin the man hefted his spade and began to dig.

He was not sure whether this was what Thomas had intended. The buried letter was a precaution against Thomas's being killed by violence, not dying of natural causes at the age of fifty-eight. Would he still have wanted the letter dug up? Merthin did not know. He would decide what to do when he had read the letter. He was irresistibly curious about what was in it.

His memory of where he had buried the bag was not perfect, and with his first try he missed the spot. He got down about eighteen inches and realized his mistake: the hole had been only about a foot deep, he was sure. He tried again a few inches to the left.

This time he got it right.

A foot down, the spade struck something that was not earth. It was soft, but unyielding. He put the spade to one side and scrabbled with his fingers in the hole. He felt a piece of ancient, rotting leather. Gently, he dislodged the earth and lifted the object. It was the wallet Thomas had worn on his belt all those years ago.

He wiped his muddy hands on his tunic and opened it.

Inside was a bag made of oiled wool, still intact. He loosened the drawstring of the bag and reached in. He pulled out a sheet of parchment, rolled into a scroll and sealed with wax.

He handled it gently, but all the same the wax crumbled as soon as he touched it. With careful fingertips he unrolled the parchment. It was intact: it had survived thirty-four years in the earth remarkably well.

He saw immediately that it was not an official document but a personal letter. He could tell by the handwriting, which was the painstaking scrawl of an educated nobleman, rather than the practised script of a clerk.

He began to read. The salutation ran:

*From Edward, the second of that name, King of England, at Berkeley Castle; by the hand of his faithful servant, Sir Thomas Langley; to his beloved eldest son, Edward; royal greeting and fatherly love.*

Merthin felt scared. This was a message from the old king to the new. The hand holding the document shook, and he looked up from it and scanned the greenery around him, as if there might be someone peering at him through the bushes.

*My beloved son, you will soon hear that I am dead. Know that it is not true.*

Merthin frowned. This was not what he had expected.

*Your mother, the queen, the wife of my heart, has corrupted and subverted Roland, earl of Shiring, and his sons, who sent murderers here; but I was forewarned by Thomas, and the murderers were killed.*

So Thomas had not been the assassin, after all, but the saviour of the king.

*Your mother, having failed to kill me once, would surely try again, for she and her adulterous consort cannot feel safe while I live. So I have changed clothes with one of the slain murderers, a man of my height and general appearance, and I have bribed several people to swear that the dead body is mine. Your mother will know the truth when she sees the body, but she will go along with the pretence; for if I am thought to be dead, I will be no threat to her, and no rebel or rival to the throne can claim my support.*

Merthin was amazed. The nation had thought Edward II to be dead. All Europe had been fooled.

But what had happened to him afterwards?

*I will not tell you where I plan to go, but know that I intend to leave my kingdom of England and never return. However, I pray that I will again see you, my son, before I die.*

Why had Thomas buried this letter instead of delivering it? Because he had feared for his own life, and had seen the letter as a powerful weapon in his defence. Once Queen Isabella had committed herself to the pretence of her husband's death, she had needed to deal with those few people who knew the truth. Merthin now recalled that while he was still an adolescent the earl of Kent had been convicted of treason and beheaded for maintaining that Edward II was still alive.

Queen Isabella had sent men to kill Thomas, and they had caught up with him just outside Kingsbridge. But Thomas had disposed of them, with the help of the ten-year-old Ralph. Afterwards, Thomas must have threatened to expose the whole deception – and he had proof, in the form of the old king's letter. That evening, as he lay in the hospital at Kingsbridge Priory, Thomas had negotiated with the queen, or more likely with Earl Roland and his sons as her agents. He had promised to keep the secret, on condition that he was accepted as a monk. He would feel safe in the monastery – and, in case the queen should be tempted to renege, he had said that the letter was in a safe place and would be revealed on his death. The queen therefore needed to keep him alive.

Old Prior Anthony had known something of this, and as he lay dying had told Mother Cecilia, who on her own deathbed had repeated part of the story to Caris. People might keep secrets for decades, Merthin reflected, but they felt compelled to tell the truth when death was near. Caris had also seen the incriminating document that gave Lynn Grange to the priory on condition Thomas was accepted as a monk. Merthin now understood why Caris's disingenuous inquiries about this document had caused such trouble. Sir Gregory Longfellow had persuaded Ralph to break into the monastery and steal all the nuns' charters in the hope of finding the incriminating letter.

Had the destructive power of this sheet of vellum been lessened by the passage of time? Isabella had lived a long life, but she had died three years ago. Edward II himself was almost certainly dead – if alive he would be seventy-seven now. Would Edward III fear the revelation that his father had remained alive when the world thought him dead? He was too strong a king, now, to be seriously threatened, but he would face great embarrassment and humiliation.

So what was Merthin to do?

He remained where he was, on the grassy floor of the forest among the wild flowers, for a long time. At last he rolled up the scroll, replaced it in the bag and put the bag back in the old leather pouch.

He put the pouch back into the ground and filled up the hole. He also filled in his first, erroneous hole. He smoothed the earth on top of both. He stripped some leaves off the bushes and scattered them in front of the oak tree. He stood back and looked at his work. He was satisfied: the excavations were no longer visible to the casual glance.

Then he turned his back on the clearing and went home.

# 90

AT THE END OF AUGUST, Earl Ralph made a tour of his landholdings around Shiring, accompanied by his long-term sidekick, Sir Alan Fernhill, and his new-found son, Sam. He enjoyed having Sam along, his child yet a grown man. His other sons, Gerry and Roley, were too young for this sort of thing. Sam did not know about his paternity, but Ralph nursed the secret with pleasure.

They were horrified by what they saw as they went around. Hundreds of Ralph's serfs were dead or dying, and the corn was standing unharvested in the fields. As they rode from one place to the next, Ralph's anger and frustration grew. His sarcastic remarks cowed his companions, and his bad temper turned his horse skittish.

In each village, as well as the serfs' landholdings, some acres were kept exclusively for the earl's personal use. They should have been cultivated by his employees and by serfs who were obliged to work for him one day a week. These lands were in the worst state of all. Many of his employees had died; so had some of the serfs who owed him labour; other serfs had negotiated more favourable tenancies after the last plague, so that they no longer had to work for the lord; and, finally, it was impossible to find labourers for hire.

When Ralph came to Wigleigh he went around the back of the manor house and looked into the big timber barn, which at this time of year should have been filling with grain ready for milling – but it was empty, and a cat had given birth to a litter of kittens in the hay loft.

'What will we do for bread?' he roared at Nathan Reeve. 'With no barley to make ale, what will we drink? You'd better have a plan, by God.'

Nate looked churlish. 'All we can do is reallocate the strips,' he said.

Ralph was surprised by his surliness. Nate was usually sycophantic. Then Nate glared at young Sam, and Ralph realized why the worm had turned. Nate hated Sam for killing Jonno, his son. Instead of punishing Sam, Ralph had first pardoned him, then made him a squire. No wonder Nate looked resentful.

Ralph said: 'There must be one or two young men in the village who could farm some extra acres.'

'Ah, yes, but they aren't willing to pay an entry fee,' Nate said.

'They want land for nothing?'

'Yes. They can see that you have too much land and not enough labour, and they know when they're in a strong bargaining position.' In the past Nate had been quick to abuse uppity peasants, but now he seemed to be enjoying Ralph's dilemma.

'They act as if England belongs to them, not to the nobility,' Ralph said angrily.

'It is disgraceful, lord,' said Nate more politely, and a sly look came over his face. 'For example, Wulfric's son Davey wants to marry Amabel and take over her mother's land. It would make sense: Annet has never been able to manage her holding.'

Sam spoke up. 'My parents won't pay the entry fee – they're against the marriage.'

Nate said: 'Davey could pay it himself, though.'

Ralph was surprised. 'How?'

'He sold that new crop he grew in the forest.'

'Madder. Obviously we didn't do a sufficiently thorough job of trampling it. How much did he get?'

'No one knows. But Gwenda has bought a young milking cow, and Wulfric has a new knife ... and Amabel wore a yellow scarf to church on Sunday.'

And Nate had been offered a fat bribe, Ralph guessed. 'I hate to reward Davey's disobedience,' he said. 'But I'm desperate. Let him have the land.'

'You would have to give him special permission to marry against his parents' will.'

Davey had asked Ralph for this, and Ralph had turned him

down, but that was before the plague decimated the peasantry. He did not like to revisit such decisions. However, it was a small price to pay. 'I shall give him permission,' he said.

'Very well.'

'But let's go and see him. I'd like to make the offer in person.'

Nate was startled, but of course made no objection.

The truth was that Ralph wanted to see Gwenda again. There was something about her that made his throat go dry. His last encounter with her, in the little hunting lodge, had not satisfied him for long. He had thought about her often in the weeks since then. He got little satisfaction nowadays from the kind of women he normally lay with: young prostitutes, tavern wenches and maidservants. They all pretended to be delighted by his advances, though he knew they just wanted the present of money that came afterwards. Gwenda, by contrast, made no secret of the fact that she loathed him and shuddered at his touch; and that pleased him, paradoxically, because it was honest and therefore real. After their meeting in the hunting lodge he had given her a purse of silver pennies, and she had thrown it back at him so hard that it had bruised his chest.

'They're in Brookfield today, turning their reaped barley,' Nate said. 'I'll take you there.'

Ralph and his men followed Nate out of the village and along the bank of the stream at the edge of the great field. Wigleigh was always windy, but today the summer breeze was soft and warm, like Gwenda's breasts.

Some of the strips of land here had been reaped, but in others Ralph despaired to see overripe oats, barley rank with weeds, and one patch of rye that had been reaped but not bundled, so that the crop lay scattered on the ground.

A year ago he had thought that all his financial troubles were over. He had come home from the most recent French war with a captive, the Marquis de Neuchatel, and had negotiated a ransom of fifty thousand pounds. But the marquis's family had not been able to raise the money. Something similar had happened to the French king, Jean II, captured by the prince of Wales at the battle of Poitiers. King Jean had stayed in London for four years, technically a prisoner, though living in comfort at the Savoy, the new palace built by the Duke of Lancaster. The king's ransom had been reduced, but still it had not been paid in full. Ralph had sent Alan Fernhill to Neuchatel to renegotiate his prisoner's ransom, and Alan had reduced the price to twenty thousand, but again the family had failed to pay it. Then the marquis had died of the plague, so Ralph was insolvent again, and had to worry about the harvest.

It was midday. The peasants were having their dinner at the side of the field. Gwenda, Wulfric and Davey were sitting on the ground under a tree eating cold pork with raw onions. They all jumped to their feet when the horses came near. Ralph went over to Gwenda's family and waved the rest away.

Gwenda wore a loose green dress that hid her shape. Her hair was tied back, making her face more rat-like. Her hands were dirty, with earth under the nails. But, when Ralph looked at her, in his imagination he saw her naked, ready, waiting for him with an expression of resigned disgust at what he was about to do; and he felt aroused.

He looked away from her to her husband. Wulfric stared back at him with a level gaze, neither defiant nor cowed. There was a little grey now in his tawny beard, but still it would not grow over the scar of the sword cut Ralph had given him. 'Wulfric, your son wants to marry Amabel and take over Annet's land.'

Gwenda responded. She had never learned to speak only when spoken to. 'You've stolen one son from me – will you take the other now?' she said bitterly.

Ralph ignored her. 'Who will pay the heriot?'

Nate put in: 'It's thirty shillings.'

Wulfric said: 'I haven't got thirty shillings.'

Davey said calmly: 'I can pay it.'

He must have done very well out of his madder crop, Ralph thought, to be so cool about such a large sum of money. 'Good,' he said. 'In that case—'

Davey interrupted him. 'But on what terms are you offering it?'

Ralph felt his face redden. 'What do you mean?'

Nate intervened again. 'The same terms as those upon which Annet holds the land, of course.'

Davey said: 'Then I thank the earl, but I will not accept his gracious offer.'

Ralph said: 'What the devil are you talking about?'

'I would like to take over the land, my lord, but only as a free tenant, paying cash rent, without customary dues.'

Sir Alan said threateningly: 'Do you dare to haggle with the earl of Shiring, you insolent young dog?'

Davey was scared but defiant. 'I've no wish to offend, lord. But I want to be free to grow whatever crop I can sell. I don't want to cultivate what Nate Reeve chooses regardless of market prices.'

Davey had inherited that streak of stubborn determination from Gwenda, Ralph thought. He said angrily: 'Nate expresses my wishes! Do you think you know better than your earl?'

'Forgive me, lord, but you neither till the soil nor go to market.'

Alan's hand went to the hilt of his sword. Ralph saw Wulfric glance at his scythe, lying on the ground, its sharp blade gleaming in the sunlight. On Ralph's other side, young Sam's horse skittered nervously, picking up its rider's tension. If it came to a fight, Ralph thought, would Sam fight for his lord, or for his family?

Ralph did not want a fight. He wanted to get the harvest in, and killing his peasants would make that harder. He restrained Alan with a gesture. 'This is how the plague undermines morality,' he said disgustedly. 'I will give you what you want, Davey, because I must.'

Davey swallowed drily and said: 'In writing, lord?'

'You're demanding a copyhold, too?'

Davey nodded, too frightened to speak.

'Do you doubt the word of your earl?'

'No, lord.'

'Then why demand a written lease?'

'For the avoidance of doubt in future years.'

They all said that when they asked for a copyhold. What they meant was that if the lease was written down the landlord could not easily alter the terms. It was yet another encroachment on time-honoured traditions. Ralph did not want to make a further concession – but, once again, he had no option if he wanted to get the harvest in.

And then he thought of a way he could use this situation to gain something else he wanted, and he cheered up.

'All right,' he said. 'I'll give you a written lease. But I don't want men leaving the fields during the harvest. Your mother can come to Earlscastle to collect the document next week.'

*

GWENDA WALKED TO Earlscastle on a baking hot day. She knew what Ralph wanted her for, and the prospect made her miserable. As she crossed the drawbridge into the castle, the rooks seemed to laugh derisively at her plight.

The sun beat down mercilessly on the compound, where the walls blocked the breeze. The squires were playing a game outside the stables. Sam was among them, and too absorbed to notice Gwenda.

They had tied a cat to a post at eye level in such a way that it could move its head and legs. A squire had to kill the cat with his hands tied behind his back. Gwenda had seen the game before. The only way for the squire to achieve his object was to headbutt the wretched animal, but the cat naturally defended itself by scratching and biting the attacker's face. The challenger, a boy of about sixteen, was hovering near the post, watched by the terrified cat. Suddenly the boy jerked his head. His forehead smashed into the cat's chest, but the animal lashed out with its clawed paws. The squire yelped with pain and jumped back, his cheeks streaming blood, and all the other squires roared with laughter. Enraged, the challenger rushed at the post and butted the cat again. He was scratched worse, and he hurt his head, which they found even funnier. The third time he was more careful. Getting close, he feinted, making the cat lash out at thin air; then he delivered a carefully aimed strike right at the beast's head. Blood poured from its mouth and nostrils and it slumped unconscious, though still breathing. He butted it a final time to kill it, and the others cheered and clapped.

Gwenda felt sickened. She did not much like cats – she preferred dogs – but it was unpleasant to see any helpless creature tormented. She supposed that boys had to do this sort of thing to prepare them for maiming and killing human beings in war. Did it have to be that way?

She moved on without speaking to her son. Perspiring, she crossed the second bridge and climbed the steps to the keep. The great hall was mercifully cool.

She was glad Sam had not seen her. She was hoping to avoid him as long as possible. She did not want him to suspect that anything was wrong. He was not notably sensitive, but he might detect his mother's distress.

She told the marshal of the hall why she was here, and he promised to let the earl know. 'Is Lady Philippa in residence?' Gwenda asked hopefully. Perhaps Ralph would be inhibited by the presence of his wife.

But the marshal shook his head. 'She's at Monmouth, with her daughter.'

Gwenda nodded grimly and settled down to wait. She could not help thinking about her encounter with Ralph at the hunting lodge. When she looked at the unadorned grey wall of the great hall she saw him, staring at her as she undressed, his mouth slightly open in anticipation. As much as the intimacy of sex was a joy with the man she loved, so much was it loathsome with one she hated.

The first time Ralph had coerced her, more than twenty years ago, her body had betrayed her, and she had felt a physical pleasure, even while experiencing a spiritual revulsion. The same thing had happened with Alwyn the outlaw in the forest. But it had not occurred this time with Ralph in the hunting lodge. She attributed the change to age. When she had been a young girl, full of desire, the physical act had triggered an automatic response – something she could not help, although it had made her even more ashamed. Now in her maturity her body was not so vulnerable, the reflex not so ready. She could at least be grateful for that.

The stairs at the far end of the hall led to the earl's chamber. Men were going up and down constantly: knights, servants, tenants, bailiffs. After an hour, the marshal told her to go up.

She was afraid Ralph would want sex there and then, but she was relieved to find that he was having a business day. With him were Sir Alan and two priest-clerks sitting at a table with writing materials. One of the clerks handed her a small vellum scroll.

She did not look at it. She could not read.

'There,' said Ralph. 'Now your son is a free tenant. Isn't that what you always wanted?'

She had wanted freedom for herself, as Ralph knew. She had never achieved it – but Ralph was right, Davey had. That meant that her life had not been completely without purpose. Her grandchildren would be free and independent, growing what crops they chose, paying their rent and keeping for themselves everything else they earned. They would never know the miserable existence of poverty and hunger that Gwenda had been born to.

Was that worth all she had been through? She did not know.

She took the scroll and went to the door.

Alan came after her and spoke in a low voice as she was going out. 'Stay here tonight, in the hall,' he said. The great hall was where most of the castle's residents slept. 'Tomorrow, be at the hunting lodge two hours after midday.'

She tried to leave without replying.

Alan barred her way with his arm. 'Understand?' he said.

'Yes,' she said in a low voice. 'I will be there in the afternoon.'

He let her go.

*

SHE DID NOT speak to Sam until late in the evening. The squires spent the whole afternoon at various violent games. She was glad to have the time to herself. She sat in the cool hall alone with her thoughts. She tried to tell herself that it was nothing for her to have sexual congress with Ralph. She was no virgin, after all. She had been married for twenty years. She had had sex thousands of times. It would all be over in a few minutes, and it would leave no scars. She would do it and forget it.

Until the next time.

That was the worst of it. He could go on coercing her indefinitely. His threat to reveal the secret of Sam's paternity would terrify her as long as Wulfric was alive.

Surely Ralph would tire of her soon, and go back to the firm young bodies of his tavern wenches?

'What's the matter with you?' Sam said when at dusk the squires came in for supper.

'Nothing,' she said quickly. 'Davey's bought me a milking cow.'

Sam looked a bit envious. He was enjoying life, but squires were not paid. They had little need of money – they were provided with food, drink, accommodation and clothing – but, all the same, a young man liked to have a few pennies in his wallet.

They talked about Davey's forthcoming wedding. 'You and Annet are going to be grandmothers together,' Sam said. 'You'll have to make your peace with her.'

'Don't be stupid,' Gwenda snapped. 'You don't know what you're talking about.'

Ralph and Alan emerged from the chamber when supper was served. All the residents and visitors assembled in the hall. The kitchen staff brought in three large pike baked with herbs. Gwenda sat near the foot of the table, well away from Ralph, and he took no notice of her.

After dinner she lay down to sleep in the straw on the floor beside Sam. It was a comfort to her to lie next to him, as she had when he was little. She remembered listening to his childish breathing, soft and contented, in the silence of the night. Drifting off, she thought about how children grew up to defy their parents' expectations. Her own father had wanted to treat her like a commodity to be traded, but she had angrily refused to be used that way. Now each of her sons was taking his own road through life, and in both cases it was not the one she had planned. Sam would be a knight, and Davey was going to marry Annet's daughter. If we knew how they would turn out, she thought, would we be so eager to have them?

She dreamed that she went to Ralph's hunting lodge and found that he was not there, but there was a cat on his bed. She knew she had to kill the cat, but she had her hands tied behind her back, so she butted it with her head until it died.

When she woke up she wondered if she could kill Ralph at the lodge.

She had killed Alwyn, all those years ago, sticking his own knife into his throat and pushing it up into his head until its point had come out through his eye. She had killed Sim Chapman, too, holding his head under the water while he wriggled and thrashed, keeping him there until he breathed the river into his lungs and died. If Ralph went to the hunting lodge alone, she might be able to kill him, if she chose her moment well.

But he would not be on his own. Earls never went anywhere alone. He would have Alan with him, as he had before. It was unusual for him to travel with only one companion. It was unlikely he would have none.

Could she kill them both? No one else knew she was going to meet them there. If she killed them and simply walked on home she would not even be suspected. No one knew of her motive – it was a secret, that was the whole point. Someone might realize she had been near the lodge at the time, but they would only ask her whether she had seen any suspicious-looking men in the vicinity – it would not occur to them that big strong Ralph might have been murdered by a small middle-aged woman.

But could she do it? She thought about it, but she knew in her heart it was hopeless. They were experienced men of violence. They had been at war, off and on, for twenty years, most recently in the campaign of the winter before last. They had quick reflexes and their reactions were deadly. Many French knights had wanted to kill them, and had died trying.

She might have killed one, using guile and surprise, but not two.

She was going to have to submit to Ralph.

Grimly she went outside and washed her face and hands. When she came back into the great hall, the kitchen staff were putting out rye bread and weak ale for breakfast. Sam was dipping the stale bread into his ale to soften it. 'You've got that look again,' he said. 'What's the matter?'

'Nothing,' she said. She drew her knife and cut a slab of the bread. 'I've got a long walk ahead of me.'

'Is that what you're worried about? You shouldn't really go on your own. Most women don't like to travel alone.'

'I'm tougher than most women.' She was pleased that he showed concern for her. It was something his real father, Ralph, would never have done. Wulfric had had some influence over the boy, after all. But she was embarrassed that he had read her expression and divined her state of mind. 'You don't need to worry about me.'

'I could come with you,' he offered. 'I'm sure the earl would let me. He doesn't need any squires today – he's going off somewhere with Alan Fernhill.'

That was the last thing she wanted. If she failed to keep her rendezvous, Ralph would let out the secret. She could readily imagine the pleasure Ralph would take in that. He would not need much provocation. 'No,' she said firmly. 'Stay here. You never know when your earl will call for you.'

'He won't call for me. I should come with you.'

'I absolutely forbid it.' Gwenda swallowed a mouthful of her bread and stuffed the rest into her wallet. 'You're a good boy to worry about me, but it's not necessary.' She kissed his cheek. 'Take care of yourself. Don't run unnecessary risks. If you want to do something for me, stay alive.'

She walked away. At the door, she turned. He was watching her thoughtfully. She forced herself to give what she hoped was a carefree smile. Then she went out.

*

ON THE ROAD, Gwenda began to worry that someone might find out about her liaison with Ralph. Such things had a way of getting out. She had met him once, she was about to do so a second time, and she feared there might be more such occasions. How long would it be before someone saw her leaving the road and heading into the woods at a certain point in her journey, and wondered why? What if someone should stumble by accident into the hunting lodge at the wrong moment? How many people would notice that Ralph went off with Alan whenever Gwenda was travelling from Earlscastle to Wigleigh?

She stopped at a tavern just before noon and had some ale and cheese. Travellers generally left such places in a group, for safety, but she made sure to wait behind so that she would be alone on the road. When she came to the point where she had to turn into the woods she looked ahead and behind, to make sure there was no one watching. She thought she saw a movement in the trees a quarter of a mile back, and she peered into the hazy distance, trying to make out more clearly what she had seen; but no one was there. She was just getting jumpy.

She thought again about killing Ralph as she waded through the summer undergrowth. If by some lucky chance Alan was not here, might she find an opportunity? But Alan was the one person in the world who knew she was meeting Ralph here. If Ralph were killed, Alan would know who had done it. She would have to kill him, too. And that seemed impossible.

There were two horses outside the lodge. Ralph and Alan were inside, sitting at the little table, with the remains of a meal in front of them: half a loaf, a ham bone, the rind of a cheese and a wine flask. Gwenda closed the door behind her.

'Here she is, as promised,' Alan said with a satisfied air. Clearly he had been given the job of getting her to come to the rendezvous, and he was relieved she had obeyed orders. 'Just perfect for your dessert,' he said. 'Like a raisin, wrinkled but sweet.'

Gwenda said to Ralph: 'Why don't you get him out of here?'

Alan stood up. 'Always the insolent remark,' he said. 'Will you never learn?' But he left the room, going into the kitchen and slamming the door behind him.

Ralph smiled at her. 'Come here,' he said. She moved obediently closer to him. 'I'll tell Alan not to be so rude, if you like.'

'Please don't!' she said, horrified. 'If he starts being nice to me, people will wonder why.'

'As you please.' He took her hand and tried to draw her closer. 'Sit on my lap.'

'Couldn't we just fuck and get it over with?'

He laughed. 'That's what I like about you – you're honest.' He stood up, held her shoulders and looked into her eyes; then he bent his head and kissed her.

It was the first time he had done this. They had had sex twice without ever kissing. Now Gwenda was revolted. As his lips pressed against hers she felt more violated than when he had thrust his penis into her. He opened his mouth, and she tasted his cheesy breath. She pulled away, disgusted. 'No,' she said.

'Remember what you stand to lose.'

'Please don't do this.'

He started to become angry. 'I will have you!' he said loudly. 'Get that dress off.'

'Please let me go,' she said. He started to say something, but she raised her voice to speak over him. The walls were thin, and she knew that Alan in the kitchen could hear her pleading, but she did not care. 'Don't force me, I beg you!'

'I don't care what you say!' he shouted. 'Get on that bed!'

'Please don't make me!'

The front door flew open.

Both Gwenda and Ralph turned and stared.

Sam stood there.

Gwenda said: 'Oh, God, no!'

The three of them were frozen still for a split second, and in that moment Gwenda guessed, all at once, what had happened. Sam had been worried about her and – disobeying her orders – he had followed her from Earlscastle, staying out of sight but never far behind. He had seen her leave the road and head into the woods – she had caught a flash of movement when she looked behind, but she had dismissed it. He had found the hut, arriving a minute or two after her. He must have stood outside and heard the shouting. It must have been obvious that Ralph was in the process of forcing Gwenda to submit to unwanted sex – although, recalling in a flash what they had said, Gwenda realized they had not mentioned the true reason she had to submit. The secret had not been revealed – yet.

Sam drew his sword.

Ralph leaped to his feet. As Sam rushed at him, Ralph managed to get his own sword out. Sam swung at Ralph's head, but Ralph raised his sword just in time to parry the stroke.

Gwenda's son was trying to kill his father.

Sam was in terrible danger. Hardly more than a boy, he was up against a battle-hardened soldier.

Ralph shouted: 'Alan!'

Then Gwenda realized Sam was up against not one but two veterans.

She dashed across the room. As the kitchen door came open, she stood on the far side of the doorway and flattened herself against the wall. She drew the long dagger from her belt.

The door flew wide and Alan stepped into the room.

He looked at the two fighters and did not see Gwenda. He paused for an instant, taking in the scene in front of him. Sam's sword swept through the air again, aimed at Ralph's neck; and again Ralph took the blow on his own sword.

Alan could see instantly that his master was under furious attack. His hand went to the hilt of his sword, and he took a pace forward. Then Gwenda stabbed him in the back.

She thrust the long dagger in and upwards as hard as she could, pushing with a fieldworker's strength, thrusting through the muscles of Alan's back, up through kidneys and stomach and lungs, hoping to reach his heart. The knife was ten inches long, pointed and sharp, and it sliced through his organs; but it did not kill him immediately.

He roared with pain then suddenly went silent. Staggering, he turned and grabbed her, pulling her to him in a wrestler's embrace. She stabbed him again, in the stomach this time, with the same upward stroke through the vital organs. Blood came out of his mouth. He went limp and his arms fell to his sides. He stared for a moment with a look of utter incredulity at the contemptible little woman who had ended his life. Then his eyes closed and he fell to the floor.

Gwenda looked at the other two.

Sam struck and Ralph parried; Ralph stepped back and Sam advanced; Sam struck again and Ralph parried again. Ralph was defending himself vigorously, but not attacking.

Ralph was fearful of killing his son.

Sam, not knowing that his opponent was his father, had no such scruples, and pressed forward, slashing with his sword.

Gwenda knew this could not go on for long. One of them would hurt the other, and then it would become a fight to the death. Holding her bloody knife ready, she looked desperately for a chance to intervene, and stab Ralph the way she had stabbed Alan.

'Wait,' Ralph said, holding up his left hand; but Sam was angry, and thrust at him regardless. Ralph parried and spoke again. 'Wait!' He was gasping from exertion, but he managed to get a few words out. 'There's something you don't know.'

'I know enough!' Sam yelled, and Gwenda could hear the note of boyish hysteria in his big man's voice. He swung again.

'You don't!' Ralph shouted.

Gwenda knew what Ralph wanted to tell Sam. He was going to say: I am your father.

It must not happen.

'Listen to me!' Ralph said, and at last Sam responded. He stepped back, though he did not lower his sword.

Ralph panted, catching his breath in preparation for speaking; and, as he paused, Gwenda ran at him.

He spun around to face her, at the same time swinging his sword to the right in a flat arc. His blade hit hers, knocking the knife out of her hand. She was completely defenceless, and she knew that if he slashed at her with the return stroke she would be killed.

But, for the first time since Sam had drawn his sword, Ralph's guard was open, leaving the front of his body undefended.

Sam stepped forward and thrust his sword into Ralph's chest.

The pointed tip of the blade passed through Ralph's light summer tunic and entered his body on the left side of his breastbone. It must have slipped between two ribs, for the blade sank farther in. Sam gave a bloodthirsty cry of triumph and pushed harder. Ralph staggered backwards under the impact. His shoulders hit the wall behind him, but still Sam came forward, pushing with all his might. The sword seemed to pass all the way through Ralph's chest. There was a strange thud as the point came out of his back and stuck into the timber of the wall.

Ralph's eyes looked into Sam's face, and Gwenda knew what he was thinking. Ralph understood that he had been wounded fatally. And, in the last few seconds of his life, he knew that he had been killed by his own son.

Sam let go of the sword, but it did not fall. It was embedded in the wall, impaling Ralph gruesomely. Sam stepped back, aghast.

Ralph was not yet dead. His arms waved feebly in an effort to grab the sword and pull it out of his chest, but he was not able to coordinate his movements. Gwenda realized in a ghastly flash that he looked a bit like the cat the squires had tied to the post.

She stooped and quickly picked up her dagger from the floor.

Then, incredibly, Ralph spoke.

'Sam,' he said. 'I am...' Then blood spurted from his mouth in a sudden flood, cutting off his speech.

Thank God, Gwenda thought.

The torrent stopped as quickly as it had started, and he spoke again. 'I am—'

This time he was stopped by Gwenda. She leaped forward and thrust her dagger into his mouth. He made a gruesome choking noise. The blade sank into his throat.

She let go of the knife and stepped back.

She stared in horror at what she had done. The man who had tormented her for so long was nailed to the wall as if crucified, with a sword through his chest and a knife in his mouth. He made no sound, but his eyes showed that he was alive, as they looked from Gwenda to Sam and back again, in agony and terror and despair.

They stood still, staring at him, silent, waiting.

At last his eyes closed.

# 91

THE PLAGUE FADED AWAY in September. Caris's hospital gradually emptied, as patients died without being replaced by new ones. The vacant rooms were swept and scrubbed, and juniper logs were burned in the fireplaces, filling the hospital with a sharp autumn fragrance. Early in October, the last victim was laid to rest in the hospital's graveyard. A smoky-red sun rose over Kingsbridge Cathedral as four strong young nuns lowered the shrouded corpse into the hole in the ground. The body was that of a crookbacked weaver from Outhenby but, as Caris gazed into the grave, she saw her old enemy, the plague, lying on the cold earth. Under her breath, she said: 'Are you really dead, or will you come back again?'

When the nuns returned to the hospital after the funeral, there was nothing to do.

Caris washed her face, brushed her hair and put on the new dress she had been saving for this day. It was the bright red of Kingsbridge Scarlet. Then she walked out of the hospital for the first time in half a year.

She went immediately into Merthin's garden.

His pear trees cast long shadows in the morning sun. The leaves were beginning to redden and crisp, while a few late fruits still hung on the boughs, round-bellied and brown. Arn, the gardener, was chopping firewood with an axe. When he saw Caris he was at first startled and frightened; then he realized what her appearance meant, and his face split in a grin. He dropped his axe and ran into the house.

In the kitchen, Em was boiling porridge over a cheerful fire. She looked at Caris as at a heavenly apparition. She was so moved that she kissed Caris's hands.

Caris went up the stairs and into Merthin's bedroom.

He was standing at the window in his undershirt, looking out at the river that flowed past the front of the house. He turned towards her, and her heart faltered to see his familiar, irregular face, the gaze of alert intelligence and the quick humour in the twist of his lips. His golden-brown eyes looked lovingly at her, and his mouth widened in a welcoming smile. He showed no surprise: he must have noticed that there had been fewer and fewer patients arriving at the hospital, and he would have been expecting her to reappear any day. He looked like a man whose hopes have been fulfilled.

She stood beside him at the window. He put his arm around her shoulders, and she put hers around his waist. There was a little more grey in his red beard than six months ago, she thought, and his halo of hair seemed to have receded a little farther, unless it was her imagination.

For a moment, they both looked out at the river. In the grey morning light, the water was the colour of iron. The surface shifted endlessly, mirror-bright or deep black in irregular patterns, always changing and always the same.

'It's over,' Caris said.

Then they kissed.

*

MERTHIN ANNOUNCED a special Autumn Fair to celebrate the reopening of the town. It was held during the last week of October. The wool-dealing season was over, but anyway fleeces were no longer the principal commodity traded in Kingsbridge, and thousands of people came to buy the scarlet cloth for which the town was now famous.

At the Saturday-night banquet that opened the fair, the guild honoured Caris. Although Kingsbridge had not totally escaped the plague, it had suffered much less than other cities, and most people felt they owed their lives to her precautions. She was everyone's hero. The guildsmen insisted on marking her achievement, and Madge Webber devised a new ceremony in which Caris was presented with a gold key, symbolizing the key to the city gate. Merthin felt very proud.

Next day, Sunday, Merthin and Caris went to the cathedral. The monks were still at St-John-in-the-Forest, so the service was taken by Father Michael from St Peter's parish church in the town. Lady Philippa, countess of Shiring, showed up.

Merthin had not seen Philippa since Ralph's funeral. Not many tears had been shed for his brother, her husband. The earl would normally have been buried at Kingsbridge Cathedral but, because the town had been closed, Ralph had been interred in Shiring.

His death remained a mystery. His body had been found in a hunting lodge, stabbed through the chest. Alan Fernhill lay on the floor nearby, also dead of stab wounds. The two men appeared to have had dinner together, for the remains of a meal were still on the table. Obviously there had been a fight, but it was not clear whether Ralph and Alan had inflicted fatal wounds on one another or someone else had been involved. Nothing had been stolen: money was found on both bodies, their costly weapons lay beside them, and two valuable horses were cropping the grass in the clearing outside. Because of that, the Shiring coroner inclined to the theory that the two men had killed one another.

In another sense, there was no mystery. Ralph had been a man of violence, and it was no surprise that he had died a violent death. They that live by the sword shall die by the sword, Jesus said, although that verse was not often quoted by the priests of King Edward III's reign. If anything was remarkable, it was that Ralph had survived so many military campaigns, so many bloody battles, and so many charges by the French cavalry, to die in a squabble a few miles from his home.

Merthin had surprised himself by weeping at the funeral. He wondered what he was sad about. His brother had been a wicked man who caused a great deal of misery, and his death was a blessing. Merthin had not been close to him since he murdered Tilly. What was there to mourn? In the end, Merthin decided he was grieving for a Ralph that might have been – a man whose violence was not indulged but controlled; whose aggression was directed, not by ambition for personal glory, but by a sense of justice. Perhaps it had once been possible for Ralph to grow into such a man. When the two of them had played together, aged five and six, floating wooden boats on a muddy puddle, Ralph had not been cruel and vengeful. That was why Merthin cried.

Philippa's two boys had been at the funeral, and they were with her today. The elder, Gerry, was Ralph's son by poor Tilly. The younger, Roley, was believed by everyone to be Ralph's son by Philippa, though in fact he was Merthin's. Fortunately, Roley was not a small, lively redhead like Merthin. He was going to be tall and dignified like his mother.

Roley was clutching a small wooden carving, which he presented solemnly to Merthin. It was a horse, and he had done it rather well for a ten-year-old, Merthin realized. Most children would have sculpted the animal standing firmly on all four feet, but Roley had made it move, its legs in different positions and its mane flying in the wind. The boy had inherited his real father's ability to visualize complex objects in three dimensions. Merthin felt an unexpected lump in his throat. He bent down and kissed Roley's forehead.

He gave Philippa a grateful smile. He guessed she had encouraged Roley to give him the horse, knowing what it would mean to him. He glanced at Caris and saw that she, too, understood its significance; though nothing was said.

The atmosphere in the great church was joyful. Father Michael was not a charismatic preacher, and he went through the mass in a mumble. But the nuns sang as beautifully as ever, and an optimistic sun shone through the rich dark colours of the stained-glass windows.

Afterwards they walked around the fair in the crisp autumn air. Caris held Merthin's arm and Philippa walked on his other side. The two boys ran on ahead while Philippa's bodyguard and lady-in-waiting followed behind. Business was good, Merthin saw. Kingsbridge craftsmen and traders were already beginning to rebuild their fortunes. The town would recover from this epidemic faster than from the last.

Senior members of the guild were going around checking weights and measures. There were standards for the weight of a woolsack, the width of a piece of cloth, the size of a bushel and so on, so that people knew what they were buying. Merthin encouraged guildsmen to perform these checks ostentatiously, so that buyers could see how carefully the town monitored its tradesmen. Of course, if they really suspected someone of cheating, they would check discreetly and then, if he was guilty, get rid of him quietly.

Philippa's two sons ran excitedly from one stall to the next. Watching Roley, Merthin said quietly to Philippa: 'Now that Ralph has gone, is there any reason why Roley should not know the truth?'

She looked thoughtful. 'I wish I could tell him – but would it be for his sake, or ours? For ten years he's believed Ralph to be his father. Two months ago he wept at Ralph's graveside. It would be a terrible shock to tell him now that he is another man's son.'

They were speaking in low voices, but Caris could hear, and she said: 'I agree with Philippa. You have to think of the child, not of yourself.'

Merthin saw the sense of what they were saying. It was a small sadness on a happy day.

'There is another reason,' Philippa said. 'Gregory Longfellow came to see me last week. The king wants to make Gerry earl of Shiring.'

'At the age of thirteen?' Merthin said.

'The title of earl is always hereditary, once it has been granted, although baronies are not. Anyway, I would administer the earldom for the next three years.'

'As you did all the time Ralph was away fighting the French. You'll be relieved the king isn't asking you to marry again.'

She made a face. 'I'm too old.'

'So Roley will be second in line for the earldom – provided we keep our secret.' If something should happen to Gerry, Merthin thought, my son will become earl of Shiring. Fancy that.

'Roley would be a good ruler,' Philippa said. 'He's intelligent and quite strong-willed, but not cruel like Ralph.'

Ralph's mean nature had been obvious at an early age: he had been ten, Roley's age now, when he shot Gwenda's dog. 'But Roley might prefer to be something else.' He looked again at the carved wooden horse.

Philippa smiled. She did not smile often, but when she did it was dazzling. She was still beautiful, he thought. She said: 'Give in to it, and be proud of him.'

Merthin recalled how proud his father had been when Ralph became the earl. But he knew he would never feel the same way. He would be proud of Roley, whatever he did, as long as he did it well. Perhaps the boy would become a stonemason, and carve saints and angels. Perhaps he would be a wise and merciful nobleman. Or he might do something else, something his parents had never anticipated.

Merthin invited Philippa and the boys to dinner, and they all left the cathedral precincts. They walked over the bridge against the flow of loaded carts coming to the fair. They crossed Leper Island together and went through the orchard into the house.

In the kitchen they found Lolla.

As soon as she saw her father, she burst into tears. He put his arms around her and she sobbed on his shoulder. Wherever she had been, she must have got out of the habit of washing, for she smelled like a pigsty, but he was too happy to care.

It was a while before they could get any sense out of her. When at last she spoke, she said: 'They all died!' Then she burst into fresh tears. After a while she calmed down, and spoke more coherently. 'They all died,' she repeated, suppressing her sobs. 'Jake, and Boyo, Netty and Hal, Joanie and Chalkie and Ferret, one by one, and nothing I did made any difference!'

They had been living in the forest, Merthin gathered, a group of youngsters pretending to be nymphs and shepherds. The details came out gradually. The boys would kill a deer every now and again, and sometimes they would go away for a day and come back with a barrel of wine and some bread. Lolla said they bought their supplies, but Merthin guessed they had robbed travellers. Lolla had somehow imagined they could live like that for ever: she had not thought about how things might be different in the winter. But, in the end, it was the plague rather than the weather that brought the idyll to an end. 'I was so frightened,' Lolla said. 'I wanted Caris.'

Gerry and Roley listened with mouths agape. They idolized their older cousin Lolla. Although she had come home in tears, the story of her adventure only enhanced her in their eyes.

'I never want to feel like that again,' Lolla said. 'So powerless, with my friends all sick and dying around me.'

'I can understand that,' Caris said. 'It's how I felt when my mother died.'

'Will you teach me to heal people?' Lolla said to her. 'I want to really help them, as you do, not just sing hymns and show them a picture of an angel. I want to understand about bones and blood, and herbs and things that make people better. I want to be able to do something when a person is sick.'

'Of course I'll teach you, if that's what you want,' Caris said. 'I would be pleased.'

Merthin was astonished. Lolla had been rebellious and bad-tempered for some years now, and part of her rejection of authority had been a pretence that Caris, her stepmother, was not really her parent, and need not be respected. He was delighted by the turnaround. It was almost worth the agony of worry he had been through.

A moment later, a nun came into the kitchen. 'Little Annie Jones is having a fit, and we don't know why,' she said to Caris. 'Can you come?'

'Of course,' Caris said.

Lolla said: 'Can I go with you?'

'No,' said Caris. 'Here's your first lesson: you have to be clean. Go and wash, now. You can come with me tomorrow.'

As she was leaving, Madge Webber came in. 'Have you heard the news?' she said, her face grim. 'Philemon is back.'

*

On that Sunday, Davey and Amabel were married at the little church in Wigleigh.

Lady Philippa gave permission for the manor house to be used for the party. Wulfric killed a pig and roasted it whole over a fire in the yard. Davey had bought sweet currants, and Annet baked them in buns. There was no ale – much of the barley harvest had rotted in the fields for want of reapers – but Philippa had sent Sam home with a present of a barrel of cider.

Gwenda still thought, every day, about that scene in the hunting lodge. In the middle of the night she stared into the darkness and saw Ralph with her knife in his mouth, the hilt sticking out between his brown teeth, and Sam's sword nailing him to the wall.

When she and Sam had retrieved their weapons, pulling them grimly out of Ralph, and the corpse had fallen to the floor, it had looked as if the two dead men had killed one another. Gwenda had smeared blood on their unstained weapons and left them where they lay. Outside, she had loosened the horses' tethers, so that they could survive for a few days, if necessary, until someone found them. Then she and Sam had walked away.

The Shiring coroner had speculated that outlaws might have been involved in the deaths, but in the end had come to the conclusion Gwenda expected. No suspicion had fallen on her or Sam. They had got away with murder.

She had told Sam an edited version of what had happened between her and Ralph. She pretended that this was the first time he had tried to coerce her, and she said he had simply threatened to kill her if she refused. Sam was awestruck to think that he had killed an earl, but he had no doubt that his action had been justified. He had the right temperament for a soldier, Gwenda realized: he would never suffer agonies of remorse over killing.

Nor did she, even though she often recalled the scene with revulsion. She had killed Alan Fernhill and finished Ralph off, but she had not a twinge of regret. The world was a better place without both of them. Ralph had died in the agony of knowing that his own son had stabbed him through the heart, and that was exactly what he deserved. In time, she felt sure, the vision of what she had done would cease to come to her by night.

She put the memory out of her mind and looked around the hall of the manor house at the carousing villagers.

The pig was eaten, and the men were drinking the last of the cider. Aaron Appletree produced his bagpipes. The village had had no drummer since the death of Annet's father, Perkin. Gwenda wondered whether Davey would take up drumming now.

Wulfric wanted to dance, as he always did when he had had a bellyful of drink. Gwenda partnered him for the first number, laughing as she tried to keep up with his cavorting. He lifted her, swung her through the air, crushed her to his body, and put her down again only to circle her with great leaps. He had no sense of rhythm, but his sheer enthusiasm was infectious. Afterwards she declared herself exhausted, and he danced with his new daughter-in-law, Amabel.

Then, of course, he danced with Annet.

His eye fell on her as soon as the tune ended and he let go of Amabel. Annet was sitting on a bench at one side of the hall of the manor house. She wore a green dress that was girlishly short and showed her dainty ankles. The dress was not new, but she had embroidered the bosom with yellow and pink flowers. As always, a few ringlets had escaped from her headdress, and they hung around her face. She was twenty years too old to dress that way, but she did not know it, and nor did Wulfric.

Gwenda smiled as they began to dance. She wanted to look happy and carefree, but she realized her expression might be more like a grimace, and she gave up trying. She tore her gaze away from them and watched Davey and Amabel. Perhaps Amabel would not turn out quite like her mother. She had some of Annet's coquettish ways, but Gwenda had never seen her actually flirting, and right now she seemed uninterested in anyone but her husband.

Gwenda scanned the room and located her other son, Sam. He was with the young men, telling a story, miming it, holding the reins of an imaginary horse and almost falling off. He had them spellbound. They probably envied his luck in becoming a squire.

Sam was still living at Earlscastle. Lady Philippa had kept on most of the squires and men-at-arms, for her son Gerry would need them to ride and hunt with him, and practise with the sword and the lance. Gwenda hoped that, during the period of Philippa's regency, Sam would learn a more intelligent and merciful code than he would have got from Ralph.

There was not much else to look at, and Gwenda's gaze returned to her husband and the woman he had once wanted to marry. As Gwenda had feared, Annet was making the most of Wulfric's exuberance and inebriation. She gave him sexy smiles when they danced apart, and when they came together she clung to him, Gwenda thought, like a wet shirt.

The dance seemed to go on for ever, Aaron Appletree repeating the bouncy melody endlessly on his bagpipes. Gwenda knew her husband's moods, and now she saw the glint in his eye that always appeared when he was about to ask her to lie with him. Annet knew exactly what she was doing, Gwenda thought furiously. She shifted restlessly on her bench, willing the music to stop, trying not to let her anger show.

However, she was seething with indignation when the tune ended with a flourish. She made up her mind to get Wulfric to calm down and sit beside her. She would keep him close for the rest of the afternoon, and there would be no trouble.

But then Annet kissed him.

While he still had his hands on her waist she stood on tiptoe and tilted her face and kissed him full on the lips, briefly but firmly; and Gwenda boiled over.

She jumped up from her bench and strode across the hall. As she passed the bridal couple her son, Davey, saw the expression on her face and tried to detain her, but she ignored him. She went up to Wulfric and Annet, who were still gazing at one another and smiling stupidly. She poked Annet's shoulder with her finger and said loudly: 'Leave my husband alone!'

Wulfric said: 'Gwenda, please—'

'Don't you say anything,' Gwenda said. 'Just stay away from this whore.'

Annet's eyes flashed defiance. 'It's not dancing that whores are paid for.'

'I'm sure you know all about what whores do.'

'How dare you!'

Davey and Amabel intervened. Amabel said to Annet: 'Please don't make a scene, Ma.'

Annet said: 'It's not me, it's Gwenda!'

Gwenda said: 'I'm not the one trying to seduce someone else's husband.'

Davey said: 'Mother, you're spoiling the wedding.'

Gwenda was too enraged to listen. 'She always does this. She jilted him twenty-three years ago, but she's never let him go!'

Annet began to cry. Gwenda was not surprised. Annet's tears were just another means of getting her way.

Wulfric reached out to pat Annet's shoulder, and Gwenda snapped: 'Don't touch her!' He jerked back his hand as if burned.

'You don't understand,' Annet sobbed.

'I understand you all too well,' Gwenda said.

'No, you don't,' Annet said. She wiped her eyes and gave Gwenda a surprisingly direct, candid look. 'You don't understand that you have won. He's yours. You don't know how he adores you, respects you, admires you. You don't see the way he looks at you when you're speaking to someone else.'

Gwenda was taken aback. 'Well,' she mumbled, but she did not know what else to say.

Annet went on: 'Does he eye younger women? Does he ever sneak away from you? How many nights have you slept apart in the last twenty years – two? Three? Can't you see that he will never love another woman as long as he lives?'

Gwenda looked at Wulfric and realized that all this was true. In fact it was obvious. She knew it and so did everyone. She tried to remember why she was so angry with Annet, but somehow the logic of it had slipped her mind.

The dancing had stopped and Aaron had put down his pipes. All the villagers now gathered around the two women, mothers of the bridal couple.

Annet said: 'I was a foolish and selfish girl, and I made a stupid decision, and lost the best man I've ever met. And you got him. Sometimes I can't resist the temptation to pretend it happened the other way around, and he's mine. So I smile at him, and I pat his arm; and he's kind to me because he knows he broke my heart.'

'You broke your own heart,' Gwenda said.

'I did. And you were the lucky girl who benefited from my folly.'

Gwenda was dumbfounded. She had never looked at Annet as a sad person. To her, Annet had always been a powerful, threatening figure, ever scheming to take Wulfric back. But that was never going to come to pass.

Annet said: 'I know it annoys you when Wulfric is nice to me. I'd like to say it won't happen again, but I know my own weakness. Do you have to hate me for it? Don't let this spoil the joy of the wedding and of the grandchildren we both want. Instead of regarding me as your lifelong enemy, couldn't you think of me as a bad sister, who sometimes misbehaves and makes you cross, but still has to be treated as one of the family?'

She was right. Gwenda had always thought of Annet as a pretty face with an empty head, but on this occasion Annet was the wiser of the two, and Gwenda felt humbled. 'I don't know,' she said. 'Perhaps I could try.'

Annet stepped forward and kissed Gwenda's cheek. Gwenda felt Annet's tears on her face. 'Thank you,' Annet said.

Gwenda hesitated, then put her arms around Annet's bony shoulders and hugged her.

All around them, the villagers clapped and cheered.

A moment later, the music began again.

*

EARLY IN NOVEMBER, Philemon arranged a service of thanksgiving for the end of the plague. Archbishop Henri came with Canon Claude. So did Sir Gregory Longfellow.

Gregory must have come to Kingsbridge to announce the king's choice of bishop, Merthin thought. Formally, he would tell the monks that the king had nominated a certain person, and it would be up to the monks to elect that person or someone else; but, in the end, the monks usually voted for whomever the king had chosen.

Merthin could read no message in Philemon's face, and he guessed that Gregory had not yet revealed the king's choice. The decision meant everything to Merthin and Caris. If Claude got the job, their troubles were over. He was moderate and reasonable. But if Philemon became bishop, they faced more years of squabbling and lawsuits.

Henri took the service, but Philemon preached the sermon. He thanked God for answering the prayers of Kingsbridge monks and sparing the town from the worst effects of the plague. He did not mention that the monks had fled to St-John-in-the-Forest and left the townspeople to fend for themselves; nor that Caris and Merthin had helped God to answer the monks' prayers by closing the town gates for six months. He made it sound as if he had saved Kingsbridge.

'It makes my blood boil,' Merthin said to Caris, not troubling to keep his voice down. 'He's completely twisting the facts!'

'Relax,' she said. 'God knows the truth, and so do the people. Philemon isn't fooling anyone.'

She was right, of course. After a battle, the soldiers on the winning side always thanked God, but all the same they knew the difference between good generals and bad.

After the service, Merthin as alderman was invited to dine at the prior's palace with the archbishop. He was seated next to Canon Claude. As soon as grace had been said, a general hubbub of conversation broke out, and Merthin spoke to Claude in a low, urgent voice. 'Does the archbishop know yet who the king has chosen as bishop?'

Claude replied with an almost imperceptible nod.

'Is it you?'

Claude's head shake was equally minimal.

'Philemon, then?'

Again the tiny nod.

Merthin's heart sank. How could the king pick a fool and coward such as Philemon in preference to someone as competent and sensible as Claude? But he knew the answer: Philemon had played his cards well. 'Has Gregory instructed the monks yet?'

'No.' Claude leaned closer. 'He will probably tell Philemon informally tonight after supper, then speak to the monks in chapter tomorrow morning.'

'So we've got until the end of the day.'

'For what?'

'To change his mind.'

'You won't do that.'

'I'm going to try.'

'You'll never succeed.'

'Bear in mind that I'm desperate.'

Merthin toyed with his food, eating little and fighting to keep his patience, until the archbishop rose from the table; then he spoke to Gregory. 'If you would walk with me in the cathedral, I would speak to you about something I feel sure will interest you deeply,' he said, and Gregory nodded assent.

They paced side by side up the nave, where Merthin could be sure no one was lurking close enough to hear. He took a deep breath. What he was about to do was dangerous. He was going to try to bend the king to his will. If he failed he could be charged with treason – and executed.

He said: 'There have long been rumours that a document exists, somewhere in Kingsbridge, that the king would dearly love to destroy.'

Gregory was stone-faced, but he said: 'Go on.' That was as good as confirmation.

'This letter was in the possession of a knight who has recently died.'

'Has he!' said Gregory, startled.

'You obviously know exactly what I'm talking about.'

Gregory answered like a lawyer. 'Let us say, for the sake of argument, that I do.'

'I would like to do the king the service of restoring that document to him – whatever it may be.' He knew perfectly well what it was, but he could adopt a cautious pretence of ignorance as well as Gregory.

'The king would be grateful,' said Gregory.

'How grateful?'

'What did you have in mind?'

'A bishop more in sympathy with the people of Kingsbridge than Philemon.'

Gregory looked hard at him. 'Are you trying to blackmail the king of England?'

Merthin knew this was the point of danger. 'We Kingsbridge folk are merchants and craftsmen,' he said, trying to sound reasonable. 'We buy, we sell, we make deals. I'm just trying to make a bargain with you. I want to sell you something, and I've told you my price. There's no blackmail, no coercion. I make no threats. If you don't want what I'm selling, that will be the end of the matter.'

They reached the altar. Gregory stared at the crucifix that surmounted it. Merthin knew exactly what he was thinking.

Should he have Merthin arrested, taken to London, and tortured until he revealed the whereabouts of the document? Or would it be simpler and more convenient to the king just to nominate a different man as bishop of Kingsbridge?

There was a long silence. The cathedral was cold, and Merthin pulled his cloak closer around him. At last Gregory said: 'Where is the document?'

'Close by. I'll take you there.'

'Very well.'

'And our bargain?'

'If the document is what you believe it to be, I will honour my side of the arrangement.'

'And make Canon Claude bishop?'

'Yes.'

'Thank you,' said Merthin. 'We'll need to walk a little way into the woods.'

They went side by side down the main street and across the bridge, their breath making clouds in the air. A wintry sun shone with little warmth as they walked into the forest. Merthin found the way easily this time, having followed the same route only a few weeks earlier. He recognized the little spring, the big rock and the boggy valley. They came quickly to the clearing with the broad oak tree, and he went straight to the spot where he had dug up the scroll.

He was dismayed to see that someone else had got here first.

He had carefully smoothed the loose earth and covered it with leaves but, despite that, someone had found the hiding place. There was a hole a foot deep, and a pile of recently excavated earth beside it. And the hole was empty.

He stared at the hole, appalled. 'Oh, hell,' he said.

Gregory said: 'I hope this isn't some kind of charade—'

'Let me think,' Merthin snapped.

Gregory shut up.

'Only two people knew about this,' Merthin said, thinking aloud. 'I haven't told anyone, so Thomas must have. He was getting senile before he died. I think he spilled the beans.'

'But to whom?'

'Thomas spent the last few months of his life at St-John-in-the-Forest, and the monks were keeping everyone else out, so it must have been a monk.'

'How many are there?'

'Twenty or so. But not many would know enough about the background to understand the significance of an old man's mumblings about a buried letter.'

'That's all very well, but where is it now?'

'I think I know,' said Merthin. 'Give me one more chance.'

'Very well.'

They walked back to the town. As they crossed the bridge, the sun was setting over Leper Island. They went into the darkening cathedral, walked to the south-west tower, and climbed the narrow spiral staircase to the little room where the costumes for the mystery play were kept.

Merthin had not been here for eleven years, but dusty storerooms did not change much, especially in cathedrals, and this was the same. He found the loose stone in the wall and pulled it out.

All Philemon's treasures were behind the stone, including the love note carved in wood. And there, among them, was a bag made of oiled wool. Merthin opened the bag and drew from it a vellum scroll.

'I thought so,' he said. 'Philemon got the secret out of Thomas when Thomas was losing his mind.' No doubt Philemon was keeping the letter to be used as a bargaining counter if the decision on the bishopric went the wrong way – but now Merthin could use it instead.

He handed the scroll to Gregory.

Gregory unrolled it. A look of awe came over his face as he read. 'Dear God,' he said. 'Those rumours were true.' He rolled it up again. He had the look of a man who has found something he has been seeking for many years.

'Is it what you expected?' Merthin said.

'Oh, yes.'

'And the king will be grateful?'

'Profoundly.'

'So your part of the bargain . . . ?'

'Will be kept,' said Gregory. 'You shall have Claude as your bishop.'

'Thank God,' said Merthin.

*

EIGHT DAYS LATER, early in the morning, Caris was at the hospital, teaching Lolla how to tie a bandage, when Merthin came in. 'I want to show you something,' he said. 'Come to the cathedral.'

It was a bright, cold winter's day. Caris wrapped herself in a heavy red cloak. As they were crossing the bridge into the city, Merthin stopped and pointed. 'The spire is finished,' he said.

Caris looked up. She could see its shape through the spider web of flimsy scaffolding that still surrounded it. The spire was immensely tall and graceful. As her eye followed its upward taper, Caris had the feeling that it might go on for ever.

She said: 'And is it the tallest building in England?'

He smiled. 'Yes.'

They walked up the main street and into the cathedral. Merthin led the way up the staircase within the walls of the central tower. He was used to the climb, but Caris was panting by the time they emerged into the open air at the summit of the tower, on the walkway that ran round the base of the spire. Up here the breeze was stiff and cold.

They looked at the view while Caris caught her breath. All Kingsbridge was laid out to the north and west: the main street, the industrial district, the river, and the island with the hospital. Smoke rose from a thousand chimneys. Miniature people hurried through the streets, walking or riding or driving carts, carrying tool bags or baskets of produce or heavy sacks; men and women and children, fat and thin, their clothing poor and worn or rich and heavy, mostly brown and green but with flashes of peacock blue and scarlet. The sight of them all made Caris marvel: each individual had a different life, every one of them rich and complex, with dramas in the past and challenges in the future, happy memories and secret sorrows, and a crowd of friends and enemies and loved ones.

'Ready?' Merthin said.

Caris nodded.

He led her up the scaffolding. It was an insubstantial affair of ropes and branches, and it always made her nervous, though she did not like to say so: if Merthin could climb it, so could she. The wind made the whole structure sway a little, and the skirts of Caris's robe flapped around her legs like the sails of a ship. The spire was as tall again as the tower, and the climb up the rope ladders was strenuous.

They stopped half way for a rest. 'The spire is very plain,' Merthin said, not needing to catch his breath. 'Just a roll moulding at the angles.' Caris realized that other spires she had seen featured decorative crochets, bands of coloured stone or tile, and window-like recesses. The simplicity of Merthin's design was what made it seem to go on for ever.

Merthin pointed down. 'Hey, look what's happening!'

'I'd rather not look down . . .'

'I think Philemon is leaving for Avignon.'

She had to see that. She was standing on a broad platform of planks, but all the same she had to hold on tight with both hands to the upright pole to convince herself that she was not falling. She swallowed hard and directed her gaze down the perpendicular side of the tower to the ground below.

It was worth the effort. A charette drawn by two oxen was outside the prior's palace. An escort consisting of a monk and a man-at-arms, both on horseback, waited patiently. Philemon stood beside the charette while the monks of Kingsbridge came forward, one by one, and kissed his hand.

When they had all done, Brother Sime handed him a black-and-white cat, and Caris recognized the descendant of Godwyn's cat Archbishop.

Philemon climbed into the carriage and the driver whipped the oxen. The vehicle lumbered slowly out of the gate and down the main street. Caris and Merthin watched it cross the double bridge and disappear into the suburbs.

'Thank God he's gone,' said Caris.

Merthin looked up. 'Not much farther to the top,' he said. 'Soon you will be higher off the ground than any woman in England has ever stood.' He began to climb again.

The wind grew stronger but, despite her anxiety, Caris felt exhilarated. This was Merthin's dream, and he had made it come true. Every day for hundreds of years people for miles around would look at this spire and think how beautiful it was.

They reached the top of the scaffolding and stood on the stage that encircled the peak of the spire. Caris tried to forget that there was no railing around the platform to stop them falling off.

At the point of the spire was a cross. It had looked small from the ground, but now Caris saw that it was taller than she.

'There's always a cross at the top of a spire,' Merthin said. 'That's conventional. Aside from that, practice varies. At Chartres, the cross bears an image of the sun. I've done something different.'

Caris saw that, at the foot of the cross, Merthin had placed a life-size stone angel. The kneeling figure was not gazing up at the cross, but out to the west, over the town. Looking more closely, Caris saw that the angel's features were not conventional. The small round face was clearly female, and looked vaguely familiar, with neat features and short hair.

Then she realized that the face was her own.

She was amazed. 'Will they let you do that?' she said.

Merthin nodded. 'Half the town thinks you're an angel already.'

'I'm not, though,' she said.

'No,' he said with the familiar grin that she loved so much. 'But you're the closest they've seen.'

The wind blustered suddenly. Caris grabbed Merthin. He held her tightly, standing confidently on spread feet. The gust died away as quickly as it had come, but Merthin and Caris remained locked together, standing there at the top of the world, for a long time afterwards.

# *Acknowledgements*

My principal historical consultants were Sam Cohn, Geoffrey Hindley and Marilyn Livingstone. The weakness in the foundations of Kingsbridge Cathedral is loosely based on that of the cathedral of Santa Maria in Vitoria-Gasteiz, Spain, and I'm grateful to the staff of the Fundacion Catedral Santa Maria for help and inspiration, especially Carlos Rodriguez de Diego, Gonzalo Arroita and interpreter Luis Rivero. I was also helped by the staff of York Minster, especially John David. Martin Allen of the Fitzwilliam Museum in Cambridge, England, kindly allowed me to handle coins from the reign of Edward III. At Le Mont-St-Michel in France I was helped by Soeur Judith and Frère François. As always, Dan Starer of Research for Writers in New York city helped with the research. My literary advisers included Amy Berkower, Leslie Gelbman, Phyllis Grann, Neil Nyren, Imogen Taylor and Al Zuckerman. I was also helped by comments and criticisms from friends and family, especially Barbara Follett, Emanuele Follett, Marie-Claire Follett, Erica Jong, Tony McWalter, Chris Manners, Jann Turner and Kim Turner.